THE WORLD'S CLASSICS

WILLIAM MAKEPEACE THACKERAY

The History of
Henry Esmond, Esq.

Edited with an Introduction by
DONALD HAWES

Oxford   New York
OXFORD UNIVERSITY PRESS
1991

Oxford University Press, Walton Street, Oxford OX2 6DP

Oxford New York Toronto
Delhi Bombay Calcutta Madras Karachi
Petaling Jaya Singapore Hong Kong Tokyo
Nairobi Dar es Salaam Cape Town
Melbourne Auckland

and associated companies in
Berlin Ibadan

Oxford is a trade mark of Oxford University Press

British Library Cataloguing in Publication Data
Thackeray, W. M. (William Makepeace) 1811–1863.
The history of Henry Esmond Esq.– (The World's classics)
I. Title II. Hawes, Donald
823.8
ISBN 0–19–282727–8

Library of Congress Cataloging in Publication Data
Thackeray, William Makepeace, 1811–1863.
The history of Henry Esmond. Esq./William Makepeace Thackeray:
edited with an introduction by Donald Hawes.
p. cm.—(The World's classics)
Reproduces the Oxford Thackeray text of 1908.
Includes bibliographical references.
1. Great Britain—History—Anne, 1702–1714—Fiction. I. Hawes,
Donald. II. Title. III. Series.
PR5612.A2H38   1991   823'.8—dc20   90–45112
ISBN 0–19–282727–8

Printed in Great Britain by
BPCC Hazell Books
Aylesbury, Bucks

CONTENTS

INTRODUCTION

WHEN George Russell, a barrister and friend of Thackeray's, asked him which was his own favourite amongst his works, he said emphatically, 'Well, I should like to stand or fall by *Esmond*'.[1] Probably one of the reasons why he treasured the novel was that he had invested in it so much intellectual and emotional capital. He had, it is true, already written historical novels: *Catherine* and *Barry Lyndon*, his first two, have eighteenth-century settings and the action of *Vanity Fair* takes place mostly in the Regency. But in late 1850 and early 1851 he read extensively in the history and literature of early eighteenth-century England (a period that had always fascinated him) for his highly successful series of lectures on *The English Humourists* and he continued to do so in preparation for *Henry Esmond*, which he had first thought of in November 1850. By the time that Eyre Crowe, a young artist and family friend, had become his secretary and amanuensis in early 1852, he found that Thackeray had completed the 'first portion' of the novel, 'written upon small slips of note-paper kept in the firm grip of an elastic band'. He would send Crowe 'to make enquiries' at the British Museum. There, thanks to the help of Antonio Pannizi, the Principal Librarian, Thackeray would dictate parts of the novel to Crowe in a secluded gallery. They also worked in 'one of the side rooms off the large library' at the Athenaeum; Crowe did not recollect 'that these utterances, not at all delivered *sotto voce*, disturbed the equanimity of either Church, law, or science dignitaries frequenting that luxuriously seated library'.[2]

---

[1] Philip Collins (ed.), *Thackeray: Interviews and Recollections* (London, 1983), ii. 311.
[2] Eyre Crowe, *With Thackeray in America* (London, 1893), 3–5.

They seem to have consulted a large number of historical sources, though to call their kind of investigation 'research' would perhaps be to dignify it overmuch. A few years later, Thackeray told one of his correspondents, S. N. Rowland, that he had used Marlborough's dispatches, the memoirs of both the Duke of Berwick and the Marquis de Torcy, French documents relating to the War of the Spanish Succession, Archibald Alison's biography of Marlborough, an anonymous poem about the Battle of Oudenarde, Swift's *Journal to Stella*, and Edward Chamberlayne's *Angliae Notitia* (a virtually annual publication of the late seventeenth and early eighteenth centuries, like *Whitaker's Almanack*). We know from the investigations of such Thackeray scholars as T. C. and William Snow and John Sutherland and from internal evidence that he drew material from many other contemporary memoirs and records as well as obvious literary sources like *The Tatler* and *The Spectator*.[3] Above all, Macaulay was a potent influence: the first two volumes (1849) of his best-selling *History of England*, covering the years 1685–9, which Thackeray 'had pondered',[4] and the *Edinburgh Review* essays on Addison (July 1843) and the Restoration Dramatists (January 1841). From Macaulay came striking details, anecdotes, and pictures: Tusher's wanting to leave the Castlewoods' dining-table when the sweetmeats were brought, Marlborough's showing Cadogan the coins in a drawer, the Jesuits' activities overseas, and much else. But Thackeray acknowledged the fact that he couldn't possibly rival the historian's phenomenal learning and memory. He wrote to his mother while he was working on the novel to say that it 'takes as much trouble as Macaulay's History

---

[3] Gordon N. Ray (ed.), *The Letters and Private Papers of William Makepeace Thackeray* (Harvard, 1945–6), iii. 446–8. See also the Snows' edition of *Henry Esmond* (Oxford, 1909; 2nd edition, 1915), p. xxvi; J. A. Sutherland, *Thackeray at Work* (London, 1974), pp. 138–43; Edgar F. Harden's edition of *Henry Esmond* (New York, 1989), 398–9, n. 15.

[4] Gordon N. Ray, *Thackeray: The Age of Wisdom* (London, 1958), 179.

almost and he has the vast advantage of remembering everything he has read, whilst everything but impressions I mean facts dates and so forth slip out of my head in wh. there is some great faculty lacking depend upon it'.[5] And indeed the pedant can find plenty of slips and anachronisms, but the wealth and ease of allusion that pervade the novel give a sense of the period which a more laboured display of learning would impede.

It is, of course, a sense of period that was acceptable to readers of the 1850s and that Thackeray had already evoked in his *English Humourists* when talking about the 'delightful volumes of the *Tatler* and the *Spectator*':

The Maypole rises in the Strand again in London; the churches are thronged with daily worshippers; the beaux are gathering in the coffee-houses; the gentry are going to the Drawing-room; the ladies are thronging to the toy-shops; the chairmen are jostling in the streets; the footmen are running with links before the chariots, or fighting round the theatre doors. In the country I see the young Squire riding to Eton with his servants behind him, and Will Wimble, the friend of the family, to see him safe.[6]

Thackeray's fictional portrait of the Old Pretender in *Henry Esmond* confirms popular ideas about the immorality and unreliability of many of the Stuarts and their supporters, Addison's gentlemanliness is contrasted with Swift's boorishness, the rakishness of the male Castlewoods and Mohun is opposed by Esmond's selfless nobility, and so on. Altogether, an early Victorian ethos is apparent, as has often been remarked: respectability, gentlemanliness, and the idealization of domestic bliss and female virtue are key characteristics, which find their full realization in the final pages of the novel—pages far removed in content and tone from any in *Tom Jones*, the masterpiece of the novelist Thackeray revered. But Thackeray presents us with historical issues and personages that tease us with uncertainty and contradiction. He openly gives one reason for this at the beginning of the novel, where he declares that he would have 'history familiar rather than heroic'. So Queen Anne on occasion was 'a hot, red-faced woman'; on another, towards the end of the novel, she 'looked very pale and ill' and 'sat with a stupefied look' (opening of Book I; Book III, Chapter X). The Battle of Blenheim, as witnessed by Esmond, was brutally different from the triumph of arms celebrated in Addison's *Campaign*—and yet thanks to it and other military victories England achieved glory. Besides, 'Esmond's own natural vanity was pleased at the little share of reputation which his good fortune had won him' in the wars and which pleased Lady Castlewood and raised him in the eyes of Beatrix (Book II, Chapter XV). Marlborough and Swift, though usually presented in terms of sharp disapproval or scorn, are, nevertheless, Esmond thinks, 'the two greatest men of that age' (Book III, Chapter V).

Macaulay's eloquent tenth chapter (written in 1848, the 'year of revolutions') in his *History of England*, where he glories in the 'stand which was made by our forefathers against the House of Stuart' in 1688, was fresh in readers' minds when *Henry Esmond* appeared. Esmond, reflecting in his mature years, owns that he has come to think that Addison's politics were right and that were his time to come again he 'would be a Whig in England and not a Tory'. This view, identical to Macaulay's, is immediately undercut by his observations that men and chance rather than principles determine our allegiances and that English history is in reality a series of compromises—of principles, party, and worship (Book III, Chapter V). Esmond's life exemplifies this philosophy of personal influence and accident since he is subjected as a child to Huguenot, Catholic, and Church of England teaching and later works for the Jacobite cause because of the two women in his life.

In *The Historical Novel*, Georg Lukács took Thackeray severely to task for this approach. He acknowledged the compelling and subtle psychology involved in the novelist's presentation of character in his concern to expose pseudo-greatness and lack of principle, but he deplored Thackeray's exclusion from his narrative of the broad, objective forces of history and of the common people. Lukács argued that Scott, in contrast, produced a picture of history that was 'grand, dramatic and rife with deep conflict in every phase'.[7] One answer to Lukács's criticisms is that for Thackeray the essential conflicts in *Henry Esmond* were those within individual people and those engendered by their relationships. This is not to say that 'history' is there merely as background or as a means of unusual colouring. Motive and action are inseparably related to political and social intrigue, although perhaps in comparatively simple ways, as in Esmond's plan to place Prince James Edward on the English throne. The text of the novel itself, as we shall see later, ingeniously suggests the linguistic patterns of the period.

But psychological and even autobiographical issues are predominant. 'The hero', Thackeray told his mother, 'is . . . a handsome likeness of an ugly son of yours.' His tone was more sombre in a letter to Lady Stanley in October 1851: 'I am writing a book of cut-throat melancholy suitable to my state.'[8] His 'state' was mainly due to the ending of his relationship with Mrs Brookfield. Thackeray had become friends with William Henry Brookfield when they were undergraduates at Cambridge in 1829. Brookfield took holy orders, married Jane Elton in 1841, and settled in London. Thackeray's friendship with Mrs Brookfield deepened into love, an emotion intensified by his loneliness after his wife's mental instability had enforced his separation from her and

---

[7] Georg Lukács, *The Historical Novel* (Harmondsworth, 1969), 240–4.
[8] Ray, *Letters*, ii. 815, 807.

by his awareness of much unhappiness in the Brookfields' marriage. Mr Brookfield's objections to their close but platonic friendship increased until a quarrel ensued between him and Thackeray in September 1851, when he was working on the novel. As a result of the breach with the Brookfields, it could be said that *Henry Esmond* became, in the words of Ann Monsarrat, 'the repository for his wounds and rages, a charting of his own passions, a text-book of desire'.[9] The tensions in the Castlewoods' married life, Esmond's yearnings, disappointments, and regrets, and the resolution of his long-borne miseries in a fulfilling love can therefore be traced, in part, to autobiographical feelings of melancholy, frustration, and wish-fulfilment. Occasionally, a direct reference can be discerned. Gordon Ray noticed that Esmond's passionate celebration of the immortality that love confers (at the end of Book II, Chapter VI) is an echo of a letter Thackeray wrote to Mrs Brookfield on 18 December 1848: 'if I [die first], I swear the best thought I have is to remember that I shall have your love surviving me and with a constant tenderness blessing my memory.'[10] The identifications between fact and fiction are not always simple one-to-one relationships. Catherine Peters has interestingly suggested that 'Thackeray's pure and spiritual love for Jane is represented by Rachel, and his unacknowledged lust for her by Beatrix'.[11] This kind of complexity of emotion divided among different women characters is a favourite fictional device of Thackeray's, previously seen in the contrasting and complementary groups formed by Amelia and Becky in *Vanity Fair* and by Laura, Blanche, and Fanny in *Pendennis*.

Another poignant memory is present in the opening of the novel, where Thackeray evokes Henry Esmond's

[9] Ann Monsarrat, *An Uneasy Victorian: Thackeray the Man* (London, 1980), 278.
[10] Ray, *Letters*, ii. 470 and n.
[11] Catherine Peters, *Thackeray's Universe: Shifting Worlds of Imagination and Reality* (London, 1987), 209.

childhood. That wonderful first chapter introduces us to 'the sad lonely little occupant of this gallery busy over his great book' and then looking up to see a golden-haired goddess. Outside, we see, with him, 'the great darkling woods with a cloud of rooks returning'. In 1848, after Thackeray had gone back to Addiscombe, where he had stayed for two summers as a boy with his mother and stepfather, he wrote in his diary: 'All sorts of recollections of my youth came back to me: dark and sad and painful with my dear good mother as a gentle angel interposing between me and misery . . . how well I remember the cawing of the rooks there of a morning! they were still talking away in the wilderness wh. is quite unaltered.'[12] How close, by the way, are the expressions of feeling in both fact and fiction.

Yet another area of emotional involvement is Thackeray's championship of General Webb and his corresponding animus against Marlborough. This partisanship arose from his belief, which he later discovered to be mistaken, that he was a direct descendant of Webb's. He obviously felt, even as he was composing the novel, that he had gone too far. A typical indication of his second thoughts is the lengthy footnote in Book II, Chapter XV, where by indicating Esmond's constancy in dislikes and attachments his grandchildren help to distance the reader a little way from the one-sided view so relentlessly expressed. Winston Churchill testified to its strength when he scornfully referred in his biography of Marlborough to 'Thackeray's malicious pages'.[13] On the other hand, it is precisely this kind of subjective response on the part of the narrator that gives truth and feeling to his participation in political intrigue and that typifies his belief that ' 'tis men rather than principles' that commonly determine loyalties.

---

[12] Ray, *Letters* ii. 361.
[13] Winston S. Churchill, *Marlborough: His Life and Times* (London, 1933–8), iii. 509.

From its first publication, *Henry Esmond* has moved, disturbed, and sometimes bewildered its readers because of Thackeray's uninhibited presentation of Esmond's love for both mother and daughter and of the controversial choice that he finally makes (though it is surely not an unexpected choice). It is the intensity of feeling that calls forth the intensity of response and it is, furthermore, an intensity that has about it a naturalness and inevitability. Leslie Stephen revealed that Thackeray wrote some of the novel in his 'own small upright handwriting' but dictated impromptu 'a considerable part of the book' (probably about 40 per cent) to Eyre Crowe and Anne Thackeray. Minor carelessnesses resulted and probably a fair amount of improvization occurred, especially since, as Stephen also indicated, 'the copy was sent straight to press as it stands, with ... remarkably little alteration'.[14] But the masterly consequences of this mode of procedure can be seen in a chapter like 'The 29th December', where setting, dialogue, reflection, and allusion blend together to give an unforgettable sense of tender reconciliation. This chapter, in turn, moves smoothly into the next, with its celebrated description of Beatrix, 'holding her dress with one fair rounded arm, and her taper before her, tripping down the stair to greet Esmond', who is consequently enslaved by her. The memorable and significant tableaux and passages of reflection (Esmond's meditations over his mother's grave, Boyle's dazzling, perfumed irruption into Addison's chamber, Beatrix's dropping 'the great gold salver' with a clang, Esmond's

---

[14] From a letter of 11 June 1889 to the Librarian, Trinity College, Cambridge, where the manuscript is deposited. The relevant passage is in the *Oxford Thackeray*, xiii. p. xxvii. Eyre Crowe said that the 'first portion' was written in 'beautiful penmanship ... with scarcely any interpolations or marginal *repentirs*' (*With Thackeray in America*, 3). John Sutherland agrees 'with Leslie Stephen that the remarkable fact is how little—rather than how much—revision we find in the manuscript' (*Thackeray at Work*, 66). But Edgar F. Harden says that 'the Esmond manuscript shows many signs of revision' (*The History of Henry Esmond*, 412).

putting Beatrix's slipper on her 'little stockinged foot') seem not to be contrived set pieces but to be inescapably part of the actual stream of experience that the narrator is recalling as his pen and voice run on.

George Saintsbury perceptively defined Thackeray's technique and effects:

There is a curious saturation with history and literature which betrays itself, not in digression or padding, but by constant allusion and suggestion; a light, current, apparently facile, sketching of scene and character which suddenly plunges (as a great phrase of Walt Whitman's has it) to 'the accepted hells beneath,' but recovers itself at once and goes placidly on; above all, a shower of original and memorable phrases, never paraded, never dwelt upon too long, but more absolutely startling in its unique felicity than the most laboured conceits of mere phrasemongers.[15]

Yet *Henry Esmond* is elegantly shaped, even though this (as John Sutherland has argued in *Thackeray at Work*) may have come about partly by accident. By means of the Preface, five chapters of 'flashback' (Book I, Chapters II–VI), the footnotes, various personages' reminiscences, and other comments, a span of time from the 1580s to about 1780 is covered, giving a perspective to the main action, which takes place between about 1685 and 1714.

Thackeray tells Lord Ashburton in his Dedication that the novel 'copies the manners and language of Queen Anne's time'. The illusion that they were reading a novel of that period was enhanced for its first readers in England by its appearance in an eighteenth-century typeface complete with the long 's'. On the title-page were the Dedication to a nobleman, a quotation from Horace, and the announcement that the book was 'printed for Smith, Elder, & Company,

[15] Introduction to *Catherine, etc.* (*Oxford Thackeray*, iii, p. xiii). Repr. in *A Consideration of Thackeray* (Oxford, 1931), 54.

over against St Peter's Church in Cornhill'. 'It came out', Anne Thackeray recalled, 'in periwig and embroidery, in beautiful type and handsome proportions.'[16] There were precedents for this sort of imitation: for example, the *Diary of Lady Willoughby*, by Hannah Rathbone, which concerned the 'domestic history' of the fictional heroine and 'the eventful period of the reign of Charles the First', was published in 1844 (and subsequently reprinted and extended) with a mock seventeenth-century title-page and typeface. Thackeray was an accomplished parodist who had thrown off some coruscating, comic pieces in his early days on *Fraser's Magazine*, *Punch*, and other periodicals. His series, 'Punch's Prize Novelists', had included 'Barbazure', which took off the historical novels of the popular and prolific G. P. R. James. He depicts a warrior and his 'noble beast': 'The arblast, the mangonel, the demi-culverin, and the cuissart of the period glittered upon the neck and chest of the war-steed; while the rider, with chamfron and catapult, with ban and arrière-ban, morion and tumbril, battle-axe and rifflard, and the other appurtenances of ancient chivalry, rode stately on his steel-clad charger, himself a tower of steel.'[17] Instinctively resistant to such absurdities as he parodies here, Thackeray in *Henry Esmond* subtly suggests an early eighteenth-century English prose style, without attempting to copy it closely (except in the imitation paper from *The Spectator*). The basic characteristics are still Thackerayan, in the way Saintsbury described them, but they are modified by a few archaic words and expressions, some oddities of grammar, and some lengthier and more Latinate sentences than usual. There are a good many Latin quotations, particularly from Horace, of whom Thackeray had a typical public schoolboy's knowledge. But oaths and coarse phrases, as can be found in Fielding, are

---

[16] Introduction to *Esmond, etc.* (*Biographical Edition* of Thackeray's works, London, 1898, vii, p. xxv).   [17] *Oxford Thackeray*, viii. 128.

excluded: by the 1850s, Englishmen were congratulating themselves on their new politeness of speech as well as manners.[18]

Unlike most of Thackeray's novels, *Henry Esmond* was not illustrated when first published, either by himself or by others. Perhaps this was because he thought that drawings would not be in keeping with the mock eighteenth-century format or with the serious historical and emotional content of the narrative. One can't help feeling that pictorial representations of scenes and incidents in this particular novel would do inadequate justice to the shifts and shades of Thackeray's descriptions, meditations, and dialogue. George du Maurier, an admirer of Thackeray's work, illustrated 1868 and 1884 reprints of the novel. The engravings are skilfully realistic, since du Maurier was at the height of his powers in that remarkable period for English illustrated books: his full-page depiction of a Victorian-looking Beatrix descending the staircase is a glorious image. But anyone who can compare his detailed, static picture of young Esmond's departure from Castlewood to Cambridge with the rhythm, colour, memories, and forebodings expressed in the prose of Thackeray's paragraph at the end of Chapter IX in Book I will have an immediate and vivid understanding of the novelist's powers.

Henry Esmond, following hard on the heels of *Vanity Fair* and *Pendennis*, may not exactly mark a new departure in Thackeray's fiction. *Pendennis*, its immediate predecessor, had also had an autobiographical element, since (leaving aside the hero's inner life) Pendennis's career at Oxbridge

---

[18] Cf. Charles Kingsley's Preface to the Fourth Edition of *Yeast* (dated 17 Feb. 1859): 'one finds, more and more, swearing banished from the hunting-field, foul songs from the universities, drunkenness and gambling from the barracks.' He also notes 'a growing moral earnestness'. There are analyses of the language of the novel in *The History of Henry Esmond*, ed. T. C. and William Snow, pp. xxvii–xxxii, and in K. C. Phillipps, *The Language of Thackeray* (London, 1978), 148–75.

and in London journalism was a fictional parallel to Thackeray's. But *Henry Esmond* differs in some ways from the previous novels. It was composed as a whole, and not in monthly parts. It is quiet, grave, and sometimes melancholy, with no comic personages, dialogue, or events. Some contemporary reviewers welcomed these changes. G. H. Lewes in *The Leader* (6 November 1852) approvingly noted the absence of 'the mocking spirit' and 'careless disrespect' which had been features of Thackeray's earlier writings. In *The Spectator* (6 November 1852), George Brimley considered that the novel would 'rank higher as a work of art than either *Vanity Fair* or *Pendennis*; because the characters are of a higher type, and drawn with greater finish, and the book is more of a complete whole'. But others deplored the central theme of Henry's love for both mother and daughter. George Eliot minced no words in a letter written on 13 November 1852 to Mr and Mrs Charles Bray: ' "Esmond" is the most uncomfortable book you can imagine . . . The hero is in love with the daughter all through the book, and marries the mother at the end.' John Forster in *The Examiner* (13 November 1852) acknowledged that there were 'many beautiful passages of emotion, much delicate writing, and here and there a subtle stroke of passionate nature', but they could not induce him 'to accept or tolerate such a set of incidents' as Esmond's vacillations between Lady Castlewood and Beatrix. As for Samuel Phillips's review in *The Times* (22 December 1852), which found the historical element unconvincing and asserted that 'the sentiment with which we take leave of [Esmond] is one of unaffected disgust', Thackeray thought that it 'absolutely stopped' the sale of the novel.[19]

Soon, however, the consensus of opinion was that *Henry Esmond* was a masterpiece. Trollope in 1879 regarded it as

[19] Geoffrey Tillotson and Donald Hawes (eds.), *Thackeray: The Critical Heritage* (London, 1968), 137, 144, 150, 151, 158–9.

'the greatest work that Thackeray did'. For Pater in 1888 it
was 'a perfect fiction', as *Lycidas* was a 'perfect poem' and
Newman's *Idea of a University* 'the perfect handling of a
theory'. Like other fine art and literature, it could be
regarded as 'a refuge, a sort of cloistral refuge, from a
certain vulgarity in the real world'. 'Of this book', Frank T.
Marzials wrote in 1891, 'it is difficult to speak in language
that shall not seem to savour of exaggeration and hyper-
bole.' Charles Whibley declared in 1903 that its supremacy
among historical novels 'is still unchallenged'. George
Saintsbury, who had read everything, was forthright in his
introductory essay in the *Oxford Thackeray*: 'A greater novel
than *Esmond* I do not know; and I do not know many greater
books.'[20] The reasons for what had so rapidly become
conventional admiration included the satisfying form of the
novel, the portrayal of the hero as the epitome of honour,
the full and lively characterization (especially of Lady
Castlewood and Beatrix), the depiction of the England of
Queen Anne, and the prose style with its eighteenth-
century colouring. From the 1850s onwards, the historical
novel was popular in England for its romanticism and
excitement and for its potential educative value. Scott,
Hugo, and Dumas, all of whom Thackeray relished, had a
wide readership, and in the years following the publication
of *Henry Esmond* there appeared *Westward Ho!* (1855), *The
Virginians* (1857–9), *A Tale of Two Cities* (1859), *The Cloister
and the Hearth* (1861), and *Romola* (1863). As Charles
Whibley pointed out, critics saw *Henry Esmond* as a near-
perfect example of the genre.

Today we may or may not accept the late-Victorian

[20] Anthony Trollope, *Thackeray* (London, 1879), 122; Walter Pater, 'Style', in
Appreciations (London, repr. 1924), 14; Herman Merivale and Frank T. Marzials, *Life
of W. M. Thackeray* (Edinburgh, 1891), 169; Charles Whibley, *William Makepeace
Thackeray* (Edinburgh and London, 1903), 193; George Saintsbury, Introduction to
Henry Esmond, etc. (*Oxford Thackeray*, xii, p. x; reprinted in *A Consideration of Thackeray*,
193).

evaluations of the book, although they cannot be easily dismissed and are in themselves indicative of literary fashion and taste. But *Henry Esmond* offers us rich possibilities for exploration in terms of twentieth-century theories and interests. There are, to begin with, the subtleties and ambiguities of Thackeray's narrative technique: Esmond and Esmond's daughter as the novelist's personae, the shifts between the first and third personal pronouns, the ever-changing timbres of the authorial voices, and the relevant or irrelevant interdependence of fact and fiction. Other features that repay analysis are the Freudian implications of Esmond's sexual dilemmas and involvements, the early Victorian readings of eighteenth-century political and social history, the bourgeois values implicit in the text and in readers' responses to it, and the relationship of the novel to the rest of Thackeray's work, especially to its sequel, *The Virginians*. In any case, the novel appeals to a fundamental human characteristic: the recollection of experience and the ways in which we reshape it as we remember and recount it to ourselves and others. G. K. Chesterton's 'approximate summary' of Thackeray's essential quality was that he 'is the novelist of memory—of our memories as well as his own'.[21]

[21] G. K. Chesterton, *The Victorian Age in Literature* (London, 1913, repr. 1961), 78.

HISTORICAL BACKGROUND

BEHIND the complexities of domestic and foreign policy of the period 1685–1714 lie deep-rooted, fundamental oppositions: Protestant and Roman Catholic, absolute and constitutional monarchy, Jacobite and Hanoverian, Whig and Tory. These oppositions are further complicated by the more fluid character of political parties than those of modern times and by personal rivalries and intrigues. Thackeray also gives his own subjective interpretation of the events of the time. Here, however, is an outline of the historical and religious background to the novel. Readers will find detailed information in two well-established histories: G. M. Trevelyan, *The England of Queen Anne*, 3 vols. (London, 1930–4) and Sir George Clark, *The Later Stuarts 1660–1714* (Oxford, 1934; 2nd edn., 1955).

James II succeeded Charles II, his brother, as King in 1685. The Duke of Monmouth, one of Charles II's illegitimate sons, led an unsuccessful rebellion against James in an attempt to seize the throne and so ensure a Protestant monarchy. He was executed in 1685 (p. 458). James appointed Roman Catholics to a number of influential offices. His two Declarations of Indulgence (1687 and 1688), the second of which the 'Seven Bishops' refused to accept, suspended penal statutes against both Dissenters and Catholics, but many people saw them as opening the way to further Catholic power and influence. His actions aroused angry controversy and opposition, including 'No Popery' demonstrations (pp. 27, 42–3). The birth of a son and heir, James Edward, to his second wife, Mary of Modena, on 10 June 1688 was one of the causes of his expulsion from England at the end of that year to live in exile in France, as it seemed to many that a Catholic monarchy would have been permanently established. In the 'Glorious Revolution', William and Mary were invited to assume the throne in James's place as joint, constitutional monarchs: 'King James had been banished, the Prince of Orange was on the throne' (p. 51).

The concluding part of the Bill of Rights (1689) declared that henceforth no Roman Catholic, nor anyone marrying a Roman Catholic, was eligible for the crown. But although William and Mary were Protestant monarchs, some clergymen of the Church of England were non-jurors, refusing to take the oath of allegiance; these clergy, who adhered to the doctrine of Divine Right, could not accept the replacement of one monarch by others in merely secular fashion (p. 268). In 1689 James landed in Ireland with a French army to try to regain the throne, but he was defeated at the Battle of the Boyne on 1 July 1690 (p. 68). The so-called Toleration Act (1689) gave certain concessions to Nonconformists but not to Catholics; Lady Castlewood's misgivings (p. 51) therefore had some justification. Conspiracies against the Protestant monarchy included the one led by the Jacobite, Sir John Fenwick (pp. 60, 120, 121, 194, 393). Queen Mary died in 1694, and William in 1702 (p. 188). By the Act of Settlement (1701), the crown passed to Anne, Mary's sister; subsequently, if Anne had no direct heirs of her own, it was to go to the Electress-Dowager Sophia of Hanover, a granddaughter of James I.

When Anne succeeded to the throne (p. 191), the War of the Spanish Succession had begun, which had the fundamental aim of curbing the power of Louis XIV in Europe. The Duke of Marlborough and Prince Eugene were the principal commanders of the Grand Alliance (eventually comprising Britain, Austria, Prussia, Denmark, Holland, Portugal, and Savoy) against France, Bavaria, and Spain. Marlborough's great victories were at Blenheim (1704), Ramillies (1706), Oudenarde (1708), and Malplaquet

(1709). These and other campaigns and battles (notably Vigo Bay and Wynendael) feature in Book II of *Henry Esmond*.

At home, Anne at first appointed Tory ministers, including Godolphin, the Lord Treasurer (p. 258), but after a time the administration became almost wholly Whig. It was the Whigs who instigated the impeachment of Sacheverell (p. 322) for his sermons attacking them and the principle of toleration; they thereby incurred widespread unpopularity. In the summer of 1710 Anne broke with her favourite, Sarah, Duchess of Marlborough, who had been replaced in her affections by Mrs Masham (p. 279). At the same time, she dismissed the Whigs from office. Instead, the Tories, Harley and St John, became her principal ministers. St John was in communication with Torcy, Louis XIV's foreign minister (p. 323), in attempts to end the war, whereas the Whigs were trying to prevent the peace. On 31 December 1711 Anne created twelve Tory peers to make certain that the moves for peace met parliamentary approval. On the same day, Marlborough was dismissed from his command; he withdrew to the Continent in November 1712 and returned to England on the accession of George I (p. 422). Hostilities were concluded by the Treaty of Utrecht (11 April 1713).

Since all Queen Anne's children had predeceased her and she was by this time in a precarious state of health, the question of the succession had become urgent. The Whigs, with their Protestant, anti-Jacobite views, kept in close contact with the Electress Sophia of Hanover and Prince George, her son. On the other hand, 'a very great body of Tory clergy, nobility, and gentry, were public partisans of the exiled prince', James Edward (p. 423). St John (who had been created Viscount Bolingbroke in 1712) and Harley (created Earl of Oxford in 1711) were now involved in bitter quarrels over questions of political leadership and influence. With the support of the Tories, Bolingbroke persuaded the Queen to dismiss Oxford a few days before her death. Bolingbroke, apparently sympathetic towards the Jacobites, seems to have been undecided whether to support the Stuart or the Hanoverian cause (pp. 423, 445–6). But the last-minute intervention of two Whig dukes, Argyll and Somerset, and Anne's appointment of the Duke of Shrewsbury as Lord Treasurer (p. 447) were decisive in ensuring the Protestant, Hanoverian succession, the establishment of the Whigs in power, and the downfall of Bolingbroke. George I was proclaimed King on 1 August 1714 (p. 461); his mother, the Electress, had died on 8 June 1714.

James Edward (1688–1766), the Old Pretender, was brought up in the exiled court at St Germains. Louis XIV recognized him as King James III on the death of James II in 1701 (p. 193). He fought with the French army at Oudenarde and Malplaquet (and see p. 324). Under the Treaty of Utrecht, Louis XIV was forbidden to let him remain in France; he therefore moved to Bar-le-Duc in the independent state of Lorraine (p. 400). In 1715 there was an uprising in Scotland in support of his claim to the throne, but this had already virtually failed by the time that he landed in Scotland in December. After about a month, he sailed to France, and eventually settled for the rest of his life in Italy. He married Maria Clementina Sobieski in 1719.

The opposition between Whigs and Tories during Queen Anne's reign was, broadly speaking, an opposition between the Low and High Church. Apart from political implications, much devotional and controversial writing on religious matters was published, such as the works of Taylor, Baxter, Law, and Tillotson (pp. 100, 141). Some of this (for example, the work of Charles Leslie, p. 403) was issued in refutation of Deist arguments. Addison, Steele, and Swift each played a part in the complex political controversies of the period. On the whole, Addison and Steele supported the Whigs in some of their writings whereas Swift, a friend of St John and Harley, supported the Tories.

NOTE ON THE TEXT

Henry Esmond was published by Smith, Elder and Co. in 3 volumes in 1852, and was reissued with minor revisions in 1853. Tauchnitz (Leipzig) and Harper (New York) editions dated 1852 were also set from the first edition with varying degrees of normalization. A one-volume cheap edition was published in 1858, with further alterations and the omission of a passage from Book II, Chapter XV. The text used in this World's Classics edition is a reproduction of George Saintsbury's *Oxford Thackeray* edition (1908), with a few minor amendments. In the *Oxford Thackeray* edition, the emendations of 1858 were followed 'in practically every case', but the omitted passage and a few errors were noted in an Appendix (p. 464). A few page-headings were changed and there was some modernization of spelling, hyphenation, and the use of capital and lower-case letters. Philip Gaskell's *From Writer to Reader* (Oxford, 1978) contains a chapter on the text of *Henry Esmond*. For a thorough re-editing of the text, based on the manuscript, see Edgar F. Harden's edition (New York, 1989), which contains a textual introduction and an authoritative record of composition and revision.

SELECT BIBLIOGRAPHY

FOR bibliographies of Thackeray's work, see Lewis Melville, *William Makepeace Thackeray* (London, 1910), ii. 143–376; *A Thackeray Library*, collected by Henry Sayre Van Duzer (New York, 1919; reissued with an introduction by Lionel Stevenson, 1965); and the *Cambridge Bibliography of English Literature*, ed. George Watson, iii. (1969), 855–64 (compiled by Lionel Stevenson).

The principal collected editions of Thackeray's works are the *Biographical Edition*, with biographical introductions by Anne Ritchie, Thackeray's daughter (13 vols., London, 1898–9); the *Works of William Makepeace Thackeray*, reprinted from the first editions and edited (from 1903) by Lewis Melville (20 vols., London, 1901–07); the *Oxford Thackeray*, edited with introductions by George Saintsbury (17 vols., London, 1908); the *Centenary Biographical Edition*, a revised and expanded reissue of the *Biographical Edition* (26 vols., London 1910–11), and the *Harry Furniss Centenary Edition* (20 vols., London, 1911). The *Thackeray Edition Project*, under the general editorship of Peter L. Shillingsburg, has begun with the publication of *Henry Esmond*, ed. Edgar F. Harden, and *Vanity Fair*, ed. Peter L. Shillingsburg, with commentary by Nicholas Pickwood and Robert Colby (both New York, 1989).

Editions of *Henry Esmond* include those by the following editors: Austin Dobson, with illustrations by Hugh Thomson (London, 1905); T. C. and William Snow, with George Saintsbury's introduction from the *Oxford Thackeray* (Oxford, 1909; new edn., 1915); G. Robert Stange, who includes 'A Note on the Composition and Text of the Novel' (New York, 1962); John Sutherland and Michael Greenfield (Harmondsworth, 1970); Gilbert Phelps (London, 1974); and Edgar F. Harden (New York, 1989).

Gordon N. Ray's books are indispensable for biographical information: *The Letters and Private Papers of William Makepeace Thackeray*, 4 vols. (Harvard, 1945–6); *The Buried Life: A Study of the Relation between Thackeray's Fiction and his Personal History* (Oxford,

1952); *Thackeray: The Uses of Adversity* and *Thackeray: The Age of Wisdom* (London, 1955, 1958). Philip Collins's collection, *Thackeray: Interviews and Recollections*, 2 vols. (London, 1983), contains numerous first-hand accounts. Two books that give psychological insights into Thackeray's life and work are Ann Monsarrat's *An Uneasy Victorian: Thackeray the Man* (London, 1980) and Catherine Peters's *Thackeray's Universe: Shifting Worlds of Imagination and Reality* (London, 1987). Robert A. Colby's *Thackeray's Canvass of Humanity: An Author and his Public* (Columbus, Ohio, 1979) places the novelist's work in its social and literary context.

K. C. Phillipps's *The Language of Thackeray* (London, 1978) includes a carefully analytical chapter on the prose of *Henry Esmond*.

The following works of comment and criticism represent a variety of approaches, ranging from those taken by Thackeray's contemporaries (in the *Critical Heritage* volume) to those of the late twentieth century: George Saintsbury, *A Consideration of Thackeray* (London, 1931); J. Y. T. Greig, *Thackeray: A Reconsideration* (London, 1950); Geoffrey Tillotson, *Thackeray the Novelist* (Cambridge, 1954; new edn., London, 1963); Geoffrey Tillotson and Donald Hawes, eds., *Thackeray: The Critical Heritage* (London, 1968); J. A. Sutherland, *Thackeray at Work* (London, 1974); John Carey, *Thackeray: Prodigal Genius* (London, 1977); Michael Lund, *Reading Thackeray* (Detroit, 1988).

A selection of modern critical essays can be found in *William Makepeace Thackeray*, edited and introduced by Harold Bloom (Modern Critical Views series, New York; 1987). On *Henry Esmond* itself, influential articles include the following: John E. Tilford, jun., 'The Love Theme of *Henry Esmond*' (*PMLA* 67 (Sept. 1952), 684–701); George J. Worth, 'The Unity of *Henry Esmond*' (*Nineteenth-Century Fiction*, 15 (Mar. 1961), 345–53); Elaine Scarry, '*Henry Esmond*: The Rookery at Castlewood' (*Literary Monographs*), (1975), 1–47.

The relationship of *Henry Esmond* to one particular genre is explored in Georg Lukács, *The Historical Novel* (1962; Harmondsworth, 1969) and Andrew Sanders, *The Victorian Historical Novel 1840–1880* (Basingstoke and London, 1978).

A CHRONOLOGY OF
WILLIAM MAKEPEACE THACKERAY

(June–October). Publishes *The Paris Sketch Book* (July). His wife's insanity revealed after an attempt to drown herself *en route* from London to Cork (September)

1841   *The Second Funeral of Napoleon* (January). Wife entrusted to a private nurse. Visits John Bowes in Co. Durham and conceives first notion for *Barry Lyndon* (June–July). *The Great Hoggarty Diamond* published in *Fraser's* (September–December)

1842   Wife placed in asylum at Chaillot near Paris. Moves to 13 Great Coram Street. First contribution to *Punch* (June). Visits Ireland (July–November)

1843   Publication of *The Irish Sketch Book* (May). Takes rooms at 27 Jermyn Street

1844   First instalment of *The Luck of Barry Lyndon* in *Fraser's Magazine* (January). Leaves Southampton for Mediterranean and Near Eastern Tour (22 August). Final instalment of *Barry Lyndon* (December)

1845   Returns to London from Rome (February). Moves to 88 St. James's Street. Wife placed in care at Camberwell

1846   *Notes of a Journey from Cornhill to Grand Cairo* published (January). First instalment of *The Book of Snobs* in *Punch* (March). Moves to 13 Young Street, Kensington (June). Publishes first Christmas Book, *Mrs. Perkins's Ball* (December)

1847   First number of *Vanity Fair* (January). Final instalment of *The Book of Snobs* (February). *Our Street* (December)

1848   *Vanity Fair* completed (June). Travels on Continent (July–August). Begins *Pendennis* (3 August) the first number of which appears in November. *Dr. Birch and his Young Friends* (December)

1849   Visits Paris (January–February, August–September). Serious illness disrupts publication of *Pendennis* (October–December). *Rebecca and Rowena* (December)

1850   *Pendennis* completed (November). *The Kickleburys on the Rhine* (December)

1851   Lectures on *The English Humourists* in London (May–July).
Begins *Esmond* (August). Resigns from *Punch* (December)

1852   Completes *Esmond* (May). *The History of Henry Esmond*
published in 3 vols (October). Leaves Liverpool for
Boston (October). Lectures in New York (November–
December)

1853   Lectures in eastern United States on *English Humourists*
(January–April). Returns to London and visits Paris
(May–July). Visits Germany and Switzerland (July–
August). Begins *The Newcomes* (9 July). First number of
The Newcomes published (October). Travels to Rome
(November)

1854   Ill at Rome (January–February). Begins *The Rose and the
Ring* (February). Moves to 36 Onslow Square, Brompton.
The Rose and the Ring published (December)

1855   *The Newcomes* finished (June, last monthly number
August). Sails from Liverpool to Boston (October).
Lectures in United States on *The Four Georges*

1856   Lectures in United States (January–April). Arrives in
London (May). Begins *The Virginians* which he shortly
abandons (July). Visits Paris. Lectures in Scotland and
north of England (November–December)

1857   Lectures in England and Scotland (January–May).
Stands unsuccessfully as Independent Liberal in parliamentary election for the City of Oxford (July). First
number of *The Virginians* (November)

1858   The 'Garrick Club Affair' provoked by an article by
Edmund Yates. Alienation from Dickens (June–July)

1859   Accepts editorship of the *Cornhill Magazine*. Last number
of *The Virginians* (October)

1860   First number of the *Cornhill Magazine* (January) containing the first of the *Roundabout Papers* and the first
instalment of *Lovel the Widower*. *The Four Georges* published
in the *Cornhill* (July–October)

1861   First instalment of *Philip* in the *Cornhill* (January)

THE HISTORY OF
HENRY ESMOND, ESQ.

A COLONEL IN THE SERVICE OF HER MAJESTY QUEEN ANNE

WRITTEN BY HIMSELF

Servetur ad imum
Qualis ab incepto processerit, et sibi constet*

THE HISTORY OF HENRY ESMOND

CONTENTS

BOOK I

**THE EARLY YOUTH OF HENRY ESMOND, UP TO THE TIME OF HIS
LEAVING TRINITY COLLEGE, IN CAMBRIDGE**

CONTENTS

BOOK II

CONTAINS MR. ESMOND'S MILITARY LIFE, AND OTHER MATTERS
APPERTAINING TO THE ESMOND FAMILY

BOOK III

CONTAINING THE END OF MR. ESMOND'S ADVENTURES IN ENGLAND

PREFACE

THE ESMONDS OF VIRGINIA

THE estate of Castlewood, in Virginia, which was given to our ancestors by King Charles the First, as some return for the sacrifices made in his Majesty's cause by the Esmond family, lies in Westmoreland county, between the rivers Potomac and Rappahannoc, and was once as great as an English Principality, though in the early times its revenues were but small. Indeed, for near eighty years after our forefathers possessed them, our plantations were in the hands of factors, who enriched themselves one after another, though a few scores of hogsheads of tobacco were all the produce that, for long after the Restoration, our family received from their Virginian estates.

My dear and honoured father, Colonel Henry Esmond, whose history, written by himself, is contained in the accompanying volume, came to Virginia in the year 1718, built his house of Castlewood, and here permanently settled. After a long stormy life in England, he passed the remainder of his many years in peace and honour in this country; how beloved and respected by all his fellow citizens, how inexpressibly dear to his family, I need not say. His whole life was a benefit to all who were connected with him. He gave the best example, the best advice, the most bounteous hospitality to his friends; the tenderest care to his dependants; and bestowed on those of his immediate family such a blessing of fatherly love and protection, as can never be thought of, by us at least, without veneration and thankfulness; and my son's children, whether established here in our Republick, or at home in the always beloved mother country, from which our late quarrel hath separated us, may surely be proud to be descended from one who in all ways was so truly noble.

My dear mother died in 1736, soon after our return from England, whither my parents took me for my education;

and where I made the acquaintance of Mr. Warrington, whom my children never saw. When it pleased Heaven, in the bloom of his youth, and after but a few months of a most happy union, to remove him from me, I owed my recovery from the grief which that calamity caused me, mainly to my dearest father's tenderness, and then to the blessing vouchsafed to me in the birth of my two beloved boys. I know the fatal differences which separated them in politics never disunited their hearts ; and as I can love them both, whether wearing the king's colours or the Republick's, I am sure that they love me, and one another, and him above all, my father and theirs, the dearest friend of their childhood, the noble gentleman who bred them from their infancy in the practice and knowledge of Truth, and Love, and Honour.

My children will never forget the appearance and figure of their revered grandfather ; and I wish I possessed the art of drawing (which my papa had in perfection), so that I could leave to our descendants a portrait of one who was so good and so respected. My father was of a dark complexion, with a very great forehead and dark hazel eyes, overhung by eyebrows which remained black long after his hair was white. His nose was aquiline, his smile extraordinary sweet. How well I remember it, and how little any description I can write can recall his image ! He was of rather low stature, not being above five feet seven inches in height ; he used to laugh at my sons, whom he called his crutches, and say they were grown too tall for him to lean upon. But small as he was he had a perfect grace and majesty of deportment, such as I have never seen in this country, except perhaps in our friend Mr. Washington, and commanded respect wherever he appeared.

In all bodily exercises he excelled, and showed an extraordinary quickness and agility. Of fencing he was especially fond, and made my two boys proficient in that art ; so much so, that when the French came to this country with Monsieur Rochambeau,* not one of his officers was superior to my Henry, and he was not the equal of my poor George, who had taken the king's side in our lamentable but glorious War of Independence.

Neither my father nor my mother ever wore powder in their hair ; both their heads were as white as silver, as I can remember them. My dear mother possessed to the

last an extraordinary brightness and freshness of complexion ;
nor would people believe that she did not wear rouge. At
sixty years of age she still looked young, and was quite
agile. It was not until after that dreadful siege of our
house by the Indians, which left me a widow ere I was
a mother, that my dear mother's health broke. She never
recovered her terror and anxiety of those days, which ended
so fatally for me, then a bride scarce six months married,
and died in my father's arms ere my own year of widow-
hood was over.

From that day, until the last of his dear and honoured
life, it was my delight and consolation to remain with him
as his comforter and companion ; and from those little
notes which my mother hath made here and there in the
volume in which my father describes his adventures in
Europe, I can well understand the extreme devotion with
which she regarded him—a devotion so passionate and
exclusive as to prevent her, I think, from loving any other
person except with an inferior regard ; her whole thoughts
being centred on this one object of affection and worship.
I know that, before her, my dear father did not show the
love which he had for his daughter ; and in her last and
most sacred moments, this dear and tender parent owned
to me her repentance that she had not loved me enough :
her jealousy even that my father should give his affection
to any but herself ; and in the most fond and beautiful
words of affection and admonition, she bade me never to
leave him, and to supply the place which she was quitting.
With a clear conscience, and a heart inexpressibly thankful,
I think I can say that I fulfilled those dying commands, and
that until his last hour my dearest father never had to
complain that his daughter's love and fidelity failed him.

And it is since I knew him entirely, for during my mother's
life he never quite opened himself to me—since I knew the
value and splendour of that affection which he bestowed
upon me, that I have come to understand and pardon what,
I own, used to anger me in my mother's lifetime, her jealousy
respecting her husband's love. 'Twas a gift so precious,
that no wonder she who had it was for keeping it all, and
could part with none of it, even to her daughter.

Though I never heard my father use a rough word, 'twas
extraordinary with how much awe his people regarded him ;
and the servants on our plantation, both those assigned

from England and the purchased negroes, obeyed him with
an eagerness such as the most severe taskmasters round
about us could never get from their people. He was never
familiar, though perfectly simple and natural ; he was the
same with the meanest man as with the greatest, and as
courteous to a black slave-girl as to the governor's wife.
No one ever thought of taking a liberty with him (except
once a tipsy gentleman from York, and I am bound to own
that my papa never forgave him) : he set the humblest
people at once on their ease with him, and brought down
the most arrogant by a grave satiric way, which made
persons exceedingly afraid of him. His courtesy was not
put on like a Sunday suit, and laid by when the company
went away ; it was always the same ; as he was always
dressed the same whether for a dinner by ourselves or for
a great entertainment. They say he liked to be the first
in his company ; but what company was there in which
he would not be first ? When I went to Europe for my
education, and we passed a winter at London with my half-
brother, my Lord Castlewood and his second lady, I saw at
her Majesty's Court some of the most famous gentlemen of
those days ; and I thought to myself, ' None of these are
better than my papa'; and the famous Lord Bolingbroke,
who came to us from Dawley,* said as much, and that the
men of that time were not like those of his youth :—' Were
your father, madam,' he said, ' to go into the woods, the
Indians would elect him Sachem ; '* and his lordship was
pleased to call me Pocahontas.*

I did not see our other relative, Bishop Tusher's lady,
of whom so much is said in my papa's memoirs—although
my mamma went to visit her in the country. I have no
pride (as I showed by complying with my mother's request,
and marrying a gentleman who was but the younger son
of a Suffolk baronet), yet I own to *a decent respect* for my
name, and wonder how one, who ever bore it, should change
it for that of Mrs. *Thomas Tusher*. I pass over as odious
and unworthy of credit those reports (which I heard in
Europe, and was then too young to understand), how this
person, having *left her family* and fled to Paris, out of
jealousy of the Pretender, betrayed his secrets to my Lord
Stair,* King George's ambassador, and nearly caused the
prince's death there ; how she came to England and married
this Mr. Tusher, and became a great favourite of King

George the Second, by whom Mr. Tusher was made a dean, and then a bishop. I did not see the lady, who chose to remain *at her palace* all the time we were in London; but after visiting her, my poor mamma said she had lost all her good looks, and warned me not to set too much store by any such gifts which nature had bestowed upon me. She grew exceedingly stout; and I remember my brother's wife, Lady Castlewood, saying—'No wonder she became a favourite, for the king likes them old and ugly, as his father did before him.' On which papa said—'All women were alike; that there was never one so beautiful as that one; and that we could forgive her everything but her beauty.' And hereupon my mamma looked vexed, and my Lord Castlewood began to laugh; and I, of course, being a young creature, could not understand what was the subject of their conversation.

After the circumstances narrated in the third book of these memoirs, my father and mother both went abroad, being advised by their friends to leave the country in consequence of the transactions which are recounted at the close of the volume of the memoirs. But my brother, hearing how the *future bishop's lady* had quitted Castlewood and joined the Pretender at Paris, pursued him, and would have killed him, prince as he was, had not the prince managed to make his escape. On his expedition to Scotland directly after, Castlewood was so enraged against him that he asked leave to serve as a volunteer, and join the Duke of Argyle's army in Scotland, which the Pretender never had the courage to face; and thenceforth my lord was quite reconciled to the present reigning family, from whom he hath even received promotion.

Mrs. Tusher was by this time as angry against the Pretender as any of her relations could be, and used to boast, as I have heard, that she not only brought back my lord to the Church of England, but procured the English peerage for him, which the *junior branch* of our family at present enjoys. She was a great friend of Sir Robert Walpole, and would not rest until her husband slept at Lambeth, my papa used laughing to say. However, the bishop died of apoplexy suddenly, and his wife erected a great monument over him; and the pair sleep under that stone, with a canopy of marble clouds and angels above them—the first Mrs. Tusher lying sixty miles off at Castlewood.

But my papa's genius and education are both greater than any a woman can be expected to have, and his adventures in Europe far more exciting than his life in this country, which was past in the tranquil offices of love and duty; and I shall say no more by way of introduction to his memoirs, nor keep my children from the perusal of a story which is much more interesting than that of their affectionate old mother,

RACHEL ESMOND WARRINGTON.

CASTLEWOOD, VIRGINIA,
November 3, 1778.

THE
HISTORY OF HENRY ESMOND

※

BOOK I

THE EARLY YOUTH OF HENRY ESMOND, UP TO THE TIME OF HIS
LEAVING TRINITY COLLEGE, IN CAMBRIDGE

THE actors in the old tragedies, as we read, piped their
iambics to a tune, speaking from under a mask, and wearing
stilts and a great head-dress. 'Twas thought the dignity
of the Tragic Muse required these appurtenances, and that
she was not to move except to a measure and cadence. So
Queen Medea slew her children to a slow music : and King
Agamemnon perished in a dying fall (to use Mr. Dryden's
words) :* the Chorus standing by in a set attitude, and
rhythmically and decorously bewailing the fates of those
great crowned persons. The Muse of History hath encumbered herself with ceremony as well as her Sister of the
Theatre. She too wears the mask and the cothurnus, and
speaks to measure. She too, in our age, busies herself with
the affairs only of kings ; waiting on them obsequiously
and stately, as if she were but a mistress of Court ceremonies,
and had nothing to do with the registering of the affairs of
the common people. I have seen in his very old age and
decrepitude the old French King Lewis the Fourteenth, the
type and model of kinghood—who never moved but to
measure, who lived and died according to the laws of his
Court-marshal, persisting in enacting through life the part
of Hero ; and, divested of poetry, this was but a little
wrinkled old man, pock-marked, and with a great periwig
and red heels to make him look tall—a hero for a book if
you like, or for a brass statue or a painted ceiling, a god

in a Roman shape, but what more than a man for Madame
Maintenon, or the barber who shaved him, or Monsieur
Fagon, his surgeon ? I wonder shall History ever pull off
her periwig and cease to be court-ridden ? Shall we see
something of France and England besides Versailles and
Windsor ? I saw Queen Anne at the latter place tearing
down the Park slopes after her staghounds, and driving
her one-horse chaise—a hot, red-faced woman, not in the
least resembling that statue of her which turns its stone
back upon St. Paul's, and faces the coaches struggling
up Ludgate Hill. She was neither better bred nor wiser
than you and me, though we knelt to hand her a letter
or a washhand-basin. Why shall History go on kneeling
to the end of time ? I am for having her rise up off her
knees, and take a natural posture : not to be for ever
performing cringes and congees like a Court-chamberlain,
and shuffling backwards out of doors in the presence of
the sovereign. In a word, I would have History familiar
rather than heroic : and think that Mr. Hogarth and Mr.
Fielding will give our children a much better idea of the
manners of the present age in England, than the *Court
Gazette* and the newspapers which we get thence.

There was a German officer of Webb's, with whom we
used to joke, and of whom a story (whereof I myself was
the author) was got to be believed in the army, that he was
eldest son of the Hereditary Grand Bootjack of the Empire,
and heir to that honour of which his ancestors had been
very proud, having been kicked for twenty generations by
one imperial foot, as they drew the boot from the other.
I have heard that the old Lord Castlewood, of part of whose
family these present volumes are a chronicle, though he
came of quite as good blood as the Stuarts whom he served
(and who as regards mere lineage are no better than a dozen
English and Scottish houses I could name), was prouder
of his post about the Court than of his ancestral honours
and valued his dignity (as Lord of the Butteries and Groom
of the King's Posset) so highly, that he cheerfully ruined
himself for the thankless and thriftless race who bestowed
it. He pawned his plate for King Charles the First, mort-
gaged his property for the same cause, and lost the greater
part of it by fines and sequestration : stood a siege of his
castle by Ireton, where his brother Thomas capitulated
(afterwards making terms with the Commonwealth, for

which the elder brother never forgave him), and where his second brother Edward, who had embraced the ecclesiastical profession, was slain on Castlewood tower, being engaged there both as preacher and artilleryman. This resolute old loyalist, who was with the king whilst his house was thus being battered down, escaped abroad with his only son, then a boy, to return and take a part in Worcester fight. On that fatal field Eustace Esmond was killed, and Castlewood fled from it once more into exile, and henceforward, and after the Restoration, never was away from the Court of the monarch (for whose return we offer thanks in the Prayer-book) who sold his country and who took bribes of the French king.

What spectacle is more august than that of a great king in exile ? Who is more worthy of respect than a brave man in misfortune ? Mr. Addison has painted such a figure in his noble piece of *Cato*.* But suppose fugitive Cato fuddling himself at a tavern with a wench on each knee, a dozen faithful and tipsy companions of defeat, and a landlord calling out for his bill ; and the dignity of misfortune is straightway lost. The Historical Muse turns away shamefaced from the vulgar scene, and closes the door— on which the exile's unpaid drink is scored up—upon him and his pots and his pipes, and the tavern-chorus which he and his friends are singing. Such a man as Charles should have had an Ostade or Mieris* to paint him. Your Knellers and Le Bruns* only deal in clumsy and impossible allegories : and it hath always seemed to me blasphemy to claim Olympus for such a wine-drabbled divinity as that.

About the king's follower the Viscount Castlewood— orphan of his son, ruined by his fidelity, bearing many wounds and marks of bravery, old and in exile, his kinsmen I suppose should be silent ; nor if this patriarch fell down in his cups, call fie upon him, and fetch passers-by to laugh at his red face and white hairs. What ! does a stream rush out of a mountain free and pure, to roll through fair pastures, to feed and throw out bright tributaries, and to end in a village gutter ? Lives that have noble commencements have often no better endings ; it is not without a kind of awe and reverence that an observer should speculate upon such careers as he traces the course of them. I have seen too much of success in life to take off my hat and huzza to it as it passes in its gilt coach : and would do my little part with my neighbours on foot, that they should not gape with too much wonder, nor applaud too loudly. Is it the Lord Mayor going in state to mince-pies and the Mansion House ? Is it poor Jack of Newgate's procession, with the sheriff and javelin-men, conducting him on his last journey to Tyburn ?* I look into my heart and think that I am as good as my Lord Mayor, and know I am as bad as Tyburn Jack. Give me a chain and red gown and a pudding before me, and I could play the part of alderman very well, and sentence Jack after dinner. Starve me, keep me from books and honest people, educate me to love dice, gin, and pleasure, and put me on Hounslow Heath, with a purse before me and I will take it. 'And I shall be deservedly hanged,' say you, wishing to put an end to this prosing. I don't say no. I can't but accept the world as I find it, including a rope's end, as long as it is in fashion.

CHAPTER I

AN ACCOUNT OF THE FAMILY OF ESMOND OF CASTLEWOOD HALL*

WHEN Francis, fourth Viscount Castlewood, came to his title, and presently after to take possession of his house of Castlewood, county Hants, in the year 1691, almost the only tenant of the place besides the domestics was a lad of twelve years of age, of whom no one seemed to take any note until my lady viscountess lighted upon him, going over the house, with the housekeeper on the day of her arrival. The boy was in the room known as the book-room, or yellow gallery, where the portraits of the family used to hang, that fine piece among others of Sir Antonio Van Dyck of George, second viscount, and that by Mr. Dobson* of my lord the third viscount, just deceased, which it seems his lady and widow did not think fit to carry away, when she sent for and carried off to her house at Chelsey, near to London, the picture of herself by Sir Peter Lely, in which her ladyship was represented as a huntress of Diana's court.

The new and fair lady of Castlewood found the sad lonely little occupant of this gallery busy over his great book, which he laid down when he was aware that a stranger was at hand. And, knowing who that person must be, the lad stood up and bowed before her, performing a shy obeisance to the mistress of his house.

She stretched out her hand—indeed when was it that that hand would not stretch out to do an act of kindness, or to protect grief and ill-fortune ? ' And this is our kinsman,' she said ; ' and what is your name, kinsman ? '

' My name is Henry Esmond,' said the lad, looking up at her in a sort of delight and wonder, for she had come upon him as a *Dea certè*,[*] and appeared the most charming object he had ever looked on. Her golden hair was shining in the gold of the sun ; her complexion was of a dazzling bloom ; her lips smiling, and her eyes beaming with a kindness which made Harry Esmond's heart to beat with surprise.

' His name is Henry Esmond, sure enough, my lady,' says Mrs. Worksop the housekeeper (an old tyrant whom Henry Esmond plagued more than he hated), and the old gentlewoman looked significantly towards the late lord's picture, as it now is in the family, noble and severe-looking, with his hand on his sword, and his order on his cloak, which he had from the emperor during the war on the Danube against the Turk.

Seeing the great and undeniable likeness between this portrait and the lad, the new viscountess, who had still hold of the boy's hand as she looked at the picture, blushed and dropped the hand quickly, and walked down the gallery, followed by Mrs. Worksop.

When the lady came back, Harry Esmond stood exactly in the same spot, and with his hand as it had fallen when he dropped it on his black coat.

Her heart melted I suppose (indeed she hath since owned as much) at the notion that she should do anything unkind to any mortal, great or small ; for, when she returned, she had sent away the housekeeper upon an errand by the door at the farther end of the gallery ; and, coming back to the lad, with a look of infinite pity and tenderness in her eyes, she took his hand again, placing her other fair hand on his head, and saying some words to him, which were so kind and said in a voice so sweet, that the boy, who had never looked upon so much beauty before, felt as if the touch of a superior being or angel smote him down to the ground, and kissed the fair protecting hand as he knelt on one knee. To the very last hour of his life, Esmond remembered the lady as she then spoke and looked, the rings on her fair hands, the very scent of her robe, the beam of her eyes lighting up with surprise and kindness, her lips blooming in a smile, the sun making a golden halo round her hair.

As the boy was yet in this attitude of humility, enters behind him a portly gentleman, with a little girl of four years old in his hand. The gentleman burst into a great laugh at the lady and her adorer, with his little queer figure, his sallow face, and long black hair. The lady blushed, and seemed to deprecate his ridicule by a look of appeal to her husband, for it was my lord viscount who now arrived, and whom the lad knew, having once before seen him in the late lord's lifetime.

' So this is the little priest ! ' says my lord, looking down at the lad ; ' welcome, kinsman.'

' He is saying his prayers to mamma,' says the little girl, who came up to her papa's knee ; and my lord burst out into another great laugh at this, and kinsman Henry looked very silly. He invented a half-dozen of speeches in reply, but 'twas months afterwards when he thought of this adventure : as it was, he had never a word in answer.

' *Le pauvre enfant, il n'a que nous*,' says the lady, looking to her lord ; and the boy, who understood her, though doubtless she thought otherwise, thanked her with all his heart for her kind speech.

' And he shan't want for friends here,' says my lord, in a kind voice, ' shall he, little Trix ? '

The little girl, whose name was Beatrix, and whom her papa called by this diminutive, looked at Henry Esmond solemnly, with a pair of large eyes, and then a smile shone over her face, which was as beautiful as that of a cherub, and she came up and put out a little hand to him. A keen and delightful pang of gratitude, happiness, affection, filled the orphan child's heart, as he received from the protectors, whom Heaven had sent to him, these touching words, and tokens of friendliness and kindness. But an hour since he had felt quite alone in the world : when he heard the great peal of bells from Castlewood church ringing that morning to welcome the arrival of the new lord and lady, it had rung only terror and anxiety to him, for he knew not how the new owner would deal with him ; and those to whom he formerly looked for protection were forgotten or dead. Pride and doubt too had kept him within doors : when the vicar and the people of the village, and the servants of the house, had gone out to welcome my Lord Castlewood—for Henry Esmond was no servant, though a dependant ; no relative, though he bore the name and inherited the blood of the house ; and in the midst of the noise and acclamations attending the arrival of the new lord (for whom you may be sure a feast was got ready, and guns were fired, and tenants and domestics huzzaed when his carriage approached and rolled into the courtyard of the hall), no one ever took any notice of young Henry Esmond, who sat unobserved and alone in the book-room, until the afternoon of that day, when his new friends found him.

When my lord and lady were going away thence, the little girl, still holding her kinsman by the hand, bade him to come too. 'Thou wilt always forsake an old friend for a new one, Trix,' says her father to her good-naturedly ; and went into the gallery, giving an arm to his lady. They passed thence through the music-gallery, long since dismantled, and Queen Elizabeth's rooms, in the clock-tower, and out into the terrace, where was a fine prospect of sunset, and the great darkling woods with a cloud of rooks returning ; and the plain and river with Castlewood village beyond, and purple hills beautiful to look at—and the little heir of Castlewood, a child of two years old, was already here on the terrace in his nurse's arms, from whom he ran across the grass instantly he perceived his mother, and came to her.

'If thou canst not be happy here,' says my lord, looking round at the scene, ' thou art hard to please, Rachel.'

'I am happy where you are,' she said, ' but we were happiest of all at Walcote Forest.' Then my lord began to describe what was before them to his wife, and what indeed little Harry knew better than he—viz., the history of the house : how by yonder gate the page ran away with the heiress of Castlewood, by which the estate came into the present family, how the Roundheads attacked the clocktower, which my lord's father was slain in defending. 'I was but two years old then,' says he, ' but take forty-six from ninety, and how old shall I be, kinsman Harry ? '

'Thirty,' says his wife, with a laugh.

'A great deal too old for you, Rachel,' answers my lord, looking fondly down at her. Indeed she seemed to be a girl ; and was at that time scarce twenty years old.

'You know, Frank, I will do anything to please you,' says she, 'and I promise you I will grow older every day.'

'You mustn't call papa Frank; you must call papa my lord, now,' says Miss Beatrix, with a toss of her little head; at which the mother smiled, and the good-natured father laughed, and the little, trotting boy laughed, not knowing why—but because he was happy no doubt—as every one seemed to be there. How those trivial incidents and words, the landscape and sunshine, and the group of people smiling and talking, remain fixed on the memory!

As the sun was setting, the little heir was sent in the arms of his nurse to bed, whither he went howling; but little Trix was promised to sit to supper that night—' and you will come too, kinsman, won't you?' she said.

Harry Esmond blushed: 'I—I have supper with Mrs. Worksop,' says he.

'D—n it,' says my lord, 'thou shalt sup with us, Harry, to-night! Shan't refuse a lady, shall he, Trix?'—and they all wondered at Harry's performance as a trencher-man, in which character the poor boy acquitted himself very remarkably; for the truth is he had no dinner, nobody thinking of him in the bustle which the house was in, during the preparations antecedent to the new lord's arrival.

'No dinner! poor dear child!' says my lady, heaping up his plate with meat, and my lord filling a bumper for him, bade him call a health; on which Master Harry, crying 'The King', tossed off the wine. My lord was ready to drink that, and most other toasts: indeed only too ready. He would not hear of Doctor Tusher (the Vicar of Castle-wood, who came to supper) going away when the sweet-meats were brought :* he had not had a chaplain long enough, he said, to be tired of him : so his reverence kept my lord company for some hours over a pipe and a punchbowl; and went away home with rather a reeling gait, and declaring a dozen of times, that his lordship's affability surpassed every kindness he had ever had from his lordship's gracious family.

As for young Esmond, when he got to his little chamber, it was with a heart full of surprise and gratitude towards the new friends whom this happy day had brought him. He was up and watching long before the house was astir, longing to see that fair lady and her children—that kind protector and patron; and only fearful lest their welcome

of the past night should in any way be withdrawn or altered.
But presently little Beatrix came out into the garden, and
her mother followed, who greeted Harry as kindly as before.
He told her at greater length the histories of the house
(which he had been taught in the old lord's time), and to
which she listened with great interest ; and then he told
her, with respect to the night before, that he understood
French, and thanked her for her protection.

'Do you ? ' says she, with a blush ; ' then, sir, you shall
teach me and Beatrix.' And she asked him many more
questions regarding himself, which had best be told more
fully and explicitly, than in those brief replies which the
lad made to his mistress's questions.

CHAPTER II

RELATES HOW FRANCIS, FOURTH VISCOUNT, ARRIVES AT CASTLEWOOD

'TIS known that the name of Esmond and the estate of
Castlewood, com. Hants, came into possession of the present
family through Dorothea, daughter and heiress of Edward,
Earl and Marquis of Esmond, and Lord of Castlewood,
which lady married, 23 Eliz., Henry Poyns, gent. ;   the
said Henry being then a page in the household of her father.
Francis, son and heir of the above Henry and Dorothea,
who took the maternal name which the family hath borne
subsequently, was made knight and baronet by King James
the First ;   and, being of a military disposition, remained
long in Germany with the Elector-Palatine, in whose service
Sir Francis incurred both expense and danger, lending large
sums of money to that unfortunate prince ;   and receiving
many wounds in the battles against the Imperialists, in
which Sir Francis engaged.

On his return home Sir Francis was rewarded for his
services and many sacrifices, by his late Majesty James the
First, who graciously conferred upon this tried servant
the post of Warden of the Butteries and Groom of the King's
Posset, which high and confidential office he filled in that
king's, and his unhappy successor's, reign.

His age, and many wounds and infirmities, obliged Sir
Francis to perform much of his duty by deputy ;   and his
son, Sir George Esmond, knight and banneret, first as his

father's lieutenant, and afterwards as inheritor of his father's title and dignity, performed this office during almost the whole of the reign of King Charles the First, and his two sons who succeeded him.

Sir George Esmond married rather beneath the rank that a person of his name and honour might aspire to, the daughter of Thos. Topham, of the city of London, alderman and goldsmith, who, taking the Parliamentary side in the troubles then commencing, disappointed Sir George of the property which he expected at the demise of his father-in-law, who devised his money to his second daughter, Barbara, a spinster.

Sir George Esmond, on his part, was conspicuous for his attachment and loyalty to the royal cause and person, and the king being at Oxford in 1642, Sir George, with the consent of his father, then very aged and infirm, and residing at his house of Castlewood, melted the whole of the family plate for his Majesty's service.

For this, and other sacrifices and merits, his Majesty, by patent under the Privy Seal, dated Oxford, Jan., 1643, was pleased to advance Sir Francis Esmond to the dignity of Viscount Castlewood, of Shandon, in Ireland : and the viscount's estate being much impoverished by loans to the king, which in those troublesome times his Majesty could not repay, a grant of land in the plantations of Virginia was given to the lord viscount ; part of which land is in possession of descendants of his family to the present day.

The first Viscount Castlewood died full of years, and within a few months after he had been advanced to his honours. He was succeeded by his eldest son, the before-named George ; and left issue besides, Thomas, a colonel in the king's army, that afterwards joined the Usurper's government ; and Francis, in holy orders, who was slain whilst defending the house of Castlewood against the Parliament, anno 1647.

George, Lord Castlewood (the second viscount) of King Charles the First's time, had no male issue save his one son Eustace Esmond, who was killed, with half of the Castlewood men beside him, at Worcester fight. The lands about Castlewood were sold and apportioned to the Commonwealth men ; Castlewood being concerned in almost all of the plots against the Protector, after the death of the king, and up to King Charles the Second's restoration. My lord followed that king's Court about in its exile, having ruined himself in its service. He had but one daughter, who was of no great comfort to her father ; for misfortune had not taught those exiles sobriety of life ; and it is said that the Duke of York and his brother the king both quarrelled about Isabel Esmond. She was maid of honour to the Queen Henrietta Maria; she early joined the Roman Church ; her father, a weak man, following her not long after at Breda.

On the death of Eustace Esmond at Worcester, Thomas Esmond, nephew to my Lord Castlewood, and then a stripling, became heir to the title. His father had taken the Parliament side in the quarrels, and so had been estranged from the chief of his house ; and my Lord Castlewood was at first so much enraged to think that his title (albeit little more than an empty one now) should pass to a rascally Roundhead, that he would have married again, and indeed proposed to do so to a vintner's daughter at Bruges, to whom his lordship owed a score for lodging when the king was there, but for fear of the laughter of the Court, and the anger of his daughter, of whom he stood in awe ; for she was in temper as imperious and violent as my lord, who was much enfeebled by wounds and drinking, was weak.

Lord Castlewood would have had a match between his daughter Isabel and her cousin, the son of that Francis Esmond who was killed at Castlewood siege. And the lady, it was said, took a fancy to the young man, who was her junior by several years (which circumstance she did not consider to be a fault in him) ; but having paid his court, and being admitted to the intimacy of the house, he suddenly flung up his suit, when it seemed to be pretty prosperous, without giving a pretext for his behaviour. His friends rallied him at what they laughingly chose to call his infidelity. Jack Churchill,* Frank Esmond's lieutenant in the royal regiment of foot guards, getting the company which Esmond vacated, when he left the Court and went to Tangier in a rage at discovering that his promotion depended on the complaisance of his elderly affianced bride. He and Churchill, who had been *condiscipuli* at St. Paul's School, had words about this matter ; and Frank Esmond said to him with an oath, ' Jack, your sister*may be so-and-so, but by Jove, my wife shan't ! ' and swords were drawn, and blood drawn, too, until friends separated them on this quarrel. Few men were so jealous about the point of honour in those

days ; and gentlemen of good birth and lineage thought
a royal blot was an ornament to their family coat. Frank
Esmond retired in the sulks, first to Tangier, whence he
returned after two years' service, settling on a small property
he had of his mother, near to Winchester, and became
a country gentleman, and kept a pack of beagles, and never
came to Court again in King Charles's time. But his uncle
Castlewood was never reconciled to him ; nor, for some
time afterwards, his cousin whom he had refused.

By places, pensions, bounties from France, and gifts
from the king, whilst his daughter was in favour, Lord
Castlewood, who had spent in the royal service his youth
and fortune, did not retrieve the latter quite, and never
cared to visit Castlewood, or repair it, since the death of
his son, but managed to keep a good house, and figure at
Court, and to save a considerable sum of ready money.

And now, his heir and nephew, Thomas Esmond, began
to bid for his uncle's favour. Thomas had served with the
emperor, and with the Dutch, when King Charles was
compelled to lend troops to the States, and against them,
when his Majesty made an alliance with the French king.
In these campaigns Thomas Esmond was more remarked
for duelling, brawling, vice, and play, than for any conspicuous gallantry in the field, and came back to England,
like many another English gentleman who has travelled, with
a character by no means improved by his foreign experience.
He had dissipated his small paternal inheritance of a younger
brother's portion, and, as truth must be told, was no better
than a hanger-on of ordinaries, and a brawler about Alsatia
and the Friars,* when he bethought him of a means of
mending his fortune.

His cousin was now of more than middle age, and had
nobody's word but her own for the beauty which she said
she once possessed. She was lean, and yellow, and long
in the tooth ; all the red and white in all the toy-shops* in
London could not make a beauty of her—Mr. Killigrew*
called her the Sibyl, the death's-head put up at the king's
feast as a *memento mori*, &c.—in fine, a woman who might
be easy of conquest, but whom only a very bold man would
think of conquering. This bold man was Thomas Esmond.
He had a fancy to my Lord Castlewood's savings, the
amount of which rumour had very much exaggerated.
Madam Isabel was said to have royal jewels of great

value ; whereas poor Tom Esmond's last coat but one was in pawn.

My lord had at this time a fine house in Lincoln's Inn Fields, nigh to the Duke's Theatre and the Portugal ambassador's chapel. Tom Esmond, who had frequented the one as long as he had money to spend among the actresses, now came to the church as assiduously. He looked so lean and shabby, that he passed without difficulty for a repentant sinner ; and so, becoming converted, you may be sure took his uncle's priest for a director.

This charitable father reconciled him with the old lord his uncle, who a short time before would not speak to him, as Tom passed under my lord's coach window, his lordship going in state to his place at Court, while his nephew slunk by with his battered hat and feather, and the point of his rapier sticking out of the scabbard—to his twopenny ordinary in Bell Yard.

Thomas Esmond, after this reconciliation with his uncle, very soon began to grow sleek, and to show signs of the benefits of good living and clean linen. He fasted rigorously twice a week to be sure ; but he made amends on the other days : and, to show how great his appetite was, Mr. Wycherley* said, he ended by swallowing that fly-blown rank old morsel his cousin. There were endless jokes and lampoons about this marriage at Court : but Tom rode thither in his uncle's coach now, called him father, and having won could afford to laugh. This marriage took place very shortly before King Charles died : whom the Viscount of Castlewood speedily followed.

The issue of this marriage was one son, whom the parents watched with an intense eagerness and care ; but who, in spite of nurses and physicians, had only a brief existence. His tainted blood did not run very long in his poor feeble little body. Symptoms of evil broke out early on him ; and, part from flattery, part superstition, nothing would satisfy my lord and lady, especially the latter, but having the poor little cripple touched by his Majesty at his church. They were ready to cry out miracle at first (the doctors and quack-salvers being constantly in attendance on the child, and experimenting on his poor little body with every conceivable nostrum)—but though there seemed from some reason a notable amelioration in the infant's health after his Majesty touched him, in a few weeks afterward the poor thing died—causing the lampooners of the Court to say, that the king in expelling evil out of the infant of Tom Esmond and Isabella his wife, expelled the life out of it, which was nothing but corruption.

The mother's natural pang at losing this poor little child must have been increased when she thought of her rival Frank Esmond's wife, who was a favourite of the whole Court, where my poor Lady Castlewood was neglected, and who had one child, a daughter, flourishing and beautiful, and was about to become a mother once more.

The Court, as I have heard, only laughed the more because the poor lady, who had pretty well passed the age when ladies are accustomed to have children, nevertheless determined not to give hope up, and even when she came to live at Castlewood, was constantly sending over to Hexton for the doctor, and announcing to her friends the arrival of an heir.   This absurdity of hers was one amongst many others which the wags used to play upon.   Indeed, to the last days of her life, my lady viscountess had the comfort of fancying herself beautiful, and persisted in blooming up to the very midst of winter, painting roses on her cheeks long after their natural season, and attiring herself like summer though her head was covered with snow.

Gentlemen who were about the Court of King Charles and King James, have told the present writer a number of stories about this queer old lady, with which it's not necessary that posterity should be entertained.   She is said to have had great powers of invective ; and, if she fought with all her rivals in King James's favour, 'tis certain she must have had a vast number of quarrels on her hands.   She was a woman of an intrepid spirit, and it appears pursued and rather fatigued his Majesty with her rights and her wrongs.   Some say that the cause of her leaving Court was jealousy of Frank Esmond's wife : others, that she was forced to retreat after a great battle which took place at Whitehall, between her ladyship and Lady Dorchester,* Tom Killigrew's daughter, whom the king delighted to honour, and in which that ill-favoured Esther got the better of our elderly Vashti.* But her ladyship for her part always averred that it was her husband's quarrel, and not her own, which occasioned the banishment of the two into the country ; and the cruel ingratitude of the sovereign in giving away, out of the family, that place of Warden of

the Butteries and Groom of the King's Posset, which the
two last Lords Castlewood had held so honourably, and
which was now conferred upon a fellow of yesterday, and
a hanger-on of that odious Dorchester creature, my Lord
Bergamot [1]; 'I never,' said my lady, 'could have come
to see his Majesty's posset carried by any other hand than
an Esmond. I should have dashed the salver out of Lord
Bergamot's hand, had I met him.' And those who knew
her ladyship are aware that she was a person quite capable
of performing this feat, had she not wisely kept out of
the way.

Holding the purse-strings in her own control, to which,
indeed, she liked to bring most persons who came near her,
Lady Castlewood could command her husband's obedience,
and so broke up her establishment at London; she had
removed from Lincoln's Inn Fields to Chelsey, to a pretty
new house she bought there; and brought her establishment, her maids, lap-dogs, and gentlewomen, her priest,
and his lordship, her husband, to Castlewood Hall, that
she had never seen since she quitted it as a child with her
father during the troubles of King Charles the First's reign.
The walls were still open in the old house as they had been
left by the shot of the Commonwealth men. A part of the
mansion was restored and furnished up with the plate,
hangings, and furniture, brought from the house in London.
My lady meant to have a triumphal entry into Castlewood
village, and expected the people to cheer as she drove over
the Green in her great coach, my lord beside her, her gentlewomen, lap-dogs, and cockatoos on the opposite seat, six
horses to her carriage, and servants armed and mounted,
following it and preceding it. But 'twas in the height of
the No-Popery cry;* the folks in the village and the neighbouring town were scared by the sight of her ladyship's
painted face and eyelids, as she bobbed her head out of the
coach window, meaning no doubt to be very gracious; and
one old woman said, 'Lady Isabel! lord-a-mercy, it's Lady

[1] Lionel Tipton, created Baron Bergamot, ann. 1686, Gentleman
Usher of the Back Stairs, and afterwards appointed Warden of the
Butteries and Groom of the King's Posset (on the decease of George,
second Viscount Castlewood), accompanied his Majesty to St.
Germains, where he died without issue. No Groom of the Posset
was appointed by the Prince of Orange, nor hath there been such an
officer in any succeeding reign.

Jezebel!' a name by which the enemies of the right
honourable viscountess were afterwards in the habit of
designating her. The country was then in a great No-
Popery fervour, her ladyship's known conversion, and her
husband's, the priest in her train, and the service performed
at the chapel of Castlewood (though the chapel had been
built for that worship before any other was heard of in the
country, and though the service was performed in the
most quiet manner), got her no favour at first in the county
or village. By far the greater part of the estate of Castlewood had been confiscated, and been parcelled out to
Commonwealth men. One or two of these old Cromwellian
soldiers were still alive in the village, and looked grimly
at first upon my lady viscountess, when she came to
dwell there.

She appeared at the Hexton Assembly, bringing her lord
after her, scaring the country folks with the splendour of her
diamonds, which she always wore in public. They said she
wore them in private, too, and slept with them round her
neck ; though the writer can pledge his word that this was
a calumny. 'If she were to take them off,' my Lady Sark
said, 'Tom Esmond, her husband, would run away with
them and pawn them.' 'Twas another calumny. My
Lady Sark was also an exile from Court, and there had been
war between the two ladies before.

The village people began to be reconciled presently to their
lady, who was generous and kind, though fantastic and
haughty, in her ways ; and whose praises Dr. Tusher, the
vicar, sounded loudly amongst his flock. As for my lord, he
gave no great trouble, being considered scarce more than
an appendage to my lady, who as daughter of the old lords
of Castlewood, and possessor of vast wealth, as the country
folks said (though indeed nine-tenths of it existed but in
rumour), was looked upon as the real queen of the Castle,
and mistress of all it contained.

CHAPTER III

WHITHER IN THE TIME OF THOMAS, THIRD VISCOUNT, I HAD PRECEDED
HIM AS PAGE TO ISABELLA

COMING up to London again some short time after this
retreat, the Lord Castlewood dispatched a retainer of his
to a little cottage in the village of Ealing, near to London,
where for some time had dwelt an old French refugee, by
name Mr. Pastoureau, one of those whom the persecution
of the Huguenots by the French king had brought over
to this country. With this old man lived a little lad, who
went by the name of Henry Thomas. He remembered to
have lived in another place a short time before, near to
London, too, amongst looms and spinning-wheels, and
a great deal of psalm-singing and church-going, and a whole
colony of Frenchmen.

There he had a dear, dear friend, who died and whom he
called aunt. She used to visit him in his dreams sometimes;
and her face, though it was homely, was a thousand times
dearer to him than that of Mrs. Pastoureau, Bon Papa
Pastoureau's new wife, who came to live with him after
aunt went away. And there, at Spittlefields, as it used
to be called, lived Uncle George, who was a weaver too,
but used to tell Harry that he was a little gentleman, and
that his father was a captain, and his mother an angel.

When he said so, Bon Papa used to look up from the
loom, where he was embroidering beautiful silk flowers, and
say, 'Angel! she belongs to the Babylonish Scarlet Woman.'
Bon Papa was always talking of the Scarlet Woman. He
had a little room where he always used to preach and sing
hymns out of his great old nose. Little Harry did not like
the preaching; he liked better the fine stories which aunt
used to tell him. Bon Papa's wife never told him pretty
stories; she quarrelled with Uncle George, and he went
away.

After this Harry's Bon Papa, and his wife and two children
of her own that she brought with her, came to live at Ealing.
The new wife gave her children the best of everything, and
Harry many a whipping, he knew not why. Besides blows,
he got ill names from her, which need not be set down here,

for the sake of old Mr. Pastoureau, who was still kind sometimes. The unhappiness of those days is long forgiven,
though they cast a shade of melancholy over the child's
youth, which will accompany him, no doubt, to the end of
his days : as those tender twigs are bent the trees grow
afterward ; and he, at least, who has suffered as a child,
and is not quite perverted in that early school of unhappiness, learns to be gentle and long-suffering with little
children.

Harry was very glad when a gentleman dressed in black,
on horseback, with a mounted servant behind him, came to
fetch him away from Ealing. The *noverca,* or unjust stepmother, who had neglected him for her own two children,
gave him supper enough the night before he went away,
and plenty in the morning. She did not beat him once, and
told the children to keep their hands off him. One was a
girl, and Harry never could bear to strike a girl ; and the
other was a boy, whom he could easily have beat, but he
always cried out, when Mrs. Pastoureau came sailing to the
rescue with arms like a flail. She only washed Harry's face
the day he went away ; nor ever so much as once boxed
his ears. She whimpered rather when the gentleman in
black came for the boy ; and old Mr. Pastoureau, as he
gave the child his blessing, scowled over his shoulder at the
strange gentleman, and grumbled out something about
Babylon and the scarlet lady. He was grown quite old,
like a child almost. Mrs. Pastoureau used to wipe his
nose as she did to the children. She was a great, big,
handsome young woman ; but, though she pretended to
cry, Harry thought 'twas only a sham, and sprung quite
delighted upon the horse upon which the lackey helped him.

He was a Frenchman ; his name was Blaise. The child
could talk to him in his own language perfectly well : he
knew it better than English indeed : having lived hitherto
chiefly among French people : and being called the little
Frenchman by other boys on Ealing Green. He soon learnt
to speak English perfectly, and to forget some of his French :
children forget easily. Some earlier and fainter recollections
the child had, of a different country ; and a town with tall
white houses ; and a ship. But these were quite indistinct
in the boy's mind, as indeed the memory of Ealing soon
became, at least of much that he suffered there.

The lackey before whom he rode was very lively and

voluble, and informed the boy that the gentleman riding
before him was my lord's chaplain, Father Holt—that he
was now to be called Master Harry Esmond—that my Lord
Viscount Castlewood was his *parrain*—that he was to live at
the great house of Castlewood, in the province of ——shire,
where he would see madame the viscountess, who was a
grand lady. And so, seated on a cloth before Blaise's
saddle, Harry Esmond was brought to London, and to a fine
square called Covent Garden, near to which his patron
lodged.

Mr. Holt the priest took the child by the hand, and
brought him to this nobleman, a grand languid nobleman
in a great cap and flowered morning-gown, sucking oranges.
He patted Harry on the head and gave him an orange.

' *C'est bien ça*,' he said to the priest after eyeing the
child, and the gentleman in black shrugged his shoulders.

'Let Blaise take him out for a holiday,' and out for a
holiday the boy and the valet went. Harry went jumping
along ; he was glad enough to go.

He will remember to his life's end the delights of those
days. He was taken to see a play by Monsieur Blaise, in
a house a thousand times greater and finer than the booth
at Ealing Fair—and on the next happy day they took water
on the river, and Harry saw London Bridge, with the
houses and booksellers' shops thereon, looking like a street,
and the Tower of London, with the armour, and the great
lions and bears in the moats—all under company of Monsieur Blaise.

Presently, of an early morning, all the party set forth for
the country, namely, my lord viscount and the other
gentleman ; Monsieur Blaise, and Harry on a pillion behind
them, and two or three men with pistols leading the baggage-
horses. And all along the road the Frenchman told little
Harry stories of brigands, which made the child's hair stand
on end, and terrified him ; so that at the great gloomy inn
on the road where they lay, he besought to be allowed to
sleep in a room with one of the servants, and was com-
passionated by Mr. Holt, the gentleman who travelled with
my lord, and who gave the child a little bed in his chamber.

His artless talk and answers very likely inclined this
gentleman in the boy's favour, for next day Mr. Holt said
Harry should ride behind him, and not with the French
lackey ; and all along the journey put a thousand questions

to the child—as to his foster-brother and relations at
Ealing ; what his old grandfather had taught him ; what
languages he knew ; whether he could read and write, and
sing, and so forth.   And Mr. Holt found that Harry could
read and write, and possessed the two languages of French
and English very well ; and when he asked Harry about
singing, the lad broke out with a hymn to the tune of
Dr. Martin Luther, which set Mr. Holt a-laughing ; and
even caused his *grand parrain* in the laced hat and periwig
to laugh too when Holt told him what the child was singing.
For it appeared that Dr. Martin Luther's hymns were not
sung in the churches Mr. Holt preached at.

' You must never sing that song any more, do you hear,
little manikin ? '   says my lord viscount, holding up a
finger.

' But we will try and teach you a better, Harry,' Mr. Holt
said ; and the child answered, for he was a docile child,
and of an affectionate nature, ' That he loved pretty songs,
and would try and learn anything the gentleman would
tell him.'   That day he so pleased the gentlemen by his
talk, that they had him to dine with them at the inn, and
encouraged him in his prattle ; and Monsieur Blaise, with
whom he rode and dined the day before, waited upon him
now.

' 'Tis well, 'tis well ! ' said Blaise, that night (in his own
language) when they lay again at an inn.   ' We are a little
lord here ; we are a little lord now : we shall see what we are
when we come to Castlewood where my lady is.'

' When shall we come to Castlewood, Monsieur Blaise ? '
says Harry.

' *Parbleu !* my lord does not press himself,' Blaise says,
with a grin ; and, indeed, it seemed as if his lordship was
not in a great hurry, for he spent three days on that journey,
which Harry Esmond hath often since ridden in a dozen
hours.   For the last two of the days, Harry rode with the
priest, who was so kind to him, that the child had grown
to be quite fond and familiar with him by the journey's
end, and had scarce a thought in his little heart which by
that time he had not confided to his new friend.

At length on the third day, at evening, they came to a
village standing on a green with elms round it, very pretty
to look at ; and the people there all took off their hats,
and made curtsies to my lord viscount, who bowed to them

all languidly; and there was one portly person that wore
a cassock and a broad-leafed hat, who bowed lower than
any one—and with this one both my lord and Mr. Holt
had a few words. 'This, Harry, is Castlewood church,'
says Mr. Holt, ' and this is the pillar thereof, learned Doctor
Tusher. Take off your hat, sirrah, and salute Doctor
Tusher.'

'Come up to supper, doctor,' says my lord; at which
the doctor made another low bow, and the party moved on
towards a grand house that was before them, with many
grey towers, and vanes on them, and windows flaming in
the sunshine; and a great army of rooks, wheeling over
their heads, made for the woods behind the house, as Harry
saw; and Mr. Holt told him that they lived at Castlewood
too.

They came to the house, and passed under an arch into
a courtyard, with a fountain in the centre, where many
men came and held my lord's stirrup as he descended, and
paid great respect to Mr. Holt likewise. And the child
thought that the servants looked at him curiously, and
smiled to one another—and he recalled what Blaise had
said to him when they were in London, and Harry had
spoken about his godpapa, when the Frenchman said,
'Parbleu! one sees well that my lord is your godfather';
words whereof the poor lad did not know the meaning then,
though he apprehended the truth in a very short time afterwards, and learned it and thought of it with no small feeling
of shame.

Taking Harry by the hand as soon as they were both
descended from their horses, Mr. Holt led him across the
court, and under a low door to rooms on a level with the
ground; one of which Father Holt said was to be the boy's
chamber, the other on the other side of the passage being
the father's own; and as soon as the little man's face was
washed, and the father's own dress arranged, Harry's guide
took him once more to the door by which my lord had entered
the hall, and up a stair, and through an ante-room to my
lady's drawing-room—an apartment than which Harry
thought he had never seen anything more grand—no, not in
the Tower of London which he had just visited. Indeed
the chamber was richly ornamented in the manner of
Queen Elizabeth's time, with great stained windows at
either end, and hangings of tapestry, which the sun shining

through the coloured glass painted of a thousand hues ;
and here in state, by the fire, sat a lady to whom the priest
took up Harry, who was indeed amazed by her appearance.

My lady viscountess's face was daubed with white and
red up to the eyes, to which the paint gave an unearthly
glare : she had a tower of lace on her head, under which
was a bush of black curls—borrowed curls—so that no
wonder little Harry Esmond was scared when he was first
presented to her—the kind priest acting as master of the
ceremonies at that solemn introduction—and he stared at
her with eyes almost as great as her own, as he had stared
at the player-woman who acted the wicked tragedy-queen,
when the players came down to Ealing Fair. She sat in
a great chair by the fire-corner ; in her lap was a spaniel-
dog that barked furiously ; on a little table by her was her
ladyship's snuff-box and her sugar-plum box. She wore
a dress of black velvet, and a petticoat of flame-coloured
brocade. She had as many rings on her fingers as the old
woman of Banbury Cross ; and pretty small feet which
she was fond of showing, with great gold clocks to her
stockings, and white pantofles with red heels ; and an
odour of musk was shook out of her garments whenever she
moved or quitted the room, leaning on her tortoiseshell
stick, little Fury barking at her heels.

Mrs. Tusher, the parson's wife, was with my lady. She
had been waiting-woman to her ladyship in the late lord's
time, and, having her soul in that business, took naturally
to it when the Viscountess of Castlewood returned to inhabit
her father's house.

' I present to your ladyship your kinsman and little page
of honour, Master Henry Esmond,' Mr. Holt said, bowing
lowly, with a sort of comical humility. ' Make a pretty
bow to my lady, monsieur ; and then another little bow,
not so low, to Madam Tusher—the fair priestess of Castlewood.'

' Where I have lived and hope to die, sir,' says Madam
Tusher, giving a hard glance at the brat, and then at my
lady.

Upon her the boy's whole attention was for a time directed.
He could not keep his great eyes off from her. Since the
Empress of Ealing he had seen nothing so awful.

' Does my appearance please you, little page ? ' asked
the lady.

'He would be very hard to please if it didn't,' cried Madam Tusher.

'Have done, you silly Maria,' said Lady Castlewood.

'Where I'm attached, I'm attached, madam—and I'd die rather than not say so.'

'*Je meurs où je m'attache*,' Mr. Holt said, with a polite grin. 'The ivy says so in the picture, and clings to the oak like a fond parasite as it is.'

'Parricide, sir!' cries Mrs. Tusher.

'Hush, Tusher—you are always bickering with Father Holt,' cried my lady. 'Come and kiss my hand, child,' and the oak held out a *branch* to little Harry Esmond, who took and dutifully kissed the lean old hand, upon the gnarled knuckles of which there glittered a hundred rings.

'To kiss that hand would make many a pretty fellow happy!' cried Mrs. Tusher: on which my lady crying out, 'Go, you foolish Tusher,' and tapping her with her great fan, Tusher ran forward to seize her hand and kiss it. Fury arose and barked furiously at Tusher; and Father Holt looked on at this queer scene, with arch grave glances.

The awe exhibited by the little boy perhaps pleased the lady to whom this artless flattery was bestowed; for having gone down on his knee (as Father Holt had directed him, and the mode then was) and performed his obeisance, she said, 'Page Esmond, my groom of the chamber will inform you what your duties are, when you wait upon my lord and me; and good Father Holt will instruct you as becomes a gentleman of our name. You will pay him obedience in everything, and I pray you may grow to be as learned and as good as your tutor.'

The lady seemed to have the greatest reverence for Mr. Holt, and to be more afraid of him than of anything else in the world. If she was ever so angry, a word or look from Father Holt made her calm: indeed he had a vast power of subjecting those who came near him; and, among the rest, his new pupil gave himself up with an entire confidence and attachment to the good father, and became his willing slave almost from the first moment he saw him.

He put his small hand into the father's as he walked away from his first presentation to his mistress, and asked many questions in his artless childish way. 'Who is that other woman?' he asked. 'She is fat and round; she is more pretty than my Lady Castlewood.'

'She is Madam Tusher, the parson's wife of Castlewood. She has a son of your age, but bigger than you.'

'Why does she like so to kiss my lady's hand ? It is not good to kiss.'

'Tastes are different, little man. Madam Tusher is attached to my lady, having been her waiting-woman, before she was married, in the old lord's time. She married Doctor Tusher the chaplain. The English household divines often marry the waiting-women.'

'You will not marry the French woman, will you ? I saw her laughing with Blaise in the buttery.'

'I belong to a church that is older and better than the English Church,' Mr. Holt said (making a sign whereof Esmond did not then understand the meaning, across his breast and forehead); 'in our Church the clergy do not marry. You will understand these things better soon.'

'Was not St. Peter the head of your Church ?—Dr. Rabbits of Ealing told us so.'

The father said, ' Yes, he was.'

'But St. Peter was married, for we heard only last Sunday that his wife's mother lay sick of a fever.' On which the father again laughed, and said he would understand this too better soon, and talked of other things, and took away Harry Esmond, and showed him the great old house which he had come to inhabit.

It stood on a rising green hill, with woods behind it, in which were rooks' nests, where the birds at morning and returning home at evening made a great cawing. At the foot of the hill was a river with a steep ancient bridge crossing it ; and beyond that a large pleasant green flat, where the village of Castlewood stood and stands, with the church in the midst, the parsonage hard by it, the inn with the blacksmith's forge beside it, and the sign of the ' Three Castles ' on the elm. The London road stretched away towards the rising sun, and to the west were swelling hills and peaks, behind which many a time Harry Esmond saw the same sun setting, that he now looks on thousands of miles away across the great ocean—in a new Castlewood by another stream, that bears, like the new country of wandering Aeneas, the fond names of the land of his youth.*

The Hall of Castlewood was built with two courts, whereof one only, the fountain court, was now inhabited, the other having been battered down in the Cromwellian wars. In the fountain court, still in good repair, was the great hall, near to the kitchen and butteries. A dozen of living-rooms looking to the north, and communicating with the little chapel that faced eastwards and the buildings stretching from that to the main gate, and with the hall (which looked to the west) into the court now dismantled. This court had been the most magnificent of the two, until the protector's cannon tore down one side of it before the place was taken and stormed. The besiegers entered at the terrace under the clock-tower, slaying every man of the garrison, and at their head my lord's brother, Francis Esmond.

The Restoration did not bring enough money to the Lord Castlewood to restore this ruined part of his house ; where were the morning parlours, above them the long music-gallery, and before which stretched the garden-terrace, where, however, the flowers grew again, which the boots of the Roundheads had trodden in their assault, and which was restored without much cost, and only a little care, by both ladies who succeeded the second viscount in the government of this mansion. Round the terrace-garden was a low wall with a wicket leading to the wooded height beyond, that is called Cromwell's battery to this day.

Young Harry Esmond learned the domestic part of his duty, which was easy enough, from the groom of her ladyship's chamber : serving the countess, as the custom commonly was in his boyhood, as page, waiting at her chair, bringing her scented water and the silver basin after dinner —sitting on her carriage step on state occasions, or on public days introducing her company to her. This was chiefly of the Catholic gentry, of whom there were a pretty many in the country and neighbouring city ; and who rode not seldom to Castlewood to partake of the hospitalities there. In the second year of their residence the company seemed especially to increase. My lord and my lady were seldom without visitors, in whose society it was curious to contrast the difference of behaviour between Father Holt, the director of the family, and Doctor Tusher, the rector of the parish—Mr. Holt moving amongst the very highest as quite their equal, and as commanding them all ; while poor Doctor Tusher, whose position was indeed a difficult one, having been chaplain once to the Hall, and still to the Protestant servants there, seemed more like an usher than an equal, and always rose to go away after the first course.

Also there came in these times to Father Holt many private visitors, whom after a little, Henry Esmond had little difficulty in recognizing as ecclesiastics of the father's persuasion ; whatever their dresses (and they adopted all) might be. These were closeted with the father constantly, and often came and rode away without paying their devoirs to my lord and lady—to the lady and lord rather—his lordship being little more than a cipher in the house, and entirely under his domineering partner. A little fowling, a little hunting, a great deal of sleep, and a long time at cards and table, carried through one day after another with his lordship. When meetings took place in this second year, which often would happen with closed doors, the page found my lord's sheet of paper scribbled over with dogs and horses, and 'twas said he had much ado to keep himself awake at these councils : the countess ruling over them, and he acting as little more than her secretary.

Father Holt began speedily to be so much occupied with these meetings as rather to neglect the education of the little lad who so gladly put himself under the kind priest's orders. At first they read much and regularly, both in Latin and French ; the father not neglecting in anything to impress his faith upon his pupil, but not forcing him violently, and treating him with a delicacy and kindness which surprised and attached the child ; always more easily won by these methods than by any severe exercise of authority. And his delight in our walks was to tell Harry of the glories of his order, of its martyrs and heroes, of its brethren converting the heathen by myriads, traversing the desert, facing the stake, ruling the courts and councils, or braving the tortures of kings ; so that Harry Esmond thought that to belong to the Jesuits was the greatest prize of life and bravest end of ambition ; the greatest career here, and in heaven the surest reward ; and began to long for the day, not only when he should enter into the one Church and receive his first communion, but when he might join that wonderful brotherhood, which was present throughout all the world, and which numbered the wisest, the bravest, the highest born, the most eloquent of men among its members. Father Holt bade him keep his views secret, and to hide them as a great treasure which would escape him if it was revealed ; and proud of this confidence and secret vested in him, the lad became fondly attached to the master who initiated him into a mystery so wonderful and awful. And when little Tom Tusher, his neighbour, came from school for his holiday, and said how he, too, was to be bred up for an English priest, and would get what he called an exhibition from his school, and then a college scholarship and fellowship, and then a good living—it tasked young Harry Esmond's powers of reticence not to say to his young companion, ' Church ! priesthood ! fat living ! My dear Tommy, do you call yours a Church and a priesthood ? What is a fat living compared to converting a hundred thousand heathens by a single sermon ? What is a scholarship at Trinity by the side of a crown of martyrdom, with angels awaiting you as your head is taken off ? Could your master at school sail over the Thames on his gown ? Have you statues in your church that can bleed, speak, walk, and cry ? My good Tommy, in dear Father Holt's Church these things take place every day. You know St. Philip of the Willows appeared to Lord Castlewood and caused him to turn to the one true Church. No saints ever come to you.' And Harry Esmond, because of his promise to Father Holt, hiding away these treasures of faith from T. Tusher, delivered himself of them nevertheless simply to Father Holt, who stroked his head, smiled at him with his inscrutable look, and told him that he did well to meditate on these great things, and not to talk of them except under direction.

CHAPTER IV

I AM PLACED UNDER A POPISH PRIEST AND BRED TO THAT RELIGION.— VISCOUNTESS CASTLEWOOD

HAD time enough been given, and his childish inclinations been properly nurtured, Harry Esmond had been a Jesuit priest ere he was a dozen years older, and might have finished his days a martyr in China or a victim on Tower Hill : for, in the few months they spent together at Castlewood, Mr. Holt obtained an entire mastery over the boy's intellect and affections ; and had brought him to think, as indeed Father Holt thought with all his heart too, that no life was so noble, no death so desirable, as that which

many brethren of his famous order were ready to undergo.
By love, by a brightness of wit and good humour that
charmed all, by an authority which he knew how to assume,
by a mystery and silence about him which increased the
child's reverence for him, he won Harry's absolute fealty,
and would have kept it, doubtless, if schemes greater and
more important than a poor little boy's admission into
orders had not called him away.

After being at home for a few months in tranquillity
(if theirs might be called tranquillity, which was, in truth,
a constant bickering), my lord and lady left the country
for London, taking their director with them : and his little
pupil scarce ever shed more bitter tears in his life than he
did for nights after the first parting with his dear friend,
as he lay in the lonely chamber next to that which the
father used to occupy. He and a few domestics were left
as the only tenants of the great house : and, though Harry
sedulously did all the tasks which the father set him, he had
many hours unoccupied, and read in the library, and
bewildered his little brains with the great books he found
there.

After a while the little lad grew accustomed to the loneliness of the place ; and in after days remembered this part
of his life as a period not unhappy. When the family was
at London the whole of the establishment travelled thither
with the exception of the porter, who was, moreover, brewer,
gardener, and woodman, and his wife and children. These
had their lodging in the gate-house: hard by, with a door
into the court and a window looking out on the green
was the chaplain's room ; and next to this a small chamber
where Father Holt had his books, and Harry Esmond his
sleeping-closet. The side of the house facing the east had
escaped the guns of the Cromwellians, whose battery was
on the height facing the western court ; so that this eastern
end bore few marks of demolition, save in the chapel, where
the painted windows surviving Edward the Sixth had been
broke by the Commonwealth men. In Father Holt's time
little Harry Esmond acted as his familiar, and faithful little
servitor ; beating his clothes, folding his vestments, fetching
his water from the well long before daylight, ready to run
anywhere for the service of his beloved priest. When the
father was away he locked his private chamber ; but the
room where the books were was left to little Harry, who,

but for the society of this gentleman, was little less solitary
when Lord Castlewood was at home.

The French wit saith that a hero is none to his valet de
chambre,* and it required less quick eyes than my lady's
little page was naturally endowed with, to see that she had
many qualities by no means heroic, however much Mrs.
Tusher might flatter and coax her. When Father Holt was
not by, who exercised an entire authority over the pair,
my lord and my lady quarrelled and abused each other so
as to make the servants laugh, and to frighten the little
page on duty. The poor boy trembled before his mistress,
who called him by a hundred ugly names, who made nothing
of boxing his ears—and tilting the silver basin in his face
which it was his business to present to her after dinner.
She hath repaired, by subsequent kindness to him, these
severities, which it must be owned made his childhood very
unhappy. She was but unhappy herself at this time, poor
soul, and I suppose made her dependants lead her own sad
life. I think my lord was as much afraid of her as her page
was, and the only person of the household who mastered
her was Mr. Holt. Harry was only too glad when the
father dined at table, and to slink away and prattle with
him afterwards, or read with him, or walk with him. Luckily
my lady viscountess did not rise till noon. Heaven help
the poor waiting-woman who had charge of her toilet!
I have often seen the poor wretch come out with red eyes
from the closet, where those long and mysterious rites of
her ladyship's dress were performed, and the backgammon-
box locked up with a rap on Mrs. Tusher's fingers when she
played ill or the game was going the wrong way.

Blessed be the king who introduced cards, and the kind
inventors of piquet and cribbage, for they employed six
hours at least of her ladyship's day, during which her family
was pretty easy. Without this occupation my lady frequently declared she should die. Her dependants one after
another relieved guard—'twas rather a dangerous post to
play with her ladyship—and took the cards turn about.
Mr. Holt would sit with her at piquet during hours together,
at which time she behaved herself properly; and, as for
Dr. Tusher, I believe he would have left a parishioner's
dying bed, if summoned to play a rubber with his patroness
at Castlewood. Sometimes, when they were pretty comfortable together, my lord took a hand. Besides these my lady

had her faithful poor Tusher, and one, two, three gentlewomen whom Harry Esmond could recollect in his time.
They could not bear that genteel service very long ; one
after another tried and failed at it. These and the housekeeper, and little Harry Esmond, had a table of their own.
Poor ladies ! their life was far harder than the page's. He
was found asleep tucked up in his little bed, whilst they
were sitting by her ladyship reading her to sleep, with the
News Letter or the *Grand Cyrus.* My lady used to have
boxes of new plays from London, and Harry was forbidden,
under the pain of a whipping, to look into them. I am
afraid he deserved the penalty pretty often, and got it
sometimes. Father Holt applied it twice or thrice, when
he caught the young scapegrace with a delightful wicked
comedy of Mr. Shadwell's or Mr. Wycherley's under his
pillow.

These, when he took any, were my lord's favourite
reading. But he was averse to much study, and, as his
little page fancied, to much occupation of any sort.

It always seemed to young Harry Esmond that my lord
treated him with more kindness when his lady was not
present, and Lord Castlewood would take the lad sometimes
on his little journeys a-hunting or a-birding ; he loved to
play at cards and tric-trac with him, which games the boy
learned to pleasure his lord : and was growing to like him
better daily, showing a special pleasure if Father Holt gave
a good report of him, patting him on the head, and promising that he would provide for the boy. However, in my
lady's presence, my lord showed no such marks of kindness,
and affected to treat the lad roughly, and rebuked him
sharply for little faults—for which he in a manner asked
pardon of young Esmond when they were private, saying
if he did not speak roughly, she would, and his tongue was
not such a bad one as his lady's—a point whereof the boy,
young as he was, was very well assured.

Great public events were happening all this while, of
which the simple young page took little count. But one
day, riding into the neighbouring town on the step of my
lady's coach, his lordship and she and Father Holt being
inside, a great mob of people came hooting and jeering
round the coach, bawling out, ' The bishops for ever ! '
' Down with the Pope ! ' ' No Popery ! no Popery ! Jezebel,
Jezebel ! ' so that my lord began to laugh, my lady's eyes

to roll with anger, for she was as bold as a lioness, and feared
nobody ; whilst Mr. Holt, as Esmond saw from his place
on the step, sank back with rather an alarmed face, crying
out to her ladyship, ' For God's sake, madam, do not speak
or look out of window, sit still.'   But she did not obey this
prudent injunction of the father ; she thrust her head out
of the coach window, and screamed out to the coachman,
' Flog your way through them, the brutes, James, and use
your whip ! '

The mob answered with a roaring jeer of laughter, and
fresh cries of, ' Jezebel ! Jezebel ! '   My lord only laughed
the more : he was a languid gentleman : nothing seemed
to excite him commonly, though I have seen him cheer
and halloo the hounds very briskly, and his face (which
was generally very yellow and calm) grow quite red and
cheerful during a burst over the Downs after a hare, and
laugh, and swear, and huzza at a cockfight, of which sport
he was very fond.   And now, when the mob began to hoot
his lady, he laughed with something of a mischievous look,
as though he expected sport, and thought that she and they
were a match.

James the coachman was more afraid of his mistress than
the mob, probably, for he whipped on his horses as he was
bidden, and the postboy that rode with the first pair (my
lady always went with her coach-and-six) gave a cut of his
thong over the shoulders of one fellow who put his hand
out towards the leading horse's rein.

It was a market day and the country people were all
assembled with their baskets of poultry, eggs, and such
things ; the postilion had no sooner lashed the man who
would have taken hold of his horse, but a great cabbage
came whirling like a bombshell into the carriage, at which
my lord laughed more, for it knocked my lady's fan out of
her hand, and plumped into Father Holt's stomach.   Then
came a shower of carrots and potatoes.

' For heaven's sake be still ! ' says Mr. Holt ; ' we are
not ten paces from the " Bell " archway, where they can
shut the gates on us, and keep out this *canaille*.'

The little page was outside the coach on the step, and
a fellow in the crowd aimed a potato at him, and hit him
in the eye, at which the poor little wretch set up a shout ;
the man laughed, a great big saddler's apprentice of the
town.   ' Ah ! you d—— little yelling Popish bastard,' he

said, and stooped to pick up another; the crowd had gathered quite between the horses and in the inn door by this time, and the coach was brought to a dead standstill. My lord jumped as briskly as a boy out of the door on his side of the coach, squeezing little Harry behind it; had hold of the potato-thrower's collar in an instant, and the next moment the brute's heels were in the air, and he fell on the stones with a thump.

'You hulking coward!' says he; 'you pack of screaming blackguards! how dare you attack children, and insult women? Fling another shot at that carriage, you sneaking pigskin cobbler, and by the Lord I'll send my rapier through you!'

Some of the mob cried, 'Huzza, my lord!' for they knew him, and the saddler's man was a known bruiser, near twice as big as my lord viscount.

'Make way, there,' says he (he spoke in a high shrill voice, but with a great air of authority). 'Make way, and let her ladyship's carriage pass.' The men that were between the coach and the gate of the 'Bell' actually did make way, and the horses went in, my lord walking after them with his hat on his head.

As he was going in at the gate, through which the coach had just rolled, another cry begins of 'No Popery—no Papists!' My lord turns round and faces them once more.

'God save the king!' says he at the highest pitch of his voice. 'Who dares abuse the king's religion? You, you d——d psalm-singing cobbler, as sure as I'm a magistrate of this county I'll commit you!' The fellow shrunk back, and my lord retreated with all the honours of the day. But when the little flurry caused by the scene was over, and the flush passed off his face, he relapsed into his usual languor, trifled with his little dog, and yawned when my lady spoke to him.

This mob was one of many thousands that were going about the country at that time, huzzaing for the acquittal of the seven bishops who had been tried just then, and about whom little Harry Esmond at that time knew scarce anything. It was assizes at Hexton, and there was a great meeting of the gentry at the 'Bell'; and my lord's people had their new liveries on, and Harry a little suit of blue and silver, which he wore upon occasions of state; and the gentlefolks came round and talked to my lord: and a judge

in a red gown, who seemed a very great personage, especially
complimented him and my lady, who was mighty grand.
Harry remembers her train borne up by her gentlewoman.
There was an assembly and ball at the great room at the
' Bell ', and other young gentlemen of the county families
looked on as he did.   One of them jeered him for his black
eye, which was swelled by the potato, and another called
him a bastard, on which he and Harry fell to fisticuffs.   My
lord's cousin, Colonel Esmond of Walcote, was there, and
separated the two lads, a great tall gentleman with a handsome, good-natured face.   The boy did not know how
nearly in after-life he should be allied to Colonel Esmond,
and how much kindness he should have to owe him.

There was little love between the two families.   My lady
used not to spare Colonel Esmond in talking of him, for
reasons which have been hinted already ; but about which,
at his tender age, Henry Esmond could be, expected to
know nothing.

Very soon afterwards my lord and lady went to London
with Mr. Holt, leaving, however, the page behind them.
The little man had the great house of Castlewood to himself ; or between him and the housekeeper, Mrs. Worksop,
an old lady who was a kinswoman of the family in some
distant way, and a Protestant, but a stanch Tory and
king's-man, as all the Esmonds were.   He used to go to
school to Dr. Tusher when he was at home, though the doctor
was much occupied too.   There was a great stir and commo-
tion everywhere, even in the little quiet village of Castlewood, whither a party of people came from the town, who
would have broken Castlewood Chapel windows, but the
village people turned out, and even old Sievewright, the republican blacksmith, along with them : for my lady, though
she was a Papist, and had many odd ways, was kind to the
tenantry, and there was always a plenty of beef, and
blankets, and medicine for the poor at Castlewood Hall.

A kingdom was changing hands whilst my lord and lady
were away.   King James was flying, the Dutchmen were
coming ; awful stories about them and the Prince of Orange
used old Mrs. Worksop to tell to the idle little page.

He liked the solitude of the great house very well ; he
had all the play-books to read, and no Father Holt to whip
him, and a hundred childish pursuits and pastimes, without
doors and within, which made this time very pleasant.

CHAPTER V

NOT having been able to sleep, for thinking of some lines
for eels which he had placed the night before, the lad was
lying in his little bed, waiting for the hour when the gate
would be open, and he and his comrade, Job Lockwood,
the porter's son, might go to the pond and see what fortune
had brought them. At daybreak Job was to awaken him,
but his own eagerness for the sport had served as a réveille
long since—so long, that it seemed to him as if the day
never would come.

It might have been four o'clock when he heard the door
of the opposite chamber, the chaplain's room, open, and
the voice of a man coughing in the passage. Harry jumped
up, thinking for certain it was a robber, or hoping perhaps
for a ghost, and, flinging open his own door, saw before
him the chaplain's door open, and a light inside, and a
figure standing in the doorway, in the midst of a great
smoke which issued from the room.

'Who's there?' cried out the boy, who was of a good
spirit.

'*Silentium!*' whispered the other; ''tis I, my boy!'
and, holding his hand out, Harry had no difficulty in
recognizing his master and friend, Father Holt. A curtain
was over the window of the chaplain's room that looked
to the court, and Harry saw that the smoke came from a
great flame of papers which were burning in a brazier when
he entered the chaplain's room. After giving a hasty
greeting and blessing to the lad, who was charmed to see
his tutor, the father continued the burning of his papers,
drawing them from a cupboard over the mantelpiece wall,
which Harry had never seen before.

Father Holt laughed, seeing the lad's attention fixed at
once on this hole. 'That is right, Harry,' he said; 'faithful
little famuli see all and say nothing. You are faithful,
I know.'

'I know I would go to the stake for you,' said Harry.

'I don't want your head,' said the father, patting it
kindly ; 'all you have to do is to hold your tongue. Let
us burn these papers, and say nothing to anybody. Should
you like to read them ? '

Harry Esmond blushed, and held down his head ; he *had*
looked as the fact was, and without thinking, at the paper
before him ; and though he had seen it, could not understand a word of it, the letters being quite clear enough, but
quite without meaning. They burned the papers, beating
down the ashes in a brazier, so that scarce any traces of
them remained.

Harry had been accustomed to see Father Holt in more
dresses than one ; it not being safe, or worth the danger,
for Popish ecclesiastics to wear their proper dress ; and he
was, in consequence, in no wise astonished that the priest
should now appear before him in a riding dress, with large
buff leather boots, and a feather to his hat, plain, but such
as gentlemen wore.

'You know the secret of the cupboard,' said he, laughing,
'and must be prepared for other mysteries ; ' and he opened
—but not a secret cupboard this time—only a wardrobe,
which he usually kept locked, and from which he now took
out two or three dresses and perukes of different colours, and
a couple of swords of a pretty make (Father Holt was an
expert practitioner with the small sword, and every day,
whilst he was at home, he and his pupil practised this
exercise, in which the lad became a very great proficient),
a military coat and cloak, and a farmer's smock, and placed
them in the large hole over the mantelpiece from which
the papers had been taken.

'If they miss the cupboard,' he said, 'they will not find
these ; if they find them, they'll tell no tales, except that
Father Holt wore more suits of clothes than one. All Jesuits
do. You know what deceivers we are, Harry.'

Harry was alarmed at the notion that his friend was about
to leave him ; but 'No', the priest said ; 'I may very likely
come back with my lord in a few days. We are to be
tolerated ; we are not to be persecuted. But they may take
a fancy to pay a visit at Castlewood ere our return ; and, as
gentlemen of my cloth are suspected, they might choose
to examine my papers, which concern nobody—at least, not
them.' And to this day, whether the papers in cipher
related to politics, or to the affairs of that mysterious society

whereof Father Holt was a member, his pupil, Harry Esmond, remains in entire ignorance.

The rest of his goods, his small wardrobe, &c., Holt left untouched on his shelves and in his cupboard, taking down —with a laugh, however—and flinging into the brazier, where he only half burned them, some theological treatises which he had been writing against the English divines. ' And now,' said he, ' Henry, my son, you may testify, with a safe conscience, that you saw me burning Latin sermons the last time I was here before I went away to London ; and it will be daybreak directly, and I must be away before Lockwood is stirring.'

' Will not Lockwood let you out, sir ? ' Esmond asked. Holt laughed ; he was never more gay or good-humoured than when in the midst of action or danger.

' Lockwood knows nothing of my being here, mind you,' he said ; ' nor would you, you little wretch, had you slept better. You must forget that I have been here ; and now farewell. Close the door, and go to your own room, and don't come out till—stay, why should you not know one secret more ? I know you will never betray me.'

In the chaplain's room were two windows ; the one looking into the court facing westwards to the fountain ; the other, a small casement strongly barred, and looking on to the green in front of the Hall. This window was too high to reach from the ground ; but, mounting on a buffet which stood beneath it, Father Holt showed me how, by pressing on the base of the window, the whole framework of lead, glass, and iron stanchions, descended into a cavity worked below, from which it could be drawn and restored to its usual place from without ; a broken pane being purposely open to admit the hand which was to work upon the spring of the machine.

' When I am gone,' Father Holt said, ' you may push away the buffet, so that no one may fancy that an exit has been made that way ; lock the door ; place the key— where shall we put the key ?—under *Chrysostom* on the book-shelf ; and if any ask for it, say I keep it there, and told you where to find it, if you had need to go to my room. The descent is easy down the wall into the ditch ; and so, once more farewell, until I see thee again, my dear son.' And with this the intrepid father mounted the buffet with great agility and briskness, stepped across the window, lifting up the bars and framework again from the other side, and only leaving room for Harry Esmond to stand on tiptoe and kiss his hand before the casement closed, the bars fixing as firm as ever seemingly in the stone arch over-head. When Father Holt next arrived at Castlewood, it was by the public gate on horseback; and he never so much as alluded to the existence of the private issue to Harry, except when he had need of a private messenger from within, for which end, no doubt, he had instructed his young pupil in the means of quitting the Hall.

Esmond, young as he was, would have died sooner than betray his friend and master, as Mr. Holt well knew; for he had tried the boy more than once, putting temptations in his way, to see whether he would yield to them and confess afterwards, or whether he would resist them, as he did sometimes, or whether he would lie, which he never did. Holt instructing the boy on this point, however, that if to keep silence is not to lie, as it certainly is not, yet silence is, after all, equivalent to a negation—and therefore a downright No, in the interest of justice or your friend, and in reply to a question that may be prejudicial to either, is not criminal, but, on the contrary, praiseworthy; and as lawful a way as the other of eluding a wrongful demand. For instance (says he), suppose a good citizen, who had seen his Majesty take refuge there, had been asked, 'Is King Charles up that oak-tree?' His duty would have been not to say, Yes—so that the Cromwellians should seize the king and murder him like his father—but No; his Majesty being private in the tree, and therefore not to be seen there by loyal eyes: all which instruction, in religion and morals, as well as in the rudiments of the tongues and sciences, the boy took eagerly and with gratitude from his tutor. When, then, Holt was gone, and told Harry not to see him, it was as if he had never been. And he had this answer pat when he came to be questioned a few days after.

The Prince of Orange was then at Salisbury, as young Esmond learned from seeing Doctor Tusher in his best cassock (though the roads were muddy, and he never was known to wear his silk, only his stuff one, a-horseback), with a great orange cockade in his broad-leafed hat, and Nahum, his clerk, ornamented with a like decoration. The doctor was walking up and down, in front of his parsonage, when little Esmond saw him, and heard him say he was going to pay

his duty to his highness the prince, as he mounted his pad
and rode away with Nahum behind. The village people
had orange cockades too, and his friend the blacksmith's
laughing daughter pinned one into Harry's old hat, which
he tore out indignantly when they bid him to cry, ' God
save the Prince of Orange and the Protestant religion ! '
but the people only laughed, for they liked the boy in the
village, where his solitary condition moved the general pity,
and where he found friendly welcomes and faces in many
houses. Father Holt had many friends there too, for he
not only would fight the blacksmith at theology, never
losing his temper, but laughing the whole time in his pleasant
way, but he cured him of an ague with quinquina,* and was
always ready with a kind word for any man that asked it,
so that they said in the village 'twas a pity the two were
Papists.

The director and the Vicar of Castlewood agreed very
well ; indeed, the former was a perfectly bred gentleman,
and it was the latter's business to agree with everybody.
Doctor Tusher and the lady's maid, his spouse, had a boy
who was about the age of little Esmond ; and there was
such a friendship between the lads, as propinquity and
tolerable kindness and good humour on either side would
be pretty sure to occasion. Tom Tusher was sent off early
however to a school in London, whither his father took him
and a volume of sermons in the first year of the reign of
King James ; and Tom returned but once, a year afterwards, to Castlewood for many years of his scholastic and
collegiate life. Thus there was less danger to Tom of a perversion of his faith by the director, who scarce ever saw him,
than there was to Harry, who constantly was in the vicar's
company ; but as long as Harry's religion was his Majesty's,
and my lord's, and my lady's, the doctor said gravely, it
should not be for him to disturb or disquiet him : it was
far from him to say that his Majesty's Church was not a
branch of the Catholic Church ; upon which Father Holt
used, according to his custom, to laugh and say, that the
Holy Church throughout all the world, and the noble army
of martyrs, were very much obliged to the doctor.

It was while Dr. Tusher was away at Salisbury that there
came a troop of dragoons with orange scarfs, and quartered
in Castlewood, and some of them came up to the Hall,
where they took possession, robbing nothing however

beyond the hen-house and the beer-cellar ; and only insisting upon going through the house and looking for papers.
The first room they asked to look at was Father Holt's
room, of which Harry Esmond brought the key, and they
opened the drawers and the cupboards, and tossed over the
papers and clothes—but found nothing except his books
and clothes, and the vestments in a box by themselves,
with which the dragoons made merry, to Harry Esmond's
horror.   And to the questions which the gentleman put to
Harry, he replied, that Father Holt was a very kind man
to him, and a very learned man, and Harry supposed
would tell him none of his secrets if he had any.   He was
about eleven years old at this time, and looked as innocent
as boys of his age.

The family were away more than six months, and when
they returned they were in the deepest state of dejection,
for King James had been banished, the Prince of Orange
was on the throne, and the direst persecutions of those of
the Catholic faith were apprehended by my lady, who
said she did not believe that there was a word of truth in
the promises of toleration that Dutch monster made, or in
a single word the perjured wretch said.   My lord and lady
were in a manner prisoners in their own house ; so her
ladyship gave the little page to know, who was by this
time growing of an age to understand what was passing
about him, and something of the characters of the people
he lived with.

' We are prisoners,' says she ; ' in everything but chains,
we are prisoners.   Let them come, let them consign me to
dungeons, or strike off my head from this poor little throat '
(and she clasped it in her long fingers).   ' The blood of the
Esmonds will always flow freely for their kings.   We are
not like the Churchills—the Judases, who kiss their master
and betray him.   We know how to suffer, how even to forgive in the royal cause ' (no doubt it was to that fatal business of losing the place of Groom of the Posset to which her
ladyship alluded, as she did half a dozen times in the day).
' Let the tyrant of Orange bring his rack and his odious
Dutch tortures—the beast ! the wretch ! I spit upon him
and defy him.   Cheerfully will I lay this head upon the
block ; cheerfully will I accompany my lord to the scaffold :
we will cry, "God save King James ! " with our dying breath,
and smile in the face of the executioner.'   And she told her

page a hundred times at least of the particulars of the last interview which she had with his Majesty.

'I flung myself before my liege's feet,' she said, 'at Salisbury. I devoted myself—my husband—my house, to his cause. Perhaps he remembered old times, when Isabella Esmond was young and fair ; perhaps he recalled the day when 'twas not *I* that knelt—at least he spoke to me with a voice that reminded *me* of days gone by. "Egad ! " said his Majesty, " you should go to the Prince of Orange, if you want anything." "No, sire, " I replied, " I would not kneel to a usurper ; the Esmond that would have served your Majesty will never be groom to a traitor's posset." The royal exile smiled, even in the midst of his misfortune ; he deigned to raise me with words of consolation. The viscount, my husband, himself, could not be angry at the august salute with which he honoured me ! '

The public misfortune had the effect of making my lord and his lady better friends than they ever had been since their courtship. My lord viscount had shown both loyalty and spirit, when these were rare qualities in the dispirited party about the king ; and the praise he got elevated him not a little in his wife's good opinion, and perhaps in his own. He wakened up from the listless and supine life which he had been leading ; was always riding to and fro in consultation with this friend or that of the king's ; the page of course knowing little of his doings, but remarking only his greater cheerfulness and altered demeanour.

Father Holt came to the Hall constantly, but officiated no longer openly as chaplain ; he was always fetching and carrying : strangers, military and ecclesiastic (Harry knew the latter though they came in all sorts of disguises), were continually arriving and departing. My lord made long absences and sudden reappearances, using sometimes the means of exit which Father Holt had employed, though how often the little window in the chaplain's room let in or let out my lord and his friends, Harry could not tell. He stoutly kept his promise to the father of not prying, and if at midnight from his little room he heard noises of persons stirring in the next chamber, he turned round to the wall and hid his curiosity under his pillow until it fell asleep. Of course he could not help remarking that the priest's journeys were constant, and understanding by a hundred signs that some active though secret business employed him : what this was may pretty well be guessed by what soon happened to my lord.

No garrison or watch was put into Castlewood when my lord came back, but a guard was in the village ; and one or other of them was always on the Green keeping a look-out on our great gate, and those who went out and in. Lockwood said that at night especially every person who came in or went out was watched by the outlying sentries. 'Twas lucky that we had a gate which their worships knew nothing about. My lord and Father Holt must have made constant journeys at night : once or twice little Harry acted as their messenger and discreet little aide de camp. He remembers he was bidden to go into the village with his fishing-rod, enter certain houses, ask for a drink of water, and tell the good man, ' There would be a horse-market at Newbury next Thursday,' and so carry the same message on to the next house on his list.

He did not know what the message meant at the time, nor what was happening : which may as well, however, for clearness' sake, be explained here. The Prince of Orange being gone to Ireland, where the king was ready to meet him with a great army, it was determined that a great rising of his Majesty's party should take place in this country : and my lord was to head the force in our county. Of late he had taken a greater lead in affairs than before, having the indefatigable Mr. Holt at his elbow, and my lady viscountess strongly urging him on ; and my Lord Sark being in the Tower a prisoner, and Sir Wilmot Crawley, of Queen's Crawley,* having gone over to the Prince of Orange's side— my lord became the most considerable person in our part of the county for the affairs of the king.

It was arranged that the regiment of Scots Greys and Dragoons, then quartered at Newbury, should declare for the king on a certain day, when likewise the gentry affected to his Majesty's cause were to come in with their tenants and adherents to Newbury, march upon the Dutch troops at Reading under Ginckel ;* and, these overthrown, and their indomitable little master away in Ireland, 'twas thought that our side might move on London itself, and a confident victory was predicted for the king.

As these great matters were in agitation, my lord lost his listless manner and seemed to gain health ; my lady did not scold him, Mr. Holt came to and fro, busy always ;

and little Harry longed to have been a few inches taller,
that he might draw a sword in this good cause.

One day, it must have been about the month of July,
1690, my lord, in a great horseman's coat, under which
Harry could see the shining of a steel breastplate he had on,
called little Harry to him, put the hair off the child's forehead, and kissed him, and bade God bless him in such an
affectionate way as he never had used before. Father Holt
blessed him too, and then they took leave of my lady
viscountess, who came from her apartment with a pocket-
handkerchief to her eyes, and her gentlewoman and Mrs.
Tusher supporting her.

'You are going to—to ride,' says she. 'Oh, that I might
come too !—but in my situation I am forbidden horse
exercise.'

'We kiss my lady marchioness's hand,' says Mr. Holt.

'My lord, God speed you !' she said, steping up and
embracing my lord in a grand manner. 'Mr. Holt, I ask
your blessing :' and she knelt down for that, whilst Mrs.
Tusher tossed her head up.

Mr. Holt gave the same benediction to the little page, who
went down and held my lord's stirrups for him to mount ;
there were two servants waiting there too—and they rode
out of Castlewood gate.

As they crossed the bridge Harry could see an officer in
scarlet ride up touching his hat, and address my lord.

The party stopped, and came to some parley or discussion,
which presently ended, my lord putting his horse into a
canter after taking off his hat and making a bow to the
officer who rode alongside him step for step : the trooper
accompanying him, falling back, and riding with my lord's
two men. They cantered over the Green, and behind the
elms (my lord waving his hand, Harry thought), and so
they disappeared.

That evening we had a great panic, the cow-boy coming
at milking-time riding one of our horses, which he had
found grazing at the outer park wall.

All night my lady viscountess was in a very quiet and
subdued mood. She scarce found fault with anybody ;
she played at cards for six hours ; little page Esmond went
to sleep. He prayed for my lord and the good cause before
closing his eyes.

It was quite in the grey of the morning when the porter's

bell rang, and old Lockwood waking up, let in one of my lord's servants, who had gone with him in the morning, and who returned with a melancholy story.

The officer who rode up to my lord had, it appeared, said to him, that it was his duty to inform his lordship that he was not under arrest, but under surveillance, and to request him not to ride abroad that day.

My lord replied that riding was good for his health, that if the captain chose to accompany him he was welcome, and it was then that he made a bow, and they cantered away together.

When he came on to Wansey Down, my lord all of a sudden pulled up, and the party came to a halt at the cross-way.

'Sir,' says he to the officer, ' we are four to two ; will you be so kind as to take that road, and leave me to go mine ? '

' Your road is mine, my lord,' says the officer.

' Then,' says my lord, but he had no time to say more, for the officer, drawing a pistol, snapped it at his lordship ; as at the same moment Father Holt, drawing a pistol, shot the officer through the head.

It was done, and the man dead in an instant of time. The orderly, gazing at the officer, looked scared for a moment, and galloped away for his life.

' Fire ! fire ! ' cries out Father Holt, sending another shot after the trooper, but the two servants were too much surprised to use their pieces, and my lord calling to them to hold their hands, the fellow got away.

' Mr. Holt, *qui pensoit à tout*,' says Blaise, ' gets off his horse, examines the pockets of the dead officer for papers, gives his money to us two, and says, " The wine is drawn, monsieur le marquis,"—why did he say marquis to monsieur le vicomte ?—" we must drink it."

' The poor gentleman's horse was a better one than that I rode,' Blaise continues ; ' Mr. Holt bids me get on him, and so I gave a cut to Whitefoot, and she trotted home. We rode on towards Newbury ; we heard firing towards midday : at two o'clock a horseman comes up to us as we were giving our cattle water at an inn—and says, All is done. The Écossois declared an hour too soon—General Ginckel was down upon them. The whole thing was at an end.

' " And we've shot an officer on duty, and let his orderly escape," says my lord.

' " Blaise," says Mr. Holt, writing two lines on his table-
book, one for my lady, and one for you, Master Harry;
" you must go back to Castlewood, and deliver these," and
behold me.'

And he gave Harry the two papers. He read that to
himself, which only said, ' Burn the papers in the cupboard,
burn this. You know nothing about anything.' Harry
read this, ran upstairs to his mistress's apartment, where
her gentlewoman slept near to the door, made her bring a
light and wake my lady, into whose hands he gave the
paper. She was a wonderful object to look at in her night
attire, nor had Harry ever seen the like.

As soon as she had the paper in her hand, Harry stepped
back to the chaplain's room, opened the secret cupboard
over the fireplace, burned all the papers in it, and, as he
had seen the priest do before, took down one of his reverence's
manuscript sermons, and half burnt that in the brazier.
By the time the papers were quite destroyed it was daylight.
Harry ran back to his mistress again. Her gentlewoman
ushered him again into her ladyship's chamber; she told
him (from behind her nuptial curtains) to bid the coach
be got ready, and that she would ride away anon.

But the mysteries of her ladyship's toilet were as awfully
long on this day as on any other, and, long after the coach
was ready, my lady was still attiring herself. And just as
the viscountess stepped forth from her room, ready for
departure, young Job Lockwood comes running up from
the village with news that a lawyer, three officers, and
twenty or four-and-twenty soldiers, were marching thence
upon the house. Job had but two minutes the start of them,
and, ere he had well told his story, the troop rode into our
courtyard.

CHAPTER VI

THE ISSUE OF THE PLOTS.—THE DEATH OF THOMAS, THIRD VISCOUNT
OF CASTLEWOOD; AND THE IMPRISONMENT OF HIS VISCOUNTESS

At first my lady was for dying like Mary, Queen of Scots (to
whom she fancied she bore a resemblance in beauty), and,
stroking her scraggy neck, said, ' They will find Isabel of
Castlewood is equal to her fate.' Her gentlewoman,
Victoire, persuaded her that her prudent course was, as she
could not fly, to receive the troops as though she suspected
nothing, and that her chamber was the best place wherein
to await them. So her black japan casket which Harry
was to carry to the coach was taken back to her ladyship's
chamber, whither the maid and mistress retired. Victoire
came out presently, bidding the page to say her ladyship was
ill, confined to her bed with the rheumatism.

By this time the soldiers had reached Castlewood.
Harry Esmond saw them from the window of the tapestry
parlour; a couple of sentinels were posted at the gate—
a half-dozen more walked towards the stable; and some
others, preceded by their commander, and a man in black,
a lawyer probably, were conducted by one of the servants
to the stair leading up to the part of the house which my
lord and lady inhabited.

So the captain, a handsome kind man, and the lawyer,
came through the ante-room to the tapestry parlour, and
where now was nobody but young Harry Esmond, the page.

' Tell your mistress, little man,' says the captain kindly,
' that we must speak to her.'

' My mistress is ill abed,' said the page.

' What complaint has she ? ' asked the captain.

The boy said, ' the rheumatism ! '

' Rheumatism! that's a sad complaint,' continues the
good-natured captain; ' and the coach is in the yard to
fetch the doctor, I suppose ? '

' I don't know,' says the boy.

' And how long has her ladyship been ill ? '

' I don't know,' says the boy.

' When did my lord go away ? '

' Yesterday night.'

' With Father Holt ? '

' With Mr. Holt.'

' And which way did they travel ? ' asks the lawyer.

' They travelled without me,' says the page.

' We must see Lady Castlewood.'

' I have orders that nobody goes in to her ladyship—she is sick,' says the page ; but at this moment Victoire came out. ' Hush ! ' says she ; and, as if not knowing that any one was near, ' What's this noise ? ' says she. ' Is this gentleman the doctor ? '

' Stuff ! we must see Lady Castlewood,' says the lawyer, pushing by.

The curtains of her ladyship's room were down, and the chamber dark, and she was in bed with a nightcap on her head, and propped up by her pillows, looking none the less ghastly because of the red which was still on her cheeks, and which she could not afford to forgo.

' Is that the doctor ? ' she said.

' There is no use with this deception, madam,' Captain Westbury said (for so he was named). ' My duty is to arrest the person of Thomas, Viscount Castlewood, a nonjuring peer—of Robert Tusher, Vicar of Castlewood—and Henry Holt, known under various other names and designations, a Jesuit priest, who officiated as chaplain here in the late king's time, and is now at the head of the conspiracy which was about to break out in this country against the authority of their Majesties King William and Queen Mary—and my orders aie to search the house for such papers or traces of the conspiracy as may be found here. Your ladyship will please to give me your keys, and it will be as well for yourself that you should help us, in every way, in our search.'

' You see, sir, that I have the rheumatism, and cannot move,' said the lady, looking uncommonly ghastly as she sat up in her bed, where however she had had her cheeks painted, and a new cap put on, so that she might at least look her best when the officers came.

' I shall take leave to place a sentinel in the chamber, so that your ladyship, in case you should wish to rise, may have an arm to lean on,' Captain Westbury said. ' Your woman will show me where I am to look ; ' and Madame Victoire, chattering in her half-French and half-English jargon, opened while the captain examined one drawer after another ; but, as Harry Esmond thought, rather carelessly, with a smile on his face, as if he was only conducting the examination for form's sake.

Before one of the cupboards Victoire flung herself down, stretching out her arms, and, with a piercing shriek, cried, ' *Non, jamais, monsieur l'officier ! Jamais !* I will rather die than let you see this wardrobe.'

But Captain Westbury would open it, still with a smile on his face, which, when the box was opened, turned into a fair burst of laughter. It contained—not papers regarding the conspiracy—but my lady's wigs, washes, and rouge-pots, and Victoire said men were monsters, as the captain went on with his perquisition. He tapped the back to see whether or no it was hollow, and as he thrust his hands into the cupboard, my lady from her bed called out with a voice that did not sound like that of a very sick woman, ' Is it your commission to insult ladies as well as to arrest gentlemen, captain ? '

' These articles are only dangerous when worn by your ladyship,' the captain said with a low bow, and a mock grin of politeness. ' I have found nothing which concerns the Government as yet—only the weapons with which beauty is authorized to kill,' says he, pointing to a wig with his sword-tip. ' We must now proceed to search the rest of the house.'

' You are not going to leave that wretch in the room with me,' cried my lady, pointing to the soldier.

' What can I do, madam ? Somebody you must have to smooth your pillow and bring your medicine—permit me——'

' Sir ! ' screamed out my lady—

' Madam, if you are too ill to leave the bed,' the captain then said, rather sternly, ' I must have in four of my men to lift you off in the sheet : I must examine this bed, in a word ; papers may be hidden in a bed as elsewhere ; we know that very well and——'

Here it was her ladyship's turn to shriek, for the captain, with his fist shaking the pillows and bolsters, at last came to ' burn ', as they say in the play of forfeits, and wrenching away one of the pillows, said, ' Look, did not I tell you so ? Here is a pillow stuffed with paper.'

' Some villain has betrayed us,' cried out my lady, sitting up in the bed, showing herself full dressed under her night-rail.

'And now your ladyship can move, I am sure ; permit me to give you my hand to rise. You will have to travel for some distance, as far as Hexton Castle to-night. Will you have your coach ? Your woman shall attend you if you like—and the japan-box ? '

'Sir ! you don't strike a *man* when he is down,' said my lady, with some dignity : ' can you not spare a woman ? '

'Your ladyship must please to rise and let me search the bed,' said the captain ; ' there is no more time to lose in bandying talk.'

And, without more ado, the gaunt old woman got up. Harry Esmond recollected to the end of his life that figure, with the brocade dress and the white night-rail, and the gold-clocked red stockings, and white red-heeled shoes sitting up in the bed, and stepping down from it. The trunks were ready packed for departure in her ante-room, and the horses ready harnessed in the stable : about all which the captain seemed to know, by information got from some quarter or other ; and, whence, Esmond could make a pretty shrewd guess in after-times, when Dr. Tusher complained that King William's Government had basely treated him for services done in that cause.

And here he may relate, though he was then too young to know all that was happening, what the papers contained, of which Captain Westbury had made a seizure, and which papers had been transferred from the japan-box to the bed when the officers arrived.

There was a list of gentlemen of the county in Father Holt's handwriting—Mr. Freeman's (King James's) friends —a similar paper being found among those of Sir John Fenwick and Mr. Coplestone,* who suffered death for this conspiracy.

There was a patent conferring the title of Marquis of Esmond on my Lord Castlewood, and the heirs male of his body ; his appointment as lord lieutenant of the county, and major-general.[1]

---

[1] To have this rank of marquis restored in the family had always been my lady viscountess's ambition ; and her old maiden aunt, Barbara Topham, the goldsmith's daughter, dying about this time, and leaving all her property to Lady Castlewood, I have heard that her ladyship sent almost the whole of the money to King James, a proceeding which so irritated my Lord Castlewood that he actually went to the parish church, and was only appeased by the marquis's

There were various letters from the nobility and gentry, some ardent and some doubtful, in the king's service; and (very luckily for him) two letters concerning Colonel Francis Esmond; one from Father Holt, which said, ' I have been to see this colonel at his house at Walcote near to Wells, where he resides since the king's departure, and pressed him very eagerly in Mr. Freeman's cause, showing him the great advantage he would have by trading with that merchant, offering him large premiums there as agreed between us. But he says no : he considers Mr. Freeman the head of the firm, will never trade against him or embark with any other trading company, but considers his duty was done when Mr. Freeman left England. This colonel seems to care more for his wife and his beagles than for affairs. He asked me much about young H. E., " that bastard," as he called him : doubting my lord's intentions respecting him. I reassured him on this head, stating what I knew of the lad, and our intentions respecting him, but with regard to Freeman he was inflexible.'

And another letter was from Colonel Esmond to his kinsman, to say that one Captain Holton had been with him offering him large bribes to join, *you know who*, and saying that the head of the house of Castlewood was deeply engaged in that quarter. But for his part he had broke his sword when the K. left the country, and would never again fight in that quarrel. The P. of O. was a man, at least, of a noble courage, and his duty and, as he thought, every Englishman's, was to keep the country quiet, and the French out of it : and, in fine, that he would have nothing to do with the scheme.

Of the existence of these two letters and the contents of the pillow, Colonel Frank Esmond, who became Viscount Castlewood, told Henry Esmond afterwards, when the letters were shown to his lordship, who congratulated himself, as he had good reason, that he had not joined in the scheme which proved so fatal to many concerned in it. But, naturally, the lad knew little about these circumstances when they happened under his eyes : only being aware that his patron and his mistress were in some trouble, which had caused the flight of the one, and the apprehension of the other by the officers of King William.

title which his exiled majesty sent to him in return for the 15,000*l.* his faithful subject lent him.

The seizure of the papers effected, the gentlemen did not
pursue their further search through Castlewood house very
rigorously. They examined Mr. Holt's room, being led
thither by his pupil, who showed, as the father had bidden him, the place where the key of his chamber lay, opened
the door for the gentlemen, and conducted them into
the room.

When the gentlemen came to the half-burned papers in
the brazier, they examined them eagerly enough, and their
young guide was a little amused at their perplexity.

'What are these?' says one.

'They're written in a foreign language,' says the lawyer.
'What are you laughing at, little whelp?' adds he, turning
round as he saw the boy smile.

'Mr. Holt said they were sermons,' Harry said, 'and bade
me to burn them;' which indeed was true of those papers.

'Sermons indeed—it's treason, I would lay a wager,'
cries the lawyer.

'Egad! it's Greek to me,' says Captain Westbury. 'Can
you read it, little boy?'

'Yes, sir, a little,' Harry said.

'Then read, and read in English, sir, on your peril,' said
the lawyer. And Harry began to translate :—

'Hath not one of your own writers said, " The children
of Adam are now labouring as much as he himself ever did,
about the tree of the knowledge of good and evil, shaking
the boughs thereof, and seeking the fruit, being for the most
part unmindful of the tree of life." O blind generation!
'tis this tree of knowledge to which the serpent has led you'
—and here the boy was obliged to stop, the rest of the page
being charred by the fire : and asked of the lawyer—' Shall
I go on, sir?'

The lawyer said—' This boy is deeper than he seems :
who knows that he is not laughing at us?'

'Let's have in Dick the Scholar,' cried Captain Westbury,
laughing; and he called to a trooper out of the window—
'Ho, Dick, come in here and construe.'

A thick-set soldier, with a square good-humoured face,
came in at the summons, saluting his officer.

'Tell us what is this, Dick,' says the lawyer.

'My name is Steele, sir,' says the soldier. 'I may be
Dick for my friends, but I don't name gentlemen of your
cloth amongst them.'

' Well then, Steele.'

' Mr. Steele, sir, if you please. When you address a gentleman of his Majesty's Horse Guards, be pleased not to be so familiar.'

' I didn't know, sir,' said the lawyer.

' How should you ? I take it you are not accustomed to meet with gentlemen,' says the trooper.

' Hold thy prate, and read that bit of paper,' says Westbury.

' 'Tis Latin,' says Dick, glancing at it, and again saluting his officer, ' and from a sermon of Mr. Cudworth's,'*and he translated the words pretty much as Henry Esmond had rendered them.

' What a young scholar you are,' says the captain to the boy.

' Depend on't, he knows more than he tells,' says the lawyer. ' I think we will pack him off in the coach with old Jezebel.'

' For construing a bit of Latin ? ' said the captain very good-naturedly.

' I would as lief go there as anywhere,' Harry Esmond said, simply, ' for there is nobody to care for me.'

There must have been something touching in the child's voice, or in this description of his solitude—for the captain looked at him very good-naturedly, and the trooper, called Steele, put his hand kindly on the lad's head, and said some words in the Latin tongue.

' What does he say ? ' says the lawyer.

' Faith, ask Dick himself,' cried Captain Westbury.

' I said I was not ignorant of misfortune myself, and had learned to succour the miserable, and that's not *your* trade, Mr. Sheepskin,' said the trooper.

' You had better leave Dick the Scholar alone, Mr. Corbet,' the captain said. And Harry Esmond, always touched by a kind face and kind word, felt very grateful to this good-natured champion.

The horses were by this time harnessed to the coach ; and the countess and Victoire came down and were put into the vehicle. This woman, who quarrelled with Harry Esmond all day, was melted at parting with him, and called him ' dear angel', and ' poor infant ', and a hundred other names.

The viscountess, giving him her lean hand to kiss, bade him always be faithful to the house of Esmond. ' If evil should happen to my lord,' says she, ' his *successor* I trust will be found, and give you protection. Situated as I am, they will not dare wreak their vengeance on me *now*.' And she kissed a medal she wore with great fervour, and Henry Esmond knew not in the least what her meaning was ; but hath since learned that, old as she was, she was for ever expecting, by the good offices of saints and relics, to have an heir to the title of Esmond.

Harry Esmond was too young to have been introduced into the secrets of politics in which his patrons were implicated ; for they put but few questions to the boy (who was little of stature, and looked much younger than his age), and such questions as they put he answered cautiously enough, and professing even more ignorance than he had, for which his examiners willingly enough gave him credit. He did not say a word about the window or the cupboard over the fireplace ; and these secrets quite escaped the eyes of the searchers.

So then my lady was consigned to her coach, and sent off to Hexton, with her woman and the man of law to bear her company, a couple of troopers riding on either side of the coach. And Harry was left behind at the Hall, belonging as it were to nobody, and quite alone in the world. The captain and a guard of men remained in possession there ; and the soldiers, who were very good-natured and kind, ate my lord's mutton and drank his wine, and made themselves comfortable, as they well might do, in such pleasant quarters.

The captains had their dinner served in my lord's tapestry parlour, and poor little Harry thought his duty was to wait upon Captain Westbury's chair, as his custom had been to serve his lord when he sat there.

After the departure of the countess, Dick the Scholar took Harry Esmond under his special protection, and would examine him in his humanities, and talk to him both of French and Latin, in which tongues the lad found, and his new friend was willing enough to acknowledge, that he was even more proficient than Scholar Dick. Hearing that he had learned them from a Jesuit, in the praise of whom, and whose goodness Harry was never tired of speaking, Dick, rather to the boy's surprise, who began to have an early shrewdness, like many children bred up alone, showed a great deal of theological science, and knowledge of the points at issue between the two Churches ; so that he and Harry would have hours of controversy together, in which the boy was certainly worsted by the arguments of this singular trooper. ' I am no common soldier,' Dick would say, and indeed it was easy to see by his learning, breeding, and many accomplishments, that he was not. ' I am of one of the most ancient families in the Empire ; I have had my education at a famous school, and a famous university; I learned my first rudiments of Latin near to Smithfield, in London, where the martyrs were roasted.'

' You hanged as many of ours,' interposed Harry ; ' and, for the matter of persecution, Father Holt told me that a young gentleman of Edinburgh, eighteen years of age, student at the college there, was hanged for heresy only last year, though he recanted, and solemnly asked pardon for his errors.'

' Faith ! there has been too much persecution on both sides : but 'twas you taught us.'

' Nay, 'twas the pagans began it,' cried the lad, and began to instance a number of saints of the Church, from the Protomartyr downwards—' this one's fire went out under him : that one's oil cooled in the cauldron : at a third holy head the executioner chopped three times and it would not come off. Show us martyrs in *your* Church for whom such miracles have been done.'

' Nay,' says the trooper gravely, ' the miracles of the first three centuries belong to my Church as well as yours, Master Papist,' and then added, with something of a smile upon his countenance, and a queer look at Harry—' And yet, my little catechizer, I have sometimes thought about those miracles, that there was not much good in them, since the victim's head always finished by coming off at the third or fourth chop, and the cauldron, if it did not boil one day, boiled the next. Howbeit, in our times, the Church has lost that questionable advantage of respites. There never was a shower to put out Ridley's fire, nor an angel to turn the edge of Campion's axe. The rack tore the limbs of Southwell the Jesuit and Sympson the Protestant alike. For faith, everywhere multitudes die willingly enough. I have read in Monsieur Rycaut's *History of the Turks*, of thousands of Mahomet's followers rushing upon death in battle as upon certain Paradise ;* and in the Great Mogul's dominions people fling themselves by hundreds under the cars of the idols annually, and the widows burn themselves on their husbands' bodies, as 'tis well known. 'Tis not the dying for a faith that's so hard, Master Harry— every man of every nation has done that—'tis the living up to it that is difficult, as I know to my cost,' he added, with a sigh. ' And ah ! ' he added, ' my poor lad, I am not strong enough to convince thee by my life—though to die for my religion would give me the greatest of joys—but I had a dear friend in Magdalen College in Oxford ; I wish Joe Addison were here to convince thee, as he quickly could —for I think he's a match for the whole College of Jesuits ; and what's more, in his life too. In that very sermon of Dr. Cudworth's which your priest was quoting from, and which suffered martyrdom in the brazier,' Dick added, with a smile, ' I had a thought of wearing the black coat (but was ashamed of my life you see, and took to this sorry red one)—I have often thought of Joe Addison—Doctor Cudworth says, " A good conscience is the best looking-glass of Heaven "—and there's a serenity in my friend's face which always reflects it—I wish you could see him, Harry.'

' Did he do you a great deal of good ? ' asked the lad, simply.

' He might have done,' said the other—' at least he taught me to see and approve better things. 'Tis my own fault, *deteriora sequi*.'*

' You seem very good,' the boy said.

' I'm not what I seem, alas ! ' answered the trooper—and indeed, as it turned out, poor Dick told the truth—for that very night, at supper in the hall, where the gentlemen of the troop took their repasts, and passed most part of their days dicing and smoking of tobacco, and singing and cursing, over the Castlewood ale—Harry Esmond found Dick the Scholar in a woful state of drunkenness. He hiccuped out a sermon ; and his laughing companions bade him sing a hymn, on which Dick, swearing he would run the scoundrel through the body who insulted his religion, made for his sword, which was hanging on the wall, and fell down flat on the floor under it, saying to Harry, who ran forward to help him, ' Ah, little Papist, I wish Joseph Addison was here ! '

Though the troopers of the king's Life Guards were all gentlemen, yet the rest of the gentlemen seemed ignorant and vulgar boors to Harry Esmond, with the exception of this good-natured Corporal Steele the Scholar, and Captain Westbury and Lieutenant Trant, who were always kind to the lad. They remained for some weeks or months encamped in Castlewood, and Harry learned from them, from time to time, how the lady at Hexton Castle was treated, and the particulars of her confinement there. 'Tis known that King William was disposed to deal very leniently with the gentry who remained faithful to the old king's cause ; and no prince usurping a crown, as his enemies said he did (righteously taking it as I think now), ever caused less blood to be shed. As for women-conspirators, he kept spies on the least dangerous, and locked up the others. Lady Castlewood had the best rooms in Hexton Castle, and the gaoler's garden to walk in ; and though she repeatedly desired to be led out to execution, like Mary Queen of Scots, there never was any thought of taking her painted old head off, or any desire to do aught but keep her person in security.

And it appeared she found that some were friends in her misfortune, whom she had, in her prosperity, considered as her worst enemies. Colonel Francis Esmond, my lord's cousin and her ladyship's, who had married the Dean of Winchester's daughter, and, since King James's departure out of England, had lived not very far away from Hexton town, hearing of his kinswoman's strait, and being friends with Colonel Brice, commanding for King William in Hexton, and with the Church dignitaries there, came to visit her ladyship in prison, offering to his uncle's daughter any friendly services which lay in his power. And he brought his lady and little daughter to see the prisoner, to the latter of whom, a child of great beauty, and many winning ways, the old viscountess took not a little liking, although between her ladyship and the child's mother there was little more love than formerly. There are some injuries which women never forgive one another; and Madam Francis Esmond, in marrying her cousin, had done one of those irretrievable wrongs to Lady Castlewood. But as she was now humiliated, and in misfortune, Madam Francis could allow a truce to her enmity, and could be kind for a while, at least, to her husband's discarded mistress. So the little Beatrix, her daughter, was permitted often to go and visit the imprisoned viscountess, who, in so far as the child and its father were concerned, got to abate in her anger towards that branch of the Castlewood family. And the letters of Colonel Esmond coming to light, as has been said, and his conduct being known to the king's council, the colonel was put in a better position with the existing Government than he had ever before been ; any suspicions regarding his loyalty were entirely done away ; and so he was enabled to be of more service to his kinswoman than he could otherwise have been.

And now there befell an event by which this lady recovered her liberty, and the house of Castlewood got a new owner, and fatherless little Harry Esmond a new and most kind protector and friend. Whatever that secret was which Harry was to hear from my lord, the boy never heard it ; for that night when Father Holt arrived, and carried my lord away with him, was the last on which Harry ever saw his patron. What happened to my lord may be briefly told here. Having found the horses at the place where they were lying, my lord and Father Holt rode together to Chatteris, where they had temporary refuge with one of the father's penitents in that city ; but the pursuit being hot for them, and the reward for the apprehension of one or the other considerable, it was deemed advisable that they should separate ; and the priest betook himself to other places of retreat known to him, whilst my lord passed over from Bristol into Ireland, in which kingdom King James had a Court and an army. My lord was but a small addition to this ; bringing, indeed, only his sword and the few pieces in his pocket ; but the king received him with some kindness and distinction in spite of his poor plight, confirmed him in his new title of marquis, gave him a regiment, and promised him further promotion. But titles or promotion were not to benefit him now. My lord was wounded at the fatal battle of the Boyne, flying from which field (long after his master had set him an example), he lay for a while concealed in the marshy country near to the town of Trim, and more from catarrh and fever caught in the bogs than from the steel of the enemy in the battle, sank and died. May the earth lie light upon Thomas of Castlewood ! He who writes this must speak in charity, though this lord did him and his two grievous wrongs : for one of these he would have made amends, perhaps, had life been spared him ; but the other lay beyond his power to repair, though

'tis to be hoped that a greater Power than a priest has
absolved him of it.   He got the comfort of this absolution,
too, such as it was : a priest of Trim writing a letter to my
lady to inform her of this calamity.

But in those days letters were slow of travelling, and our
priest's took two months or more on its journey from
Ireland to England : where, when it did arrive, it did not
find my lady at her own house ; she was at the king's
house of Hexton Castle when the letter came to Castlewood,
but it was opened for all that by the officer in command
there.

Harry Esmond well remembered the receipt of this letter,
which Lockwood brought in as Captain Westbury and
Lieutenant Trant were on the green playing at bowls, young
Esmond looking on at the sport, or reading his book in the
arbour.

' Here's news for Frank Esmond,' says Captain Westbury ;
' Harry, did you ever see Colonel Esmond ? '   And Captain
Westbury looked very hard at the boy as he spoke.

Harry said he had seen him but once when he was at
Hexton, at the ball there.

' And did he say anything ? '

' He said what I don't care to repeat,' Harry answered.
For he was now twelve years of age : he knew what his
birth was and the disgrace of it ; and he felt no love towards
the man who had most likely stained his mother's honour
and his own.

' Did you love my Lord Castlewood ? '

' I wait until I know my mother, sir, to say,' the boy
answered, his eyes filling with tears.

' Something has happened to Lord Castlewood,' Captain
Westbury said, in a very grave tone—' something which
must happen to us all.   He is dead of a wound received
at the Boyne, fighting for King James.'

' I am glad my lord fought for the right cause,' the boy
said.

' It was better to meet death on the field like a man, than
face it on Tower Hill, as some of them may,' continued
Mr. Westbury.   ' I hope he has made some testament, or
provided for thee somehow. This letter says, he recommends
*unicum filium suum dilectissimum**to his lady.   I hope he
has left you more than that.'

Harry did not know, he said.   He was in the hands of

Heaven and Fate ; but more lonely now, as it seemed to him, than he had been all the rest of his life ; and that night, as he lay in his little room which he still occupied, the boy thought with many a pang of shame and grief of his strange and solitary condition :—how he had a father and no father ; a nameless mother that had been brought to ruin, perhaps, by that very father whom Harry could only acknowledge in secret and with a blush, and whom he could neither love nor revere. And he sickened to think how Father Holt, a stranger, and two or three soldiers, his acquaintances of the last six weeks, were the only friends he had in the great wide world, where he was now quite alone. The soul of the boy was full of love, and he longed as he lay in the darkness there for some one upon whom he could bestow it. He remembers, and must to his dying day, the thoughts and tears of that long night, the hours tolling through it. Who was he and what ? Why here rather than elsewhere ? I have a mind, he thought, to go to that priest at Trim, and find out what my father said to him on his death-bed confession. Is there any child in the whole world so un-protected as I am ? Shall I get up and quit this place, and run to Ireland ? With these thoughts and tears the lad passed that night away until he wept himself to sleep.

The next day, the gentlemen of the guard who had heard what had befallen him were more than usually kind to the child, especially his friend Scholar Dick, who told him about his own father's death, which had happened when Dick was a child at Dublin, not quite five years of age. ' That was the first sensation of grief,' Dick said, ' I ever knew.* I remember I went into the room where his body lay, and my mother sat weeping beside it. I had my battle-dore in my hand, and fell a-beating the coffin, and calling papa ; on which my mother caught me in her arms, and told me in a flood of tears papa could not hear me, and would play with me no more, for they were going to put him under ground, whence he could never come to us again. And this,' said Dick kindly, ' has made me pity all children ever since ; and caused me to love thee, my poor fatherless, motherless lad. And if ever thou wantest a friend, thou shalt have one in Richard Steele.'

Harry Esmond thanked him, and was grateful. But what could Corporal Steele do for him ? take him to ride a spare horse, and be servant to the troop ? Though there might be a bar in Harry Esmond's shield, it was a noble one. The counsel of the two friends was, that little Harry should stay where he was, and abide his fortune : so Esmond stayed on at Castlewood, awaiting with no small anxiety the fate, whatever it was, which was over him.

CHAPTER VII

I AM LEFT AT CASTLEWOOD AN ORPHAN, AND FIND MOST KIND PROTECTORS THERE

DURING the stay of the soldiers in Castlewood, honest Dick the Scholar was the constant companion of the lonely little orphan lad Harry Esmond : and they read together, and they played bowls together, and when the other troopers or their officers, who were free-spoken over their cups (as was the way of that day, when neither men nor women were over-nice), talked unbecomingly of their amours and gallantries before the child, Dick, who very likely was setting the whole company laughing, would stop their jokes with a *maxima debetur pueris reverentia*,* and once offered to lug out against another trooper called Hulking Tom, who wanted to ask Harry Esmond a ribald question.

Also, Dick seeing that the child had, as he said, a sensibility above his years, and a great and praiseworthy discretion, confided to Harry his love for a vintner's daughter, near to the Tollyard, Westminster, whom Dick addressed as Saccharissa in many verses of his composition, and without whom he said it would be impossible that he could continue to live. He vowed this a thousand times in a day, though Harry smiled to see the lovelorn swain had his health and appetite as well as the most heart-whole trooper in the regiment : and he swore Harry to secrecy too, which vow the lad religiously kept, until he found that officers and privates were all taken into Dick's confidence, and had the benefit of his verses. And it must be owned likewise that, while Dick was sighing after Saccharissa in London, he had consolations in the country ; for there came a wench out of Castlewood village who had washed his linen, and who cried sadly when she heard he was gone : and without paying her bill too, which Harry Esmond took upon himself to discharge by giving the girl a silver pocket-piece, which Scholar Dick had presented to him, when, with many embraces and prayers for his prosperity, Dick parted from him, the garrison of Castlewood being ordered away. Dick the Scholar said he would never forget his young friend, nor indeed did he : and Harry was sorry when the kind soldiers vacated Castlewood, looking forward with no small anxiety (for care and solitude had made him thoughtful beyond his years) to his fate when the new lord and lady of the house came to live there. He had lived to be past twelve years old now ; and had never had a friend, save this wild trooper perhaps, and Father Holt ; and had a fond and affectionate heart, tender to weakness, that would fain attach itself to somebody, and did not seem at rest until it had found a friend who would take charge of it.

The instinct which led Henry Esmond to admire and love the gracious person, the fair apparition of whose beauty and kindness had so moved him when he first beheld her, became soon a devoted affection and passion of gratitude, which entirely filled his young heart, that as yet, except in the case of dear Father Holt, had had very little kindness for which to be thankful. *O Dea certè*, thought he, remembering the lines out of the *Aeneis* which Mr. Holt had taught him. There seemed, as the boy thought, in every look or gesture of this fair creature, an angelical softness and bright pity—in motion or repose she seemed gracious alike ; the tone of her voice, though she uttered words ever so trivial, gave him a pleasure that amounted almost to anguish. It cannot be called love, that a lad of twelve years of age, little more than a menial, felt for an exalted lady, his mistress : but it was worship. To catch her glance, to divine her errand and run on it before she had spoken it ; to watch, to follow, adore her ; became the business of his life. Meanwhile, as is the way often, his idol had idols of her own, and never thought of or suspected the admiration of her little pigmy adorer.

My lady had on her side her three idols : first and foremost, Jove and supreme ruler, was her lord, Harry's patron, the good Viscount of Castlewood. All wishes of his were laws with her. If he had a headache, she was ill. If he frowned, she trembled. If he joked, she smiled and was charmed. If he went a-hunting, she was always at the window to see him ride away, her little son crowing on her

arm, or on the watch till his return. She made dishes for
his dinner : spiced his wine for him : made the toast for
his tankard at breakfast : hushed the house when he slept
in his chair, and watched for a look when he woke. If my
lord was not a little proud of his beauty, my lady adored it.
She clung to his arm as he paced the terrace, her two fair
little hands clasped round his great one ; her eyes were
never tired of looking in his face and wondering at its
perfection. Her little son was his son, and had his father's
look and curly brown hair. Her daughter Beatrix was his
daughter, and had his eyes—were there ever such beautiful
eyes in the world ? All the house was arranged so as to
bring him ease and give him pleasure. She liked the small
gentry round about to come and pay him court, never
caring for admiration for herself ; those who wanted to
be well with the lady must admire him. Not regarding
her dress, she would wear a gown to rags, because he
had once liked it : and, if he brought her a brooch or a
ribbon, would prefer it to all the most costly articles of her
wardrobe.

My lord went to London every year for six weeks, and the
family being too poor to appear at Court with any figure,
he went alone. It was not until he was out of sight that
her face showed any sorrow : and what a joy when he came
back ! What preparation before his return ! The fond
creature had his arm-chair at the chimney-side—delighting
to put the children in it, and look at them there. Nobody
took his place at the table ; but his silver tankard stood
there as when my lord was present.

A pretty sight it was to see, during my lord's absence, or
on those many mornings when sleep or headache kept him
abed, this fair young lady of Castlewood, her little daughter
at her knee, and her domestics gathered round her reading
the Morning Prayer of the English Church. Esmond long
remembered how she looked and spoke kneeling reverently
before the sacred book, the sun shining upon her golden
hair until it made a halo round about her. A dozen of
the servants of the house kneeled in a line opposite their
mistress ; for awhile Harry Esmond kept apart from these
mysteries, but Doctor Tusher showing him that the prayers
read were those of the Church of all ages, and the boy's
own inclination prompting him to be always as near as he
might to his mistress, and to think all things she did right,

from listening to the prayers in the antechamber, he came presently to kneel down with the rest of the household in the parlour ; and before a couple of years my lady had made a thorough convert. Indeed, the boy loved his catechizer so much that he would have subscribed to anything she bade him, and was never tired of listening to her fond discourse and simple comments upon the book, which she read to him in a voice of which it was difficult to resist the sweet persuasion and tender appealing kindness. This friendly controversy, and the intimacy which it occasioned, bound the lad more fondly than ever to his mistress. The happiest period of all his life was this ; and the young mother, with her daughter and son, and the orphan lad whom she protected, read and worked and played, and were children together. If the lady looked forward—as what fond woman does not ?—towards the future, she had no plans from which Harry Esmond was left out ; and a thousand and a thousand times in his passionate and impetuous way he vowed that no power should separate him from his mistress, and only asked for some chance to happen by which he might show his fidelity to her. Now, at the close of his life, as he sits and recalls in tranquillity the happy and busy scenes of it, he can think, not ungratefully, that he has been faithful to that early vow. Such a life is so simple that years may be chronicled in a few lines. But few men's life-voyages are destined to be all prosperous ; and this calm of which we are speaking was soon to come to an end.

As Esmond grew, and observed for himself, he found of necessity much to read and think of outside that fond circle of kinsfolk who had admitted him to join hand with them. He read more books than they cared to study with him ; was alone in the midst of them many a time, and passed nights over labours, futile perhaps, but in which they could not join him. His dear mistress divined his thoughts with her usual jealous watchfulness of affection : began to forebode a time when he would escape from his home-nest ; and, at his eager protestations to the contrary, would only sigh and shake her head. Before those fatal decrees in life are executed, there are always secret previsions and warning omens. When everything yet seems calm, we are aware that the storm is coming. Ere the happy days were over, two at least of that home-party felt that they were

drawing to a close ; and were uneasy, and on the look-out
for the cloud which was to obscure their calm.

'Twas easy for Harry to see, however much his lady persisted in obedience and admiration for her husband, that my
lord tired of his quiet life, and grew weary, and then testy,
at those gentle bonds with which his wife would have held
him. As they say the Grand Lama of Thibet is very much
fatigued by his character of divinity, and yawns on his altar
as his bonzes kneel and worship him, many a home-god
grows heartily sick of the reverence with which his family
devotees pursue him, and sighs for freedom and for his old
life, and to be off the pedestal on which his dependants
would have him sit for ever, whilst they adore him, and ply
him with flowers, and hymns, and incense, and flattery ;—
so, after a few years of his marriage, my honest Lord Castlewood began to tire ; all the high-flown raptures and devotional ceremonies with which his wife, his chief priestess,
treated him, first sent him to sleep, and then drove him out
of doors ; for the truth must be told, that my lord was a
jolly gentleman, with very little of the august or divine in
his nature, though his fond wife persisted in revering it—
and, besides, he had to pay a penalty for this love, which
persons of his disposition seldom like to defray : and, in
a word, if he had a loving wife, had a very jealous and exacting one. Then he wearied of this jealousy : then he broke
away from it ; then came, no doubt, complaints and
recriminations ; then, perhaps, promises of amendment
not fulfilled ; then upbraidings not the more pleasant
because they were silent, and only sad looks and tearful
eyes conveyed them. Then, perhaps, the pair reached that
other stage which is not uncommon in married life, when
the woman perceives that the god of the honeymoon is a god
no more ; only a mortal like the rest of us—and so she looks
into her heart, and lo ! *vacuae sedes et inania arcana*.* And
now, supposing our lady to have a fine genius and a brilliant
wit of her own, and the magic spell and infatuation removed
from her which had led her to worship as a god a very
ordinary mortal—and what follows ? They live together,
and they dine together, and they say ' my dear ' and ' my
love ' as heretofore ; but the man is himself, and the
woman herself : that dream of love is over, as everything
else is over in life ; as flowers and fury, and griefs and
pleasures, are over.

Very likely the Lady Castlewood had ceased to adore her husband herself long before she got off her knees, or would allow her household to discontinue worshipping him. To do him justice, my lord never exacted this subservience : he laughed and joked, and drank his bottle, and swore when he was angry, much too familiarly for any one pretending to sublimity ; and did his best to destroy the ceremonial with which his wife chose to surround him. And it required no great conceit on young Esmond's part to see that his own brains were better than his patron's, who, indeed, never assumed any airs of superiority over the lad, or over any dependant of his, save when he was displeased, in which case he would express his mind, in oaths, very freely ; and who, on the contrary, perhaps, spoiled ' Parson Harry ', as he called young Esmond, by constantly praising his parts, and admiring his boyish stock of learning.

It may seem ungracious in one who has received a hundred favours from his patron to speak in any but a reverential manner of his elders ; but the present writer has had descendants of his own, whom he has brought up with as little as possible of the servility at present exacted by parents from children (under which mask of duty there often lurks indifference, contempt, or rebellion) : and as he would have his grandsons believe or represent him to be not an inch taller than Nature has made him : so, with regard to his past acquaintances, he would speak without anger, but with truth, as far as he knows it, neither extenuating nor setting down aught in malice.*

So long, then, as the world moved according to Lord Castlewood's wishes, he was good-humoured enough ; of a temper naturally sprightly and easy, liking to joke, especially with his inferiors, and charmed to receive the tribute of their laughter. All exercises of the body he could perform to perfection—shooting at a mark and flying, breaking horses, riding at the ring, pitching the quoit, playing at all games with great skill. And not only did he do these things well, but he thought he did them to perfection ; hence he was often tricked about horses, which he pretended to know better than any jockey ; was made to play at ball and billiards by sharpers who took his money ; and came back from London wofully poorer each time than he went, as the state of his affairs testified, when the sudden accident came by which his career was brought to an end.

He was fond of the parade of dress, and passed as many hours daily at his toilette as an elderly coquette. A tenth part of his day was spent in the brushing of his teeth and the oiling of his hair, which was curling and brown, and which he did not like to conceal under a periwig, such as almost everybody of that time wore (we have the liberty of our hair back now, but powder and pomatum along with it. When, I wonder, will these monstrous poll-taxes of our age be withdrawn, and men allowed to carry their colours, black, red, or grey, as nature made them ?) And, as he liked her to be well dressed, his lady spared no pains in that matter to please him ; indeed, she would dress her head or cut it off if he had bidden her.

It was a wonder to young Esmond, serving as page to my lord and lady, to hear, day after day, to such company as came, the same boisterous stories told by my lord, at which his lady never failed to smile or hold down her head, and Doctor Tusher to burst out laughing at the proper point, or cry, ' Fie, my lord, remember my cloth,' but with such a faint show of resistance, that it only provoked my lord further. Lord Castlewood's stories rose by degrees, and became stronger after the ale at dinner and the bottle after- wards ; my lady always taking flight after the very first glass to Church and King, and leaving the gentlemen to drink the rest of the toasts by themselves.

And, as Harry Esmond was her page, he also was called from duty at this time. ' My lord has lived in the army and with soldiers,' she would say to the lad, ' amongst whom great licence is allowed. You have had a different nurture, and I trust these things will change as you grow older ; not that any fault attaches to my lord, who is one of the best and most religious men in this kingdom.' And very likely she believed so. 'Tis strange what a man may do, and a woman yet think him an angel.

And as Esmond has taken truth for his motto, it must be owned, even with regard to that other angel, his mistress, that she had a fault of character, which flawed her perfec- tions. With the other sex perfectly tolerant and kindly, of her own she was invariably jealous, and a proof that she had this vice is, that though she would acknowledge a thousand faults that she had not, to this which she had she could never be got to own. But if there came a woman with even a semblance of beauty to Castlewood, she was so sure to find out some wrong in her, that my lord, laughing in his jolly way, would often joke with her concerning her foible. Comely servant-maids might come for hire, but none were taken at Castlewood. The housekeeper was old ; my lady's own waiting-woman squinted, and was marked with the small-pox ; the housemaids and scullion were ordinary country wenches, to whom Lady Castlewood was kind, as her nature made her to everybody almost ; but as soon as ever she had to do with a pretty woman, she was cold, retiring, and haughty. The country ladies found this fault in her ; and though the men all admired her, their wives and daughters complained of her coldness and airs, and said that Castlewood was pleasanter in Lady Jezebel's time (as the dowager was called) than at present. Some few were of my mistress's side. Old Lady Blenkinsop Jointure, who had been at Court in King James the First's time, always took her side ; and so did old Mistress Crookshank, Bishop Crookshank's daughter, of Hexton, who, with some more of their like, pronounced my lady an angel ; but the pretty women were not of this mind ; and the opinion of the country was, that my lord was tied to his wife's apron-strings, and that she ruled over him.

The second fight which Harry Esmond had, was at fourteen years of age, with Bryan Hawkshaw, Sir John Hawkshaw's son, of Bramblebrook, who advancing this opinion, that my lady was jealous, and henpecked my lord, put Harry into such a fury, that Harry fell on him, and with such rage, that the other boy, who was two years older, and by far bigger than he, had by far the worst of the assault, until it was interrupted by Doctor Tusher walking out of the dinner room.

Bryan Hawkshaw got up, bleeding at the nose, having, indeed, been surprised, as many a stronger man might have been, by the fury of the assault upon him.

'You little bastard beggar!' he said, 'I'll murder you for this!' And indeed he was big enough.

'Bastard or not,' said the other, grinding his teeth, 'I have a couple of swords, and if you like to meet me, as a man, on the terrace to-night——'

And here the doctor coming up, the colloquy of the young champions ended. Very likely, big as he was, Hawkshaw did not care to continue a fight with such a ferocious opponent as this had been.

CHAPTER VIII

AFTER GOOD FORTUNE COMES EVIL

SINCE my Lady Mary Wortley Montagu brought home the
custom of inoculation from Turkey (a perilous practice
many deem it, and only a useless rushing into the jaws of
danger), I think the severity of the small-pox, that dreadful
scourge of the world, has somewhat been abated in our part
of it ; and remembering in my time hundreds of the young
and beautiful who have been carried to the grave, or have
only risen from their pillows frightfully scarred and disfigured by this malady. Many a sweet face hath left its
roses on the bed, on which this dreadful and withering blight
has laid them. In my early days this pestilence would enter
a village and destroy half its inhabitants : at its approach
it may well be imagined not only the beautiful but the
strongest were alarmed, and those fled who could. One
day in the year 1694 (I have good reason to remember it),
Doctor Tusher ran into Castlewood House, with a face of
consternation, saying that the malady had made its appearance at the blacksmith's house in the village, and that one
of the maids there was down in the small-pox.

The blacksmith, beside his forge and irons for horses, had
an alehouse for men, which his wife kept, and his company
sat on benches before the inn door, looking at the smithy
while they drank their beer. Now, there was a pretty girl
at this inn, the landlord's men called Nancy Sievewright,
a bouncing fresh-looking lass, whose face was as red as the
hollyhocks over the pales of the garden behind the inn.
At this time Harry Esmond was a lad of sixteen, and
somehow in his walks and rambles it often happened that
he fell in with Nancy Sievewright's bonny face ; if he did
not want something done at the blacksmith's he would go
and drink ale at the ' Three Castles ', or find some pretext
for seeing this poor Nancy. Poor thing, Harry meant or
imagined no harm ; and she, no doubt, as little, but the
truth is they were always meeting—in the lanes, or by the
brook, or at the garden-palings, or about Castlewood : it
was, ' Lord, Mr. Henry ! ' and ' How do you do, Nancy ? '
many and many a time in the week. 'Tis surprising the

magnetic attraction which draws people together from ever
so far. I blush as I think of poor Nancy now, in a red
bodice and buxom purple cheeks and a canvas petticoat ;
and that I devised schemes, and set traps, and made
speeches in my heart, which I seldom had courage to say
when in presence of that humble enchantress, who knew
nothing beyond milking a cow, and opened her black eyes
with wonder when I made one of my fine speeches out of
Waller* or Ovid. Poor Nancy ! from the mist of far-off
years thine honest country face beams out ; and I remember
thy kind voice as if I had heard it yesterday.

When Doctor Tusher brought the news that the small-
pox was at the ' Three Castles ', whither a tramper, it was
said, had brought the malady, Henry Esmond's first thought
was of alarm for poor Nancy, and then of shame and disquiet for the Castlewood family, lest he might have brought
this infection ; for the truth is that Mr. Harry had been
sitting in a back room for an hour that day, where Nancy
Sievewright was with a little brother who complained of
headache, and was lying stupefied and crying, either in a
chair by the corner of the fire, or in Nancy's lap, or on
mine.

Little Lady Beatrix screamed out at Dr. Tusher's news ;
and my lord cried out, 'God bless me ! ' He was a brave
man, and not afraid of death in any shape but this. He
was very proud of his pink complexion and fair hair—but
the idea of death by small-pox scared him beyond all other
ends. ' We will take the children and ride away to-morrow
to Walcote : ' this was my lord's small house, inherited from
his mother, near to Winchester.

' That is the best refuge in case the disease spreads,' said
Dr. Tusher. ' 'Tis awful to think of it beginning at the
alehouse. Half the people of the village have visited that
to-day, or the blacksmith's, which is the same thing. My
clerk Simons lodges with them—I can never go into my
reading-desk and have that fellow so near me. I *won't* have
that man near me.'

' If a parishioner dying in the small-pox sent to you,
would you not go ? ' asked my lady, looking up from her
frame of work, with her calm blue eyes.

' By the Lord, *I* wouldn't,' said my lord.

' We are not in a Popish country : and a sick man doth
not absolutely need absolution and confession,' said the

doctor. ' 'Tis true they are a comfort and a help to him when attainable, and to be administered with hope of good. But in a case where the life of a parish priest in the midst of his flock is highly valuable to them, he is not called upon to risk it (and therewith the lives, future prospects, and temporal, even spiritual welfare of his own family) for the sake of a single person, who is not very likely in a condition even to understand the religious message whereof the priest is the bringer—being uneducated, and likewise stupefied or delirious by disease. If your ladyship or his lordship, my excellent good friend and patron, were to take it——'

' God forbid ! ' cried my lord.

' Amen,' continued Dr. Tusher. ' Amen to that prayer, my very good lord ! for your sake I would lay my life down ' —and, to judge from the alarmed look of the doctor's purple face, you would have thought that that sacrifice was about to be called for instantly.

To love children, and be gentle with them, was an instinct, rather than a merit, in Henry Esmond, so much so, that he thought almost with a sort of shame of his liking for them, and of the softness into which it betrayed him ; and on this day the poor fellow had not only had his young friend, the milkmaid's brother, on his knee, but had been drawing pictures, and telling stories to the little Frank Esmond, who had occupied the same place for an hour after dinner, and was never tired of Henry's tales, and his pictures of soldiers and horses. As luck would have it, Beatrix had not on that evening taken her usual place, which generally she was glad enough to have, upon her tutor's lap. For Beatrix, from the earliest time, was jealous of every caress which was given to her little brother Frank. She would fling away even from the maternal arms, if she saw Frank had been there before her ; insomuch that Lady Castlewood was obliged not to show her love for her son in the presence of the little girl, and embrace one or the other alone. She would turn pale and red with rage if she caught signs of intelligence or affection between Frank and his mother ; would sit apart, and not speak for a whole night, if she thought the boy had a better fruit or a larger cake than hers ; would fling away a ribbon if he had one ; and from the earliest age, sitting up in her little chair by the great fireplace opposite to the corner where Lady Castlewood

commonly sat at her embroidery, would utter infantine
sarcasms about the favour shown to her brother. These, if
spoken in the presence of Lord Castlewood, tickled and
amused his humour ; he would pretend to love Frank best,
and dandle and kiss him, and roar with laughter at Beatrix's
jealousy. But the truth is, my lord did not often witness
these scenes, nor very much trouble the quiet fireside at
which his lady passed many long evenings. My lord was
hunting all day when the season admitted ; he frequented
all the cockfights and fairs in the country, and would ride
twenty miles to see a main fought, or two clowns break their
heads at a cudgelling match ; and he liked better to sit in
his parlour drinking ale and punch with Jack and Tom,
than in his wife's drawing-room : whither, if he came, he
brought only too often bloodshot eyes, a hiccuping voice,
and a reeling gait. The management of the house and the
property, the care of the few tenants and the village poor,
and the accounts of the estate, were in the hands of his lady
and her young secretary, Harry Esmond. My lord took
charge of the stables, the kennel, and the cellar—and he
filled this and emptied it too.

So it chanced that upon this very day, when poor Harry
Esmond had had the blacksmith's son, and the peer's son,
alike upon his knee, little Beatrix, who would come to her
tutor willingly enough with her book and her writing, had
refused him, seeing the place occupied by her brother, and,
luckily for her, had sat at the further end of the room,
away from him, playing with a spaniel dog which she had
(and for which, by fits and starts, she would take a great
affection), and talking at Harry Esmond over her shoulder,
as she pretended to caress the dog, saying, that Fido would
love her, and she would love Fido, and nothing but Fido,
all her life.

When, then, the news was brought that the little boy at
the ' Three Castles ' was ill with the small-pox, poor Harry
Esmond felt a shock of alarm, not so much for himself as for
his mistress's son, whom he might have brought into peril.
Beatrix, who had pouted sufficiently (and who whenever
a stranger appeared began, from infancy almost, to play off
little graces to catch his attention), her brother being now
gone to bed, was for taking her place upon Esmond's knee :
for, though the doctor was very obsequious to her, she did
not like him, because he had thick boots and dirty hands

(the pert young miss said), and because she hated learning the catechism.

But as she advanced towards Esmond from the corner where she had been sulking, he started back and placed the great chair on which he was sitting between him and her—saying in the French language to Lady Castlewood, with whom the young lad had read much, and whom he had perfected in this tongue—'Madam, the child must not approach me; I must tell you that I was at the blacksmith's to-day, and had his little boy upon my lap.'

'Where you took my son afterwards,' Lady Castlewood said, very angry, and turning red. 'I thank you, sir, for giving him such company. Beatrix,' she said in English, 'I forbid you to touch Mr. Esmond. Come away, child—come to your room. Come to your room—I wish your reverence good night—and you, sir, had you not better go back to your friends at the alehouse?' Her eyes, ordinarily so kind, darted flashes of anger as she spoke; and she tossed up her head (which hung down commonly) with the mien of a princess.

'Hey-day!' says my lord, who was standing by the fireplace—indeed he was in the position to which he generally came by that hour of the evening—'Hey-day! Rachel, what are you in a passion about? Ladies ought never to be in a passion. Ought they, Doctor Tusher? though it does good to see Rachel in a passion—Damme, Lady Castlewood, you look dev'lish handsome in a passion.'

'It is, my lord, because Mr. Henry Esmond, having nothing to do with his time here, and not having a taste for our company, has been to the alehouse, where he has *some friends*.'

My lord burst out with a laugh and an oath—'You young sly-boots, you've been at Nancy Sievewright. D—— the young hypocrite, who'd have thought it in him? I say, Tusher, he's been after——'

'Enough, my lord,' said my lady, 'don't insult me with this talk.'

'Upon my word,' said poor Harry, ready to cry with shame and mortification, 'the honour of that young person is perfectly unstained for me.'

'Oh, of course, of course,' says my lord, more and more laughing and tipsy. 'Upon his *honour*, doctor—Nancy Sieve——'

'Take Mistress Beatrix to bed,' my lady cried at this moment to Mrs. Tucker her woman, who came in with her ladyship's tea. 'Put her into my room—no, into yours,' she added quickly. 'Go, my child: go, I say: not a word!' And Beatrix, quite surprised at so sudden a tone of authority from one who was seldom accustomed to raise her voice, went out of the room with a scared countenance and waited even to burst out a-crying, until she got to the door with Mrs. Tucker.

For once her mother took little heed of her sobbing, and continued to speak eagerly—'My lord,' she said, 'this young man—your dependant—told me just now in French—he was ashamed to speak in his own language—that he had been at the ale-house all day, where he has had that little wretch who is now ill of the small-pox on his knee. And he comes home reeking from that place—yes, reeking from it—and takes my boy into his lap without shame, and sits down by me, yes, by *me*. He may have killed Frank for what I know—killed our child. Why was he brought in to disgrace our house? Why is he here? Let him go—let him go, I say, to-night, and pollute the place no more.'

She had never once uttered a syllable of unkindness to Harry Esmond; and her cruel words smote the poor boy, so that he stood for some moments bewildered with grief and rage at the injustice of such a stab from such a hand. He turned quite white from red, which he had been.

'I cannot help my birth, madam,' he said, 'nor my other misfortune. And as for your boy, if—if my coming nigh to him pollutes him now, it was not so always. Good night, my lord. Heaven bless you and yours for your goodness to me. I have tired her ladyship's kindness out, and I will go;' and, sinking down on his knee, Harry Esmond took the rough hand of his benefactor and kissed it.

'He wants to go to the ale-house—let him go,' cried my lady.

'I'm d——d if he shall,' said my lord. 'I didn't think you could be so d——d ungrateful, Rachel.'

Her reply was to burst into a flood of tears, and to quit the room with a rapid glance at Harry Esmond. As my lord, not heeding them, and still in great good humour, raised up his young client from his kneeling posture (for a thousand kindnesses had caused the lad to revere my lord as a father), and put his broad hand on Harry Esmond's shoulder—

' She was always so,' my lord said ; ' the very notion of a woman drives her mad. I took to liquor on that very account, by Jove, for no other reason than that ; for she can't be jealous of a beer-barrel or a bottle of rum, can she, doctor ? D—— it, look at the maids—just look at the maids in the house ' (my lord pronounced all the words together—just-look-at-the-maze-in-the-house : jever-see-such-maze ?) ' You wouldn't take a wife out of Castlewood now, would you, doctor ? ' and my lord burst out laughing.

The doctor, who had been looking at my Lord Castlewood from under his eyelids, said, ' But joking apart, and, my lord, as a divine, I cannot treat the subject in a jocular light, nor, as a pastor of this congregation, look with anything but sorrow at the idea of so very young a sheep going astray.'

' Sir,' said young Esmond, bursting out indignantly, ' she told me that you yourself were a horrid old man, and had offered to kiss her in the dairy.'

' For shame, Henry,' cried Doctor Tusher, turning as red as a turkey-cock, while my lord continued to roar with laughter. ' If you listen to the falsehoods of an abandoned girl—— '

' She is as honest as any woman in England, and as pure for me,' cried out Henry, ' and as kind, and as good. For shame on you to malign her ! '

' Far be it from me to do so,' cried the doctor. ' Heaven grant I may be mistaken in the girl, and in you, sir, who have a truly *precocious* genius ; but that is not the point at issue at present. It appears that the small-pox broke out in the little boy at the " Three Castles " ; that it was on him when you visited the ale-house, for your *own* reasons ; and that you sat with the child for some time, and immediately afterwards with my young lord.' The doctor raised his voice as he spoke, and looked towards my lady, who had now come back, looking very pale, with a handkerchief in her hand.

' This is all very true, sir,' said Lady Esmond, looking at the young man.

' 'Tis to be feared that he may have brought the infection with him.'

' From the ale-house—yes,' said my lady.

' D—— it, I forgot when I collared you, boy,' cried my

lord, stepping back. ' Keep off, Harry, my boy ; there's no good in running into the wolf's jaws, you know.'

My lady looked at him with some surprise, and instantly advancing to Henry Esmond, took his hand. ' I beg your pardon, Henry,' she said ; ' I spoke very unkindly. I have no right to interfere with you—with your——'

My lord broke out into an oath. ' Can't you leave the boy alone, my lady ? ' She looked a little red, and faintly pressed the lad's hand as she dropped it.

' There is no use, my lord,' she said ; ' Frank was on his knee as he was making pictures, and was running constantly from Henry to me. The evil is done, if any.'

' Not with me, damme,' cried my lord. ' I've been smoking '—and he lighted his pipe again with a coal—' and it keeps off infection ; and as the disease is in the village— plague take it—I would have you leave it. We'll go to-morrow to Walcote, my lady.'

' I have no fear,' said my lady ; ' I may have had it as an infant, it broke out in our house then ; and when four of my sisters had it at home, two years before our marriage, I escaped it, and two of my dear sisters died.'

' I won't run the risk,' said my lord ; ' I'm as bold as any man, but I'll not bear that.'

' Take Beatrix with you and go,' said my lady. ' For us the mischief is done ; and Tucker can wait upon us, who has had the disease.'

' You take care to choose 'em ugly enough,' said my lord, at which her ladyship hung down her head and looked foolish : and my lord, calling away Tusher, bade him come to the oak parlour and have a pipe. The doctor made a low bow to her ladyship (of which salaams he was profuse), and walked off on his creaking square-toes after his patron.

When the lady and the young man were alone, there was a silence of some moments, during which he stood at the fire, looking rather vacantly at the dying embers, whilst her ladyship busied herself with her tambour-frame and needles.

' I am sorry,' she said, after a pause, in a hard, dry voice, —' I *repeat* I am sorry that I showed myself so ungrateful for the safety of my son. It was not at all my wish that you should leave us, I am sure, unless you found pleasure else-where. But you must perceive, Mr. Esmond, that at your age, and with your tastes, it is impossible that you can continue to stay upon the intimate footing in which you have been in this family. You have wished to go to the University, and I think 'tis quite as well that you should be sent thither. I did not press this matter, thinking you a child, as you are, indeed, in years—quite a child ; and I should never have thought of treating you otherwise until—until these *circumstances* came to light. And I shall beg my lord to dispatch you as quick as possible : and will go on with Frank's learning as well as I can (I owe my father thanks for a little grounding, and you, I'm sure, for much that you have taught me),—and—and I wish you a good night, Mr. Esmond.'

And with this she dropped a stately curtsy, and, taking her candle, went away through the tapestry door, which led to her apartments. Esmond stood by the fireplace, blankly staring after her. Indeed, he scarce seemed to see until she was gone ; and then her image was impressed upon him, and remained for ever fixed upon his memory. He saw her retreating, the taper lighting up her marble face, her scarlet lip quivering, and her shining golden hair. He went to his own room, and to bed, where he tried to read, as his custom was ; but he never knew what he was reading until afterwards he remembered the appearance of the letters of the book (it was in Montaigne's *Essays*), and the events of the day passed before him—that is, of the last hour of the day ; for as for the morning, and the poor milkmaid yonder, he never so much as once thought. And he could not get to sleep until daylight, and woke with a violent headache, and quite unrefreshed.

He had brought the contagion with him from the ' Three Castles' sure enough, and was presently laid up with the small-pox, which spared the Hall no more than it did the cottage.

CHAPTER IX

I HAVE THE SMALL-POX, AND PREPARE TO LEAVE CASTLEWOOD

WHEN Harry Esmond passed through the crisis of that malady, and returned to health again, he found that little Frank Esmond had also suffered and rallied after the disease, and the lady his mother was down with it, with a couple more of the household. ' It was a providence, for which we all ought to be thankful,' Doctor Tusher said, 'that my lady and her son were spared, while Death carried off the poor domestics of the house ; ' and rebuked Harry for asking, in his simple way—for which we ought to be thankful—that the servants were killed, or the gentlefolks were saved ? Nor could young Esmond agree in the doctor's vehement protestations to my lady, when he visited her during her convalescence, that the malady had not in the least impaired her charms, and had not been churl enough to injure the fair features of the Viscountess of Castlewood, whereas in spite of these fine speeches, Harry thought that her ladyship's beauty was very much injured by the small-pox. When the marks of the disease cleared away, they did not, it is true, leave furrows or scars on her face (except one, perhaps, on her forehead over her left eyebrow) ; but the delicacy of her rosy colour and complexion were gone : her eyes had lost their brilliancy, her hair fell, and her face looked older. It was as if a coarse hand had rubbed off the delicate tints of that sweet picture, and brought it, as one has seen unskilful painting-cleaners do, to the dead colour. Also, it must be owned, that for a year or two after the malady, her ladyship's nose was swollen and redder.

There would be no need to mention these trivialities, but that they actually influenced many lives, as trifles will in the world, where a gnat often plays a greater part than an elephant, and a mole-hill, as we know in King William's case, can upset an empire.* When Tusher in his courtly way (at which Harry Esmond always chafed and spoke scornfully) vowed and protested that my lady's face was none the worse—the lad broke out and said, ' It *is* worse : and my mistress is not near so handsome as she was ' ; on which poor Lady Esmond gave a rueful smile, and a look into a

little Venice glass she had, which showed her I suppose
that what the stupid boy said was only too true, for she
turned away from the glass and her eyes filled with tears.

The sight of these in Esmond's heart always created a sort
of rage of pity, and seeing them on the face of the lady whom
he loved best, the young blunderer sank down on his knees,
and besought her to pardon him, saying that he was a fool
and an idiot, that he was a brute to make such a speech, he
who had caused her malady, and Doctor Tusher told him
that a bear he was indeed, and a bear he would remain, at
which speech poor young Esmond was so dumb-stricken that
he did not even growl.

'He is *my* bear, and I will not have him baited, doctor,'
my lady said, patting her hand kindly on the boy's head,
as he was still kneeling at her feet. 'How your hair has
come off! And mine, too,' she added with another sigh.

'It is not for myself that I cared,' my lady said to Harry,
when the parson had taken his leave; 'but *am* I very much
changed? Alas! I fear 'tis too true.'

'Madam, you have the dearest, and kindest, and sweetest
face in the world, I think,' the lad said; and indeed he
thought and thinks so.

'Will my lord think so when he comes back?' the
lady asked, with a sigh, and another look at her Venice
glass. 'Suppose he should think as you do, sir, that I am
hideous—yes, you said hideous—he will cease to care for me.
'Tis all men care for in women, our little beauty. Why did
he select me from among my sisters? 'Twas only for that.
We reign but for a day or two: and be sure that Vashti knew
Esther was coming.'

'Madam,' said Mr. Esmond, 'Ahasuerus was the Grand
Turk, and to change was the manner of his country, and
according to his law.'

'You are all Grand Turks for that matter,' said my lady,
'or would be if you could. Come, Frank, come, my child.
You are well, praised be Heaven. *Your* locks are not
thinned by this dreadful small-pox: nor your poor face
scarred—is it, my angel?'

Frank began to shout and whimper at the idea of such
a misfortune. From the very earliest time the young lord
had been taught to admire his beauty by his mother: and
esteemed it as highly as any reigning toast valued hers.

One day, as he himself was recovering from his fever and

illness, a pang of something like shame shot across young
Esmond's breast as he remembered that he had never once,
during his illness, given a thought to the poor girl at the
smithy, whose red cheeks but a month ago he had been so
eager to see.   Poor Nancy ! her cheeks had shared the fate
of roses, and were withered now.   She had taken the illness
on the same day with Esmond—she and her brother were
both dead of the small-pox, and buried under the Castlewood
yew-trees.   There was no bright face looking now from the
garden, or to cheer the old smith at his lonely fireside.
Esmond would have liked to have kissed her in her shroud
(like the lass in Mr. Prior's pretty poem),* but she rested
many foot below the ground, when Esmond after his malady
first trod on it.

Doctor Tusher brought the news of this calamity, about
which Harry Esmond longed to ask, but did not like.   He
said almost the whole village had been stricken with the
pestilence ; seventeen persons were dead of it, among them
mentioning the names of poor Nancy and her little brother.
He did not fail to say how thankful we survivors ought to
be.   It being this man's business to flatter and make
sermons, it must be owned he was most industrious in it,
and was doing the one or the other all day.

And so Nancy was gone ; and Harry Esmond blushed that
he had not a single tear for her, and fell to composing an
elegy in Latin verses over the rustic little beauty.   He bade
the dryads mourn and the river-nymphs deplore her.   As
her father followed the calling of Vulcan, he said that surely
she was like a daughter of Venus, though Sievewright's
wife was an ugly shrew, as he remembered to have heard
afterwards.   He made a long face, but, in truth, felt scarcely
more sorrowful than a mute at a funeral.   These first
passions of men and women are mostly abortive ; and are
dead almost before they are born.   Esmond could repeat,
to his last day, some of the doggerel lines in which his muse
bewailed his pretty lass ; not without shame to remember
how bad the verses were, and how good he thought them ;
how false the grief, and yet how he was rather proud of it.
'Tis an error, surely, to talk of the simplicity of youth.
I think no persons are more hypocritical, and have a more
affected behaviour to one another, than the young.   They
deceive themselves and each other with artifices that do
not impose upon men of the world ; and so we get to

understand truth better, and grow simpler as we grow older.

When my lady heard of the fate which had befallen poor Nancy, she said nothing so long as Tusher was by, but when he was gone, she took Harry Esmond's hand and said—

'Harry, I beg your pardon for those cruel words I used on the night you were taken ill. I am shocked at the fate of the poor creature, and am sure that nothing had happened of that with which, in my anger, I charged you. And the very first day we go out, you must take me to the blacksmith, and we must see if there is anything I can do to console the poor old man. Poor man! to lose both his children! What should I do without mine!'

And this was, indeed, the very first walk which my lady took, leaning on Esmond's arm, after her illness. But her visit brought no consolation to the old father; and he showed no softness, or desire to speak. 'The Lord gave and took away,' he said; and he knew what His servant's duty was. He wanted for nothing—less now than ever before, as there were fewer mouths to feed. He wished her ladyship and Master Esmond good morning—he had grown tall in his illness, and was but very little marked; and with this, and a surly bow, he went in from the smithy to the house, leaving my lady, somewhat silenced and shamefaced, at the door. He had a handsome stone put up for his two children, which may be seen in Castlewood churchyard to this very day; and before a year was out his own name was upon the stone. In the presence of Death, that sovereign ruler, a woman's coquetry is scared; and her jealousy will hardly pass the boundaries of that grim kingdom. 'Tis entirely of the earth that passion, and expires in the cold blue air, beyond our sphere.

At length, when the danger was quite over, it was announced that my lord and his daughter would return. Esmond well remembered the day. The lady, his mistress, was in a flurry of fear: before my lord came, she went into her room, and returned from it with reddened cheeks. Her fate was about to be decided. Her beauty was gone— was her reign, too, over? A minute would say. My lord came riding over the bridge—he could be seen from the great window, clad in scarlet, and mounted on his grey hackney—his little daughter ambled by him in a bright riding-dress of blue, on a shining chestnut horse. My lady

leaned against the great mantelpiece, looking on, with one
hand on her heart—she seemed only the more pale for
those red marks on either cheek. She put her handkerchief
to her eyes, and withdrew it, laughing hysterically—the
cloth was quite red with the rouge when she took it away.
She ran to her room again, and came back with pale cheeks
and red eyes—her son in her hand—just as my lord entered,
accompanied by young Esmond, who had gone out to meet
his protector, and to hold his stirrup as he descended from
horseback.

'What, Harry, boy!' my lord said good-naturedly,
'you look as gaunt as a greyhound. The small-pox hasn't
improved your beauty, and your side of the house hadn't
never too much of it—ho, ho!'

And he laughed, and sprang to the ground with no small
agility, looking handsome and red, with a jolly face and
brown hair, like a beef-eater; Esmond kneeling again, as
soon as his patron had descended, performed his homage,
and then went to greet the little Beatrix, and help her
from her horse.

'Fie! how yellow you look,' she said; 'and there are
one, two, red holes in your face;' which, indeed, was very
true; Harry Esmond's harsh countenance bearing, as long
as it continued to be a human face, the marks of the disease.

My lord laughed again, in high good humour.

'D—— it!' said he, with one of his usual oaths, 'the
little slut sees everything. She saw the dowager's paint
t'other day, and asked her why she wore that red stuff—
didn't you, Trix? and the Tower; and St. James's; and
the play; and the Prince George, and the Princess Anne—
didn't you, Trix?'

'They are both very fat, and smelt of brandy,' the child
said.

Papa roared with laughing.

'Brandy!' he said. 'And how do you know, Miss
Pert?'

'Because your lordship smells of it after supper, when
I embrace you before you go to bed,' said the young lady,
who, indeed, was as pert as her father said, and looked as
beautiful a little gipsy as eyes ever gazed on.

'And now for my lady,' said my lord, going up the stairs,
and passing under the tapestry curtain that hung before
the drawing-room door. Esmond remembered that noble

figure handsomely arrayed in scarlet. Within the last few
months he himself had grown from a boy to be a man, and
with his figure, his thoughts had shot up, and grown manly.

My lady's countenance, of which Harry Esmond was
accustomed to watch the changes, and with a solicitous
affection to note and interpret the signs of gladness or care,
wore a sad and depressed look for many weeks after her
lord's return : during which it seemed as if, by caresses and
entreaties, she strove to win him back from some ill humour
he had, and which he did not choose to throw off. In her
eagerness to please him she practised a hundred of those
arts which had formerly charmed him, but which seemed
now to have lost their potency. Her songs did not amuse
him ; and she hushed them and the children when in his
presence. My lord sat silent at his dinner, drinking greatly,
his lady opposite to him, looking furtively at his face,
though also speechless. Her silence annoyed him as much
as her speech ; and he would peevishly, and with an oath,
ask her why she held her tongue and looked so glum, or
he would roughly check her when speaking, and bid her
not talk nonsense. It seemed as if, since his return, nothing
she could do or say could please him.

When a master and mistress are at strife in a house, the
subordinates in the family take the one side or the other.
Harry Esmond stood in so great fear of my lord, that he
would run a league barefoot to do a message for him ; but
his attachment for Lady Esmond was such a passion of
grateful regard, that to spare her a grief, or to do her
a service, he would have given his life daily : and it was
by the very depth and intensity of this regard that he began
to divine how unhappy his adored lady's life was, and that
a secret care (for she never spoke of her anxieties) was
weighing upon her.

Can any one, who has passed through the world and
watched the nature of men and women there, doubt what
had befallen her ? I have seen, to be sure, some people
carry down with them into old age the actual bloom of their
youthful love, and I know that Mr. Thomas Parr*lived to
be a hundred and sixty years old. But, for all that, three-
score and ten is the age of men, and few get beyond it ; and
'tis certain that a man who marries for mere *beaux yeux*,
as my lord did, considers his part of the contract at end
when the woman ceases to fulfil hers, and his love does

not survive her beauty. I know 'tis often otherwise, I say; and can think (as most men in their own experience may) of many a house, where, lighted in early years, the sainted lamp of love hath never been extinguished; but so there is Mr. Parr, and so there is the great giant at the fair that is eight feet high—exceptions to men—and that poor lamp whereof I speak, that lights at first the nuptial chamber, is extinguished by a hundred winds and draughts down the chimney, or sputters out for want of feeding. And then—and then it is Chloe, in the dark, stark awake, and Strephon snoring unheeding; or *vice versa*, 'tis poor Strephon that has married a heartless jilt, and awoke out of that absurd vision of conjugal felicity, which was to last for ever, and is over like any other dream. One and other has made his bed, and so must lie in it, until that final day when life ends, and they sleep separate.

About this time young Esmond, who had a knack of stringing verses, turned some of Ovid's epistles into rhymes, and brought them to his lady for her delectation. Those which treated of forsaken women touched her immensely, Harry remarked; and when Oenone called after Paris, and Medea bade Jason come back again, the lady of Castlewood sighed, and said she thought that part of the verses was the most pleasing. Indeed, she would have chopped up the dean, her old father, in order to bring her husband back again. But her beautiful Jason was gone, as beautiful Jasons will go, and the poor enchantress had never a spell to keep him.

My lord was only sulky as long as his wife's anxious face or behaviour seemed to upbraid him. When she had got to master these, and to show an outwardly cheerful countenance and behaviour, her husband's good humour returned partially, and he swore and stormed no longer at dinner, but laughed sometimes, and yawned unrestrainedly; absenting himself often from home, inviting more company thither, passing the greater part of his days in the hunting-field, or over the bottle as before; but, with this difference, that the poor wife could no longer see now, as she had done formerly, the light of love kindled in his eyes. He was with her, but that flame was out; and that once welcome beacon no more shone there.

What were this lady's feelings when forced to admit the truth whereof her foreboding glass had given her only too true warning, that with her beauty her reign had ended, and the days of her love were over ? What does a seaman do in a storm if mast and rudder are carried away ? He ships a jurymast, and steers as he best can with an oar. What happens if your roof falls in a tempest ? After the first stun of the calamity the sufferer starts up, gropes around to see that the children are safe, and puts them under a shed out of the rain. If the palace burns down, you take shelter in the barn. What man's life is not overtaken by one or more of these tornadoes that send us out of the course, and fling us on rocks to shelter as best we may ?

When Lady Castlewood found that her great ship had gone down, she began as best she might, after she had rallied from the effects of the loss, to put out small ventures of happiness ; and hope for little gains and returns, as a merchant on 'Change, *indocilis pauperiem pati*,* having lost his thousands, embarks a few guineas upon the next ship. She laid out her all upon her children, indulging them beyond all measure, as was inevitable with one of her kindness of disposition ; giving all her thoughts to their welfare—learning, that she might teach them, and improving her own many natural gifts and feminine accomplishments, that she might impart them to her young ones. To be doing good for some one else, is the life of most good women. They are exuberant of kindness, as it were, and must impart it to some one. She made herself a good scholar of French, Italian, and Latin, having been grounded in these by her father in her youth : hiding these gifts from her husband out of fear, perhaps, that they should offend him, for my lord was no bookman—pish'd and psha'd at the notion of learned ladies, and would have been angry that his wife could construe out of a Latin book of which he could scarce understand two words. Young Esmond was usher, or house tutor, under her or over her, as it might happen. During my lord's many absences, these schooldays would go on uninterruptedly : the mother and daughter learning with surprising quickness ; the latter by fits and starts only, and as suited her wayward humour. As for the little lord, it must be owned that he took after his father in the matter of learning—liked marbles and play, and the great horse, and the little one which his father brought him, and on which he took him out a-hunting—a great deal better than

Corderius and Lily ;* marshalled the village boys, and had
a little court of them, already flogging them, and domineering over them with a fine imperious spirit, that made his
father laugh when he beheld it, and his mother fondly warn
him. The cook had a son, the woodman had two, the big
lad at the porter's lodge took his cuffs and his orders.
Doctor Tusher said he was a young nobleman of gallant
spirit ; and Harry Esmond, who was his tutor, and eight
years his little lordship's senior, had hard work sometimes
to keep his own temper, and hold his authority over his
rebellious little chief and kinsman.

In a couple of years after that calamity had befallen
which had robbed Lady Castlewood of a little—a very
little—of her beauty, and her careless husband's heart (if
the truth must be told, my lady had found not only that
her reign was over, but that her successor was appointed,
a princess of a noble house in Drury Lane somewhere, who
was installed and visited by my lord at the town eight miles
off—*pudet haec opprobria dicere nobis*)*—a great change had
taken place in her mind, which, by struggles only known to
herself, at least never mentioned to any one, and unsuspected
by the person who caused the pain she endured—had been
schooled into such a condition as she could not very likely
have imagined possible a score of months since, before her
misfortunes had begun.

She had oldened in that time as people do who suffer
silently great mental pain ; and learned much that she had
never suspected before. She was taught by that bitter
teacher Misfortune. A child, the mother of other children,
but two years back her lord was a god to her ; his words
her law ; his smile her sunshine ; his lazy commonplaces
listened to eagerly, as if they were words of wisdom—all
his wishes and freaks obeyed with a servile devotion. She
had been my lord's chief slave and blind worshipper. Some
women bear farther than this, and submit not only to
neglect but to unfaithfulness too—but here this lady's allegiance had failed her. Her spirit rebelled and disowned any
more obedience. First she had to bear in secret the passion
of losing the adored object ; then to get a farther initiation,
and to find this worshipped being was but a clumsy idol :
then to admit the silent truth, that it was she was superior,
and not the monarch her master : that she had thoughts
which his brains could never master, and was the better

of the two ; quite separate from my lord although tied to
him, and bound as almost all people (save a very happy few)
to work all her life alone. My lord sat in his chair, laughing
his laugh, cracking his joke, his face flushing with wine—
my lady in her place over against him—he never suspecting
that his superior was there, in the calm resigned lady, cold
of manner, with downcast eyes. When he was merry in
his cups, he would make jokes about her coldness, and,
' D—— it, now my lady is gone, we will have t'other bottle,'
he would say. He was frank enough in telling his thoughts,
such as they were. There was little mystery about my
lord's words or actions. His fair Rosamond did not live
in a labyrinth, like the lady of Mr. Addison's opera,* but
paraded with painted cheeks and a tipsy retinue in the
country town. Had she a mind to be revenged, Lady
Castlewood could have found the way to her rival's house
easily enough ; and, if she had come with bowl and dagger,
would have been routed off the ground by the enemy with
a volley of Billingsgate, which the fair person always kept
by her.

Meanwhile, it has been said, that for Harry Esmond his
benefactress's sweet face had lost none of its charms. It
had always the kindest of looks and smiles for him—smiles,
not so gay and artless perhaps as those which Lady Castlewood had formerly worn, when, a child herself, playing
with her children, her husband's pleasure and authority
were all she thought of ; but out of her griefs and cares,
as will happen I think when these trials fall upon a kindly
heart, and are not too unbearable, grew up a number of
thoughts and excellences which had never come into
existence, had not her sorrow and misfortunes engendered
them. Sure, occasion is the father of most that is good
in us. As you have seen the awkward fingers and clumsy
tools of a prisoner cut and fashion the most delicate little
pieces of carved work ; or achieve the most prodigious
underground labours, and cut through walls of masonry,
and saw iron bars and fetters ; 'tis misfortune that awakens
ingenuity, or fortitude, or endurance, in hearts where these
qualities had never come to life but for the circumstance
which gave them a being.

' 'Twas after Jason left her, no doubt,' Lady Castlewood
once said with one of her smiles to young Esmond (who
was reading to her a version of certain lines out of Euripides)*

' that Medea became a learned woman and a great enchantress.'

' And she could conjure the stars out of heaven,' the young tutor added, ' but she could not bring Jason back again.'

' What do you mean ? ' asked my lady, very angry.

' Indeed I mean nothing,' said the other, ' save what I've read in books. What should I know about such matters ? I have seen no woman save you and little Beatrix, and the parson's wife and my late mistress, and your ladyship's woman here.'

' The men who wrote your books,' says my lady, ' your Horaces, and Ovids, and Virgils, as far as I know of them, all thought ill of us, as all the heroes they wrote about used us basely. We were bred to be slaves always ; and even of our own times, as you are still the only lawgivers, I think our sermons seem to say that the best woman is she who bears her master's chains most gracefully. 'Tis a pity there are no nunneries permitted by our Church : Beatrix and I would fly to one, and end our days in peace there away from you.'

' And is there no slavery in a convent ? ' says Esmond.

' At least if women are slaves there, no one sees them,' answered the lady. ' They don't work in street-gangs with the public to jeer them : and if they suffer, suffer in private. Here comes my lord home from hunting. Take away the books. My lord does not love to see them. Lessons are over for to-day, Mr. Tutor.' And with a curtsy and a smile she would end this sort of colloquy.

Indeed ' Mr. Tutor ', as my lady called Esmond, had now business enough on his hands in Castlewood House. He had three pupils, his lady and her two children, at whose lessons she would always be present ; besides writing my lord's letters, and arranging his accompts for him—when these could be got from Esmond's indolent patron.

Of the pupils the two young people were but lazy scholars, and as my lady would admit no discipline such as was then in use, my lord's son only learned what he liked, which was but little, and never to his life's end could be got to construe more than six lines of Virgil. Mistress Beatrix chattered French prettily from a very early age ; and sang sweetly, but this was from her mother's teaching—not Harry Esmond's, who could scarce distinguish between ' Green

Sleeves' and 'Lillabullero'; although he had no greater delight in life than to hear the ladies sing. He sees them now (will he ever forget them?) as they used to sit together of the summer evenings—the two golden heads over the page—the child's little hand and the mother's beating the time, with their voices rising and falling in unison.

But if the children were careless, 'twas a wonder how eagerly the mother learned from her young tutor—and taught him too. The happiest instinctive faculty was this lady's—a faculty for discerning latent beauties and hidden graces of books, especially books of poetry, as in a walk she would spy out field-flowers and make posies of them, such as no other hand could. She was a critic not by reason but by feeling; the sweetest commentator of those books they read together; and the happiest hours of young Esmond's life, perhaps, were those passed in the company of this kind mistress and her children.

These happy days were to end soon, however; and it was by the Lady Castlewood's own decree that they were brought to a conclusion. It happened about Christmas-time, Harry Esmond being now past sixteen years of age, that his old comrade, adversary, and friend, Tom Tusher, returned from his school in London, a fair, well-grown, and sturdy lad, who was about to enter college, with an exhibition from his school, and a prospect of after promotion in the Church. Tom Tusher's talk was of nothing but Cambridge, now; and the boys, who were good friends, examined each other eagerly about their progress in books. Tom had learned some Greek and Hebrew, besides Latin, in which he was pretty well skilled, and also had given himself to mathematical studies under his father's guidance, who was a proficient in those sciences, of which Esmond knew nothing, nor could he write Latin so well as Tom, though he could talk it better, having been taught by his dear friend the Jesuit father, for whose memory the lad ever retained the warmest affection, reading his books, keeping his swords clean in the little crypt where the father had shown them to Esmond on the night of his visit; and often of a night sitting in the chaplain's room, which he inhabited, over his books, his verses, and rubbish, with which the lad occupied himself, he would look up at the window, thinking he wished it might open and let in the good father. He had come and passed away like a dream; but for the swords and books Harry might almost think the father was an imagination of his mind—and for two letters which had come to him, one from abroad full of advice and affection, another soon after he had been confirmed by the Bishop of Hexton, in which Father Holt deplored his falling away. But Harry Esmond felt so confident now of his being in the right, and of his own powers as a casuist, that he thought he was able to face the father himself in argument, and possibly convert him.

To work upon the faith of her young pupil, Esmond's kind mistress sent to the library of her father the dean, who had been distinguished in the disputes of the late king's reign ; and, an old soldier now, had hung up his weapons of controversy. These he took down from his shelves willingly for young Esmond, whom he benefited by his own personal advice and instruction. It did not require much persuasion to induce the boy to worship with his beloved mistress. And the good old nonjuring dean flattered himself with a conversion which in truth was owing to a much gentler and fairer persuader.

Under her ladyship's kind eyes (my lord's being sealed in sleep pretty generally), Esmond read many volumes of the works of the famous British divines of the last age, and was familiar with Wake and Sherlock, with Stillingfleet and Patrick. His mistress never tired to listen or to read, to pursue the text with fond comments, to urge those points which her fancy dwelt on most, or her reason deemed most important. Since the death of her father the dean, this lady hath admitted a certain latitude of theological reading, which her orthodox father would never have allowed ; his favourite writers appealing more to reason and antiquity than to the passions or imaginations of their readers, so that the works of Bishop Taylor, nay, those of Mr. Baxter and Mr. Law, have in reality found more favour with my Lady Castlewood than the severer volumes of our great English schoolmen.*

In later life, at the University, Esmond reopened the controversy, and pursued it in a very different manner, when his patrons had determined for him that he was to embrace the ecclesiastical life. But though his mistress's heart was in this calling, his own never was much. After that first fervour of simple devotion, which his beloved Jesuit priest had inspired in him, speculative theology took but little hold upon the young man's mind. When his early credulity was disturbed, and his saints and virgins taken out of his worship, to rank little higher than the divinities of Olympus, his belief became acquiescence rather than ardour ; and he made his mind up to assume the cassock and bands, as another man does to wear a breast-plate and jack-boots, or to mount a merchant's desk for a livelihood, and from obedience and necessity, rather than from choice. There were scores of such men in Mr. Esmond's time at the Universities, who were going to the Church with no better calling than his.

When Thomas Tusher was gone, a feeling of no small depression and disquiet fell upon young Esmond, of which, though he did not complain, his kind mistress must have divined the cause : for soon after she showed not only that she understood the reason of Harry's melancholy, but could provide a remedy for it. Her habit was thus to watch, unobservedly, those to whom duty or affection bound her, and to prevent their designs, or to fulfil them, when she had the power. It was this lady's disposition to think kindnesses, and devise silent bounties, and to scheme benevolence for those about her. We take such goodness, for the most part, as if it was our due ; the Marys who bring ointment for our feet get but little thanks. Some of us never feel this devotion at all, or are moved by it to gratitude or acknowledgement ; others only recall it years after, when the days are past in which those sweet kindnesses were spent on us, and we offer back our return for the debt by a poor tardy payment of tears. Then forgotten tones of love recur to us, and kind glances shine out of the past— oh, so bright and clear !—oh, so longed after !—because they are out of reach ; as holiday music from withinside a prison wall—or sunshine seen through the bars ; more prized because unattainable—more bright because of the contrast of present darkness and solitude, whence there is no escape.

All the notice, then, which Lady Castlewood seemed to take of Harry Esmond's melancholy, upon Tom Tusher's depar-ture, was, by a gaiety unusual to her, to attempt to dispel his gloom. She made his three scholars (herself being the chief one) more cheerful than ever they had been before, and more docile too, all of them learning and reading much more than they had been accustomed to do. ' For who knows,'

said the lady, ' what may happen, and whether we may be
able to keep such a learned tutor long ? '

Frank Esmond said he for his part did not want to learn
any more, and Cousin Harry might shut up his book whenever he liked, if he would come out a-fishing ; and little
Beatrix declared she would send for Tom Tusher, and *he*
would be glad enough to come to Castlewood, if Harry chose
to go away.

At last comes a messenger from Winchester one day,
bearer of a letter with a great black seal from the dean there,
to say that his sister was dead, and had left her fortune
of 2,000*l.* among her six nieces, the dean's daughters ; and
many a time since has Harry Esmond recalled the flushed
face and eager look wherewith, after this intelligence, his
kind lady regarded him.   She did not pretend to any grief
about the deceased relative, from whom she and her family
had been many years parted.

When my lord heard of the news, he also did not make
any very long face.   ' The money will come very handy to
furnish the music-room and the cellar, which is getting low,
and buy your ladyship a coach and a couple of horses that
will do indifferent to ride or for the coach.   And Beatrix,
you shall have a spinet : and Frank, you shall have a little
horse from Hexton Fair ; and Harry, you shall have five
pounds to buy some books,' said my lord, who was generous
with his own, and indeed with other folks' money.   ' I wish
your aunt would die once a year, Rachel ; we could spend
your money, and all your sisters', too.'

' I have but one aunt—and—and I have another use for
the money, my lord,' says my lady, turning very red.

' Another use, my dear ; and what do you know about
money ? ' cries my lord.   ' And what the devil is there that
I don't give you which you want ? '

' I intend to give this money—can't you fancy how, my
lord ? '

My lord swore one of his large oaths that he did not know
in the least what she meant.

' I intend it for Harry Esmond to go to college.—Cousin
Harry,' says my lady, ' you mustn't stay longer in this
dull place, but make a name to yourself, and for us too,
Harry.'

' D—n it, Harry's well enough here,' says my lord, for
a moment looking rather sulky.

' Is Harry going away ?   You don't mean to say you will go away ? ' cry out Frank and Beatrix at one breath.

' But he will come back : and this will always be his home,' cries my lady, with blue eyes looking a celestial kindness : ' and his scholars will always love him ; won't they ? '

' By G——d, Rachel, you're a good woman ! ' says my lord, seizing my lady's hand, at which she blushed very much, and shrank back, putting her children before her.   ' I wish you joy, my kinsman,' he continued, giving Harry Esmond a hearty slap on the shoulder. ' I won't balk your luck. Go to Cambridge, boy ; and when Tusher dies you shall have the living here, if you are not better provided by that time.   We'll furnish the dining-room and buy the horses another year.   I'll give thee a nag out of the stable : take any one except my hack and the bay gelding and the coach-horses ; and God speed thee, my boy ! '

' Have the sorrel, Harry ; 'tis a good one.   Father says 'tis the best in the stable,' says little Frank, clapping his hands, and jumping up.   ' Let's come and see him in the stable.'   And the other, in his delight and eagerness, was for leaving the room that instant to arrange about his journey.

The Lady Castlewood looked after him with sad pene-trating glances.   ' He wishes to be gone already, my lord,' said she to her husband.

The young man hung back abashed.   ' Indeed, I would stay for ever, if your ladyship bade me,' he said.

' And thou wouldst be a fool for thy pains, kinsman,' said my lord.   ' Tut, tut, man.   Go and see the world. Sow thy wild oats ; and take the best luck that Fate sends thee.   I wish I were a boy again that I might go to college, and taste the Trumpington ale.'

' Ours indeed is but a dull home,' cries my lady, with a little of sadness, and maybe of satire, in her voice : ' an old glum house, half ruined, and the rest only half furnished ; a woman and two children are but poor company for men that are accustomed to better.   We are only fit to be your worship's handmaids, and your pleasures must of necessity lie elsewhere than at home.'

' Curse me, Rachel, if I know now whether thou art in earnest or not,' said my lord.

' In earnest, my lord ! ' says she, still clinging by one of

her children. ' Is there much subject here for joke ? '
And she made him a grand curtsy, and, giving a stately
look to Harry Esmond, which seemed to say, ' Remember ;
you understand me, though he does not,' she left the room
with her children.

' Since she found out that confounded Hexton business,'
my lord said—' and be hanged to them that told her !—
she has not been the same woman. She, who used to be
as humble as a milkmaid, is as proud as a princess,' says
my lord. ' Take my counsel, Harry Esmond, and keep
clear of women. Since I have had anything to do with
the jades, they have given me nothing but disgust. I had
a wife at Tangier, with whom, as she couldn't speak a word
of my language, you'd have thought I might lead a quiet
life. But she tried to poison me, because she was jealous
of a Jew girl. There was your aunt, for aunt she is—aunt
Jezebel, a pretty life your father led with *her*, and here's
my lady. When I saw her on a pillion riding behind the
dean her father, she looked and was such a baby, that a
sixpenny doll might have pleased her. And now you see
what she is—hands off, highty-tighty, high and mighty,
an empress couldn't be grander. Pass us the tankard,
Harry, my boy. A mug of beer and a toast at morn, says
my host. A toast and a mug of beer at noon, says my dear.
D—n it, Polly loves a mug of ale, too, and laced with
brandy, by Jove ! ' Indeed, I suppose they drank it together ; for my lord was often thick in his speech at midday dinner ; and at night at supper, speechless altogether.

Harry Esmond's departure resolved upon, it seemed as
if the Lady Castlewood, too, rejoiced to lose him ; for
more than once, when the lad, ashamed perhaps at his own
secret eagerness to go away (at any rate stricken with
sadness at the idea of leaving those from whom he had
received so many proofs of love and kindness inestimable),
tried to express to his mistress his sense of gratitude to her,
and his sorrow at quitting those who had so sheltered and
tended a nameless and houseless orphan, Lady Castlewood
cut short his protests of love and his lamentations, and
would hear of no grief, but only look forward to Harry's
fame and prospects in life. ' Our little legacy will keep
you for four years like a gentleman. Heaven's Providence,
your own genius, industry, honour, must do the rest for
you. Castlewood will always be a home for you ; and these

children, whom you have taught and loved, will not forget
to love you. And Harry,' said she (and this was the only
time when she spoke with a tear in her eye, or a tremor in
her voice), ' it may happen in the course of nature that
I shall be called away from them : and their father—and—
and they will need true friends and protectors. Promise
me that you will be true to them—as—as I think I have
been to you—and a mother's fond prayer and blessing go
with you.'

' So help me God, madam, I will,' said Harry Esmond,
falling on his knees, and kissing the hand of his dearest
mistress. ' If you will have me stay now, I will. What
matters whether or no I make my way in life, or whether
a poor bastard dies as unknown as he is now ? 'Tis enough
that I have your love and kindness surely ; and to make
you happy is duty enough for me.'

' Happy ! ' says she ; ' but indeed I ought to be, with my
children, and——'

' Not happy ! ' cried Esmond (for he knew what her life
was, though he and his mistress never spoke a word concerning it). ' If not happiness, it may be ease. Let me stay
and work for you—let me stay and be your servant.'

' Indeed, you are best away,' said my lady, laughing, as
she put her hand on the boy's head for a moment. ' You
shall stay in no such dull place. You shall go to college
and distinguish yourself as becomes your name. That is
how you shall please me best ; and—and if my children
want you, or I want you, you shall come to us ; and I
know we may count on you.'

' May Heaven forsake me if you may not,' Harry said,
getting up from his knee.

' And my knight longs for a dragon this instant that he
may fight,' said my lady, laughing ; which speech made
Harry Esmond start, and turn red ; for indeed the very
thought was in his mind, that he would like that some
chance should immediately happen whereby he might show
his devotion. And it pleased him to think that his lady
had called him 'her knight', and often and often he recalled
this to his mind, and prayed that he might be her true
knight, too.

My lady's bedchamber window looked out over the
country, and you could see from it the purple hills beyond
Castlewood village, the green common betwixt that and the

Hall, and the old bridge which crossed over the river. When Harry Esmond went away for Cambridge, little Frank ran alongside his horse as far as the bridge, and there Harry stopped for a moment, and looked back at the house where the best part of his life had been passed.   It lay before him with its grey familiar towers, a pinnacle or two shining in the sun, the buttresses and terrace walls casting great blue shades on the grass.   And Harry remembered all his life after how he saw his mistress at the window looking out on him, in a white robe, the little Beatrix's chestnut curls resting at her mother's side.   Both waved a farewell to him, and little Frank sobbed to leave him.   Yes, he *would* be his lady's true knight, he vowed in his heart ; he waved her an adieu with his hat.   The village people had good-bye to say to him too.   All knew that Master Harry was going to college, and most of them had a kind word and a look of farewell.   I do not stop to say what adventures he began to imagine, or what career to devise for himself, before he had ridden three miles from home.   He had not read Monsieur Galland's ingenious Arabian tales as yet ; but be sure that there are other folks who build castles in the air, and have fine hopes, and kick them down too, besides honest Alnaschar.*

CHAPTER X

I GO TO CAMBRIDGE, AND DO BUT LITTLE GOOD THERE

MY lord, who said he should like to revisit the old haunts of his youth, kindly accompanied Harry Esmond in his first journey to Cambridge.   Their road lay through London, where my lord viscount would also have Harry stay a few days to show him the pleasures of the town, before he entered upon his University studies, and whilst here Harry's patron conducted the young man to my lady dowager's house at Chelsey near London : the kind lady at Castlewood having specially ordered that the young gentleman and the old should pay a respectful visit in that quarter.

Her ladyship the viscountess dowager occupied a handsome new house in Chelsey, with a garden behind it, and facing the river, always a bright and animated sight with its swarms of sailors, barges, and wherries. Harry laughed at recognizing in the parlour the well-remembered old piece of Sir Peter Lely,* wherein his father's widow was represented as a virgin huntress, armed with a gilt bow and arrow, and encumbered only with that small quantity of drapery which it would seem the virgins in King Charles's day were accustomed to wear.

My lady dowager had left off this peculiar habit of huntress when she married. But though she was now considerably past sixty years of age, I believe she thought that airy nymph of the picture could still be easily recognized in the venerable personage who gave an audience to Harry and his patron.

She received the young man with even more favour than she showed to the elder, for she chose to carry on the conversation in French, in which my Lord Castlewood was no great proficient, and expressed her satisfaction at finding that Mr. Esmond could speak fluently in that language. ' 'Twas the only one fit for polite conversation,' she condescended to say, ' and suitable to persons of high breeding.'

My lord laughed afterwards, as the gentlemen went away, at his kinswoman's behaviour. He said he remembered the time when she could speak English fast enough, and joked in his jolly way at the loss he had had of such a lovely wife as that.

My lady viscountess deigned to ask his lordship news of his wife and children ; she had heard that Lady Castlewood had had the small-pox ; she hoped she was not so *very* much disfigured as people said.

At this remark about his wife's malady, my lord viscount winced and turned red ; but the dowager, in speaking of the disfigurement of the young lady, turned to her looking-glass and examined her old wrinkled countenance in it with such a grin of satisfaction, that it was all her guests could do to refrain from laughing in her ancient face.

She asked Harry what his profession was to be ; and my lord, saying that the lad was to take orders, and have the living of Castlewood when old Dr. Tusher vacated it ; she did not seem to show any particular anger at the notion of Harry's becoming a Church of England clergyman, nay, was rather glad than otherwise, that the youth should be so provided for. She bade Mr. Esmond not to forget to pay her a visit whenever he passed through London, and carried her graciousness so far as to send a purse with twenty guineas for him, to the tavern at which my lord put up (the 'Greyhound', in Charing Cross) ; and, along with this welcome gift for her kinsman, she sent a little doll for a present to my lord's little daughter Beatrix, who was growing beyond the age of dolls by this time, and was as tall almost as her venerable relative.

After seeing the town, and going to the plays, my Lord Castlewood and Esmond rode together to Cambridge, spending two pleasant days upon the journey. Those rapid new coaches were not established as yet, that performed the whole journey between London and the University in a single day ; however, the road was pleasant and short enough to Harry Esmond, and he always gratefully remembered that happy holiday, which his kind patron gave him.

Mr. Esmond was entered a pensioner of Trinity College in Cambridge, to which famous college my lord had also in his youth belonged. Dr. Montague was master at this time, and received my lord viscount with great politeness : so did Mr. Bridge, who was appointed to be Harry's tutor. Tom Tusher, who was of Emmanuel College, and was by this time a junior soph, came to wait upon my lord, and to take Harry under his protection ; and comfortable rooms being provided for him in the great court close by the gate, and near to the famous Mr. Newton's lodgings, Harry's patron took leave of him with many kind words and blessings, and an admonition to him to behave better at the University than my lord himself had ever done.*

'Tis needless in these memoirs to go at any length into the particulars of Harry Esmond's college career. It was like that of a hundred young gentlemen of that day. But he had the ill fortune to be older by a couple of years than most of his fellow students ; and by his previous solitary mode of bringing up, the circumstances of his life, and the peculiar thoughtfulness and melancholy that had naturally engendered, he was, in a great measure, cut off from the society of comrades who were much younger and higher-spirited than he. His tutor, who had bowed down to the ground, as he walked my lord over the college grass-plats, changed his behaviour as soon as the nobleman's back was turned, and was—at least Harry thought so—harsh and overbearing. When the lads used to assemble in their *greges* in hall, Harry found himself alone in the midst of that little flock of boys ; they raised a great laugh at him when he was set on to read Latin, which he did with the foreign pronunciation taught to him by his old master, the Jesuit, than which he knew no other. Mr. Bridge, the tutor, made him the object of clumsy jokes, in which he was fond of indulging. The young man's spirit was chafed, and his vanity mortified ; and he found himself, for some time, as lonely in this place as ever he had been at Castlewood, whither he longed to return. His birth was a source of shame to him, and he fancied a hundred slights and sneers from young and old, who, no doubt, had treated him better had he met them himself more frankly. And as he looks back, in calmer days, upon this period of his life, which he thought so unhappy, he can see that his own pride and vanity caused no small part of the mortifications which he attributed to others' ill will. The world deals good-naturedly with good-natured people, and I never knew a sulky misanthropist who quarrelled with it, but it was he, and not it, that was in the wrong. Tom Tusher gave Harry plenty of good advice on this subject, for Tom had both good sense and good humour ; but Mr. Harry chose to treat his senior with a great deal of superfluous disdain and absurd scorn, and would by no means part from his darling injuries, in which, very likely, no man believed but himself. As for honest Doctor Bridge, the tutor found, after a few trials of wit with the pupil, that the younger man was an ugly subject for wit, and that the laugh was often turned against him. This did not make tutor and pupil any better friends ; but had, so far, an advantage for Esmond, that Mr. Bridge was induced to leave him alone ; and so long as he kept his chapels, and did the college exercises required of him, Bridge was content not to see Harry's glum face in his class, and to leave him to read and sulk for himself in his own chamber.

A poem or two in Latin and English, which were pronounced to have some merit, and a Latin oration (for Mr. Esmond could write that language better than pronounce it), got him a little reputation both with the authorities of the University and amongst the young men, with whom he began to pass for more than he was worth. A few victories over their common enemy Mr. Bridge, made them incline towards him, and look upon him as the champion of their order against the seniors. Such of the lads as he took into

his confidence, found him not so gloomy and haughty as
his appearance led them to believe ; and Don Dismallo,* as
he was called, became presently a person of some little
importance in his college, and was, as he believes, set down
by the seniors there as rather a dangerous character.

Don Dismallo was a stanch young Jacobite, like the rest
of his family ; gave himself many absurd airs of loyalty ;
used to invite young friends to burgundy, and give the
king's health on King James's birthday ; wore black on the
day of his abdication ; fasted on the anniversary of King
William's coronation ; and performed a thousand absurd
antics, of which he smiles now to think.

These follies caused many remonstrances on Tom Tusher's
part, who was always a friend to the powers that be, as
Esmond was always in opposition to them. Tom was a
Whig, while Esmond was a Tory. Tom never missed a
lecture, and capped the proctor with the profoundest of
bows. No wonder he sighed over Harry's insubordinate
courses, and was angry when the others laughed at him.
But that Harry was known to have my lord viscount's
protection, Tom no doubt would have broken with him altogether. But honest Tom never gave up a comrade as long
as he was the friend of a great man. This was not out of
scheming on Tom's part, but a natural inclination towards
the great. 'Twas no hypocrisy in him to flatter, but the
bent of his mind, which was always perfectly good-
humoured, obliging, and servile.

Harry had very liberal allowances, for his dear mistress
of Castlewood not only regularly supplied him, but the
dowager at Chelsey made her donation annual, and received
Esmond at her house near London every Christmas ; but,
in spite of these benefactions, Esmond was constantly
poor ; whilst 'twas a wonder with how small a stipend
from his father, Tom Tusher contrived to make a good
figure. 'Tis true that Harry both spent, gave, and lent
his money very freely, which Thomas never did. I think
he was like the famous Duke of Marlborough in this instance, who, getting a present of fifty pieces, when a young
man, from some foolish woman who fell in love with his
good looks, showed the money to Cadogan in a drawer
scores of years after, where it had lain ever since he had
sold his beardless honour to procure it.* I do not mean to
say that Tom ever let out his good looks so profitably, for

nature had not endowed him with any particular charms of
person, and he ever was a pattern of moral behaviour, losing
no opportunity of giving the very best advice to his younger
comrade ; with which article, to do him justice, he parted
very freely. Not but that he was a merry fellow, too, in his
way ; he loved a joke, if by good fortune he understood it,
and took his share generously of a bottle if another paid for
it, and especially if there was a young lord in company to
drink it. In these cases there was not a harder drinker
in the University than Mr. Tusher could be ; and it was
edifying to behold him, fresh shaved and with smug face,
singing out ' Amen ! ' at early chapel in the morning. In
his reading, poor Harry permitted himself to go a-gadding
after all the Nine Muses, and so very likely had but little
favour from any one of them ; whereas Tom Tusher, who
had no more turn for poetry than a ploughboy, nevertheless,
by a dogged perseverance and obsequiousness in courting
the divine Calliope,* got himself a prize, and some credit
in the University, and a fellowship at his college, as a
reward for his scholarship. In this time of Mr. Esmond's
life, he got the little reading which he ever could boast of,
and passed a good part of his days greedily devouring all
the books on which he could lay hand. In this desultory
way the works of most of the English, French, and Italian
poets came under his eyes, and he had a smattering of the
Spanish tongue likewise, besides the ancient languages, of
which, at least of Latin, he was a tolerable master.

Then, about midway in his University career, he fell to
reading for the profession to which worldly prudence rather
than inclination called him, and was perfectly bewildered
in theological controversy. In the course of his reading
(which was neither pursued with that seriousness or that
devout mind which such a study requires), the youth found
himself, at the end of one month, a Papist, and was about
to proclaim his faith ; the next month a Protestant, with
Chillingworth ; and the third a sceptic, with Hobbs and
Bayle.* Whereas honest Tom Tusher never permitted his
mind to stray out of the prescribed University path,
accepted the Thirty-nine Articles with all his heart, and
would have signed and sworn to other nine-and-thirty
with entire obedience. Harry's wilfulness in this matter,
and disorderly thoughts and conversation, so shocked and
afflicted his senior, that there grew up a coldness and

estrangement between them, so that they became scarce
more than mere acquaintances, from having been intimate
friends when they came to college first.   Politics ran high,
too, at the University ; and here, also, the young men were
at variance.   Tom professed himself, albeit a High Churchman, a strong King William's-man ; whereas Harry brought
his family Tory politics to college with him, to which he
must add a dangerous admiration for Oliver Cromwell,
whose side, or King James's by turns, he often chose to take
in the disputes which the young gentlemen used to hold in
each other's rooms, where they debated on the state of the
nation, crowned and deposed kings, and toasted past and
present heroes or beauties in flagons of college ale.

Thus, either from the circumstances of his birth, or the
natural melancholy of his disposition, Esmond came to live
very much by himself during his stay at the University,
having neither ambition enough to distinguish himself in
the college career, nor caring to mingle with the mere pleasures and boyish frolics of the students, who were, for the
most part, two or three years younger than he.   He fancied
that the gentlemen of the common-room of his college
slighted him on account of his birth, and hence kept aloof
from their society.   It may be that he made the ill will,
which he imagined came from them, by his own behaviour,
which, as he looks back on it in after-life, he now sees was
morose and haughty.   At any rate, he was as tenderly
grateful for kindness as he was susceptible of slight and
wrong ; and, lonely as he was generally, yet had one or two
very warm friendships for his companions of those days.

One of these was a queer gentleman that resided in the
University, though he was no member of it, and was the
professor of a science scarce recognized in the common course
of college education.   This was a French refugee officer,
who had been driven out of his native country at the time of
the Protestant persecutions there, and who came to Cambridge, where he taught the science of the small-sword, and
set up a saloon-of-arms.   Though he declared himself a
Protestant, 'twas said Mr. Moreau was a Jesuit in disguise ;
indeed, he brought very strong recommendations to the
Tory party, which was pretty strong in that University,
and very likely was one of the many agents whom King
James had in this country.   Esmond found this gentleman's
conversation very much more agreeable, and to his taste,

than the talk of the college divines in the common-room ; he never wearied of Moreau's stories of the wars of Turenne and Condé, in which he had borne a part ;* and being familiar with the French tongue from his youth, and in a place where but few spoke it, his company became very agreeable to the brave old professor of arms, whose favourite pupil he was, and who made Mr. Esmond a very tolerable proficient in the noble science of *escrime*.*

At the next term Esmond was to take his degree of Bachelor of Arts, and afterwards, in proper season, to assume the cassock and bands which his fond mistress would have him wear. Tom Tusher himself was a parson and a fellow of his college by this time ; and Harry felt that he would very gladly cede his right to the living of Castlewood to Tom, and that his own calling was in no way the pulpit. But as he was bound, before all things in the world, to his dear mistress at home, and knew that a refusal on his part would grieve her, he determined to give her no hint of his unwillingness to the clerical office ; and it was in this unsatisfactory mood of mind that he went to spend the last vacation he should have at Castlewood before he took orders.

CHAPTER XI

I COME HOME FOR A HOLIDAY TO CASTLEWOOD, AND FIND A SKELETON IN THE HOUSE

At his third long vacation, Esmond came as usual to Castlewood, always feeling an eager thrill of pleasure when he found himself once more in the house where he had passed so many years, and beheld the kind familiar eyes of his mistress looking upon him. She and her children (out of whose company she scarce ever saw him) came to greet him. Miss Beatrix was grown so tall that Harry did not quite know whether he might kiss her or no ; and she blushed and held back when he offered that salutation, though she took it, and even courted it, when they were alone. The young lord was shooting up to be like his gallant father in look, though with his mother's kind eyes : the Lady of Castlewood herself seemed grown, too, since Harry saw her—in her look more stately, in her person fuller, in her face, still as ever most tender and friendly, a greater air of command and decision than had appeared in that guileless sweet countenance which Harry remembered so gratefully. The tone of her voice was so much deeper and sadder when she spoke and welcomed him, that it quite startled Esmond, who looked up at her surprised as she spoke, when she withdrew her eyes from him ; nor did she ever look at him afterwards when his own eyes were gazing upon her. A something hinting at grief and secret, and filling his mind with alarm undefinable, seemed to speak with that low thrilling voice of hers, and look out of those clear sad eyes. Her greeting to Esmond was so cold that it almost pained the lad (who would have liked to fall on his knees and kiss the skirt of her robe, so fond and ardent was his respect and regard for her), and he faltered in answering the questions which she, hesitating on her side, began to put to him. Was he happy at Cambridge ? Did he study too hard ? She hoped not. He had grown very tall, and looked very well.

' He has got a moustache ! ' cries out Master Esmond.

' Why does he not wear a peruke like my Lord Mohun ? '* asked Miss Beatrix. 'My lord says that nobody wears their own hair.'

' I believe you will have to occupy your old chamber,' says my lady. ' I hope the housekeeper has got it ready.'

' Why, mamma, you have been there ten times these three days yourself ! ' exclaims Frank.

' And she cut some flowers which you planted in my garden—do you remember, ever so many years ago ?— when I was quite a little girl,' cries out Miss Beatrix, on tiptoe. ' And mamma put them in your window.'

' I remember when you grew well after you were ill that you used to like roses,' said the lady, blushing like one of them. They all conducted Harry Esmond to his chamber ; the children running before, Harry walking by his mistress hand-in-hand.

The old room had been ornamented and beautified not a little to receive him. The flowers were in the window in a china vase ; and there was a fine new counterpane on the bed, which chatterbox Beatrix said mamma had made too. A fire was crackling on the hearth, although it was June. My lady thought the room wanted warming ; everything was done to make him happy and welcome : ' And you are not to be a page any longer, but a gentleman and kinsman, and to walk with papa and mamma,' said the children. And as soon as his dear mistress and children had left him to himself, it was with a heart overflowing with love and gratefulness that he flung himself down on his knees by the side of the little bed, and asked a blessing upon those who were so kind to him.

The children, who are always house tell-tales, soon made him acquainted with the little history of the house and family. Papa had been to London twice. Papa often went away now. Papa had taken Beatrix to Westlands, where she was taller than Sir George Harper's second daughter, though she was two years older. Papa had taken Beatrix and Frank both to Bellminster, where Frank had got the better of Lord Bellminster's son in a boxing-match—my lord, laughing, told Harry afterwards. Many gentlemen came to stop with papa, and papa had gotten a new game from London, a French game, called a billiard—that the French king played it very well : and the Dowager Lady Castlewood had sent Miss Beatrix a present ; and papa had gotten a new chaise, with two little horses, which he drove himself, beside the coach, which mamma went in ; and Dr. Tusher was a cross old plague, and they did not like to learn from him at all ; and papa did not care about them learning, and laughed when they were at their books, but mamma liked them to learn, and taught them ; and ' I don't think papa is fond of mamma ', said Miss Beatrix, with her great eyes. She had come quite close up to Harry Esmond by the time this prattle took place, and was on his knee, and had examined all the points of his dress, and all the good or bad features of his homely face.

' You shouldn't say that papa is not fond of mamma,' said the boy, at this confession. ' Mamma never said so ; and mamma forbade you to say it, Miss Beatrix.'

'Twas this, no doubt, that accounted for the sadness in Lady Castlewood's eyes, and the plaintive vibrations of her voice. Who does not know of eyes, lighted by love once, where the flame shines no more ?—of lamps extinguished, once properly trimmed and tended ? Every man has such in his house. Such mementoes make our splendidest chambers look blank and sad ; such faces seen in a day cast a gloom upon our sunshine. So oaths mutually sworn, and invocations of Heaven, and priestly ceremonies, and fond belief, and love, so fond and faithful that it never doubted but that it should live for ever, are all of no avail towards making love eternal : it dies, in spite of the banns and the priest ; and I have often thought there should be a visitation of the sick for it, and a funeral service, and an extreme unction, and an *abi in pace.** It has its course, like all mortal things—its beginning, progress, and decay. It buds and it blooms out into sunshine, and it withers and ends. Strephon and Chloe languish apart ; join in a rapture : and presently you hear that Chloe is crying, and Strephon has broken his crook across her back. Can you mend it so as to show no marks of rupture ? Not all the priests of Hymen, not all the incantations to the gods, can make it whole !

Waking up from dreams, books, and visions of college honours, in which, for two years, Harry Esmond had been immersed, he found himself instantly, on his return home, in the midst of this actual tragedy of life, which absorbed and interested him more than all his tutor taught him. The persons whom he loved best in the world, and to whom he owed most, were living unhappily together. The gentlest and kindest of women was suffering ill-usage and shedding tears in secret : the man who made her wretched by neglect, if not by violence, was Harry's benefactor and patron. In houses where, in place of that sacred, inmost flame of love, there is discord at the centre, the whole household becomes hypocritical, and each lies to his neighbour. The husband (or it may be the wife) lies when the visitor comes in, and wears a grin of reconciliation or politeness before him. The wife lies (indeed, her business is to do that, and to smile, however much she is beaten), swallows her tears, and lies to her lord and master ; lies in bidding little Jacky respect dear papa ; lies in assuring grandpapa that she is perfectly happy. The servants lie, wearing grave faces behind their master's chair, and pretending to be unconscious of the fighting ; and so, from morning till bedtime, life is passed in falsehood. And wiseacres call this a proper regard of morals, and point out Baucis and Philemon* as examples of a good life.

If my lady did not speak of her griefs to Harry Esmond, my lord was by no means reserved when in his cups, and spoke his mind very freely, bidding Harry in his coarse way, and with his blunt language, beware of all women as cheats, jades, jilts, and using other unmistakable monosyllables in speaking of them. Indeed, 'twas the fashion of the day as I must own ; and there's not a writer of my time of any note, with the exception of poor Dick Steele, that does not speak of a woman as of a slave, and scorn and use her as such. Mr. Pope, Mr. Congreve, Mr. Addison, Mr. Gay, every one of 'em, sing in this key, each according to his nature and politeness ; and louder and fouler than all in abuse is Dr. Swift, who spoke of them as he treated them, worst of all.

Much of the quarrels and hatred which arise between married people come in my mind from the husband's rage and revolt at discovering that his slave and bedfellow, who is to minister to all his wishes, and is church-sworn to honour and obey him—is his superior ; and that *he*, and not she, ought to be the subordinate of the twain ; and in these controversies, I think, lay the cause of my lord's anger against his lady. When he left her, she began to think for herself, and her thoughts were not in his favour. After the illumination, when the love-lamp is put out that anon we spoke of, and by the common daylight we look at the picture, what a daub it looks ! what a clumsy effigy ! How many men and wives come to this knowledge, think you ? And if it be painful to a woman to find herself mated for life to a boor, and ordered to love and honour a dullard ; it is worse still for the man himself perhaps, whenever in his dim comprehension the idea dawns that his slave and drudge yonder is, in truth, his superior ; that the woman who does his bidding, and submits to his humour, should be his lord ; that she can think a thousand things beyond the power of his muddled brains ; and that in yonder head, on the pillow opposite to him, lie a thousand feelings, mysteries of thought, latent scorns and rebellions, whereof he only dimly perceives the existence as they look out furtively from her eyes : treasures of love doomed to perish without a hand to gather them ; sweet fancies and images of beauty that would grow and unfold themselves into flower ; bright wit that would shine like diamonds could it be brought into the sun : and the tyrant in possession crushes the outbreak of all these, drives them back like slaves into the dungeon and darkness, and chafes without that his prisoner is rebellious, and his sworn subject undutiful and refractory. So the lamp was out in Castlewood Hall, and the lord and lady there saw each other as they were. With her illness and altered beauty my lord's fire for his wife disappeared ; with

his selfishness and faithlessness her foolish fiction of love
and reverence was rent away. Love !—who is to love what
is base and unlovely ? Respect !—who is to respect what is
gross and sensual ? Not all the marriage oaths sworn before
all the parsons, cardinals, ministers, muftis, and rabbins in
the world, can bind to that monstrous allegiance. This
couple was living apart then ; the woman happy to be
allowed to love and tend her children (who were never of
her own goodwill away from her) and thankful to have
saved such treasures as these out of the wreck in which the
better part of her heart went down.

These young ones had had no instructors save their
mother, and Doctor Tusher for their theology occasionally,
and had made more progress than might have been expected
under a tutor so indulgent and fond as Lady Castlewood.
Beatrix could sing and dance like a nymph. Her voice
was her father's delight after dinner. She ruled over the
house with little imperial ways, which her parents coaxed
and laughed at. She had long learned the value of her
bright eyes, and tried experiments in coquetry, *in corpore
vili,** upon rustics and country squires, until she should
prepare to conquer the world and the fashion. She put on
a new ribbon to welcome Harry Esmond, made eyes at him,
and directed her young smiles at him, not a little to the
amusement of the young man, and the joy of her father,
who laughed his great laugh, and encouraged her in her
thousand antics. Lady Castlewood watched the child
gravely and sadly : the little one was pert in her replies to
her mother, yet eager in her protestations of love and
promises of amendment ; and as ready to cry (after a little
quarrel brought on by her own giddiness) until she had won
back her mamma's favour, as she was to risk the kind lady's
displeasure by fresh outbreaks of restless vanity. From
her mother's sad looks she fled to her father's chair and
boozy laughter. She already set the one against the other :
and the little rogue delighted in the mischief which she
knew how to make so early.

The young heir of Castlewood was spoiled by father and
mother both. He took their caresses as men do, and as if
they were his right. He had his hawks and his spaniel
dog, his little horse and his beagles. He had learned to ride
and to drink, and to shoot flying : and he had a small court,
the sons of the huntsman and woodman, as became the

heir-apparent, taking after the example of my lord his father. If he had a headache, his mother was as much frightened as if the plague were in the house : my lord laughed and jeered in his abrupt way—(indeed, 'twas on the day after New Year's Day, and an excess of mince-pie)— and said with some of his usual oaths—' D—n it, Harry Esmond—you see how my lady takes on about Frank's megrim. She used to be sorry about me, my boy (pass the tankard, Harry), and to be frightened if I had a headache once. She don't care about my head now. They're like that—women are—all the same, Harry, all jilts in their hearts. Stick to college—stick to punch and buttery ale : and never see a woman that's handsomer than an old cinder-faced bedmaker. That's my counsel.'

It was my lord's custom to fling out many jokes of this nature, in presence of his wife and children, at meals— clumsy sarcasms which my lady turned many a time, or which, sometimes, she affected not to hear, or which now and again would hit their mark and make the poor victim wince (as you could see by her flushing face and eyes filling with tears), or which again worked her up to anger and retort, when, in answer to one of these heavy bolts, she would flash back with a quivering reply. The pair were not happy ; nor indeed was it happy to be with them. Alas that youthful love and truth should end in bitterness and bankruptcy ! To see a young couple loving each other is no wonder ; but to see an old couple loving each other is the best sight of all. Harry Esmond became the confidant of one and the other—that is, my lord told the lad all his griefs and wrongs (which were indeed of Lord Castlewood's own making), and Harry divined my lady's ; his affection leading him easily to penetrate the hypocrisy under which Lady Castlewood generally chose to go disguised, and see her heart aching whilst her face wore a smile. 'Tis a hard task for women in life, that mask which the world bids them wear. But there is no greater crime than for a woman who is ill used and unhappy to show that she is so. The world is quite relentless about bidding her to keep a cheerful face ; and our women, like the Malabar wives,* are forced to go smiling and painted to sacrifice themselves with their husbands ; their relations being the most eager to push them on to their duty, and, under their shouts and applauses, to smother and hush their cries of pain.

So, into the sad secret of his patron's household, Harry Esmond became initiated, he scarce knew how. It had passed under his eyes two years before, when he could not understand it ; but reading, and thought, and experience of men, had oldened him ; and one of the deepest sorrows of a life which had never, in truth, been very happy, came upon him now, when he was compelled to understand and pity a grief which he stood quite powerless to relieve.

It hath been said my lord would never take the oath of allegiance, nor his seat as a peer of the kingdom of Ireland, where, indeed, he had but a nominal estate ; and refused an English peerage which King William's Government offered him as a bribe to secure his loyalty.

He might have accepted this, and would doubtless, but for the earnest remonstrances of his wife (who ruled her husband's opinions better than she could govern his conduct), and who being a simple-hearted woman, with but one rule of faith and right, never thought of swerving from her fidelity to the exiled family, or of recognizing any other sovereign but King James ; and, though she acquiesced in the doctrine of obedience to the reigning power, no temptation, she thought, could induce her to acknowledge the Prince of Orange as rightful monarch, nor to let her lord so acknowledge him. So my Lord Castlewood remained a nonjuror all his life nearly, though his self-denial caused him many a pang, and left him sulky and out of humour.

The year after the Revolution, and all through King William's life, 'tis known there were constant intrigues for the restoration of the exiled family ; but if my Lord Castlewood took any share of these, as is probable, 'twas only for a short time, and when Harry Esmond was too young to be introduced into such important secrets.

But in the year 1695, when that conspiracy of Sir John Fenwick, Colonel Lowick, and others, was set on foot, for waylaying King William as he came from Hampton Court to London, and a secret plot was formed, in which a vast number of the nobility and people of honour were engaged ; Father Holt appeared at Castlewood, and brought a young friend with him, a gentleman whom 'twas easy to see that both my lord and the father treated with uncommon deference. Harry Esmond saw this gentleman, and knew and recognized him in after-life, as shall be shown in its place ;

and he has little doubt now that my lord viscount was implicated somewhat in the transactions which always kept
Father Holt employed and travelling hither and thither
under a dozen of different names and disguises. The
father's companion went by the name of Captain James ;
and it was under a very different name and appearance
that Harry Esmond afterwards saw him.

It was the next year that the Fenwick conspiracy blew up,
which is a matter of public history now, and which ended
in the execution of Sir John and many more, who suffered
manfully for their treason, and who were attended to Tyburn
by my lady's father, Dean Armstrong, Mr. Collier, and other
stout nonjuring clergymen, who absolved them at the
gallows' foot.*

'Tis known that when Sir John was apprehended, discovery
was made of a great number of names of gentlemen engaged
in the conspiracy ; when, with a noble wisdom and clemency,
the prince burned the list of conspirators furnished to him,
and said he would know no more. Now it was, after this,
that Lord Castlewood swore his great oath, that he would
never, so help him Heaven, be engaged in any transaction
against that brave and merciful man ; and so he told Holt
when the indefatigable priest visited him, and would have
had him engage in a farther conspiracy. After this my
lord ever spoke of King William as he was—as one of the
wisest, the bravest, and the greatest of men. My Lady
Esmond (for her part) said she could never pardon the king,
first, for ousting his father-in-law from his throne, and
secondly, for not being constant to his wife, the Princess
Mary. Indeed, I think if Nero were to rise again, and be
king of England, and a good family man, the ladies would
pardon him. My lord laughed at his wife's objections—
the standard of virtue did not fit him much.

The last conference which Mr. Holt had with his lordship
took place when Harry was come home for his first vacation
from college (Harry saw his old tutor but for a half-hour,
and exchanged no private words with him), and their talk,
whatever it might be, left my lord viscount very much
disturbed in mind—so much so, that his wife, and his young
kinsman, Henry Esmond, could not but observe his disquiet.
After Holt was gone, my lord rebuffed Esmond, and again
treated him with the greatest deference ; he shunned his
wife's questions and company, and looked at his children

with such a face of gloom and anxiety, muttering, ' Poor children—poor children ! ' in a way that could not but fill those whose life it was to watch him and obey him, with great alarm.   For which gloom, each person interested in the Lord Castlewood, framed in his or her own mind an interpretation.

My lady, with a laugh of cruel bitterness, said, ' I suppose the person at Hexton has been ill, or has scolded him ' (for my lord's infatuation about Mrs. Marwood was known only too well).   Young Esmond feared for his money affairs, into the condition of which he had been initiated ; and that the expenses, always greater than his revenue, had caused Lord Castlewood disquiet.

One of the causes why my lord viscount had taken young Esmond into his special favour was a trivial one, that hath not before been mentioned, though it was a very lucky accident in Henry Esmond's life.   A very few months after my lord's coming to Castlewood, in the winter-time—the little boy, being a child in a petticoat, trotting about—it happened that little Frank was with his father after dinner, who fell asleep over his wine, heedless of the child, who crawled to the fire ; and, as good fortune would have it, Esmond was sent by his mistress for the boy just as the poor little screaming urchin's coat was set on fire by a log ; when Esmond, rushing forward, tore the dress off the infant, so that his own hands were burned more than the child's, who was frightened rather than hurt, by this accident. But certainly 'twas providential that a resolute person should have come in at that instant, or the child had been burned to death probably, my lord sleeping very heavily after drinking, and not waking so cool as a man should who had a danger to face.

Ever after this the father, loud in his expressions of remorse and humility for being a tipsy good-for-nothing, and of admiration for Harry Esmond, whom his lordship would style a hero for doing a very trifling service, had the tenderest regard for his son's preserver, and Harry became quite as one of the family.   His burns were tended with the greatest care by his kind mistress, who said that Heaven had sent him to be the guardian of her children, and that she would love him all her life.

And it was after this, and from the very great love and tenderness which had grown up in this little household, rather than to the exhortations of Dean Armstrong (though these had no small weight with him), that Harry came to be quite of the religion of his house and his dear mistress, of which he has ever since been a professing member. As for Dr. Tusher's boasts that he was the cause of this conversion—even in these young days Mr. Esmond had such a contempt for the doctor, that had Tusher bade him believe anything (which he did not—never meddling at all), Harry would that instant have questioned the truth on't.

My lady seldom drank wine; but on certain days of the year, such as birthdays (poor Harry had never a one) and anniversaries, she took a little; and this day, the 29th December, was one. At the end, then, of this year, '96, it might have been a fortnight after Mr. Holt's last visit, Lord Castlewood being still very gloomy in mind, and sitting at table—my lady bidding a servant bring her a glass of wine, and looking at her husband with one of her sweet smiles, said—

' My lord, will you not fill a bumper too, and let me call a toast ? '

' What is it, Rachel ? ' says he, holding out his empty glass to be filled.

' 'Tis the 29th of December,' says my lady, with her fond look of gratitude : ' and my toast is, " Harry—and God bless him, who saved my boy's life ! " '

My lord looked at Harry hard, and drank the glass, but clapped it down on the table in a moment, and, with a sort of groan, rose up, and went out of the room. What was the matter ? We all knew that some great grief was over him.

Whether my lord's prudence had made him richer, or legacies had fallen to him, which enabled him to support a greater establishment than that frugal one which had been too much for his small means, Harry Esmond knew not ; but the house of Castlewood was now on a scale much more costly than it had been during the first year of his lordship's coming to the title. There were more horses in the stable and more servants in the hall, and many more guests coming and going now than formerly, when it was found difficult enough by the strictest economy to keep the house as befitted one of his lordship's rank, and the estate out of debt. And it did not require very much penetration to find, that many of the new acquaintances

at Castlewood were not agreeable to the lady there : not
that she ever treated them or any mortal with anything
but courtesy ; but they were persons who could not be
welcome to her ; and whose society a lady so refined and
reserved could scarce desire for her children.   There came
fuddling squires from the country round, who bawled their
songs under her windows and drank themselves tipsy with
my lord's punch and ale : there came officers from Hexton,
in whose company our little lord was made to hear talk
and to drink, and swear too in a way that made the delicate
lady tremble for her son.   Esmond tried to console her by
saying what he knew of his college experience ; that with
this sort of company and conversation a man must fall in
sooner or later in his course through the world : and it
mattered very little whether he heard it at twelve years old
or twenty—the youths who quitted mother's apron-strings
the latest being not uncommonly the wildest rakes.   But
it was about her daughter that Lady Castlewood was the
most anxious, and the danger which she thought menaced
the little Beatrix from the indulgences which her father
gave her (it must be owned that my lord, since these unhappy
domestic differences especially, was at once violent in his
language to the children when angry, as he was too familiar,
not to say coarse, when he was in a good humour), and from
the company into which the careless lord brought the ch

Not very far off from Castlewood is Sark Castle, where
the Marchioness of Sark lived, who was known to have
been a mistress of the late King Charles—and to this house,
whither indeed a great part of the country gentry went,
my lord insisted upon going, not only himself, but on
taking his little daughter and son to play with the children
there.   The children were nothing loath, for the house was
splendid, and the welcome kind enough.   But my lady,
justly no doubt, thought that the children of such a mother
as that noted Lady Sark had been, could be no good
company for her two ; and spoke her mind to her lord.
His own language when he was thwarted was not indeed
of the gentlest : to be brief, there was a family dispute
on this, as there had been on many other points—and the
lady was not only forced to give in, for the other's will was
law—nor could she, on account of their tender age, tell
her children what was the nature of her objection to their
visit of pleasure, or indeed mention to them any objection

at all—but she had the additional secret mortification to find them returning delighted with their new friends, loaded with presents from them, and eager to be allowed to go back to a place of such delights as Sark Castle. Every year she thought the company there would be more dangerous to her daughter, as from a child Beatrix grew to a woman, and her daily increasing beauty, and many faults of character too, expanded.

It was Harry Esmond's lot to see one of the visits which the old lady of Sark paid to the lady of Castlewood Hall : whither she came in state with six chestnut horses and blue ribbons, a page on each carriage step, a gentleman of the horse, and armed servants riding before and behind her. And, but that it was unpleasant to see Lady Castlewood's face, it was amusing to watch the behaviour of the two enemies : the frigid patience of the younger lady, and the unconquerable good humour of the elder—who would see no offence whatever her rival intended, and who never ceased to smile and to laugh, and to coax the children, and to pay compliments to every man, woman, child, nay dog, or chair and table, in Castlewood, so bent was she upon admiring everything there. She lauded the children, and wished—as indeed she well might—that her own family had been brought up as well as those cherubs. She had never seen such a complexion as dear Beatrix's—though to be sure she had a right to it from father and mother— Lady Castlewood's was indeed a wonder of freshness, and Lady Sark sighed to think she had not been born a fair woman ; and remarking Harry Esmond, with a fascinating superannuated smile, she complimented him on his wit, which she said she could see from his eyes and forehead ; and vowed that she would never have *him* at Sark until her daughter were out of the way.

CHAPTER XII

MY LORD MOHUN COMES AMONG US FOR NO GOOD

THERE had ridden along with this old princess's cavalcade,
two gentlemen ; her son, my Lord Firebrace, and his friend,
my Lord Mohun, who both were greeted with a great deal
of cordiality by the hospitable Lord of Castlewood.   My
Lord Firebrace was but a feeble-minded and weak-limbed
young nobleman, small in stature and limited in understanding—to judge from the talk young Esmond had with
him ; but the other was a person of a handsome presence,
with the *bel air*, and a bright daring warlike aspect, which,
according to the chronicle of those days, had already
achievèd for him the conquest of several beauties and
toasts.   He had fought and conquered in France, as well
as in Flanders ; he had served a couple of campaigns with
the Prince of Baden on the Danube, and witnessed the
rescue of Vienna from the Turk.   And he spoke of his
military exploits pleasantly, and with the manly freedom of
a soldier, so as to delight all his hearers at Castlewood, who
were little accustomed to meet a companion so agreeable.

On the first day this noble company came, my lord would
not hear of their departure before dinner, and carried away
the gentlemen to amuse them, whilst his wife was left to
do the honours of her house to the old marchioness and her
daughter within.   They looked at the stables, where my
Lord Mohun praised the horses, though there was but
a poor show there : they walked over the old house and
gardens, and fought the siege of Oliver's time over again :
they played a game of rackets in the old court, where my
Lord Castlewood beat my Lord Mohun, who said he loved
ball of all things, and would quickly come back to Castlewood for his revenge.   After dinner they played bowls, and
drank punch in the green alley ;   and when they parted
they were sworn friends, my Lord Castlewood kissing the
other lord before he mounted on horseback, and pronouncing
him the best companion he had met for many a long day.
All night long, over his tobacco-pipe Castlewood did not
cease to talk to Harry Esmond in praise of his new friend,
and in fact did not leave off speaking of him until his

lordship was so tipsy that he could not speak plainly any more.

At breakfast next day it was the same talk renewed; and when my lady said there was something free in the Lord Mohun's looks and manner of speech which caused her to mistrust him, her lord burst out with one of his laughs and oaths; said that he never liked man, woman, or beast, but what she was sure to be jealous of it; that Mohun was the prettiest fellow in England; that he hoped to see more of him whilst in the country; and that he would let Mohun know what my Lady Prude said of him.

'Indeed,' Lady Castlewood said, 'I liked his conversation well enough. 'Tis more amusing than that of most people I know. I thought it, I own, too free; not from what he said, as rather from what he implied.'

'Psha! your ladyship does not know the world,' said her husband; 'and you have always been as squeamish as when you were a miss of fifteen.'

'You found no fault when I was a miss at fifteen.'

'Begad, madam, you are grown too old for a pinafore now; and I hold that 'tis for me to judge what company my wife shall see,' said my lord, slapping the table.

'Indeed, Francis, I never thought otherwise,' answered my lady, rising and dropping him a curtsy, in which stately action, if there was obedience, there was defiance too; and in which a bystander, deeply interested in the happiness of that pair as Harry Esmond was, might see how hopelessly separated they were; what a great gulf of difference and discord had run between them.

'By G—d! Mohun is the best fellow in England; and I'll invite him here, just to plague that woman. Did you ever see such a frigid insolence as it is, Harry? That's the way she treats me,' he broke out, storming, and his face growing red as he clenched his fists and went on. 'I'm nobody in my own house. I'm to be the humble servant of that parson's daughter. By Jove! I'd rather she should fling the dish at my head than sneer at me as she does. She puts me to shame before the children with her d—d airs; and, I'll swear, tells Frank and Beaty that papa's a reprobate, and that they ought to despise me.'

'Indeed and indeed, sir, I never heard her say a word but of respect regarding you,' Harry Esmond interposed.

'No, curse it! I wish she would speak. But she never

does. She scorns me, and holds her tongue. She keeps off from me, as if I was a pestilence. By George! she was fond enough of her pestilence once. And when I came a-courting, you would see miss blush—blush red, by George! for joy. Why, what do you think she said to me, Harry? She said herself, when I joked with her about her d—d smiling red cheeks: " 'Tis as they do at St. James's; I put up my red flag when my king comes." I was the king, you see, she meant. But now, sir, look at her! I believe she would be glad if I was dead; and dead I've been to her these five years—ever since you all of you had the small-pox: and she never forgave me for going away.'

'Indeed, my lord, though 'twas hard to forgive, I think my mistress forgave it,' Harry Esmond said; 'and remember how eagerly she watched your lordship's return, and how sadly she turned away when she saw your cold looks.'

'Damme!' cries out my lord; 'would you have had me wait and catch the small-pox? Where the deuce had been the good of that? I'll bear danger with any man—but not useless danger—no, no. Thank you for nothing. And—you nod your head, and I know very well, Parson Harry, what you mean. There was the—the other affair to make her angry. But is a woman never to forgive a husband who goes a-tripping? Do you take me for a saint?'

'Indeed, sir, I do not,' says Harry, with a smile.

'Since that time my wife's as cold as the statue at Charing Cross. I tell thee she has no forgiveness in her, Henry. Her coldness blights my whole life, and sends me to the punch-bowl, or driving about the country. My children are not mine, but hers, when we are together. 'Tis only when she is out of sight with her abominable cold glances, that run through me, that they'll come to me, and that I dare to give them so much as a kiss; and that's why I take 'em and love 'em in other people's houses, Harry. I'm killed by the very virtue of that proud woman. Virtue! give me the virtue that can forgive; give me the virtue that thinks not of preserving itself, but of making other folks happy. Damme, what matters a scar or two if 'tis got in helping a friend in ill fortune?'

And my lord again slapped the table, and took a great draught from the tankard. Harry Esmond admired as he listened to him, and thought how the poor preacher of this self-sacrifice had fled from the small-pox, which the lady had borne so cheerfully, and which had been the cause of so much disunion in the lives of all in this house. ' How well men preach,' thought the young man, ' and each is the example in his own sermon. How each has a story in a dispute, and a true one, too, and both are right, or wrong as you will ! ' Harry's heart was pained within him, to watch the struggles and pangs that tore the breast of this kind, manly friend and protector.

' Indeed, sir,' said he, ' I wish to God that my mistress could hear you speak as I have heard you ; she would know much that would make her life the happier, could she hear it.' But my lord flung away with one of his oaths, and a jeer ; he said that Parson Harry was a good fellow ; but that as for women, all women were alike—all jades and heartless. So a man dashes a fine vase down and despises it for being broken. It may be worthless—true : but who had the keeping of it, and who shattered it ?

Harry, who would have given his life to make his bene-factress and her husband happy, bethought him, now that he saw what my lord's state of mind was, and that he really had a great deal of that love left in his heart, and ready for his wife's acceptance if she would take it, whether he could not be a means of reconciliation between these two persons, whom he revered the most in the world. And he cast about how he should break a part of his mind to his mistress, and warn her that in his, Harry's opinion, at least, her husband was still her admirer, and even her lover.

But he found the subject a very difficult one to handle, when he ventured to remonstrate, which he did in the very gravest tone (for long confidence and reiterated proofs of devotion and loyalty had given him a sort of authority in the house, which he resumed as soon as ever he returned to it) ; and with a speech that should have some effect, as, indeed, it was uttered with the speaker's own heart, he ventured most gently to hint to his adored mistress, that she was doing her husband harm by her ill opinion of him, and that the happiness of all the family depended upon setting her right.

She, who was ordinarily calm and most gentle, and full of smiles and soft attentions, flushed up when young Esmond so spoke to her, and rose from her chair, looking at him with a haughtiness and indignation that he had never before known her to display. She was quite an altered being for that moment ; and looked an angry princess insulted by a vassal.

' Have you ever heard me utter a word in my lord's disparagement ? ' she asked hastily, hissing out her words, and stamping her foot.

' Indeed, no,' Esmond said, looking down.

' Are you come to me as his ambassador—*You* ? ' she continued.

' I would sooner see peace between you than anything else in the world,' Harry answered, ' and would go of any embassy that had that end.'

' So *you* are my lord's go-between ? ' she went on, not regarding this speech. ' You are sent to bid me back into slavery again, and inform me that my lord's favour is graciously restored to his handmaid ? He is weary of Covent Garden, is he, that he comes home and would have the fatted calf killed ? '

' There's good authority for it, surely,' said Esmond.

' For a son, yes ; but my lord is not my son. It was he who cast me away from him. It was he who broke our happiness down, and he bids me to repair it. It was he who showed himself to me at last, as he was, not as I had thought him. It is he who comes before my children stupid and senseless with wine—who leaves our company for that of frequenters of taverns and bagnios—who goes from his home to the city yonder and his friends there, and when he is tired of them returns hither, and expects that I shall kneel and welcome him. And he sends *you* as his chamberlain ! What a proud embassy ! Monsieur, I make you my compliment of the new place.'

' It would be a proud embassy, and a happy embassy too, could I bring you and my lord together,' Esmond replied.

' I presume you have fulfilled your mission now, sir. 'Twas a pretty one for you to undertake. I don't know whether 'tis your Cambridge philosophy, or time, that has altered your ways of thinking,' Lady Castlewood continued, still in a sarcastic tone. ' Perhaps you too have learned to love drink, and to hiccup over your wine or punch ;—which is your worship's favourite liquor ? Perhaps you too put up at the ' Rose '*on your way through London, and have your acquaintances in Covent Garden. My services

to you, sir, to principal and ambassador, to master and—
and lackey.'

'Great Heavens, madam,' cried Harry, 'what have I
done that thus, for a second time, you insult me ? Do
you wish me to blush for what I used to be proud of, that
I lived on your bounty ? Next to doing you a service
(which my life would pay for), you know that to receive
one from you is my highest pleasure. What wrong have
I done you that you should wound me so, cruel woman ?'

'What wrong ?' she said, looking at Esmond with wild
eyes. 'Well, none—none that you know of, Harry, or
could help. Why did you bring back the small-pox,' she
added, after a pause, ' from Castlewood village ? You could
not help it, could you ? Which of us knows whither fate
leads us ? But we were all happy, Henry, till then.' And
Harry went away from this colloquy, thinking still that
the estrangement between his patron and his beloved
mistress was remediable, and that each had at heart a strong
attachment to the other.

The intimacy between the Lords Mohun and Castlewood
appeared to increase as long as the former remained in the
country ; and my Lord of Castlewood especially seemed
never to be happy out of his new comrade's sight. They
sported together, they drank, they played bowls and tennis :
my Lord Castlewood would go for three days to Sark, and
bring back my Lord Mohun to Castlewood—where indeed
his lordship made himself very welcome to all persons,
having a joke or a new game at romps for the children,
all the talk of the town for my lord, and music and gallantry
and plenty of the *beau langage* for my lady, and for Harry
Esmond, who was never tired of hearing his stories of his
campaigns and his life at Vienna, Venice, Paris, and the
famous cities of Europe which he had visited both in peace
and war. And he sang at my lady's harpsichord, and
played cards or backgammon, or his new game of billiards
with my lord (of whom he invariably got the better) ;
always having a consummate good humour, and bearing
himself with a certain manly grace, that might exhibit
somewhat of the camp and Alsatia perhaps, but that had
its charm and stamped him a gentleman : and his manner
to Lady Castlewood was so devoted and respectful, that
she soon recovered from the first feelings of dislike which
she had conceived against him—nay, before long, began to

be interested in his spiritual welfare, and hopeful of his
conversion, lending him books of piety, which he promised
dutifully to study. With her my lord talked of reform,
of settling into quiet life, quitting the Court and town, and
buying some land in the neighbourhood—though it must
be owned that, when the two lords were together over their
burgundy after dinner, their talk was very different, and
there was very little question of conversion on my Lord
Mohun's part. When they got to their second bottle,
Harry Esmond used commonly to leave these two noble
topers, who, though they talked freely enough, Heaven
knows, in his presence (Good Lord, what a set of stories,
of Alsatia and Spring Garden,* of the taverns and gaming-
houses, of the ladies of the Court, and mesdames of the
theatres, he can recall out of their godly conversation !)—
although I say they talked before Esmond freely, yet they
seemed pleased when he went away, and then they had
another bottle, and then they fell to cards, and then my
Lord Mohun came to her ladyship's drawing-room ; leaving
his boon companion to sleep off his wine.

'Twas a point of honour with the fine gentlemen of those
days to lose or win magnificently at their horse-matches,
or games of cards and dice—and you could never tell,
from the demeanour of these two lords afterwards, which
had been successful and which the loser at their games.
And when my lady hinted to my lord that he played more
than she liked, he dismissed her with a ' pish ', and swore
that nothing was more equal than play betwixt gentlemen,
if they did but keep it up long enough. And these kept
it up long enough you may be sure. A man of fashion
of that time often passed a quarter of his day at cards,
and another quarter at drink : I have known many a pretty
fellow, who was a wit too, ready of repartee, and possessed
of a thousand graces, who would be puzzled if he had to
write more than his name.

There is scarce any thoughtful man or woman, I suppose,
but can look back upon his course of past life, and remember
some point, trifling as it may have seemed at the time of
occurrence, which has nevertheless turned and altered his
whole career. 'Tis with almost all of us, as in Monsieur
Massillon's magnificent image regarding King William, a
grain de sable that perverts or perhaps overthrows us ;* and
so it was but a light word flung in the air, a mere freak of

a perverse child's temper, that brought down a whole heap
of crushing woes upon that family whereof Harry Esmond
formed a part.

Coming home to his dear Castlewood in the third year
of his academical course (wherein he had now obtained
some distinction, his Latin Poem on the death of the Duke
of Gloucester, Princess Anne of Denmark's son, having
gained him a medal, and introduced him to the society of
the University wits), Esmond found his little friend and
pupil Beatrix grown to be taller than her mother, a slim
and lovely young girl, with cheeks mantling with health
and roses : with eyes like stars shining out of azure, with
waving bronze hair clustered about the fairest young forehead ever seen : and a mien and shape haughty and beautiful, such as that of the famous antique statue of the huntress
Diana—at one time haughty, rapid, imperious, with eyes
and arrows that dart and kill. Harry watched and wondered
at this young creature, and likened her in his mind to
Artemis with the ringing bow and shafts flashing death
upon the children of Niobe ; at another time she was coy
and melting as Luna shining tenderly upon Endymion.
This fair creature, this lustrous Phoebe, was only young as
yet, nor had nearly reached her full splendour : but crescent
and brilliant, our young gentleman of the University, his
head full of poetical fancies, his heart perhaps throbbing
with desires undefined, admired this rising young divinity ;
and gazed at her (though only as at some ' bright particular
star ', far above his earth) with endless delight and wonder.
She had been a coquette from the earliest times almost,
trying her freaks and jealousies, her wayward frolics and
winning caresses, upon all that came within her reach ;
she set her women quarrelling in the nursery, and practised
her eyes on the groom as she rode behind him on the pillion.

She was the darling and torment of father and mother.
She intrigued with each secretly ; and bestowed her fondness and withdrew it, plied them with tears, smiles, kisses,
cajolements ;—when the mother was angry, as happened
often, flew to the father, and sheltering behind him, pursued
her victim ; when both were displeased, transferred her
caresses to the domestics, or watched until she could win
back her parents' good graces, either by surprising them
into laughter and good humour, or appeasing them by
submission and artful humility. She was *saevo laeta negotio*,

like that fickle goddess Horace describes, and of whose 'malicious joy' a great poet of our own has written so nobly*—who, famous and heroic as he was, was not strong enough to resist the torture of women.

It was but three years before, that the child, then but ten years old, had nearly managed to make a quarrel between Harry Esmond and his comrade, good-natured, phlegmatic Thomas Tusher, who never of his own seeking quarrelled with anybody : by quoting to the latter some silly joke which Harry had made regarding him—(it was the merest, idlest jest, though it near drove two old friends to blows, and I think such a battle would have pleased her)—and from that day Tom kept at a distance from her ; and she respected him, and coaxed him sedulously whenever they met. But Harry was much more easily appeased, because he was fonder of the child : and when she made mischief, used cutting speeches, or caused her friends pain, she excused herself for her fault, not by admitting and deploring it, but by pleading not guilty, and asserting innocence so constantly, and with such seeming artlessness, that it was impossible to question her plea. In her childhood, they were but mischiefs then which she did ; but her power became more fatal as she grew older—as a kitten first plays with a ball, and then pounces on a bird and kills it. 'Tis not to be imagined that Harry Esmond had all this experience at this early stage of his life, whereof he is now writing the history—many things here noted were but known to him in later days. Almost everything Beatrix did or undid seemed good, or at least pardonable, to him then, and years afterwards.

It happened, then, that Harry Esmond came home to Castlewood for his last vacation, with good hopes of a fellowship at his college, and a contented resolve to advance his fortune that way. 'Twas in the first year of the present century, Mr. Esmond (as far as he knew the period of his birth) being then twenty-two years old. He found his quondam pupil shot up into this beauty of which we have spoken, and promising yet more : her brother, my lord's son, a handsome high-spirited brave lad, generous and frank, and kind to everybody, save perhaps his sister, with whom Frank was at war (and not from his but her fault)—adoring his mother, whose joy he was : and taking her side in the unhappy matrimonial differences which

were now permanent, while of course Mistress Beatrix
ranged with her father.   When heads of families fall out,
it must naturally be that their dependants wear the one
or the other party's colour ; and even in the parliaments
in the servants' hall or the stables, Harry, who had an
early observant turn, could see which were my lord's
adherents and which my lady's, and conjecture pretty
shrewdly how their unlucky quarrel was debated.   Our
lackeys sit in judgement on us.   My lord's intrigues may
be ever so stealthily conducted, but his valet knows them ;
and my lady's woman carries her mistress's private history
to the servants' scandal-market, and exchanges it against
the secrets of other abigails.

CHAPTER XIII

MY LORD LEAVES US AND HIS EVIL BEHIND HIM

My Lord Mohun (of whose exploits and fame some of the
gentlemen of the University had brought down but ugly
reports) was once more a guest at Castlewood, and seemingly
more intimately allied with my lord even than before.
Once in the spring those two noblemen had ridden to Cambridge from Newmarket, whither they had gone for the
horse-racing, and had honoured Harry Esmond with a visit
at his rooms ; after which Doctor Montague, the master
of the college, who had treated Harry somewhat haughtily,
seeing his familiarity with these great folks, and that my
Lord Castlewood laughed and walked with his hand on
Harry's shoulder, relented to Mr. Esmond, and condescended
to be very civil to him ; and some days after his arrival,
Harry, laughing, told this story to Lady Esmond, remarking
how strange it was that men famous for learning and
renowned over Europe, should, nevertheless, so bow down
to a title, and cringe to a nobleman ever so poor.   At this,
Mistress Beatrix flung up her head, and said, it became
those of low origin to respect their betters ; that the parsons
made themselves a great deal too proud, she thought ; and
that she liked the way at Lady Sark's best, where the
chaplain, though he loved pudding, as all parsons do,
always went away before the custard.

'And when I am a parson,' says Mr. Esmond, 'will you give me no custard, Beatrix?'

'You—you are different,' Beatrix answered. 'You are of our blood.'

'My father was a parson, as you call him,' said my lady.

'But mine is a peer of Ireland,' says Mistress Beatrix, tossing her head. 'Let people know their places. I suppose you will have me go down on my knees and ask a blessing of Mr. Thomas Tusher, that has just been made a curate, and whose mother was a waiting-maid.'

And she tossed out of the room, being in one of her flighty humours then.

When she was gone, my lady looked so sad and grave, that Harry asked the cause of her disquietude. She said it was not merely what he said of Newmarket, but what she had remarked, with great anxiety and terror, that my lord, ever since his acquaintance with the Lord Mohun especially, had recurred to his fondness for play, which he had renounced since his marriage.

'But men promise more than they are able to perform in marriage,' said my lady, with a sigh. 'I fear he has lost large sums; and our property, always small, is dwindling away under this reckless dissipation. I heard of him in London with very wild company. Since his return letters and lawyers are constantly coming and going: he seems to me to have a constant anxiety, though he hides it under boisterousness and laughter. I looked through—through the door last night, and—and before,' said my lady, 'and saw them at cards after midnight; no estate will bear that extravagance, much less ours, which will be so diminished that my son will have nothing at all, and my poor Beatrix no portion!'

'I wish I could help you, madam,' said Harry Esmond, sighing, and wishing that unavailingly, and for the thousandth time in his life.

'Who can? Only God,' said Lady Esmond—'only God, in whose hands we are.' And so it is, and for his rule over his family, and for his conduct to wife and children—subjects over whom his power is monarchical—any one who watches the world must think with trembling sometimes of the account which many a man will have to render. For in our society there's no law to control the King of the

Fireside.   He is master of property, happiness—life almost.
He is free to punish, to make happy or unhappy—to ruin
or to torture.   He may kill a wife gradually, and be no
more questioned than the Grand Seignior who drowns a
slave at midnight.   He may make slaves and hypocrites
of his children ; or friends and freemen ; or drive them into
revolt and enmity against the natural law of love.   I have
heard politicians and coffee-house wiseacres talking over
the newspaper, and railing at the tyranny of the French
king, and the emperor, and wondered how these (who are
monarchs, too, in their way) govern their own dominions
at home, where each man rules absolute ?   When the annals
of each little reign are shown to the Supreme Master, under
whom we hold sovereignty, histories will be laid bare of
household tyrants as cruel as Amurath,* and as savage as
Nero, and as reckless and dissolute as Charles.

If Harry Esmond's patron erred, 'twas in the latter way,
from a disposition rather self-indulgent than cruel ; and he
might have been brought back to much better feelings, had
time been given to him to bring his repentance to a lasting
reform.

As my lord and his friend Lord Mohun were such close
companions, Mistress Beatrix chose to be jealous of the
latter ; and the two gentlemen often entertained each other
by laughing, in their rude boisterous way, at the child's
freaks of anger and show of dislike.   ' When thou art old
enough, thou shalt marry Lord Mohun,' Beatrix's father
would say : on which the girl would pout and say, ' I would
rather marry Tom Tusher.'   And because the Lord Mohun
always showed an extreme gallantry to my Lady Castlewood, whom he professed to admire devotedly, one day, in
answer to this old joke of her father's, Beatrix said, ' I think
my lord would rather marry mamma than marry me ; and
is waiting till you die to ask her.'

The words were said lightly and pertly by the girl one
night before supper, as the family party were assembled
near the great fire.   The two lords, who were at cards, both
gave a start ; my lady turned as red as scarlet, and bade
Mistress Beatrix go to her own chamber ; whereupon the
girl, putting on, as her wont was, the most innocent air, said,
' I am sure I meant no wrong ; I am sure mamma talks a
great deal more to Harry Esmond than she does to papa—
and she cried when Harry went away, and she never does

when papa goes away ; and last night she talked to Lord
Mohun for ever so long, and sent us out of the room, and
cried when we came back, and——'

'D——n!' cried out my Lord Castlewood, out of all
patience. 'Go out of the room, you little viper !' and he
started up and flung down his cards.

'Ask Lord Mohun what I said to him, Francis,' her ladyship said, rising up with a scared face, but yet with a great
and touching dignity and candour in her look and voice.
'Come away with me, Beatrix.' Beatrix sprung up too ;
she was in tears now.

'Dearest mamma, what have I done ?' she asked. 'Sure
I meant no harm.' And she clung to her mother, and the
pair went out sobbing together.

'I will tell you what your wife said to me, Frank,' my
Lord Mohun cried—'Parson Harry may hear it ; and, as
I hope for heaven, every word I say is true. Last night,
with tears in her eyes, your wife implored me to play no
more with you at dice or at cards, and you know best
whether what she asked was not for your good.'

'Of course it was, Mohun,' says my lord, in a dry hard
voice. 'Of course, you are a model of a man : and the
world knows what a saint you are.'

My Lord Mohun was separated from his wife, and had had
many affairs of honour : of which women as usual had been
the cause.

'I am no saint, though your wife is—and I can answer
for my actions as other people must for their words,' said
my Lord Mohun.

'By G—, my lord, you shall,' cried the other, starting up.

'We have another little account to settle first, my lord,'
says Lord Mohun. Whereupon Harry Esmond, filled with
alarm for the consequences to which this disastrous dispute
might lead, broke out into the most vehement expostulations
with his patron and his adversary. 'Gracious Heavens !'
he said, 'my lord, are you going to draw a sword upon your
friend in your own house ? Can you doubt the honour of
a lady who is as pure as Heaven, and would die a thousand
times rather than do you a wrong ? Are the idle words of
a jealous child to set friends at variance ? Has not my
mistress, as much as she dared to, besought your lordship.
as the truth must be told, to break your intimacy with my
Lord Mohun ; and to give up the habit which may bring

ruin on your family ? But for my Lord Mohun's illness, had he not left you ? '

' Faith, Frank, a man with a gouty toe can't run after other men's wives,' broke out my Lord Mohun, who indeed was in that way, and with a laugh and a look at his swathed limb so frank and comical, that the other dashing his fist across his forehead was caught by that infectious good humour, and said with his oath, ' —— it, Harry, I believe thee,' and so this quarrel was over, and the two gentlemen, at swords drawn but just now, dropped their points, and shook hands.

Beati pacifici. ' Go, bring my lady back,' said Harry's patron. Esmond went away only too glad to be the bearer of such good news. He found her at the door ; she had been listening there, but went back as he came. She took both his hands, hers were marble cold. She seemed as if she would fall on his shoulder. ' Thank you, and God bless you, my dear brother Harry,' she said. She kissed his hand, Esmond felt her tears upon it : and leading her into the room, and up to my lord, the Lord Castlewood with an outbreak of feeling and affection, such as he had not exhibited for many a long day, took his wife to his heart, and bent over and kissed her and asked her pardon.

' 'Tis time for me to go to roost. I will have my gruel abed,' said my Lord Mohun : and limped off comically on Harry Esmond's arm. ' By George, that woman is a pearl !' he said ; ' and 'tis only a pig that wouldn't value her. Have you seen the vulgar trapesing orange-girl whom Esmond '—but here Mr. Esmond interrupted him, saying, that these were not affairs for him to know.

My lord's gentleman came in to wait upon his master, who was no sooner in his nightcap and dressing-gown than he had another visitor whom his host insisted on sending to him : and this was no other than the Lady Castlewood herself with the toast and gruel, which her husband bade her make and carry with her own hands in to her guest.

Lord Castlewood stood looking after his wife as she went on this errand, and as he looked, Harry Esmond could not but gaze on him, and remarked in his patron's face an expression of love, and grief, and care, which very much moved and touched the young man. Lord Castlewood's hands fell down at his sides, and his head on his breast, and presently he said—

' You heard what Mohun said, parson ? '

' That my lady was a saint ? '

' That there are two accounts to settle.   I have been going
wrong these five years, Harry Esmond.   Ever since you
brought that damned small-pox into the house, there has
been a fate pursuing me, and I had best have died of it, and
not run away from it like a coward.   I left Beatrix with her
relations, and went to London ; and I fell among thieves,
Harry, and I got back to confounded cards and dice, which
I hadn't touched since my marriage—no, not since I was in
the duke's guard, with those wild Mohocks.*   And I have
been playing worse and worse, and going deeper and deeper
into it ; and I owe Mohun two thousand pounds now ; and
when it's paid I am little better than a beggar.   I don't
like to look my boy in the face ; he hates me, I know he does.
And I have spent Beaty's little portion ; and the Lord
knows what will come if I live ; the best thing I can do is to
die, and release what portion of the estate is redeemable for
the boy.'

Mohun was as much master at Castlewood as the owner
of the Hall itself ; and his equipages filled the stables, where,
indeed, there was room in plenty for many more horses than
Harry Esmond's impoverished patron could afford to keep.
He had arrived on horseback with his people ; but when his
gout broke out my Lord Mohun sent to London for a light
chaise he had, drawn by a pair of small horses, and running
as swift, wherever roads were good, as a Laplander's sledge.
When this carriage came, his lordship was eager to drive
the Lady Castlewood abroad in it, and did so many times,
and at a rapid pace, greatly to his companion's enjoyment,
who loved the swift motion and the healthy breezes over
the downs which lie hard upon Castlewood, and stretch
thence towards the sea.   As this amusement was very
pleasant to her, and her lord, far from showing any mistrust
of her intimacy with Lord Mohun, encouraged her to be
his companion ; as if willing, by his present extreme confidence, to make up for any past mistrust which his jealousy
had shown ; the Lady Castlewood enjoyed herself freely in
this harmless diversion, which, it must be owned, her guest
was very eager to give her ; and it seemed that she grew
the more free with Lord Mohun, and pleased with his company, because of some sacrifice which his gallantry was
pleased to make in her favour.

Seeing the two gentlemen constantly at cards still of evenings, Harry Esmond one day deplored to his mistress that this fatal infatuation of her lord should continue ; and now they seemed reconciled together, begged his lady to hint to her husband that he should play no more.

But Lady Castlewood, smiling archly and gaily, said she would speak to him presently, and that, for a few nights more at least, he might be let to have his amusement.

' Indeed, madam,' said Harry, ' you know not what it costs you ; and 'tis easy for any observer who knows the game, to see that Lord Mohun is by far the stronger of the two.'

' I know he is,' says my lady, still with exceeding good humour ; ' he is not only the best player, but the kindest player in the world.'

' Madam, madam,' Esmond cried, transported and provoked. ' Debts of honour must be paid some time or other ; and my master will be ruined if he goes on.'

' Harry, shall I tell you a secret ? ' my lady replied, with kindness and pleasure still in her eyes. ' Francis will not be ruined if he goes on ; he will be rescued if he goes on. I repent of having spoken and thought unkindly of the Lord Mohun when he was here in the past year. He is full of much kindness and good ; and 'tis my belief that we shall bring him to better things. I have lent him Tillotson and your favourite Bishop Taylor,* and he is much touched, he says ; and as a proof of his repentance—(and herein lies my secret)—what do you think he is doing with Francis ? He is letting poor Frank win his money back again. He hath won already at the last four nights ; and my Lord Mohun says that he will not be the means of injuring poor Frank and my dear children.'

' And in God's name, what do you return him for this sacrifice ? ' asked Esmond, aghast ; who knew enough of men, and of this one in particular, to be aware that such a finished rake gave nothing for nothing. ' How, in Heaven's name, are you to pay him ? '

' Pay him ! With a mother's blessing and a wife's prayers ! ' cries my lady, clasping her hands together. Harry Esmond did not know whether to laugh, to be angry, or to love his dear mistress more than ever for the obstinate innocency with which she chose to regard the conduct of a man of the world, whose designs he knew better how to interpret. He told the lady, guardedly, but so as to make

his meaning quite clear to her, what he knew in respect of
the former life and conduct of this nobleman ; of other
women against whom he had plotted, and whom he had
overcome ; of the conversation which he Harry himself
had had with Lord Mohun, wherein the lord made a boast
of his libertinism, and frequently avowed that he held all
women to be fair game (as his lordship styled this pretty
sport), and that they were all, without exception, to be won.
And the return Harry had for his entreaties and remonstrances was a fit of anger on Lady Castlewood's part, who
would not listen to his accusations, she said, and retorted
that he himself must be very wicked and perverted, to suppose evil designs, where she was sure none were meant.
' And this is the good meddlers get of interfering,' Harry
thought to himself with much bitterness ; and his perplexity
and annoyance were only the greater, because he could not
speak to my Lord Castlewood himself upon a subject of this
nature, or venture to advise or warn him regarding a
matter so very sacred as his own honour, of which my lord
was naturally the best guardian.

But though Lady Castlewood would listen to no advice
from her young dependant, and appeared indignantly to
refuse it when offered, Harry had the satisfaction to find
that she adopted the counsel which she professed to reject ;
for the next day she pleaded a headache, when my Lord
Mohun would have had her drive out, and the next day
the headache continued ; and next day, in a laughing gay
way she proposed that the children should take her place
in his lordship's car, for they would be charmed with a ride
of all things ; and she must not have all the pleasure for
herself.   My lord gave them a drive with a very good grace,
though I dare say with rage and disappointment inwardly—
not that his heart was very seriously engaged in his designs
upon this simple lady : but the life of such men is often one
of intrigue, and they can no more go through the day without
a woman to pursue, than a fox-hunter without his sport
after breakfast.

Under an affected carelessness of demeanour, and though
there was no outward demonstration of doubt upon his
patron's part since the quarrel between the two lords,
Harry yet saw that Lord Castlewood was watching his guest
very narrowly ; and caught signs of distrust and smothered
rage (as Harry thought) which foreboded no good.   On the

cries the Lord Mohun. ' Did Frank Esmond commission you ? '

' No one did. 'Twas the honour of my family that commissioned me.'

' And you are prepared to answer this ? ' cries the other, furiously lashing his horses.

' Quite, my lord : your lordship will upset the carriage if you whip so hotly.'

' By George, you have a brave spirit ! ' my lord cried out, bursting into a laugh. ' I suppose 'tis that infernal *botte de Jésuite**that makes you so bold,' he added.

' 'Tis the peace of the family I love best in the world,' Harry Esmond said warmly—' 'tis the honour of a noble benefactor—the happiness of my dear mistress and her children. I owe them everything in life, my lord ; and would lay it down for any one of them. What brings you here to disturb this quiet household ? What keeps you lingering month after month in the country ? What makes you feign illness and invent pretexts for delay ? Is it to win my poor patron's money ? Be generous, my lord, and spare his weakness for the sake of his wife and children. Is it to practise upon the simple heart of a virtuous lady ? You might as well storm the Tower single-handed. But you may blemish her name by light comments on it, or by lawless pursuits—and I don't deny that 'tis in your power to make her unhappy. Spare these innocent people, and leave them.'

' By the Lord, I believe thou hast an eye to the pretty Puritan thyself, Master Harry,' says my lord, with his reckless, good-humoured laugh, and as if he had been listening with interest to the passionate appeal of the young man. ' Whisper, Harry. Art thou in love with her thyself ? Hath tipsy Frank Esmond come by the way of all flesh ? '

' My lord, my lord,' cried Harry, his face flushing and his eyes filling as he spoke, ' I never had a mother, but I love this lady as one. I worship her as a devotee worships a saint. To hear her name spoken lightly seems blasphemy to me. Would you dare think of your own mother so, or suffer any one so to speak of her ! It is a horror to me to fancy that any man should think of her impurely. I implore you, I beseech you, to leave her. Danger will come out of it.'

' Danger, psha ! ' says my lord, giving a cut to the horses, which at this minute—for we were got on to the Downs— fairly ran off into a gallop that no pulling could stop.   The rein broke in Lord Mohun's hands, and the furious beasts scampered madly forwards, the carriage swaying to and fro, and the persons within it holding on to the sides as best they might, until seeing a great ravine before them, where an upset was inevitable, the two gentlemen leapt for their lives, each out of his side of the chaise.   Harry Esmond was quit for a fall on the grass, which was so severe that it stunned him for a minute ; but he got up presently very sick, and bleeding at the nose, but with no other hurt. The Lord Mohun was not so fortunate ; he fell on his head against a stone, and lay on the ground dead to all appearance.

This misadventure happened as the gentlemen were on their return homewards ; and my Lord Castlewood, with his son and daughter, who were going out for a ride, met the ponies as they were galloping with the car behind, the broken traces entangling their heels, and my lord's people turned and stopped them.   It was young Frank who spied out Lord Mohun's scarlet coat as he lay on the ground, and the party made up to that unfortunate gentleman and Esmond, who was now standing over him.   His large peri-wig and feathered hat had fallen off, and he was bleeding profusely from a wound on the forehead, and looking, and being, indeed, a corpse.

' Great God ! he's dead ! ' says my lord.   ' Ride, some one : fetch a doctor—stay.   I'll go home and bring back Tusher ; he knows surgery,' and my lord, with his son after him, galloped away.

They were scarce gone when Harry Esmond, who was indeed but just come to himself, bethought him of a similar accident which he had seen on a ride from Newmarket to Cambridge, and taking off a sleeve of my lord's coat, Harry, with a penknife, opened a vein in his arm, and was greatly relieved, after a moment, to see the blood flow.   He was near half an hour before he came to himself, by which time Doctor Tusher and little Frank arrived, and found my lord not a corpse indeed, but as pale as one.

After a time, and when he was able to bear motion, they put my lord upon a groom's horse, and gave the other to Esmond, the men walking on each side of my lord, to support him, if need were, and worthy Doctor Tusher with them. Little Frank and Harry rode together at a foot pace.

When we rode together home, the boy said : ' We met mamma, who was walking on the terrace with the doctor, and papa frightened her, and told her you were dead——'

' That I was dead ? ' asks Harry.

' Yes. Papa says : " Here's poor Harry killed, my dear ; ' on which mamma gives a great scream ; and oh, Harry ! she drops down ; and I thought she was dead, too. And you never saw such a way as papa was in : he swore one of his great oaths : and he turned quite pale ; and then he began to laugh somehow, and he told the doctor to take his horse, and me to follow him ; and we left him. And I looked back, and saw him dashing water out of the fountain on to mamma. Oh, she was so frightened ! '

Musing upon this curious history—for my Lord Mohun's name was Henry too, and they called each other Frank and Harry often—and not a little disturbed and anxious, Esmond rode home. His dear lady was on the terrace still, one of her women with her, and my lord no longer there. There are steps and a little door thence down into the road. My lord passed, looking very ghastly, with a handkerchief over his head, and without his hat and periwig, which a groom carried, but his politeness did not desert him, and he made a bow to the lady above.

' Thank Heaven you are safe,' she said.

' And so is Harry, too, mamma,' says little Frank,— ' huzzay ! '

Harry Esmond got off the horse to run to his mistress, as did little Frank, and one of the grooms took charge of the two beasts, while the other, hat and periwig in hand, walked by my lord's bridle to the front gate, which lay half a mile away.

' Oh, my boy ! what a fright you have given me ! ' Lady Castlewood said, when Harry Esmond came up, greeting him with one of her shining looks, and a voice of tender welcome ; and she was so kind as to kiss the young man ('twas the second time she had so honoured him), and she walked into the house between him and her son, holding a hand of each.

CHAPTER XIV

WE RIDE AFTER HIM TO LONDON

AFTER a repose of a couple of days, the Lord Mohun was so
far recovered of his hurt as to be able to announce his
departure for the next morning ; when, accordingly, he
took leave of Castlewood, proposing to ride to London by
easy stages, and lie two nights upon the road. His host
treated him with a studied and ceremonious courtesy,
certainly different from my lord's usual frank and careless
demeanour ; but there was no reason to suppose that the
two lords parted otherwise than good friends, though Harry
Esmond remarked that my lord viscount only saw his
guest in company with other persons, and seemed to avoid
being alone with him. Nor did he ride any distance with
Lord Mohun, as his custom was with most of his friends,
whom he was always eager to welcome and unwilling to lose ;
but contented himself, when his lordship's horses were
announced, and their owner appeared booted for his journey,
to take a courteous leave of the ladies of Castlewood, by
following the Lord Mohun downstairs to his horses, and by
bowing and wishing him a good day, in the courtyard.
' I shall see you in London before very long, Mohun,' my
lord said, with a smile ; ' when we will settle our accounts
together.'

' Do not let them trouble you, Frank,' said the other
good-naturedly, and, holding out his hand, looked rather
surprised at the grim and stately manner in which his host
received his parting salutation : and so, followed by his
people, he rode away.

Harry Esmond was witness of the departure. It was
very different to my lord's coming, for which great preparation had been made (the old house putting on its best
appearance to welcome its guest), and there was a sadness
and constraint about all persons that day, which filled
Mr. Esmond with gloomy forebodings, and sad indefinite
apprehensions. Lord Castlewood stood at the door watching his guest and his people as they went out under the
arch of the outer gate. When he was there, Lord Mohun
turned once more, my lord viscount slowly raised his beaver

and bowed. His face wore a peculiar livid look, Harry
thought. He cursed and kicked away his dogs, which came
jumping about him—then he walked up to the fountain in
the centre of the court, and leaned against a pillar and
looked into the basin. As Esmond crossed over to his
own room, late the chaplain's, on the other side of the
court, and turned to enter in at the low door, he saw Lady
Castlewood looking through the curtains of the great
window of the drawing-room overhead, at my lord as he
stood regarding the fountain. There was in the court
a peculiar silence somehow ; and the scene remained long
in Esmond's memory ;—the sky bright overhead ; the
buttresses of the building and the sundial casting shadow
over the gilt *memento mori* inscribed underneath ; the two
dogs, a black greyhound and a spaniel nearly white, the one
with his face up to the sun, and the other snuffing amongst
the grass and stones, and my lord leaning over the fountain,
which was plashing audibly. 'Tis strange how that scene
and the sound of that fountain remain fixed on the memory
of a man who has beheld a hundred sights of splendour, and
danger too, of which he has kept no account.

It was Lady Castlewood, she had been laughing all the
morning, and especially gay and lively before her husband
and his guest, who, as soon as the two gentlemen went
together from her room, ran to Harry, the expression of her
countenance quite changed now, and with a face and eyes
full of care, and said, ' Follow them, Harry, I am sure
something has gone wrong.' And so it was that Esmond
was made an eavesdropper at this lady's orders : and
retired to his own chamber, to give himself time in truth to
try and compose a story which would soothe his mistress,
for he could not but have his own apprehension that some
serious quarrel was pending between the two gentlemen.

And now for several days the little company at Castlewood sat at table as of evenings : this care, though unnamed
and invisible, being nevertheless present alway, in the minds
of at least three persons there. My lord was exceeding
gentle and kind. Whenever he quitted the room, his wife's
eyes followed him. He behaved to her with a kind of mourn-
ful courtesy and kindness remarkable in one of his blunt
ways and ordinary rough manner. He called her by her
Christian name often and fondly, was very soft and gentle
with the children, especially with the boy, whom he did not

love, and being lax about church generally, he went thither
and performed all the offices (down even to listening to
Doctor Tusher's sermon) with great devotion.

' He paces his room all night; what is it ? Henry, find
out what it is,' Lady Castlewood said constantly to her
young dependant. ' He has sent three letters to London,'
she said, another day.

' Indeed, madam, they were to a lawyer,' Harry answered,
who knew of these letters, and had seen a part of the
correspondence, which related to a new loan my lord was
raising ; and when the young man remonstrated with his
patron, my lord said, ' He was only raising money to
pay off an old debt on the property, which must be
discharged.'

Regarding the money, Lady Castlewood was not in the
least anxious. Few fond women feel money-distressed ;
indeed you can hardly give a woman a greater pleasure than
to bid her pawn her diamonds for the man she loves ; and
I remember hearing Mr. Congreve say of my Lord Marlborough, that the reason why my lord was so successful
with women as a young man was, because he took money of
them. ' There are few men who will make such a sacrifice
for them,' says Mr. Congreve, who knew a part of the sex
pretty well.

Harry Esmond's vacation was just over, and, as hath
been said, he was preparing to return to the University for
his last term before taking his degree and entering into the
Church. He had made up his mind for this office, not
indeed with that reverence which becomes a man about
to enter upon a duty so holy, but with a worldly spirit of
acquiescence in the prudence of adopting that profession
for his calling. But his reasoning was that he owed all to
the family of Castlewood, and loved better to be near them
than anywhere else in the world ; that he might be useful
to his benefactors, who had the utmost confidence in him
and affection for him in return ; that he might aid in bringing
up the young heir of the house and acting as his governor ;
that he might continue to be his dear patron's and mistress's
friend and adviser, who both were pleased to say that they
should ever look upon him as such : and so, by making himself useful to those he loved best, he proposed to console
himself for giving up of any schemes of ambition which he
might have had in his own bosom. Indeed, his mistress had

told him that she would not have him leave her ; and whatever she commanded was will to him.

The Lady Castlewood's mind was greatly relieved in the last few days of this well-remembered holiday time, by my lord's announcing one morning, after the post had brought him letters from London, in a careless tone, that the Lord Mohun was gone to Paris, and was about to make a great journey in Europe ; and though Lord Castlewood's own gloom did not wear off, or his behaviour alter, yet this cause of anxiety being removed from his lady's mind, she began to be more hopeful and easy in her spirits ; striving too, with all her heart, and by all the means of soothing in her power, to call back my lord's cheerfulness and dissipate his moody humour.

He accounted for it himself, by saying that he was out of health ; that he wanted to see his physician ; that he would go to London, and consult Doctor Cheyne.* It was agreed that his lordship and Harry Esmond should make the journey as far as London together ; and of a Monday morning, the 10th of October, in the year 1700, they set forwards towards London on horseback. The day before being Sunday, and the rain pouring down, the family did not visit church ; and at night my lord read the service to his family, very finely, and with a peculiar sweetness and gravity—speaking the parting benediction, Harry thought, as solemn as ever he heard it. And he kissed and embraced his wife and children before they went to their own chambers with more fondness than he was ordinarily wont to show, and with a solemnity and feeling of which they thought in after days with no small comfort.

They took horse the next morning (after adieux from the family as tender as on the night previous), lay that night on the road, and entered London at nightfall ; my lord going to the ' Trumpet ', in the Cockpit, Whitehall, a house used by the military in his time as a young man, and accustomed by his lordship ever since.

An hour after my lord's arrival (which showed that his visit had been arranged beforehand), my lord's man of business arrived from Gray's Inn ; and thinking that his patron might wish to be private with the lawyer, Esmond was for leaving them : but my lord said his business was short ; introduced Mr. Esmond particularly to the lawyer, who had been engaged for the family in the old lord's time ;

who said that he had paid the money, as desired that day, to my Lord Mohun himself, at his lodgings in Bow Street ; that his lordship had expressed some surprise, as it was not customary to employ lawyers, he said, in such transactions between men of honour ; but, nevertheless, he had returned my lord viscount's note of hand, which he held at his client's disposition.

'I thought the Lord Mohun had been in Paris ! ' cried Mr. Esmond, in great alarm and astonishment.

'He is come back at my invitation,' said my lord viscount. 'We have accounts to settle together.'

'I pray Heaven they are over, sir,' says Esmond.

'Oh, quite,' replied the other, looking hard at the young man. 'He was rather troublesome about that money which I told you I had lost to him at play. And now 'tis paid, and we are quits on that score, and we shall meet good friends again.'

'My lord,' cried out Esmond, 'I am sure you are deceiving me, and that there is a quarrel between the Lord Mohun and you.'

'Quarrel—pish ! We shall sup together this very night, and drink a bottle. Every man is ill-humoured who loses such a sum as I have lost. But now 'tis paid, and my anger is gone with it.'

'Where shall we sup, sir ? ' says Harry.

'We ! Let some gentlemen wait till they are asked,' says my lord viscount, with a laugh. 'You go to Duke Street, and see Mr. Betterton.* You love the play, I know. Leave me to follow my own devices ; and in the morning we'll breakfast together, with what appetite we may, as the play says.'*

'By G— ! my lord, I will not leave you this night,' says Harry Esmond. 'I think I know the cause of your dispute. I swear to you 'tis nothing. On the very day the accident befell Lord Mohun, I was speaking to him about it. I know that nothing has passed but idle gallantry on his part.'

'You know that nothing has passed but idle gallantry between Lord Mohun and my wife,' says my lord, in a thundering voice—' you knew of this, and did not tell me ? '

'I knew more of it than my dear mistress did herself, sir—a thousand times more. How was she, who was as innocent as a child, to know what was the meaning of the covert addresses of a villain ? '

'A villain he is, you allow, and would have taken my wife away from me.'

'Sir, she is as pure as an angel,' cried young Esmond.

'Have I said a word against her?' shrieks out my lord. 'Did I ever doubt that she was pure? It would have been the last day of her life when I did. Do you fancy I think that *she* would go astray? No, she hasn't passion enough for that. She neither sins nor forgives. I know her temper—and now I've lost her: by Heaven I love her ten thousand times more than ever I did—yes, when she was young and as beautiful as an angel—when she smiled at me in her old father's house, and used to lie in wait for me there as I came from hunting—when I used to fling my head down on her little knees and cry like a child on her lap—and swear I would reform and drink no more, and play no more, and follow women no more; when all the men of the Court used to be following her—when she used to look with her child more beautiful, by George, than the Madonna in the Queen's Chapel. I am not good like her, I know it. Who is—by Heaven, who is? I tired and wearied her, I know that very well. I could not talk to her. You men of wit and books could do that, and I couldn't—I felt I couldn't. Why, when you was but a boy of fifteen I could hear you two together talking your poetry and your books till I was in such a rage that I was fit to strangle you. But you were always a good lad, Harry, and I loved you, you know I did. And I felt she didn't belong to me: and the children don't. And I besotted myself, and gambled, and drank, and took to all sorts of devilries out of despair and fury. And now comes this Mohun, and she likes him, I know she likes him.'

'Indeed, and on my soul, you are wrong, sir,' Esmond cried.

'She takes letters from him,' cries my lord—'look here Harry,' and he pulled out a paper with a brown stain of blood upon it. 'It fell from him that day he wasn't killed. One of the grooms picked it up from the ground and gave it me. Here it is in their d——d comedy jargon. "Divine Gloriana—Why look so coldly on your slave who adores you? Have you no compassion on the tortures you have seen me suffering? Do you vouchsafe no reply to billets that are written with the blood of my heart." She had more letters from him.'

'But she answered none,' cries Esmond.

'That's not Mohun's fault,' says my lord, 'and I will be revenged on him, as God's in heaven, I will.'

'For a light word or two, will you risk your lady's honour and your family's happiness, my lord?' Esmond interposed beseechingly.

'Psha—there shall be no question of my wife's honour,' said my lord; 'we can quarrel on plenty of grounds beside. If I live, that villain will be punished; if I fall, my family will be only the better: there will only be a spendthrift the less to keep in the world: and Frank has better teaching than his father. My mind is made up, Harry Esmond, and whatever the event is I am easy about it. I leave my wife and you as guardians to the children.'

Seeing that my lord was bent upon pursuing this quarrel, and that no entreaties would draw him from it, Harry Esmond (then of a hotter and more impetuous nature than now, when care, and reflection, and grey hairs have calmed him) thought it was his duty to stand by his kind generous patron, and said—'My lord, if you are determined upon war, you must not go into it alone. 'Tis the duty of our house to stand by its chief: and I should neither forgive myself nor you if you did not call me, or I should be absent from you at a moment of danger.'

'Why, Harry, my poor boy, you are bred for a parson,' says my lord, taking Esmond by the hand very kindly: 'and it were a great pity that you should meddle in the matter.'

'Your lordship thought of being a churchman once,' Harry answered, 'and your father's orders did not prevent him fighting at Castlewood against the Roundheads. Your enemies are mine, sir: I can use the foils, as you have seen, indifferently well, and don't think I shall be afraid when the buttons are taken off 'em.' And then Harry explained with some blushes and hesitation (for the matter was delicate, and he feared lest, by having put himself forward in the quarrel, he might have offended his patron), how he had himself expostulated with the Lord Mohun, and proposed to measure swords with him if need were, and he could not be got to withdraw peaceably in this dispute. 'And I should have beat him, sir,' says Harry, laughing. 'He never could parry that *botte* I brought from Cambridge. Let us have half an hour of it, and rehearse—I can teach it your lordship : 'tis the most delicate point in the world, and if you miss it your adversary's sword is through you.'

' By George, Harry ! you ought to be the head of the house,' says my lord gloomily. ' You had been better Lord Castlewood than a lazy sot like me,' he added, drawing his hand across his eyes, and surveying his kinsman with very kind and affectionate glances.

' Let us take our coats off and have half an hour's practice before nightfall,' says Harry, after thankfully grasping his patron's manly hand.

' You are but a little bit of a lad,' says my lord good-humouredly ; ' but, in faith, I believe you could do for that fellow. No, my boy,' he continued, ' I'll have none of your feints and tricks of stabbing : I can use my sword pretty well too, and will fight my own quarrel my own way.'

' But I shall be by to see fair play,' cries Harry.

' Yes, God bless you—you shall be by.'

' When is it, sir ? ' says Harry, for he saw that the matter had been arranged privately, and beforehand, by my lord.

' 'Tis arranged thus : I sent off a courier to Jack Westbury to say that I wanted him specially. He knows for what, and will be here presently, and drink part of that bottle of sack. Then we shall go to the theatre in Duke Street, where we shall meet Mohun ; and then we shall all go sup at the 'Rose' or the 'Greyhound'. Then we shall call for cards, and there will be probably a difference over the cards— and then, God help us !—either a wicked villain and traitor shall go out of the world, or a poor worthless devil, that doesn't care to remain in it. I am better away, Hal—my wife will be all the happier when I am gone,' says my lord, with a groan, that tore the heart of Harry Esmond so that he fairly broke into a sob over his patron's kind hand.

' The business was talked over with Mohun before he left home—Castlewood I mean '—my lord went on. ' I took the letter in to him, which I had read, and I charged him with his villany, and he could make no denial of it, only he said that my wife was innocent.'

' And so she is ; before Heaven, my lord, she is ! ' cries Harry.

' No doubt, no doubt. They always are,' says my lord. ' No doubt, when she heard he was killed, she fainted from accident.'

' But, my lord, *my* name is Harry,' cried out Esmond,
burning red. ' You told my lady, " Harry was killed ! " '

' Damnation ! shall I fight you too ? ' shouts my lord,
in a fury. ' Are you, you little serpent, warmed by my
fire, going to sting—*you ?*—No, my boy, you're an honest
boy ; you are a good boy.' (And here he broke from rage
into tears even more cruel to see.) ' You are an honest boy.
and I love you ; and, by Heavens, I am so wretched that
I don't care what sword it is that ends me. Stop, here's
Jack Westbury. Well, Jack ! Welcome, old boy ! This
is my kinsman, Harry Esmond.'

' Who brought your bowls for you at Castlewood, sir.'
says Harry, bowing ; and the three gentlemen sat down
and drank of that bottle of sack which was prepared for
them.

' Harry is number three,' says my lord. ' You needn't
be afraid of him, Jack.' And the colonel gave a look, as
much as to say, ' Indeed, he don't look as if I need.' And
then my lord explained what he had only told by hints
before. When he quarrelled with Lord Mohun he was
indebted to his lordship in a sum of sixteen hundred pounds.
for which Lord Mohun said he proposed to wait until my lord
viscount should pay him. My lord had raised the sixteen
hundred pounds and sent them to Lord Mohun that morning,
and before quitting home had put his affairs into order,
and was now quite ready to abide the issue of the quarrel.

When we had drunk a couple of bottles of sack, a coach
was called, and the three gentlemen went to the Duke's
Playhouse, as agreed. The play was one of Mr. Wycherley's
—*Love in a Wood.*

Harry Esmond has thought of that play ever since with
a kind of terror, and of Mrs. Bracegirdle,* the actress who
performed the girl's part in the comedy. She was disguised
as a page, and came and stood before the gentlemen as
they sat on the stage, and looked over her shoulder with
a pair of arch black eyes, and laughed at my lord, and
asked what ailed the gentlemen from the country, and had
he had bad news from Bullock Fair ?*

Between the acts of the play the gentlemen crossed over
and conversed freely. There were two of Lord Mohun's
party, Captain Macartney,* in a military habit, and a gentleman in a suit of blue velvet and silver in a fair periwig.
with a rich fall of point of Venice lace—my lord the Earl of

Warwick and Holland. My lord had a paper of oranges, which he ate and offered to the actresses, joking with them. And Mrs. Bracegirdle, when my Lord Mohun said something rude, turned on him, and asked him what he did there, and whether he and his friends had come to stab anybody else, as they did poor Will Mountford? My lord's dark face grew darker at this taunt, and wore a mischievous fatal look.* They that saw it remembered it, and said so afterward.

When the play was ended the two parties joined company; and my Lord Castlewood then proposed that they should go to a tavern and sup. Lockit's, the 'Greyhound', in Charing Cross, was the house selected. All six marched together that way; the three lords going ahead, Lord Mohun's captain, and Colonel Westbury, and Harry Esmond, walking behind them. As they walked, Westbury told Harry Esmond about his old friend Dick the Scholar, who had got promotion, and was cornet of the Guards, and had wrote a book called the *Christian Hero*,* and had all the Guards to laugh at him for his pains, for the Christian Hero was breaking the commandments constantly, Westbury said, and had fought one or two duels already. And, in a lower tone, Westbury besought young Mr. Esmond to take no part in the quarrel. 'There was no need for more seconds than one,' said the colonel, 'and the captain or Lord Warwick might easily withdraw.' But Harry said no; he was bent on going through with the business. Indeed, he had a plan in his head, which, he thought, might prevent my lord viscount from engaging.

They went in at the bar of the tavern, and desired a private room and wine and cards, and when the drawer had brought these, they began to drink and call healths, and as long as the servants were in the room appeared very friendly.

Harry Esmond's plan was no other than to engage in talk with Lord Mohun, to insult him, and so get the first of the quarrel. So when cards were proposed he offered to play. 'Psha!' says my Lord Mohun (whether wishing to save Harry, or not choosing to try the *botte de Jésuite*, it is not to be known)—'young gentlemen from college should not play these stakes. You are too young.'

'Who dares say I am too young?' broke out Harry. 'Is your lordship afraid?'

'Afraid!', cries out Mohun.

But my good lord viscount saw the move—' I'll play you
for ten moidores, Mohun,' says he—' You silly boy, we don't
play for groats here as you do at Cambridge : ' and Harry,
who had no such sum in his pocket (for his half-year's
salary was always pretty well spent before it was due), fell
back with rage and vexation in his heart that he had not
money enough to stake.

' I'll stake the young gentleman a crown,' says the Lord
Mohun's captain.

' I thought crowns were rather scarce with the gentlemen
of the army,' says Harry.

' Do they birch at college ? ' says the captain.

' They birch fools,' says Harry, ' and they cane bullies,
and they fling puppies into the water.'

' Faith, then, there's some escapes drowning,' says the
captain, who was an Irishman ; and all the gentlemen
began to laugh, and made poor Harry only more angry.

My Lord Mohun presently snuffed a candle.   It was when
the drawers brought in fresh bottles and glasses and were
in the room—on which my lord viscount said—' The deuce
take you, Mohun, how damned awkward you are !   Light
the candle, you drawer.'

' Damned awkward is a damned awkward expression, my
lord,' says the other.   ' Town gentlemen don't use such
words—or ask pardon if they do.'

' I'm a country gentleman,' says my lord viscount.

' I see it by your manner,' says my Lord Mohun.   ' No
man shall say " damned awkward " to me.'

' I fling the words in your face, my lord,' says the other ;
' shall I send the cards too ? '

' Gentlemen, gentlemen ! before the servants ? ' cry out
Colonel Westbury and my Lord Warwick in a breath.
The drawers go out of the room hastily.   They tell the
people below of the quarrel upstairs.

' Enough has been said,' says Colonel Westbury.   ' Will
your lordships meet to-morrow morning ? '

' Will my Lord Castlewood withdraw his words ? ' asks
the Earl of Warwick.

' My Lord Castlewood will be —— first,' says Colonel
Westbury.

' Then we have nothing for it.   Take notice, gentlemen,
there have been outrageous words—reparation asked and
refused.'

' And refused,' says my Lord Castlewood, putting on his hat. ' Where shall the meeting be ? and when ? '

' Since my lord refuses me satisfaction, which I deeply regret, there is no time so good as now,' says my Lord Mohun. ' Let us have chairs and go to Leicester Field.'

' Are your lordship and I to have the honour of exchanging a pass or two ? ' says Colonel Westbury, with a low bow to my Lord of Warwick and Holland.

' It is an honour for me,' says my lord, with a profound congée, ' to be matched with a gentleman who has been at Mons and Namur.'*

' Will your reverence permit me to give you a lesson ? ' says the captain.

' Nay, nay, gentlemen, two on a side are plenty,' says Harry's patron. ' Spare the boy, Captain Macartney,' and he shook Harry's hand—for the last time, save one, in his life.

At the bar of the tavern all the gentlemen stopped, and my lord viscount said, laughing, to the barwoman, that those cards set people sadly a-quarrelling ; but that the dispute was over now, and the parties were all going away to my Lord Mohun's house, in Bow Street, to drink a bottle more before going to bed.

A half-dozen of chairs were now called, and the six gentlemen stepping into them, the word was privately given to the chairmen to go to Leicester Field, where the gentlemen were set down opposite the 'Standard' Tavern. It was midnight, and the town was abed by this time, and only a few lights in the windows of the houses ; but the night was bright enough for the unhappy purpose which the disputants came about ; and so all six entered into that fatal square, the chairmen standing without the railing and keeping the gate, lest any persons should disturb the meeting.

All that happened there hath been matter of public notoriety, and is recorded, for warning to lawless men, in the annals of our country. After being engaged for not more than a couple of minutes, as Harry Esmond thought (though being occupied at the time with his own adversary's point, which was active, he may not have taken a good note of time), a cry from the chairmen without, who were smoking their pipes, and leaning over the railings of the field as they watched the dim combat within, announced that some catastrophe had happened which caused Esmond

to drop his sword and look round, at which moment his
enemy wounded him in the right hand. But the young
man did not heed this hurt much, and ran up to the place
where he saw his dear master was down.

My Lord Mohun was standing over him.

' Are you much hurt, Frank ? ' he asked, in a hollow voice.

' I believe I'm a dead man,' my lord said from the ground.

' No, no, not so,' says the other ; ' and I call God to
witness, Frank Esmond, that I would have asked your
pardon, had you but given me a chance. In—in the first
cause of our falling out, I swear that no one was to blame
but me, and—and that my lady—— '

' Hush ! ' says my poor lord viscount, lifting himself on
his elbow, and speaking faintly. ' 'Twas a dispute about
the cards—the cursed cards. Harry, my boy, are you
wounded, too ?   God help thee !   I loved thee, Harry, and
thou must watch over my little Frank—and—and carry
this little heart to my wife.'

And here my dear lord felt in his breast for a locket he
wore there, and, in the act, fell back, fainting.

We were all at this terrified, thinking him dead ; but
Esmond and Colonel Westbury bade the chairmen to come
into the field ; and so my lord was carried to one Mr. Aimes,
a surgeon, in Long Acre, who kept a bath,* and there the
house was wakened up, and the victim of this quarrel
carried in.

My lord viscount was put to bed, and his wound looked
to by the surgeon, who seemed both kind and skilful.
When he had looked to my lord, he bandaged up Harry
Esmond's hand (who, from loss of blood, had fainted too,
in the house, and may have been some time unconscious) ;
and when the young man came to himself, you may be sure
he eagerly asked what news there were of his dear patron ;
on which the surgeon carried him to the room where the
Lord Castlewood lay ; who had already sent for a priest ;
and desired earnestly, they said, to speak with his kinsman.
He was lying on a bed, very pale and ghastly, with that
fixed, fatal look in his eyes, which betokens death ; and
faintly beckoning all the other persons away from him with
his hand, and crying out ' Only Harry Esmond ', the hand
fell powerless down on the coverlet, as Harry came forward,
and knelt down and kissed it.

' Thou art all but a priest, Harry,' my lord viscount

gasped out, with a faint smile, and pressure of his cold hand. 'Are they all gone ? Let me make thee a death-bed confession.'

And with sacred Death waiting, as it were, at the bed-foot, as an awful witness of his words, the poor dying soul gasped out his last wishes in respect of his family ;—his humble profession of contrition for his faults ;—and his charity towards the world he was leaving. Some things he said concerned Harry Esmond as much as they astonished him. And my lord viscount, sinking visibly, was in the midst of these strange confessions, when the ecclesiastic for whom my lord had sent, Mr. Atterbury,* arrived.

This gentleman had reached to no great church dignity as yet, but was only preacher at St. Bride's, drawing all the town thither by his eloquent sermons. He was godson to my lord, who had been pupil to his father ; had paid a visit to Castlewood from Oxford more than once ; and it was by his advice, I think, that Harry Esmond was sent to Cambridge, rather than to Oxford, of which place Mr. Atterbury, though a distinguished member, spoke but ill.

Our messenger found the good priest already at his books, at five o'clock in the morning, and he followed the man eagerly to the house where my poor lord viscount lay— Esmond watching him, and taking his dying words from his mouth.

My lord, hearing of Mr. Atterbury's arrival, and squeezing Esmond's hand, asked to be alone with the priest ; and Esmond left them there for this solemn interview. You may be sure that his own prayers and grief accompanied that dying benefactor. My lord had said to him that which confounded the young man—informed him of a secret which greatly concerned him. Indeed, after hearing it, he had had good cause for doubt and dismay ; for mental anguish as well as resolution. While the colloquy between Mr. Atterbury and his dying penitent took place within, an immense contest of perplexity was agitating Lord Castlewood's young companion.

At the end of an hour—it may be more—Mr. Atterbury came out of the room looking very hard at Esmond, and holding a paper.

'He is on the brink of God's awful judgement,' the priest whispered. 'He has made his breast clean to me.

He forgives and believes, and makes restitution. Shall it be in public ? Shall we call a witness to sign it ? '

' God knows,' sobbed out the young man, ' my dearest lord has only done me kindness all his life.'

The priest put the paper into Esmond's hand. He looked at it. It swam before his eyes.

' 'Tis a confession,' he said.

' 'Tis as you please,' said Mr. Atterbury.

There was a fire in the room, where the cloths were drying for the baths, and there lay a heap in a corner, saturated with the blood of my dear lord's body. Esmond went to the fire, and threw the paper into it. 'Twas a great chimney with glazed Dutch tiles. How we remember such trifles in such awful moments !—the scrap of the book that we have read in a great grief—the taste of that last dish that we have eaten before a duel or some such supreme meeting or parting. On the Dutch tiles at the bagnio was a rude picture representing Jacob in hairy gloves, cheating Isaac of Esau's birthright. The burning paper lighted it up.

' 'Tis only a confession, Mr. Atterbury,' said the young man. He leaned his head against the mantelpiece : a burst of tears came to his eyes. They were the first he had shed as he sat by his lord, scared by this calamity and more yet by what the poor dying gentleman had told him, and shocked to think that he should be the agent of bringing this double misfortune on those he loved best.

' Let us go to him,' said Mr. Esmond. And accordingly they went into the next chamber, where, by this time, the dawn had broke, which showed my lord's poor pale face and wild appealing eyes, that wore that awful fatal look of coming dissolution. The surgeon was with him. He went into the chamber as Atterbury came out thence. My lord viscount turned round his sick eyes towards Esmond. It choked the other to hear that rattle in his throat.

' My lord viscount,' says Mr. Atterbury, ' Mr. Esmond wants no witnesses, and hath burned the paper.'

' My dearest master ! ' Esmond said, kneeling down, and taking his hand and kissing it.

My lord viscount sprang up in his bed, and flung his arms round Esmond. ' God bl—bless . . . .,' was all he said. The blood rushed from his mouth, deluging the young man. My dearest lord was no more. He was gone with a blessing on his lips, and love and repentance and kindness in his manly heart.

' *Benedicti benedicentes*,' says Mr. Atterbury, and the young man kneeling at the bedside, groaned out an Amen.

' Who shall take the news to her ? ' was Mr. Esmond's next thought. And on this he besought Mr. Atterbury to bear the tidings to Castlewood. He could not face his mistress himself with those dreadful news. Mr. Atterbury complying kindly, Esmond writ a hasty note on his table-book to my lord's man, bidding him get the horses for Mr. Atterbury, and ride with him, and send Esmond's own valise to the Gatehouse prison, whither he resolved to go and give himself up.

BOOK II

CHAPTER I

I AM IN PRISON, AND VISITED, BUT NOT CONSOLED THERE

THOSE may imagine, who have seen death untimely strike down persons revered and beloved, and know how unavailing consolation is, what was Harry Esmond's anguish after being an actor in that ghastly midnight scene of blood and homicide. He could not, he felt, have faced his dear mistress, and told her that story. He was thankful that kind Atterbury consented to break the sad news to her; but, besides his grief, which he took into prison with him, he had that in his heart which secretly cheered and consoled him.

A great secret had been told to Esmond by his unhappy stricken kinsman, lying on his death-bed. Were he to disclose it, as in equity and honour he might do, the discovery would but bring greater grief upon those whom he loved best in the world, and who were sad enough already. Should he bring down shame and perplexity upon all those beings to whom he was attached by so many tender ties of affection and gratitude? degrade his father's widow? impeach and sully his father's and kinsman's honour? and for what? for a barren title, to be worn at the expense of an innocent boy, the son of his dearest benefactress. He had debated this matter in his conscience, whilst his poor lord was making his dying confession. On one side were ambition, temptation, justice even; but love, gratitude, and fidelity, pleaded on the other. And when the struggle was over in Harry's mind, a glow of righteous happiness filled it; and it was with grateful tears in his eyes that he returned thanks to God for that decision which he had been enabled to make.

' When I was denied by my own blood,' thought he; ' these dearest friends received and cherished me. When

I was a nameless orphan myself, and needed a protector. I found one in yonder kind soul, who has gone to his account repenting of the innocent wrong he has done.'

And with this consoling thought he went away to give himself up at the prison, after kissing the cold lips of his benefactor.

It was on the third day after he had come to the Gatehouse prison (where he lay in no small pain from his wound, which inflamed and ached severely) ; and with those thoughts and resolutions that have been just spoke of, to depress, and yet to console him, that H. Esmond's keeper came and told him that a visitor was asking for him, and though he could not see her face, which was enveloped in a black hood, her whole figure, too, being veiled and covered with the deepest mourning, Esmond knew at once that his visitor was his dear mistress.

He got up from his bed, where he was lying, being very weak ; and advancing towards her, as the retiring keeper shut the door upon him and his guest in that sad place, he put forward his left hand (for the right was wounded and bandaged), and he would have taken that kind one of his mistress, which had done so many offices of friendship for him for so many years.

But the Lady Castlewood went back from him, putting back her hood, and leaning against the great stanchioned door which the gaoler had just closed upon them. Her face was ghastly white, as Esmond saw it, looking from the hood ; and her eyes, ordinarily so sweet and tender, were fixed at him with such a tragic glance of woe and anger, as caused the young man, unaccustomed to unkindness from that person, to avert his own glances from her face.

' And this, Mr. Esmond,' she said, ' is where I see you ; and 'tis to this you have brought me ! '

' You have come to console me in my calamity, madam,' said he (though, in truth, he scarce knew how to address her, his emotions at beholding her, so overpowered him).

She advanced a little, but stood silent and trembling, looking out at him from her black draperies, with her small white hands clasped together, and quivering lips and hollow eyes.

' Not to reproach me,' he continued, after a pause. ' My grief is sufficient as it is.'

' Take back your hand—do not touch me with it ! ' she cried. ' Look ! there's blood on it ! '

' I wish they had taken it all,' said Esmond ; ' if you are unkind to me.'

' Where is my husband ? ' she broke out. ' Give me back my husband, Henry ? Why did you stand by at midnight and see him murdered ? Why did the traitor escape who did it ? You, the champion of your house, who offered to die for us ! You that he loved and trusted, and to whom I confided him—you that vowed devotion and gratitude, and I believed you—yes, I believed you—why are you here, and my noble Francis gone ? Why did you come among us ? You have only brought us grief and sorrow ; and repentance, bitter, bitter repentance, as a return for our love and kindness. Did I ever do you a wrong, Henry ? You were but an orphan child when I first saw you—when *he* first saw you, who was so good, and noble, and trusting. He would have had you sent away, but, like a foolish woman, I besought him to let you stay. And you pretended to love us, and we believed you— and you made our house wretched, and my husband's heart went from me : and I lost him through you—I lost him—the husband of my youth, I say. I worshipped him : you know I worshipped him—and he was changed to me. He was no more my Francis of old—my dear, dear soldier. He loved me before he saw you ; and I loved him ; oh, God is my witness how I loved him ! Why did he not send you from among us ? 'Twas only his kindness, that could refuse me nothing then. And, young as you were—yes, and weak and alone—there was evil, I knew there was evil in keeping you. I read it in your face and eyes. I saw that they boded harm to us—and it came, I knew it would. Why did you not die when you had the small-pox—and I came myself and watched you, and you called out for me in your delirium—and you called out for me, though I was there at your side. All that has happened since, was a just judgement on my wicked heart—my wicked jealous heart. Oh, I am punished—awfully punished ! My husband lies in his blood—murdered for defending me, my kind, kind, generous lord—and you were by, and you let him die, Henry ! '

These words, uttered in the wildness of her grief, by one who was ordinarily quiet, and spoke seldom except with

a gentle smile and a soothing tone, rung in Esmond's ear;
and 'tis said that he repeated many of them in the fever
into which he now fell from his wound, and perhaps from
the emotion which such passionate, undeserved upbraidings
caused him.   It seemed as if his very sacrifices and love
for this lady and her family were to turn to evil and reproach:
as if his presence amongst them was indeed a cause of grief,
and the continuance of his life but woe and bitterness to
theirs.   As the Lady Castlewood spoke bitterly, rapidly,
without a tear, he never offered a word of appeal or remonstrance; but sat at the foot of his prison-bed, stricken only
with the more pain at thinking it was that soft and beloved
hand which should stab him so cruelly, and powerless against
her fatal sorrow.   Her words as she spoke struck the chords
of all his memory, and the whole of his boyhood and youth
passed within him; whilst this lady, so fond and gentle but
yesterday—this good angel whom he had loved and worshipped—stood before him, pursuing him with keen words
and aspect malign.

' I wish I were in my lord's place,' he groaned out.   ' It
was not my fault that I was not there, madam.   But Fate
is stronger than all of us, and willed what has come to pass.
It had been better for me to have died when I had the
illness.'

' Yes, Henry,' said she—and as she spoke she looked at
him with a glance that was at once so fond and so sad,
that the young man, tossing up his arms, wildly fell back,
hiding his head in the coverlet of the bed.   As he turned
he struck against the wall with his wounded hand, displacing
the ligature; and he felt the blood rushing again from the
wound.   He remembered feeling a secret pleasure at the
accident—and thinking, ' Suppose I were to end now, who
would grieve for me ? '

This haemorrhage, or the grief and despair in which the
luckless young man was at the time of the accident, must
have brought on a deliquium presently; for he had scarce
any recollection afterwards, save of some one, his mistress
probably, seizing his hand—and then of the buzzing noise
in his ears as he awoke, with two or three persons of the
prison around his bed, whereon he lay in a pool of blood
from his arm.

It was now bandaged up again by the prison surgeon,
who happened to be in the place; and the governor's wife

and servant, kind people both, were with the patient.
Esmond saw his mistress still in the room when he awoke
from his trance; but she went away without a word;
though the governor's wife told him that she sat in her
room for some time afterward, and did not leave the prison
until she heard that Esmond was likely to do well.

Days afterwards, when Esmond was brought out of a
fever which he had, and which attacked him that night
pretty sharply, the honest keeper's wife brought her patient
a handkerchief fresh washed and ironed, and at the corner of
which he recognized his mistress's well-known cipher and
viscountess's crown. 'The lady had bound it round his
arm when he fainted, and before she called for help,' the
keeper's wife said; 'poor lady; she took on sadly about her
husband. He has been buried to-day, and a many of the
coaches of the nobility went with him,—my Lord Marlborough's and my Lord Sunderland's, and many of the
officers of the Guards, in which he served in the old king's
time; and my lady has been with her two children to the
king at Kensington, and asked for justice against my Lord
Mohun, who is in hiding, and my lord the Earl of Warwick
and Holland, who is ready to give himself up and take his
trial.'

Such were the news, coupled with assertions about her
own honesty and that of Molly her maid, who would never
have stolen a certain trumpery gold sleeve-button of Mr.
Esmond's that was missing after his fainting fit, that the
keeper's wife brought to her lodger. His thoughts followed
to that untimely grave, the brave heart, the kind friend,
the gallant gentleman, honest of word and generous of
thought (if feeble of purpose, but are his betters much
stronger than he?) who had given him bread and shelter
when he had none; home and love when he needed them;
and who, if he had kept one vital secret from him, had done
that of which he repented ere dying—a wrong indeed, but
one followed by remorse, and occasioned by almost irresistible temptation.

Esmond took his handkerchief when his nurse left him,
and very likely kissed it, and looked at the bauble em-
broidered in the corner. 'It has cost thee grief enough,'
he thought, 'dear lady, so loving and so tender. Shall
I take it from thee and thy children? No, never! Keep
it, and wear it, my little Frank, my pretty boy. If I cannot

make a name for myself, I can die without one. Some day,
when my dear mistress sees my heart, I shall be righted ;
or if not here or now, why, elsewhere ; where Honour doth
not follow us, but where Love reigns perpetual.'

'Tis needless to narrate here, as the reports of the lawyers
already have chronicled them, the particulars or issue of
that trial which ensued upon my Lord Castlewood's melancholy homicide. Of the two lords engaged in that said
matter, the second, my lord the Earl of Warwick and Holland, who had been engaged with Colonel Westbury, and
wounded by him, was found not guilty by his peers, before
whom he was tried (under the presidence of the Lord
Steward, Lord Somers) ; and the principal, the Lord
Mohun, being found guilty of the manslaughter (which,
indeed, was forced upon him, and of which he repented
most sincerely), pleaded his clergy ; and so was discharged
without any penalty. The widow of the slain nobleman,
as it was told us in prison, showed an extraordinary spirit ;
and, though she had to wait for ten years before her son was
old enough to compass it, declared she would have revenge
of her husband's murderer. So much and suddenly had
grief, anger, and misfortune appeared to change her. But
fortune, good or ill, as I take it, does not change men and
women. It but develops their characters. As there are
a thousand thoughts lying within a man that he does not
know till he takes up the pen to write, so the heart is a
secret even to him (or her) who has it in his own breast.
Who hath not found himself surprised into revenge, or
action, or passion, for good or evil ; whereof the seeds lay
within him, latent and unsuspected, until the occasion
called them forth ? With the death of her lord, a change
seemed to come over the whole conduct and mind of Lady
Castlewood ; but of this we shall speak in the right season
and anon.

The lords being tried then before their peers at Westminster, according to their privilege, being brought from
the Tower with state processions and barges, and accompanied by lieutenants and axe-men, the commoners engaged
in that melancholy fray took their trial at Newgate, as
became them ; and, being all found guilty, pleaded likewise their benefit of clergy. The sentence, as we all know,
in these cases is, that the culprit lies a year in prison, or
during the king's pleasure, and is burned in the hand, or

only stamped with a cold iron; or this part of the punishment is altogether remitted at the grace of the sovereign.
So Harry Esmond found himself a criminal and a prisoner
at two-and-twenty years old; as for the two colonels, his
comrades, they took the matter very lightly. Duelling
was a part of their business; and they could not in honour
refuse any invitations of that sort.

But the case was different with Mr. Esmond. His life
was changed by that stroke of the sword which destroyed
his kind patron's. As he lay in prison, old Dr. Tusher fell
ill and died; and Lady Castlewood appointed Thomas
Tusher to the vacant living; about the filling of which she
had a thousand times fondly talked to Harry Esmond:
how they never should part; how he should educate her
boy; how to be a country clergyman, like saintly George
Herbert, or pious Dr. Ken,* was the happiness and greatest
lot in life; how (if he were obstinately bent on it, though,
for her part, she owned rather to holding Queen Bess's
opinion, that a bishop should have no wife, and if not a
bishop why a clergyman?) she would find a good wife for
Harry Esmond: and so on, with a hundred pretty prospects
told by fireside evenings, in fond prattle, as the children
played about the hall. All these plans were overthrown now.
Thomas Tusher wrote to Esmond, as he lay in prison,
announcing that his patroness had conferred upon him the
living his reverend father had held for many years; that
she never, after the tragical events which had occurred
(whereof Tom spoke with a very edifying horror), could
see in the revered Tusher's pulpit, or at her son's table, the
man who was answerable for the father's life; that her
ladyship bade him to say that she prayed for her kinsman's
repentance and his worldly happiness; that he was free
to command her aid for any scheme of life which he might
propose to himself; but that on this side of the grave she
would see him no more. And Tusher, for his own part,
added that Harry should have his prayers as a friend of his
youth, and commended him whilst he was in prison to read
certain works of theology, which his reverence pronounced
to be very wholesome for sinners in his lamentable condition.

And this was the return for a life of devotion—this the
end of years of affectionate intercourse and passionate
fidelity! Harry would have died for his patron, and was
held as little better than his murderer: he had sacrificed,

she did not know how much, for his mistress, and she threw him aside—he had endowed her family with all they had, and she talked about giving him alms as to a menial! The grief for his patron's loss: the pains of his own present position, and doubts as to the future: all these were forgotten under the sense of the consummate outrage which he had to endure, and overpowered by the superior pang of that torture.

He writ back a letter to Mr. Tusher from his prison, congratulating his reverence upon his appointment to the living of Castlewood: sarcastically bidding him to follow in the footsteps of his admirable father, whose gown had descended upon him—thanking her ladyship for her offer of alms, which he said he should trust not to need; and beseeching her to remember that, if ever her determination should change towards him, he would be ready to give her proofs of a fidelity which had never wavered, and which ought never to have been questioned by that house. ' And if we meet no more, or only as strangers in this world,' Mr. Esmond concluded, ' a sentence against the cruelty and injustice of which I disdain to appeal; hereafter she will know who was faithful to her, and whether she had any cause to suspect the love and devotion of her kinsman and servant.'

After the sending of this letter, the poor young fellow's mind was more at ease than it had been previously. The blow had been struck, and he had borne it. His cruel goddess had shaken her wings and fled: and left him alone and friendless, but *virtute sua*.* And he had to bear him up, at once the sense of his right and the feeling of his wrongs, his honour and his misfortune. As I have seen men waking and running to arms at a sudden trumpet; before emergency a manly heart leaps up resolute; meets the threatening danger with undaunted countenance; and, whether conquered or conquering, faces it always. Ah! no man knows his strength or his weakness, till occasion proves them. If there be some thoughts and actions of his life from the memory of which a man shrinks with shame, sure there are some which he may be proud to own and remember; forgiven injuries, conquered temptations (now and then), and difficulties vanquished by endurance.

It was these thoughts regarding the living, far more than

any great poignancy of grief respecting the dead, which affected Harry Esmond whilst in prison after his trial : but it may be imagined that he could take no comrade of misfortune into the confidence of his feelings, and they thought it was remorse and sorrow for his patron's loss which affected the young man, in error of which opinion he chose to leave them. As a companion he was so moody and silent that the two officers, his fellow sufferers, left him to himself mostly, liked little very likely what they knew of him, consoled themselves with dice, cards, and the bottle, and whiled away their own captivity in their own way. It seemed to Esmond as if he lived years in that prison : and was changed and aged when he came out of it. At certain periods of life we live years of emotion in a few weeks—and look back on those times, as on great gaps between the old life and the new. You do not know how much you suffer in those critical maladies of the heart, until the disease is over and you look back on it afterwards. During the time, the suffering is at least sufferable. The day passes in more or less of pain, and the night wears away somehow. 'Tis only in after-days that we see what the danger has been—as a man out a-hunting or riding for his life looks at a leap, and wonders how he should have survived the taking of it. O dark months of grief and rage ! of wrong and cruel endurance ! He is old now who recalls you. Long ago he has forgiven and blest the soft hand that wounded him : but the mark is there, and the wound is cicatrized only—no time, tears, caresses, or repentance, can obliterate the scar. We are indocile to put up with grief, however. *Reficimus rates quassas :* we tempt the ocean again and again, and try upon new ventures. Esmond thought of his early time as a novitiate, and of this past trial as an initiation before entering into life—as our young Indians undergo tortures silently before they pass to the rank of warriors in the tribe.

The officers, meanwhile, who were not let into the secret of the grief which was gnawing at the side of their silent young friend, and being accustomed to such transactions, in which one comrade or another was daily paying the forfeit of the sword, did not of course bemoan themselves very inconsolably about the fate of their late companion in arms. This one told stories of former adventures of love, or war, or pleasure, in which poor Frank Esmond had been engaged ; t'other recollected how a constable had been bilked, or a

tavern-bully beaten : whilst my lord's poor widow was
sitting at his tomb worshipping him as an actual saint and
spotless hero—so the visitors said who had news of Lady
Castlewood ; and Westbury and Macartney had pretty
nearly had all the town to come and see them.

The duel, its fatal termination, the trial of the two peers
and the three commoners concerned, had caused the
greatest excitement in the town. The prints and News
Letters were full of them. The three gentlemen in Newgate
were almost as much crowded as the bishops in the Tower,
or a highwayman before execution. We were allowed to
live in the governor's house, as hath been said, both before
trial and after condemnation, waiting the king's pleasure ;
nor was the real cause of the fatal quarrel known, so closely
had my lord and the two other persons who knew it kept
the secret, but every one imagined that the origin of the
meeting was a gambling dispute. Except fresh air, the
prisoners had, upon payment, most things they could desire.
Interest was made that they should not mix with the vulgar
convicts, whose ribald choruses and loud laughter and
curses could be heard from their own part of the prison,
where they and the miserable debtors were confined pell-
mell.

CHAPTER II

I COME TO THE END OF MY CAPTIVITY, BUT NOT OF MY TROUBLE

AMONG the company which came to visit the two officers
was an old acquaintance of Harry Esmond ; that gentleman
of the Guards, namely, who had been so kind to Harry
when Captain Westbury's troop had been quartered at
Castlewood more than seven years before. Dick the
Scholar was no longer Dick the Trooper now, but Captain
Steele of Lucas's Fusiliers, and secretary to my Lord Cutts,
that famous officer of King William's, the bravest and most
beloved man of the English army.* The two jolly prisoners
had been drinking with a party of friends (for our cellar
and that of the keepers of Newgate, too, were supplied with
endless hampers of burgundy and champagne that the
friends of the colonels sent in) ; and Harry, having no wish
for their drink or their conversation, being too feeble in

health for the one and too sad in spirits for the other, was sitting apart in his little room, reading such books as he had, one evening, when honest Colonel Westbury, flushed with liquor, and always good-humoured in and out of his cups, came laughing into Harry's closet, and said, ' Ho, young Killjoy ! here's a friend come to see thee ; he'll pray with thee, or he'll drink with thee ; or he'll drink and pray turn about. Dick, my Christian hero, here's the little scholar of Castlewood.'

Dick came up and kissed Esmond on both cheeks, imparting a strong perfume of burnt sack along with his caress to the young man.

' What ! is this the little man that used to talk Latin and fetch our bowls ? How tall thou art grown ! I protest I should have known thee anywhere. And so you have turned ruffian and fighter ; and wanted to measure swords with Mohun, did you ? I protest that Mohun said at the Guard dinner yesterday, where there was a pretty company of us, that the young fellow wanted to fight him, and was the better man of the two.'

' I wish we could have tried and proved it, Mr. Steele,' says Esmond, thinking of his dead benefactor, and his eyes filling with tears.

With the exception of that one cruel letter which he had from his mistress, Mr. Esmond heard nothing from her, and she seemed determined to execute her resolve of parting from him and disowning him. But he had news of her, such as it was, which Mr. Steele assiduously brought him from the prince's and princesses' Court, where our honest captain had been advanced to the post of gentleman waiter. When off duty there, Captain Dick often came to console his friends in captivity ; a good nature and a friendly disposition towards all who were in ill fortune no doubt prompting him to make his visits, and good fellowship and good wine to prolong them.

' Faith,' says Westbury, ' the little scholar was the first to begin the quarrel—I mind me of it now—at Lockit's. I always hated that fellow Mohun. What was the real cause of the quarrel betwixt him and poor Frank ? I would wager 'twas a woman.'

' 'Twas a quarrel about play—on my word, about play,' Harry said. ' My poor lord lost great sums to his guest at Castlewood. Angry words passed between them ; and, though Lord Castlewood was the kindest and most pliable soul alive, his spirit was very high ; and hence that meeting which has brought us all here,' says Mr. Esmond, resolved never to acknowledge that there had ever been any other but cards for the duel.

'I do not like to use bad words of a nobleman,' says Westbury ; 'but if my Lord Mohun were a commoner, I would say, 'twas a pity he was not hanged.   He was familiar with dice and women at a time other boys are at school, being birched ; he was as wicked as the oldest rake, years ere he had done growing ; and handled a sword and a foil, and a bloody one too, before ever he used a razor. He held poor Will Mountford in talk that night, when bloody Dick Hill ran him through.   He will come to a bad end, will that young lord ; and no end is bad enough for him,' says honest Mr. Westbury : whose prophecy was fulfilled twelve years after, upon that fatal day when Mohun fell, dragging down one of the bravest and greatest gentlemen in England in his fall.

From Mr. Steele, then, who brought the public rumour, as well as his own private intelligence, Esmond learned the movements of his unfortunate mistress.   Steele's heart was of very inflammable composition ; and the gentleman usher spoke in terms of boundless admiration both of the widow (that most beautiful woman, as he said) and of her daughter, who, in the captain's eyes, was a still greater paragon.   If the pale widow, whom Captain Richard, in his poetic rapture, compared to a Niobe in tears—to a Sigismunda—to a weeping Belvidera,* was an object the most lovely and pathetic which his eyes had ever beheld, or for which his heart had melted, even her ripened perfections and beauty were as nothing compared to the promise of that extreme loveliness which the good captain saw in her daughter.   It was *matre pulcra filia pulcrior.*   Steele composed sonnets whilst he was on duty in his prince's antechamber, to the maternal and filial charms.   He would speak for hours about them to Harry Esmond ; and, indeed, he could have chosen few subjects more likely to interest the unhappy young man, whose heart was now as always devoted to these ladies ; and who was thankful to all who loved them, or praised them, or wished them well.

Not that his fidelity was recompensed by any answering kindness, or show of relenting even, on the part of a mistress

obdurate now after ten years of love and benefactions. The
poor young man getting no answer, save Tusher's, to that
letter which he had written, and being too proud to write
more, opened a part of his heart to Steele, than whom no
man, when unhappy, could find a kinder hearer or more
friendly emissary ;   described (in words which were no
doubt pathetic, for they came *imo pectore*,* and caused honest
Dick to weep plentifully) his youth, his constancy, his fond
devotion to that household which had reared him ;   his
affection how earned, and how tenderly requited until but
yesterday, and (as far as he might) the circumstances and
causes for which that sad quarrel had made of Esmond a
prisoner under sentence, a widow and orphans of those whom
in life he held dearest. In terms that might well move
a harder-hearted man than young Esmond's confidant—for,
indeed, the speaker's own heart was half broke as he uttered
them ; he described a part of what had taken place in that
only sad interview which his mistress had granted him ;
how she had left him with anger and almost imprecation,
whose words and thoughts until then had been only blessing
and kindness ; how she had accused him of the guilt of that
blood, in exchange for which he would cheerfully have
sacrificed his own (indeed, in this the Lord Mohun, the
Lord Warwick, and all the gentlemen engaged, as well as
the common rumour out of doors—Steele told him—bore
out the luckless young man) ; and with all his heart, and
tears, he besought Mr. Steele to inform his mistress of her
kinsman's unhappiness, and to deprecate that cruel anger
she showed him. Half frantic with grief at the injustice
done him, and contrasting it with a thousand soft recollections of love and confidence gone by, that made his present
misery inexpressibly more bitter, the poor wretch passed
many a lonely day and wakeful night in a kind of powerless
despair and rage against his iniquitous fortune. It was
the softest hand that struck him, the gentlest and most
compassionate nature that persecuted him. ' I would as
lief,' he said, ' have pleaded guilty to the murder, and
have suffered for it like any other felon, as have to endure
the torture to which my mistress subjects me.'

Although the recital of Esmond's story, and his passionate
appeals and remonstrances, drew so many tears from Dick
who heard them, they had no effect upon the person whom
they were designed to move. Esmond's ambassador came

back from the mission with which the poor young gentleman
had charged him, with a sad blank face and a shake of the
head, which told that there was no hope for the prisoner ;
and scarce a wretched culprit in that prison of Newgate
ordered for execution, and trembling for a reprieve, felt
more cast down than Mr. Esmond, innocent and condemned.

As had been arranged between the prisoner and his
counsel in their consultations, Mr. Steele had gone to the
dowager's house in Chelsey, where it has been said the
widow and her orphans were, had seen my lady viscountess
and pleaded the cause of her unfortunate kinsman. 'And
I think I spoke well, my poor boy,' says Mr. Steele ; 'for
who would not speak well in such a cause, and before so
beautiful a judge ? I did not see the lovely Beatrix (sure
her famous namesake of Florence was never half so beautiful), only the young viscount was in the room with the Lord
Churchill, my Lord of Marlborough's eldest son. But these
young gentlemen went off to the garden, I could see them
from the window tilting at each other with poles in a mimic
tournament (grief touches the young but lightly, and I
remember that I beat a drum at the coffin of my own father).
My lady viscountess looked out at the two boys at their
game, and said—" You see, sir, children are taught to use
weapons of death as toys, and to make a sport of murder " ;
and as she spoke she looked so lovely, and stood there in
herself so sad and beautiful an instance of that doctrine
whereof I am a humble preacher, that had I not dedicated
my little volume of the *Christian Hero* (I perceive, Harry,
thou hast not cut the leaves of it. The sermon is good,
believe me, though the preacher's life may not answer it)—
I say, hadn't I dedicated the volume to Lord Cutts, I would
have asked permission to place her ladyship's name on the
first page. I think I never saw such a beautiful violet
as that of her eyes, Harry. Her complexion is of the pink
of the blush-rose, she hath an exquisite turned wrist and
dimpled hand, and I make no doubt——'

'Did you come to tell me about the dimples on my lady's
hand ? ' broke out Mr. Esmond, sadly.

'A lovely creature in affliction seems always doubly
beautiful to me,' says the poor captain, who indeed was
but too often in a state to see double, and so checked he
resumed the interrupted thread of his story. 'As I spoke

my business,' Mr. Steele said, ' and narrated to your
mistress what all the world knows, and the other side hath
been eager to acknowledge—that you had tried to put
yourself between the two lords, and to take your patron's
quarrel on your own point ; I recounted the general praises
of your gallantry, besides my Lord Mohun's particular
testimony to it ; I thought the widow listened with some
interest, and her eyes—I have never seen such a violet,
Harry—looked up at mine once or twice. But after
I had spoken on this theme for a while she suddenly broke
away with a cry of grief. "I would to God, sir," she
said, "I had never heard that word gallantry which
you use, or known the meaning of it. My lord might
have been here but for that ; my home might be happy ;
my poor boy have a father. It was what you gentlemen call gallantry came into my home, and drove my
husband on to the cruel sword that killed him. You
should not speak the word to a Christian woman, sir—
a poor widowed mother of orphans, whose home was
happy until the world came into it—the wicked godless
world, that takes the blood of the innocent, and lets the
guilty go free."

' As the afflicted lady spoke in this strain, sir,' Mr. Steele
continued, ' it seemed as if indignation moved her, even
more than grief. " Compensation ! " she went on passion-
ately, her cheeks and eyes kindling ; " what compensation
does your world give the widow for her husband, and the
children for the murderer of their father ? The wretch
who did the deed has not even a punishment. Conscience !
what conscience has he, who can enter the house of a friend,
whisper falsehood and insult to a woman that never harmed
him, and stab the kind heart that trusted him ? My lord—
my Lord Wretch, my Lord Villain's, my Lord Murderer's
peers meet to try him, and they dismiss him with a word
or two of reproof, and send him into the world again, to
pursue women with lust and falsehood, and to murder
unsuspecting guests that harbour him. That day, my
lord—my Lord Murderer—(I will never name him)—was
let loose, a woman was executed at Tyburn for stealing in
a shop. But a man may rob another of his life, or a lady
of her honour, and shall pay no penalty ! I take my
child, run to the throne, and on my knees ask for justice,
and the king refuses me. The king ! he is no king of

mine—he never shall be. He, too, robbed the throne from the king his father—the true king—and he has gone unpunished, as the great do."

'I then thought to speak for you,' Mr. Steele continued, 'and I interposed by saying, "There was one, madam, who, at least, would have put his own breast between your husband's and my Lord Mohun's sword. Your poor young kinsman, Harry Esmond, hath told me that he tried to draw the quarrel on himself."

' "Are you come from *him* ? " asked the lady' (so Mr. Steele went on), 'rising up with a great severity and stateliness. "I thought you had come from the princess. I saw Mr. Esmond in his prison, and bade him farewell. He brought misery into my house. He never should have entered it."

' "Madam, madam, he is not to blame," I interposed,' continued Mr. Steele.

' "Do I blame him to you, sir ? " asked the widow. "If 'tis he who sent you, say that I have taken counsel, where "—she spoke with a very pallid cheek now, and a break in her voice—" where all who ask may have it ;—and that it bids me to part from him, and to see him no more. We met in the prison for the last time—at least for years to come. It may be, in years hence, when—when our knees and our tears and our contrition have changed our sinful hearts, sir, and wrought our pardon, we may meet again—but not now. After what has passed, I could not bear to see him. I wish him well, sir ; but I wish him farewell, too ; and if he has that—that regard towards us which he speaks of, I beseech him to prove it by obeying me in this."

' "I shall break the young man's heart, madam, by this hard sentence," ' Mr. Steele said.

'The lady shook her head,' continued my kind scholar. ' "The hearts of young men, Mr. Steele, are not so made," she said. "Mr. Esmond will find other—other friends. The mistress of this house has relented very much towards the late lord's son," she added, with a blush, " and has promised me, that is, has promised that she will care for his fortune. Whilst I live in it, after the horrid, horrid deed which has passed, Castlewood must never be a home to him—never. Nor would I have him write to me— except—no—I would have him never write to me, nor see him more. ˙ Give him, if you will, my parting—Hush ! not a word of this before my daughter."

' Here the fair Beatrix entered from the river, with her cheeks flushing with health, and looking only the more lovely and fresh for the mourning habiliments which she wore. And my lady viscountess said—

' " Beatrix, this is Mr. Steele, gentleman-usher to the prince's highness. When does your new comedy appear, Mr. Steele ? " I hope thou wilt be out of prison for the first night, Harry.'

The sentimental captain concluded his sad tale, saying, ' Faith, the beauty of *Filia pulcrior* drove *pulcram matrem* out of my head ; and yet as I came down the river, and thought about the pair, the pallid dignity and exquisite grace of the matron had the uppermost, and I thought her even more noble than the virgin ! '

The party of prisoners lived very well in Newgate, and with comforts very different to those which were awarded to the poor wretches there (his insensibility to their misery, their gaiety still more frightful, their curses and blasphemy, hath struck with a kind of shame since—as proving how selfish, during his imprisonment, his own particular grief was, and how entirely the thoughts of it absorbed him) : if the three gentlemen lived well under the care of the warden of Newgate, it was because they paid well : and indeed the cost at the dearest ordinary or the grandest tavern in London could not have furnished a longer reckoning, than our host of the ' Handcuff Inn '—as Colonel Westbury called it. Our rooms were the three in the gate over Newgate—on the second story looking up Newgate Street towards Cheapside and Paul's Church. And we had leave to walk on the roof, and could see thence Smithfield and the Bluecoat Boys' School, Gardens, and the Chartreux, where, as Harry Esmond remembered, Dick the Scholar, and his friend Tom Tusher, had had their schooling.

Harry could never have paid his share of that prodigious heavy reckoning which my landlord brought to his guests once a week : for he had but three pieces in his pockets that fatal night before the duel, when the gentlemen were at cards, and offered to play five. But whilst he was yet ill at the Gatehouse, after Lady Castlewood had visited him there, and before his trial, there came one in an orange-tawny coat and blue lace, the livery which the Esmonds always wore, and brought a sealed packet for Mr. Esmond, which contained twenty guineas, and a note saying that a counsel had been appointed for him, and that more money would be forthcoming whenever he needed it.

'Twas a queer letter from the scholar as she was, or as she called herself : the Dowager Viscountess Castlewood, written in the strange barbarous French which she and many other fine ladies of that time—witness Her Grace of Portsmouth*—employed. Indeed, spelling was not an article of general commodity in the world then, and my Lord Marlborough's letters can show that he, for one, had but a little share of this part of grammar.

Mong Coussin (my lady viscountess dowager wrote), je scay que vous vous etes bravement batew et grievement bléssay—du costé de feu M. le Vicomte. M. le Compte de Varique ne se playt qua parlay de vous : M. de Moon aucy. Il di que vous avay voulew vous bastre avecque luy—que vous estes plus fort que luy sur l'ayscrimme—quil'y a surtout certaine Botte que vous scavay quil n'a jammay sceu pariay : et que c'en eut été fay de luy si vouseluy vous vous fussiay battews ansamb. Aincy ce pauv Vicompte est mort. Mort et peutayt—Mon coussin, mon coussin ! jay dans la tayste que vous n'estes quung pety Monst—angcy que les Esmonds ong tousjours esté. La veuve est chay moy. J'ay recuilly cet' pauve famme. Elle est furieuse cont vous, allans tous les jours chercher le Roy (d'icy) démandant à gran cri revanche pour son Mary. Elle ne veux voyre ni entende parlay de vous : pourtant elle ne fay qu'en parlay milfoy par jour. Quand vous seray hor prison venay me voyre. J'auray soing de vous. Si cette petite Prude veut se défaire de song pety Monste (Hélas je craing qùil ne soy trotar !) je m'en chargeray. J'ay encor quelqu interay et quelques escus de costay.

La Veuve se raccommode avec Miladi Marlboro qui est tout puiçante avecque la Reine Anne. Cet dam sentéraysent pour la vetite prude ; qui pourctant a un fi du mesme asge que vous savay.

En sortant de prisong venez icy. Je ne puy vous recevoir chay-moy à cause des méchansetés du monde, may pre du moy vous aurez logement.

ISABELLE VICOMPTESSE D'ESMOND.*

Marchioness of Esmond this lady sometimes called herself, in virtue of that patent which had been given by the late King James to Harry Esmond's father ; and in this state she had her train carried by a knight's wife, a cup and cover of assay to drink from, and fringed cloth.

He who was of the same age as little Francis, whom we

shall henceforth call Viscount Castlewood here, was H.R.H.
the Prince of Wales, born in the same year and month with
Frank, and just proclaimed at St. Germains, King of Great
Britain, France, and Ireland.

CHAPTER III

I TAKE THE QUEEN'S PAY IN QUIN'S REGIMENT

THE fellow in the orange-tawny livery with blue lace
and facings was in waiting when Esmond came out of
prison, and, taking the young gentleman's slender baggage,
led the way out of that odious Newgate, and by Fleet
Conduit, down to the Thames, where a pair of oars was
called, and they went up the river to Chelsea. Esmond
thought the sun had never shone so bright ; nor the air
felt so fresh and exhilarating. Temple Garden, as they
rowed by, looked like the garden of Eden to him, and the
aspect of the quays, wharves, and buildings by the river,
Somerset House, and Westminster (where the splendid
new bridge was just beginning), Lambeth tower and palace,
and that busy shining scene of the Thames swarming with
boats and barges, filled his heart with pleasure and cheerfulness—as well such a beautiful scene might to one who had
been a prisoner so long, and with so many dark thoughts
deepening the gloom of his captivity. They rowed up at
length to the pretty village of Chelsey, where the nobility
have many handsome country-houses ; and so came to
my lady viscountess's house, a cheerful new house in the
row facing the river, with a handsome garden behind it,
and a pleasant look-out both towards Surrey and Kensington, where stands the noble ancient palace of the Lord
Warwick, Harry's reconciled adversary.

Here in her ladyship's saloon, the young man saw again
some of those pictures which had been at Castlewood, and
which she had removed thence on the death of her lord,
Harry's father. Specially, and in the place of honour,
was Sir Peter Lely's picture of the Honourable Mistress
Isabella Esmond as Diana, in yellow satin, with a bow
in her hand and a crescent in her forehead ; and dogs
frisking about her. 'Twas painted about the time when

royal Endymions were said to find favour with this virgin
huntress ; and, as goddesses have youth perpetual, this
one believed to the day of her death that she never grew
older : and always persisted in supposing the picture was
still like her.

After he had been shown to her room by the groom of
the chamber, who filled many offices besides in her ladyship's modest household ; and after a proper interval, his
elderly goddess Diana vouchsafed to appear to the young
man. A blackamoor in a Turkish habit, with red boots
and a silver collar, on which the viscountess's arms were
engraven, preceded her and bore her cushion ; then came
her gentlewoman ; a little pack of spaniels barking and
frisking about preceded the austere huntress—then, behold,
the viscountess herself ' dropping odours '.* Esmond recollected from his childhood that rich aroma of musk which
his mother-in-law (for she may be called so) exhaled. As
the sky grows redder and redder towards sunset, so, in the
decline of her years, the cheeks of my lady dowager blushed
more deeply. Her face was illuminated with vermilion, which
appeared the brighter from the white paint employed to
set it off. She wore the ringlets which had been in fashion
in King Charles's time ; whereas the ladies of King William's
had head-dresses like the towers of Cybele.* Her eyes
gleamed out from the midst of this queer structure of
paint, dyes, and pomatums. Such was my lady viscountess,
Mr. Esmond's father's widow.

He made her such a profound bow as her dignity and
relationship merited : and advanced with the greatest
gravity, and once more kissed that hand, upon the trembling
knuckles of which glittered a score of rings—remembering
old times when that trembling hand made him tremble.
' Marchioness,' says he, bowing, and on one knee, ' is it only
the hand I may have the honour of saluting ? ' For,
accompanying that inward laughter, which the sight of
such an astonishing old figure might well produce in the
young man, there was goodwill too, and the kindness of
consanguinity. She had been his father's wife, and was his
grandfather's daughter. She had suffered him in old days,
and was kind to him now after her fashion. And now
that bar-sinister was removed from Esmond's thought, and
that secret opprobrium no longer cast upon his mind, he
was pleased to feel family ties and own them—perhaps

secretly vain of the sacrifice he had made, and to think that he, Esmond, was really the chief of his house, and only prevented by his own magnanimity from advancing his claim.

At least, ever since he had learned that secret from his poor patron on his dying bed, actually as he was standing beside it, he had felt an independency which he had never known before, and which since did not desert him. So he called his old aunt marchioness, but with an air as if he was the Marquis of Esmond who so addressed her.

Did she read in the young gentleman's eyes, which had now no fear of hers or their superannuated authority, that he knew or suspected the truth about his birth ? She gave a start of surprise at his altered manner : indeed, it was quite a different bearing to that of the Cambridge student who had paid her a visit two years since, and whom she had dismissed with five pieces sent by the groom of the chamber. She eyed him, then trembled a little more than was her wont, perhaps, and said, ' Welcome, cousin ', in a frightened voice.

His resolution, as has been said before, had been quite different, namely, so to bear himself through life as if the secret of his birth was not known to him ; but he suddenly and rightly determined on a different course. He asked that her ladyship's attendants should be dismissed, and when they were private—' Welcome, nephew, at least, madam, it should be,' he said, ' A great wrong has been done to me and to you, and to my poor mother, who is no more.'

' I declare before Heaven that I was guiltless of it,' she cried out, giving up her cause at once. ' It was your wicked father who——'

' Who brought this dishonour on our family,' says Mr. Esmond. ' I know it full well. I want to disturb no one. Those who are in present possession have been my dearest benefactors, and are quite innocent of intentional wrong to me. The late lord, my dear patron, knew not the truth until a few months before his death, when Father Holt brought the news to him.'

' The wretch ! he had it in confession ! He had it in confession ! ' cried out the dowager lady.

' Not so. He learned it elsewhere as well as in confession,' Mr. Esmond answered. ' My father, when wounded at the

Boyne, told the truth to a French priest, who was in hiding after the battle, as well as to the priest there, at whose house he died. This gentleman did not think fit to divulge the story till he met with Mr. Holt at St. Omer's. And the latter kept it back for his own purpose, and until he had learned whether my mother was alive or no. She is dead years since : my poor patron told me with his dying breath ; and I doubt him not. I do not know even whether I could prove a marriage. I would not if I could. I do not care to bring shame on our name, or grief upon those whom I love, however hardly they may use me. My father's son, madam, won't aggravate the wrong my father did you. Continue to be his widow, and give me your kindness. 'Tis all I ask from you ; and I shall never speak of this matter again.'

'*Mais vous êtes un noble jeune homme!*' breaks out my lady, speaking, as usual with her when she was agitated, in the French language.

'*Noblesse oblige*,' says Mr. Esmond, making her a low bow. 'There are those alive to whom, in return for their love to me, I often fondly said I would give my life away. Shall I be their enemy now, and quarrel about a title ? What matters who has it ? 'Tis with the family still.'

'What can there be in that little prude of a woman, that makes men so *raffoler* about her ?' cries out my lady dowager. 'She was here for a month petitioning the king. She is pretty, and well conserved ; but she has not the *bel air*. In his late Majesty's Court all the men pretended to admire her ; and she was no better than a little wax doll. She is better now, and looks the sister of her daughter : but what mean you all by bepraising her ? Mr. Steele, who was in waiting on Prince George, seeing her with her two children going to Kensington, writ a poem about her ; and says he shall wear her colours, and dress in black for the future. Mr. Congreve says he will write a *Mourning Widow*, that shall be better than his *Mourning Bride*. Though their husbands quarrelled and fought when that wretch Churchill deserted the king (for which he deserved to be hung), Lady Marlborough has again gone wild about the little widow ; insulted me in my own drawing-room, by saying that 'twas not the *old* widow, but the young viscountess, she had come to see. Little Castlewood and little Lord Churchill are to be sworn friends, and have boxed

each other twice or thrice like brothers already. 'Twas
that wicked young Mohun who, coming back from the
provinces last year, where he had disinterred her, raved
about her all the winter ; said she was a pearl set before
swine ; and killed poor stupid Frank. The quarrel was
all about his wife. I know 'twas all about her. Was there
anything between her and Mohun, nephew ? Tell me now ;
was there anything ? About yourself, I do not ask you
to answer questions.' Mr. Esmond blushed up. ' My
lady's virtue is like that of a saint in heaven, madam,' he
cried out.

' Eh !—*mon neveu*. Many saints get to Heaven after
having a deal to repent of. I believe you are like all the
rest of the fools, and madly in love with her.'

' Indeed, I loved and honoured her before all the world,'
Esmond answered. ' I take no shame in that.'

' And she has shut her door on you—given the living to
that horrid young cub, son of that horrid old bear, Tusher,
and says she will never see you more. *Monsieur mon neveu*
—we are all like that. When I was a young woman, I'm
positive that a thousand duels were fought about me. And
when poor Monsieur de Souchy drowned himself in the
canal at Bruges because I danced with Count Springbock,
I couldn't squeeze out a single tear, but danced till five
o'clock the next morning. 'Twas the count—no, 'twas my
Lord Ormonde that paid the fiddles, and his Majesty did
me the honour of dancing all night with me.—How you are
grown ! You have got the *bel air*. You are a black man.
Our Esmonds are all black. The little prude's son is fair ; so
was his father—fair and stupid. You were an ugly little
wretch when you came to Castlewood—you were all eyes,
like a young crow. We intended you should be a priest.
That awful Father Holt—how he used to frighten me when
I was ill ! I have a comfortable director now—the Abbé
Douillette—a dear man. We make meagre on Fridays
always. My cook is a devout pious man. You, of course,
are of the right way of thinking. They say the Prince
of Orange is very ill indeed.'

In this way the old dowager rattled on remorselessly to
Mr. Esmond, who was quite astounded with her present
volubility, contrasting it with her former haughty behaviour
to him. But she had taken him into favour for the moment,
and chose not only to like him, as far as her nature permitted,

but to be afraid of him ; and he found himself to be as
familiar with her now as a young man, as when a boy,
he had been timorous and silent. She was as good as her
word respecting him. She introduced him to her company,
of which she entertained a good deal—of the adherents of
King James of course—and a great deal of loud intriguing
took place over her card-tables. She presented Mr. Esmond
as her kinsman to many persons of honour ; she supplied
him not illiberally with money, which he had no scruple
in accepting from her, considering the relationship which
he bore to her, and the sacrifices which he himself was
making in behalf of the family. But he had made up his
mind to continue at no woman's apron-strings longer ; and
perhaps had cast about how he should distinguish himself,
and make himself a name, which his singular fortune had
denied him. A discontent with his former bookish life and
quietude,—a bitter feeling of revolt at that slavery in which
he had chosen to confine himself for the sake of those whose
hardness towards him made his heart bleed,—a restless wish
to see men and the world,—led him to think of the military
profession : at any rate, to desire to see a few campaigns,
and accordingly he pressed his new patroness to get him
a pair of colours ; and one day had the honour of finding
himself appointed an ensign in Colonel Quin's regiment of
Fusiliers on the Irish establishment.

Mr. Esmond's commission was scarce three weeks old
when that accident befell King William which ended the
life of the greatest, the wisest, the bravest, and most clement
sovereign whom England ever knew. 'Twas the fashion
of the hostile party to assail this great prince's reputation
during his life ; but the joy which they and all his enemies
in Europe showed at his death, is a proof of the terror in
which they held him. Young as Esmond was, he was wise
enough (and generous enough too, let it be said) to scorn
that indecency of gratulation which broke out amongst the
followers of King James in London, upon the death of this
illustrious prince, this invincible warrior, this wise and
moderate statesman. Loyalty to the exiled king's family
was traditional, as has been said, in that house to which
Mr. Esmond belonged. His father's widow had all her
hopes, sympathies, recollections, prejudices, engaged on
King James's side ; and was certainly as noisy a conspirator
as ever asserted the king's rights, or abused his opponent's,

over a quadrille table or a dish of bohea. Her ladyship's
house swarmed with ecclesiastics, in disguise and out ; with
tale-bearers from St. Germains ; and quidnuncs that knew
the last news from Versailles ; nay, the exact force and
number of the next expedition which the French king was
to send from Dunkirk, and which was to swallow up the
Prince of Orange, his army, and his Court. She had
received the Duke of Berwick when he landed here in '96.
She kept the glass he drank from, vowing she never would
use it till she drank King James the Third's health in it
on his Majesty's return ; she had tokens from the queen,
and relics of the saint who, if the story was true, had not
always been a saint as far as she and many others were concerned. She believed in the miracles wrought at his tomb,
and had a hundred authentic stories of wondrous cures
effected by the blessed king's rosaries, the medals which he
wore, the locks of his hair, or what not. Esmond remembered
a score of marvellous tales which the credulous old woman
told him. There was the Bishop of Autun, that was healed
of a malady he had for forty years, and which left him
after he said mass for the repose of the king's soul. There
was Monsieur Marais, a surgeon in Auvergne, who had a
palsy in both his legs, which was cured through the king's
intercession. There was Philip Pitet, of the Benedictines,
who had a suffocating cough, which wellnigh killed him, but
he besought relief of Heaven through the merits and intercession of the blessed king, and he straightway felt a profuse
sweat breaking out all over him, and was recovered perfectly.
And there was the wife of Monsieur Lepervier, dancing-
master to the Duke of Saxe-Gotha, who was entirely eased
of a rheumatism by the king's intercession, of which miracle
there could be no doubt, for her surgeon and his apprentice
had given their testimony, under oath, that they did not
in any way contribute to the cure. Of these tales, and
a thousand like them, Mr. Esmond believed as much as
he chose. His kinswoman's greater faith had swallow for
them all.*

The English High Church party did not adopt these
legends. But truth and honour, as they thought, bound
them to the exiled king's side ; nor had the banished
family any warmer supporter than that kind lady of Castlewood, in whose house Esmond was brought up. She influenced her husband, very much more perhaps than my

lord knew, who admired his wife prodigiously though he might be inconstant to her, and who, adverse to the trouble of thinking himself, gladly enough adopted the opinions which she chose for him.   To one of her simple and faithful heart, allegiance to any sovereign but the one was impossible. To serve King William for interest's sake would have been a monstrous hypocrisy and treason.   Her pure conscience could no more have consented to it than to a theft, a forgery, or any other base action.   Lord Castlewood might have been won over, no doubt, but his wife never could : and he submitted his conscience to hers in this case as he did in most others, when he was not tempted too sorely.   And it was from his affection and gratitude most likely, and from that eager devotion for his mistress, which characterized all Esmond's youth, that the young man subscribed to this, and other articles of faith, which his fond benefactress set him.   Had she been a Whig, he had been one ; had she followed Mr. Fox,* and turned Quaker, no doubt he would have abjured ruffles and a periwig, and have forsworn swords, lace coats, and clocked stockings.   In the scholars' boyish disputes at the University, where parties ran very high, Esmond was noted as a Jacobite, and very likely from vanity as much as affection took the side of his family.

Almost the whole of the clergy of the country and more than a half of the nation were on this side.   Ours is the most loyal people in the world surely ; we admire our kings, and are faithful to them long after they have ceased to be true to us.   'Tis a wonder to any one who looks back at the history of the Stuart family to think how they kicked their crowns away from them ; how they flung away chances after chances ; what treasures of loyalty they dissipated, and how fatally they were bent on consummating their own ruin.   If ever men had fidelity, 'twas they ; if ever men squandered opportunity, 'twas they ; and, of all the enemies they had, they themselves were the most fatal.[1]

When the Princess Anne succeeded, the wearied nation was glad enough to cry a truce from all these wars, controversies, and conspiracies, and to accept in the person of

---

[1] Ὦ πόποι, οἷον δή νυ θεοὺς βροτοὶ αἰτιόωνται,
ἐξ ἡμέων γάρ φασι κάκ᾽ ἔμμεναι· οἱ δὲ καὶ αὐτοὶ
σφῇσιν ἀτασθαλίῃσιν ὑπὲρ μόρον ἄλγε᾽ ἔχουσιν.*

a princess of the blood royal a compromise between the parties into which the country was divided. The Tories could serve under her with easy consciences; though a Tory herself, she represented the triumph of the Whig opinion. The people of England, always liking that their princes should be attached to their own families, were pleased to think the princess was faithful to hers; and up to the very last day and hour of her reign, and but for that fatality which he inherited from his fathers along with their claims to the English crown, King James the Third might have worn it. But he neither knew how to wait an opportunity, nor to use it when he had it; he was venturesome when he ought to have been cautious, and cautious when he ought to have dared everything. 'Tis with a sort of rage at his inaptitude that one thinks of his melancholy story. Do the Fates deal more specially with kings than with common men? One is apt to imagine so, in considering the history of that royal race, in whose behalf so much fidelity, so much valour, so much blood were desperately and bootlessly expended.

The king dead then, the Princess Anne (ugly Anne Hyde's daughter, our dowager at Chelsey called her) was proclaimed by trumpeting heralds all over the town from Westminster to Ludgate Hill, amidst immense jubilations of the people.

Next week my Lord Marlborough was promoted to the Garter, and to be captain-general of her Majesty's forces at home and abroad. This appointment only inflamed the dowager's rage, or, as she thought it, her fidelity to her rightful sovereign. 'The princess is but a puppet in the hands of that fury of a woman, who comes into my drawing-room and insults me to my face. What can come to a country that is given over to such a woman?' says the dowager: 'As for that double-faced traitor, my Lord Marlborough, he has betrayed every man and every woman with whom he has had to deal, except his horrid wife, who makes him tremble. 'Tis all over with the country when it has got into the clutches of such wretches as these.'

Esmond's old kinswoman saluted the new powers in this way; but some good fortune at least occurred to a family which stood in great need of it, by the advancement of these famous personages who benefited humbler people that had the luck of being in their favour. Before Mr. Esmond

left England in the month of August, and being then at
Portsmouth, where he had joined his regiment, and was
busy at drill, learning the practice and mysteries of the
musket and pike, he heard that a pension on the Stamp
Office had been got for his late beloved mistress, and that
the young Mistress Beatrix was also to be taken into Court.
So much good, at least, had come of the poor widow's visit
to London, not revenge upon her husband's enemies, but
reconcilement to old friends, who pitied, and seemed inclined
to serve her.   As for the comrades in prison and the late
misfortune ; Colonel Westbury was with the captain-general
gone to Holland; Captain Macartney was now at Portsmouth,
with his regiment of Fusiliers and the force under command
of his grace the Duke of Ormonde, bound for Spain it was
said ; my Lord Warwick was returned home ; and Lord
Mohun, so far from being punished for the homicide which
had brought so much grief and change into the Esmond
family, was gone in company of my Lord Macclesfield's
splendid embassy to the Elector of Hanover, carrying the
Garter to his highness, and a complimentary letter from the
queen.*

CHAPTER IV

RECAPITULATIONS

FROM such fitful lights as could be cast upon his dark
history by the broken narrative of his poor patron, torn
by remorse and struggling in the last pangs of dissolution,
Mr. Esmond had been made to understand so far, that his
mother was long since dead ; and so there could be no
question as regarded her or her honour, tarnished by her
husband's desertion and injury, to influence her son in any
steps which he might take either for prosecuting or relin-
quishing his own just claims. It appeared from my poor
lord's hurried confession, that he had been made acquainted
with the real facts of the case only two years since, when
Mr. Holt visited him, and would have implicated him in
one of those many conspiracies by which the secret leaders
of King James's party in this country were ever endeavour-
ing to destroy the Prince of Orange's life or power ; conspiracies so like murder, so cowardly in the means used,

so wicked in the end, that our nation has sure done well in throwing off all allegiance and fidelity to the unhappy family that could not vindicate its right except by such treachery—by such dark intrigue and base agents. There were designs against King William that were no more honourable than the ambushes of cut-throats and footpads. 'Tis humiliating to think that a great prince, possessor of a great and sacred right, and upholder of a great cause, should have stooped to such baseness of assassination and treasons as are proved by the unfortunate King James's own warrant and sign-manual given to his supporters in this country. What he and they called levying war was, in truth, no better than instigating murder. The noble Prince of Orange burst magnanimously through those feeble meshes of conspiracy in which his enemies tried to envelop him : it seemed as if their cowardly daggers broke upon the breast of his undaunted resolution. After King James's death, the queen and her people at St. Germains—priests and women for the most part—continued their intrigues in behalf of the young prince, James the Third, as he was called in France and by his party here (this prince, or Chevalier de St. George, was born in the same year with Esmond's young pupil Frank, my lord viscount's son) : and the prince's affairs, being in the hands of priests and women, were conducted as priests and women will conduct them, artfully, cruelly, feebly, and to a certain bad issue. The moral of the Jesuit's story I think as wholesome a one as ever was writ : the artfullest, the wisest, the most toilsome, and dexterous plot-builders in the world—there always comes a day when the roused public indignation kicks their flimsy edifice down, and sends its cowardly enemies a-flying. Mr. Swift hath finely described that passion for intrigue, that love of secrecy, slander, and lying, which belongs to weak people, hangers-on of weak courts.* 'Tis the nature of such to hate and envy the strong, and conspire their ruin ; and the conspiracy succeeds very well, and every-thing presages the satisfactory overthrow of the great victim ; until one day Gulliver rouses himself, shakes off the little vermin of an enemy, and walks away unmolested. Ah ! the Irish soldiers might well say after the Boyne, ' Change kings with us, and we will fight it over again.' Indeed, the fight was not fair between the two. 'Twas a weak priest-ridden, woman-ridden man, with such puny

allies and weapons as his own poor nature led him to choose,
contending against the schemes, the generalship, the wisdom,
and the heart of a hero.

On one of these many coward's errands, then (for, as
I view them now, I can call them no less), Mr. Holt had
come to my lord at Castlewood, proposing some infallible
plan for the Prince of Orange's destruction, in which my
lord viscount, loyalist as he was, had indignantly refused
to join.   As far as Mr. Esmond could gather from his dying
words, Holt came to my lord with a plan of insurrection,
and offer of the renewal, in his person, of that marquis's
title which King James had conferred on the preceding
viscount ; and on refusal of this bribe, a threat was made,
on Holt's part, to upset my lord viscount's claim to his
estate and title of Castlewood altogether.   To back this
astounding piece of intelligence, of which Henry Esmond's
patron now had the first light, Holt came armed with the
late lord's dying declaration, after the affair of the Boyne,
at Trim, in Ireland, made both to the Irish priest and a
French ecclesiastic of Holt's order, that was with King
James's army.   Holt showed, or pretended to show, the
marriage certificate of the late Viscount Esmond with my
mother, in the city of Brussels, in the year 1677, when the
viscount, then Thomas Esmond, was serving with the
English army in Flanders ; he could show, he said, that
this Gertrude, deserted by her husband long since, was
alive, and a professed nun in the year 1685, at Brussels,
in which year Thomas Esmond married his uncle's daughter,
Isabella, now called Viscountess Dowager of Castlewood ;
and leaving him, for twelve hours, to consider this astounding news (so the poor dying lord said), disappeared with
his papers in the mysterious way in which he came.   Esmond
knew how, well enough : by that window from which he
had seen the father issue :—but there was no need to explain
to my poor lord, only to gather from his parting lips the
words which he would soon be able to utter no more.

Ere the twelve hours were over, Holt himself was a
prisoner, implicated in Sir John Fenwick's conspiracy, and
locked up at Hexton first, whence he was transferred to the
Tower ; leaving the poor lord viscount, who was not aware
of the others being taken, in daily apprehension of his return,
when (as my Lord Castlewood declared, calling God to
witness, and with tears in his dying eyes) it had been his

intention at once to give up his estate and his title to their proper owner, and to retire to his own house at Walcote with his family. ' And would to God I had done it,' the poor lord said ; ' I would not be here now, wounded to death, a miserable, stricken man ! '

My lord waited day after day, and, as may be supposed, no messenger came ; but at a month's end Holt got means to convey to him a message out of the Tower, which was to this effect : that he should consider all unsaid that had been said, and that things were as they were.

' I had a sore temptation,' said my poor lord. ' Since I had come into this cursed title of Castlewood, which hath never prospered with me, I have spent far more than the income of that estate and my paternal one, too. I calculated all my means down to the last shilling, and found I never could pay you back, my poor Harry, whose fortune I had had for twelve years. My wife and children must have gone out of the house dishonoured, and beggars. God knows, it hath been a miserable one for me and mine. Like a coward, I clung to that respite which Holt gave me. I kept the truth from Rachel and you. I tried to win money of Mohun, and only plunged deeper into debt ; I scarce dared look thee in the face when I saw thee. This sword hath been hanging over my head these two years. I swear I felt happy when Mohun's blade entered my side.'

After lying ten months in the Tower, Holt, against whom nothing could be found except that he was a Jesuit priest, known to be in King James's interest, was put on shipboard by the incorrigible forgiveness of King William, who promised him, however, a hanging if ever he should again set foot on English shore. More than once, whilst he was in prison himself, Esmond had thought where those papers could be, which the Jesuit had shown to his patron, and which had such an interest for himself. They were not found on Mr. Holt's person when that father was apprehended, for had such been the case my lords of the council had seen them, and this family history had long since been made public. However, Esmond cared not to seek the papers. His resolution being taken ; his poor mother dead ; what matter to him that documents existed proving his right to a title which he was determined not to claim, and of which he vowed never to deprive that family which he loved best in the world ? Perhaps he took a greater pride out of his

sacrifice than he would have had in those honours which
he was resolved to forgo.   Again, as long as these titles
were not forthcoming, Esmond's kinsman, dear young
Francis, was the honourable and undisputed owner of the
Castlewood estate and title. The mere word of a Jesuit could
not overset Frank's right of occupancy, and so Esmond's
mind felt actually at ease to think the papers were missing,
and in their absence his dear mistress and her son the lawful lady and lord of Castlewood.

Very soon after his liberation, Mr. Esmond made it his
business to ride to that village of Ealing where he had
passed his earliest years in this country, and to see if his
old guardians were still alive and inhabitants of that place.
But the only relic which he found of old Monsieur Pastoureau
was a stone in the churchyard, which told that Athanasius
Pastoureau, a native of Flanders, lay there buried, aged
87 years. The old man's cottage, which Esmond perfectly
recollected, and the garden (where in his childhood he had
passed many hours of play and reverie, and had many
a beating from his termagant of a foster-mother), were now
in the occupation of quite a different family ; and it was
with difficulty that he could learn in the village what had
come of Pastoureau's widow and children.   The clerk of the
parish recollected her—the old man was scarce altered in
the fourteen years that had passed since last Esmond set
eyes on him.   It appeared she had pretty soon consoled
herself after the death of her old husband, whom she ruled
over, by taking a new one younger than herself, who spent
her money and ill-treated her and her children.   The girl
died ; one of the boys 'listed ; the other had gone apprentice.   Old Mr. Rogers, the clerk, said he had heard that
Mrs. Pastoureau was dead too. She and her husband had
left Ealing this seven year ; and so Mr. Esmond's hopes
of gaining any information regarding his parentage from
this family, were brought to an end.   He gave the old clerk
a crown-piece for his news, smiling to think of the time
when he and his little playfellows had slunk out of the
churchyard, or hidden behind the gravestones, at the
approach of this awful authority.

Who was his mother ? What had her name been ?
When did she die ? Esmond longed to find some one who
could answer these questions to him, and thought even of
putting them to his aunt the viscountess, who had inno-

cently taken the name which belonged of right to Henry's
mother. But she knew nothing, or chose to know nothing,
on this subject, nor, indeed, could Mr. Esmond press her
much to speak on it. Father Holt was the only man who
could enlighten him, and Esmond felt he must wait until
some fresh chance or new intrigue might put him face to
face with his old friend, or bring that restless indefatigable
spirit back to England again.

The appointment to his ensigncy, and the preparations
necessary for the campaign, presently gave the young gentleman other matters to think of. His new patroness treated
him very kindly and liberally ; she promised to make
interest and pay money, too, to get him a company speedily ;
she bade him procure a handsome outfit, both of clothes
and of arms, and was pleased to admire him when he made
his first appearance in his laced scarlet coat, and to permit
him to salute her on the occasion of this interesting inves
titure. ' Red,' says she, tossing up her old head, ' hath
always been the colour worn by the Esmonds.' And so her
ladyship wore it on her own cheeks very faithfully to the
last. She would have him be dressed, she said, as became
his father's son, and paid cheerfully for his five-pound
beaver, his black buckled periwig, and his fine holland
shirts, and his swords, and his pistols, mounted with silver.
Since the day he was born, poor Harry had never looked
such a fine gentleman : his liberal stepmother filled his
purse with guineas, too, some of which Captain Steele and
a few choice spirits helped Harry to spend in an entertainment which Dick ordered (and, indeed, would have paid
for, but that he had no money when the reckoning was
called for ; nor would the landlord give him any more
credit) at the ' Garter ', over against the gate of the Palace,
in Pall Mall.

The old viscountess, indeed, if she had done Esmond any
wrong formerly, seemed inclined to repair it by the present
kindness of her behaviour : she embraced him copiously
at parting, wept plentifully, bade him write by every packet,
and gave him an inestimable relic, which she besought him
to wear round his neck—a medal, blessed by I know not
what Pope, and worn by his late sacred Majesty King James.
So Esmond arrived at his regiment with a better equipage
than most young officers could afford. He was older than
most of his seniors, and had a further advantage which

belonged but to very few of the army gentlemen in his day
—many of whom could do little more than write their
names—that he had read much, both at home and at the
University, was master of two or three languages, and had
that further education which neither books nor years will
give, but which some men get from the silent teaching of
adversity. She is a great schoolmistress, as many a poor
fellow knows, that hath held his hand out to her ferule,
and whimpered over his lesson before her awful chair.

CHAPTER V

I GO ON THE VIGO BAY EXPEDITION, TASTE SALT WATER AND SMELL POWDER*

THE first expedition in which Mr. Esmond had the honour
to be engaged, rather resembled one of the invasions projected by the redoubted Captain Avory or Captain Kid,*
than a war between crowned heads, carried on by generals
of rank and honour. On the 1st day of July, 1702, a great
fleet, of a hundred and fifty sail, set sail from Spithead,
under the command of Admiral Shovell, having on board
12,000 troops, with his grace the Duke of Ormond as the
captain-general of the expedition. One of these 12,000
heroes having never been to sea before, or, at least, only
once in his infancy, when he made the voyage to England
from that unknown country where he was born—one of
those 12,000—the junior ensign of Colonel Quin's regiment
of Fusiliers—was in a quite unheroic state of corporal pros-
tration a few hours after sailing; and an enemy, had he
boarded the ship, would have had easy work of him.   From
Portsmouth we put into Plymouth, and took in fresh rein-
forcements. We were off Finisterre on the 31st of July,
so Esmond's table-book informs him ; and on the 8th of
August made the rock of Lisbon. By this time the ensign
was grown as bold as an admiral, and a week afterwards
had the fortune to be under fire for the first time—and
under water, too—his boat being swamped in the surf in
Toros Bay, where the troops landed. The ducking of his
new coat was all the harm the young soldier got in this
expedition, for, indeed, the Spaniards made no stand before
our troops, and were not in strength to do so.

But the campaign, if not very glorious, was very pleasant.
New sights of nature, by sea and land—a life of action,
beginning now for the first time—occupied and excited the
young man. The many accidents, and the routine of shipboard—the military duty—the new acquaintances, both of
his comrades in arms, and of the officers of the fleet—
served to cheer and occupy his mind, and waken it out of
that selfish depression into which his late unhappy fortunes
had plunged him. He felt as if the ocean separated him
from his past care, and welcomed the new era of life which
was dawning for him. Wounds heal rapidly in a heart
of two-and-twenty; hopes revive daily; and courage
rallies, in spite of a man. Perhaps, as Esmond thought of
his late despondency and melancholy, and how irremediable
it had seemed to him, as he lay in his prison a few months
back, he was almost mortified in his secret mind at finding
himself so cheerful.

To see with one's own eyes men and countries, is better
than reading all the books of travel in the world : and it
was with extreme delight and exultation that the young
man found himself actually on his grand tour, and in the
view of people and cities which he had read about as a boy.
He beheld war for the first time—the pride, pomp, and
circumstance of it, at least, if not much of the danger. He
saw actually, and with his own eyes, those Spanish cavaliers
and ladies whom he had beheld in imagination in that
immortal story of Cervantes, which had been the delight
of his youthful leisure. 'Tis forty years since Mr. Esmond
witnessed those scenes, but they remain as fresh in his
memory as on the day when first he saw them as a young
man. A cloud, as of grief, that had lowered over him, and
had wrapped the last years of his life in gloom, seemed to
clear away from Esmond during this fortunate voyage and
campaign. His energies seemed to awaken and to expand,
under a cheerful sense of freedom. Was his heart secretly
glad to have escaped from that fond but ignoble bondage
at home ? Was it that the inferiority to which the idea
of his base birth had compelled him, vanished with the
knowledge of that secret, which though, perforce, kept to
himself, was yet enough to cheer and console him ? At
any rate, young Esmond of the army was quite a different
being to the sad little dependant of the kind Castlewood
household, and the melancholy student of Trinity Walks ;

discontented with his fate, and with the vocation into
which that drove him, and thinking, with a secret indignation, that the cassock and bands, and the very sacred office
with which he had once proposed to invest himself, were, in
fact, but marks of a servitude which was to continue all his
life long. For, disguise it as he might to himself, he had
all along felt that to be Castlewood's chaplain was to be
Castlewood's inferior still, and that his life was but to be
a long, hopeless servitude. So, indeed, he was far from
grudging his old friend Tom Tusher's good fortune (as Tom,
no doubt, thought it). Had it been a mitre and Lambeth
which his friends offered him, and not a small living and
a country parsonage, he would have felt as much a slave
in one case as in the other, and was quite happy and thankful to be free.

The bravest man I ever knew in the army, and who had
been present in most of King William's actions, as well as
in the campaigns of the great Duke of Marlborough, could
never be got to tell us of any achievement of his, except
that once Prince Eugene ordered him up a tree to reconnoitre
the enemy, which feat he could not achieve on account of
the horseman's boots he wore ; and on another day that
he was very nearly taken prisoner because of these jack-
boots, which prevented him from running away. The
present narrator shall imitate this laudable reserve, and
doth not intend to dwell upon his military exploits, which
were in truth not very different from those of a thousand
other gentlemen. This first campaign of Mr. Esmond's
lasted but a few days ; and as a score of books have been
written concerning it, it may be dismissed very briefly here.

When our fleet came within view of Cadiz, our commander
sent a boat with a white flag and a couple of officers to the
Governor of Cadiz, Don Scipio de Brancaccio, with a letter
from his grace, in which he hoped that as Don Scipio had
formerly served with the Austrians against the French in
England, 'twas to be hoped that his excellency would now
declare himself against the French king and for the Austrian
in the war between King Philip and King Charles. But his
excellency, Don Scipio, prepared a reply, in which he
announced that, having served his former king with honour
and fidelity, he hoped to exhibit the same loyalty and
devotion towards his present sovereign, King Philip V ;
and by the time this letter was ready, the officers who had

been taken to see the town, and the Alameda, and the theatre, where bull-fights are fought, and the convents, where the admirable works of Don Bartholomew Murillo inspired one of them with a great wonder and delight—such as he had never felt before—concerning this divine art of painting; and these sights over, and a handsome refection and chocolate being served to the English gentlemen, they were accompanied back to their shallop with every courtesy, and were the only two officers of the English army that saw at that time that famous city.

The general tried the power of another proclamation on the Spaniards, in which he announced that we only came in the interest of Spain and King Charles, and for ourselves wanted to make no conquest nor settlement in Spain at all. But all this eloquence was lost upon the Spaniards, it would seem : the Captain-General of Andalusia would no more listen to us than the Governor of Cadiz ; and in reply to his grace's proclamation, the Marquis of Villadarias fired off another, which those who knew the Spanish thought rather the best of the two ; and of this number was Harry Esmond, whose kind Jesuit in old days had instructed him, and now had the honour of translating for his grace these harmless documents of war. There was a hard touch for his grace, and, indeed, for other generals in her Majesty's service, in the concluding sentence of the Don : 'That he and his council had the generous example of their ancestors to follow, who had never yet sought their elevation in the blood or in the flight of their kings. " *Mori pro patria* "* was his device, which the duke might communicate to the princess who governed England.'

Whether the troops were angry at this repartee or no, 'tis certain something put them in a fury ; for, not being able to get possession of Cadiz, our people seized upon Port St. Mary's and sacked it, burning down the merchants' storehouses, getting drunk with the famous wines there, pillaging and robbing quiet houses and convents, murdering and doing worse. And the only blood which Mr. Esmond drew in this shameful campaign, was the knocking down an English sentinel with a half-pike, who was offering insult to a poor trembling nun. Is she going to turn out a beauty ? or a princess ? or perhaps Esmond's mother that he had lost and never seen ? Alas no, it was but a poor wheezy old dropsical woman, with a wart on

her nose. But having been early taught a part of the
Roman religion, he never had the horror of it that some
Protestants have shown, and seem to think to be a part
of ours.

After the pillage and plunder of St. Mary's, and an
assault upon a fort or two, the troops all took shipping, and
finished their expedition, at any rate, more brilliantly
than it had begun. Hearing that the French fleet with
a great treasure was in Vigo Bay, our admirals, Rooke
and Hopson, pursued the enemy thither ; the troops
landed and carried the forts that protected the bay, Hopson
passing the boom first on board his ship the *Torbay*, and
the rest of the ships, English and Dutch, following him.
Twenty ships were burned or taken in the port of Redondilla, and a vast deal more plunder than was ever accounted
for ; but poor men before that expedition were rich afterwards, and so often was it found and remarked that the
Vigo officers came home with pockets full of money, that
the notorious Jack Shafto, who made such a figure at the
coffee-houses and gaming-tables in London, and gave out
that he had been a soldier at Vigo, owned, when he was
about to be hanged, that Bagshot Heath had been *his*
Vigo, and that he only spoke of La Redondilla to turn
away people's eyes from the real place where the booty lay.
Indeed, Hounslow or Vigo—which matters much ? The
latter was a bad business, though Mr. Addison did sing its
praises in Latin. That honest gentleman's muse had an
eye to the main chance ; and I doubt whether she saw
much inspiration in the losing side.

But though Esmond, for his part, got no share of this
fabulous booty, one great prize which he had out of the
campaign was, that excitement of action and change of
scene, which shook off a great deal of his previous melancholy. He learnt at any rate to bear his fate cheerfully.
He brought back a browned face, a heart resolute enough,
and a little pleasant store of knowledge and observation,
from that expedition, which was over with the autumn,
when the troops were back in England again ; and Esmond
giving up his post of secretary to General Lumley,* whose
command was over, and parting with that officer with
many kind expressions of goodwill on the general's side,
had leave to go to London, to see if he could push his
fortunes any way further, and found himself once more

in his dowager aunt's comfortable quarters at Chelsey, and in greater favour than ever with the old lady. He propitiated her with a present of a comb, a fan, and a black mantle, such as the ladies of Cadiz wear, and which my lady viscountess pronounced became her style of beauty mightily. And she was greatly edified at hearing of that story of his rescue of the nun, and felt very little doubt but that her King James's relic, which he had always dutifully worn in his desk, had kept him out of danger, and averted the shot of the enemy. My lady made feasts for him, introduced him to more company, and pushed his fortunes with such enthusiasm and success, that she got a promise of a company for him through the Lady Marlborough's interest, who was graciously pleased to accept of a diamond worth a couple of hundred guineas, which Mr. Esmond was enabled to present to her ladyship through his aunt's bounty, and who promised that she would take charge of Esmond's fortune. He had the honour to make his appearance at the queen's drawing-room occasionally, and to frequent my Lord Marlborough's levees. That great man received the young one with very especial favour, so Esmond's comrades said, and deigned to say that he had received the best reports of Mr. Esmond, both for courage and ability, whereon you may be sure the young gentleman made a profound bow, and expressed himself eager to serve under the most distinguished captain in the world.

Whilst his business was going on thus prosperously, Esmond had his share of pleasure, too, and made his appearance along with other young gentlemen at the coffee-houses, the theatres, and the Mall. He longed to hear of his dear mistress and her family : many a time, in the midst of the gaieties and pleasures of the town, his heart fondly reverted to them ; and often as the young fellows of his society were making merry at the tavern, and calling toasts (as the fashion of that day was) over their wine, Esmond thought of persons—of two fair women, whom he had been used to adore almost, and emptied his glass with a sigh.

By this time the elder viscountess had grown tired again of the younger, and whenever she spoke of my lord's widow, 'twas in terms by no means complimentary towards that poor lady : the younger woman not needing her protection any longer, the elder abused her. Most of the family quarrels that I have seen in life (saving always those arising from money disputes, when a division of twopence-halfpenny will often drive the dearest relatives into war and estrangement), spring out of jealousy and envy. Jack and Tom, born of the same family and to the same fortune, live very cordially together, not until Jack is ruined when Tom deserts him, but until Tom makes a sudden rise in prosperity, which Jack can't forgive. Ten times to one 'tis the unprosperous man that is angry, not the other who is in fault. 'Tis Mrs. Jack, who can only afford a chair, that sickens at Mrs. Tom's new coach-and-six, cries out against her sister's airs, and sets her husband against his brother. 'Tis Jack who sees his brother shaking hands with a lord (with whom Jack would like to exchange snuff-boxes himself), that goes home and tells his wife how poor Tom is spoiled, he fears, and no better than a sneak, parasite, and beggar on horseback. I remember how furious the coffee-house wits were with Dick Steele when he set up his coach, and fine house in Bloomsbury : they began to forgive him when the bailiffs were after him, and abused Mr. Addison for selling Dick's country-house. And yet Dick in the spunging-house, or Dick in the Park, with his four mares and plated harness, was exactly the same gentle, kindly, improvident, jovial Dick Steele : and yet Mr. Addison was perfectly right in getting the money which was his, and not giving up the amount of his just claim, to be spent by Dick upon champagne and fiddlers, laced clothes, fine furniture, and parasites, Jew and Christian, male and female, who clung to him. As, according to the famous maxim of Monsieur de Rochefoucault, ' in our friends' misfortunes there's something secretly pleasant to us ' ;* so, on the other hand, their good fortune is disagreeable. If 'tis hard for a man to bear his own good luck, 'tis harder still for his friends to bear it for him ; and but few of them ordinarily can stand that trial : whereas one of the ' precious uses ' of adversity is, that it is a great reconciler ;* that it brings back averted kindness, disarms animosity, and causes yesterday's enemy to fling his hatred aside, and hold out a hand to the fallen friend of old days. There's pity and love, as well as envy, in the same heart and towards the same person. The rivalry stops when the competitor tumbles ;

and, as I view it, we should look at these agreeable and disagreeable qualities of our humanity humbly alike. They are consequent and natural, and our kindness and meanness both manly.

So you may either read the sentence, that the elder of Esmond's two kinswomen pardoned the younger her beauty, when that had lost somewhat of its freshness, perhaps; and forgot most her grievances against the other, when the subject of them was no longer prosperous and enviable; or we may say more benevolently (but the sum comes to the same figures, worked either way), that Isabella repented of her unkindness towards Rachel, when Rachel was unhappy; and, bestirring herself in behalf of the poor widow and her children, gave them shelter and friendship. The ladies were quite good friends as long as the weaker one needed a protector. Before Esmond went away on his first campaign, his mistress was still on terms of friendship (though a poor little chit, a woman that had evidently no spirit in her, &c.) with the elder Lady Castlewood; and Mistress Beatrix was allowed to be a beauty.

But between the first year of Queen Anne's reign, and the second, sad changes for the worse had taken place in the two younger ladies, at least in the elder's description of them. Rachel, Viscountess Castlewood, had no more face than a dumpling, and Mrs. Beatrix was grown quite coarse, and was losing all her beauty. Little Lord Bland-ford (she never would call him Lord Blandford; his father was Lord Churchill—the king, whom she betrayed, had made him Lord Churchill, and he was Lord Churchill still)—might be making eyes at her; but his mother, that vixen of a Sarah Jennings, would never hear of such a folly. Lady Marlborough had got her to be a maid of honour at Court to the princess, but she would repent of it. The widow Francis (she was but Mrs. Francis Esmond) was a scheming, artful, heartless hussy. She was spoiling her brat of a boy, and she would end by marrying her chaplain.

'What, Tusher?' cried Mr. Esmond, feeling a strange pang of rage and astonishment.

'Yes—Tusher, my maid's son; and who has got all the qualities of his father, the lackey in black, and his accomplished mamma, the waiting-woman,' cries my lady. 'What, do you suppose that a sentimental widow, who will live down in that dingy dungeon of a Castlewood, where she spoils her boy, kills the poor with her drugs, has prayers twice a day and sees nobody but the chaplain— what do you suppose she can do, *mon cousin*, but let the horrid parson, with his great square toes, and hideous little green eyes, make love to her ? *Cela c'est vu, mon cousin.* When I was a girl at Castlewood, all the chaplains fell in love with me—they've nothing else to do.'

My lady went on with more talk of this kind, though, in truth, Esmond had no idea of what she said further, so entirely did her first words occupy his thought. Were they true ? Not all, nor half, nor a tenth part of what the garrulous old woman said, was true. Could this be so ? No ear had Esmond for anything else, though his patroness chattered on for an hour.

Some young gentlemen of the town, with whom Esmond had made acquaintance, had promised to present him to that most charming of actresses, and lively and agreeable of women, Mrs. Bracegirdle, about whom Harry's old adversary Mohun had drawn swords, a few years before my poor lord and he fell out. The famous Mr. Congreve had stamped with his high approval, to the which there was no gainsaying, this delightful person : and she was acting in Dick Steele's comedies, and finally, and for twenty-four hours after beholding her, Mr. Esmond felt himself, or thought himself, to be as violently enamoured of this lovely brunette, as were a thousand other young fellows about the city. To have once seen her was to long to behold her again ; and to be offered the delightful privilege of her acquaintance, was a pleasure the very idea of which set the young lieutenant's heart on fire. A man cannot live with comrades under the tents without finding out that he too is five-and-twenty. A young fellow cannot be cast down by grief and misfortune ever so severe but some night he begins to sleep sound, and some day when dinner-time comes to feel hungry for a beefsteak. Time, youth, and good health, new scenes and the excitement of action and a campaign, had pretty well brought Esmond's mourning to an end ; and his comrades said that Don Dismal, as they called him, was Don Dismal no more. So when a party was made to dine at the ' Rose ', and go to the playhouse afterward, Esmond was as pleased as another to take his share of the bottle and the play.

How was it that the old aunt's news, or it might be

scandal, about Tom Tusher, caused such a strange and sudden excitement in Tom's old playfellow ? Hadn't he sworn a thousand times in his own mind that the lady of Castlewood, who had treated him with such kindness once, and then had left him so cruelly, was, and was to remain henceforth, indifferent to him for ever ? Had his pride and his sense of justice not long since helped him to cure the pain of that desertion—was it even a pain to him now ? Why, but last night as he walked across the fields and meadows to Chelsey from Pall Mall, had he not composed two or three stanzas of a song, celebrating Bracegirdle's brown eyes, and declaring them a thousand times more beautiful than the brightest blue ones that ever languished under the lashes of an insipid fair beauty ! But Tom Tusher ! Tom Tusher, the waiting-woman's son, raising up his little eyes to his mistress ! Tom Tusher presuming to think of Castlewood's widow ! Rage and contempt filled Mr. Harry's heart at the very notion ; the honour of the family, of which he was the chief, made it his duty to prevent so monstrous an alliance, and to chastise the upstart who could dare to think of such an insult to their house. 'Tis true Mr. Esmond often boasted of republican principles, and could remember many fine speeches he had made at college and elsewhere, with *worth* and not *birth* for a text : but Tom Tusher to take the place of the noble Castlewood—faugh ! 'twas as monstrous as King Hamlet's widow taking off her weeds for Claudius. Esmond laughed at all widows, all wives, all women ; and were the banns about to be published, as no doubt they were, that very next Sunday at Walcote Church, Esmond swore that he would be present to shout No ! in the face of the congregation, and to take a private revenge upon the ears of the bridegroom.

Instead of going to dinner then at the ' Rose ' that night, Mr. Esmond bade his servant pack a portmanteau and get horses, and was at Farnham, half-way on the road to Walcote, thirty miles off, before his comrades had got to their supper after the play. He bade his man give no hint to my lady dowager's household of the expedition on which he was going : and as Chelsey was distant from London, the roads bad, and infested by footpads, and Esmond often in the habit, when engaged in a party of pleasure, of lying at a friend's lodging in town, there was no need that his old aunt should be disturbed at his absence —indeed, nothing more delighted the old lady than to fancy that *mon cousin*, the incorrigible young sinner, was abroad boxing the watch, or scouring St. Giles's. When she was not at her books of devotion, she thought Etheridge and Sedley very good reading. She had a hundred pretty stories about Rochester, Harry Jermyn, and Hamilton ; * and if Esmond would but have run away with the wife even of a citizen, 'tis my belief she would have pawned her diamonds (the best of them went to our Lady of Chaillot) * to pay his damages.

My lord's little house of Walcote, which he inhabited before he took his title and occupied the house of Castle-wood—lies about a mile from Winchester, and his widow had returned to Walcote after my lord's death as a place always dear to her, and where her earliest and happiest days had been spent, cheerfuller than Castlewood, which was too large for her straitened means, and giving her, too, the protection of the ex-dean, her father. The young viscount had a year's schooling at the famous college there, with Mr. Tusher as his governor. So much news of them Mr. Esmond had had during the past year from the old viscountess, his own father's widow ; from the young one there had never been a word.

Twice or thrice in his benefactor's lifetime, Esmond had been to Walcote ; and now, taking but a couple of hours' rest only at the inn on the road, he was up again long before daybreak, and made such good speed that he was at Walcote by two o'clock of the day. He rid to the inn of the village, where he alighted and sent a man thence to Mr. Tusher, with a message that a gentleman from London would speak with him on urgent business. The messenger came back to say the doctor was in town, most likely at prayers in the cathedral. My lady viscountess was there too ; she always went to cathedral prayers every day.

The horses belonged to the post-house at Winchester. Esmond mounted again, and rode on to the ' George '; whence he walked, leaving his grumbling domestic at last happy with a dinner, straight to the cathedral. The organ was playing : the winter's day was already growing grey : as he passed under the street-arch into the cathedral-yard, and made his way into the ancient solemn edifice.

CHAPTER VI

THE 29TH DECEMBER

THERE was scarce a score of persons in the Cathedral
besides the dean and some of his clergy, and the choristers,
young and old, that performed the beautiful evening
prayer. But Dr. Tusher was one of the officiants, and read
from the eagle, in an authoritative voice, and a great
black periwig; and in the stalls, still in her black widow's
hood, sat Esmond's dear mistress, her son by her side,
very much grown, and indeed a noble-looking youth, with
his mother's eyes, and his father's curling brown hair, that
fell over his *point de Venise*—a pretty picture such as
Vandyke might have painted. Monsieur Rigaud's portrait*
of my lord viscount, done at Paris afterwards, gives but
a French version of his manly, frank, English face. When
he looked up there were two sapphire beams out of his
eyes, such as no painter's palette has the colour to match,
I think. On this day there was not much chance of seeing
that particular beauty of my young lord's countenance;
for the truth is, he kept his eyes shut for the most part,
and, the anthem being rather long, was asleep.

But the music ceasing, my lord woke up, looking about
him, and his eyes lighting on Mr. Esmond, who was sitting
opposite him, gazing with no small tenderness and melancholy upon two persons who had had so much of his heart
for so many years; Lord Castlewood, with a start, pulled
at his mother's sleeve (her face had scarce been lifted from
her book), and said, 'Look, mother!' so loud, that Esmond
could hear on the other side of the church, and the old
dean on his throned stall. Lady Castlewood looked for
an instant as her son bade her, and held up a warning
finger to Frank; Esmond felt his whole face flush, and
his heart throbbing, as that dear lady beheld him once
more. The rest of the prayers were speedily over: Mr.
Esmond did not hear them; nor did his mistress, very
likely, whose hood went more closely over her face, and
who never lifted her head again until the service was over,
the blessing given, and Mr. Dean, and his procession of
ecclesiastics, out of the inner chapel.

Young Castlewood came clambering over the stalls before the clergy were fairly gone, and, running up to Esmond, eagerly embraced him. 'My dear, dearest old Harry,' he said, 'are you come back? Have you been to the wars? You'll take me with you when you go again? Why didn't you write to us? Come to mother.'

Mr. Esmond could hardly say more than a 'God bless you, my boy', for his heart was very full and grateful at all this tenderness on the lad's part; and he was as much moved at seeing Frank, as he was fearful about that other interview which was now to take place; for he knew not if the widow would reject him as she had done so cruelly a year ago.

'It was kind of you to come back to us, Henry,' Lady Esmond said, 'I thought you might come.'

'We read of the fleet coming to Portsmouth. Why did you not come from Portsmouth?' Frank asked, or my lord viscount, as he now must be called.

Esmond had thought of that too. He would have given one of his eyes so that he might see his dear friends again once more; but believing that his mistress had forbidden him her house, he had obeyed her, and remained at a distance.

'You had but to ask, and you knew I would be here,' he said.

She gave him her hand, her little fair hand: there was only her marriage ring on it. The quarrel was all over. The year of grief and estrangement was passed. They never had been separated. His mistress had never been out of his mind all that time. No, not once. No, not in the prison; nor in the camp; nor on shore before the enemy; nor at sea under the stars of solemn midnight, nor as he watched the glorious rising of the dawn: not even at the table, where he sat carousing with friends, or at the theatre yonder, where he tried to fancy that other eyes were brighter than hers. Brighter eyes there might be, and faces more beautiful, but none so dear—no voice so sweet as that of his beloved mistress, who had been sister, mother, goddess to him during his youth—goddess now no more, for he knew of her weaknesses; and by thought, by suffering, and that experience it brings, was older now than she; but more fondly cherished as woman perhaps than ever she had been adored as divinity.

What is it ? Where lies it ? the secret which makes one little hand the dearest of all ? Whoever can unriddle that mystery ? Here she was, her son by his side, his dear boy. Here she was, weeping and happy. She took his hand in both hers ; he felt her tears. It was a rapture of reconciliation.

' Here comes Squaretoes,' says Frank. ' Here's Tusher.'

Tusher, indeed, now appeared, creaking on his great heels. Mr. Tom had divested himself of his alb or surplice, and came forward habited in his cassock and great black periwig. How had Harry Esmond ever been for a moment jealous of this fellow ?

' Give us thy hand, Tom Tusher,' he said. The chaplain made him a very low and stately bow. ' I am charmed to see Captain Esmond,' says he. ' My lord and I have read the *Reddas incolumem precor*,* and applied it, I am sure, to you. You come back with Gaditanian laurels : when I heard you were bound thither, I wished, I am sure, I was another Septimius. My lord viscount, your lordship remembers *Septimi, Gades aditure mecum ?* '*

' There's an angle of earth that I love better than Gades, Tusher,' says Mr. Esmond. ' 'Tis that one where your reverence hath a parsonage, and where our youth was brought up.'

' A house that has so many sacred recollections to me,' says Mr. Tusher (and Harry remembered how Tom's father used to flog him there)—' a house near to that of my respected patron, my most honoured patroness, must ever be a dear abode to me. But, madam, the verger waits to close the gates on your ladyship.'

' And Harry's coming home to supper. Huzzay ! huzzay !' cries my lord. ' Mother, shall I run home and bid Beatrix put her ribbons on ? Beatrix is a maid of honour, Harry. Such a fine set-up minx ! '

' Your heart was never in the Church, Harry,' the widow said, in her sweet low tone, as they walked away together. (Now, it seemed they had never been parted, and again, as if they had been ages asunder.) ' I always thought you had no vocation that way ; and that 'twas a pity to shut you out from the world. You would but have pined and chafed at Castlewood : and 'tis better you should make a name for yourself. I often said so to my dear lord. How he loved you ! 'Twas my lord that made you stay with us.'

'I asked no better than to stay near you always,' said Mr. Esmond.

'But to go was best, Harry. When the world cannot give peace, you will know where to find it; but one of your strong imagination and eager desires must try the world first before he tires of it. 'Twas not to be thought of, or if it once was, it was only by my selfishness that you should remain as chaplain to a country gentleman and tutor to a little boy. You are of the blood of the Esmonds, kinsman; and that was always wild in youth. Look at Francis. He is but fifteen, and I scarce can keep him in my nest. His talk is all of war and pleasure, and he longs to serve in the next campaign. Perhaps he and the young Lord Churchill shall go the next. Lord Marlborough has been good to us. You know how kind they were in my misfortune. And so was your—your father's widow. No one knows how good the world is, till grief comes to try us. 'Tis through my Lady Marlborough's goodness that Beatrix hath her place at Court; and Frank is under my Lord Chamberlain. And the dowager lady, your father's widow, has promised to provide for you—has she not?'

Esmond said, 'Yes. As far as present favour went, Lady Castlewood was very good to him. And should her mind change,' he added gaily, 'as ladies' minds will, I am strong enough to bear my own burden, and make my way somehow. Not by the sword very likely. Thousands have a better genius for that than I, but there are many ways in which a young man of good parts and education can get on in the world; and I am pretty sure, one way or other, of promotion!' Indeed, he had found patrons already in the army, and amongst persons very able to serve him, too; and told his mistress of the flattering aspect of fortune. They walked as though they had never been parted, slowly, with the grey twilight closing round them.

'And now we are drawing near to home,' she continued. 'I knew you would come, Harry, if—if it was but to forgive me for having spoken unjustly to you after that horrid—horrid misfortune. I was half frantic with grief then when I saw you. And I know now—they have told me. That wretch, whose name I can never mention, even has said it: how you tried to avert the quarrel, and would have taken it on yourself, my poor child: but it was God's will that I should be punished, and that my dear lord should fall.'

'He gave me his blessing on his death-bed,' Esmond said. 'Thank God for that legacy!'

'Amen, amen! dear Henry,' says the lady, pressing his arm. 'I knew it. Mr. Atterbury, of St. Bride's, who was called to him, told me so. And I thanked God, too, and in my prayers ever since remembered it.'

'You had spared me many a bitter night, had you told me sooner,' Mr. Esmond said.

'I know it, I know it,' she answered, in a tone of such sweet humility, as made Esmond repent that he should ever have dared to reproach her. 'I know how wicked my heart has been; and I have suffered too, my dear. I confessed to Mr. Atterbury—I must not tell any more. He—I said I would not write to you or go to you—and it was better even that, having parted, we should part. But I knew you would come back—I own that. That is no one's fault. And to-day, Henry, in the anthem, when they sang it, "When the Lord turned the captivity of Zion, we were like them that dream", I thought, yes, like them that dream—them that dream. And then it went, "They that sow in tears shall reap in joy; and he that goeth forth and weepeth, shall doubtless come home again with rejoicing, bringing his sheaves with him";* I looked up from the book, and saw you. I was not surprised when I saw you. I knew you would come, my dear, and saw the gold sunshine round your head.'

She smiled an almost wild smile as she looked up at him. The moon was up by this time, glittering keen in the frosty sky. He could see, for the first time now clearly, her sweet careworn face.

'Do you know what day it is?' she continued. 'It is the 29th of December—it is your birthday! But last year we did not drink it—no, no. My lord was cold, and my Harry was likely to die; and my brain was in a fever; and we had no wine. But now—now you are come again, bringing your sheaves with you, my dear.' She burst into a wild flood of weeping as she spoke; she laughed and sobbed on the young man's heart, crying out wildly, 'bringing your sheaves with you—your sheaves with you!'

As he had sometimes felt, gazing up from the deck at midnight into the boundless starlit depths overhead, in a rapture of devout wonder at that endless brightness and beauty—in some such a way as now, the depth of this pure devotion (which was, for the first time, revealed to him quite) smote upon him, and filled his heart with thanksgiving. Gracious God, who was he, weak and friendless creature, that such a love should be poured out upon him ? Not in vain, not in vain has he lived—hard and thankless should he be to think so—that has such a treasure given him. What is ambition compared to that ? but selfish vanity. To be rich, to be famous ? What do these profit a year hence, when other names sound louder than yours, when you lie hidden away under the ground, along with the idle titles engraven on your coffin ? But only true love lives after you—follows your memory with secret blessing—or precedes you, and intercedes for you. *Non omnis moriar*—if dying, I yet live in a tender heart or two ; nor am lost and hopeless living, if a sainted departed soul still loves and prays for me.

' If—if 'tis so, dear lady,' Mr. Esmond said, ' why should I ever leave you ? If God hath given me this great boon— and near or far from me, as I know now—the heart of my dearest mistress follows me ; let me have that blessing near me, nor ever part with it till life separate us. Come away— leave this Europe, this place which has so many sad recollections for you. Begin a new life in a new world. My good lord often talked of visiting that land in Virginia which King Charles gave us—gave his ancestor. Frank will give us that. No man there will ask if there is a blot on my name, or inquire in the woods what my title is.'

' And my children—and my duty—and my good father ? —Henry,' she broke out. ' He has none but me now ; for soon my sister will leave him, and the old man will be alone. He has conformed since the new queen's reign ; and here in Winchester, where they love him, they have found a church for him. When the children leave me, I will stay with him. I cannot follow them into the great world, where their way lies—it scares me. They will come and visit me ; and you will, sometimes, Henry—yes, sometimes, as now, in the holy Advent season, when I have seen and blessed you once more.'

' I would leave all to follow you,' said Mr. Esmond ; ' and can you not be as generous for me, dear lady ? '

' Hush, boy !' she said, and it was with a mother's sweet

plaintive tone and look that she spoke. 'The world is beginning for you. For me, I have been so weak and sinful that I must leave it, and pray out an expiation, dear Henry. Had we houses of religion as there were once, and many divines of our Church would have them again, I often think I would retire to one and pass my life in penance. But I would love you still—yes, there is no sin in such a love as mine now; and my dear lord in heaven may see my heart; and knows the tears that have washed my sin away—and now—now my duty is here, by my children whilst they need me, and by my poor old father, and——'

'And not by me?' Henry said.

'Hush!' she said again, and raised her hand up to his lip. 'I have been your nurse. You could not see me, Harry, when you were in the small-pox, and I came and sat by you. Ah! I prayed that I might die, but it would have been in sin, Henry. Oh, it is horrid to look back to that time. It is over now and past, and it has been forgiven me. When you need me again I will come ever so far. When your heart is wounded, then come to me, my dear. Be silent! let me say all. You never loved me, dear Henry—no, you do not now, and I thank Heaven for it. I used to watch you, and knew by a thousand signs that it was so. Do you remember how glad you were to go away to college? 'Twas I sent you. I told my papa that, and Mr. Atterbury too, when I spoke to him in London. And they both gave me absolution—both—and they are godly men, having authority to bind and to loose. And they forgave me, as my dear lord forgave me before he went to heaven.'

'I think the angels are not all in heaven,' Mr. Esmond said. And as a brother folds a sister to his heart; and as a mother cleaves to her son's breast—so for a few moments Esmond's beloved mistress came to him and blessed him.

CHAPTER VII

I AM MADE WELCOME AT WALCOTE

As they came up to the house at Walcote, the windows
from within were lighted up with friendly welcome ; the
supper-table was spread in the oak-parlour ; it seemed as if
forgiveness and love were awaiting the returning prodigal.
Two or three familiar faces of domestics were on the look-
out at the porch—the old housekeeper was there, and young
Lockwood from Castlewood in my lord's livery of tawny
and blue. His dear mistress pressed his arm as they passed
into the hall. Her eyes beamed out on him with affection
indescribable. 'Welcome,' was all she said : as she looked
up, putting back her fair curls and black hood. A sweet
rosy smile blushed on her face : Harry thought he had
never seen her look so charming. Her face was lighted
with a joy that was brighter than beauty—she took a hand
of her son who was in the hall waiting his mother—she
did not quit Esmond's arm.

'Welcome, Harry !' my young lord echoed after her.
'Here, we are all come to say so. Here's old Pincot,
hasn't she grown handsome ? ' and Pincot, who was older,
and no handsomer than usual, made a curtsy to the captain,
as she called Esmond, and told my lord to 'Have done,
now '.

'And here's Jack Lockwood. He'll make a famous
grenadier, Jack ; and so shall I ; we'll both 'list under you,
cousin. As soon as I am seventeen, I go to the army—
every gentleman goes to the army. Look ! who comes
here—ho, ho ! ' he burst into a laugh. ' 'Tis Mistress Trix,
with a new ribbon ; I knew she would put one on as soon
as she heard a captain was coming to supper.'

This laughing colloquy took place in the hall of Walcote
House : in the midst of which is a staircase that leads from
an open gallery, where are the doors of the sleeping-cham-
bers : and from one of these, a wax candle in her hand,
and illuminating her, came Mistress Beatrix—the light
falling indeed upon the scarlet ribbon which she wore, and
upon the most brilliant white neck in the world.

Esmond had left a child and found a woman, grown

beyond the common height; and arrived at such a dazzling completeness of beauty, that his eyes might well show surprise and delight at beholding her. In hers there was a brightness so lustrous and melting, that I have seen a whole assembly follow her as if by an attraction irresistible: and that night the great duke was at the playhouse after Ramillies, every soul turned and looked (she chanced to enter at the opposite side of the theatre at the same moment) at her, and not at him. She was a brown beauty: that is, her eyes, hair, and eyebrows and eyelashes, were dark: her hair curling with rich undulations, and waving over her shoulders; but her complexion was as dazzling white as snow in sunshine; except her cheeks, which were a bright red, and her lips, which were of a still deeper crimson. Her mouth and chin, they said, were too large and full, and so they might be for a goddess in marble, but not for a woman whose eyes were fire, whose look was love, whose voice was the sweetest low song, whose shape was perfect symmetry, health, decision, activity, whose foot as it planted itself on the ground, was firm but flexible, and whose motion, whether rapid or slow, was always perfect grace —agile as a nymph, lofty as a queen—now melting, now imperious, now sarcastic, there was no single movement of hers but was beautiful. As he thinks of her, he who writes feels young again, and remembers a paragon.

So she came holding her dress with one fair rounded arm, and her taper before her, tripping down the stair to greet Esmond.

'She hath put on her scarlet stockings and white shoes,' says my lord, still laughing. 'Oh, my fine mistress! is this the way you set your cap at the captain!' She approached, shining smiles upon Esmond, who could look at nothing but her eyes. She advanced holding forward her head, as if she would have him kiss her as he used to do when she was a child.

'Stop,' she said, 'I am grown too big! Welcome, cousin Harry,' and she made him an arch curtsy, sweeping down to the ground almost, with the most gracious bend, looking up the while with the brightest eyes and sweetest smile. Love seemed to radiate from her. Harry eyed her with such a rapture as the first lover is described as having by Milton.*

'N'est-ce pas?' says my lady, in a low, sweet voice, still hanging on his arm.

Esmond turned round with a start and a blush, as he
met his mistress's clear eyes. He had forgotten her, wrapt
in admiration of the *filia pulcrior*.

' Right foot forward, toe turned out, so : now drop the
curtsy, and show the red stockings, Trix. They've silver
clocks, Harry. The dowager sent 'em. She went to put
'em on,' cries my lord.

' Hush, you stupid child ! ' says miss, smothering her
brother with kisses ; and then she must come and kiss her
mamma, looking all the while at Harry, over his mistress's
shoulder. And if she did not kiss him, she gave him both
her hands, and then took one of his in both hands, and said,
' Oh, Harry, we're so, *so* glad you're come ! '

' There are woodcocks for supper,' says my lord : ' huzzay ! It was such a hungry sermon.'

' And it is the 29th of December ; and our Harry has
come home.'

' Huzzay, old Pincot ! ' again says my lord ; and my
dear lady's lips looked as if they were trembling with
a prayer. She would have Harry lead in Beatrix to the
supper-room, going herself with my young lord viscount ;
and to this party came Tom Tusher directly, whom four
at least out of the company of five wished away. Away
he went, however, as soon as the sweetmeats were put
down, and then, by the great crackling fire, his mistress
or Beatrix, with her blushing graces, filling his glass for him,
Harry told the story of his campaign, and passed the most
delightful night his life had ever known. The sun was up
long ere he was, so deep, sweet, and refreshing was his
slumber. He woke as if angels had been watching at his
bed all night. I dare say one that was as pure and loving
as an angel had blest his sleep with her prayers.

Next morning the chaplain read prayers to the little
household at Walcote, as the custom was ; Esmond thought
Mistress Beatrix did not listen to Tusher's exhortation
much : her eyes were wandering everywhere during the
service, at least whenever he looked up he met them.
Perhaps he also was not very attentive to his reverence the
chaplain. ' This might have been my life,' he was thinking ;
' this might have been my duty from now till old age.
Well, were it not a pleasant one to be with these dear
friends and part from 'em no more ? Until—until the
destined lover comes and takes away pretty Beatrix '—

and the best part of Tom Tusher's exposition, which may have been very learned and eloquent, was quite lost to poor Harry by this vision of the destined lover, who put the preacher out.

All the while of the prayers, Beatrix knelt a little way before Harry Esmond. The red stockings were changed for a pair of grey, and black shoes, in which her feet looked to the full as pretty. All the roses of spring could not vie with the brightness of her complexion ; Esmond thought he had never seen anything like the sunny lustre of her eyes. My lady viscountess looked fatigued, as if with watching, and her face was pale.

Miss Beatrix remarked these signs of indisposition in her mother, and deplored them. ' I am an old woman,' says my lady, with a kind smile ; ' I cannot hope to look as young as you do, my dear.'

' She'll never look as good as you do if she lives till she's a hundred,' says my lord, taking his mother by the waist, and kissing her hand.

' Do I look very wicked, cousin ? ' says Beatrix, turning full round on Esmond, with her pretty face so close under his chin, that the soft perfumed hair touched it. She laid her finger-tips on his sleeve as she spoke ; and he put his other hand over hers.

' I'm like your looking-glass,' says he, ' and that can't flatter you.'

' He means that you are always looking at him, my dear,' says her mother, archly. Beatrix ran away from Esmond at this, and flew to her mamma, whom she kissed, stopping my lady's mouth with her pretty hand.

' And Harry is very good to look at,' says my lady, with her fond eyes regarding the young man.

' If 'tis good to see a happy face,' says he, ' you see that.' My lady said ' Amen ', with a sigh ; and Harry thought the memory of her dead lord rose up and rebuked her back again into sadness ; for her face lost the smile, and resumed its look of melancholy.

' Why, Harry, how fine we look in our scarlet and silver, and our black periwig,' cries my lord. ' Mother, I am tired of my own hair. When shall I have a peruke ? Where did you get your steenkirk, Harry ? '

' It's some of my lady dowager's lace,' says Harry ; ' she gave me this and a number of other fine things.'

'My lady dowager isn't such a bad woman,' my lord continued.

'She's not so—so red as she's painted,' says Miss Beatrix. Her brother broke into a laugh. 'I'll tell her you said so; by the lord, Trix, I will,' he cries out.

'She'll know that you hadn't the wit to say it, my lord,' says Miss Beatrix.

'We won't quarrel the first day Harry's here, will we, mother?' said the young lord. 'We'll see if we can get on to the new year without a fight. Have some of this Christmas pie? and here comes the tankard; no, it's Pincot with the tea.'

'Will the captain choose a dish?' asks Mistress Beatrix.

'I say, Harry,' my lord goes on, 'I'll show thee my horses after breakfast; and we'll go a bird-netting to-night, and on Monday there's a cock-match at Winchester—do you love cock-fighting, Harry?—between the gentlemen of Sussex and the gentlemen of Hampshire, at ten pound the battle, and fifty pound the odd battle to show one-and-twenty cocks.'

'And what will you do, Beatrix, to amuse our kinsman?' asks my lady.

'I'll listen to him,' says Beatrix; 'I am sure he has a hundred things to tell us. And I'm jealous already of the Spanish ladies. Was that a beautiful nun at Cadiz that you rescued from the soldiers? Your man talked of it last night in the kitchen, and Mrs. Betty told me this morning as she combed my hair. And he says you must be in love, for you sat on deck all night, and scribbled verses all day in your table-book.' Harry thought if he had wanted a subject for verses yesterday, to-day he had found one: and not all the Lindamiras and Ardelias of the poets were half so beautiful as this young creature; but he did not say so, though some one did for him.

This was his dear lady who, after the meal was over, and the young people were gone, began talking of her children with Mr. Esmond, and of the characters of one and the other, and of her hopes and fears for both of them. ''Tis not while they are at home,' she said, 'and in their mother's nest, I fear for them—'tis when they are gone into the world, whither I shall not be able to follow them. Beatrix will begin her service next year. You may have heard a rumour about—about my Lord Blandford. They were both chil-

dren ; and it is but idle talk. I know my kinswoman would
never let him make such a poor marriage as our Beatrix
would be. There's scarce a princess in Europe that she
thinks is good enough for him or for her ambition.'

'There's not a princess in Europe to compare with her,'
says Esmond.

'In beauty ? No, perhaps not,' answered my lady.
'She is most beautiful, isn't she ? 'Tis not a mother's
partiality that deceives me. I marked you yesterday when
she came down the stair : and read it in your face. We
look when you don't fancy us looking, and see better than
you think, dear Harry : and just now when they spoke
about your poems—you writ pretty lines when you were
but a boy—you thought Beatrix was a pretty subject for
verse, did not you, Harry ? ' (The gentleman could only
blush for a reply.) 'And so she is—nor are you the first
her pretty face has captivated. 'Tis quickly done. Such
a pair of bright eyes as hers learn their power very soon,
and use it very early.' And, looking at him keenly with
hers, the fair widow left him.

And so it is—a pair of bright eyes with a dozen glances
suffice to subdue a man ; to enslave him, and inflame him ;
to make him even forget ; they dazzle him so that the past
becomes straightway dim to him ; and he so prizes them
that he would give all his life to possess 'em. What is the
fond love of dearest friends compared to this treasure ?
Is memory as strong as expectancy ? fruition, as hunger ?
gratitude, as desire ? I have looked at royal diamonds in
the jewel-rooms in Europe, and thought how wars have been
made about 'em : Mogul sovereigns deposed and strangled
for them, or ransomed with them : millions expended to
buy them ; and daring lives lost in digging out the little
shining toys that I value no more than the button in my
hat. And so there are other glittering baubles (of rare
water too) for which men have been set to kill and quarrel
ever since mankind began ; and which last but for a score
of years, when their sparkle is over. Where are those
jewels now that beamed under Cleopatra's forehead, or
shone in the sockets of Helen ?

The second day after Esmond's coming to Walcote, Tom
Tusher had leave to take a holiday, and went off in his very
best gown and bands to court the young woman whom his
reverence desired to marry, and who was not a viscount's

widow, as it turned out, but a brewer's relict at South-ampton, with a couple of thousand pounds to her fortune : for honest Tom's heart was under such excellent control, that Venus herself without a portion would never have caused it to flutter. So he rode away on his heavy-paced gelding to pursue his jog-trot loves, leaving Esmond to the society of his dear mistress and her daughter, and with his young lord for a companion, who was charmed not only to see an old friend, but to have the tutor and his Latin books put out of the way.

The boy talked of things and people, and not a little about himself, in his frank artless way. 'Twas easy to see that he and his sister had the better of their fond mother, for the first place in whose affections, though they fought constantly, and though the kind lady persisted that she loved both equally, 'twas not difficult to understand that Frank was his mother's darling and favourite. He ruled the whole household (always excepting rebellious Beatrix) not less now than when he was a child marshalling the village boys in playing at soldiers, and caning them lustily too, like the sturdiest corporal. As for Tom Tusher, his reverence treated the young lord with that politeness and deference which he always showed for a great man, what-ever his age or his stature was. Indeed, with respect to this young one, it was impossible not to love him, so frank and winning were his manners, his beauty, his gaiety, the ring of his laughter, and the delightful tone of his voice. Wherever he went, he charmed and domineered. I think his old grandfather, the dean, and the grim old housekeeper, Mrs. Pincot, were as much his slaves as his mother was : and as for Esmond, he found himself presently submitting to a certain fascination the boy had, and slaving it like the rest of the family. The pleasure which he had in Frank's mere company and converse exceeded that which he ever enjoyed in the society of any other man, however delightful in talk, or famous for wit. His presence brought sunshine into a room, his laugh, his prattle, his noble beauty and brightness of look cheered and charmed indescribably. At the least tale of sorrow, his hands were in his purse, and he was eager with sympathy and bounty. The way in which women loved and petted him, when, a year or two after-wards, he came upon the world, yet a mere boy, and the follies which they did for him (as indeed he for them), recalled the career of Rochester, and outdid the successes of Grammont.* His very creditors loved him ; and the hardest usurers, and some of the rigid prudes of the other sex too, could deny him nothing. He was no more witty than another man, but what he said, he said and looked as no man else could say or look it. I have seen the women at the comedy at Bruxelles crowd round him in the lobby : and as he sat on the stage more people looked at him than at the actors, and watched him ; and I remember at Ramillies, when he was hit and fell, a great big red-haired Scotch sergeant flung his halbert down, burst out a-crying like a woman, seizing him up as if he had been an infant, and carrying him out of the fire. This brother and sister were the most beautiful couple ever seen ; though after he winged away from the maternal nest this pair were seldom together.

Sitting at dinner two days after Esmond's arrival (it was the last day of the year), and so happy a one to Harry Esmond, that to enjoy it was quite worth all the previous pain which he had endured and forgot : my young lord, filling a bumper, and bidding Harry take another, drank to his sister, saluting her under the title of ' marchioness'.

' Marchioness ! ' says Harry, not without a pang of wonder, for he was curious and jealous already.

' Nonsense, my lord,' says Beatrix, with a toss of her head. My lady viscountess looked up for a moment at Esmond, and cast her eyes down.

' The Marchioness of Blandford,' says Frank, ' don't you know—hath not Rouge Dragon told you ? ' (My lord used to call the dowager at Chelsey by this and other names.) ' Blandford has a lock of her hair : the duchess found him on his knees to Mistress 'Trix, and boxed his ears, and said Dr. Hare* should whip him.'

' I wish Mr. Tusher would whip you too,' says Beatrix.

My lady only said : ' I hope you will tell none of these silly stories elsewhere than at home, Francis.'

' 'Tis true, on my word,' continues Frank : ' look at Harry scowling, mother, and see how Beatrix blushes as red as the silver-clocked stockings.'

' I think we had best leave the gentlemen to their wine and their talk,' says Mistress Beatrix, rising up with the air of a young queen, tossing her rustling, flowing draperies about her, and quitting the room, followed by her mother.

Lady Castlewood again looked at Esmond, as she stooped down and kissed Frank. ' Do not tell those silly stories, child,' she said : ' do not drink much wine, sir ; Harry never loved to drink wine.' And she went away, too, in her black robes, looking back on the young man with her fair, fond face.

' Egad ! it's true,' says Frank, sipping his wine with the air of a lord. ' What think you of this Lisbon—real Collares ? 'Tis better than your heady port : we got it out of one of the Spanish ships that came from Vigo last year : my mother bought it at Southampton, as the ship was lying there—the *Rose*, Captain Hawkins.'

' Why, I came home in that ship,' says Harry.

' And it brought home a good fellow and good wine,' says my lord. ' I say, Harry, I wish thou hadst not that cursed bar sinister.'

' And why not the bar sinister ? ' asks the other.

' Suppose I go to the army and am killed—every gentle-man goes to the army—who is to take care of the women ? 'Trix will never stop at home ; mother's in love with you,— yes, I think mother's in love with you. She was always praising you, and always talking about you ; and when she went to Southampton, to see the ship, I found her out. But you see it is impossible : we are of the oldest blood in England ; we came in with the Conqueror ; we were only baronets,—but what then ? we were forced · into that. James the First forced our great-grandfather. We are above titles ; we old English gentry don't want 'em ; the queen can make a duke any day. Look at Blandford's father, Duke Churchill, and Duchess Jennings, what were they, Harry ? Damn it, sir, what are they, to turn up their noses at us ? Where were they, when our ancestor rode with King Henry at Agincourt, and filled up the French king's cup after Poictiers ? 'Fore George, sir, why shouldn't Blandford marry Beatrix ? By G—! he *shall* marry Beatrix, or tell me the reason why. We'll marry with the best blood of England, and none but the best blood of England. You are an Esmond, and you can't help your birth, my boy. Let's have another bottle. What ! no more ? I've drunk three parts of this myself. I had many a night with my father ; you stood to him like a man, Harry. You backed your blood ; you can't help your mis-fortune, you know,—no man can help that.'

The elder said he would go in to his mistress's tea-table. The young lad, with a heightened colour and voice, began singing a snatch of a song, and marched out of the room. Esmond heard him presently calling his dogs about him, and cheering and talking to them; and by a hundred of his looks and gestures, tricks of voice and gait, was reminded of the dead lord, Frank's father.

And so, the Sylvester Night passed away; the family parted long before midnight, Lady Castlewood remembering, no doubt, former New-Year's Eves, when healths were drunk, and laughter went round in the company of him to whom years, past, and present, and future, were to be as one; and so cared not to sit with her children and hear the cathedral bells ringing the birth of the year 1703. Esmond heard the chimes as he sat in his own chamber, ruminating by the blazing fire there, and listened to the last notes of them, looking out from his window towards the city, and the great grey towers of the cathedral lying under the frosty sky, with the keen stars shining above.

The sight of these brilliant orbs no doubt made him think of other luminaries. 'And so her eyes have already done execution,' thought Esmond—'on whom?—who can tell me?' Luckily his kinsman was by, and Esmond knew he would have no difficulty in finding out Mistress Beatrix's history from the simple talk of the boy.

CHAPTER VIII

FAMILY TALK

WHAT Harry admired and submitted to in the pretty lad, his kinsman, was (for why should he resist it?) the calmness of patronage which my young lord assumed, as if to command was his undoubted right, and all the world (below his degree) ought to bow down to Viscount Castlewood.

'I know my place, Harry,' he said. 'I'm not proud— the boys at Winchester College say I'm proud: but I'm not proud. I am simply Francis James Viscount Castlewood in the peerage of Ireland. I might have been (do you know that?) Francis James Marquis and Earl of Esmond in that of England. The late lord refused the title which was

offered to him by my godfather, his late Majesty. You
should know that—you are of our family, you know—you
cannot help your bar sinister, Harry, my dear fellow ; and
you belong to one of the best families in England, in spite of
that ; and you stood by my father, and by G— ! I'll stand
by you. You shall never want a friend, Harry, while
Francis James Viscount Castlewood has a shilling. It's
now 1703—I shall come of age in 1709. I shall go back
to Castlewood ; I shall live at Castlewood ; I shall build
up the house. My property will be pretty well restored
by then. The late viscount mismanaged my property, and
left it in a very bad state. My mother is living close, as
you see, and keeps me in a way hardly befitting a peer of
these realms ; for I have but a pair of horses, a governor,
and a man that is valet and groom. But when I am of
age, these things will be set right, Harry. Our house will
be as it should be. You'll always come to Castlewood,
won't you ? You shall always have your two rooms in
the court kept for you ; and if anybody slights you, d——
them ! let them have a care of *me*. I shall marry early—
'Trix will be a duchess by that time, most likely ; for
a cannon-ball may knock over his grace any day, you
know.'

'How ? ' says Harry.

'Hush, my dear ! ' says my lord viscount. ' You are of
the family—you are faithful to us, by George, and I tell
you everything. Blandford will marry her—or —— ' and
here he put his little hand on his sword—' you understand
the rest. Blandford knows which of us two is the best
weapon. At small-sword, or back-sword, or sword and
dagger, if he likes : I can beat him. I have tried him,
Harry ; and begad, he knows I am a man not to be trifled
with.'

'But you do not mean,' says Harry, concealing his
laughter, but not his wonder, ' that you can force my Lord
Blandford, the son of the first man of this kingdom, to
marry your sister at sword's point ? '

'I mean to say that we are cousins by the mother's side,
though that's nothing to boast of. I mean to say that an
Esmond is as good as a Churchill ; and when the king comes
back, the Marquis of Esmond's sister may be a match for
any nobleman's daughter in the kingdom. There are but
two marquises in all England, William Herbert, Marquis of

Powis, and Francis James, Marquis of Esmond; and hark you, Harry, now swear you'll never mention this. Give me your honour as a gentleman, for you *are* a gentleman, though you are a——'

'Well, well,' says Harry, a little impatient.

'Well, then, when after my late viscount's misfortune, my mother went up with us to London, to ask for justice against you all (as for Mohun, I'll have his blood, as sure as my name is Francis Viscount Esmond), we went to stay with our cousin my Lady Marlborough, with whom we had quarrelled for ever so long. But when misfortune came, she stood by her blood:—so did the dowager viscountess stand by her blood,—so did you. Well, sir, whilst my mother was petitioning the late Prince of Orange—for I will never call him king—and while you were in prison, we lived at my Lord Marlborough's house, who was only a little there, being away with the army in Holland. And then ... I say, Harry, you won't tell, now?'

Harry again made a vow of secrecy.

'Well, there used to be all sorts of fun, you know: my Lady Marlborough was very fond of us, and she said I was to be her page; and she got 'Trix to be a maid of honour, and while she was up in her room crying, we used to be always having fun, you know; and the duchess used to kiss me, and so did her daughters, and Blandford fell tremendous in love with 'Trix, and she liked him; and one day he—he kissed her behind a door—he did though,—and the duchess caught him, and she banged such a box of the ear both to 'Trix and Blandford—you should have seen it! And then she said that we must leave directly, and abused my mamma, who was cognizant of the business; but she wasn't—never thinking about anything but father. And so we came down to Walcote. Blandford being locked up, and not allowed to see 'Trix. But *I* got at him. I climbed along the gutter, and in through the window, where he was crying.

' "Marquis," says I, when he had opened it and helped me in, " you know I wear a sword," for I had brought it.

' "Oh, viscount," says he—" oh, my dearest Frank! " and he threw himself into my arms and burst out a-crying. " I do love Mistress Beatrix so, that I shall die if I don't have her."

' " My dear Blandford," says I, " you are young to think

of marrying;" for he was but fifteen, and a young fellow of that age can scarce do so, you know.

' "But I'll wait twenty years, if she'll have me," says he. "I'll never marry—no never, never, never, marry anybody but her. No, not a princess, though they would have me do it ever so. If Beatrix will wait for me, her Blandford swears he will be faithful." And he wrote a paper (it wasn't spelt right, for he wrote : "I'm ready to *sine with my blode*", which you know, Harry, isn't the way of spelling it), and vowing that he would marry none other but the Honourable Mistress Gertrude Beatrix Esmond, only sister of his dearest friend Francis James, fourth Viscount Esmond. And so I gave him a locket of her hair.'

' A locket of her hair !' cries Esmond.

' Yes. 'Trix gave me one after the fight with the duchess that very day. I am sure I didn't want it ; and so I gave it him, and we kissed at parting, and said—" Good-bye, brother." And I got back through the gutter ; and we set off home that very evening. And he went to King's College, in Cambridge, and *I'm* going to Cambridge soon ; and if he doesn't stand to his promise (for he's only wrote once),—he knows I wear a sword, Harry. Come along, and let's go see the cocking-match at Winchester.

' . . . . But I say,' he added laughing, after a pause, ' I don't think 'Trix will break her heart about him. Law bless you ! Whenever she sees a man, she makes eyes at him ; and young Sir Wilmot Crawley of Queen's Crawley, and Anthony Henley of Alresford, were at swords drawn about her, at the Winchester Assembly, a month ago.'

That night Mr. Harry's sleep was by no means so pleasant or sweet as it had been on the first two evenings after his arrival at Walcote. ' So the bright eyes have been already shining on another,' thought he, ' and the pretty lips, or the cheeks at any rate, have begun the work which they were made for. Here's a girl not sixteen, and one young gentleman is already whimpering over a lock of her hair, and two country squires are ready to cut each other's throats that they may have the honour of a dance with her. What a fool am I to be dallying about this passion, and singeing my wings in this foolish flame. Wings !—why not say crutches ? There is but eight years' difference between us, to be sure ; but in life I am thirty years older. How could I ever hope to please such a sweet creature as that, with my rough ways and glum face ? Say that I have merit ever so much, and won myself a name, could she ever listen to me? She must be my lady marchioness, and I remain a nameless bastard. O my master, my master ! ' (here he fell to thinking with a passionate grief of the vow which he had made to his poor dying lord) ; ' O my mistress, dearest and kindest, will you be contented with the sacrifice which the poor orphan makes for you, whom you love, and who so loves you ? '

And then came a fiercer pang of temptation. ' A word from me,' Harry thought, ' a syllable of explanation, and all this might be changed ; but no, I swore it over the dying bed of my benefactor. For the sake of him and his ; for the sacred love and kindness of old days ; I gave my promise to him, and may kind Heaven enable me to keep my vow ! '

The next day, although Esmond gave no sign of what was going on in his mind, but strove to be more than ordinarily gay and cheerful when he met his friends at the morning meal, his dear mistress, whose clear eyes it seemed no emotion of his could escape, perceived that something troubled him, for she looked anxiously towards him more than once during the breakfast, and when he went up to his chamber afterwards she presently followed him, and knocked at his door.

As she entered, no doubt the whole story was clear to her at once, for she found our young gentleman packing his valise, pursuant to the resolution which he had come to over-night of making a brisk retreat out of this temptation.

She closed the door very carefully behind her, and then leant against it, very pale, her hands folded before her, looking at the young man, who was kneeling over his work of packing. ' Are you going so soon ? ' she said.

He rose up from his knees, blushing, perhaps, to be so discovered, in the very act, as it were, and took one of her fair little hands—it was that which had her marriage ring on—and kissed it.

' It is best that it should be so, dearest lady,' he said.

' I knew you were going, at breakfast. I—I thought you might stay. What has happened ? Why can't you remain longer with us ? What has Frank told you—you were talking together late last night ? '

' I had but three days' leave from Chelsea,' Esmond said,

as gaily as he could. ' My aunt—she lets me call her aunt—
is my mistress now; I owe her my lieutenancy and my
laced coat. She has taken me into high favour; and my
new general is to dine at Chelsea to-morrow—General
Lumley, madam—who has appointed me his aide de camp,
and on whom I must have the honour of waiting. See,
here is a letter from the dowager; the post brought it last
night; and I would not speak of it, for fear of disturbing
our last merry meeting.'

My lady glanced at the letter, and put it down with
a smile that was somewhat contemptuous. ' I have no
need to read the letter,' says she—(indeed, 'twas as well
she did not; for the Chelsea missive, in the poor dowager's
usual French jargon, permitted him a longer holiday than
he said. ' *Je vous donne*,' quoth her ladyship, ' *oui jour,
pour vous fatigay parfaictement de vos parens fatigans*')—
' I have no need to read the letter,' says she. ' What was
it Frank told you last night ? '

' He told me little I did not know,' Mr. Esmond answered.
' But I have thought of that little, and here's the result;
I have no right to the name I bear, dear lady; and it is
only by your sufferance that I am allowed to keep it. If
I thought for an hour of what has perhaps crossed your
mind too—— '

' Yes, I did, Harry,' said she; 'I thought of it; and think
of it. I would sooner call you my son than the greatest
prince in Europe—yes, than the greatest prince. For who
is there so good and so brave, and who would love her as
you would ? But there are reasons a mother can't tell.'

' I know them,' said Mr. Esmond, interrupting her with
a smile.—' I know there's Sir Wilmot Crawley of Queen's
Crawley, and Mr. Anthony Henley of the Grange, and my
Lord Marquis of Blandford, that seems to be the favoured
suitor. You shall ask me to wear my lady marchioness's
favours and to dance at her ladyship's wedding.'

' Oh, Harry, Harry, it is none of these follies that
frighten me,' cried out Lady Castlewood. ' Lord Churchill
is but a child, his outbreak about Beatrix was a mere boyish
folly. His parents would rather see him buried than
married to one below him in rank. And do you think that
I would stoop to sue for a husband for Francis Esmond's
daughter; or submit to have my girl smuggled into that
proud family to cause a quarrel between son and parents,

and to be treated only as an inferior ? I would disdain such
a meanness. Beatrix would scorn it. Ah ! Henry, 'tis
not with you the fault lies, 'tis with her. I know you both,
and love you : need I be ashamed of that love now ? No,
never, never, and 'tis not you, dear Harry, that is unworthy.
'Tis for my poor Beatrix I tremble—whose headstrong will
frightens me ; whose jealous temper (they say I was jealous
too, but, pray God, I am cured of that sin) and whose vanity
no words or prayers of mine can cure—only suffering, only
experience, and remorse afterwards. Oh, Henry, she will
make no man happy who loves her. Go away, my son .
leave her : love us always, and think kindly of us : and for
me, my dear, you know that these walls contain all that
I love in the world.'

In after-life, did Esmond find the words true which his
fond mistress spoke from her sad heart ? Warning he had :
but I doubt others had warning before his time, and since :
and he benefited by it as most men do.

My young lord viscount was exceeding sorry when he
heard that Harry could not come to the cock-match with
him, and must go to London, but no doubt my lord consoled himself when the Hampshire cocks won the match ;
and he saw every one of the battles, and crowed properly
over the conquered Sussex gentlemen.

As Esmond rode towards town his servant, coming up
to him, informed him with a grin, that Mistress Beatrix had
brought out a new gown and blue stockings for that day's
dinner, in which she intended to appear, and had flown into
a rage and given her maid a slap on the face soon after she
heard he was going away. Mistress Beatrix's woman, the
fellow said, came down to the servants' hall, crying, and
with the mark of a blow still on her cheek : but Esmond
peremptorily ordered him to fall back and be silent, and
rode on with thoughts enough of his own to occupy him—
some sad ones, some inexpressibly dear and pleasant.

His mistress, from whom he had been a year separated,
was his dearest mistress again. The family from which he
had been parted, and which he loved with the fondest devotion, was his family once more. If Beatrix's beauty shone
upon him, it was with a friendly lustre, and he could regard
it with much such a delight as he brought away after
seeing the beautiful pictures of the smiling Madonnas in
the convent at Cadiz, when he was dispatched thither with

a flag : and as for his mistress, 'twas difficult to say with
what a feeling he regarded her. 'Twas happiness to have
seen her : 'twas no great pang to part ; a filial tenderness,
a love that was at once respect and protection, filled his
mind as he thought of her ; and near her or far from her,
and from that day until now, and from now till death
is past, and beyond it, he prays that sacred flame may
ever burn.

CHAPTER IX

I MAKE THE CAMPAIGN OF 1704*

MR. ESMOND rode up to London then, where, if the dowager
had been angry at the abrupt leave of absence he took, she
was mightily pleased at his speedy return.

He went immediately and paid his court to his new
general, General Lumley, who received him graciously,
having known his father, and also, he was pleased to say,
having had the very best accounts of Mr. Esmond from the
officer whose aide de camp he had been at Vigo. During
this winter Mr. Esmond was gazetted to a lieutenancy in
Brigadier Webb's regiment of Fusiliers,* then with their
colonel in Flanders ; but being now attached to the suite
of Mr. Lumley, Esmond did not join his own regiment until
more than a year afterwards, and after his return from the
campaign of Blenheim, which was fought the next year.
The campaign began very early, our troops marching out of
their quarters before the winter was almost over, and invest-
ing the city of Bonn, on the Rhine, under the duke's command. His grace joined the army in deep grief of mind,
with crape on his sleeve, and his household in mourning ;
and the very same packet which brought the commander-
in-chief over, brought letters to the forces which preceded
him, and one from his dear mistress to Esmond, which
interested him not a little.

The young Marquis of Blandford, his grace's son, who
had been entered in King's College in Cambridge (whither
my lord viscount had also gone, to Trinity, with Mr. Tusher
as his governor), had been seized with small-pox, and was
dead at sixteen years of age, and so poor Frank's schemes

for his sister's advancement were over, and that innocent childish passion nipped in the birth.

Esmond's mistress would have had him return, at least her letters hinted as much ; but in the presence of the enemy this was impossible, and our young man took his humble share in the siege, which need not be described here, and had the good luck to escape without a wound of any sort, and to drink his general's health after the surrender. He was in constant military duty this year, and did not think of asking for a leave of absence, as one or two of his less fortunate friends did, who were cast away in that tremendous storm which happened towards the close of November, that ' which of late o'er pale Britannia past ' (as Mr. Addison sang of it), and in which scores of our greatest ships and 15,000 of our seamen went down.[*]

They said that our duke was quite heartbroken by the calamity which had befallen his family ; but his enemies found that he could subdue them, as well as master his grief. Successful as had been this great general's operations in the past year, they were far enhanced by the splendour of his victory in the ensuing campaign. His grace the captain-general went to England after Bonn, and our army fell back into Holland, where, in April, 1704, his grace again found the troops embarking from Harwich and landing at Maesland Sluys : thence his grace came immediately to the Hague, where he received the foreign ministers, general officers, and other people of quality. The greatest honours were paid to his grace everywhere—at the Hague, Utrecht, Ruremonde, and Maestricht ; the civic authorities coming to meet his coaches : salvos of cannon saluting him, canopies of state being erected for him where he stopped, and feasts prepared for the numerous gentlemen following in his suite. His grace reviewed the troops of the States-General between Liége and Maestricht, and afterwards the English forces, under the command of General Churchill,[*] near Bois-le-Duc. Every preparation was made for a long march ; and the army heard, with no small elation, that it was the commander-in-chief's intention to carry the war out of the Low Countries, and to march on the Mozelle. Before leaving our camp at Maestricht, we heard that the French, under the Marshal Villeroy, were also bound towards the Mozelle.

Towards the end of May, the army reached Coblentz ; and

next day, his grace, and the generals accompanying him, went to visit the Elector of Treves at his Castle of Ehrenbreitstein, the horse and dragoons passing the Rhine whilst the duke was entertained at a grand feast by the Elector. All as yet was novelty, festivity, and splendour—a brilliant march of a great and glorious army through a friendly country, and sure through some of the most beautiful scenes of nature which I ever witnessed.

The foot and artillery, following after the horse as quick as possible, crossed the Rhine under Ehrenbreitstein, and so to Castel, over against Mayntz, in which city his grace, his generals, and his retinue were received at the landing-place by the Elector's coaches, carried to his highness's palace amidst the thunder of cannon, and then once more magnificently entertained.   Gidlingen, in Bavaria, was appointed as the general rendezvous of the army, and thither, by different routes, the whole forces of English, Dutch, Danes, and German auxiliaries took their way.   The foot and artillery under General Churchill passed the Neckar, at Heidelberg ; and Esmond had an opportunity of seeing that city and palace, once so famous and beautiful (though shattered and battered by the French, under Turenne, in the late war), where his grandsire had served the beautiful and unfortunate Electress-Palatine, the first King Charles's sister.

At Mindelsheim, the famous Prince of Savoy*came to visit our commander, all of us crowding eagerly to get a sight of that brilliant and intrepid warrior ; and our troops were drawn up in battalia before the prince, who was pleased to express his admiration of this noble English army.   At length we came in sight of the enemy between Dillingen and Lawingen, the Brentz lying between the two armies.   The Elector, judging that Donauwort would be the point of his grace's attack, sent a strong detachment of his best troops to Count Darcos, who was posted at Schellenberg, near that place, where great entrenchments were thrown up, and thousands of pioneers employed to strengthen the position.

On the 2nd of July, his grace stormed the post, with what success on our part need scarce be told.   His grace advanced with six thousand foot, English and Dutch, thirty squadrons, and three regiments of Imperial cuirassiers, the duke crossing the river at the head of the cavalry.   Although our

troops made the attack with unparalleled courage and fury
—rushing up to the very guns of the enemy, and being
slaughtered before their works—we were driven back many
times, and should not have carried them, but that the
Imperialists came up under the Prince of Baden, when the
enemy could make no head against us : we pursued him
into the trenches, making a terrible slaughter there, and
into the very Danube, where a great part of his troops,
following the example of their generals, Count Darcos
and the Elector himself, tried to save themselves by swimming. Our army entered Donauwort, which the Bavarians
evacuated ; and where 'twas said the Elector purposed to
have given us a warm reception, by burning us in our beds ;
the cellars of the houses, when we took possession of them,
being found stuffed with straw. But though the links
were there, the link-boys had run away. The townsmen
saved their houses, and our general took possession of the
enemy's ammunition in the arsenals, his stores, and maga-
zines. Five days afterwards a great *Te Deum* was sung
in Prince Lewis's army, and a solemn day of thanksgiving
held in our own ; the Prince of Savoy's compliments coming
to his grace the captain-general during the day's religious
ceremony, and concluding, as it were, with an amen.

And now, having seen a great military march through
a friendly country ; the pomps and festivities of more than
one German court ; the severe struggle of a hotly-contested
battle, and the triumph of victory ; Mr. Esmond beheld
another part of military duty ; our troops entering the
enemy's territory, and putting all around them to fire and
sword ; burning farms, wasted fields, shrieking women,
slaughtered sons and fathers, and drunken soldiery, cursing
and carousing in the midst of tears, terror, and murder.
Why does the stately Muse of History, that delights in
describing the valour of heroes and the grandeur of conquest,
leave out these scenes, so brutal, mean, and degrading,
that yet form by far the greater part of the drama of war?*
You, gentlemen of England, who live at home at ease,* and
compliment yourselves in the songs of triumph with which
our chieftains are bepraised—you pretty maidens, that come
tumbling down the stairs when the fife and drum call you,
and huzzah for the British Grenadiers—do you take account
that these items go to make up the amount of the triumph
you admire, and form part of the duties of the heroes you

fondle ? Our chief, whom England and all Europe, saving only the Frenchmen, worshipped almost, had this of the godlike in him, that he was impassible before victory, before danger, before defeat. Before the greatest obstacle or the most trivial ceremony ; before a hundred thousand men drawn in battalia, or a peasant slaughtered at the door of his burning hovel ; before a carouse of drunken German lords, or a monarch's court, or a cottage-table, where his plans were laid, or an enemy's battery, vomiting flame and death, and strewing corpses round about him ;—he was always cold, calm, resolute, like fate. He performed a treason or a court-bow, he told a falsehood as black as Styx, as easily as he paid a compliment or spoke about the weather. He took a mistress, and left her ; he betrayed his benefactor, and supported him, or would have murdered him, with the same calmness always, and having no more remorse than Clotho when she weaves the thread, or Lachesis when she cuts it.* In the hour of battle I have heard the Prince of Savoy's officers say, the prince became possessed with a sort of warlike fury ; his eyes lighted up ; he rushed hither and thither, raging ; he shrieked curses and encouragement, yelling and harking his bloody war-dogs on, and himself always at the first of the hunt. Our duke was as calm at the mouth of the cannon as at the door of a drawing-room. Perhaps he could not have been the great man he was, had he had a heart either for love or hatred, or pity or fear, or regret, or remorse. He achieved the highest deed of daring, or deepest calculation of thought, as he performed the very meanest action of which a man is capable ; told a lie, or cheated a fond woman, or robbed a poor beggar of a half-penny, with a like awful serenity and equal capacity of the highest and lowest acts of our nature.

His qualities were pretty well known in the army, where there were parties of all politics, and of plenty of shrewdness and wit ; but there existed such a perfect confidence in him, as the first captain of the world, and such a faith and admiration in his prodigious genius and fortune, that the very men whom he notoriously cheated of their pay, the chiefs whom he used and injured—(for he used all men, great and small, that came near him, as his instruments alike, and took something of theirs, either some quality or some property— the blood of a soldier, it might be, or a jewelled hat, or a hundred thousand crowns from a king, or a portion out of a starving sentinel's three farthings ; or (when he was young) a kiss from a woman, and the gold chain off her neck, taking all he could from woman or man, and having, as I have said, this of the godlike in him, that he could see a hero perish or a sparrow fall, with the same amount of sympathy for either. Not that he had no tears ; he could always order up this reserve at the proper moment to battle ; he could draw upon tears or smiles alike, and whenever need was for using this cheap coin. He would cringe to a shoeblack, as he would flatter a minister or a monarch ; be haughty, be humble, threaten, repent, weep, grasp your hand, or stab you whenever he saw occasion)—But yet those of the army, who knew him best and had suffered most from him, admired him most of all : and as he rode along the lines to battle or galloped up in the nick of time to a battalion reeling from before the enemy's charge or shot, the fainting men and officers got new courage as they saw the splendid calm of his face, and felt that his will made them irresistible.

After the great victory of Blenheim the enthusiasm of the army for the duke, even of his bitterest personal enemies in it, amounted to a sort of rage—nay, the very officers who cursed him in their hearts, were among the most frantic to cheer him. Who could refuse his meed of admiration to such a victory and such a victor ? Not he who writes : a man may profess to be ever so much a philosopher ; but he who fought on that day must feel a thrill of pride as he recalls it.

The French right was posted near to the village of Blenheim, on the Danube, where the Marshal Tallard's quarters were ; their line extending through, it may be a league and a half, before Lutzingen and up to a woody hill, round the base of which, and acting against the Prince of Savoy, were forty of his squadrons. Here was a village that the Frenchmen had burned, the wood being, in fact, a better shelter and easier of guard than any village.

Before these two villages and the French lines ran a little stream, not more than two foot broad, through a marsh (that was mostly dried up from the heats of the weather), and this stream was the only separation between the two armies—ours coming up and ranging themselves in line of battle before the French, at six o'clock in the morning ; so that our line was quite visible to theirs ; and the whole of this great plain was black and swarming with troops for hours before the cannonading began.

On one side and the other this cannonading lasted many hours. The French guns being in position in front of their line, and doing severe damage among our horse especially, and on our right wing of Imperialists under the Prince of Savoy, who could neither advance his artillery nor his lines, the ground before him being cut up by ditches, morasses, and very difficult of passage for the guns.

It was past midday when the attack began on our left, where Lord Cutts commanded, the bravest and most beloved officer in the English army. And now, as if to make his experience in war complete, our young aide de camp having seen two great armies facing each other in line of battle, and had the honour of riding with orders from one end to other of the line, came in for a not uncommon accompaniment of military glory, and was knocked on the head, along with many hundred of brave fellows, almost at the very commencement of this famous day of Blenheim. A little after noon, the disposition for attack being completed with much delay and difficulty, and under a severe fire from the enemy's guns, that were better posted and more numerous than ours, a body of English and Hessians, with Major-General Wilkes commanding at the extreme left of our line, marched upon Blenheim, advancing with great gallantry, the major-general on foot, with his officers, at the head of the column, and marching, with his hat off, intrepidly in the face of the enemy, who was pouring in a tremendous fire from his guns and musketry, to which our people were instructed not to reply, except with pike and bayonet when they reached the French palisades.. To these Wilkes walked intrepidly, and struck the woodwork with his sword before our people charged it. He was shot down at the instant, with his colonel, major, and several officers ; and our troops cheering and huzzaing, and coming on, as they did, with immense resolution and gallantry, were nevertheless stopped by the murderous fire from behind the enemy's defences, and then attacked in flank by a furious charge of French horse which swept out of Blenheim, and cut down our men in great numbers. Three fierce and desperate assaults of our foot were made and repulsed by the enemy ; so that our columns of foot were quite shattered, and fell back, scrambling over the little rivulet, which we had crossed so resolutely an hour before, and pursued by the French cavalry, slaughtering us and cutting us down.

And now the conquerors were met by a furious charge of English horse under Esmond's general, General Lumley, behind whose squadrons the flying foot found refuge, and formed again, whilst Lumley drove back the French horse, charging up to the village of Blenheim and the palisades where Wilkes, and many hundred more gallant Englishmen, lay in slaughtered heaps. Beyond this moment, and of this famous victory, Mr. Esmond knows nothing ; for a shot brought down his horse and our young gentleman on it, who fell crushed and stunned under the animal ; and came to his senses he knows not how long after, only to lose them again from pain and loss of blood. A dim sense, as of people groaning round about him, a wild incoherent thought or two for her who occupied so much of his heart now, and that here his career, and his hopes, and misfortunes were ended, he remembers in the course of these hours. When he woke up it was with a pang of extreme pain, his breast-plate was taken off, his servant was holding his head up, the good and faithful lad of Hampshire [1] was blubbering over his master, whom he found and had thought dead, and a surgeon was probing a wound in the shoulder, which he must have got at the same moment when his horse was shot and fell over him. The battle was over at this end of the field, by this time : the village was in possession of the English, its brave defenders prisoners, or fled, or drowned, many of them, in the neighbouring waters of the Donau. But for honest Lockwood's faithful search after his master, there had no doubt been an end of Esmond here, and of this his story. The marauders were out rifling the bodies as they lay on the field, and Jack had brained one of these gentry with the club-end of his musket, who had eased Esmond of his hat and periwig, his purse, and fine silver-mounted pistols which the dowager gave him, and was fumbling in his pockets for further treasure, when Jack Lockwood came up and put an end to the scoundrel's triumph.

Hospitals for our wounded were established at Blenheim, and here for several weeks Esmond lay in very great danger of his life ; the wound was not very great from which he suffered, and the ball extracted by the surgeon on the spot

[1] My mistress before I went this campaign sent me John Lockwood out of Walcote, who hath ever since remained with me.—H. E.

where our young gentleman received it ; but a fever set in
next day, as he was lying in hospital, and that almost
carried him away. Jack Lockwood said he talked in the
wildest manner during his delirium ; that he called himself
the Marquis of Esmond, and seizing one of the surgeon's
assistants who came to dress his wounds, swore that he was
Madam Beatrix, and that he would make her a duchess if she
would but say yes. He was passing the days in these crazy
fancies, and *vana somnia*,* whilst the army was singing *Te
Deum* for the victory, and those famous festivities were
taking place at which our duke, now made a Prince of the
Empire, was entertained by the King of the Romans and his
nobility. His grace went home by Berlin and Hanover,
and Esmond lost the festivities which took place at those
cities, and which his general shared in company of the other
general officers who travelled with our great captain. When
he could move it was by the Duke of Wirtemburg's city of
Stuttgard that he made his way homewards, revisiting
Heidelberg again, whence he went to Manheim, and hence
had a tedious but easy water journey down the river of
Rhine, which he had thought a delightful and beautiful
voyage indeed, but that his heart was longing for home, and
something far more beautiful and delightful.

As bright and welcome as the eyes almost of his mistress
shone the lights of Harwich, as the packet came in from
Holland. It was not many hours ere he, Esmond, was in
London, of that you may be sure, and received with open
arms by the old dowager of Chelsea, who vowed, in her
jargon of French and English, that he had the *air noble*,
that his pallor embellished him, that he was an Amadis and
deserved a Gloriana ;* and, O flames and darts ! what
was his joy at hearing that his mistress was come into
waiting, and was now with her Majesty at Kensington !
Although Mr. Esmond had told Jack Lockwood to get horses
and they would ride for Winchester that night ; when he
heard this news he countermanded the horses at once ; his
business lay no longer in Hants ; all his hope and desire lay
within a couple of miles of him in Kensington Park wall.
Poor Harry had never looked in the glass before so eagerly
to see whether he had the *bel air*, and his paleness really did
become him ; he never took such pains about the curl of
his periwig, and the taste of his embroidery and point-lace,
as now, before Mr. Amadis presented himself to Madam

Gloriana.   Was the fire of the French lines half so murderous
as the killing glances from her ladyship's eyes ?   O darts
and raptures, how beautiful were they !

And as, before the blazing sun of morning, the moon fades
away in the sky almost invisible ; Esmond thought, with
a blush perhaps, of another sweet pale face, sad and faint,
and fading out of sight, with its sweet fond gaze of affection ;
such a last look it seemed to cast as Eurydice might have
given, yearning after her lover, when Fate and Pluto summoned her, and she passed away into the shades.

CHAPTER X

AN OLD STORY ABOUT A FOOL AND A WOMAN

ANY taste for pleasure which Esmond had (and he liked to
desipere in loco,* neither more nor less than most young men
of his age) he could now gratify to the utmost extent, and
in the best company which the town afforded.   When the
army went into winter quarters abroad, those of the officers
who had interest or money easily got leave of absence, and
found it much pleasanter to spend their time in Pall Mall
and Hyde Park, than to pass the winter away behind the
fortifications of the dreary old Flanders towns, where the
English troops were gathered.   Yatches and packets passed
daily between the Dutch and Flemish ports and Harwich ;
the roads thence to London and the great inns were crowded
with army gentlemen ;   the taverns and ordinaries of the
town swarmed with red-coats ;   and our great duke's levees
at St. James's were as thronged as they had been at Ghent
and Brussels, where we treated him, and he us, with the
grandeur and ceremony of a sovereign.   Though Esmond
had been appointed to a lieutenancy in the Fusilier regiment,
of which that celebrated officer, Brigadier John Richmond
Webb, was colonel, he had never joined the regiment, nor
been introduced to its excellent commander, though they
had made the same campaign together, and been engaged
in the same battle.   But being aide de camp to General
Lumley, who commanded the division of horse, and the
army marching to its point of destination on the Danube
by different routes, Esmond had not fallen in, as yet, with

his commander and future comrades of the fort; and it was in London, in Golden Square, where Major-General Webb lodged, that Captain Esmond had the honour of first paying his respects to his friend, patron, and commander of after-days.

Those who remember this brilliant and accomplished gentleman may recollect his character, upon which he prided himself, I think, not a little, of being the handsomest man in the army; a poet who writ a dull copy of verses upon the battle of Oudenarde three years after, describing Webb, says:—

> To noble danger Webb conducts the way,
> His great example all his troops obey;
> Before the front the general sternly rides,
> With such an air as Mars to battle strides:
> Propitious Heaven must sure a hero save,
> Like Paris handsome, and like Hector brave.*

Mr. Webb thought these verses quite as fine as Mr. Addison's on the Blenheim campaign, and, indeed, to be Hector *à la mode de Paris*, was part of this gallant gentleman's ambition. It would have been difficult to find an officer in the whole army, or amongst the splendid courtiers and cavaliers of the Maison-du-Roy,*that fought under Vendosme and Villeroy*in the army opposed to ours, who was a more accomplished soldier and perfect gentleman, and either braver or better-looking. And, if Mr. Webb believed of himself what the world said of him, and was deeply convinced of his own indisputable genius, beauty, and valour, who has a right to quarrel with him very much? This self-content of his kept him in general good humour, of which his friends and dependants got the benefit.

He came of a very ancient Wiltshire family, which he respected above all families in the world: he could prove a lineal descent from King Edward the First, and his first ancestor, Roaldus de Richmond, rode by William the Conqueror's side on Hastings field. 'We were gentlemen, Esmond,' he used to say, 'when the Churchills were horse-boys.' He was a very tall man, standing in his pumps six feet three inches (in his great jack-boots, with his tall, fair periwig, and hat and feather, he could not have been less than eight feet high). 'I am taller than Churchill,' he would say, surveying himself in the glass, 'and I am a better made man ; and if the women won't like a man that hasn't a wart on his nose, faith, I can't help myself, and Churchill has the better of me there.' Indeed, he was always measuring himself with the duke, and always asking his friends to measure them. And talking in this frank way, as he would do, over his cups, wags would laugh and encourage him ; friends would be sorry for him ; schemers and flatterers would egg him on, and tale-bearers carry the stories to head quarters, and widen the difference which already existed there between the great captain and one of the ablest and bravest lieutenants he ever had.

His rancour against the duke was so apparent, that one saw it in the first half-hour's conversation with General Webb ; and his lady, who adored her general, and thought him a hundred times taller, handsomer, and braver than a prodigal nature had made him, hated the great duke with such an intensity as it becomes faithful wives to feel against their husbands' enemies. Not that my lord duke was so yet ; Mr. Webb had said a thousand things against him, which his superior had pardoned ; and his grace, whose spies were everywhere, had heard a thousand things more that Webb had never said. But it cost this great man no pains to pardon ; and he passed over an injury or a benefit alike easily.

Should any child of mine take the pains to read these, his ancestor's memoirs, I would not have him judge of the great duke [1] by what a contemporary has written of him. No man hath been so immensely lauded and decried as this great statesman and warrior ; as, indeed, no man ever deserved better the very greatest praise and the strongest censure. If the present writer joins with the latter faction, very likely a private pique of his own may be the cause of his ill-feeling.

On presenting himself at the commander-in-chief's levee, his grace had not the least remembrance of General Lumley's aide de camp, and though he knew Esmond's family perfectly well, having served with both lords (my Lord Francis and the viscount, Esmond's father) in Flanders, and in the Duke of York's Guard, the Duke of Marlborough, who was friendly and serviceable to the (so-styled) legitimate

---

[1] This passage in the memoirs of Esmond is written on a leaf inserted into the MS. book, and dated 1744, probably after he had heard of the duchess's death.

representatives of the Viscount Castlewood, took no sort of
notice of the poor lieutenant who bore their name. A word
of kindness or acknowledgement, or a single glance of approbation, might have changed Esmond's opinion of the great
man ; and instead of a satire, which his pen cannot help
writing, who knows but that the humble historian might
have taken the other side of panegyric ? We have but
to change the point of view, and the greatest action looks
mean ; as we turn the perspective-glass, and a giant appears
a pigmy. You may describe, but who can tell whether
your sight is clear or not, or your means of information
accurate ? Had the great man said but a word of kindness
to the small one (as he would have stepped out of his gilt
chariot to shake hands with Lazarus in rags and sores, if he
thought Lazarus could have been of any service to him), no
doubt Esmond would have fought for him with pen and
sword to the utmost of his might ; but my lord the lion did
not want master mouse at this moment, and so Muscipulus
went off and nibbled in opposition.

So it was, however, that a young gentleman, who, in the
eyes of his family, and in his own, doubtless, was looked upon
as a consummate hero, found that the great hero of the day
took no more notice of him than of the smallest drummer
in his grace's army. The dowager at Chelsea was furious
against this neglect of her family, and had a great battle
with Lady Marlborough (as Lady Castlewood insisted on
calling the duchess). Her grace was now mistress of the
robes to her Majesty, and one of the greatest personages in
this kingdom, as her husband was in all Europe, and the
battle between the two ladies took place in the queen's
drawing-room.

The duchess, in reply to my aunt's eager clamour, said
haughtily, that she had done her best for the legitimate
branch of the Esmonds, and could not be expected to provide for the bastard brats of the family.

' Bastards,' says the viscountess, in a fury, ' there are
bastards amongst the Churchills, as your grace knows, and
the Duke of Berwick is provided for well enough.'

' Madam,' says the duchess, ' you know whose fault it is
that there are no such dukes in the Esmond family too, and
how that little scheme of a certain lady miscarried.'

Esmond's friend, Dick Steele, who was in waiting on the
prince, heard the controversy between the ladies at Court,

' And faith,' says Dick, ' I think, Harry, thy kinswoman
had the worst of it.'

He could not keep the story quiet ; 'twas all over the
coffee-houses ere night ; it was printed in a News Letter
before a month was over, and ' The Reply of her Grace the
Duchess of M-rlb-r-gh, to a Popish Lady of the Court, once
a favourite of the late K— J-m-s,' was printed in half a dozen
places, with a note stating that this duchess, when the head
of this lady's family came by his death lately in a fatal
duel, never rested until she got a pension for the orphan
heir, and widow, from her Majesty's bounty.'   The squabble
did not advance poor Esmond's promotion much, and indeed
made him so ashamed of himself that he dared not show his
face at the commander-in-chief's levees again.

During those eighteen months which had passed since
Esmond saw his dear mistress, her good father, the old
dean, quitted this life, firm in his principles to the very last,
and enjoining his family always to remember that the
queen's brother, King James the Third, was their rightful
sovereign. He made a very edifying end, as his daughter
told Esmond, and, not a little to her surprise, after his
death (for he had lived always very poorly) my lady found
that her father had left no less a sum than 3,000*l.* behind
him, which he bequeathed to her.

With this little fortune Lady Castlewood was enabled,
when her daughter's turn at Court came, to come to London,
where she took a small genteel house at Kensington, in the
neighbourhood of the Court, bringing her children with her,
and here it was that Esmond found his friends.

As for the young lord, his University career had ended
rather abruptly. Honest Tusher, his governor, had found
my young gentleman quite ungovernable. My lord worried
his life away with tricks ; and broke out, as home-bred lads
will, into a hundred youthful extravagances, so that
Dr. Bentley,* the new master of Trinity, thought fit to write
to the Viscountess Castlewood, my lord's mother, and beg
her to remove the young nobleman from a college where he
declined to learn, and where he only did harm by his riotous
example. Indeed, I believe he nearly set fire to Nevil's
Court, that beautiful new quadrangle of our college, which
Sir Christopher Wren had lately built. He knocked down
a proctor's man that wanted to arrest him in a midnight

prank ; he gave a dinner party on the Prince of Wales's
birthday, which was within a fortnight of his own, and the
twenty young gentlemen then present sallied out after their
wine, having toasted King James's health with open windows, and sung cavalier songs, and shouted, ' God save the
King ! ' in the great court, so that the master came out of
his lodge at midnight, and dissipated the riotous assembly.

This was my lord's crowning freak, and the Rev. Thomas
Tusher, domestic chaplain to the Right Honourable the
Lord Viscount Castlewood, finding his prayers and sermons
of no earthly avail to his lordship, gave up his duties of
governor ; went and married his brewer's widow at
Southampton, and took her and her money to his parsonage-
house at Castlewood.

My lady could not be angry with her son for drinking
King James's health, being herself a loyal Tory, as all the
Castlewood family were, and acquiesced with a sigh,
knowing, perhaps, that her refusal would be of no avail to
the young lord's desire for a military life. She would have
liked him to be in Mr. Esmond's regiment, hoping that
Harry might act as guardian and adviser to his wayward
young kinsman ; but my young lord would hear of nothing
but the Guards, and a commission was got for him in the
Duke of Ormonde's regiment ; so Esmond found my lord,
ensign and lieutenant, when he returned from Germany
after the Blenheim campaign.

The effect produced by both Lady Castlewood's children
when they appeared in public was extraordinary, and the
whole town speedily rang with their fame ; such a beautiful
couple, it was declared, never had been seen ; the young
maid of honour was toasted at every table and tavern,
and as for my young lord, his good looks were even more
admired than his sister's. A hundred songs were written
about the pair, and as the fashion of that day was, my
young lord was praised in these Anacreontics as warmly
as Bathyllus.* You may be sure that he accepted very
complacently the town's opinion of him,- and acquiesced
with that frankness and charming good humour he always
showed in the idea that he was the prettiest fellow in all
London.

The old dowager at Chelsea, though she could never be
got to acknowledge that Mrs. Beatrix was any beauty at all
(in which opinion, as it may be imagined, a vast number

of the ladies agreed with her), yet, on the very first sight of young Castlewood, she owned she fell in love with him ; and Henry Esmond, on his return to Chelsea, found himself quite superseded in her favour by her younger kinsman. That feat of drinking the king's health at Cambridge would have won her heart, she said, if nothing else did. ' How had the dear young fellow got such beauty ? ' she asked. ' Not from his father—certainly not from his mother. How had he come by such noble manners, and the perfect *bel air ?* That countrified Walcote widow could never have taught him.' Esmond had his own opinion about the countrified Walcote widow, who had a quiet grace, and serene kindness, that had always seemed to him the perfection of good breeding, though he did not try to argue this point with his aunt. But he could agree in most of the praises which the enraptured old dowager bestowed on my lord viscount, than whom he never beheld a more fascinating and charming gentleman. Castlewood had not wit so much as enjoyment. ' The lad looks good things,' Mr. Steele used to say ; ' and his laugh lights up a conversation as much as ten repartees from Mr. Congreve. I would as soon sit over a bottle with him as with Mr. Addison ; and rather listen to his talk than hear Nicolini.* Was ever man so gracefully drunk as my Lord Castlewood ? I would give anything to carry my wine (though, indeed, Dick bore his very kindly, and plenty of it, too) like this incomparable young man. When he is sober he is delightful ; and when tipsy, perfectly irresistible.' And referring to his favourite, Shakespeare (who was quite out of fashion until Steele brought him back into the mode), Dick compared Lord Castlewood to Prince Hal, and was pleased to dub Esmond as ancient Pistol.

The mistress of the robes, the greatest lady in England after the queen, or even before her Majesty, as the world said, though she never could be got to say a civil word to Beatrix, whom she had promoted to her place as maid of honour, took her brother into instant favour. When young Castlewood, in his new uniform, and looking like a prince out of a fairy-tale, went to pay his duty to her grace, she looked at him for a minute in silence, the young man blushing and in confusion before her, then fairly burst out a-crying, and kissed him before her daughters

and company. ' He was my boy's friend,' she said, through
her sobs. ' My Blandford might have been like him.'
And everybody saw, after this mark of the duchess's
favour, that my young lord's promotion was secure, and
people crowded round the favourite's favourite, who became
vainer and gayer, and more good-humoured than ever.

Meanwhile Madam Beatrix was making her conquests on
her own side, and amongst them was one poor gentleman,
who had been shot by her young eyes two years before,
and had never been quite cured of that wound ; he knew,
to be sure, how hopeless any passion might be, directed in
that quarter, and had taken that best, though ignoble,
remedium amoris,* a speedy retreat from before the charmer,
and a long absence from her ; and not being dangerously
smitten in the first instance, Esmond pretty soon got the
better of his complaint, and if he had it still, did not know
he had it, and bore it easily. But when he returned after
Blenheim, the young lady of sixteen, who had appeared
the most beautiful object his eyes had ever looked on two
years back, was now advanced to a perfect ripeness and
perfection of beauty, such as instantly enthralled the poor
devil, who had already been a fugitive from her charms.
Then he had seen her but for two days, and fled ; now he
beheld her day after day, and when she was at Court,
watched after her ; when she was at home, made one of
the family party ; when she went abroad, rode after her
mother's chariot ; when she appeared in public places,
was in the box near her, or in the pit looking at her ; when
she went to church was sure to be there, though he might
not listen to the sermon, and be ready to hand her to her
chair if she deigned to accept of his services, and select
him from a score of young men who were always hanging
round about her. When she went away, accompanying
her Majesty to Hampton Court, a darkness fell over London.
Gods, what nights has Esmond passed, thinking of her,
rhyming about her, talking about her ! His friend Dick
Steele was at this time courting the young lady, Mrs.
Scurlock, whom he married ; she had a lodging in Kensington Square, hard by my Lady Castlewood's house there.
Dick and Harry, being on the same errand, used to meet
constantly at Kensington. They were always prowling
about that place, or dismally walking thence, or eagerly
running thither. They emptied scores of bottles at the

'King's Arms', each man prating of his love, and allowing the other to talk on condition that he might have his own turn as a listener. Hence arose an intimacy between them, though to all the rest of their friends they must have been insufferable. Esmond's verses to 'Gloriana at the Harpsichord', to 'Gloriana's Nosegay', to 'Gloriana at Court', appeared this year in the *Observator.*—Have you never read them ? They were thought pretty poems, and attributed by some to Mr. Prior.*

This passion did not escape—how should it ?—the clear eyes of Esmond's mistress : he told her all ; what will a man not do when frantic with love ? To what baseness will he not demean himself ? What pangs will he not make others suffer, so that he may ease his selfish heart of a part of its own pain ? Day after day he would seek his dear mistress, pour insane hopes, supplications, rhapsodies, raptures, into her ear. She listened, smiled, consoled, with untiring pity and sweetness. Esmond was the eldest of her children, so she was pleased to say ; and as for her kindness, who ever had or would look for aught else from one who was an angel of goodness and pity ? After what has been said, 'tis needless almost to add that poor Esmond's suit was unsuccessful. What was a nameless, penniless lieutenant to do, when some of the greatest in the land were in the field ? Esmond never so much as thought of asking permission to hope so far above his reach as he knew this prize was—and passed his foolish, useless life in mere abject sighs and impotent longing. What nights of rage, what days of torment, of passionate unfulfilled desire, of sickening jealousy, can he recall ! Beatrix thought no more of him than of the lackey that followed her chair. His complaints did not touch her in the least ; his raptures rather fatigued her ; she cared for his verses no more than for Dan Chaucer's, who's dead these ever so many hundred years ; she did not hate him ; she rather despised him, and just suffered him.

One day, after talking to Beatrix's mother, his dear, fond, constant mistress—for hours—for all day long—pouring out his flame and his passion, his despair and rage, returning again and again to the theme, pacing the room, tearing up the flowers on the table, twisting and breaking into bits the wax out of the standish, and performing a hundred mad freaks of passionate folly ; seeing his mistress at last quite pale and tired out with sheer weariness of compassion, and watching over his fever for the hundredth time, Esmond seized up his hat, and took his leave. As he got into Kensington Square, a sense of remorse came over him for the wearisome pain he had been inflicting upon the dearest and kindest friend ever man had. He went back to the house, where the servant still stood at the open door, ran up the stairs, and found his mistress where he had left her in the embrasure of the window, looking over the fields towards Chelsea. She laughed, wiping away at the same time the tears which were in her kind eyes ; he flung himself down on his knees, and buried his head in her lap. She had in her hand the stalk of one of the flowers, a pink, that he had torn to pieces. 'Oh, pardon me, pardon me, my dearest and kindest,' he said ; 'I am in hell, and you are the angel that brings me a drop of water.'

'I am your mother, you are my son, and I love you always,' she said, holding her hands over him ; and he went away comforted and humbled in mind, as he thought of that amazing and constant love and tenderness with which this sweet lady ever blessed and pursued him.

CHAPTER XI

THE FAMOUS MR. JOSEPH ADDISON*

THE gentlemen ushers had a table at Kensington, and the Guard a very splendid dinner daily at St. James's, at either of which ordinaries Esmond was free to dine. Dick Steele liked the Guard-table better than his own at the gentleman ushers', where there was less wine and more ceremony ; and Esmond had many a jolly afternoon in company of his friend, and a hundred times at least saw Dick into his chair. If there is verity in wine, according to the old adage, what an amiable-natured character Dick's must have been ! In proportion as he took in wine he over-flowed with kindness. His talk was not witty so much as charming. He never said a word that could anger any-body, and only became the more benevolent the more tipsy he grew. Many of the wags derided the poor fellow in his cups, and chose him as a butt for their satire ; but there was a kindness about him, and a sweet playful fancy, that seemed to Esmond far more charming than the pointed talk of the brightest wits, with their elaborate repartees and affected severities. I think Steele shone rather than sparkled. Those famous *beaux-esprits* of the coffee-houses (Mr. William Congreve, for instance, when his gout and his grandeur permitted him to come among us) would make many brilliant hits—half a dozen in a night sometimes— but, like sharpshooters, when they had fired their shot, they were obliged to retire under cover till their pieces were loaded again, and wait till they got another chance at their enemy ; whereas Dick never thought that his bottle-companion was a butt to aim at—only a friend to shake by the hand. The poor fellow had half the town in his confidence ; everybody knew everything about his loves and his debts, his creditors or his mistress's obduracy. When Esmond first came on to the town, honest Dick was all flames and raptures for a young lady, a West India fortune, whom he married. In a couple of years the lady was dead, the fortune was all but spent, and the honest widower was as eager in pursuit of a new paragon of beauty as if he had never courted and married and buried the last one.

Quitting the Guard-table on one sunny afternoon, when by chance Dick had a sober fit upon him, he and his friend were making their way down Germain Street, and Dick all of a sudden left his companion's arm, and ran after a gentleman who was poring over a folio volume at the book-shop near to St. James's Church. He was a fair, tall man, in a snuff-coloured suit, with a plain sword, very sober, and almost shabby in appearance—at least when compared to Captain Steele, who loved to adorn his jolly round person with the finest of clothes, and shone in scarlet and gold lace. The captain rushed up, then, to the student of the bookstall, took him in his arms, hugged him, and would have kissed him—for Dick was always hugging and bussing his friends—but the other stepped back with a flush on his pale face, seeming to decline this public manifestation of Steele's regard.

'My dearest Joe, where hast thou hidden thyself this age ? ' cries the captain, still holding both his friend's hands ; ' I have been languishing for thee this fortnight.'

'A fortnight is not an age, Dick,' says the other, very good-humouredly. (He had light blue eyes, extraordinary bright, and a face perfectly regular and handsome, like a tinted statue.) 'And I have been hiding myself—where do you think?'

'What! not across the water, my dear Joe?' says Steele, with a look of great alarm: 'thou knowest I have always——'

'No,' says his friend, interrupting him with a smile: 'we are not come to such straits as that, Dick. I have been hiding, sir, at a place where people never think of finding you—at my own lodgings, whither I am going to smoke a pipe now and drink a glass of sack; will your honour come?'

'Harry Esmond, come hither,' cries out Dick. 'Thou hast heard me talk over and over again at my dearest Joe, my guardian angel.'

'Indeed,' says Mr. Esmond, with a bow, 'it is not from you only that I have learnt to admire Mr. Addison. We loved good poetry at Cambridge, as well as at Oxford; and I have some of yours by heart, though I have put on a red-coat . . . "*O qui canoro blandius Orpheo vocale ducis carmen*"; shall I go on, sir?' says Mr. Esmond, who indeed had read and loved the charming Latin poems of Mr. Addison, as every scholar of that time knew and admired them.*

'This is Captain Esmond who was at Blenheim,' says Steele.

'Lieutenant Esmond,' says the other, with a low bow; 'at Mr. Addison's service.'

'I have heard of you,' says Mr. Addison, with a smile; as, indeed, everybody about town had heard that unlucky story about Esmond's dowager aunt and the duchess.

'We were going to the "George", to take a bottle before the play,' says Steele; 'wilt thou be one, Joe?'

Mr. Addison said his own lodgings were hard by, where he was still rich enough to give a good bottle of wine to his friends; and invited the two gentlemen to his apartment in the Haymarket, whither we accordingly went.

'I shall get credit with my landlady,' says he, with a smile, 'when she sees two such fine gentlemen as you come up my stair.' And he politely made his visitors welcome to his apartment, which was indeed but a shabby one, though no grandee of the land could receive his guests with a more perfect and courtly grace than this gentleman. A frugal dinner, consisting of a slice of meat and a penny loaf, was awaiting the owner of the lodgings. ' My wine is better than my meat,' says Mr. Addison ; ' my Lord Halifax sent me the burgundy.' And he set a bottle and glasses before his friends, and eat his simple dinner in a very few minutes, after which the three fell to, and began to drink. ' You see,' says Mr. Addison, pointing to his writing-table, whereon was a map of the action at Hochstedt, and several other gazettes and pamphlets relating to the battle, ' that I, too, am busy about your affairs, captain. I am engaged as a poetical gazetteer, to say truth, and am writing a poem on the campaign.'

So Esmond, at the request of his host, told him what he knew about the famous battle, drew the river on the table, *aliquo mero*, and with the aid of some bits of tobacco-pipe, showed the advance of the left wing, where he had been engaged.

A sheet or two of the verses lay already on the table beside our bottles and glasses, and Dick having plentifully refreshed himself from the latter, took up the pages of manuscript, writ out with scarce a blot or correction, in the author's slim, neat handwriting, and began to read therefrom with great emphasis and volubility. At pauses of the verse the enthusiastic reader stopped and fired off a great salvo of applause.

Esmond smiled at the enthusiasm of Addison's friend. You are like the German burghers,' says he, ' and the princes on the Mozelle ; when our army came to a halt, they always sent a deputation to compliment the chief, and fired a salute with all their artillery from their walls.'

' And drunk the great chief's health afterward, did not they ? ' says Captain Steele, gaily filling up a bumper ;— he never was tardy at that sort of acknowledgement of a friend's merit.

' And the duke, since you will have me act his grace's part,' says Mr. Addison, with a smile and something of a blush, ' pledged his friends in return. Most serene Elector of Covent Garden, I drink to your highness's health,' and he filled himself a glass. Joseph required scarce more pressing than Dick to that sort of amusement ; but the wine never seemed at all to fluster Mr. Addison's

brains; it only unloosed his tongue, whereas Captain
Steele's head and speech were quite overcome by a single
bottle.

No matter what the verses were, and, to say truth, Mr.
Esmond found some of them more than indifferent, Dick's
enthusiasm for his chief never faltered, and in every line
from Addison's pen, Steele found a master-stroke. By the
time Dick had come to that part of the poem, wherein the
bard describes as blandly as though he were recording
a dance at the Opera, or a harmless bout of bucolic cudgelling
at a village fair, that bloody and ruthless part of our
campaign, with the remembrance whereof every soldier who
bore a part in it must sicken with shame—when we were
ordered to ravage and lay waste the Elector's country;
and with fire and murder, slaughter and crime, a great
part of his dominions was overrun: when Dick çame to
the lines—*

> In vengeance roused the soldier fills his hand
> With sword and fire, and ravages the land.
> In crackling flames a thousand harvests burn,
> A thousand villages to ashes turn.
> To the thick woods the woolly flocks retreat,
> And mixed with bellowing herds confusedly bleat.
> Their trembling lords the common shade partake,
> And cries of infants found in every brake.
> The listening soldier fixed in sorrow stands,
> Loath to obey his leader's just commands.
> The leader grieves, by generous pity swayed,
> To see his just commands so well obeyed:

by this time wine and friendship had brought poor Dick
to a perfectly maudlin state, and he hiccuped out the
last line with a tenderness that set one of his auditors
a-laughing.

'I admire the licence of you poets,' says Esmond to Mr.
Addison. (Dick, after reading of the verses, was fain to
go off, insisting on kissing his two dear friends before his
departure, and reeling away with his periwig over his
eyes.) 'I admire your art: the murder of the campaign
is done to military music, like a battle at the Opera, and
the virgins shriek in harmony, as our victorious grenadiers
march into their villages. Do you know what a scene it
was' (by this time, perhaps, the wine had warmed Mr.
Esmond's head too),—' what a triumph you are celebrating?

what scenes of shame and horror were enacted, over which the commander's genius presided, as calm as though he didn't belong to our sphere ? You talk of the " listening soldier fixed in sorrow", the " leader's grief swayed by generous pity " ; to my belief the leader cared no more for bleating flocks than he did for infants' cries, and many of our ruffians butchered one or the other with equal alacrity. I was ashamed of my trade when I saw those horrors perpetrated, which came under every man's eyes. You hew out of your polished verses a stately image of smiling victory ; I tell you 'tis an uncouth, distorted, savage idol ; hideous, bloody, and barbarous. The rites performed before it are shocking to think of. You great poets should show it as it is—ugly and horrible, not beautiful and serene. Oh, sir, had you made the campaign, believe me, you never would have sung it so.'

During this little outbreak, Mr. Addison was listening, smoking out of his long pipe, and smiling very placidly. ' What would you have ? ' says he. ' In our polished days, and according to the rules of art, 'tis impossible that the Muse should depict tortures or begrime her hands with the horrors of war. These are indicated rather than described ; as in the Greek tragedies, that, I dare say, you have read (and sure there can be no more elegant specimens of composition) ; Agamemnon is slain, or Medea's children destroyed, away from the scene ;—the chorus occupying the stage and singing of the action to pathetic music. Something of this I attempt, my dear sir, in my humble way : 'tis a panegyric I mean to write, and not a satire. Were I to sing as you would have me, the town would tear the poet in pieces, and burn his book by the hands of the common hangman. Do you not use tobacco ? Of all the weeds grown on earth, sure the nicotian is the most soothing and salutary. We must paint our great duke,' Mr. Addison went on, ' not as a man, which no doubt he is, with weaknesses like the rest of us, but as a hero. 'Tis in a triumph, not a battle, that your humble servant is riding his sleek Pegasus. We college-poets trot, you know, on very easy nags ; it hath been, time out of mind, part of the poet's profession to celebrate the actions of heroes in verse, and to sing the deeds which you men of war perform. I must follow the rules of my art, and the composition of such a strain as this must be harmonious and majestic, not

familiar, or too near the vulgar truth. *Si parva licet :** if
Virgil could invoke the divine Augustus, a humbler poet
from the banks of the Isis may celebrate a victory and a conqueror of our own nation, in whose triumphs every Briton
has a share, and whose glory and genius contributes to every
citizen's individual honour. When hath there been, since
our Henrys' and Edwards' days, such a great feat of arms
as that from which you yourself have brought away marks
of distinction ? If 'tis in my power to sing that song
worthily, I will do so, and be thankful to my Muse. If
I fail as a poet, as a Briton at least I will show my loyalty
and fling up my cap and huzzah for the conqueror :

> ——————'Rheni pacator et Istri
> Omnis in hoc uno variis discordia cessit
> Ordinibus ; laetatur eques, plauditque senator,
> Votaque patricio certant plebeia favori.'*

'There were as brave men on that field,' says Mr.
Esmond (who never could be made to love the Duke of
Marlborough, nor to forget those stories which he used to
hear in his youth regarding that great chief's selfishness
and treachery)—'there were men at Blenheim as good as
the leader, whom neither knights nor senators applauded,
nor voices plebeian or patrician favoured, and who lie there
forgotten, under the clods. What poet is there to sing
them ? '

'To sing the gallant souls of heroes sent to Hades ! '
says Mr. Addison, with a smile : ' would you celebrate
them all ? If I may venture to question anything in such
an admirable work, the catalogue of the ships in Homer
hath always appeared to me as somewhat wearisome ;
what had the poem been, supposing the writer had chronicled the names of captains, lieutenants, rank and file ?
One of the greatest of a great man's qualities is success ;
'tis the result of all the others ; 'tis a latent power in him
which compels the favour of the gods, and subjugates
fortune. Of all his gifts I admire that one in the great
Marlborough. To be brave ? every man is brave. But
in being victorious, as he is, I fancy there is something
divine. In presence of the occasion, the great soul of
the leader shines out, and the god is confessed. Death
itself respects him, and passes by him to lay others low.
War and carnage flee before him to ravage other parts of

the field, as Hector from before the divine Achilles. You
say he hath no pity ; no more have the gods, who are
above it, and superhuman. The fainting battle gathers
strength at his aspect ; and, wherever he rides, victory
charges with him.'

A couple of days after, when Mr. Esmond revisited his
poetic friend, he found this thought, struck out in the
fervour of conversation, improved and shaped into those
famous lines, which are in truth the noblest in the poem
of the *Campaign*.* As the two gentlemen sat engaged
in talk, Mr. Addison solacing himself with his customary
pipe ; the little maidservant that waited on his lodging
came up, preceding a gentleman in fine laced clothes, that
had evidently been figuring at Court or a great man's
levee. The courtier coughed a little at the smoke of the
pipe, and looked round the room curiously, which was
shabby enough, as was the owner in his worn snuff-coloured
suit and plain tie-wig.

'How goes on the *magnum opus*, Mr. Addison ?' says
the Court gentleman on looking down at the papers that
were on the table.

'We were but now over it,' says Addison (the greatest
courtier in the land could not have a more splendid politeness, or greater dignity of manner) ; 'here is the plan,'
says he, 'on the table ; *hac ibat Simois*, here ran the little
river Nebel : *hic est Sigeia tellus*,* here are Tallard's quarters,
at the bowl of this pipe, at the attack of which Captain
Esmond was present. I have the honour to introduce him
to Mr. Boyle ; and Mr. Esmond was but now depicting
aliquo praelia mixta mero,* when you came in.' In truth
the two gentlemen had been so engaged when the visitor
arrived, and Addison, in his smiling way, speaking of
Mr. Webb, colonel of Esmond's regiment (who commanded
a brigade in the action, and greatly distinguished himself
there), was lamenting that he could find never a suitable
rhyme for Webb, otherwise the brigade should have had
a place in the poet's verses. 'And for you, you are but
a lieutenant,' says Addison, 'and the Muse can't occupy
herself with any gentleman under the rank of a field-
officer.'

Mr. Boyle was all impatient to hear, saying that my
Lord Treasurer and my Lord Halifax were equally anxious ;
and Addison, blushing, began reading of his verses, and,

I suspect, knew their weak parts as well as the most critical hearer.   When he came to the lines describing the
angel, that

> Inspired repulsed battalions to engage,
> And taught the doubtful battle where to rage,*

he read with great animation, looking at Esmond, as much
as to say, ' You know where that simile came from—from
our talk, and our bottle of burgundy, the other day.'
The poet's two hearers were caught with enthusiasm,
and applauded the verses with all their might.   The
gentleman of the Court sprang up in great delight.   ' Not
a word more, my dear sir,' says he.   ' Trust me with the
papers—I'll defend them with my life.   Let me read them
over to my Lord Treasurer, whom I am appointed to see
in half an hour.   I venture to promise, the verses shall
lose nothing by my reading, and then, sir, we shall see
whether Lord Halifax has a right to complain that his
friend's pension is no longer paid.'   And without more
ado, the courtier in lace seized the manuscript pages,
placed them in his breast with his ruffled hand over his
heart, executed a most gracious wave of the hat with the
disengaged hand, and smiled and bowed out of the room,
leaving an odour of pomander behind him.
' Does not the chamber look quite dark,' says Addison,
surveying it, ' after the glorious appearance and disappearance of that gracious messenger ?   Why, he illuminated the
whole room.   Your scarlet, Mr. Esmond, will bear any
light ; but this threadbare old coat of mine, how very
worn it looked under the glare of that splendour !   I wonder
whether they will do anything for me,' he continued.
' When I came out of Oxford into the world, my patrons
promised me great things ; and you see where their promises have landed me, in a lodging up two pair of stairs,
with a sixpenny dinner from the cook's shop.   Well,
I suppose this promise will go after the others, and fortune
will jilt me, as the jade has been doing any time these
seven years.   " I puff the prostitute away,"* says he,
smiling, and blowing a cloud out of his pipe.   ' There is
no hardship in poverty, Esmond, that is not bearable ; no
hardship even in honest dependence that an honest man
may not put up with.   I came out of the lap of Alma
Mater, puffed up with her praises of me, and thinking to

make a figure in the world with the parts and learning which had got me no small name in our college. The world is the ocean, and Isis and Charwell are but little drops, of which the sea takes no account. My reputation ended a mile beyond Maudlin Tower ; no one took note of me ; and I learned this, at least, to bear up against evil fortune with a cheerful heart. Friend Dick hath made a figure in the world, and has passed me in the race long ago. What matters a little name or a little fortune ? There is no fortune that a philosopher cannot endure. I have been not unknown as a scholar, and yet forced to live by turning bear-leader, and teaching a boy to spell. What then ? The life was not pleasant, but possible—the bear was bearable. Should this venture fail, I will go back to Oxford ; and some day, when you are a general, you shall find me a curate in a cassock and bands, and I shall welcome your honour to my cottage in the country, and to a mug of penny ale. 'Tis not poverty that's the hardest to bear, or the least happy lot in life,' says Mr. Addison, shaking the ash out of his pipe. ' See, my pipe is smoked out. Shall we have another bottle ? I have still a couple in the cupboard, and of the right sort. No more ?—let us go abroad and take a turn on the Mall, or look in at the theatre and see Dick's comedy. 'Tis not a masterpiece of wit ; but Dick is a good fellow, though he doth not set the Thames on fire.'

Within a month after this day, Mr. Addison's ticket had come up a prodigious prize in the lottery of life. All the town was in an uproar of admiration of his poem, the *Campaign*, which Dick Steele was spouting at every coffee-house in Whitehall and Covent Garden. The wits on the other side of Temple Bar saluted him at once as the greatest poet the world had seen for ages ; the people huzza'ed for Marlborough and for Addison, and, more than this, the party in power provided for the meritorious poet, and Mr. Addison got the appointment of Commissioner of Excise, which the famous Mr. Locke vacated, and rose from this place to other dignities and honours ; his prosperity from henceforth to the end of his life being scarce ever interrupted. But I doubt whether he was not happier in his garret in the Haymarket, than ever he was in his splendid palace at Kensington ; and I believe the fortune that came to him in the shape of

the countess his wife, was no better than a shrew and
a vixen.

Gay as the town was, 'twas but a dreary place for Mr.
Esmond, whether his charmer was in it or out of it, and
he was glad when his general gave him notice that he was
going back to his division of the army which lay in winter
quarters at Bois-le-Duc. His dear mistress bade him
farewell with a cheerful face ; her blessing he knew he had
always, and wheresoever fate carried him. Mrs. Beatrix
was away in attendance on her Majesty at Hampton Court,
and kissed her fair finger-tips to him, by way of adieu,
when he rode thither to take his leave. She received her
kinsman in a waiting-room where there were half a dozen
more ladies of the Court, so that his high-flown speeches,
had he intended to make any (and very likely he did),
were impossible ; and she announced to her friends that
her cousin was going to the army, in as easy a manner
as she would have said he was going to a chocolate-house.
He asked with a rather rueful face, if she had any orders
for the army ? and she was pleased to say that she would
like a mantle of Mechlin lace. She made him a saucy
curtsy in reply to his own dismal bow. She deigned to
kiss her finger-tips from the window, where she stood
laughing with the other ladies, and chanced to see him
as he made his way to the 'Toy'.* The dowager at Chelsea
was not sorry to part with him this time. 'Mon cher,
vous êtes triste comme un sermon,' she did him the honour
to say to him ; indeed, gentlemen in his condition are by
no means amusing companions, and besides, the fickle old
woman had now found a much more amiable favourite,
and raffolé'd for her darling lieutenant of the Guard. Frank
remained behind for a while, and did not join the army
till later, in the suite of his grace the commander-in-chief.
His dear mother, on the last day before Esmond went
away, and when the three dined together, made Esmond
promise to befriend her boy, and besought Frank to take
the example of his kinsman as of a loyal gentleman and
brave soldier, so she was pleased to say ; and at parting,
betrayed not the least sign of faltering or weakness, though,
God knows, that fond heart was fearful enough when others
were concerned, though so resolute in bearing its own pain.
Esmond's general embarked at Harwich. 'Twas a grand

sight to see Mr. Webb dressed in scarlet on the deck, waving his hat as our yacht put off, and the guns saluted from the shore. Harry did not see his viscount again, until three months after, at Bois-le-Duc, when his grace the duke came to take the command, and Frank brought a budget of news from home : how he had supped with this actress, and got tired of that ; how he had got the better of Mr. St. John, both over the bottle, and with Mrs. Mountford,* of the Haymarket Theatre (a veteran charmer of fifty, with whom the young scapegrace chose to fancy himself in love) ; how his sister was always at her tricks, and had jilted a young baron for an old earl. ' I can't make out Beatrix,' he said ; ' she cares for none of us—she only thinks about herself ; she is never happy unless she is quarrelling ; but as for my mother—my mother, Harry, is an angel.' Harry tried to impress on the young fellow the necessity of doing everything in his power to please that angel ; not to drink too much ; not to go into debt ; not to run after the pretty Flemish girls, and so forth, as became a senior speaking to a lad. ' But Lord bless thee ! ' the boy said ; ' I may do what I like, and I know she will love me all the same ; ' and so, indeed, he did what he liked. Everybody spoiled him, and his grave kinsman as much as the rest.

CHAPTER XII

I GET A COMPANY IN THE CAMPAIGN OF 1706

On Whit Sunday, the famous 23rd of May, 1706,* my young lord first came under the fire of the enemy, whom we found posted in order of battle, their lines extending three miles or more, over the high ground behind the little Gheet river, and having on his left the little village of Anderkirk or Autre-église, and on his right Ramillies, which has given its name to one of the most brilliant and disastrous days of battle that history ever hath recorded.

Our duke here once more met his old enemy of Blenheim, the Bavarian Elector and the Mareschal Villeroy, over whom the Prince of Savoy had gained the famous victory of Chiari. What Englishman or Frenchman doth not know the issue of that day ? Having chosen his own ground, having a force superior to the English, and besides the excellent Spanish and Bavarian troops, the whole Maison-du-Roy with him, the most splendid body of horse in the world,—in an hour (and in spite of the prodigious gallantry of the French Royal Household, who charged through the centre of our line and broke it), this magnificent army of Villeroy was utterly routed by troops that had been marching for twelve hours, and by the intrepid skill of a commander, who did, indeed, seem in the presence of the enemy to be the very Genius of Victory.

I think it was more from conviction than policy, though that policy was surely the most prudent in the world, that the great duke always spoke of his victories with an extraordinary modesty, and as if it was not so much his own admirable genius and courage which achieved these amazing successes, but as if he was a special and fatal instrument in the hands of Providence, that willed irresistibly the enemy's overthrow. Before his actions he always had the church service read solemnly, and professed an undoubting belief that our queen's arms were blessed and our victory sure. All the letters which he writ after his battles show awe rather than exultation ; and he attributes the glory of these achievements, about which I have heard mere petty officers and men bragging with a pardonable vainglory, in no wise to his own bravery or skill, but to the superintending protection of Heaven, which he ever seemed to think was our especial ally. And our army got to believe so, and the enemy learnt to think so too ; for we never entered into a battle without a perfect confidence that it was to end in a victory ; nor did the French, after the issue of Blenheim, and that astonishing triumph of Ramillies, ever meet us without feeling that the game was lost before it was begun to be played, and that our general's fortune was irresistible. Here, as at Blenheim, the duke's charger was shot, and 'twas thought for a moment he was dead. As he mounted another, Binfield, his master of the horse, kneeling to hold his grace's stirrup, had his head shot away by a cannon-ball. A French gentleman of the Royal Household, that was a prisoner with us, told the writer that at the time of the charge of the Household, when their horse and ours were mingled, an Irish officer recognized the Prince-Duke, and calling out—' Marlborough, Marlborough ! ' fired his pistol at him *à bout portant*, and that a score more carbines and pistols were discharged at him. Not one touched him : he rode through the French Cuirassiers sword in hand, and entirely unhurt, and calm and smiling rallied the German horse, that was reeling before the enemy, brought these and twenty squadrons of Orkney's back upon them, and drove the French across the river again—leading the charge himself, and defeating the only dangerous move the French made that day.

Major-General Webb commanded on the left of our line, and had his own regiment under the orders of their beloved colonel. Neither he nor they belied their character for gallantry on this occasion ; but it was about his dear young lord that Esmond was anxious, never having sight of him save once, in the whole course of the day, when he brought an order from the commander-in-chief to Mr. Webb. When our horse, having charged round the right flank of the enemy by Overkirk, had thrown him into entire confusion, a general advance was made, and our whole line of foot, crossing the little river and the morass, ascended the high ground where the French were posted, cheering as they went, the enemy retreating before them. 'Twas a service of more glory than danger, the French battalions never waiting to exchange push of pike or bayonet with ours ; and the gunners flying from their pieces which our line left behind us as they advanced, and the French fell back.

At first it was a retreat orderly enough ; but presently the retreat became a rout, and a frightful slaughter of the French ensued on this panic ; so that an army of sixty thousand men was utterly crushed and destroyed in the course of a couple of hours. It was as if a hurricane had seized a compact and numerous fleet, flung it all to the winds, shattered, sunk, and annihilated it ; *afflavit Deus, et dissipati sunt.*[*] The French army of Flanders was gone, their artillery, their standards, their treasure, provisions, and ammunition were all left behind them : the poor devils had even fled without their soup-kettles, which are as much the palladia of the French infantry as of the Grand Signor's Janizaries,[*] and round which they rally even more than round their lilies.

The pursuit, and a dreadful carnage which ensued (for the dregs of a battle, however brilliant, are ever a base residue of rapine, cruelty, and drunken plunder), was carried far beyond the field of Ramillies.

Honest Lockwood, Esmond's servant, no doubt wanted to be among the marauders himself and take his share of the booty ; for when, the action over, and the troops got to their ground for the night, the captain bade Lockwood get a horse, he asked, with a very rueful countenance, whether his honour would have him come too ; but his honour only bade him go about his own business, and Jack hopped away quite delighted as soon as he saw his master mounted. Esmond made his way, and not without danger and difficulty, to his grace's head quarters, and found for himself very quickly where the aides de camp's quarters were, in an outbuilding of a farm, where several of these gentlemen were seated, drinking and singing, and at supper. If he had any anxiety about his boy, 'twas relieved at once. One of the gentlemen was singing a song to a tune that Mr. Farquhar and Mr. Gay both had used in their admirable comedies, and very popular in the army of that day ; after the song came a chorus, ' Over the hills and far away ' ; and Esmond heard Frank's fresh voice soaring, as it were, over the songs of the rest of the young men—a voice that had always a certain artless, indescribable pathos with it, and indeed which caused Mr. Esmond's eyes to fill with tears now, out of thankfulness to God the child was safe and still alive to laugh and sing.

When the song was over Esmond entered the room, where he knew several of the gentlemen present, and there sat my young lord, having taken off his cuirass, his waistcoat open, his face flushed, his long yellow hair hanging over his shoulders, drinking with the rest ; the youngest, gayest, handsomest there. As soon as he saw Esmond, he clapped down his glass, and running towards his friend, put both his arms round him and embraced him. The other's voice trembled with joy as he greeted the lad ; he had thought but now as he stood in the courtyard under the clear-shining moonlight : ' Great God ! what a scene of murder is here within a mile of us ; what hundreds and thousands have faced danger to-day ; and here are these lads singing over their cups, and the same moon that is shining over yonder horrid field is looking down on Walcote very likely, while my lady sits and thinks about her boy that is at the war.' As Esmond embraced his young pupil now, 'twas with the feeling of quite religious thankfulness, and an almost paternal pleasure that he beheld him.

Round his neck was a star with a striped ribbon, that was made of small brilliants and might be worth a hundred crowns. 'Look,' says he, 'won't that be a pretty present for mother?'

'Who gave you the Order? says Harry, saluting the gentleman: 'did you win it in battle?'

'I won it,' cried the other, 'with my sword and my spear. There was a mousquetaire that had it round his neck—such a big mousquetaire, as big as General Webb. I called out to him to surrender, and that I'd give him quarter: he called me a *petit polisson*, and fired his pistol at me, and then sent it at my head with a curse. I rode at him, sir, drove my sword right under his arm-hole, and broke it in the rascal's body. I found a purse in his holster with sixty-five louis in it, and a bundle of love-letters, and a flask of Hungary-water. *Vive la guerre!* there are the ten pieces you lent me. I should like to have a fight every day;' and he pulled at his little moustache and bade a servant bring a supper to Captain Esmond.

Harry fell to with a very good appetite; he had tasted nothing since twenty hours ago, at early dawn. Master Grandson, who read this, do you look for the history of battles and sieges? Go, find them in the proper books; this is only the story of your grandfather and his family. Far more pleasant to him than the victory, though for that too he may say *meminisse juvat,* it was to find that the day was over, and his dear young Castlewood was unhurt.

And would you, sirrah, wish to know how it was that a sedate captain of foot, a studious and rather solitary bachelor of eight or nine and twenty years of age, who did not care very much for the jollities which his comrades engaged in, and was never known to lose his heart in any garrison town—should you wish to know why such a man had so prodigious a tenderness, and tended so fondly a boy of eighteen, wait, my good friend, until thou art in love with thy schoolfellow's sister, and then see how mighty tender thou wilt be towards him. Esmond's general and his grace the prince-duke were notoriously at variance, and the former's friendship was in no wise likely to advance any man's promotion, of whose services Webb spoke well; but rather likely to injure him, so the army said, in the favour of the greater man. However, Mr. Esmond had the good fortune to be mentioned very advantageously by

Major-General Webb in his report after the action; and the major of his regiment and two of the captains having been killed upon the day of Ramillies, Esmond, who was second of the lieutenants, got his company, and had the honour of serving as Captain Esmond in the next campaign.

My lord went home in the winter, but Esmond was afraid to follow him. His dear mistress wrote him letters more than once, thanking him, as mothers know how to thank, for his care and protection of her boy, extolling Esmond's own merits with a great deal more praise than they deserved; for he did his duty no better than any other officer; and speaking sometimes, though gently and cautiously, of Beatrix. News came from home of at least half a dozen grand matches that the beautiful maid of honour was about to make. She was engaged to an earl, our gentlemen of St. James's said, and then jilted him for a duke, who, in his turn, had drawn off. Earl or duke it might be who should win this Helen, Esmond knew she would never bestow herself on a poor captain. Her conduct, it was clear, was little satisfactory to her mother, who scarcely mentioned her, or else the kind lady thought it was best to say nothing, and leave time to work out its cure. At any rate, Harry was best away from the fatal object which always wrought him so much mischief; and so he never asked for leave to go home, but remained with his regiment that was garrisoned in Brussels, which city fell into our hands when the victory of Ramillies drove the French out of Flanders.

CHAPTER XIII

I MEET AN OLD ACQUAINTANCE IN FLANDERS, AND FIND MY MOTHER'S GRAVE AND MY OWN CRADLE THERE

BEING one day in the Church of St. Gudule, at Brussels, admiring the antique splendour of the architecture (and always entertaining a great tenderness and reverence for the Mother Church, that hath been as wickedly persecuted in England as ever she herself persecuted in the days of her prosperity), Esmond saw kneeling at a side altar, an officer in a green uniform coat, very deeply engaged in devotion. Something familiar in the figure and posture of the kneeling man struck Captain Esmond, even before he saw the

officer's face. As he rose up, putting away into his pocket
a little black breviary, such as priests use, Esmond beheld
a countenance so like that of his friend and tutor of early
days, Father Holt, that he broke out into an exclamation of
astonishment and advanced a step towards the gentleman,
who was making his way out of church. The German
officer too looked surprised when he saw Esmond, and his
face from being pale grew suddenly red. By this mark
of recognition, the Englishman knew that he could not be
mistaken; and though the other did not stop, but on the
contrary rather hastily walked away towards the door,
Esmond pursued him and faced him once more, as the
officer helping himself to holy water, turned mechanically
towards the altar to bow to it ere he quitted the sacred
edifice.

'My father!' says Esmond in English.

'Silence! I do not understand. I do not speak English,'
says the other in Latin.

Esmond smiled at this sign of confusion, and replied in
the same language. 'I should know my father in any
garment, black or white, shaven or bearded:' for the
Austrian officer was habited quite in the military manner,
and had as warlike a moustachio as any Pandour.*

He laughed—we were on the church steps by this time,
passing through the crowd of beggars that usually is there
holding up little trinkets for sale and whining for alms.
'You speak Latin,' says he, 'in the English way, Harry
Esmond; you have forsaken the old true Roman tongue
you once knew.' His tone was very frank, and friendly
quite; the kind voice of fifteen years back; he gave Esmond
his hand as he spoke.

'Others have changed their coats too, my father,' says
Esmond, glancing at his friend's military decoration.

'Hush! I am Mr. or Captain von Holtz, in the Bavarian
Elector's service, and on a mission to his highness the
Prince of Savoy. You can keep a secret I know from
old times.'

'Captain von Holtz,' says Esmond, 'I am your very
humble servant.'

'And you, too, have changed your coat,' continues the
other, in his laughing way; 'I have heard of you at Cambridge and afterwards: we have friends everywhere; and
I am told that Mr. Esmond at Cambridge was as good a

fencer as he was a bad theologian.' (So, thinks Esmond, my old *maitre d'armes* was a Jesuit as they said.)

'Perhaps you are right,' says the other, reading his thoughts quite as he used to do in old days : ' you were all but killed at Hochstedt of a wound in the left side. You were before that at Vigo, aide de camp to the Duke of Ormonde. You got your company the other day after Ramillies ; your general and the prince-duke are not friends ; he is of the Webbs of Lydiard Tregoze, in the county of York, a relation of my Lord St. John. Your cousin, Monsieur de Castlewood, served his first campaign this year in the Guard ; yes, I do know a few things as you see.'

Captain Esmond laughed in his turn. ' You have indeed a curious knowledge,' he says. A foible of Mr. Holt's, who did know more about books and men than, perhaps, almost any person Esmond had ever met, was omniscience ; thus in every point he here professed to know, he was nearly right, but not quite. Esmond's wound was in the right side, not the left, his first general was General Lumley ; Mr. Webb came out of Wiltshire, not out of Yorkshire ; and so forth. Esmond did not think fit to correct his old master in these trifling blunders, but they served to give him a knowledge of the other's character, and he smiled to think that this was his oracle of early days ; only now no longer infallible or divine.

' Yes,' continues Father Holt, or Captain von Holtz, ' for a man who has not been in England these eight years, I know what goes on in London very well. The old dean is dead, my Lady Castlewood's father. Do you know that your recusant bishops wanted to consecrate him Bishop of Southampton, and that Collier is Bishop of Thetford by the same imposition ? The Princess Anne has the gout and eats too much ; when the king returns, Collier will be an archbishop.'

' Amen ! ' says Esmond, laughing ; ' and I hope to see your eminence no longer in jack-boots, but red stockings, at Whitehall.'

' You are always with us—I know that—I heard of that when you were at Cambridge ; so was the late lord ; so is the young viscount.'

' And so was my father before me,' said Mr. Esmond, looking calmly at the other, who did not, however, show the

least sign of intelligence in his impenetrable grey eyes—
how well Harry remembered them and their look! only
crows' feet were wrinkled round them—marks of black old
Time had settled there.

Esmond's face chose to show no more sign of meaning
than the father's. There may have been on the one side and
the other just the faintest glitter of recognition, as you see
a bayonet shining out of an ambush; but each party fell
back, when everything was again dark.

'And you, *mon capitaine*, where have you been?' says
Esmond, turning away the conversation from this dangerous
ground, where neither chose to engage.

'I may have been in Pekin,' says he, 'or I may have
been in Paraguay—who knows where?* I am now Captain
von Holtz, in the service of his electoral highness, come to
negotiate exchange of prisoners with his highness of Savoy.'

'Twas well known that very many officers in our army
were well-affected towards the young king at St. Germains,
whose right to the throne was undeniable, and whose
accession to it, at the death of his sister, by far the greater
part of the English people would have preferred, to the
having a petty German prince for a sovereign, about whose
cruelty, rapacity, boorish manners, and odious foreign ways,
a thousand stories were current. It wounded our English pride
to think, that a shabby High-Dutch duke, whose revenues
were not a tithe as great as those of many of the princes
of our ancient English nobility, who could not speak a word
of our language, and whom we chose to represent as a sort
of German boor, feeding on train-oil and sauerkraut, with
a bevy of mistresses in a barn, should come to reign over the
proudest and most polished people in the world. Were we,
the conquerors of the Grand Monarch, to submit to that
ignoble domination? What did the Hanoverian's Protes-
tantism matter to us? Was it not notorious (we were told
and led to believe so) that one of the daughters of this
Protestant hero was being bred up with no religion at all,
as yet, and ready to be made Lutheran or Roman, according
as the husband might be, whom her parents should find for
her?* This talk, very idle and abusive much of it was, went
on at a hundred mess-tables in the army; there was scarce
an ensign that did not hear it, or join in it, and everybody
knew, or affected to know, that the commander-in-chief
himself had relations with his nephew, the Duke of Berwick

('twas by an Englishman, thank God, that we were beaten at Almanza), and that his grace was most anxious to restore the royal race of his benefactors, and to repair his former treason.

This is certain, that for a considerable period no officer in the duke's army lost favour with the commander-in-chief for entertaining or proclaiming his loyalty towards the exiled family. When the Chevalier de St. George, as the King of England called himself, came with the dukes of the French blood royal, to join the French army under Vendosme, hundreds of ours saw him and cheered him, and we all said he was like his father in this, who, seeing the action of La Hogue fought between the French ships and ours, was on the side of his native country during the battle. But this, at least the chevalier knew, and every one knew, that, however well our troops and their general might be inclined towards the prince personally, in the face of the enemy there was no question at all. Wherever my lord duke found a French army, he would fight and beat it, as he did at Oudenarde,* two years after Ramillies, where his grace achieved another of his transcendent victories ; and the noble young prince, who charged gallantly along with the magnificent Maison-du-Roy, sent to compliment his conquerors after the action.

In this battle, where the young Electoral Prince of Hanover behaved himself very gallantly, fighting on our side, Esmond's dear General Webb distinguished himself prodigiously, exhibiting consummate skill and coolness as a general, and fighting with the personal bravery of a common soldier. Esmond's good luck again attended him ; he escaped without a hurt, although more than a third of his regiment was killed, had again the honour to be favourably mentioned in his commander's report, and was advanced to the rank of major. But of this action there is little need to speak, as it hath been related in every *Gazette*, and talked of in every hamlet in this country. To return from it to the writer's private affairs, which here, in his old age, and at a distance, he narrates for his children who come after him. Before Oudenarde, and after that chance rencontre with Captain von Holtz at Brussels, a space of more than a year elapsed, during which the captain of Jesuits and the captain of Webb's Fusiliers were thrown very much together. Esmond had no difficulty in finding out (indeed, the other made no secret of it to him, being assured from old times of his pupil's fidelity), that the negotiator of prisoners was an agent from St. Germains, and that he carried intelligence between great personages in our camp and that of the French. ' My business,' said he, ' and I tell you, both because I can trust you, and your keen eyes have already discovered it, is between the King of England and his subjects, here engaged in fighting the French king. As between you and them, all the Jesuits in the world will not prevent your quarrelling : fight it out, gentlemen. St. George for England, I say—and you know who says so, wherever he may be.'

I think Holt loved to make a parade of mystery, as it were, and would appear and disappear at our quarters as suddenly as he used to return and vanish in the old days at Castlewood. He had passes between both armies, and seemed to know (but with that inaccuracy which belonged to the good father's omniscience) equally well what passed in the French camp and in ours. One day he would give Esmond news of a great *feste* that took place in the French quarters, of a supper of Monsieur de Rohan's, where there was play and violins, and then dancing and masques : the king drove thither in Marshal Villar's own guinguette.* Another day he had the news of his Majesty's ague, the king had not had a fit these ten days, and might be said to be well. Captain Holtz made a visit to England during this time, so eager was he about negotiating prisoners ; and 'twas on returning from this voyage that he began to open himself more to Esmond, and to make him, as occasion served, at their various meetings, several of those confidences which are here set down all together.

The reason of his increased confidence was this : upon going to London, the old director of Esmond's aunt, the dowager, paid her ladyship a visit at Chelsey, and there learnt from her that Captain Esmond was acquainted with the secret of his family, and was determined never to divulge it. The knowledge of this fact raised Esmond in his old tutor's eyes, so Holt was pleased to say, and he admired Harry very much for his abnegation.

' The family at Castlewood have done far more for me than my own ever did,' Esmond said. ' I would give my life for them. Why should I grudge the only benefit that 'tis in my power to confer on them ? ' The good father's

eyes filled with tears at this speech, which to the other
seemed very simple : he embraced Esmond, and broke out
into many admiring expressions ; he said he was a *noble
cœur*, that he was proud of him, and fond of him as his pupil
and friend—regretted more than ever that he had lost him,
and been forced to leave him in those early times, when he
might have had an influence over him, have brought him
into that only true Church to which the father belonged,
and enlisted him in the noblest army in which a man ever
engaged—meaning his own Society of Jesus, which numbers
(says he) in its troops the greatest heroes the world ever
knew ;—warriors, brave enough to dare or endure anything,
to encounter any odds, to die any death ;—soldiers that
have won triumphs a thousand times more brilliant than
those of the greatest general ; that have brought nations
on their knees to their sacred banner, the Cross ; that have
achieved glories and palms incomparably brighter than
those awarded to the most splendid earthly conquerors—
crowns of immortal light, and seats in the high places of
Heaven.

Esmond was thankful for his old friend's good opinion,
however little he might share the Jesuit father's enthusiasm.
' I have thought of that question, too,' says he, ' dear father,'
and he took the other's hand—' thought it out for myself,
as all men must, and contrive to do the right, and trust to
Heaven as devoutly in my way as you in yours. Another
six months of you as a child, and I had desired no better.
I used to weep upon my pillow at Castlewood as I thought
of you, and I might have been a brother of your order ;
and who knows,' Esmond added, with a smile, ' a priest in
full orders, and with a pair of moustachios, and a Bavarian
uniform.'

' My son,' says Father Holt, turning red, ' in the cause
of religion and loyalty all disguises are fair.'

' Yes,' broke in Esmond, ' all disguises are fair, you say ;
and all uniforms, say I, black or red,—a black cockade or
a white one—or a laced hat, or a sombrero, with a tonsure
under it. I cannot believe that St. Francis Xavier sailed
over the sea in a cloak, or raised the dead—I tried ; and
very nearly did once, but cannot. Suffer me to do the
right, and to hope for the best in my own way.'

Esmond wished to cut short the good father's theology,
and succeeded ; and the other, sighing over his pupil's

invincible ignorance, did not withdraw his affection from him, but gave him his utmost confidence—as much, that is to say, as a priest can give : more than most do ; for he was naturally garrulous, and too eager to speak.

Holt's friendship encouraged Captain Esmond to ask, what he long wished to know, and none could tell him, some history of the poor mother whom he had often imagined in his dreams, and whom he never knew. He described to Holt those circumstances which are already put down in the first part of this story—the promise he had made to his dear lord, and that dying friend's confession ; and he besought Mr. Holt to tell him what he knew regarding the poor woman from whom he had been taken.

' She was of this very town,' Holt said, and took Esmond to see the street where her father lived, and where, as he believed, she was born. ' In 1676, when your father came hither in the retinue of the late king, then Duke of York, and banished hither in disgrace, Captain Thomas Esmond became acquainted with your mother, pursued her, and made a victim of her ; he hath told me in many subsequent conversations, which I felt bound to keep private then, that she was a woman of great virtue and tenderness, and in all respects a most fond, faithful creature. He called himself Captain Thomas, having good reason to be ashamed of his conduct towards her, and hath spoken to me many times with sincere remorse for that, as with fond love for her many amiable qualities. He owned to having treated her very ill ; and that at this time his life was one of pro- fligacy, gambling, and poverty. She became with child of you ; was cursed by her own parents at that discovery ; though she never upbraided, except by her involuntary tears, and the misery depicted on her countenance, the author of her wretchedness and ruin.

' Thomas Esmond—Captain Thomas, as he was called— became engaged in a gaming-house brawl, of which the consequence was a duel, and a wound so severe that he never—his surgeon said—could outlive it. Thinking his death certain, and touched with remorse, he sent for a priest of the very Church of St. Gudule where I met you ; and on the same day, after his making submission to our Church, was married to your mother a few weeks before you were born. My Lord Viscount Castlewood, Marquis of Esmond, by King James's patent, which I myself took to your father,

your lordship was christened at St. Gudule by the same
curé who married your parents, and by the name of Henry
Thomas, son of E. Thomas, officier Anglais, and Gertrude
Maes.   You see you belong to us from your birth, and why
I did not christen you when you became my dear little pupil
at Castlewood.

' Your father's wound took a favourable turn—perhaps
his conscience was eased by the right he had done—and to
the surprise of the doctors he recovered.   But as his health
came back, his wicked nature, too, returned.   He was tired
of the poor girl, whom he had ruined ; and receiving some
remittance from his uncle, my lord the old viscount then in
England, he pretended business, promised return, and never
saw your poor mother more.

' He owned to me, in confession first, but afterwards in
talk before your aunt, his wife, else I never could have
disclosed what I now tell you, that on coming to London
he writ a pretended confession to poor Gertrude Maes—
Gertrude Esmond—of his having been married in England
previously, before uniting himself with her ; said that his
name was not Thomas ; that he was about to quit Europe
for the Virginia plantations, where, indeed, your family
had a grant of land from King Charles the First ; sent her
a supply of money, the half of the last hundred guineas he
had, entreated her pardon, and bade her farewell.

' Poor Gertrude never thought that the news in this letter
might be untrue as the rest of your father's conduct to her.
But though a young man of her own degree, who knew her
history, and whom she liked before she saw the English
gentleman who was the cause of all her misery, offered to
marry her, and to adopt you as his own child, and give you
his name, she refused him.   This refusal only angered her
father, who had taken her home ; she never held up her
head there, being the subject of constant unkindness after
her fall ; and some devout ladies of her acquaintance
offering to pay a little pension for her, she went into a convent, and you were put out to nurse.

' A sister of the young fellow, who would have adopted
you as his son, was the person who took charge of you.
Your mother and this person were cousins.   She had just
lost a child of her own, which you replaced, your own mother
being too sick and feeble to feed you ; and presently your
nurse grew so fond of you, that she even grudged letting

you visit the convent where your mother was, and where the nuns petted the little infant, as they pitied and loved its unhappy parent. Her vocation became stronger every day, and at the end of two years she was received as a sister of the house.

'Your nurse's family were silk-weavers out of France, whither they returned to Arras in French Flanders, shortly before your mother took her vows, carrying you with them, then a child of three years old. 'Twas a town, before the late vigorous measures of the French king, full of Protestants, and here your nurse's father, old Pastoureau, he with whom you afterwards lived at Ealing, adopted the reformed doctrines, perverting all his house with him. They were expelled thence by the edict of his most Christian Majesty, and came to London, and set up their looms in Spittlefields. The old man brought a little money with him, and carried on his trade, but in a poor way. He was a widower; by this time his daughter, a widow too, kept house for him, and his son and he laboured together at their vocation. Meanwhile your father had publicly owned his conversion just before King Charles's death (in whom our Church had much such another convert), was reconciled to my Lord Viscount Castlewood, and married, as you know, to his daughter.

'It chanced that the younger Pastoureau, going with a piece of brocade to the mercer, who employed him, on Ludgate Hill, met his old rival coming out of an ordinary there. Pastoureau knew your father at once, seized him by the collar, and upbraided him as a villain, who had seduced his mistress, and afterwards deserted her and her son. Mr. Thomas Esmond also recognized Pastoureau at once, besought him to calm his indignation, and not to bring a crowd round about them; and bade him to enter into the tavern, out of which he had just stepped, when he would give him any explanation. Pastoureau entered, and heard the landlord order the drawer to show Captain Thomas to a room; it was by his Christian name that your father was familiarly called at his tavern haunts, which, to say the truth, were none of the most reputable.

'I must tell you that Captain Thomas, or my lord viscount afterwards, was never at a loss for a story, and could cajole a woman or a dun with a volubility, and an air of simplicity at the same time, of which many a creditor of

his has been the dupe. His tales used to gather verisimili-
tude as he went on with them. He strung together fact after
fact with a wonderful rapidity and coherence. It required,
saving your presence, a very long habit of acquaintance
with your father to know when his lordship was l——,——
telling the truth or no.

' He told me with rueful remorse when he was ill—for the
fear of death set him instantly repenting, and with shrieks
of laughter when he was well, his lordship having a very
great sense of humour—how in half an hour's time, and
before a bottle was drunk, he had completely succeeded in
biting poor Pastoureau. The seduction he owned too :
that he could not help : he was quite ready with tears at
a moment's warning, and shed them profusely to melt his
credulous listener. He wept for your mother even more
than Pastoureau did, who cried very heartily, poor fellow,
as my lord informed me ; he swore upon his honour that
he had twice sent money to Brussels, and mentioned the
name of the merchant with whom it was lying for poor
Gertrude's use. He did not even know whether she had a
child or no, or whether she was alive or dead ; but got these
facts easily out of honest Pastoureau's answers to him.
When he heard that she was in a convent, he said he hoped
to end his days in one himself, should he survive his wife,
whom he hated, and had been forced by a cruel father to
marry ; and when he was told that Gertrude's son was alive,
and actually in London, " I started," says he ; " for then,
damme, my wife was expecting to lie-in, and I thought
should this old Put, my father-in-law, run rusty, here would
be a good chance to frighten him."

' He expressed the deepest gratitude to the Pastoureau
family for their care of the infant ; you were now near six
years old ; and on Pastoureau bluntly telling him, when he
proposed to go that instant and see the darling child, that
they never wished to see his ill-omened face again within
their doors ; that he might have the boy, though they should
all be very sorry to lose him ; and that they would take his
money, they being poor, if he gave it ; or bring him up,
by God's help, as they had hitherto done, without : he
acquiesced in this at once, with a sigh, said, " Well, 'twas
better that the dear child should remain with friends who
had been so admirably kind to him " ; and in his talk to
me afterwards, honestly praised and admired the weaver's

conduct and spirit ; owned that the Frenchman was a right fellow, and he, the Lord have mercy upon him, a sad villain.

'Your father,' Mr. Holt went on to say, 'was good-natured with his money when he had it ; and having that day received a supply from his uncle, gave the weaver ten pieces with perfect freedom, and promised him further remittances. He took down eagerly Pastoureau's name and place of abode in his table-book, and when the other asked him for his own, gave, with the utmost readiness, his name as Captain Thomas, New Lodge, Penzance, Cornwall ; he said he was in London for a few days only on business connected with his wife's property; described her as a shrew, though a woman of kind disposition ; and depicted his father as a Cornish squire, in an infirm state of health, at whose death he hoped for something handsome, when he promised richly to reward the admirable protector of his child, and to provide for the boy. " And by Gad, sir," he said to me in his strange laughing way, " I ordered a piece of brocade of the very same pattern as that which the fellow was carrying, and presented it to my wife for a morning wrapper, to receive company after she lay-in of our little boy."

'Your little pension was paid regularly enough ; and when your father became Viscount Castlewood on his uncle's demise, I was employed to keep a watch over you, and 'twas at my instance that you were brought home. Your foster-mother was dead ; her father made acquaintance with a woman whom he married, who quarrelled with his son. The faithful creature came back to Brussels to be near the woman he loved, and died, too, a few months before her. Will you see her cross in the convent cemetery ? The superior is an old penitent of mine, and remembers Sœur Marie Madeleine fondly still.'

Esmond came to this spot in one sunny evening of spring, and saw, amidst a thousand black crosses, casting their shadows across the grassy mounds, that particular one which marked his mother's resting-place. Many more of those poor creatures that lay there had adopted that same name, with which sorrow had rebaptized her, and which fondly seemed to hint their individual story of love and grief. He fancied her in tears and darkness, kneeling at the foot of her cross, under which her cares were buried.

Surely he knelt down, and said his own prayer there, not in sorrow so much as in awe (for even his memory had no recollection of her), and in pity for the pangs which the gentle soul in life had been made to suffer. To this cross she brought them; for this heavenly bridegroom she exchanged the husband who had wooed her, the traitor who had left her. A thousand such hillocks lay round about, the gentle daisies springing out of the grass over them, and each bearing its cross and requiescat. A nun, veiled in black, was kneeling hard by, at a sleeping sister's bedside (so fresh made, that the spring had scarce had time to spin a coverlid for it); beyond the cemetery walls you had glimpses of life and the world, and the spires and gables of the city. A bird came down from a roof opposite, and lit first on a cross, and then on the grass below it, whence it flew away presently with a leaf in its mouth: then came a sound as of chanting, from the chapel of the sisters hard by; others had long since filled the place, which poor Mary Magdalene once had there, were kneeling at the same stall, and hearing the same hymns and prayers in which her stricken heart had found consolation. Might she sleep in peace—might she sleep in peace; and we, too, when our struggles and pains are over! But the earth is the Lord's as the heaven is; we are alike His creatures here and yonder. I took a little flower off the hillock, and kissed it, and went my way, like the bird that had just lighted on the cross by me, back into the world again. Silent receptacle of death! tranquil depth of calm, out of reach of tempest and trouble! I felt as one who had been walking below the sea, and treading amidst the bones of shipwrecks.

CHAPTER XIV

THE CAMPAIGN OF 1707, 1708

DURING the whole of the year which succeeded that in which the glorious battle of Ramillies had been fought, our army made no movement of importance, much to the disgust of very many of our officers remaining inactive in Flanders, who said that his grace the captain-general had had fighting enough, and was all for money now, and the enjoyment of his five thousand a year and his splendid palace at Woodstock, which was now being built. And his grace had sufficient occupation fighting his enemies at home this year, where it begun to be whispered that his favour was decreasing, and his duchess losing her hold on the queen, who was transferring her royal affections to the famous Mrs. Masham*, and Mrs. Masham's humble servant, Mr. Harley. Against their intrigues, our duke passed a great part of his time intriguing. Mr. Harley was got out of office, and his grace, in so far, had a victory. But her Majesty, convinced against her will, was of that opinion still, of which the poet says people are when so convinced,* and Mr. Harley before long had his revenge.

Meanwhile the business of fighting did not go on any way to the satisfaction of Marlborough's gallant lieutenants. During all 1707, with the French before us, we had never so much as a battle; our army in Spain was utterly routed at Almanza by the gallant Duke of Berwick; and we of Webb's, which regiment the young duke had commanded before his father's abdication, were a little proud to think that it was our colonel who had achieved this victory. 'I think if I had had Galway's place, and my Fusiliers,' says our general, 'we would not have laid down our arms, even to our old colonel, as Galway*did; and Webb's officers swore if we had had Webb, at least we would not have been taken prisoners.' Our dear old general talked incautiously of himself and of others; a braver or a more brilliant soldier never lived than he; but he blew his honest trumpet rather more loudly than became a commander of his station, and, mighty man of valour as he was, shook his great spear, and blustered before the army too fiercely.

Mysterious Mr. Holtz went off on a secret expedition in the early part of 1708, with great elation of spirits, and a prophecy to Esmond that a wonderful something was about to take place. This secret came out on my friend's return to the army, whither he brought a most rueful and dejected countenance, and owned that the great something he had been engaged upon had failed utterly. He had been indeed with that luckless expedition of the Chevalier de St. George, who was sent by the French king with ships and an army from Dunkirk, and was to have invaded and conquered Scotland. But that ill wind which ever opposed all the projects upon which the prince ever embarked, prevented the Chevalier's invasion of Scotland, as 'tis known, and blew poor Monsieur von Holtz back into our camp again, to scheme and foretell, and to pry about as usual. The Chevalier (the King of England, as some of us held him) went from Dunkirk to the French army to make the campaign against us. The Duke of Burgundy had the command this year, having the Duke of Berry with him, and the famous Mareschal Vendosme and the Duke of Matignon to aid him in the campaign. Holtz, who knew everything that was passing in Flanders and France (and the Indies for what I know), insisted that there would be no more fighting in 1708 than there had been in the previous year, and that our commander had reasons for keeping him quiet. Indeed, Esmond's general, who was known as a grumbler, and to have a hearty mistrust of the great duke, and hundreds more officers besides, did not scruple to say that these private reasons came to the duke in the shape of crown-pieces from the French king, by whom the general-issimo was bribed to avoid a battle. There were plenty of men in our lines, quidnuncs, to whom Mr. Webb listened only too willingly, who could specify the exact sums the duke got, how much fell to Cadogan's share,* and what was the precise fee given to Doctor Hare.

And the successes with which the French began the campaign of 1708, served to give strength to these reports of treason, which were in everybody's mouth. Our general allowed the enemy to get between us and Ghent, and declined to attack him, though for eight-and-forty hours the armies were in presence of each other. Ghent was taken, and on the same day Monsieur de la Mothe summoned Bruges ; and these two great cities fell into the hands of

the French without firing a shot. A few days afterwards
La Mothe seized upon the fort of Plashendall : and it began
to be supposed that all Spanish Flanders, as well as Brabant,
would fall into the hands of the French troops ; when the
Prince Eugene arrived from the Mozelle, and then there was
no more shilly-shallying.

The Prince of Savoy always signalized his arrival at the
army by a great feast (my lord duke's entertainments
were both seldom and shabby) : and I remember our general
returning from this dinner with the two commanders-in-
chief ; his honest head a little excited by wine, which was
dealt out much more liberally by the Austrian than by the
English commander :—' Now,' says my general, slapping the
table, with an oath, ' he must fight ; and when he is forced
to it, d—— it, no man in Europe can stand up against
Jack Churchill.' Within a week the battle of Oudenarde
was fought, when, hate each other as they might, Esmond's
general and the commander-in-chief were forced to admire
each other, so splendid was the gallantry of each upon
this day.

The brigade commanded by Major-General Webb gave
and received about as hard knocks as any that were delivered
in that action, in which Mr. Esmond had the fortune to serve
at the head of his own company in his regiment, under the
command of their own colonel as major-general ; and it
was his good luck to bring the regiment out of action as
commander of it, the four senior officers above him being
killed in the prodigious slaughter which happened on that
day. I like to think that Jack Haythorn, who sneered at
me for being a bastard and a parasite of Webb's, as he chose
to call me, and with whom I had had words, shook hands
with me the day before the battle begun. Three days
before, poor Brace, our lieutenant-colonel, had heard of his
elder brother's death, and was heir to a baronetcy in Norfolk,
and four thousand a year. Fate, that had left him harmless
through a dozen campaigns, seized on him just as the world
was worth living for, and he went into action, knowing, as
he said, that the luck was going to turn against him. The
major had just joined us—a creature of Lord Marlborough,
put in much to the dislike of the other officers, and to be
a spy upon us, as it was said. I know not whether the
truth was so, nor who took the tattle of our mess to head
quarters, but Webb's regiment, as its colonel, was known

to be in the commander-in-chief's black books : 'And if
he did not dare to break it up at home,' our gallant old
chief used to say, 'he was determined to destroy it before
the enemy ; ' so that poor Major Proudfoot was put into
a post of danger.

Esmond's dear young viscount, serving as aide de camp
to my lord duke, received a wound, and won an honourable
name for himself in the *Gazette ;* and Captain Esmond's
name was sent in for promotion by his general, too, whose
favourite he was. It made his heart beat to think that
certain eyes at home, the brightest in the world, might read
the page on which his humble services were recorded ; but
his mind was made up steadily to keep out of their dangerous
influence, and to let time and absence conquer that passion
he had still lurking about him. Away from Beatrix, it did
not trouble him ; but he knew as certain that if he returned
home, his fever would break out again, and avoided Walcote
as a Lincolnshire man avoids returning to his fens, where
he is sure that the ague is lying in wait for him.

We of the English party in the army, who were inclined
to sneer at everything that came out of Hanover, and to
treat as little better than boors and savages the Elector's
court and family, were yet forced to confess that, on the
day of Oudenarde, the young electoral prince, then making
his first campaign, conducted himself with the spirit and
courage of an approved soldier. On this occasion his
electoral highness had better luck than the King of England,
who was with his cousins in the enemy's camp, and had
to run with them at the ignominious end of the day. With
the most consummate generals in the world before them,
and an admirable commander on their own side, they chose
to neglect the councils, and to rush into a combat with the
former, which would have ended in the utter annihilation
of their army but for the great skill and bravery of the Duke
of Vendosme, who remedied, as far as courage and genius
might, the disasters occasioned by the squabbles and follies
of his kinsmen, the legitimate princes of the blood royal.

'If the Duke of Berwick had but been in the army, the
fate of the day would have been very different,' was all
that poor Mr. von Holtz could say ; 'and you would have
seen that the hero of Almanza was fit to measure swords
with the conqueror of Blenheim.'

The business relative to the exchange of prisoners was

always going on, and was at least that ostensible one which
kept Mr. Holtz perpetually on the move between the forces
of the French and the Allies. I can answer for it, that he
was once very near hanged as a spy by Major-General
Wayne, when he was released and sent on to head quarters
by a special order of the commander-in-chief. He came
and went, always favoured, wherever he was, by some high
though occult protection. He carried messages between
the Duke of Berwick and his uncle, our duke. He seemed
to know as well what was taking place in the prince's quarter
as our own : he brought the compliments of the King of
England to some of our officers, the gentlemen of Webb's
among the rest, for their behaviour on that great day ; and
after Wynendael, when our general was chafing at the
neglect of our commander-in-chief, he said he knew how
that action was regarded by the chiefs of the French army,
and that the stand made before Wynendael wood was the
passage by which the Allies entered Lille.

' Ah ! ' says Holtz (and some folks were very willing to
listen to him), ' if the king came by his own, how changed
the conduct of affairs would be ! His Majesty's very exile
has this advantage, that he is enabled to read England
impartially, and to judge honestly of all the eminent men.
His sister is always in the hand of one greedy favourite or
another, through whose eyes she sees, and to whose flattery
or dependants she gives away everything. Do you suppose
that his Majesty, knowing England so well as he does,
would neglect such a man as General Webb ? He ought to
be in the House of Peers as Lord Lydiard. The enemy and
all Europe know his merit ; it is that very reputation
which certain great people, who hate all equality and independence, can never pardon.' It was intended that these
conversations should be carried to Mr. Webb. They were
welcome to him, for great as his services were, no man could
value them more than John Richmond Webb did himself,
and the differences between him and Marlborough being
notorious, his grace's enemies in the army and at home
began to court Webb, and set him up against the all-grasping
domineering chief. And soon after the victory of Oudenarde,
a glorious opportunity fell into General Webb's way, which
that gallant warrior did not neglect, and which gave him
the means of immensely increasing his reputation at home.

After Oudenarde, and against the counsels of Marlborough,

it was said, the Prince of Savoy sat down before Lille, the capital of French Flanders, and commenced that siege, the most celebrated of our time, and almost as famous as the siege of Troy itself, for the feats of valour performed in the assault and the defence. The enmity of that Prince of Savoy against the French king was a furious personal hate, quite unlike the calm hostility of our great English general, who was no more moved by the game of war than that of billiards, and pushed forward his squadrons, and drove his red battalions hither and thither as calmly as he would combine a stroke or make a cannon with the balls. The game over (and he played it so as to be pretty sure to win it), not the least animosity against the other party remained in the breast of this consummate tactician. Whereas between the Prince of Savoy and the French it was *guerre à mort*. Beaten off in one quarter, as he had been at Toulon in the last year, he was back again on another frontier of France, assailing it with his indefatigable fury. When the prince came to the army, the smouldering fires of war were lighted up and burst out into a flame. Our phlegmatic Dutch allies were made to advance at a quick march—our calm duke forced into action. The prince was an army in himself against the French ; the energy of his hatred prodigious, indefatigable— infectious over hundreds of thousands of men. The emperor's general was repaying, and with a vengeance, the slight the French king had put upon the fiery little Abbé of Savoy.* Brilliant and famous as a leader himself, and beyond all measure daring and intrepid, and enabled to cope with almost the best of those famous men of war who commanded the armies of the French king, Eugene had a weapon, the equal of which could not be found in France, since the cannon-shot of Sasbach laid low the noble Turenne, and could hurl Marlborough at the heads of the French host, and crush them as with a rock, under which all the gathered strength of their strongest captains must go down.

The English duke took little part in that vast siege of Lille, which the Imperial generalissimo pursued with all his force and vigour, further than to cover the besieging lines from the Duke of Burgundy's army, between which and the Imperialists our duke lay. Once, when Prince Eugene was wounded, our duke took his highness's place in the trenches ; but the siege was with the Imperialists, not with us. A division under Webb and Rantzau was detached into Artois and Picardy upon the most painful and odious service that Mr. Esmond ever saw in the course of his military life. The wretched towns of the defenceless provinces, whose young men had been drafted away into the French armies, which year after year the insatiable war devoured, were left at our mercy; and our orders were to show them none. We found places garrisoned by invalids, and children and women: poor as they were, and as the costs of this miserable war had made them, our commission was to rob these almost starving wretches—to tear the food out of their granaries, and strip them of their rags. 'Twas an expedition of rapine and murder we were sent on: our soldiers did deeds such as an honest man must blush to remember. We brought back money and provisions in quantity to the duke's camp; there had been no one to resist us, and yet who dares to tell with what murder and violence, with what brutal cruelty, outrage, insult, that ignoble booty had been ravished from the innocent and miserable victims of the war?

Meanwhile, gallantly as the operations before Lille had been conducted, the Allies had made but little progress, and 'twas said when we returned to the Duke of Marlborough's camp, that the siege would never be brought to a satisfactory end, and that the Prince of Savoy would be forced to raise it. My Lord Marlborough gave this as his opinion openly; those who mistrusted him, and Mr. Esmond owns himself to be of the number, hinted that the duke had his reasons why Lille should not be taken, and that he was paid to that end by the French king. If this was so, and I believe it, General Webb had now a remarkable opportunity of gratifying his hatred of the commander-in-chief, of balking that shameful avarice, which was one of the basest and most notorious qualities of the famous duke, and of showing his own consummate skill as a commander. And when I consider all the circumstances preceding the event which will now be related, that my lord duke was actually offered certain millions of crowns provided that the siege of Lille should be raised; that the Imperial army before it was without provisions and ammunition, and must have decamped but for the supplies that they received; that the march of the convoy destined to relieve the siege was accurately known to the French; and that the force covering it was shamefully inadequate to that end, and by

six times inferior to Count de la Mothe's army, which was
sent to intercept the convoy ; when 'tis certain that the
Duke of Berwick, de la Mothe's chief, was in constant
correspondence with his uncle, the English generalissimo :
I believe on my conscience that 'twas my Lord Marlborough's
intention to prevent those supplies, of which the Prince of
Savoy stood in absolute need, from ever reaching his highness ; that he meant to sacrifice the little army which
covered this convoy, and to betray it as he had betrayed
Tollemache at Brest ; as he betrayed every friend he had,
to further his own schemes of avarice or ambition.   But
for the miraculous victory which Esmond's general won over
an army six or seven times greater than his own, the siege
of Lille must have been raised ; and it must be remembered
that our gallant little force was under the command of
a general whom Marlborough hated, that he was furious
with the conqueror, and tried by the most open and shame-
less injustice afterwards to rob him of the credit of his
victory.

CHAPTER XV

GENERAL WEBB WINS THE BATTLE OF WYNENDAEL*

By the besiegers and besieged of Lille, some of the most
brilliant feats of valour were performed that ever illustrated
any war.   On the French side (whose gallantry was prodigious, the skill and bravery of Marshal Boufflers actually
eclipsing those of his conqueror, the Prince of Savoy) may
be mentioned that daring action of Messieurs de Luxembourg
and Tournefort, who, with a body of horse and dragoons,
carried powder into the town, of which the besieged were
in extreme want, each soldier bringing a bag with forty
pounds of powder behind him ; with which perilous provision
they engaged our own horse, faced the fire of the foot brought
out to meet them : and though half of the men were blown
up in the dreadful errand they rode on, a part of them got
into the town with the succours of which the garrison was
so much in want. A French officer, Monsieur du Bois,
performed an act equally daring, and perfectly successful.
The duke's great army lying at Helchin, and covering the
siege, and it being necessary for Monsieur de Vendosme to get

news of the condition of the place, Captain du Bois performed
his famous exploit : not only passing through the lines of
the siege, but swimming afterwards no less than seven moats
and ditches : and coming back the same way, swimming
with his letters in his mouth.

By these letters Monsieur de Boufflers said that he could
undertake to hold the place till October ; and that, if one
of the convoys of the Allies could be intercepted, they must
raise the siege altogether.

Such a convoy as hath been said was now prepared at
Ostend, and about to march for the siege ; and on the
27th September, we (and the French too) had news that it was
on its way. It was composed of 700 waggons, containing
ammunition of all sorts, and was escorted out of Ostend
by 2,000 infantry and 300 horse. At the same time
Monsieur de la Mothe quitted Bruges, having with him
five-and-thirty battalions, and upwards of sixty squadrons
and forty guns, in pursuit of the convoy.

Major-General Webb had meanwhile made up a force of
twenty battalions, and three squadrons of dragoons, at
Turout, whence he moved to cover the convoy and pursue
la Mothe : with whose advanced guard ours came up upon
the great plain of Turout, and before the little wood
and castle of Wynendael ; behind which the convoy was
marching.

As soon as they came in sight of the enemy, our advanced
troops were halted, with the wood behind them, and the
rest of our force brought up as quickly as possible, our little
body of horse being brought forward to the opening of the
plain, as our general said, to amuse the enemy. When
Monsieur la Mothe came up he found us posted in two lines
in front of the wood ; and formed his own army in battle
facing ours, in eight lines, four of infantry in front, and
dragoons and cavalry behind.

The French began the action, as usual, with a cannonade
which lasted three hours, when they made their attack,
advancing in twelve lines, four of foot and four of horse,
upon the allied troops in the wood where we were posted.
Their infantry behaved ill ; they were ordered to charge
with the bayonet, but, instead, began to fire, and almost
at the very first discharge from our men, broke and fled.
The cavalry behaved better ; with these alone, who were
three or four times as numerous as our whole force, Monsieur

de la Mothe might have won victory : but only two of our battalions were shaken in the least ; and these speedily rallied : nor could the repeated attacks of the French horse cause our troops to budge an inch from the position in the wood in which our general had placed them.

After attacking for two hours, the French retired at nightfall entirely foiled. With all the loss we had inflicted upon him, the enemy was still three times stronger than we : and it could not be supposed that our general could pursue M. de la Mothe, or do much more than hold our ground about the wood, from which the Frenchman had in vain attempted to dislodge us. La Mothe retired behind his forty guns, his cavalry protecting them better than it had been enabled to annoy us ; and meanwhile the convoy, which was of more importance than all our little force, and the safe passage of which we would have dropped to the last man to accomplish, marched away in perfect safety during the action, and joyfully reached the besieging camp before Lille.

Major-General Cadogan, my lord duke's quartermaster-general (and between whom and Mr. Webb there was no love lost), accompanied the convoy, and joined Mr. Webb with a couple of hundred horse just as the battle was over, and the enemy in full retreat. He offered, readily enough, to charge with his horse upon the French as they fell back ; but his force was too weak to inflict any damage upon them ; and Mr. Webb, commanding as Cadogan's senior, thought enough was done in holding our ground before an enemy that might still have overwhelmed us had we engaged him in the open territory, and in securing the safe passage of the convoy. Accordingly, the horse brought up by Cadogan did not draw a sword ; and only prevented, by the good countenance they showed, any disposition the French might have had to renew the attack on us. And no attack coming, at nightfall General Cadogan drew off with his squadron, being bound for head quarters, the two generals at parting grimly saluting each other.

'He will be at Roncq time enough to lick my lord duke's trenchers at supper,' says Mr. Webb.

Our own men lay out in the woods of Wynendael that night, and our general had his supper in the little castle there.

'If I was Cadogan, I would have a peerage for this day's

work,' General Webb said; 'and Harry, thou shouldst
have a regiment. Thou hast been reported in the last two
actions : thou wert near killed in the first. I shall mention
thee in my dispatch to his grace the commander-in-chief,
and recommend thee to poor Dick Harwood's vacant
majority. Have you ever a hundred guineas to give
Cardonnel ?* Slip them into his hand to-morrow, when you
go to head quarters with my report.'

In this report the major-general was good enough to
mention Captain Esmond's name with particular favour;
and that gentleman carried the dispatch to head quarters
the next day, and was not a little pleased to bring back
a letter by his grace's secretary, addressed to Lieutenant-
General Webb. The Dutch officer dispatched by Count
Nassau Woudenbourg, Vælt-Mareschal Auverquerque's son,
brought back also a complimentary letter to his commander,
who had seconded Mr. Webb in the action with great valour
and skill.

Esmond, with a low bow and a smiling face, presented
his dispatch, and saluted Mr. Webb as Lieutenant-General,
as he gave it in. The gentlemen round about him—he was
riding with his suite on the road to Menin as Esmond
came up with him—gave a cheer, and he thanked them,
and opened the dispatch with rather a flushed eager face.

He slapped it down on his boot in a rage after he had
read it. ' 'Tis not even writ with his own hand. Read it
out, Esmond.' And Esmond read it out :—

' Sir—Mr. Cadogan is just now come in, and has acquainted me
with the success of the action you had yesterday in the afternoon
against the body of troops commanded by Monsieur de la Mothe, at
Wynendael, which must be attributed chiefly to your good conduct
and resolution. You may be sure I shall do you justice at home,
and be glad on all occasions to own the service you have done in
securing this convoy.—Yours, &c., M.'

' Two lines by that d——d Cardonnel, and no more, for
the taking of Lille—for beating five times our number—
for an action as brilliant as the best he ever fought,' says
poor Mr. Webb. ' Lieutenant-General ! That's not his
doing. I was the oldest major-general. By ——, I believe
he had been better pleased if I had been beat.'

The letter to the Dutch officer was in French, and longer
and more complimentary than that to Mr. Webb.

'And this is the man,' he broke out, 'that's gorged with gold—that's covered with titles and honours that we won for him—and that grudges even a line of praise to a comrade in arms! Hasn't he enough? Don't we fight that he may roll in riches? Well, well, wait for the *Gazette*, gentlemen. The queen and the country will do us justice if his grace denies it us.' There were tears of rage in the brave warrior's eyes as he spoke; and he dashed them off his face on to his glove. He shook his fist in the air. 'Oh, by the Lord!' says he, 'I know what I had rather have than a peerage!'

'And what is that, sir?' some of them asked.

'I had rather have a quarter of an hour with John Churchill, on a fair green field, and only a pair of rapiers between my shirt and his——'

'Sir!' interposes one.

'Tell him so! I know that's what you mean. I know every word goes to him that's dropped from every general officer's mouth. I don't say he's not brave. Curse him! he's brave enough; but we'll wait for the *Gazette*, gentlemen. God save her Majesty! she'll do us justice.'

The *Gazette* did not come to us till a month afterwards; when my general and his officers had the honour to dine with Prince Eugene in Lille; his highness being good enough to say that we had brought the provisions, and ought to share in the banquet. 'Twas a great banquet. His grace of Marlborough was on his highness's right, and on his left the Mareschal de Boufflers, who had so bravely defended the place. The chief officers of either army were present; and you may be sure Esmond's general was splendid this day: his tall noble person, and manly beauty of face, made him remarkable anywhere; he wore, for the first time, the star of the Order of Generosity,* that his Prussian Majesty had sent to him for his victory. His Highness, the Prince of Savoy, called a toast to the conqueror of Wynendael. My lord duke drank it with rather a sickly smile. The aides de camp were present; and Harry Esmond and his dear young lord were together, as they always strove to be when duty would permit: they were over against the table where the generals were, and could see all that passed pretty well. Frank laughed at my lord duke's glum face: the affair of Wynendael, and the captain-general's conduct to Webb, had been the talk of the whole army. When his

highness spoke, and gave—'*Le vainqueur de Wynendael;
son armée et sa victoire,*' adding, '*qui nous font dîner à
Lille aujourdhuy*'—there was a great cheer through the
hall; for Mr. Webb's bravery, generosity, and very weaknesses of character caused him to be beloved in the army.

'Like Hector, handsome, and like Paris, brave!' whispers
Frank Castlewood. 'A Venus, an elderly Venus, couldn't
refuse him a pippin. Stand up, Harry. See, we are drinking the army of Wynendael. Ramillies is nothing to it.
Huzzay! Huzzay!'

At this very time, and just after our general had made
his acknowledgement, some one brought in an English
Gazette—and was passing it from hand to hand down the
table. Officers were eager enough to read it; mothers and
sisters at home must have sickened over it. There scarce
came out a *Gazette* for six years that did not tell of some
heroic death or some brilliant achievement.

'Here it is—Action of Wynendael—here you are, general,'
says Frank, seizing hold of the little dingy paper that
soldiers love to read so; and, scrambling over from our
bench, he went to where the general sat, who knew him,
and had seen many a time at his table his laughing, handsome face, which everybody loved who saw. The generals
in their great perukes made way for him. He handed the
paper over General Dohna's buff coat to our general on the
opposite side.

He came hobbling back, and blushing at his feat: 'I
thought he'd like it, Harry,' the young fellow whispered.
'Didn't I like to read my name after Ramillies, in the
London Gazette?—Viscount Castlewood serving a volunteer
——I say, what's yonder?'

Mr. Webb, reading the *Gazette*, looked very strange—
slapped it down on the table—then sprung up in his place,
and began,—'Will your highness please to——'

His grace the Duke of Marlborough here jumped up too—
'There's some mistake, my dear General Webb.'

'Your grace had better rectify it,' says Mr. Webb, holding
out the letter; but he was five off his grace the prince
duke, who, besides, was higher than the general (being
seated with the Prince of Savoy, the Electoral Prince of
Hanover, and the envoys of Prussia and Denmark, under
a baldaquin), and Webb could not reach him, tall as
he was.

'Stay,' says he, with a smile, as if catching at some idea, and then, with a perfect courtesy, drawing his sword, he ran the *Gazette* through with the point, and said, ' Permit me to hand it to your grace.'

The duke looked very black. ' Take it,' says he, to his master of the horse, who was waiting behind him.

The lieutenant-general made a very low bow, and retired and finished his glass. The *Gazette* in which Mr. Cardonnel, the duke's secretary, gave an account of the victory of Wynendael, mentioned Mr. Webb's name, but gave the sole praise and conduct of the action to the duke's favourite, Mr. Cadogan.

There was no little talk and excitement occasioned by this strange behaviour of General Webb, who had almost drawn a sword upon the commander-in-chief ; but the general, after the first outbreak of his anger, mastered it outwardly altogether ; and, by his subsequent behaviour, had the satisfaction of even more angering the commander-in-chief, than he could have done by any public exhibition of resentment.

On returning to his quarters, and consulting with his chief adviser, Mr. Esmond, who was now entirely in the general's confidence, and treated by him as a friend, and almost a son, Mr. Webb writ a letter to his grace the commander-in-chief, in which he said :—

Your grace must be aware that the sudden perusal of the *London Gazette,* in which your grace's secretary, Mr. Cardonnel, hath mentioned Major-General Cadogan's name, as the officer commanding in the late action of Wynendael, must have caused a feeling of anything but pleasure to the general who fought that action.

Your grace must be aware that Mr. Cadogan was not even present at the battle, though he arrived with squadrons of horse at its close, and put himself under the command of his superior officer. And as the result of the battle of Wynendael, in which Lieutenant-General Webb had the good fortune to command, was the capture of Lille, the relief of Brussels, then invested by the enemy under the Elector of Bavaria, the restoration of the great cities of Ghent and Bruges, of which the enemy (by treason within the walls) had got possession in the previous year : Mr. Webb cannot consent to forgo the honours of such a success and service, for the benefit of Mr. Cadogan, or any other person.

As soon as the military operations of the year are over, Lieutenant-General Webb will request permission to leave the army, and return to his place in Parliament, where he gives notice to his grace the commander-in-chief, that he shall lay his case before the House of Commons, the country, and her majesty the queen.

By his eagerness to rectify that false statement of the *Gazette*, which had been written by his grace's secretary, Mr. Cardonnel, Mr. Webb, not being able to reach his grace the commander-in-chief on account of the gentlemen seated between them, placed the paper containing the false statement on his sword, so that it might more readily arrive in the hands of his Grace the Duke of Marlborough, who surely would wish to do justice to every officer of his army.

Mr. Webb knows his duty too well to think of insubordination to his superior officer, or of using his sword in a campaign against any but the enemies of her majesty. He solicits permission to return to England immediately the military duties will permit, and take with him to England Captain Esmond, of his regiment, who acted as his aide de camp, and was present during the entire action, and noted by his watch the time when Mr. Cadogan arrived at its close.

The commander-in-chief could not but grant this permission, nor could he take notice of Webb's letter, though it was couched in terms the most insulting. Half the army believed that the cities of Ghent and Bruges were given up by a treason, which some in our army very well understood; that the commander-in-chief would not have relieved Lille if he could have helped himself; that he would not have fought that year had not the Prince of Savoy forced him. When the battle once began, then, for his own renown, my Lord Marlborough would fight as no man in the world ever fought better; and no bribe on earth could keep him from beating the enemy.[1]

---

[1] Our grandfather's hatred of the Duke of Marlborough appears all through his account of these campaigns. He always persisted that the duke was the greatest traitor and soldier history ever told of: and declared that he took bribes on all hands during the war. My lord marquis (for so we may call him here, though he never went by any other name than Colonel Esmond) was in the habit of telling many stories which he did not set down in his memoirs, and which he had from his friend the Jesuit, who was not always correctly informed, and who persisted that Marlborough was looking for a bribe of two millions of crowns before the campaign of Ramillies.

And our grandmother used to tell us children, that on his first presentation to my lord duke, the duke turned his back upon my grandfather; and said to the duchess, who told my lady dowager at Chelsea, who afterwards told Colonel Esmond—'Tom Esmond's bastard has been to my levee: he has the hang-dog look of his rogue of a father'—an expression which my grandfather never forgave. He was as constant in his dislikes as in his attachments;

But the matter was taken up by the subordinates; and half the army might have been by the ears, if the quarrel had not been stopped. General Cadogan sent an intimation to General Webb to say that he was ready if Webb liked, and would meet him. This was a kind of invitation our stout old general was always too ready to accept, and 'twas with great difficulty we got the general to reply that he had no quarrel with Mr. Cadogan, who had behaved with perfect gallantry, but only with those at head quarters, who had belied him. Mr. Cardonnel offered General Webb reparation; Mr. Webb said he had a cane at the service of Mr. Cardonnel, and the only satisfaction he wanted from him was one he was not likely to get, namely, the truth. The officers in our staff of Webb's, and those in the immediate suite of the general, were ready to come to blows; and hence arose the only affair in which Mr. Esmond ever engaged as principal, and that was from a revengeful wish to wipe off an old injury.

My Lord Mohun, who had a troop in Lord Macclesfield's regiment of the Horse Guards, rode this campaign with the duke. He had sunk by this time to the very worst reputation; he had had another fatal duel in Spain; he had married, and forsaken his wife; he was a gambler, a profligate, and debauchee. He joined just before Oudenarde; and, as Esmond feared, as soon as Frank Castlewood heard of his arrival, Frank was for seeking him out, and killing him. The wound my lord got at Oudenarde prevented their meeting, but that was nearly healed, and Mr. Esmond trembled daily lest any chance should bring his boy and this known assassin together. They met at the mess-table of Handyside's regiment at Lille; the officer commanding not knowing of the feud between the two noblemen.

Esmond had not seen the hateful handsome face of Mohun for nine years, since they had met on that fatal night in Leicester Field. It was degraded with crime and passion now; it wore the anxious look of a man who has three deaths—and who knows how many hidden shames and lusts, and crimes, on his conscience. He bowed with a sickly low bow, and slunk away when our host presented

and exceedingly partial to Webb, whose side he took against the more celebrated general. We have General Webb's portrait now at Castlewood, Va.

us round to one another. Frank Castlewood had not known
him till then, so changed was he. He knew the boy well
enough.

'Twas curious to look at the two—especially the young
man, whose face flushed up when he heard the hated
name of the other ; and who said in his bad French and
his brave boyish voice—' He had long been anxious to
meet my Lord Mohun.' The other only bowed, and moved
away from him. I do him justice, he wished to have no
quarrel with the lad.

Esmond put himself between them at table. ' D—— it,'
says Frank, ' why do you put yourself in the place of
a man who is above you in degree ? My Lord Mohun
should walk after me. I want to sit by my Lord Mohun.'

Esmond whispered to Lord Mohun, that Frank was hurt
in the leg at Oudenarde ; and besought the other to be
quiet. Quiet enough he was for some time ; disregarding
the many taunts which young Castlewood flung at him,
until after several healths, when my Lord Mohun got to be
rather in liquor.

' Will you go away, my lord ? ' Mr. Esmond said to him,
imploring him to quit the table.

' No, by G——,' says my Lord Mohun. ' I'll not go
away for any man ; ' he was quite flushed with wine by
this time.

The talk got round to the affairs of yesterday. Webb
had offered to challenge the commander-in-chief : Webb
had been ill-used : Webb was the bravest, handsomest,
vainest man in the army. Lord Mohun did not know that
Esmond was Webb's aide de camp. He began to tell some
stories against the general ; which, from t'other side of
Esmond, young Castlewood contradicted.

' I can't bear any more of this,' says my Lord Mohun.

' Nor can I, my lord,' says Mr. Esmond, starting up.
' The story my Lord Mohun has told respecting General
Webb is false, gentlemen—false, I repeat,' and making
a low bow to Lord Mohun, and without a single word more,
Esmond got up and left the dining-room. These affairs
were common enough among the military of those days.
There was a garden behind the house, and all the party
turned instantly into it ; and the two gentlemen's coats
were off and their points engaged within two minutes after
Esmond's words had been spoken. If Captain Esmond

had put Mohun out of the world, as he might, a villain
would have been punished and spared further villanies—
but who is one man to punish another ?   I declare upon
my honour that my only thought was to prevent Lord
Mohun from mischief with Frank, and the end of this
meeting was, that after half a dozen passes my lord went
home with a hurt which prevented him from lifting his
right arm for three months.

' Oh, Harry, why didn't you kill the villain ? ' young
Castlewood asked.   ' I can't walk without a crutch : but
I could have met him on horseback with sword and pistol.'
But Harry Esmond said, ' 'Twas best to have no man's
life on one's conscience, not even that villain's ' ; and this
affair, which did not occupy three minutes, being over,
the gentlemen went back to their wine, and my Lord
Mohun to his quarters, where he was laid up with a fever
which had spared mischief had it proved fatal.   And very
soon after this affair Harry Esmond and his general left
the camp for London ; whither a certain reputation had
preceded the captain, for my Lady Castlewood of Chelsea
received him as if he had been a conquering hero.   She
gave a great dinner to Mr. Webb, where the general's
chair was crowned with laurels ; and her ladyship called
Esmond's health in a toast, to which my kind general was
graciously pleased to bear the strongest testimony : and
took down a mob of at least forty coaches to cheer our
general as he came out of the House of Commons, the day
when he received the thanks of Parliament for his action.
The mob huzza'ed and applauded him, as well as the fine
company : it was splendid to see him waving his hat, and
bowing, and laying his hand upon his Order of Generosity.
He introduced Mr. Esmond to Mr. St. John and the Right
Honourable Robert Harley, Esquire, as he came out of the
House walking between them ; and was pleased to make
many flattering observations regarding Mr. Esmond's
behaviour during the three last campaigns.

Mr. St. John (who had the most winning presence of any
man I ever saw, excepting always my peerless young
Frank Castlewood) said he had heard of Mr. Esmond
before from Captain Steele, and how he had helped Mr.
Addison to write his famous poem of the *Campaign*.

' 'Twas as great an achievement as the victory of Blenheim itself,' Mr. Harley said, who was famous as a judge

and patron of letters, and so, perhaps, it may be—though for my part I think there are twenty beautiful lines, but all the rest is commonplace, and Mr. Addison's hymn worth a thousand such poems.

All the town was indignant at my lord duke's unjust treatment of General Webb, and applauded the vote of thanks which the House of Commons gave to the general for his victory at Wynendael. 'Tis certain that the capture of Lille was the consequence of that lucky achievement, and the humiliation of the old French king, who was said to suffer more at the loss of this great city, than from any of the former victories our troops had won over him. And, I think, no small part of Mr. Webb's exultation at his victory, arose from the idea that Marlborough had been disappointed of a great bribe the French king had promised him, should the siege be raised. The very sum of money offered to him was mentioned by the duke's enemies; and honest Mr. Webb chuckled at the notion, not only of beating the French, but of beating Marlborough too, and intercepting a convoy of three millions of French crowns, that were on their way to the generalissimo's insatiable pockets. When the general's lady went to the queen's drawing-room, all the Tory women crowded round her with congratulations, and made her a train greater than the Duchess of Marlborough's own. Feasts were given to the general by all the chiefs of the Tory party, who vaunted him as the duke's equal in military skill; and perhaps used the worthy soldier as their instrument, whilst he thought they were but acknowledging his merits as a commander. As the general's aide de camp, and favourite officer, Mr. Esmond came in for a share of his chief's popularity, and was presented to her Majesty, and advanced to the rank of lieutenant-colonel, at the request of his grateful chief.

We may be sure there was one family in which any good fortune that happened to Esmond, caused such a sincere pride and pleasure, that he, for his part, was thankful he could make them so happy. With these fond friends, Blenheim and Oudenarde seemed to be mere trifling incidents of the war; and Wynendael was its crowning victory. Esmond's mistress never tired to hear accounts of the battle; and I think General Webb's lady grew jealous of her, for the general was for ever at Kensington, and talking on that delightful theme. As for his aide de camp, though, no doubt, Esmond's own natural vanity was pleased at the little share of reputation which his good fortune had won him, yet it was chiefly precious to him (he may say so, now that he hath long since outlived it) because it pleased his mistress, and, above all, because Beatrix valued it.

As for the old dowager of Chelsea, never was an old woman in all England more delighted nor more gracious than she. Esmond had his quarters in her ladyship's house, where the domestics were instructed to consider him as their master. She bade him give entertainments, of which she defrayed the charges, and was charmed when his guests were carried away tipsy in their coaches. She must have his picture taken; and accordingly he was painted by Mr. Jervas,* in his red coat, and smiling upon a bombshell, which was bursting at the corner of the piece. She vowed that unless he made a great match, she should never die easy, and was for ever bringing young ladies to Chelsea, with pretty faces and pretty fortunes, at the disposal of the colonel. He smiled to think how times were altered with him, and of the early days in his father's lifetime, when a trembling page he stood before her, with her ladyship's basin and ewer, or crouched in her coach-step. The only fault she found with him was, that he was more sober than an Esmond ought to be; and would neither be carried to bed by his valet, nor lose his heart to any beauty, whether of St. James's or Covent Garden.

What is the meaning of fidelity in love, and whence the birth of it ? 'Tis a state of mind that men fall into, and depending on the man rather than the woman. We love being in love, that's the truth on't. If we had not met Joan, we should have met Kate, and adored her. We know our mistresses are no better than many other women, nor no prettier, nor no wiser, nor no wittier. 'Tis not for these reasons we love a woman, or for any special quality or charm I know of; we might as well demand that a lady should be the tallest woman in the world, like the Shropshire giantess,[1] as that she should be a paragon in any other character, before we began to love her. Esmond's mistress had a thousand faults beside her charms : he knew both perfectly well! She was imperious, she was light-

[1] 'Tis not thus *woman loves :* Col. E. hath owned to this folly for a *score of women* besides.—R.

minded, she was flighty, she was false, she had no reverence in her character ; she was in everything, even in beauty, the contrast of her mother, who was the most devoted and the least selfish of women. Well, from the very first moment he saw her on the stairs at Walcote, Esmond knew he loved Beatrix. There might be better women— he wanted that one. He cared for none other. Was it because she was gloriously beautiful ? Beautiful as she was, he had heard people say a score of times in their company, that Beatrix's mother looked as young, and was the handsomer of the two. Why did her voice thrill in his ear so ? She could not sing near so well as Nicolini or Mrs. Tofts ;* nay, she sang out of tune, and yet he liked to hear her better than St. Cecilia. She had not a finer complexion than Mrs. Steele (Dick's wife, whom he had now got, and who ruled poor Dick with a rod of pickle), and yet to see her dazzled Esmond ; he would shut his eyes, and the thought of her dazzled him all the same. She was brilliant and lively in talk, but not so incomparably witty as her mother, who, when she was cheerful, said the finest things ; but yet to hear her, and to be with her, was Esmond's greatest pleasure. Days passed away between him and these ladies, he scarce knew how. He poured his heart out to them, so as he never could in any other company, where he hath generally passed for being moody, or supercilious and silent. This society [1] was more delightful than that of the greatest wits to him. May Heaven pardon him the lies he told the dowager at Chelsea, in order to get a pretext for going away to Kensington ; the business at the Ordnance which he invented ; the interview with his general, the courts and statesman's levees which he *didn't* frequent and describe ; who wore a new suit on Sunday at St. James's or at the queen's birthday ; how many coaches filled the street at Mr. Harley's levee ; how many bottles he had had the honour to drink overnight with Mr. St. John at the ' Cocoa Tree,' or at the ' Garter ' with Mr. Walpole and Mr. Steele.

Mistress Beatrix Esmond had been a dozen times on the point of making great matches, so the Court scandal said ; but for his part Esmond never would believe the stories against her ; and came back, after three years' absence

---

[1] And, indeed, so was his to them, a thousand, thousand times more charming, for where was his equal ?—R.

from her, not so frantic as he had been perhaps, but still hungering after her and no other ; still hopeful, still kneeling, with his heart in his hand for the young lady to take. We were now got to 1709. She was near twenty-two years old, and three years at Court, and without a husband.

' 'Tis not for want of being asked,' Lady Castlewood said, looking into Esmond's heart, as she could, with that perceptiveness affection gives. 'But she will make no mean match, Harry : she will not marry as I would have her ; the person whom I should like to call my son, and Henry Esmond knows who that is, is best served by my not pressing his claim. Beatrix is so wilful, that what I would urge on her, she would be sure to resist. The man who would marry her will not be happy with her, unless he be a great person, and can put her in a great position. Beatrix loves admiration more than love ; and longs, beyond all things, for command. Why should a mother speak so of her child ? You are my son, too, Harry. You should know the truth about your sister. I thought you might cure yourself of your passion,' my lady added fondly. 'Other people can cure themselves of that folly, you know. But I see you are still as infatuated as ever. When we read your name in the *Gazette*, I pleaded for you, my poor boy. Poor boy, indeed ! You are growing a grave old gentleman now, and I am an old woman. She likes your fame well enough, and she likes your person. She says you have wit, and fire, and good breeding, and are more natural than the fine gentlemen of the Court. But this is not enough. She wants a commander-in-chief, and not a colonel. Were a duke to ask her, she would leave an earl whom she had promised. I told you so before. I know not how my poor girl is so worldly.'

' Well,' says Esmond, ' a man can but give his best and his all. She has that from me. What little reputation I have won, I swear I cared for it because I thought Beatrix would be pleased with it. What care I to be a colonel or a general ? Think you 'twill matter a few score years hence, what our foolish honours to-day are ? I would have had a little fame, that she might wear it in her hat. If I had anything better, I would endow her with it. If she wants my life, I would give it her. If she marries another, I will say God bless him. I make no boast, nor no complaint. I think my fidelity is folly, perhaps. But

so it is. I cannot help myself. I love her. You are
a thousand times better : the fondest, the fairest, the
dearest, of women. Sure, my dear lady, I see all Beatrix's
faults as well as you do. But she is my fate. 'Tis endur-
able. I shall not die for not having her. I think I should
be no happier if I won her. *Que voulez-vous ?* as my lady
of Chelsea would say. *Je l'aime.*'

' I wish she would have you,' said Harry's fond mistress,
giving a hand to him. He kissed the fair hand ('twas the
prettiest dimpled little hand in the world, and my Lady
Castlewood, though now almost forty years old, did not
look to be within ten years of her age). He kissed and
kept her fair hand, as they talked together.

' Why,' says he, ' should she hear me ? She knows
what I would say. Far or near, she knows I'm her slave.
I have sold myself for nothing, it may be. Well, 'tis the
price I choose to take. I am worth nothing, or I am
worth all.'

' You are such a treasure,' Esmond's mistress was pleased
to say, ' that the woman who has your love, shouldn't
change it away against a kingdom, I think. I am a country-
bred woman, and cannot say but the ambitions of the
town seem mean to me. I never was awe-stricken by my
lady duchess's rank and finery, or afraid,' she added,
with a sly laugh, ' of anything but her temper. I hear of
Court ladies who pine because her Majesty looks cold on
them ; and great noblemen who would give a limb that
they might wear a garter on the other. This worldliness,
which I can't comprehend, was born with Beatrix, who,
on the first day of her waiting, was a perfect courtier.
We are like sisters, and she the eldest sister, somehow.
She tells me I have a mean spirit. I laugh, and say she
adores a coach-and-six. I cannot reason her out of her
ambition. 'Tis natural to her, as to me to love quiet,
and be indifferent about rank and riches. What are they,
Harry ? and for how long do they last ? Our home is
not here.' She smiled as she spoke, and looked like an
angel that was only on earth on a visit. ' Our home is
where the just are, and where our sins and sorrows enter
not. My father used to rebuke me, and say that I was
too hopeful about Heaven. But I cannot help my nature,
and grow obstinate as I grow to be an old woman ; and
as I love my children so, sure our Father loves us with

a thousand and a thousand times greater love. It must
be that we shall meet yonder, and be happy. Yes, you—
and my children, and my dear lord. Do you know, Harry,
since his death, it has always seemed to me as if his love
came back to me, and that we are parted no more. Perhaps
he is here now, Harry—I think he is. Forgiven I am sure
he is : even Mr. Atterbury absolved him, and he died
forgiving. Oh, what a noble heart he had ! How generous
he was ! I was but fifteen, and a child when he married
me. How good he was to stoop to me ! He was always
good to the poor and humble.' She stopped, then presently,
with a peculiar expression, as if her eyes were looking into
Heaven, and saw my lord there, she smiled, and gave a little
laugh. 'I laugh to see you, sir,' she says ; 'when you
come, it seems as if you never were away.' One may
put her words down, and remember them, but how describe
her sweet tones, sweeter than music.

My young lord did not come home at the end of the
campaign, and wrote that he was kept at Bruxelles on
military duty. Indeed, I believe he was engaged in laying
siege to a certain lady, who was of the suite of Madame
de Soissons, the Prince of Savoy's mother,* who was just
dead, and who, like the Flemish fortresses, was taken and
retaken a great number of times during the war, and
occupied by French, English, and Imperialists. Of course,
Mr. Esmond did not think fit to enlighten Lady Castlewood
regarding the young scapegrace's doings : nor had he said
a word about the affair with Lord Mohun, knowing how
abhorrent that man's name was to his mistress. Frank
did not waste much time or money on pen and ink ; and,
when Harry came home with his general, only writ two
lines to his mother, to say his wound in the leg was almost
healed, that he would keep his coming of age next year—
that the duty aforesaid would keep him at Bruxelles, and
that Cousin Harry would tell all the news.

But from Bruxelles, knowing how the Lady Castlewood
always liked to have a letter about the famous 29th of
December, my lord writ her a long and full one, and in this
he must have described the affair with Mohun ; for when
Mr. Esmond came to visit his mistress one day, early in
the new year, to his great wonderment, she and her daughter
both came up and saluted him, and after them the dowager
of Chelsea, too, whose chairman had just brought her

ladyship from her village to Kensington across the fields. After this honour, I say, from the two ladies of Castlewood, the dowager came forward in great state, with her grand tall head-dress of King James's reign, that she never forsook, and said, ' Cousin Henry, all our family have met ; and we thank you, cousin, for your noble conduct towards the head of our house.' And pointing to her blushing cheek, she made Mr. Esmond aware that he was to enjoy the rapture of an embrace there. Having saluted one cheek, she turned to him the other. ' Cousin Harry,' said both the other ladies, in a little chorus, ' we thank you for your noble conduct ; ' and then Harry became aware that the story of the Lille affair had come to his kinswomen's ears. It pleased him to hear them all saluting him as one of their family.

The tables of the dining-room were laid for a great entertainment ; and the ladies were in gala dresses—my lady of Chelsea in her highest *tour*, my lady viscountess out of black, and looking fair and happy, *à ravir ;* and the maid of honour attired with that splendour which naturally distinguished her, and wearing on her beautiful breast the French officer's star which Frank had sent home after Ramillies.

' You see, 'tis a gala day with us,' says she, glancing down to the star complacently, ' and we have our orders on. Does not mamma look charming ? 'Twas I dressed her ! ' Indeed, Esmond's dear mistress, blushing as he looked at her, with her beautiful fair hair and an elegant dress, according to the *mode*, appeared to have the shape and complexion of a girl of twenty.

On the table was a fine sword, with a red velvet scabbard, and a beautiful chased silver handle, with a blue ribbon for a sword-knot. ' What is this ? ' says the captain, going up to look at this pretty piece.

Mrs. Beatrix advanced towards it. ' Kneel down,' says she : ' we dub you our knight with this '—and she waved the sword over his head—' my lady dowager hath given the sword ; and I give the ribbon, and mamma hath sewn on the fringe.'

' Put the sword on him, Beatrix,' says her mother. ' You are our knight, Harry—our true knight. Take a mother's thanks and prayers for defending her son, my dear, dear friend.' She could say no more, and even the dowager was affected, for a couple of rebellious tears made sad marks down those wrinkled old roses which Esmond had just been allowed to salute.

'We had a letter from dearest Frank,' his mother said, 'three days since, whilst you were on your visit to your friend Captain Steele, at Hampton. He told us all that you had done, and how nobly you had put yourself between him and that—that wretch.'

'And I adopt you from this day,' says the dowager; 'and I wish I was richer, for your sake, son Esmond,' she added, with a wave of her hand; and as Mr. Esmond dutifully went down on his knee before her ladyship, she cast her eyes up to the ceiling (the gilt chandelier, and the twelve wax candles in it, for the party was numerous), and invoked a blessing from that quarter upon the newly adopted son.

'Dear Frank,' says the other viscountess, 'how fond he is of his military profession! He is studying fortification very hard. I wish he were here. We shall keep his coming of age at Castlewood next year.'

'If the campaign permit us,' says Mr. Esmond.

'I am never afraid when he is with you,' cries the boy's mother. 'I am sure my Henry will always defend him.'

'But there will be a peace before next year; we know it for certain,' cries the maid of honour. 'Lord Marlborough will be dismissed, and that horrible duchess turned out of all her places. Her Majesty won't speak to her now. Did you see her at Bushy, Harry? she is furious, and she ranges about the park like a lioness, and tears people's eyes out.'

'And the Princess Anne will send for somebody,' says my lady of Chelsea, taking out her medal and kissing it.

'Did you see the king at Oudenarde, Harry?' his mistress asked. She was a stanch Jacobite, and would no more have thought of denying her king than her God.

'I saw the young Hanoverian only,' Harry said. 'The Chevalier de St. George.'

'The king, sir, the king!' said the ladies and Miss Beatrix; and she clapped her pretty hands, and cried, 'Vive le Roy!'

By this time there came a thundering knock, that drove in the doors of the house almost. It was three o'clock, and the company were arriving; and presently the servant announced Captain Steele and his lady.

Captain and Mrs. Steele, who were the first to arrive, had driven to Kensington from their country-house, the Hovel at Hampton Wick, ' Not from our mansion in Bloomsbury Square,' as Mrs. Steele took care to inform the ladies. Indeed Harry had ridden away from Hampton that very morning, leaving the couple by the ears ; for from the chamber where he lay, in a bed that was none of the cleanest, and kept awake by the company which he had in his own bed, and the quarrel which was going on in the next room, he could hear both night and morning the curtain lecture which Mrs. Steele was in the habit of administering to poor Dick.

At night it did not matter so much for the culprit ; Dick was fuddled, and when in that way no scolding could interrupt his benevolence. Mr. Esmond could hear him coaxing and speaking in that maudlin manner, which punch and claret produce, to his beloved Prue, and beseeching her to remember that there was a *distiwisht officer ithe nex roob*, who would overhear her. She went on, nevertheless, calling him a drunken wretch, and was only interrupted in her harangues by the captain's snoring.

In the morning, the unhappy victim awoke to a headache and consciousness, and the dialogue of the night was resumed. ' Why do you bring captains home to dinner when there's not a guinea in the house ? How am I to give dinners when you leave me without a shilling ? How am I to go trapesing to Kensington in my yellow satin sack before all the fine company ? I've nothing fit to put on ; I never have : ' and so the dispute went on—Mr. Esmond interrupting the talk when it seemed to be growing too intimate by blowing his nose as loudly as ever he could, at the sound of which trumpet there came a lull. But Dick was charming, though his wife was odious, and 'twas to give Mr. Steele pleasure, that the ladies of Castlewood, who were ladies of no small fashion, invited Mrs. Steele.

Besides the captain and his lady, there was a great and notable assemblage of company : my lady of Chelsea having sent her lackeys and liveries to aid the modest attendance at Kensington. There was Lieutenant-General Webb, Harry's kind patron, of whom the dowager took possession, and who resplended in velvet and gold lace ; there was Harry's new acquaintance, the Right Honourable Henry St. John, Esquire, the general's kinsman, who was

charmed with the Lady Castlewood, even more than with
her daughter; there was one of the greatest noblemen in
the kingdom, the Scots Duke of Hamilton,* just created
Duke of Brandon in England; and two other noble lords
of the Tory party, my Lord Ashburnham,* and another
I have forgot; and for ladies, her grace the Duchess of
Ormonde and her daughters, the Lady Mary and the Lady
Betty, the former one of Mistress Beatrix's colleagues in
waiting on the queen.

'What a party of Tories!' whispered Captain Steele to
Esmond, as we were assembled in the parlour before
dinner. Indeed, all the company present, save Steele, were
of that faction.

Mr. St. John made his special compliments to Mrs. Steele,
and so charmed her that she declared she would have Steele
a Tory too.

'Or will you have me a Whig?' says Mr. St. John.
'I think, madam, you could convert a man to anything.'

'If Mr. St. John ever comes to Bloomsbury Square I will
teach him what I know,' says Mrs. Steele, dropping her
handsome eyes. 'Do you know Bloomsbury Square?'

'Do I know the Mall? Do I know the Opera? Do
I know the reigning toast? Why, Bloomsbury is the very
height of the mode,' says Mr. St. John. ''Tis *rus in urbe*.
You have gardens all the way to Hampstead, and palaces
round about you—Southampton House and Montague
House.'

'Where you wretches go and fight duels,' cries Mrs. Steele.

'Of which the ladies are the cause!' says her entertainer.
'Madam, is Dick a good swordsman? How charming the
Tatler is! We all recognized your portrait in the 49th
number, and I have been dying to know you ever since
I read it. "Aspasia must be allowed to be the first of the
beauteous order of love." Doth not the passage run so?
"In this accomplished lady love is the constant effect,
though it is never the design; yet though her mien carries
much more invitation than command, to behold her is an
immediate check to loose behaviour, and to love her is
a liberal education."'*

'Oh, indeed!' says Mrs. Steele, who did not seem to
understand a word of what the gentleman was saying.

'Who could fail to be accomplished under such a mistress?' says Mr. St. John, still gallant and bowing.

' Mistress! upon my word, sir!' cries the lady. 'If
you mean me, sir, I would have you know that I am the
captain's wife.'

' Sure we all know it,' answers Mr. St. John, keeping his
countenance very gravely; and Steele broke in, saying,
' 'Twas not about Mrs. Steele I writ that paper—though
I am sure she is worthy of any compliment I can pay her—
but of the Lady Elizabeth Hastings.' [1]

' I hear Mr. Addison is equally famous as a wit and
a poet,' says Mr. St. John. ' Is it true that his hand is to
be found in your *Tatler*, Mr. Steele?'

' Whether 'tis the sublime or the humorous, no man can
come near him,' cries Steele.

' A fig, Dick, for your Mr. Addison!' cries out his lady:
' a gentleman who gives himself such airs and holds his head
so high now. I hope your ladyship thinks as I do: I can't
bear those very fair men with white eyelashes—a black
man for me.' (All the black men at table applauded, and
made Mrs. Steele a bow for this compliment.) ' As for this
Mr. Addison,' she went on, ' he comes to dine with the
captain sometimes, never says a word to me, and then
they walk upstairs, both tipsy, to a dish of tea. I remember
your Mr. Addison when he had but one coat to his back,
and that with a patch at the elbow.'

' Indeed—a patch at the elbow! You interest me,' says
Mr. St. John. ' 'Tis charming to hear of one man of letters
from the charming wife of another.'

' Law, I could tell you ever so much about 'em,' continues the voluble lady. ' What do you think the captain
has got now?—a little hunchback fellow—a little hop-o'-
my-thumb creature that he calls a poet—a little Popish
brat!'

' Hush, there are two in the room,' whispers her companion.

' Well, I call him Popish because his name is Pope,' says
the lady. ' 'Tis only my joking way. And this little
dwarf of a fellow has wrote a pastoral poem—all about
shepherds and shepherdesses, you know.'

' A shepherd should have a little crook,' says my mistress,
laughing from her end of the table: on which Mrs. Steele
said, ' She did not know, but the captain brought home
this queer little creature when she was in bed with her

[1] See Appendix, p. 464.

first boy, and it was a mercy he had come no sooner ; and Dick raved about his *genus*, and was always raving about some nonsense or other.'

' Which of the *Tatlers* do you prefer, Mrs. Steele ? ' asked Mr. St. John.

' I never read but one, and think it all a pack of rubbish, sir,' says the lady. ' Such stuff about Bickerstaffe, and Distaff, and Quarterstaff, as it all is ! There's the captain going on still with the burgundy—I know he'll be tipsy before he stops—Captain Steele ! '

' I drink to your eyes, my dear,' says the captain, who seemed to think his wife charming, and to receive as genuine all the satiric compliments which Mr. St. John paid her.

All this while the maid of honour had been trying to get Mr. Esmond to talk, and no doubt voted him a dull fellow. For, by some mistake, just as he was going to pop into the vacant place, he was placed far away from Beatrix's chair, who sat between his grace and my Lord Ashburnham, and shrugged her lovely white shoulders, and cast a look as if to say, ' Pity me,' to her cousin. My lord duke and his young neighbour were presently in a very animated and close conversation. Mrs. Beatrix could no more help using her eyes than the sun can help shining, and setting those it shines on a-burning. By the time the first course was done the dinner seemed long to Esmond : by the time the soup came he fancied they must have been hours at table : and as for the sweets and jellies he thought they never would be done.

At length the ladies rose, Beatrix throwing a Parthian glance at her duke as she retreated ; a fresh bottle and glasses were fetched, and toasts were called. Mr. St. John asked his grace the Duke of Hamilton and the company to drink to the health of his grace the Duke of Brandon. Another lord gave General Webb's health, ' and may he get the command the bravest officer in the world deserves.' Mr. Webb thanked the company, complimented his aide de camp, and fought his famous battle over again.

' *Il est fatiguant*,' whispers Mr. St. John, ' *avec sa trompette de Wynendael.*'

Captain Steele, who was not of our side, loyally gave the health of the Duke of Marlborough, the greatest general of the age.

'I drink to the greatest general with all my heart,' says Mr. Webb; 'there can be no gainsaying that character of him. My glass goes to the general, and not to the duke, Mr. Steele.' And the stout old gentleman emptied his bumper; to which Dick replied by filling and emptying a pair of brimmers, one for the general and one for the duke.

And now his grace of Hamilton, rising up, with flashing eyes (we had all been drinking pretty freely), proposed a toast to the lovely, to the incomparable Mrs. Beatrix Esmond; we all drank it with cheers, and my Lord Ashburnham especially, with a shout of enthusiasm.

'What a pity there is a Duchess of Hamilton,' whispers St. John, who drank more wine and yet was more steady than most of the others, and we entered the drawing-room where the ladies were at their tea. As for poor Dick, we were obliged to leave him alone at the dining-table, where he was hiccupping out the lines from the *Campaign*, in which the greatest poet had celebrated the greatest general in the world; and Harry Esmond found him, half an hour afterwards, in a more advanced stage of liquor, and weeping about the treachery of Tom Boxer.*

The drawing-room was all dark to poor Harry, in spite of the grand illumination. Beatrix scarce spoke to him. When my lord duke went away, she practised upon the next in rank, and plied my young Lord Ashburnham with all the fire of her eyes and the fascinations of her wit. Most of the party were set to cards, and Mr. St. John, after yawning in the face of Mrs. Steele, whom he did not care to pursue any more, and talking in his most brilliant animated way to Lady Castlewood, whom he pronounced to be beautiful, of a far higher order of beauty than her daughter, presently took his leave, and went his way. The rest of the company speedily followed, my Lord Ashburnham the last, throwing fiery glances at the smiling young temptress, who had bewitched more hearts than his in her thrall.

No doubt, as a kinsman of the house, Mr. Esmond thought fit to be the last of all in it; he remained after the coaches had rolled away—after his dowager aunt's chair and flambeaux had marched off in the darkness towards Chelsea, and the town's-people had gone to bed, who had been drawn into the square to gape at the unusual assemblage of chairs and chariots, lackeys and torchmen. The poor mean wretch lingered yet for a few minutes, to see whether the girl would vouchsafe him a smile, or a parting word of consolation. But her enthusiasm of the morning was quite died out, or she chose to be in a different mood. She fell to joking about the dowdy appearance of Lady Betty, and mimicked the vulgarity of Mrs. Steele ; and then she put up her little hand to her mouth and yawned, lighted a taper, and shrugged her shoulders, and dropping Mr. Esmond a saucy curtsy, sailed off to bed.

'The day began so well, Henry, that I had hoped it might have ended better,' was all the consolation that poor Esmond's fond mistress could give him ; and as he trudged home through the dark alone, he thought, with bitter rage in his heart, and a feeling of almost revolt against the sacrifice he had made :—' She would have me,' thought he, ' had I but a name to give her. But for my promise to her father, I might have my rank and my mistress too.'

I suppose a man's vanity is stronger than any other passion in him ; for I blush, even now, as I recall the humiliation of those distant days, the memory of which still smarts, though the fever of baulked desire has passed away more than a score of years ago. When the writer's descendants come to read this memoir, I wonder will they have lived to experience a similar defeat and shame ? Will they ever have knelt to a woman, who has listened to them, and played with them, and laughed at them—who beckoning them with lures and caresses, and with Yes, smiling from her eyes, has tricked them on to their knees, and turned her back and left them ? All this shame Mr. Esmond had to undergo ; and he submitted, and revolted, and presently came crouching back for more.

After this *feste*, my young Lord Ashburnham's coach was for ever rolling in and out of Kensington Square ; his lady-mother came to visit Esmond's mistress, and at every assembly in the town, wherever the maid of honour made her appearance, you might be pretty sure to see the young gentleman in a new suit every week, and decked out in all the finery that his tailor or embroiderer could furnish for him. My lord was for ever paying Mr. Esmond compliments : bidding him to dinner, offering him horses to ride, and giving him a thousand uncouth marks of respect and goodwill. At last, one night at the coffee-house, whither my lord came considerably flushed and excited with drink, he rushes up to Mr. Esmond, and cries out—' Give me joy, my dearest colonel ; I am the happiest of men.'

' The happiest of men needs no dearest colonel to give him joy,' says Mr. Esmond. ' What is the cause of this supreme felicity ? '

' Haven't you heard ? ' says he. ' Don't you know ? I thought the family told you everything : the adorable Beatrix hath promised to be mine.'

' What ! ' cries out Mr. Esmond, who had spent happy hours with Beatrix that very morning—had writ verses for her, that she had sung at the harpsichord.

' Yes,' says he ; ' I waited on her to-day. I saw you walking towards Knightsbridge as I passed in my coach ; and she looked so lovely, and spoke so kind, that I couldn't help going down on my knees, and—and—sure I'm the happiest of men in all the world ; and I'm very young ; but she says I shall get older : and you know I shall be of age in four months ; and there's very little difference between us ; and I'm so happy. I should like to treat the company to something. Let us have a bottle—a dozen bottles— and drink the health of the finest woman in England.'

Esmond left the young lord tossing off bumper after bumper, and strolled away to Kensington to ask whether the news was true. 'Twas only too sure: his mistress's sad, com- passionate face told him the story ; and then she related what particulars of it she knew, and how my young lord had made his offer, half an hour after Esmond went away that morning, and in the very room where the song lay yet on the harpsichord, which Esmond had writ, and they had sung together.

BOOK III

CHAPTER I

I COME TO AN END OF MY BATTLES AND BRUISES

THAT feverish desire to gain a little reputation which Esmond had had, left him now perhaps that he had attained some portion of his wish, and the great motive of his ambition was over. His desire for military honour was that it might raise him in Beatrix's eyes. 'Twas next to nobility and wealth the only kind of rank she valued. It was the stake quickest won or lost too ; for law is a very long game that requires a life to practise ; and to be distinguished in letters or the Church would not have forwarded the poor gentleman's plans in the least. So he had no suit to play but the red one, and he played it ; and this, in truth, was the reason of his speedy promotion ; for he exposed himself more than most gentlemen do, and risked more to win more. Is he the only man that hath set his life against a stake which may be not worth the winning ? Another risks his life (and his honour, too, sometimes) against a bundle of bank-notes, or a yard of blue ribbon, or a seat in Parliament ; and some for the mere pleasure and excitement of the sport ; as a field of a hundred huntsmen will do, each out-bawling and out-galloping the other at the tail of a dirty fox, that is to be the prize of the foremost happy conqueror.

When he heard this news of Beatrix's engagement in marriage, Colonel Esmond knocked under to his fate, and resolved to surrender his sword, that could win him nothing now he cared for ; and in this dismal frame of mind he determined to retire from the regiment, to the great delight of the captain next in rank to him, who happened to be a young gentleman of good fortune, who eagerly paid Mr. Esmond a thousand guineas for his majority in Webb's regiment, and was knocked on the head the next campaign. Perhaps Esmond would not have been sorry to share his fate. He was more the Knight of the Woful Countenance than ever he had been. His moodiness must have made him perfectly odious to his friends under the tents, who like a jolly fellow, and laugh at a melancholy warrior always sighing after Dulcinea at home.

Both the ladies of Castlewood approved of Mr. Esmond quitting the army, and his kind general coincided in his wish of retirement, and helped in the transfer of his commission, which brought a pretty sum into his pocket. But when the commander-in-chief came home, and was forced, in spite of himself, to appoint Lieutenant-General Webb to the command of a division of the army in Flanders, the lieutenant-general prayed Colonel Esmond so urgently to be his aide de camp and military secretary, that Esmond could not resist his kind patron's entreaties, and again took the field, not attached to any regiment, but under Webb's orders. What must have been the continued agonies of fears [1] and apprehensions which racked the gentle breasts of wives and matrons in those dreadful days, when every *Gazette* brought accounts of deaths and battles, and when the present anxiety over, and the beloved person escaped, the doubt still remained that a battle might be fought, possibly, of which the next Flanders letter would bring the account ; so they, the poor tender creatures, had to go on sickening and trembling through the whole campaign. Whatever these terrors were on the part of Esmond's mistress (and that tenderest of women must have felt them most keenly for both her sons, as she called them), she never allowed them outwardly to appear, but hid her apprehension as she did her charities and devotion. 'Twas only by chance that Esmond, wandering in Kensington, found his mistress coming out of a mean cottage there, and heard that she had a score of poor retainers, whom she visited and comforted in their sickness and poverty, and who blessed her daily. She attended the early church daily (though of a Sunday especially, she encouraged and advanced all sorts of cheerfulness and innocent gaiety in her little household) : and by notes entered into a table-book of hers at this time, and devotional compositions writ with a sweet artless fervour, such as the best divines could not surpass, showed

[1] What indeed ? Ps. xci. 2, 3, 7.—R. E.

how fond her heart was, how humble and pious her spirit, what pangs of apprehension she endured silently, and with what a faithful reliance she committed the care of those she loved to the awful Dispenser of death and life.

As for her ladyship at Chelsea, Esmond's newly-adopted mother, she was now of an age when the danger of any second party doth not disturb the rest much. She cared for trumps more than for most things in life. She was firm enough in her own faith, but no longer very bitter against ours. She had a very good-natured, easy French director, Monsieur Gauthier by name,* who was a gentleman of the world, and would take a hand of cards with Dean Atterbury, my lady's neighbour at Chelsea, and was well with all the High Church party. No doubt Monsieur Gauthier knew what Esmond's peculiar position was, for he corresponded with Holt, and always treated Colonel Esmond with particular respect and kindness; but for good reasons the colonel and the abbé never spoke on this matter together, and so they remained perfect good friends.

All the frequenters of my lady of Chelsea's house were of the Tory and High Church party. Madame Beatrix was as frantic about the king as her elderly kinswoman: she wore his picture on her heart; she had a piece of his hair; she vowed he was the most injured, and gallant, and accomplished, and unfortunate, and beautiful of princes. Steele, who quarrelled with very many of his Tory friends, but never with Esmond, used to tell the colonel that his kinswoman's house was a rendezvous of Tory intrigues; that Gauthier was a spy; that Atterbury was a spy; that letters were constantly going from that house to the queen at St. Germains; on which Esmond, laughing, would reply, that they used to say in the army the Duke of Marlborough was a spy too, and as much in correspondence with that family as any Jesuit. And without entering very eagerly into the controversy, Esmond had frankly taken the side of his family. It seemed to him that King James the Third was undoubtedly King of England by right: and at his sister's death it would be better to have him than a foreigner over us. No man admired King William more; a hero and a conqueror, the bravest, justest, wisest of men—but 'twas by the sword he conquered the country, and held and governed it by the very same right that the great Cromwell held it, who was truly and greatly a sovereign. But that

a foreign despotic prince, out of Germany, who happened
to be descended from King James the First, should take
possession of this empire, seemed to Mr. Esmond a monstrous
injustice—at least, every Englishman had a right to protest,
and the English prince, the heir-at-law, the first of all.
What man of spirit with such a cause would not back it ?
What man of honour with such a crown to win would not
fight for it ? But that race was destined. That prince
had himself against him, an enemy he could not overcome.
He never dared to draw his sword, though he had it. He
let his chances slip by as he lay in the lap of opera-girls,
or snivelled at the knees of priests asking pardon ; and the
blood of heroes, and the devotedness of honest hearts, and
endurance, courage, fidelity, were all spent for him in vain.

But let us return to my lady of Chelsea, who, when her
son Esmond announced to her ladyship that he proposed
to make the ensuing campaign, took leave of him with
perfect alacrity, and was down to piquet with her gentlewoman before he had well quitted the room on his last visit.
' Tierce to a king,' were the last words he ever heard her
say : the game of life was pretty nearly over for the good
lady, and three months afterwards she took to her bed,
where she flickered out without any pain, so the Abbé
Gauthier wrote over to Mr. Esmond, then with his general
on the frontier of France. The Lady Castlewood was with
her at her ending, and had written too, but these letters must
have been taken by a privateer in the packet that brought
them ; for Esmond knew nothing of their contents until
his return to England.

My Lady Castlewood had left everything to Colonel
Esmond, ' as a reparation for the wrong done to him ' ;
'twas writ in her will. But her fortune was not much, for
it never had been large, and the honest viscountess had
wisely sunk most of the money she had upon an annuity
which terminated with her life. However, there was the
house and furniture, plate and pictures at Chelsea, and
a sum of money lying at her merchant's, Sir Josiah Child,
which altogether would realize a sum of near three hundred
pounds per annum, so that Mr. Esmond found himself, if
not rich, at least easy for life. Likewise, there were the
famous diamonds which had been said to be worth fabulous
sums, though the goldsmith pronounced they would fetch
no more than four thousand pounds. These diamonds,

however, Colonel Esmond reserved, having a special use for them : but the Chelsea house, plate, goods, &c., with the exception of a few articles which he kept back, were sold by his orders ; and the sums resulting from the sale invested in the public securities so as to realize the aforesaid annual income of three hundred pounds.

Having now something to leave, he made a will, and dispatched it home. The army was now in presence of the enemy ; and a great battle expected every day. 'Twas known that the general-in-chief was in disgrace, and the parties at home strong against him ; and there was no stroke this great and resolute player would not venture to recall his fortune when it seemed desperate. Frank Castle-wood was with Colonel Esmond ; his general having gladly taken the young nobleman on to his staff. His studies of fortifications at Bruxelles were over by this time. The fort he was besieging had yielded, I believe, and my lord had not only marched in with flying colours, but marched out again. He used to tell his boyish wickednesses with admirable humour, and was the most charming young scapegrace in the army.

'Tis needless to say that Colonel Esmond had left every penny of his little fortune to this boy. It was the colonel's firm conviction that the next battle would put an end to him : for he felt aweary of the sun,* and quite ready to bid that and the earth farewell. Frank would not listen to his comrade's gloomy forebodings, but swore they would keep his birthday at Castlewood that autumn, after the campaign. He had heard of the engagement at home. ' If Prince Eugene goes to London,' says Frank, ' and Trix can get hold of him, she'll jilt Ashburnham for his highness. I tell you, she used to make eyes at the Duke of Marlborough, when she was only fourteen and ogling poor little Blandford. *I* wouldn't marry her, Harry, no not if her eyes were twice as big. I'll take my fun. I'll enjoy for the next three years every possible pleasure. I'll sow my wild oats then, and marry some quiet, steady, modest, sensible viscountess ; hunt my harriers ; and settle down at Castlewood. Perhaps I'll represent the county—no, damme, *you* shall represent the county. You have the brains of the family. By the Lord, my dear old Harry, you have the best head and the kindest heart in all the army ; and every man says so—and when the queen dies, and the king comes back, why shouldn't

you go to the House of Commons and be a minister, and
be made a peer, and that sort of thing ? *You* be shot in the
next action ! I wager a dozen of burgundy you are not
touched. Mohun is well of his wound. He is always with
Corporal John now. As soon as ever I see his ugly face I'll
spit in it. I took lessons of Father—of Captain Holtz at
Bruxelles. What a man that is ! He knows everything.'
Esmond bade Frank have a care ; that Father Holt's knowledge was rather dangerous ; not, indeed, knowing as yet
how far the father had pushed his instructions with his
young pupil.

The gazetteers and writers, both of the French and
English side, have given accounts sufficient of that bloody
battle of Blarignies or Malplaquet,* which was the last and
the hardest-earned of the victories of the great Duke of
Marlborough. In that tremendous combat, near upon two
hundred and fifty thousand men were engaged, more than
thirty thousand of whom were slain or wounded (the Allies
lost twice as many men as they killed of the French, whom
they conquered) : and this dreadful slaughter very likely
took place because a great general's credit was shaken at
home, and he thought to restore it by a victory. If such
were the motives which induced the Duke of Marlborough
to venture that prodigious stake, and desperately sacrifice
thirty thousand brave lives, so that he might figure once
more in a *Gazette*, and hold his places and pensions a little
longer, the event defeated the dreadful and selfish design,
for the victory was purchased at a cost which no nation,
greedy of glory as it may be, would willingly pay for any
triumph. The gallantry of the French was as remarkable
as the furious bravery of their assailants. We took a few
score of their flags, and a few pieces of their artillery ; but
we left twenty thousand of the bravest soldiers of the world
round about the entrenched lines, from which the enemy
was driven. He retreated in perfect good order ; the panic-
spell seemed to be broke, under which the French had
laboured ever since the disaster of Hochstedt ; and, fighting
now on the threshold of their country, they showed an
heroic ardour of resistance, such as had never met us in the
course of their aggressive war. Had the battle been more
successful, the conqueror might have got the price for which
he waged it. As it was (and justly, I think), the party
adverse to the duke in England were indignant at the lavish

extravagance of slaughter, and demanded more eagerly than ever the recall of a chief, whose cupidity and desperation might urge him further still. After this bloody fight of Malplaquet, I can answer for it, that in the Dutch quarters and our own, and amongst the very regiments and commanders, whose gallantry was most conspicuous upon this frightful day of carnage, the general cry was, that there was enough of the war. The French were driven back into their own boundary, and all their conquests and booty of Flanders disgorged. As for the Prince of Savoy, with whom our commander-in-chief, for reasons of his own, consorted more closely than ever, 'twas known that he was animated not merely by a political hatred, but by personal rage against the old French king : the Imperial Generalissimo never forgot the slight put by Lewis upon the Abbé de Savoie ; and in the humiliation or ruin of his most Christian Majesty, the Holy Roman Emperor found his account. But what were these quarrels to us, the free citizens of England and Holland ? Despot as he was, the French monarch was yet the chief of European civilization, more venerable in his age and misfortunes than at the period of his most splendid successes ; whilst his opponent was but a semi-barbarous tyrant, with a pillaging murderous horde of Croats and Pandours, composing a half of his army, filling our camp with their strange figures, bearded like the miscreant Turks their neighbours, and carrying into Christian warfare their native heathen habits of rapine, lust, and murder. Why should the best blood in England and France be shed in order that the Holy Roman and Apostolic master of these ruffians should have his revenge over the Christian king ? And it was to this end we were fighting ; for this that every village and family in England was deploring the death of beloved sons and fathers. We dared not speak to each other, even at table, of Malplaquet, so frightful were the gaps left in our army by the cannon of that bloody action. 'Twas heartrending, for an officer who had a heart, to look down his line on a parade-day afterwards, and miss hundreds of faces of comrades—humble or of high rank—that had gathered but yesterday full of courage and cheerfulness round the torn and blackened flags. Where were our friends ? As the great duke reviewed us, riding along our lines with his fine suite of prancing aides de camp and generals, stopping here and

there to thank an officer with those eager smiles and bows
of which his grace was always lavish, scarce a huzzah could
be got for him, though Cadogan, with an oath, rode up and
cried—' D—n you, why don't you cheer ? ' But the men
had no heart for that : not one of them but was thinking,
' Where's my comrade ?—where's my brother that fought
by me, or my dear captain that led me yesterday ? ' 'Twas
the most gloomy pageant I ever looked on ; and the *Te
Deum*, sung by our chaplains, the most woful and dreary
satire.

Esmond's general added one more to the many marks of
honour which he had received in the front of a score of
battles, and got a wound in the groin, which laid him on
his back ; and you may be sure he consoled himself by
abusing the commander-in-chief, as he lay groaning :—
' Corporal John's as fond of me,' he used to say, ' as King
David was of General Uriah ;* and so he always gives me the
post of danger.'   He persisted, to his dying day, in believing
that the duke intended he should be beat at Wynendael,
and sent him purposely with a small force, hoping that he
might be knocked on the head there.   Esmond and Frank
Castlewood both escaped without hurt, though the division
which our general commanded suffered even more than any
other, having to sustain not only the fury of the enemy's
cannonade, which was very hot and well-served, but the
furious and repeated charges of the famous Maison-du-Roy,
which we had to receive and beat off again and again, with
volleys of shot and hedges of iron, and our four lines of
musketeers and pikemen.   They said the King of England
charged us no less than twelve times that day, along with
the French Household.   Esmond's late regiment, General
Webb's own Fusiliers, served in the division which their
colonel commanded.   The general was thrice in the centre of
the square of the Fusiliers, calling the fire at the French
charges ; and, after the action, his grace the Duke of Berwick sent his compliments to his old regiment and their
colonel for their behaviour on the field.

We drank my Lord Castlewood's health and majority,
the 25th of September, the army being then before Mons :
and here Colonel Esmond was not so fortunate as he had
been in actions much more dangerous, and was hit by a
spent ball just above the place where his former wound was,
which caused the old wound to open again, fever, spitting

of blood, and other ugly symptoms, to ensue ; and, in a word, brought him near to death's door. The kind lad, his kinsman, attended his elder comrade with a very praiseworthy affectionateness and care until he was pronounced out of danger by the doctors, when Frank went off, passed the winter at Bruxelles, and besieged, no doubt, some other fortress there. Very few lads would have given up their pleasures so long and so gaily as Frank did ; his cheerful prattle soothed many long days of Esmond's pain and languor. Frank was supposed to be still at his kinsman's bedside for a month after he had left it, for letters came from his mother at home full of thanks to the younger gentleman for his care of his elder brother (so it pleased Esmond's mistress now affectionately to style him) ; nor was Mr. Esmond in a hurry to undeceive her, when the good young fellow was gone for his Christmas holiday. It was as pleasant to Esmond on his couch to watch the young man's pleasure at the idea of being free, as to note his simple efforts to disguise his satisfaction on going away. There are days when a flask of champagne at a cabaret, and a red-cheeked partner to share it, are too strong temptations for any young fellow of spirit. I am not going to play the moralist, and cry ' Fie ! ' For ages past, I know how old men preach, and what young men practise ; and that patriarchs have had their weak moments, too, long since Father Noah toppled over after discovering the vine. Frank went off, then, to his pleasures at Bruxelles, in which capital many young fellows of our army declared they found infinitely greater diversion even than in London : and Mr. Henry Esmond remained in his sick-room, where he writ a fine comedy, that his mistress pronounced to be sublime, and that was acted no less than three successive nights in London in the next year.

Here, as he lay nursing himself, ubiquitous Mr. Holtz reappeared, and stopped a whole month at Mons, where he not only won over Colonel Esmond to the king's side in politics (that side being always held by the Esmond family) ; but where he endeavoured to reopen the controversial question between the Churches once more, and to recall Esmond to that religion in which, in his infancy, he had been baptized. Holtz was a casuist, both dexterous and learned, and presented the case between the English Church and his own in such a way that those who granted his premisses ought certainly to allow his conclusions. He touched on Esmond's delicate state of health, chance of dissolution, and so forth ; and enlarged upon the immense benefits that the sick man was likely to forgo—benefits which the Church of England did not deny to those of the Roman communion, as how should she, being derived from that Church, and only an offshoot from it. But Mr. Esmond said that his Church was the church of his country, and to that he chose to remain faithful : other people were welcome to worship and to subscribe any other set of articles, whether at Rome or at Augsburg. But if the good father meant that Esmond should join the Roman communion for fear of consequences, and that all England ran the risk of being damned for heresy, Esmond, for one, was perfectly willing to take his chance of the penalty along with the countless millions of his fellow countrymen, who were bred in the same faith, and along with some of the noblest, the truest, the purest, the wisest, the most pious and learned men and women in the world.

As for the political question, in that Mr. Esmond could agree with the father much more readily, and had come to the same conclusion, though, perhaps, by a different way. The right-divine, about which Dr. Sacheverel*and the High Church party in England were just now making a bother, they were welcome to hold as they chose. If Henry Cromwell and his father before him, had been crowned and anointed (and bishops enough would have been found to do it), it seemed to Mr. Esmond that they would have had the right-divine just as much as any Plantagenet, or Tudor, or Stuart. But the desire of the country being unquestionably for an hereditary monarchy, Esmond thought an English king out of St. Germains was better and fitter than a German prince from Herrenhausen, and that if he failed to satisfy the nation, some other Englishman might be found to take his place ; and so, though with no frantic enthusiasm, or worship of that monstrous pedigree which the Tories chose to consider divine, he was ready to say, ' God save King James ! ' when Queen Anne went the way of kings and commoners.

' I fear, colonel, you are no better than a republican at heart,' says the priest, with a sigh.

' I am an Englishman,' says Harry, ' and take my country as I find her. The will of the nation being for Church and

King, I am for Church and King, too ; but English Church, and English King ; and that is why your Church isn't mine, though your king is.'

Though they lost the day at Malplaquet, it was the French who were elated by that action, whilst the conquerors were dispirited by it ; and the enemy gathered together a larger army than ever, and made prodigious efforts for the next campaign. Marshal Berwick was with the French this year ; and we heard that Mareschal Villars was still suffering of his wound, was eager to bring our duke to action, and vowed he would fight us in his coach. Young Castlewood came flying back from Bruxelles, as soon as he heard that fighting was to begin ; and the arrival of the Chevalier de St. George was announced about May. 'It's the king's third campaign, and it's mine,' Frank liked saying. He was come back a greater Jacobite than ever, and Esmond suspected that some fair conspirators at Bruxelles had been inflaming the young man's ardour. Indeed, he owned that he had a message from the queen, Beatrix's godmother, who had given her name to Frank's sister the year before he and his sovereign were born.

However desirous Marshal Villars might be to fight, my lord duke did not seem disposed to indulge him this campaign. Last year his grace had been all for the Whigs and Hano-verians ; but finding, on going to England, his country cold towards himself, and the people in a ferment of High-Church loyalty, the duke comes back to his army cooled towards the Hanoverians, cautious with the Imperialists, and par-ticularly civil and polite towards the Chevalier de St. George. 'Tis certain that messengers and letters were continually passing between his grace and his brave nephew, the Duke of Berwick, in the opposite camp. No man's caresses were more opportune than his grace's, and no man ever uttered expressions of regard and affection more generously. He professed to Monsieur de Torcy,* so Mr. St. John told the writer, quite an eagerness to be cut in pieces for the exiled queen and her family ; nay more, I believe, this year he parted with a portion of the most precious part of himself—his money—which he sent over to the royal exiles. Mr. Tunstal,* who was in the prince's service, was twice or thrice in and out of our camp ; the French, in theirs of Arlieu and about Arras. A little river, the Canihe, I think 'twas called (but this is writ away from books and Europe ; and the

only map the writer hath of these scenes of his youth, bears
no mark of this little stream), divided our pickets from the
enemy's.   Our sentries talked across the stream, when they
could make themselves understood to each other, and when
they could not, grinned, and handed each other their
brandy-flasks or their pouches of tobacco.   And one fine
day of June, riding thither with the officer who visited the
outposts (Colonel Esmond was taking an airing on horseback, being too weak for military duty), they came to this
river, where a number of English and Scots were assembled, talking to the good-natured enemy on the other
side.

Esmond was especially amused with the talk of one long
fellow, with a great curling red moustache, and blue eyes,
that was half a dozen inches taller than his swarthy little
comrades on the French side of the stream, and being asked
by the colonel, saluted him, and said that he belonged to
the Royal Cravats.

From his way of saying ' Royal Cravat ', Esmond at once
knew that the fellow's tongue had first wagged on the banks
of the Liffey, and not the Loire ; and the poor soldier—
a deserter probably—did not like to venture very deep into
French conversation, lest his unlucky brogue should peep
out.   He chose to restrict himself to such few expressions
in the French language as he thought he had mastered
easily ; and his attempt at disguise was infinitely amusing.
Mr. Esmond whistled ' Lillibullero,' at which Teague's eyes
began to twinkle, and then flung him a dollar, when the
poor boy broke out with a ' God bless—that is, *Dieu
bénisse votre honor* ', that would infallibly have sent him
to the provost-marshal had he been on our side of the
river.

Whilst this parley was going on, three officers on horseback, on the French side, appeared at some little distance,
and stopped as if eyeing us, when one of them left the other
two, and rode close up to us who were by the stream.   ' Look,
look ! ' says the Royal Cravat, with great agitation, ' *pas
lui*, that's he ; not him, *l'autre*,' and pointed to the distant
officer on a chestnut horse, with a cuirass shining in the sun,
and over it a broad blue ribbon.

' Please to take Mr. Hamilton's services to my Lord
Marlborough—my lord duke,' says the gentleman in
English ; and, looking to see that the party were not

hostilely disposed, he added, with a smile, ' There's a friend of yours, gentlemen, yonder ; he bids me to say that he saw some of your faces on the 11th of September last year.'*

As the gentleman spoke, the other two officers rode up, and came quite close. We knew at once who it was. It was the king, then two-and-twenty years old, tall and slim, with deep brown eyes, that looked melancholy, though his lips wore a smile. We took off our hats and saluted him. No man, sure, could see for the first time, without emotion, the youthful inheritor of so much fame and misfortune. It seemed to Mr. Esmond that the prince was not unlike young Castlewood, whose age and figure he resembled. The Chevalier de St. George acknowledged the salute, and looked at us hard. Even the idlers on our side of the river set up a hurrah. As for the Royal Cravat, he ran to the prince's stirrup, knelt down and kissed his boot, and bawled and looked a hundred ejaculations and blessings. The prince bade the aide de camp give him a piece of money; and when the party saluting us had ridden away, Cravat spat upon the piece of gold by way of benediction, and swaggered away, pouching his coin and twirling his honest carroty moustache.

The officer in whose company Esmond was, the same little captain of Handyside's regiment, Mr. Sterne,* who had proposed the garden at Lille, when my Lord Mohun and Esmond had their affair, was an Irishman too, and as brave a little soul as ever wore a sword. ' Bedad,' says Roger Sterne, ' that long fellow spoke French so beautiful that I shouldn't have known he wasn't a foreigner, till he broke out with his hulla-balloing, and only an Irish calf can bellow like that.'—And Roger made another remark in his wild way, in which there was sense as well as absurdity—' If that young gentleman,' says he, ' would but ride over to our camp instead of Villars's, toss up his hat and say, " Here am I, the king, who'll follow me ? " by the Lord, Esmond, the whole army would rise and carry him home again, and beat Villars, and take Paris by the way.'

The news of the prince's visit was all through the camp quickly, and scores of ours went down in hopes to see him. Major Hamilton, whom we had talked with, sent back by a trumpet several silver pieces for officers with us. Mr. Esmond received one of these : and that medal, and a recompense not uncommon amongst princes, were the only rewards he ever had from a royal person, whom he endeavoured not very long after to serve.

Esmond quitted the army almost immediately after this, following his general home ; and, indeed, being advised to travel in the fine weather and attempt to take no further part in the campaign. But he heard from the army, that of the many who crowded to see the Chevalier de St. George, Frank Castlewood had made himself most conspicuous : my lord viscount riding across the little stream bareheaded to where the prince was, and dismounting and kneeling before him to do him homage. Some said that the prince had actually knighted him, but my lord denied that statement, though he acknowledged the rest of the story, and said :—' From having been out of favour with Corporal John,' as he called the duke, ' before, his grace warned him not to commit those follies, and smiled on him cordially ever after.

' And he was so kind to me,' Frank writ, ' that I thought I would put in a good word for Master Harry, but when I mentioned your name he looked as black as thunder, and said he had never heard of you.'

CHAPTER II

I GO HOME, AND HARP ON THE OLD STRING

AFTER quitting Mons and the army, and as he was waiting for a packet at Ostend, Esmond had a letter from his young kinsman Castlewood at Bruxelles, conveying intelligence whereof Frank besought him to be the bearer to London, and which caused Colonel Esmond no small anxiety.

The young scapegrace, being one-and-twenty years old, and being anxious to sow his ' wild otes ', as he wrote, had married Mademoiselle de Wertheim, daughter of Count de Wertheim, Chamberlain to the Emperor, and having a post in the Household of the Governor of the Netherlands.

PS. (the young gentleman wrote): Clotilda is *older than me*, which perhaps may be objected to her : but I am so *old a raik*

that the age makes no difference, and I am *determined* to reform.
We were married at St. Gudule, by Father Holt. She is heart
and soul for the *good cause*. And here the cry is *Vif-le-Roy*, which
my mother will *join in*, and Trix *too*. Break this news to 'em
gently: and tell Mr. Finch, my agent, to press the people for
their rents, and send me the *ryno* anyhow. Clotilda sings, and
plays on the Spinet *beautifully*. She is a fair beauty. And if it's
a son, you shall stand *Godfather*. I'm going to leave the army,
having had *enuf of soldering ;* and my lord duke *recommends* me.
I shall pass the winter here : and stop at least until Clo's lying-in.
I call her *old Clo*, but nobody else shall. She is the cleverest woman
in all Bruxelles : understanding painting, music, poetry, and perfect
at *cookery and puddens*. I borded with the count, that's how
I came to know her. There are four counts her brothers. One
an abbey—three with the prince's army. They have a lawsuit
for *an immense fortune :* but are now in *a pore way*. Break this
to mother, who'll take anything from *you*. And write, and bid
Finch write *amediately*. Hostel de ' l'Aigle Noire,' Bruxelles,
Flanders.

So Frank had married a Roman Catholic lady, and an
heir was expected, and Mr. Esmond was to carry this intelligence to his mistress at London. 'Twas a difficult embassy ;
and the colonel felt not a little tremor as he neared the
capital.

He reached his inn late, and sent a messenger to Kensington to announce his arrival and visit the next morning.
The messenger brought back news that the Court was at
Windsor, and the fair Beatrix absent and engaged in her
duties there. Only Esmond's mistress remained in her
house at Kensington. She appeared in Court but once in
the year ; Beatrix was quite the mistress and ruler of the
little mansion, inviting the company thither, and engaging
in every conceivable frolic of town pleasure. Whilst her
mother, acting as the young lady's protectress and elder
sister, pursued her own path, which was quite modest and
secluded.

As soon as ever Esmond was dressed (and he had been
awake long before the town), he took a coach for Kensington,
and reached it so early that he met his dear mistress coming
home from morning prayers. She carried her Prayer-book,
never allowing a footman to bear it, as everybody else did :
and it was by this simple sign Esmond knew what her
occupation had been. He called to the coachman to stop,
and jumped out as she looked towards him. She wore her
hood as usual, and she turned quite pale when she saw him.

To feel that kind little hand near to his heart seemed to give him strength. They soon were at the door of her ladyship's house—and within it.

With a sweet sad smile she took his hand and kissed it.

'How ill you have been : how weak you look, my dear Henry,' she said.

'Tis certain the colonel did look like a ghost, except that ghosts do not look very happy, 'tis said. Esmond always felt so on returning to her after absence, indeed whenever he looked in her sweet kind face.

'I am come back to be nursed by my family,' says he. 'If Frank had not taken care of me after my wound, very likely I should have gone altogether.'

'Poor Frank, good Frank !' says his mother. 'You'll always be kind to him, my lord,' she went on. 'The poor child never knew he was doing you a wrong.'

'My lord !' cries out Colonel Esmond. 'What do you mean, dear lady ?'

'I am no lady,' says she ; 'I am Rachel Esmond, Francis Esmond's widow, my lord. I cannot bear that title. Would we never had taken it from him who has it now. But we did all in our power, Henry : we did all in our power ; and my lord and I—that is——'

'Who told you this tale, dearest lady ?' asked the colonel.

'Have you not had the letter I writ you ? I writ to you at Mons directly I heard it,' says Lady Esmond.

'And from whom ?' again asked Colonel Esmond—and his mistress then told him that on her death-bed the dowager countess, sending for her, had presented her with this dismal secret as a legacy. ''Twas very malicious of the dowager,' Lady Esmond said, 'to have had it so long, and to have kept the truth from me. "Cousin Rachel," she said,' and Esmond's mistress could not forbear smiling as she told the story, '"cousin Rachel," cries the dowager, "I have sent for you, as the doctors say I may go off any day in this dysentery ; and to ease my conscience of a great load that has been on it. You always have been a poor creature and unfit for great honour, and what I have to say won't, therefore, affect you so much. You must know, cousin Rachel, that I have left my house, plate, and furniture, three thousand pounds in money, and my diamonds that my late revered saint and sovereign, King James, presented me with, to my Lord Viscount Castlewood."

' "To my Frank ? " ' says Lady Castlewood : ' " I was in hopes——"

' " To Viscount Castlewood, my dear, Viscount Castlewood, and Baron Esmond of Shandon in the kingdom of Ireland, Earl and Marquis of Esmond under patent of his Majesty King James the Second, conferred upon my husband the late marquis—for I am Marchioness of Esmond before God and man."

' " And have you left poor Harry nothing, dear marchioness ? " ' asks Lady Castlewood (she hath told me the story completely since with her quiet arch way ; the most charming any woman ever had : and I set down the narrative here at length so as to have done with it). ' "And have you left poor Harry nothing ? " ' asks my dear lady : ' for you know, Henry,' she says with her sweet smile, ' I used always to pity Esau—and I think I am on his side—though papa tried very hard to convince me the other way.

' " Poor Harry ! " says the old lady. " So you want something left to poor Harry : he, he ! (reach me the drops, cousin). Well then, my dear, since you want poor Harry to have a fortune : you must understand that ever since the year 1691, a week after the battle of the Boyne, where the Prince of Orange defeated his royal sovereign and father, for which crime he is now suffering in flames (ugh, ugh), Henry Esmond hath been Marquis of Esmond and Earl of Castlewood in the United Kingdom, and Baron and Viscount Castlewood of Shandon in Ireland, and a baronet— and his eldest son will be, by courtesy, styled Earl of Castlewood—he! he! What do you think of that, my dear? "

' " Gracious mercy ! how long have you known this ? " ' cries the other lady (thinking perhaps that the old marchioness was wandering in her wits).

' " My husband, before he was converted, was a wicked wretch," ' the sick sinner continued. ' " When he was in the Low Countries he seduced a weaver's daughter ; and added to his wickedness by marrying her. And then he came to this country and married me—a poor girl—a poor innocent young thing—I say," though she was past forty, you know, Harry, when she married : and as for being innocent— "Well," she went on, " I knew nothing of my lord's wickedness for three years after our marriage, and after the burial of our poor little boy I had it done over again, my dear. I had myself married by Father Holt in Castlewood chapel, as soon as ever I heard the creature was dead—and having a great illness then, arising from another sad disappointment I had, the priest came and told me that my lord had a son before our marriage, and that the child was at nurse in England ; and I consented to let the brat be brought home, and a queer little melancholy child it was when it came.

' " Our intention was to make a priest of him : and he was bred for this, until you perverted him from it, you wicked woman. And I had again hopes of giving an heir to my lord, when he was called away upon the king's business, and died fighting gloriously at the Boyne Water.

' " Should I be disappointed—I owed your husband no love, my dear, for he had jilted me in the most scandalous way ; and I thought there would be time to declare the little weaver's son for the true heir. But I was carried off to prison, where your husband was so kind to me— urging all his friends to obtain my release, and using all his credit in my favour—that I relented towards him, especially as my director counselled me to be silent ; and that it was for the good of the king's service that the title of our family should continue with your husband the late viscount, whereby his fidelity would be always secured to the king. And a proof of this is, that a year before your husband's death, when he thought of taking a place under the Prince of Orange, Mr. Holt went to him, and told him what the state of the matter was, and obliged him to raise a large sum for his Majesty : and engaged him in the true cause so heartily, that we were sure of his support on any day when it should be considered advisable to attack the usurper. Then his sudden death came ; and there was a thought of declaring the truth. But 'twas determined to be best for the king's service to let the title still go with the younger branch ; and there's no sacrifice a Castlewood wouldn't make for that cause, my dear.

' " As for Colonel Esmond, he knew the truth already " (and then, Harry,' my mistress said, ' she told me of what had happened at my dear husband's death-bed). " He doth not intend to take the title, though it belongs to him. But it eases my conscience that you should know the truth, my dear. And your son is lawfully Viscount Castlewood so long as his cousin doth not claim the rank." '

This was the substance of the dowager's revelation.

Dean Atterbury had knowledge of it, Lady Castlewood said, and Esmond very well knows how : that divine being the clergyman for whom the late lord had sent on his death-bed : and when Lady Castlewood would instantly have written to her son, and conveyed the truth to him, the dean's advice was that a letter should be writ to Colonel Esmond rather ; that the matter should be submitted to his decision, by which alone the rest of the family were bound to abide.

' And can my dearest lady doubt what that will be ? ' says the colonel.

' It rests with you, Harry, as the head of our house.'

' It was settled twelve years since, by my dear lord's bedside,' says Colonel Esmond. ' The children must know nothing of this. Frank and his heirs after him must bear our name. 'Tis his rightfully ; I have not even a proof of that marriage of my father and mother, though my poor lord, on his death-bed, told me that Father Holt had brought such a proof to Castlewood. I would not seek it when I was abroad. I went and looked at my poor mother's grave in her convent. What matter to her now ? No court of law on earth, upon my mere word, would deprive my lord viscount and set me up. I am the head of the house, dear lady ; but Frank is Viscount of Castlewood still. And rather than disturb him, I would turn monk, or disappear in America.'

As he spoke so to his dearest mistress, for whom he would have been willing to give up his life, or to make any sacrifice any day, the fond creature flung herself down on her knees before him, and kissed both his hands in an outbreak of passionate love and gratitude, such as could not but melt his heart, and make him feel very proud and thankful that God had given him the power to show his love for her, and to prove it by some little sacrifice on his own part. To be able to bestow benefits or happiness on those one loves is sure the greatest blessing conferred upon a man—and what wealth or name, or gratification of ambition or vanity, could compare with the pleasure Esmond now had of being able to confer some kindness upon his best and dearest friends ?

' Dearest saint,' says he—' purest soul, that has had so much to suffer, that has blest the poor lonely orphan with such a treasure of love. 'Tis for me to kneel, not for you : 'tis for me to be thankful that I can make you happy. Hath

my life any other aim ?   Blessed be God that I can serve
you !   What pleasure, think you, could all the world give
me compared to that ? '

'Don't raise me,' she said, in a wild way, to Esmond, who
would have lifted her.   'Let me kneel—let me kneel, and—
and—worship you.'

Before such a partial judge, as Esmond's dear mistress
owned herself to be, any cause which he might plead was
sure to be given in his favour ; and accordingly he found
little difficulty in reconciling her to the news whereof he
was bearer, of her son's marriage to a foreign lady, Papist
though she was.   Lady Castlewood never could be brought
to think so ill of that religion as other people in England
thought of it : she held that ours was undoubtedly a branch
of the Church Catholic, but that the Roman was one of the
main stems on which, no doubt, many errors had been grafted
(she was, for a woman, extraordinarily well versed in this
controversy, having acted, as a girl, as secretary to her
father, the late dean, and written many of his sermons,
under his dictation) ; and if Frank had chosen to marry
a lady of the Church of South Europe, as she would call the
Roman communion, that was no need why she should not
welcome her as a daughter-in-law : and accordingly she
writ to her new daughter a very pretty, touching letter
(as Esmond thought, who had cognizance of it before it
went), in which the only hint of reproof was a gentle
remonstrance that her son had not written to herself, to
ask a fond mother's blessing for that step which he was
about taking.   'Castlewood knew very well,' so she wrote
to her son, 'that she never denied him anything in her
power to give, much less would she think of opposing
a marriage that was to make his happiness, as she trusted,
and keep him out of wild courses, which had alarmed her
a good deal : and she besought him to come quickly to
England, to settle down in his family house of Castlewood
('It is his family house,' says she, to Colonel Esmond,
'though only his own house by your forbearance '), and to
receive the accompt of her stewardship during his ten years'
minority.'   By care and frugality, she had got the estate
into a better condition than ever it had been since the
Parliamentary wars ; and my lord was now master of a
pretty, small income, not encumbered of debts, as it had

been, during his father's ruinous time. 'But in saving my
son's fortune,' says she, 'I fear I have lost a great part of
my hold on him.' And, indeed, this was the case; her
ladyship's daughter complaining that their mother did all
for Frank, and nothing for her; and Frank himself being
dissatisfied at the narrow, simple way of his mother's
living at Walcote, where he had been brought up more like
a poor parson's son, than a young nobleman that was to
make a figure in the world. 'Twas this mistake in his early
training, very likely, that set him so eager upon pleasure
when he had it in his power; nor is he the first lad that
has been spoiled by the over-careful fondness of women.
No training is so useful for children, great or small, as the
company of their betters in rank or natural parts; in whose
society they lose the overweening sense of their own importance, which stay-at-home people very commonly learn.

But, as a prodigal that's sending in a schedule of his debts
to his friends, never puts all down, and, you may be sure,
the rogue keeps back some immense swingeing bill, that he
doesn't dare to own; so the poor Frank had a very heavy
piece of news to break to his mother, and which he hadn't
the courage to introduce into his first confession. Some
misgivings Esmond might have, upon receiving Frank's
letter, and knowing into what hands the boy had fallen;
but whatever these misgivings were, he kept them to himself, not caring to trouble his mistress with any fears that
might be groundless.

However, the next mail which came from Bruxelles, after
Frank had received his mother's letter there, brought back
a joint composition from himself and his wife, who could
spell no better than her young scapegrace of a husband,
full of expressions of thanks, love, and duty to the dowager
viscountess, as my poor lady now was styled; and along
with this letter (which was read in a family council, namely,
the viscountess, Mistress Beatrix, and the writer of this
memoir, and which was pronounced to be vulgar by the
maid of honour, and felt to be so by the other two), there
came a private letter for Colonel Esmond from poor Frank,
with another dismal commission for the colonel to execute,
at his best opportunity; and this was to announce that
Frank had seen fit, ' by the exhortation of Mr. Holt, the
influence of his Clotilda, and the blessing of Heaven and
the saints,' says my lord, demurely, ' to change his religion,

and be received into the bosom of that Church of which
his sovereign, many of his family, and the greater part of
the civilized world, were members.' And his lordship added
a postscript, of which Esmond knew the inspiring genius
very well, for it had the genuine twang of the seminary,
and was quite unlike poor Frank's ordinary style of writing
and thinking ; in which he reminded Colonel Esmond that
he too was, by birth, of that Church ; and that his mother
and sister should have his lordship's prayers to the saints
(an inestimable benefit, truly !) for their conversion.

If Esmond had wanted to keep this secret he could not ;
for a day or two after receiving this letter, a notice from
Bruxelles appeared in the *Post-Boy*,* and other prints,
announcing that ' a young Irish lord, the Viscount C—stle-
w—d, just come to his majority, and who had served the
last campaigns with great credit, as aide de camp to his
grace the Duke of Marlborough, had declared for the Popish
religion at Bruxelles, and had walked in a procession
barefoot, with a wax taper in his hand.' The notorious
Mr. Holt, who had been employed as a Jacobite agent
during the last reign, and many times pardoned by King
William, had been, the *Post-Boy* said, the agent of this
conversion.

The Lady Castlewood was as much cast down by this
news as Miss Beatrix was indignant at it. ' So,' says she,
' Castlewood is no longer a home for us, mother. Frank's
foreign wife will bring her confessor, and there will be
frogs for dinner ; and all Tusher's and my grandfather's
sermons are flung away upon my brother. I used to tell
you that you killed him with the Catechism, and that he
would turn wicked as soon as he broke from his mammy's
leading-strings. Oh, mother, you would not believe that
the young scapegrace was playing you tricks, and that
sneak of a Tusher was not a fit guide for him. Oh, those
parsons ! I hate 'em all,' says Mistress Beatrix, clapping
her hands together ; ' yes, whether they wear cassocks
and buckles, or beards and bare feet. There's a horrid
Irish wretch who never misses a Sunday at Court, and who
pays me compliments there, the horrible man ; and if you
want to know what parsons are, you should see his behaviour, and hear him talk of his own cloth. They're all
the same, whether they're bishops or bonzes, or Indian
fakirs. They try to domineer, and they frighten us with

kingdom come; and they wear a sanctified air in public, and expect us to go down on our knees and ask their blessing; and they intrigue, and they grasp, and they backbite, and they slander worse than the worst courtier or the wickedest old woman. I heard this Mr. Swift sneering at my Lord Duke of Marlborough's courage the other day. He! that Teague from Dublin! because his grace is not in favour, dares to say this of him; and he says this that it may get to her Majesty's ear, and to coax and wheedle Mrs. Masham. They say the Elector of Hanover has a dozen of mistresses in his Court at Herrenhausen, and if he comes to be king over us, I wager that the bishops and Mr. Swift, that wants to be one, will coax and wheedle them. Oh, those priests and their grave airs! I'm sick of their square toes and their rustling cassocks. I should like to go to a country where there was not one, or turn Quaker, and get rid of 'em; and I would, only the dress is not becoming, and I've much too pretty a figure to hide it. Haven't I, cousin?' and here she glanced at her person and the looking-glass, which told her rightly that a more beautiful shape and face never were seen.

'I made that onslaught on the priests,' says Miss Beatrix, afterwards, 'in order to divert my poor dear mother's anguish about Frank. Frank is as vain as a girl, cousin. Talk of us girls being vain, what are *we* to you? It was easy to see that the first woman who chose would make a fool of him, or the first robe—I count a priest and a woman all the same. We are always caballing; we are not answerable for the fibs we tell; we are always cajoling and coaxing, or threatening; and we are always making mischief, Colonel Esmond—mark my word for that, who know the the world, sir, and have to make my way in it. I see as well as possible how Frank's marriage hath been managed. The count, our papa-in-law, is always away at the coffee-house. The countess, our mother, is always in the kitchen looking after the dinner. The countess, our sister, is at the spinet. When my lord comes to say he is going on the campaign, the lovely Clotilda bursts into tears, and faints so; he catches her in his arms—no, sir, keep your distance, cousin, if you please—she cries on his shoulder, and he says, "Oh, my divine, my adored, my beloved Clotilda, are you sorry to part with me?" "Oh, my Francisco," says she, "oh, my lord!" and at this very instant mamma and a couple of young brothers, with moustachios and long rapiers, come in from the kitchen, where they have been eating bread and onions. Mark my word, you will have all this woman's relations at Castlewood three months after she has arrived there. The old count and countess, and the young counts and all the little countesses her sisters. Counts! every one of these wretches says he is a count. Guiscard, that stabbed Mr. Harvy,* said he was a count; and I believe he was a barber. All Frenchmen are barbers—Fiddle-dee! don't contradict me—or else dancing-masters, or else priests;' and so she rattled on.

'Who was it taught *you* to dance, cousin Beatrix?' says the colonel.

She laughed out the air of a minuet, and swept a low curtsy, coming up to the recover with the prettiest little foot in the world pointed out. Her mother came in as she was in this attitude; my lady had been in her closet, having taken poor Frank's conversion in a very serious way; the madcap girl ran up to her mother, put her arms round her waist, kissed her, tried to make her dance, and said: 'Don't be silly, you kind little mamma, and cry about Frank turning Papist. What a figure he must be, with a white sheet and a candle walking in a procession barefoot!' And she kicked off her little slippers (the wonderfullest little shoes with wonderful tall red heels, Esmond pounced upon one as it fell close beside him), and she put on the drollest little *moue*, and marched up and down the room holding Esmond's cane by way of taper. Serious as her mood was, Lady Castlewood could not refrain from laughing; and as for Esmond he looked on with that delight with which the sight of this fair creature always inspired him: never had he seen any woman so arch, so brilliant, and so beautiful.

Having finished her march, she put out her foot for her slipper. The colonel knelt down: 'If you will be Pope I will turn Papist,' says he; and her holiness gave him gracious leave to kiss the little stockinged foot before he put the slipper on.

Mamma's feet began to pat on the floor during this operation, and Beatrix, whose bright eyes nothing escaped, saw that little mark of impatience. She ran up and embraced her mother, with her usual cry of, 'Oh, you silly little mamma: your feet are quite as pretty as mine,' says she: ' they are,

cousin, though she hides 'em ; but the shoemaker will tell
you that he makes for both off the same last.'

' You are taller than I am, dearest,' says her mother,
blushing over her whole sweet face—' and—and it is your
hand, my dear, and not your foot he wants you to give him,'
and she said it with a hysteric laugh, that had more of tears
than laughter in it ; laying her head on her daughter's
fair shoulder, and hiding it there.   They made a very pretty
picture together, and looked like a pair of sisters—the
sweet simple matron seeming younger than her years, and
her daughter, if not older, yet somehow, from a commanding
manner and grace which she possessed above most women,
her mother's superior and protectress.

' But, oh ! ' cries my mistress, recovering herself after
this scene, and returning to her usual sad tone, ' 'tis a shame
that we should laugh and be making merry on a day when
we ought to be down on our knees and asking pardon.'

' Asking pardon for what ? ' says saucy Mrs. Beatrix,—
' because Frank takes it into his head to fast on Fridays,
and worship images ?   You know if you had been born
a Papist, mother, a Papist you would have remained to
the end of your days.   'Tis the religion of the king and of
some of the best quality.   For my part, I'm no enemy to
it, and think Queen Bess was not a penny better than Queen
Mary.'

' Hush, Beatrix !   Do not jest with sacred things, and
remember of what parentage you come,' cries my lady.
Beatrix was ordering her ribbons, and adjusting her tucker,
and performing a dozen provoking pretty ceremonies, before
the glass.   The girl was no hypocrite at least.   She never
at that time could be brought to think but of the world
and her beauty ; and seemed to have no more sense of
devotion than some people have of music, that cannot
distinguish one air from another.   Esmond saw this fault
in her, as he saw many others—a bad wife would Beatrix
Esmond make, he thought, for any man under the degree
of a prince.   She was born to shine in great assemblies,
and to adorn palaces, and to command everywhere—to
conduct an intrigue of politics, or to glitter in a queen's
train.   But to sit at a homely table, and mend the stockings
of a poor man's children ! that was no fitting duty for her,
or at least one that she wouldn't have broke her heart in
trying to do.   She was a princess, though she had scarce

a shilling to her fortune ; and one of her subjects—the most abject and devoted wretch, sure, that ever drivelled at a woman's knees—was this unlucky gentleman ; who bound his good sense, and reason, and independence, hand and foot ; and submitted them to her.

And who does not know how ruthlessly women will tyrannize when they are let to domineer ? and who does not know how useless advice is ? I could give good counsel to my descendants, but I know they'll follow their own way, for all their grandfather's sermon. A man gets his own experience about women, and will take nobody's hearsay ; nor, indeed, is the young fellow worth a fig that would. 'Tis I that am in love with my mistress, not my old grandmother that counsels me ; 'tis I that have fixed the value of the thing I would have, and know the price I would pay for it. It may be worthless to you, but 'tis all my life to me. Had Esmond possessed the Great Mogul's crown and all his diamonds, or all the Duke of Marlborough's money, or all the ingots sunk at Vigo, he would have given them all for this woman. A fool he was, if you will ; but so is a sovereign a fool, that will give half a principality for a little crystal as big as a pigeon's egg, and called a diamond : so is a wealthy nobleman a fool, that will face danger or death, and spend half his life, and all his tranquillity, caballing for a blue ribbon : so is a Dutch merchant a fool, that hath been known to pay ten thousand crowns for a tulip. There's some particular prize we all of us value, and that every man of spirit will venture his life for. With this, it may be to achieve a great reputation for learning ; with that, to be a man of fashion, and the admiration of the town ; with another, to consummate a great work of art or poetry, and go to immortality that way ; and with another, for a certain time of his life, the sole object and aim is a woman.

Whilst Esmond was under the domination of this passion, he remembers many a talk he had with his intimates, who used to rally our Knight of the Rueful Countenance at his devotion, whereof he made no disguise, to Beatrix ; and it was with replies such as the above he met his friends' satire. ' Granted, I am a fool,' says he, ' and no better than you ; but you are no better than I. You have your folly you labour for ; give me the charity of mine. What flatteries do you, Mr. St. John, stoop to whisper in the ears of a queen's favourite ? What nights of labour doth not the laziest man in the world endure, forgoing his bottle, and his boon companions, forgoing Lais,* in whose lap he would like to be yawning, that he may prepare a speech full of lies, to cajole three hundred stupid country gentlemen in the House of Commons, and get the hiccuping cheers of the October Club !* What days will you spend in your jolting chariot ! ' (Mr. Esmond often rode to Windsor, and especially, of later days, with the secretary.) ' What hours will you pass on your gouty feet—and how humbly will you kneel down to present a dispatch—you, the proudest man in the world, that has not knelt to God since you were a boy, and in that posture whisper, flatter, adore almost, a stupid woman, that's often boozy with too much meat and drink, when Mr. Secretary goes for his audience ! If my pursuit is vanity, sure yours is too.' And then the secretary would fly out in such a rich flow of eloquence, as this pen cannot pretend to recall ; advocating his scheme of ambition, showing the great good he would do for his country when he was the undisputed chief of it ; backing his opinion with a score of pat sentences from Greek and Roman authorities (of which kind of learning he made rather an ostentatious display), and scornfully vaunting the very arts and meannesses by which fools were to be made to follow him, opponents to be bribed or silenced, doubters converted, and enemies overawed.

' I am Diogenes,' says Esmond, laughing, ' that is taken up for a ride in Alexander's chariot. I have no desire to vanquish Darius or to tame Bucephalus. I do not want what you want, a great name or a high place : to have them would bring me no pleasure. But my moderation is taste, not virtue ; and I know that what I do want, is as vain as that which you long after. Do not grudge me my vanity, if I allow yours ; or rather, let us laugh at both indifferently, and at ourselves, and at each other.'

' If your charmer holds out,' says St. John, ' at this rate, she may keep you twenty years besieging her, and surrender by the time you are seventy, and she is old enough to be a grandmother. I do not say the pursuit of a particular woman is not as pleasant a pastime as any other kind of hunting,' he added ; ' only, for my part, I find the game won't run long enough. They knock under too soon—that's the fault I find with 'em.'

'The game which you pursue is in the habit of being caught, and used to being pulled down,' says Mr. Esmond.

'But Dulcinea del Toboso is peerless, eh?' says the other. 'Well, honest Harry, go and attack windmills—perhaps thou art not more mad than other people,' St. John added, with a sigh.

CHAPTER III

A PAPER OUT OF THE 'SPECTATOR'

DOTH any young gentleman of my progeny, who may read his old grandfather's papers, chance to be presently suffering under the passion of Love? There is a humiliating cure, but one that is easy and almost specific for the malady—which is, to try an alibi. Esmond went away from his mistress and was cured a half-dozen times; he came back to her side, and instantly fell ill again of the fever. He vowed that he could leave her and think no more of her, and so he could pretty well, at least, succeed in quelling that rage and longing he had whenever he was with her; but as soon as he returned he was as bad as ever again. Truly a ludicrous and pitiable object, at least exhausting everybody's pity but his dearest mistress's, Lady Castlewood's, in whose tender breast he reposed all his dreary confessions, and who never tired of hearing him and pleading for him.

Sometimes Esmond would think there was hope. Then again he would be plagued with despair, at some impertinence or coquetry of his mistress. For days they would be like brother and sister, or the dearest friends—she, simple, fond, and charming—he, happy beyond measure at her good behaviour. But this would all vanish on a sudden. Either he would be too pressing, and hint his love, when she would rebuff him instantly, and give his vanity a box on the ear: or he would be jealous, and with perfect good reason, of some new admirer that had sprung up, or some rich young gentleman newly arrived in the town, that this incorrigible flirt would set her nets and baits to draw in. If Esmond remonstrated, the little rebel would say—'Who are you? I shall go my own way, sirrah, and that way is towards a husband, and I don't want *you* on the

way. I am for your betters, colonel, for your betters:
do you hear that? You might do if you had an estate
and were younger; only eight years older than I, you say!
pish, you are a hundred years older. You are an old, old
Graveairs, and I should make you miserable, that would be
the only comfort I should have in marrying you. But
you have not money enough to keep a cat decently after
you have paid your man his wages, and your landlady
her bill. Do you think I'm going to live in a lodging, and
turn the mutton at a string whilst your honour nurses the
baby? Fiddlestick, and why did you not get this nonsense
knocked out of your head when you were in the wars?
You are come back more dismal and dreary than ever.
You and mamma are fit for each other. You might be
Darby and Joan, and play cribbage to the end of your
lives.'

'At least you own to your worldliness, my poor Trix,'
says her mother.

'Worldliness—O my pretty lady! Do you think that
I am a child in the nursery, and to be frightened by Bogey?
Worldliness, to be sure; and pray, madam, where is the
harm of wishing to be comfortable? When you are gone,
you dearest old woman, or when I am tired of you and
have run away from you, where shall I go? Shall I go
and be head nurse to my Popish sister-in-law, take the
children their physic, and whip 'em, and put 'em to bed
when they are naughty? Shall I be Castlewood's upper
servant, and perhaps marry Tom Tusher? *Merci!* I have
been long enough Frank's humble servant. Why am I not
a man? I have ten times his brains, and had I worn the—
well, don't let your ladyship be frightened—had I worn
a sword and periwig instead of this mantle and commode,
to which nature has condemned me—(though 'tis a pretty
stuff, too—cousin Esmond! you will go to the Exchange
to-morrow, and get the exact counterpart of this ribbon,
sir, do you hear?)—I would have made our name talked
about. So would Graveairs here have made something
out of our name if he had represented it. My Lord Graveairs would have done very well. Yes, you have a very
pretty way, and would have made a very decent, grave
speaker;' and here she began to imitate Esmond's way
of carrying himself, and speaking to his face, and so
ludicrously that his mistress burst out a-laughing, and even

he himself could see there was some likeness in the fantas-
tical malicious caricature.

'Yes,' says she, 'I solemnly vow, own, and confess, that
I want a good husband. Where's the harm of one ? My
face is my fortune. Who'll come ?—buy, buy, buy!
I cannot toil, neither can I spin, but I can play twenty-three
games on the cards. I can dance the last dance, I can
hunt the stag, and I think I could shoot flying. I can
talk as wicked as any woman of my years, and know
enough stories to amuse a sulky husband for at least one
thousand and one nights. I have a pretty taste for dress,
diamonds, gambling, and old china. I love sugar-plums,
Malines lace (that you brought me, cousin, is very pretty),
the opera, and everything that is useless and costly. I have
got a monkey and a little black boy—Pompey, sir, go and
give a dish of chocolate to Colonel Graveairs,—and a parrot
and a spaniel, and I must have a husband. Cupid, you
hear ? '

'Iss, missis,' says Pompey, a little grinning negro Lord
Peterborow gave her, with a bird of Paradise in his turbant,
and a collar with his mistress's name on it.

'Iss, missis ! ' says Beatrix, imitating the child. 'And
if husband not come, Pompey must go fetch one.'

And Pompey went away grinning with his chocolate
tray, as Miss Beatrix ran up to her mother and ended her
sally of mischief in her common way, with a kiss—no
wonder that upon paying such a penalty her fond judge
pardoned her.

When Mr. Esmond came home, his health was still
shattered ; and he took a lodging near to his mistress's,
at Kensington, glad enough to be served by them, and to
see them day after day. He was enabled to see a little
company—and of the sort he liked best. Mr. Steele and
Mr. Addison both did him the honour to visit him : and
drank many a flask of good claret at his lodging, whilst
their entertainer, through his wound, was kept to diet
drink and gruel. These gentlemen were Whigs, and great
admirers of my Lord Duke of Marlborough ; and Esmond
was entirely of the other party. But their different views
of politics did not prevent the gentlemen from agreeing in
private, nor from allowing, on one evening when Esmond's
kind old patron, Lieutenant-General Webb, with a stick

and a crutch, hobbled up to the colonel's lodging (which was prettily situate at Knightsbridge, between London and Kensington, and looking over the Gardens), that the lieutenant-general was a noble and gallant soldier—and even that he had been hardly used in the Wynendael affair. He took his revenge in talk, that must be confessed; and if Mr. Addison had had a mind to write a poem about Wynendael, he might have heard from the commander's own lips the story a hundred times over.

Mr. Esmond, forced to be quiet, betook himself to literature for a relaxation, and composed his comedy, whereof the prompter's copy lieth in my walnut escritoire, sealed up and docketed, *The Faithful Fool*, a Comedy, as it was performed by her Majesty's servants. 'Twas a very sentimental piece; and Mr. Steele, who had more of that kind of sentiment than Mr. Addison, admired it, whilst the other rather sneered at the performance; though he owned that, here and there, it contained some pretty strokes. He was bringing out his own play of *Cato* at the time, the blaze of which quite extinguished Esmond's farthing candle: and his name was never put to the piece, which was printed as by a Person of Quality. Only nine copies were sold, though Mr. Dennis, the great critic,* praised it, and said 'twas a work of great merit; and Colonel Esmond had the whole impression burned one day in a rage, by Jack Lockwood, his man.

All this comedy was full of bitter satiric strokes against a certain young lady. The plot of the piece was quite a new one. A young woman was represented with a great number of suitors, selecting a pert fribble of a peer, in place of the hero (but ill-acted, I think, by Mr. Wilks,* the Faithful Fool), who persisted in admiring her. In the fifth act, Teraminta was made to discover the merits of Eugenio (the F. F.), and to feel a partiality for him too late; for he announced that he had bestowed his hand and estate upon Rosaria, a country lass, endowed with every virtue. But it must be owned that the audience yawned through the play; and that it perished on the third night, with only half a dozen persons to behold its agonies. Esmond and his two mistresses came to the first night, and Miss Beatrix fell asleep; whilst her mother, who had not been to a play since King James the Second's time, thought the piece, though not brilliant, had a very pretty moral.

Mr. Esmond dabbled in letters, and wrote a deal of prose and verse at this time of leisure. When displeased with the conduct of Miss Beatrix, he would compose a satire, in which he relieved his mind. When smarting under the faithlessness of women, he dashed off a copy of verses, in which he held the whole sex up to scorn. One day, in one of these moods, he made a little joke, in which (swearing him to secrecy) he got his friend Dick Steele to help him ; and, composing a paper, he had it printed exactly like Steele's paper, and by his printer, and laid on his mistress's breakfast-table the following :—

'SPECTATOR.'

No. 341   'Tuesday, April 1, 1712.

Mutato nomine de te Fabula narratur.—HORACE.
Thyself the moral of the Fable see.—CREECH.

Jocasta is known as a woman of learning and fashion, and as one of the most amiable persons of this Court and country. She is at home two mornings of the week, and all the wits and a few of the beauties of London flock to her assemblies. When she goes abroad to Tunbridge or the Bath, a retinue of adorers rides the journey with her ; and, besides the London beaux, she has a crowd of admirers at the Wells, the polite amongst the natives of Sussex and Somerset pressing round her tea-tables, and being anxious for a nod from her chair. Jocasta's acquaintance is thus very numerous. Indeed, 'tis one smart writer's work to keep her visiting-book—a strong footman is engaged to carry it ; and it would require a much stronger head, even than Jocasta's own, to remember the names of all her dear friends.

' Either at Epsom Wells or at Tunbridge (for of this important matter Jocasta cannot be certain) it was her ladyship's fortune to become acquainted with a young gentleman, whose conversation was so sprightly, and manners amiable, that she invited the agreeable young spark to visit her if ever he came to London, where her house in Spring Garden should be open to him. Charming as he was, and without any manner of doubt a pretty fellow, Jocasta hath such a regiment of the like continually marching round her standard, that 'tis no wonder her attention is distracted amongst them. And so, though this gentleman made a considerable impression upon her, and touched her heart for at least three-and-twenty minutes, it must be owned that she has forgotten his name. He is a dark man, and may be eight-and-twenty years old. His dress is sober, though of rich materials. He has a mole on his forehead over his left eye ; has a blue ribbon to his cane and sword, and wears his own hair.

' Jocasta was much flattered by beholding her admirer (for that everybody admires who sees her is a point which she never can for a moment doubt) in the next pew to her at St. James's Church last Sunday ; and the manner in which he appeared to go to sleep during the sermon— though from under his fringed eyelids it was evident he was casting glances of respectful rapture towards Jocasta— deeply moved and interested her. On coming out of church, he found his way to her chair, and made her an elegant bow as she stepped into it. She saw him at Court afterwards, where he carried himself with a most distinguished air, though none of her acquaintances knew his name ; and the next night he was at the play, where her ladyship was pleased to acknowledge him from the side-box.

' During the whole of the comedy she racked her brains so to remember his name, that she did not hear a word of the piece : and having the happiness to meet him once more in the lobby of the playhouse, she went up to him in a flutter, and bade him remember that she kept two nights in the week, and that she longed to see him at Spring Garden.

' He appeared on Tuesday, in a rich suit, showing a very fine taste both in the tailor and wearer ; and though a knot of us were gathered round the charming Jocasta, fellows who pretended to know every face upon the town, not one could tell the gentleman's name in reply to Jocasta's eager inquiries, flung to the right and left of her as he advanced up the room with a bow that would become a duke.

' Jocasta acknowledged this salute with one of those smiles and curtsies of which that lady hath the secret. She curtsies with a languishing air, as if to say, " You are come at last. I have been pining for you : " and then she finishes her victim with a killing look, which declares : " O Philander ! I have no eyes but for you." Camilla

hath as good a curtsy perhaps, and Thalestris much such
another look ; but the glance and the curtsy together
belong to Jocasta of all the English beauties alone.

' " Welcome to London, sir," says she.   " One can see
you are from the country by your looks."   She would have
said " Epsom ", or " Tunbridge ", had she remembered
rightly at which place she had met the stranger ; but,
alas ! she had forgotten.

' The gentleman said, " he had been in town but three
days ; and one of his reasons for coming hither was to
have the honour of paying his court to Jocasta."

' She said, " the waters had agreed with her but indifferently."

' " The waters were for the sick," the gentleman said :
' the young and beautiful came but to make them sparkle.
And, as the clergyman read the service on Sunday," he
added, " your ladyship reminded me of the angel that
visited the pool."* A murmur of approbation saluted this
sally.   Manilio, who is a wit when he is not at cards, was
in such a rage that he revoked when he heard it.

' Jocasta was an angel visiting the waters ; but at which
of the Bethesdas ?   She was puzzled more and more ; and,
as her way always is, looked the more innocent and simple,
the more artful her intentions were.

' " We were discoursing," says she, " about spelling of
names and words when you came.   Why should we say
goold and write gold, and call c h i n a chayny, and Caven-
dish Candish, and Cholmondeley Chumley ?   If we call
Pulteney Poltney, why shouldn't we call poultry pultry—
and——"

' " Such an enchantress as your ladyship," says he, " is
mistress of all sorts of spells."   But this was Dr. Swift's
pun,* and we all knew it.

' " And—and how do you spell your name ? " says she,
coming to the point, at length ; for this sprightly conversation had lasted much longer than is here set down,
and been carried on through at least three dishes of tea.

' " Oh, madam," says he, " *I spell my name with the y.*"
And laying down his dish, my gentleman made another
elegant bow, and was gone in a moment.

' Jocasta hath had no sleep since this mortification, and
the stranger's disappearance.   If balked in anything, she
is sure to lose her health and temper ; and we, her servants,

suffer, as usual, during the angry fits of our queen. Can you help us, Mr. Spectator, who know everything, to read this riddle for her, and set at rest all our minds ? We find in her list, Mr. Berty, Mr. Smith, Mr. Pike, Mr. Tyler—who may be Mr. Bertie, Mr. Smyth, Mr. Pyke, Mr. Tiler, for what we know. She hath turned away the clerk of her visiting-book, a poor fellow with a great family of children. Read me this riddle, good Mr. Shortface, and oblige your admirer—OEDIPUS.'

'THE 'TRUMPET' COFFEE-HOUSE, Whitehall.

' MR. SPECTATOR—I am a gentleman but little acquainted with the town, though I have had a university education, and passed some years serving my country abroad, where my name is better known than in the coffee-houses and St. James's.

' Two years since my uncle died, leaving me a pretty estate in the county of Kent; and being at Tunbridge Wells last summer, after my mourning was over, and on the look-out, if truth must be told, for some young lady who would share with me the solitude of my great Kentish house, and be kind to my tenantry (for whom a woman can do a great deal more good than the best-intentioned man can), I was greatly fascinated by a young lady of London, who was the toast of all the company at the Wells. Everyone knows Saccharissa's beauty; and I think, Mr. Spectator, no one better than herself.

' My table-book informs me that I danced no less than seven-and-twenty sets with her at the assembly. I treated her to the fiddles twice. I was admitted on several days to her lodging, and received by her with a great deal of distinction, and, for a time, was entirely her slave. It was only when I found, from common talk of the company at the Wells, and from narrowly watching one, who I once thought of asking the most sacred question a man can put to a woman, that I became aware how unfit she was to be a country gentleman's wife; and that this fair creature was but a heartless worldly jilt, playing with affections that she never meant to return, and, indeed, incapable of returning them. 'Tis admiration such women want, not love that touches them; and I can conceive, in her old age, no more wretched creature than this lady will be, when her beauty hath deserted her, when her admirers have left her, and she hath neither friendship nor religion to console her.

' Business calling me to London, I went to St. James's Church last Sunday, and there opposite me sat my beauty of the Wells. Her behaviour during the whole service was so pert, languishing, and absurd ; she flirted her fan, and ogled and eyed me in a manner so indecent, that I was obliged to shut my eyes, so as actually not to see her, and whenever I opened them beheld hers (and very bright they are) still staring at me. I fell in with her afterwards at Court, and at the playhouse ; and here nothing would satisfy her but she must elbow through the crowd and speak to me, and invite me to the assembly, which she holds at her house, nor very far from Ch-r-ng Cr-ss.

' Having made her a promise to attend, of course I kept my promise ; and found the young widow in the midst of a half-dozen of card-tables, and a crowd of wits and admirers. I made the best bow I could, and advanced towards her ; and saw by a peculiar puzzled look in her face, though she tried to hide her perplexity, that she had forgotten even my name.

' Her talk, artful as it was, convinced me that I had guessed aright. She turned the conversation most ridiculously upon the spelling of names and words ; and I replied with as ridiculous, fulsome compliments as I could pay her : indeed, one in which I compared her to an angel visiting the sick-wells, went a little too far ; nor should I have employed it, but that the allusion came from the Second Lesson last Sunday, which we both had heard, and I was pressed to answer her.

' Then she came to the question, which I knew was awaiting me, and asked how I *spelt* my name ? " Madam," says I, turning on my heel, " I spell it with the *y*." And so I left her, wondering at the light-heartedness of the town-people, who forget and make friends so easily, and resolved to look elsewhere for a partner for your constant reader,

' CYMON WYLDOATS.

' You know my real name, Mr. Spectator, in which there is no such a letter as *hupsilon*. But if the lady, whom I have called Saccharissa, wonders that I appear no more at the tea-tables, she is hereby respectfully informed the reason *y*.'

The above is a parable, whereof the writer will now expound the meaning. Jocasta was no other than Miss Esmond, maid of honour to her Majesty. She had told Mr. Esmond this little story of having met a gentleman, somewhere, and forgetting his name, when the gentleman, with no such malicious intentions as those of ' Cymon ' in the above fable, made the answer simply as above ; and we all laughed to think how little Mistress Jocasta-Beatrix had profited by her artifice and precautions.

As for Cymon he was intended to represent yours and her very humble servant, the writer of the apologue and of this story, which we had printed on a *Spectator* paper at Mr. Steele's office, exactly as those famous journals were printed, and which was laid on the table at breakfast in place of the real newspaper. Mistress Jocasta, who had plenty of wit, could not live without her *Spectator* to her tea ; and this sham *Spectator* was intended to convey to the young woman that she herself was a flirt, and that Cymon was a gentleman of honour and resolution, seeing all her faults, and determined to break the chains once and for ever.

For though enough hath been said about this love business already—enough, at least, to prove to the writer's heirs what a silly fond fool their old grandfather was, who would like them to consider him as a very wise old gentleman ; yet not near all has been told concerning this matter, which, if it were allowed to take in Esmond's journal the space it occupied in his time, would weary his kinsmen and women of a hundred years' time beyond all endurance ; and form such a diary of folly and drivelling, raptures and rage, as no man of ordinary vanity would like to leave behind him.

The truth is, that, whether she laughed at him or encouraged him ; whether she smiled or was cold, and turned her smiles on another—worldly and ambitious, as he knew her to be ; hard and careless, as she seemed to grow with her Court life, and a hundred admirers that came to her and left her ; Esmond, do what he would, never could get Beatrix out of his mind ; thought of her constantly at home or away. If he read his name in a *Gazette*, or

escaped the shot of a cannon-ball or a greater danger in
the campaign, as has happened to him more than once,
the instant thought after the honour achieved or the
danger avoided, was ' What will *she* say of it ? ' ' Will
this distinction or the idea of this peril elate her or touch
her, so as to be better inclined towards me ? ' He could
no more help this passionate fidelity of temper than he
could help the eyes he saw with—one or the other seemed
a part of his nature ; and knowing every one of her faults
as well as the keenest of her detractors, and the folly of
an attachment to such a woman, of which the fruition
could never bring him happiness for above a week, there
was yet a charm about this Circe from which the poor
deluded gentleman could not free himself ; and for a much
longer period than Ulysses (another middle-aged officer,
who had travelled much, and been in the foreign wars),
Esmond felt himself enthralled and besotted by the wiles
of this enchantress. Quit her ! He could no more quit
her, as the Cymon of this story was made to quit his false
one, than he could lose his consciousness of yesterday.
She had but to raise her finger, and he would come back
from ever so far ; she had but to say, ' I have discarded
such-and-such an adorer,' and the poor infatuated wretch
would be sure to come and *rôder* about her mother's house,
willing to be put on the ranks of suitors, though he knew
he might be cast off the next week. If he were like Ulysses
in his folly at least, she was in so far like Penelope, that
she had a crowd of suitors, and undid day after day and
night after night the handiwork of fascination and the
web of coquetry with which she was wont to allure and
entertain them.

Part of her coquetry may have come from her position
about the Court, where the beautiful maid of honour was
the light about which a thousand beaux came and fluttered ;
where she was sure to have a ring of admirers round her,
crowding to listen to her repartees as much as to admire
her beauty ; and where she spoke and listened to much
free talk, such as one never would have thought the lips
or ears of Rachel Castlewood's daughter would have uttered
or heard. When in waiting at Windsor or Hampton, the
Court ladies and gentlemen would be making riding parties
together ; Mrs. Beatrix in a horseman's coat and hat, the
foremost after the staghounds and over the park fences,

a crowd of young fellows at her heels. If the English
country ladies at this time were the most pure and modest
of any ladies in the world—the English town and Court
ladies permitted themselves words and behaviour that were
neither modest nor pure ; and claimed, some of them,
a freedom which those who love that sex most would never
wish to grant them. The gentlemen of my family that
follow after me (for I don't encourage the ladies to pursue
any such studies), may read in the works of Mr. Congreve,
and Dr. Swift, and others, what was the conversation and
what the habits of our time.

The most beautiful woman in England in 1712, when
Esmond returned to this country, a lady of high birth,
and though of no fortune to be sure, with a thousand
fascinations of wit and manners—Beatrix Esmond—was
now six-and-twenty years old, and Beatrix Esmond still.
Of her hundred adorers she had not chosen one for a husband ; and those who had asked had been jilted by her ;
and more still had left her. A succession of near ten
years' crops of beauties had come up since her time, and
had been reaped by proper *husband*men, if we may make
an agricultural simile, and had been housed comfortably
long ago. Her own contemporaries were sober mothers by
this time ; girls with not a tithe of her charms, or her wit,
having made good matches, and now claiming precedence
over the spinster who but lately had derided and outshone
them. The young beauties were beginning to look down
on Beatrix as an old maid, and sneer, and call her one of
Charles the Second's ladies, and ask whether her portrait
was not in the Hampton Court Gallery ? But still she
reigned, at least in one man's opinion, superior over all the
little misses that were the toasts of the young lads ; and
in Esmond's eyes was ever perfectly lovely and young.

Who knows how many were nearly made happy by
possessing her, or, rather, how many were fortunate in
escaping this siren ? 'Tis a marvel to think that her
mother was the purest and simplest woman in the whole
world, and that this girl should have been born from her.
I am inclined to fancy, my mistress, who never said a harsh
word to her children (and but twice or thrice only to one
person), must have been too fond and pressing with the
maternal authority ; for her son and her daughter both
revolted early ; nor after their first flight from the nest

could they ever be brought back quite to the fond mother's bosom. Lady Castlewood, and perhaps it was as well, knew little of her daughter's life and real thoughts. How was she to apprehend what passed in queens' antechambers and at Court tables ? Mrs. Beatrix asserted her own authority so resolutely that her mother quickly gave in. The maid of honour had her own equipage ; went from home and came back at her own will : her mother was alike powerless to resist her or to lead her, or to command or to persuade her.

She had been engaged once, twice, thrice, to be married, Esmond believed. When he quitted home, it hath been said, she was promised to my Lord Ashburnham, and now, on his return, behold his lordship was just married to Lady Mary Butler, the Duke of Ormonde's daughter, and his fine houses, and twelve thousand a year of fortune, for which Miss Beatrix had rather coveted him, was out of her power. To her Esmond could say nothing in regard to the breaking of this match ; and, asking his mistress about it, all Lady Castlewood answered was : ' Do not speak to me about it, Harry. I cannot tell you how or why they parted, and I fear to inquire. I have told you before, that with all her kindness, and wit, and generosity, and that sort of splendour of nature she has ; I can say but little good of poor Beatrix, and look with dread at the marriage she will form. Her mind is fixed on ambition only, and making a great figure : and, this achieved, she will tire of it as she does of everything. Heaven help her husband, whoever he shall be ! My Lord Ashburnham was a most excellent young man, gentle and yet manly, of very good parts, so they told me, and as my little conversation would enable me to judge : and a kind temper— kind and enduring I'm sure he must have been, from all that he had to endure. But he quitted her at last, from some crowning piece of caprice or tyranny of hers ; and now he has married a young woman that will make him a thousand times happier than my poor girl ever could.'

The rupture, whatever its cause was (I heard the scandal, but indeed shall not take pains to repeat at length in this diary the trumpery coffee-house story), caused a good deal of low talk ; and Mr. Esmond was present at my lord's appearance at the birthday with his bride, over whom the revenge that Beatrix took was to look so imperial and lovely that the modest downcast young lady could not appear beside her, and Lord Ashburnham, who had his reasons for wishing to avoid her, slunk away quite shame-faced, and very early. This time his grace the Duke of Hamilton, whom Esmond had seen about her before, was constant at Miss Beatrix's side : he was one of the most splendid gentlemen of Europe, accomplished by books, by travel, by long command of the best company, distin-guished as a statesman, having been ambassador in King William's time, and a noble speaker in the Scots Parlia-ment, where he had led the party that was against the union, and though now five- or six-and-forty years of age, a gentleman so high in stature, accomplished in wit, and favoured in person, that he might pretend to the hand of any princess in Europe.

'Should you like the duke for a cousin ? ' says Mr. Secretary St. John, whispering to Colonel Esmond in French ; ' it appears that the widower consoles himself.'

But to return to our little *Spectator* paper and the conversation which grew out of it. Miss Beatrix at first was quite *bit* (as the phrase of that day was) and did not 'smoke' the authorship of the story : indeed Esmond had tried to imitate as well as he could Mr. Steele's manner (as for the other author of the *Spectator*, his prose style I think is altogether inimitable) ; and Dick, who was the idlest and best-natured of men, would have let the piece pass into his journal and go to posterity as one of his own lucubra-tions, but that Esmond did not care to have a lady's name whom he loved sent forth to the world in a light so unfavour-able. Beatrix pished and psha'd over the paper ; Colonel Esmond watching with no little interest her countenance as she read it.

' How stupid your friend Mr. Steele becomes ! ' cries Miss Beatrix. ' Epsom and Tunbridge ! Will he never have done with Epsom and Tunbridge, and with beaux at church, and Jocastas and Lindamiras ? Why does he not call women Nelly and Betty, as their godfathers and god-mothers did for them in their baptism ? '

' Beatrix, Beatrix ! ' says her mother, ' speak gravely of grave things.'

'Mamma thinks the Church Catechism came from Heaven, I believe,' says Beatrix, with a laugh, ' and was brought down by a bishop from a mountain. Oh, how I used to

break my heart over it ! Besides, I had a Popish godmother, mamma ; why did you give me one ? '

' I gave you the queen's name,' says her mother, blushing.
' And a very pretty name it is,' said somebody else.

Beatrix went on reading—' Spell my name with a *y*—
why, you wretch,' says she, turning round to Colonel
Esmond, ' you have been telling my story to Mr. Steele—
or stop—you have written the paper yourself to turn me
into ridicule. For shame, sir ! '

Poor Mr. Esmond felt rather frightened, and told a truth,
which was nevertheless an entire falsehood. ' Upon my
honour,' says he, ' I have not even read the *Spectator* of
this morning.' Nor had he, for that was not the *Spectator*,
but a sham newspaper put in its place.

She went on reading : her face rather flushed as she
read. ' No,' she says, ' I think you couldn't have written
it. I think it must have been Mr. Steele when he was
drunk—and afraid of his horrid vulgar wife. Whenever
I see an enormous compliment to a woman, and some
outrageous panegyric about female virtue, I always feel
sure that the captain and his better half have fallen out
overnight, and that he has been brought home tipsy, or
has been found out in ——'

' Beatrix ! ' cries the Lady Castlewood.

' Well, mamma ! Do not cry out before you are hurt.
I am not going to say anything wrong. I won't give you
more annoyance than I can help, you pretty kind mamma.
Yes, and your little Trix is a naughty little Trix, and she
leaves undone those things which she ought to have done,
and does those things which she ought not to have done,
and there's——well now—I won't go on. Yes, I will,
unless you kiss me.' And with this the young lady
lays aside her paper, and runs up to her mother and
performs a variety of embraces with her ladyship, saying
as plain as eyes could speak to Mr. Esmond—' There,
sir : would not *you* like to play the very same pleasant
game ? '

' Indeed, madam, I would,' says he.

' Would what ? ' asked Miss Beatrix.

' What you meant when you looked at me in that provoking way,' answers Esmond.

' What a confessor ! ' cries Beatrix, with a laugh.

' What is it Henry would like, my dear ? ' asks her

mother, the kind soul, who was always thinking what we
would like, and how she could please us.

The girl runs up to her—' Oh, you silly kind mamma,' she
says, kissing her again, ' that's what Harry would like ; '
and she broke out into a great joyful laugh : and
Lady Castlewood blushed as bashful as a maid of
sixteen.

' Look at her, Harry,' whispers Beatrix, running up, and
speaking in her sweet low tones. ' Doesn't the blush become
her ? Isn't she pretty ? She looks younger than I am :
and I am sure she is a hundred million thousand times
better.'

Esmond's kind mistress left the room, carrying her
blushes away with her.

' If we girls at Court could grow such roses as that,'
continues Beatrix, with her laugh, ' what wouldn't we do
to preserve 'em ? We'd clip their stalks and put 'em in
salt and water. But those flowers don't bloom at Hampton
Court and Windsor, Henry.' She paused for a minute,
and the smile fading away from her April face, gave place
to a menacing shower of tears : ' Oh, how good she is,
Harry,' Beatrix went on to say. ' Oh, what a saint she is !
Her goodness frightens me. I'm not fit to live with her.
I should be better, I think, if she were not so perfect. She
has had a great sorrow in her life, and a great secret ; and
repented of it. It could not have been my father's death.
She talks freely about that ; nor could she have loved him
very much—though who knows what we women do love,
and why ? '

' What, and why, indeed,' says Mr. Esmond.

' No one knows,' Beatrix went on, without noticing this
interruption except by a look, ' what my mother's life is.
She hath been at early prayer this morning : she passes
hours in her closet ; if you were to follow her thither, you
would find her at prayers now. She tends the poor of the
place—the horrid dirty poor ! She sits through the curate's
sermons—oh, those dreary sermons ! And you see, *on a beau
dire ;* but good as they are, people like her are not fit to
commune with us of the world. There is always, as it
were, a third person present, even when I and my mother
are alone. She can't be frank with me quite ; who is always
thinking of the next world, and of her guardian angel,
perhaps that's in company. Oh, Harry, I'm jealous of

that guardian angel!' here broke out Mistress Beatrix. 'It's horrid, I know ; but my mother's life is all for Heaven, and mine—all for earth. We can never be friends quite ; and then, she cares more for Frank's little finger than she does for me—I know she does : and she loves you, sir, a great deal too much ; and I hate you for it. I would have had her all to myself ; but she wouldn't. In my childhood, it was my father she loved—(Oh, how could she ? I remember him kind and handsome, but so stupid, and not being able to speak after drinking wine). And then, it was Frank ; and now, it is Heaven and the clergyman. How I would have loved her ! From a child I used to be in a rage that she loved anybody but me ; but she loved you all better— all, I know she did. And now, she talks of the blessed consolation of religion. Dear soul ! she thinks she is happier for believing, as she must, that we are all of us wicked and miserable sinners ; and this world is only a *pied à terre* for the good, where they stay for a night, as we do, coming from Walcote, at that great, dreary, uncomfortable Hounslow inn, in those horrid beds. Oh, do you remember those horrid beds ?—and the chariot comes and fetches them to Heaven the next morning.'

'Hush, Beatrix,' says Mr. Esmond.

'Hush, indeed. You are a hypocrite, too, Henry, with your grave airs and your glum face. We are all hypocrites. Oh dear me ! We are all alone, alone, alone,' says poor Beatrix, her fair breast heaving with a sigh.

'It was I that writ every line of that paper, my dear,' says Mr. Esmond. 'You are not so worldly as you think yourself, Beatrix, and better than we believe you. The good we have in us we doubt of ; and the happiness that's to our hand we throw away. You bend your ambition on a great marriage and establishment—and why ? You'll tire of them when you win them ; and be no happier with a coronet on your coach——'

'Than riding pillion with Lubin to market,' says Beatrix. 'Thank you, Lubin ! '

'I'm a dismal shepherd, to be sure,' answers Esmond, with a blush ; 'and require a nymph that can tuck my bed-clothes up, and make me water-gruel. Well, Tom Lockwood can do that. He took me out of the fire upon his shoulders,* and nursed me through my illness as love will scarce ever do. Only good wages, and a hope of my clothes,

and the contents of my portmanteau. How long was it
that Jacob served an apprenticeship for Rachel ? '

' For mamma ? ' says Beatrix. ' Is it mamma your
honour wants, and that I should have the happiness of
calling you papa ? '

Esmond blushed again. ' I spoke of a Rachel that a
shepherd courted five thousand years ago ; when shepherds
were longer lived than now. And my meaning was, that
since I saw you first after our separation—a child you were
then——'

' And I put on my best stockings to captivate you,
I remember, sir.'

' You have had my heart ever since then, such as it was ;
and such as you were, I cared for no other woman. What
little reputation I have won, it was that you might be
pleased with it : and, indeed, it is not much ; and I think
a hundred fools in the army have got and deserved quite
as much. Was there something in the air of that dismal
old Castlewood that made us all gloomy, and dissatisfied,
and lonely under its ruined old roof ? We were all so, even
when together and united, as it seemed, following our
separate schemes, each as we sat round the table.'

' Dear, dreary old place ! ' cries Beatrix. ' Mamma hath
never had the heart to go back thither since we left it, when
—never mind how many years ago,' and she flung back
her curls, and looked over her fair shoulder at the mirror
superbly, as if she said, ' Time, I defy you.'

' Yes,' says Esmond, who had the art, as she owned, of
divining many of her thoughts. ' You can afford to look
in the glass still ; and only be pleased by the truth it tells
you. As for me, do you know what my scheme is ? I think
of asking Frank to give me the Virginia estate King Charles
gave our grandfather.' (She gave a superb curtsy, as much
as to say, ' Our grandfather, indeed ! Thank you, Mr.
Bastard.') ' Yes, I know you are thinking of my bar-
sinister, and so am I. A man cannot get over it in this
country ; unless, indeed, he wears it across a king's arms,
when 'tis a highly honourable coat ; and I am thinking of
retiring into the plantations, and building myself a wigwam
in the woods, and perhaps, if I want company, suiting myself
with a squaw. We will send your ladyship furs over for
the winter ; and, when you are old, we'll provide you with
tobacco. I am not quite clever enough, or not rogue enough

—I know not which—for the Old World. I may make a
place for myself in the new, which is not so full ; and found
a family there. When you are a mother yourself, and a
great lady, perhaps I shall send you over from the plantation some day a little barbarian that is half Esmond half
Mohock, and you will be kind to him for his father's sake,
who was, after all, your kinsman ; and whom you loved
a little.'

'What folly you are talking, Harry !' says Miss Beatrix,
looking with her great eyes.

''Tis sober earnest,' says Esmond. And, indeed, the
scheme had been dwelling a good deal in his mind for some
time past, and especially since his return home, when he
found how hopeless, and even degrading to himself, his
passion was. 'No,' says he, then, 'I have tried half a
dozen times now. I can bear being away from you well
enough ; but being with you is intolerable' (another low
curtsy on Mrs. Beatrix's part), 'and I will go. I have enough
to buy axes and guns for my men, and beads and blankets
for the savages ; and I'll go and live amongst them.'

'*Mon ami*,' she says, quite kindly, and taking Esmond's
hand, with an air of great compassion. 'You can't think
that in our position anything more than our present friendship is possible. You are our elder brother—as such we
view you, pitying your misfortune, not rebuking you with
it. Why, you are old enough and grave enough to be our
father. I always thought you a hundred years old, Harry,
with your solemn face and grave air. I feel as a sister to
you, and can no more. Isn't that enough, sir ?' And she
put her face quite close to his—who knows with what
intention ?

'It's too much,' says Esmond, turning away. 'I can't
bear this life, and shall leave it. I shall stay, I think, to
see you married, and then freight a ship, and call it the
Beatrix, and bid you all——'

Here the servant, flinging the door open, announced his
grace the Duke of Hamilton, and Esmond started back
with something like an imprecation on his lips, as the nobleman entered, looking splendid in his star and green ribbon.
He gave Mr. Esmond just that gracious bow which he would
have given to a lackey who fetched him a chair or took
his hat, and seated himself by Miss Beatrix, as the poor
colonel went out of the room with a hang-dog look.

Esmond's mistress was in the lower room as he passed downstairs. She often met him as he was coming away from Beatrix ; and she beckoned him into the apartment.

' Has she told you, Harry ? ' Lady Castlewood said.

' She has been very frank—very,' says Esmond.

' But—but about what is going to happen ? '

' What is going to happen ? ' says he, his heart beating.

' His grace the Duke of Hamilton has proposed to her,' says my lady. ' He made his offer yesterday. They will marry as soon as his mourning is over ; and you have heard his grace is appointed ambassador to Paris ; and the ambassadress goes with him.'

CHAPTER IV

BEATRIX'S NEW SUITOR

THE gentleman whom Beatrix had selected was, to be sure, twenty years older than the colonel, with whom she quarrelled for being too old ; but this one was but a nameless adventurer, and the other the greatest duke in Scotland, with pretensions even to a still higher title. My Lord Duke of Hamilton had, indeed, every merit belonging to a gentleman, and he had had the time to mature his accomplishments fully, being upwards of fifty years old when Madam Beatrix selected him for a bridegroom. Duke Hamilton, then Earl of Arran, had been educated at the famous Scottish University of Glasgow, and, coming to London, became a great favourite of Charles the Second, who made him a lord of his bedchamber, and afterwards appointed him ambassador to the French king, under whom the earl served two campaigns as his Majesty's aide de camp ; and he was absent on this service when King Charles died.

King James continued my lord's promotion—made him master of the wardrobe, and colonel of the Royal Regiment of Horse ; and his lordship adhered firmly to King James, being of the small company that never quitted that unfortunate monarch till his departure out of England ; and then it was, in 1688, namely, that he made the friendship with Colonel Francis Esmond, that had always been, more or less, maintained in the two families.

The earl professed a great admiration for King William

always, but never could give him his allegiance ; and was
engaged in more than one of the plots in the late great king's
reign, which always ended in the plotters' discomfiture,
and generally in their pardon, by the magnanimity of the
king. Lord Arran was twice prisoner in the Tower during
this reign, undauntedly saying, when offered his release,
upon parole not to engage against King William, that he
would not give his word, because ' he was sure he could
not keep it '; but, nevertheless, he was both times discharged
without any trial ; and the king bore this noble enemy so
little malice, that when his mother, the Duchess of Hamilton, of her own right, resigned her claim on her husband's
death, the earl was, by patent signed at Loo, 1690, created
Duke of Hamilton, Marquis of Clydesdale, and Earl of
Arran, with precedency from the original creation. His
grace took the oaths and his seat in the Scottish Parliament
in 1700 : was famous there for his patriotism and eloquence,
especially in the debates about the Union Bill, which Duke
Hamilton opposed with all his strength, though he would
not go the length of the Scottish gentry, who were for
resisting it by force of arms. 'Twas said he withdrew his
opposition all of a sudden, and in consequence of letters
from the king at St. Germains, who entreated him on his
allegiance not to thwart the queen, his sister, in this measure;
and the duke, being always bent upon effecting the king's
return to his kingdom through a reconciliation between his
Majesty and Queen Anne, and quite averse to his landing
with arms and French troops, held aloof, and kept out of
Scotland during the time when the Chevalier de St. George's
descent from Dunkirk was projected, passing his time in
England in his great estate of Staffordshire.

When the Whigs went out of office in 1710, the queen
began to show his grace the very greatest marks of her
favour. He was created Duke of Brandon and Baron of
Dutton in England ; having the Thistle already originally
bestowed on him by King James the Second, his grace was
now promoted to the honour of the Garter—a distinction
so great and illustrious, that no subject hath ever borne
them hitherto together. When this objection was made to
her Majesty, she was pleased to say, ' Such a subject as the
Duke of Hamilton has a pre-eminent claim to every mark
of distinction which a crowned head can confer. I will
henceforth wear both orders myself.'

At the Chapter held at Windsor in October, 1712, the duke and other knights, including Lord-Treasurer, the new-created Earl of Oxford and Mortimer, were installed; and a few days afterwards his grace was appointed Ambassador-Extraordinary to France, and his equipages, plate, and liveries commanded, of the most sumptuous kind, not only for his excellency the ambassador, but for her excellency the ambassadress, who was to accompany him. Her arms were already quartered on the coach panels, and her brother was to hasten over on the appointed day to give her away.

His lordship was a widower, having married, in 1698, Elizabeth, daughter of Digby, Lord Gerard, by which marriage great estates came into the Hamilton family; and out of these estates came, in part, that tragic quarrel which ended the duke's career.

From the loss of a tooth to that of a mistress there's no pang that is not bearable. The apprehension is much more cruel than the certainty; and we make up our mind to the misfortune when 'tis irremediable, part with the tormentor, and mumble our crust on t'other side of the jaws. I think Colonel Esmond was relieved when a ducal coach-and-six came and whisked his charmer away out of his reach, and placed her in a higher sphere. As you have seen the nymph in the opera-machine go up to the clouds at the end of the piece where Mars, Bacchus, Apollo, and all the divine company of Olympians are seated, and quaver out her last song as a goddess: so when this portentous elevation was accomplished in the Esmond family, I am not sure that every one of us did not treat the divine Beatrix with special honours; at least, the saucy little beauty carried her head with a toss of supreme authority, and assumed a touch-me-not air, which all her friends very good-humouredly bowed to.

An old army acquaintance of Colonel Esmond's, honest Tom Trett, who had sold his company, married a wife, and turned merchant in the city, was dreadfully gloomy for a long time, though living in a fine house on the river, and carrying on a great trade to all appearance. At length Esmond saw his friend's name in the *Gazette* as a bankrupt; and a week after this circumstance my bankrupt walks into Mr. Esmond's lodging with a face perfectly radiant with

good humour, and as jolly and careless as when they had
sailed from Southampton ten years before for Vigo. 'This
bankruptcy,' says Tom, 'has been hanging over my head
these three years ; the thought hath prevented my sleeping,
and I have looked at poor Polly's head on t'other pillow,
and then towards my razor on the table, and thought to
put an end to myself, and so give my woes the slip. But
now we are bankrupts : Tom Trett pays as many shillings
in the pound as he can; his wife has a little cottage at Fulham,
and her fortune secured to herself. I am afraid neither of
bailiff nor of creditor ; and for the last six nights have slept
easy.' So it was that when Fortune shook her wings and
left him, honest Tom cuddled himself up in his ragged
virtue, and fell asleep.

Esmond did not tell his friend how much his story
applied to Esmond too ; but he laughed at it, and used it ;
and having fairly struck his docket in this love transaction,
determined to put a cheerful face on his bankruptcy.
Perhaps Beatrix was a little offended at his gaiety. 'Is
this the way, sir, that you receive the announcement of
your misfortune,' says she, 'and do you come smiling before
me as if you were glad to be rid of me ?'

Esmond would not be put off from his good humour, but
told her the story of Tom Trett and his bankruptcy. 'I
have been hankering after the grapes on the wall,' says he,
'and lost my temper because they were beyond my reach ;
was there any wonder ? They're gone now, and another has
them—a taller man than your humble servant has won
them.' And the colonel made his cousin a low bow.

'A taller man, cousin Esmond !' says she. 'A man of
spirit would have scaled the wall, sir, and seized them !
A man of courage would have fought for 'em, not gaped
for 'em.'

'A duke has but to gape and they drop into his mouth,'
says Esmond, with another low bow.

'Yes, sir,' says she, 'a duke *is* a taller man than you.
And why should I not be grateful to one such as his grace,
who gives me his heart and his great name ? It is a great
gift he honours me with ; I know 'tis a bargain between us ;
and I accept it, and will do my utmost to perform my part
of it. 'Tis no question of sighing and philandering between
a nobleman of his grace's age and a girl who hath little of
that softness in her nature. Why should I not own that

I am ambitious, Harry Esmond ; and if it be no sin in a man
to covet honour, why should a woman too not desire it ?
Shall I be frank with you, Harry, and say that if you had
not been down on your knees, and so humble, you might
have fared better with me ? A woman of my spirit, cousin,
is to be won by gallantry, and not by sighs and rueful faces.
All the time you are worshipping and singing hymns to me,
I know very well I am no goddess, and grow weary of the
incense. So would you have been weary of the goddess
too—when she was called Mrs. Esmond, and got out of
humour because she had not pin-money enough, and was
forced to go about in an old gown. Eh ! cousin, a goddess
in a mob-cap, that has to make her husband's gruel, ceases
to be divine—I am sure of it. I should have been sulky
and scolded ; and of all the proud wretches in the world
Mr. Esmond is the proudest, let me tell him that. You
never fall into a passion ; but you never forgive, I think.
Had you been a great man, you might have been good
humoured ; but being nobody, sir, you are too great a man
for me ; and I'm afraid of you, cousin—there ; and I won't
worship you, and you'll never be happy except with a
woman who will. Why, after I belonged to you, and after
one of my tantrums, you would have put the pillow over
my head some night, and smothered me, as the black man
does the woman in the play that you're so fond of. What's
the creature's name ?—Desdemona. You would, you little
black-eyed Othello ! '

' I think I should, Beatrix,' says the colonel.

' And I want no such ending. I intend to live to be a
hundred, and to go to ten thousand routs and balls, and
to play cards every night of my life till the year eighteen
hundred. And I like to be the first of my company, sir ; and
I like flattery and compliments, and you give me none ; and
I like to be made to laugh, sir, and who's to laugh at *your*
dismal face, I should like to know; and I like a coach-and-
six or a coach-and-eight ; and I like diamonds, and a new
gown every week ; and people to say—" That's the duchess
—How well her grace looks—Make way for Madame l'Am-
bassadrice d'Angleterre—Call her excellency's people "—
that's what I like. And as for you, you want a woman to
bring your slippers and cap, and to sit at your feet, and cry,
" O caro ! O bravo ! " whilst you read your Shakespeares,
and Miltons, and stuff. Mamma would have been the wife

for you, had you been a little older, though you look ten
years older than she does—you do, you glum-faced, blue-
bearded, little old man ! You might have sat, like Darby
and Joan, and flattered each other ; and billed and cooed
like a pair of old pigeons on a perch. I want my wings and
to use them, sir.' And she spread out her beautiful arms,
as if indeed she could fly off like the pretty 'Gawrie',* whom
the man in the story was enamoured of.

' And what will your Peter Wilkins say to your flight ? '
says Esmond, who never admired this fair creature more
than when she rebelled and laughed at him.

' A duchess knows her place,' says she, with a laugh.
' Why, I have a son already made for me, and thirty years
old (my Lord Arran), and four daughters. How they will
scold, and what a rage they will be in, when I come to
take the head of the table ! But I give them only a month
to be angry ; at the end of that time they shall love me
every one, and so shall Lord Arran, and so shall all his
grace's Scots vassals and followers in the Highlands. I'm
bent on it ; and, when I take a thing in my head, 'tis done.
His grace is the greatest gentleman in Europe, and I'll try
and make him happy ; and, when the king comes back,
you may count on my protection, Cousin Esmond—for
come back the king will and shall : and I'll bring him back
from Versailles, if he comes under my hoop.'

' I hope the world will make you happy, Beatrix,' says
Esmond, with a sigh. ' You'll be Beatrix till you are my
lady duchess—will you not ? I shall then make your
grace my very lowest bow.'

' None of these sighs and this satire, cousin,' she says.
' I take his grace's great bounty thankfully—yes, thankfully ; and will wear his honours becomingly. I do not say
he hath touched my heart ; but he has my gratitude,
obedience, admiration—I have told him that, and no more ;
and with that his noble heart is content. I have told him
all—even the story of that poor creature that I was engaged
to—and that I could not love ; and I gladly gave his word
back to him, and jumped for joy to get back my own.
I am twenty-five years old.'

' Twenty-six, my dear,' says Esmond.

' Twenty-five, sir—I choose to be twenty-five ; and, in
eight years, no man hath ever touched my heart. Yes—
you did once, for a little, Harry, when you came back after

Lille, and engaging with that murderer, Mohun, and saving
Frank's life. I thought I could like you; and mamma
begged me hard, on her knees, and I did—for a day. But
the old chill came over me, Henry, and the old fear of you
and your melancholy; and I was glad when you went
away, and engaged with my Lord Ashburnham, that I might
hear no more of you, that's the truth. You are too good for
me somehow. I could not make you happy, and should
break my heart in trying, and not being able to love you.
But if you had asked me when we gave you the sword, you
might have had me, sir, and we both should have been
miserable by this time. I talked with that silly lord all
night just to vex you and mamma, and I succeeded,
didn't I ? How frankly we can talk of these things ! It
seems a thousand years ago : and, though we are here
sitting in the same room, there's a great wall between us.
My dear, kind, faithful, gloomy old cousin ! I can like you
now, and admire you too, sir, and say that you are brave,
and very kind, and very true, and a fine gentleman for all—
for all your little mishap at your birth,' says she, wagging
her arch head.

'And now, sir,' says she, with a curtsy, ' we must have no
more talk except when mamma is by, as his grace is with
us ; for he does not half like you, cousin, and is as jealous
as the black man in your favourite play.'

Though the very kindness of the words stabbed Mr.
Esmond with the keenest pang, he did not show his sense
of the wound by any look of his (as Beatrix, indeed, afterwards owned to him), but said, with a perfect command
of himself and an easy smile, ' The interview must not end
yet, my dear, until I have had my last word. Stay, here
comes your mother ' (indeed she came in here with her sweet
anxious face, and Esmond, going up, kissed her hand
respectfully). ' My dear lady may hear, too, the last words,
which are no secrets, and are only a parting benediction
accompanying a present for your marriage from an old
gentleman your guardian ; for I feel as if I was the guardian
of all the family, and an old, old fellow that is fit to be the
grandfather of you all ; and in this character let me make
my lady duchess her wedding present. They are the
diamonds my father's widow left me. I had thought
Beatrix might have had them a year ago ; but they are
good enough for a duchess, though not bright enough for

the handsomest woman in the world.' And he took the
case out of his pocket in which the jewels were, and presented them to his cousin.

She gave a cry of delight, for the stones were indeed very
handsome, and of great value ; and the next minute the
necklace was where Belinda's cross is in Mr. Pope's admirable poem, and glittering on the whitest and most perfectly-
shaped neck in all England.*

The girl's delight at receiving these trinkets was so great,
that after rushing to the looking-glass and examining the
effect they produced upon that fair neck which they sur-
rounded, Beatrix was running back with her arms extended,
and was perhaps for paying her cousin with a price, that he
would have liked no doubt to receive from those beautiful
rosy lips of hers, but at this moment the door opened, and
his grace the bridegroom elect was announced.

He looked very black upon Mr. Esmond, to whom he made
a very low bow indeed, and kissed the hand of each lady in
his most ceremonious manner. He had come in his chair
from the palace hard by, and wore his two stars of the
Garter and the Thistle.

' Look, my lord duke,' says Mrs. Beatrix, advancing to
him, and showing the diamonds on her breast.

' Diamonds,' says his grace. ' Hm ! they seem pretty.'

' They are a present on my marriage,' says Beatrix.

' From her Majesty ? ' asks the duke. ' The queen is
very good.'

' From my cousin Henry—from our cousin Henry '—cry
both the ladies in a breath.

' I have not the honour of knowing the gentleman.
I thought that my Lord Castlewood had no brother : and
that on your ladyship's side there were no nephews.'

' From our cousin, Colonel Henry Esmond, my lord,' says
Beatrix, taking the colonel's hand very bravely—' who
was left guardian to us by our father, and who has
a hundred times shown his love and friendship for our
family.'

' The Duchess of Hamilton receives no diamonds but from
her husband, madam,' says the duke—' may I pray you to
restore these to Mr. Esmond ? '

' Beatrix Esmond may receive a present from our kinsman
and benefactor, my lord duke,' says Lady Castlewood,
with an air of great dignity. ' She is my daughter yet :

and if her mother sanctions the gift—no one else hath the right to question it.'

'Kinsman and benefactor!' says the duke. 'I know of no kinsman : and I do not choose that my wife should have for benefactor a—— '

'My lord,' says Colonel Esmond.

'I am not here to bandy words,' says his grace : 'frankly I tell you that your visits to this house are too frequent, and that I choose no presents for the Duchess of Hamilton from gentlemen that bear a name they have no right to.'

'My lord!' breaks out Lady Castlewood, 'Mr. Esmond hath the best right to that name of any man in the world : and 'tis as old and as honourable as your grace's.'

My lord duke smiled, and looked as if Lady Castlewood was mad, that was so talking to him.

'If I called him benefactor,' said my mistress, 'it is because he has been so to us—yes, the noblest, the truest, the bravest, the dearest of benefactors. He would have saved my husband's life from Mohun's sword. He did save my boy's, and defended him from that villain. Are those no benefits ?'

'I ask Colonel Esmond's pardon,' says his grace, if possible more haughty than before ; 'I would say not a word that should give him offence, and thank him for his kindness to your ladyship's family. My Lord Mohun and I are connected, you know, by marriage—though neither by blood nor friendship ; but I must repeat what I said, that my wife can receive no presents from Colonel Esmond.'

'My daughter may receive presents from the Head of our House : my daughter may thankfully take kindness from her father's, her mother's, her brother's dearest friend ; and be grateful for one more benefit besides the thousand we owe him,' cries Lady Esmond. 'What is a string of diamond stones compared to that affection he hath given us—our dearest preserver and benefactor ? We owe him not only Frank's life, but our all—yes, our all,' says my mistress, with a heightened colour and a trembling voice. 'The title we bear is his, if he would claim it. 'Tis we who have no right to our name : not he that's too great for it. He sacrificed his name at my dying lord's bedside—sacrificed it to my orphan children ; gave up rank and honour because he loved us so nobly. His father was Viscount of Castlewood and Marquis of Esmond before him ; and he is his father's lawful son and true heir, and we are the recipients of his bounty, and he the chief of a house that's as old as your own. And if he is content to forgo his name that my child may bear it, we love him and honour him and bless him under whatever name he bears'—and here the fond and affectionate creature would have knelt to Esmond again, but that he prevented her ; and Beatrix, running up to her with a pale face and a cry of alarm, embraced her and said, ' Mother, what is this ? '

' 'Tis a family secret, my lord duke,' says Colonel Esmond : ' poor Beatrix knew nothing of it : nor did my lady till a year ago. And I have as good a right to resign my title as your grace's mother to abdicate hers to you.'

' I should have told everything to the Duke of Hamilton,' said my mistress, ' had his grace applied to me for my daughter's hand, and not to Beatrix. I should have spoken with you this very day in private, my lord, had not your words brought about this sudden explanation—and now 'tis fit Beatrix should hear it ; and know, as I would have all the world know, what we owe to our kinsman and patron.'

And then in her touching way, and having hold of her daughter's hand, and speaking to her rather than my lord duke, Lady Castlewood told the story which you know already—lauding up to the skies her kinsman's behaviour. On his side Mr. Esmond explained the reasons that seemed quite sufficiently cogent with him, why the succession in the family, as at present it stood, should not be disturbed ; and he should remain, as he was, Colonel Esmond.

' And Marquis of Esmond, my lord,' says his grace, with a low bow. ' Permit me to ask your lordship's pardon for words that were uttered in ignorance ; and to beg for the favour of your friendship. To be allied to you, sir, must be an honour under whatever name you are known ' (so his grace was pleased to say) : ' and in return for the splendid present you make my wife, your kinswoman, I hope you will please to command any service that James Douglas can perform. I shall never be easy until I repay you a part of my obligations at least ; and ere very long, and with the mission her Majesty hath given me,' says the duke, ' that may perhaps be in my power. I shall esteem it as a favour, my lord, if Colonel Esmond will give away the bride.'

' And if he will take the usual payment in advance, he is welcome,' says Beatrix, stepping up to him ; and as Esmond kissed her, she whispered, ' Oh, why didn't I know you before ? '

My lord duke was as hot as a flame at this salute, but said never a word : Beatrix made him a proud curtsy, and the two ladies quitted the room together.

' When does your excellency go for Paris ? ' asks Colonel Esmond.

' As soon after the ceremony as may be,' his grace answered. ' 'Tis fixed for the first of December : it cannot be sooner. The equipage will not be ready till then. The queen intends the embassy should be very grand—and I have law business to settle. That ill-omened Mohun has come, or is coming, to London again : we are in a lawsuit about my late Lord Gerard's property ; and he hath sent to me to meet him.'

CHAPTER V

MOHUN APPEARS FOR THE LAST TIME IN THIS HISTORY

BESIDES my Lord Duke of Hamilton and Brandon, who, for family reasons, had kindly promised his protection and patronage to Colonel Esmond, he had other great friends in power now, both able and willing to assist him, and he might, with such allies, look forward to as fortunate advancement in civil life at home as he had got rapid promotion abroad. His grace was magnanimous enough to offer to take Mr. Esmond as secretary on his Paris embassy, but no doubt he intended that proposal should be rejected ; at any rate, Esmond could not bear the thoughts of attending his mistress farther than the church-door after her marriage, and so declined that offer which his generous rival made him.

Other gentlemen, in power, were liberal at least of compliments and promises to Colonel Esmond. Mr. Harley, now become my Lord Oxford and Mortimer, and installed Knight of the Garter on the same day as his grace of Hamilton had received the same honour, sent to the colonel to say that a seat in Parliament should be at his

disposal presently, and Mr. St. John held out many flattering hopes of advancement to the colonel when he should
enter the House. Esmond's friends were all successful, and
the most successful and triumphant of all was his dear old
commander, General Webb, who was now appointed
Lieutenant-General of the Land Forces, and received with
particular honour by the ministry, by the queen, and the
people out of doors, who huzza'd the brave chief when they
used to see him in his chariot, going to the House or to
the Drawing-room, or hobbling on foot to his coach from
St. Stephen's upon his glorious old crutch and stick, and
cheered him as loud as they had ever done Marlborough.

That great duke was utterly disgraced; and honest old
Webb dated all his grace's misfortunes from Wynendael,
and vowed that Fate served the traitor right. Duchess
Sarah had also gone to ruin; she had been forced to give
up her keys, and her places, and her pensions :—' Ah, ah ! '
says Webb, ' she would have locked up three millions of
French crowns with her keys had I but been knocked on
the head, but I stopped that convoy at Wynendael.' Our
enemy Cardonnel was turned out of the House of Commons
(along with Mr. Walpole) for malversation of public money.
Cadogan lost his place of Lieutenant of the Tower. Marlborough's daughters resigned their posts of ladies of the
bedchamber; and so complete was the duke's disgrace,
that his son-in-law, Lord Bridgewater, was absolutely
obliged to give up his lodging at St. James's, and had his
half-pension, as Master of the Horse, taken away. But
I think the lowest depth of Marlborough's fall was when he
humbly sent to ask General Webb when he might wait upon
him; he who had commanded the stout old general, who
had injured him and sneered at him, who had kept him
dangling in his antechamber, who could not even after his
great service condescend to write him a letter in his own
hand. The nation was as eager for peace, as ever it had been
hot for war. The Prince of Savoy came amongst us, had
his audience of the queen, and got his famous Sword of
Honour, and strove with all his force to form a Whig party
together, to bring over the young Prince of Hanover—to
do anything which might prolong the war, and consummate
the ruin of the old sovereign whom he hated so implacably.
But the nation was tired of the struggle; so completely
wearied of it that not even our defeat at Denain could rouse

us into any anger, though such an action so lost two years
before, would have set all England in a fury. 'Twas easy
to see that the great Marlborough was not with the army.
Eugene was obliged to fall back in a rage, and forgo the
dazzling revenge of his life. 'Twas in vain the duke's side
asked, ' Would we suffer our arms to be insulted ? Would
we not send back the only champion who could repair our
honour ? ' The nation had had its bellyful of fighting ; nor
could taunts or outcries goad up our Britons any more.

For a statesman, that was always prating of liberty, and
had the grandest philosophic maxims in his mouth, it must
be owned that Mr. St. John sometimes rather acted like
a Turkish than a Greek philosopher, and especially fell foul
of one unfortunate set of men, the men of letters, with
a tyranny a little extraordinary in a man who professed
to respect their calling so much.   The literary controversy
at this time was very bitter, the Government side was the
winning one, the popular one, and I think might have been
the merciful one. 'Twas natural that the Opposition should
be peevish and cry out ; some men did so from their hearts,
admiring the Duke of Marlborough's prodigious talents, and
deploring the disgrace of the greatest general the world
ever knew : 'twas the stomach that caused other patriots
to grumble, and snch men cried out because they were poor,
and paid to do so. Against these my Lord Bolingbroke
never showed the slightest mercy, whipping a dozen into
prison or into the pillory without the least commiseration.

From having been a man of arms Mr. Esmond had now
come to be a man of letters, but on a safer side than that
in which the above-cited poor fellows ventured their liberties and ears.   There was no danger on ours, which was
the winning side ; besides, Mr. Esmond pleased himself by
thinking that he writ like a gentleman if he did not always
succeed as a wit.

Of the famous wits of that age, who have rendered Queen
Anne's reign illustrious, and whose works will be in all
Englishmen's hands in ages yet to come, Mr. Esmond saw
many, but at public places chiefly ; never having a great
intimacy with any of them, except with honest Dick Steele
and Mr. Addison, who parted company with Esmond, however, when that gentleman became a declared Tory, and
lived on close terms with the leading persons of that party.
Addison kept himself to a few friends, and very rarely

opened himself except in their company. A man more upright and conscientious than he, it was not possible to find in public life, and one whose conversation was so various, easy, and delightful. Writing now in my mature years, I own that I think Addison's politics were the right, and were my time to come over again, I would be a Whig in England and not a Tory; but with people that take a side in politics, 'tis men rather than principles that commonly bind them. A kindness or a slight puts a man under one flag or the other, and he marches with it to the end of the campaign. Esmond's master in war was injured by Marlborough, and hated him : and the lieutenant fought the quarrels of his leader. Webb coming to London was used as a weapon by Marlborough's enemies (and true steel he was, that honest chief) ; nor was his aide de camp, Mr. Esmond, an unfaithful or unworthy partisan. 'Tis strange here, and on a foreign soil, and in a land that is independent in all but the name (for that the North American colonies shall remain dependants on yonder little island for twenty years more, I never can think), to remember how the nation at home seemed to give itself up to the domination of one or other aristocratic party, and took a Hanoverian king, or a French one, according as either prevailed. And while the Tories, the October Club gentlemen, the High Church parsons that held by the Church of England, were for having a Papist king, for whom many of their Scottish and English leaders, firm churchmen all, laid down their lives with admirable loyalty and devotion ; they were governed by men who had notoriously no religion at all, but used it as they would use any opinion for the purpose of forwarding their own ambition. The Whigs, on the other hand, who professed attachment to religion and liberty too, were compelled to send to Holland or Hanover for a monarch around whom they could rally. A strange series of compromises is that English history ; compromise of principle, compromise of party, compromise of worship ! The lovers of English freedom and independence submitted their religious consciences to an Act of Parliament ; could not consolidate their liberty without sending to Zell or the Hague for a king to live under ; and could not find amongst the proudest people in the world a man speaking their own language, and understanding their laws, to govern them. The Tory and High Church patriots were ready to die in defence of a Papist family that had sold us to France ; the great Whig nobles, the sturdy Republican recusants who had cut off Charles Stuart's head for treason, were fain to accept a king whose title came to him through a royal grandmother, whose own royal grandmother's head had fallen under Queen Bess's hatchet. And our proud English nobles sent to a petty German town for a monarch to come and reign in London ; and our prelates kissed the ugly hands of his Dutch mistresses, and thought it no dishonour. In England you can but belong to one party or t'other, and you take the house you live in with all its encumbrances, its retainers, its antique discomforts, and ruins even ; you patch up, but you never build up anew. Will we of the New World submit much longer, even nominally, to this ancient British superstition ? There are signs of the times which make me think that ere long we shall care as little about King George here, and peers temporal and peers spiritual, as we do for King Canute or the Druids.

This chapter began about the wits, my grandson may say, and hath wandered very far from their company. The pleasantest of the wits I knew were the Doctors Garth and Arbuthnot,* and Mr. Gay, the author of *Trivia*, the most charming kind soul that ever laughed at a joke or cracked a bottle. Mr. Prior I saw, and he was the earthen pot swimming with the pots of brass down the stream, and always and justly frightened lest he should break in the voyage. I met him both at London and Paris, where he was performing piteous congees to the Duke of Shrewsbury, not having courage to support the dignity which his undeniable genius and talent had won him, and writing coaxing letters to Secretary St. John, and thinking about his plate and his place, and what on earth should become of him should his party go out. The famous Mr. Congreve I saw a dozen of times at Button's,* a splendid wreck of a man, magnificently attired, and though gouty, and almost blind, bearing a brave face against fortune.

The great Mr. Pope (of whose prodigious genius I have no words to express my admiration) was quite a puny lad at this time, appearing seldom in public places. There were hundreds of men, wits, and pretty fellows frequenting the theatres and coffee-houses of that day—whom *nunc prescribere longum est.** Indeed I think the most brilliant of that sort I ever saw was not till fifteen years afterwards, when I paid my last visit in England, and met young Harry Fielding, son of the Fielding that served in Spain and afterwards in Flanders with us, and who for fun and humour seemed to top them all. As for the famous Dr. Swift, I can say of him, ' *vidi tantum*.'* He was in London all these years up to the death of the queen ; and in a hundred public places where I saw him, but no more ; he never missed Court of a Sunday, where once or twice he was pointed out to your grandfather. He would have sought me out eagerly enough had I been a great man with a title to my name, or a star on my coat. At Court the doctor had no eyes but for the very greatest. Lord Treasurer and St. John used to call him Jonathan, and they paid him with this cheap coin for the service they took of him. He writ their lampoons, fought their enemies, flogged and bullied in their service, and it must be owned with a consummate skill and fierceness. 'Tis said he hath lost his intellect now, and forgotten his wrongs and his rage against mankind. I have always thought of him and of Marlborough as the two greatest men of that age. I have read his books (who doth not know them ?) here in our calm woods, and imagine a giant to myself as I think of him, a lonely fallen Prometheus, groaning as the vulture tears him. Prometheus I saw, but when first I ever had any words with him, the giant stepped out of a sedan-chair in the Poultry, whither he had come with a tipsy Irish servant parading before him, who announced him, bawling out his reverence's name, whilst his master below was as yet haggling with the chairman. I disliked this Mr. Swift, and heard many a story about him, of his conduct to men, and his words to women. He could flatter the great as much as he could bully the weak ; and Mr. Esmond, being younger and hotter in that day than now, was determined, should he ever meet this dragon, not to run away from his teeth and his fire.

Men have all sorts of motives which carry them onwards in life, and are driven into acts of desperation, or it may be of distinction, from a hundred different causes. There was one comrade of Esmond's, an honest little Irish lieutenant of Handyside's,* who owed so much money to a camp sutler, that he began to make love to the man's daughter, intending to pay his debt that way ; and at the battle of Malplaquet, flying away from the debt and lady too, he rushed so

desperately on the French lines, that he got his company ;
and came a captain out of the action, and had to marry the
sutler's daughter after all, who brought him his cancelled
debt to her father as poor Rogers's fortune. To run out of
the reach of bill and marriage, he ran on the enemy's pikes ;
and as these did not kill him he was thrown back upon
t'other horn of his dilemma. Our great duke at the same
battle was fighting, not the French, but the Tories in England ; and risking his life and the army's, not for his country
but for his pay and places ; and for fear of his wife at home,
that only being in life whom he dreaded. I have asked
about men in my own company (new drafts of poor country
boys were perpetually coming over to us during the wars,
and brought from the ploughshare to the sword), and found
that a half of them under the flags were driven thither on
account of a woman : one fellow was jilted by his mistress
and took the shilling in despair ; another jilted the girl,
and fled from her and the parish to the tents where the
law could not disturb him. Why go on particularizing ?
What can the sons of Adam and Eve expect, but to continue
in that course of love and trouble their father and mother
set out on ? O my grandson! I am drawing nigh to the
end of that period of my history, when I was acquainted
with the great world of England and Europe, my years
are past the Hebrew poet's limit, and I say unto thee, all
my troubles and joys too, for that matter, have come from
a woman ; as thine will when thy destined course begins.
'Twas a woman that made a soldier of me, that set me
intriguing afterwards ; I believe I would have spun smocks
for her had she so bidden me ; what strength I had in
my head I would have given her ; hath not every man
in his degree had his Omphale and Delilah ?* Mine befooled
me on the banks of the Thames, and in dear old England ;
thou mayest find thine own by Rappahannoc.

To please that woman then I tried to distinguish myself
as a soldier, and afterwards as a wit and a politician ; as
to please another I would have put on a black cassock and
a pair of bands, and had done so but that a superior fate
intervened to defeat that project. And I say, I think the
world is like Captain Esmond's company I spoke of anon ;
and, could you see every man's career in life, you would
find a woman clogging him ; or clinging round his march
and stopping him ; or cheering him and goading him ; or

beckoning him out of her chariot, so that he goes up to her, and leaves the race to be run without him; or bringing him the apple, and saying 'Eat'; or fetching him the daggers and whispering 'Kill! yonder lies Duncan, and a crown, and an opportunity'.

Your grandfather fought with more effect as a politician than as a wit; and having private animosities and grievances of his own and his general's against the great duke in command of the army, and more information on military matters than most writers, who had never seen beyond the fire of a tobacco-pipe at Wills's,* he was enabled to do good service for that cause which he embarked in, and for Mr. St. John and his party. But he disdained the abuse in which some of the Tory writers indulged; for instance, Dr. Swift, who actually chose to doubt the Duke of Marlborough's courage, and was pleased to hint that his grace's military capacity was doubtful: nor were Esmond's performances worse for the effect they were intended to produce (though no doubt they could not injure the Duke of Marlborough nearly so much in the public eyes as the malignant attacks of Swift did, which were carefully directed so as to blacken and degrade him), because they were writ openly and fairly by Mr. Esmond, who made no disguise of them, who was now out of the army, and who never attacked the prodigious courage and talents, only the selfishness and rapacity, of the chief.

The colonel then, having writ a paper for one of the Tory journals, called the *Post-Boy* (a letter upon Bouchain,* that the town talked about for two whole days, when the appearance of an Italian singer supplied a fresh subject for conversation), and having business at the Exchange, where Mrs. Beatrix wanted a pair of gloves or a fan very likely, Esmond went to correct his paper, and was sitting at the printer's, when the famous Dr. Swift came in, his Irish fellow with him that used to walk before his chair, and bawled out his master's name with great dignity.

Mr. Esmond was waiting for the printer too, whose wife had gone to the tavern to fetch him, and was meantime engaged in drawing a picture of a soldier on horseback for a dirty little pretty boy of the printer's wife, whom she had left behind her.

'I presume you are the editor of the *Post-Boy*, sir?' says the doctor, in a grating voice that had an Irish twang;

and he looked at the colonel from under his two bushy
eyebrows with a pair of very clear blue eyes. His complexion was muddy, his figure rather fat, his chin double.
He wore a shabby cassock, and a shabby hat over his black
wig, and he pulled out a great gold watch, at which he looks
very fierce.*

'I am but a contributor, Dr. Swift,' says Esmond, with
the little boy still on his knee. He was sitting with his
back in the window, so that the doctor could not see him.

'Who told you I was Dr. Swift?' says the doctor,
eyeing the other very haughtily.

'Your reverence's valet bawled out your name,' says the
colonel. 'I should judge you brought him from Ireland.'

'And pray, sir, what right have you to judge whether
my servant came from Ireland or no? I want to speak
with your employer, Mr. Leach.* I'll thank ye go fetch
him.'

'Where's your papa, Tommy?' asks the colonel of the
child, a smutty little wretch in a frock.

Instead of answering, the child begins to cry; the doctor's
appearance had no doubt frightened the poor little imp.

'Send that squalling little brat about his business, and
do what I bid ye, sir,' says the doctor.

'I must finish the picture first for Tommy,' says the
colonel, laughing. 'Here, Tommy, will you have your
Pandour with whiskers or without?'

'Whisters,' says Tommy, quite intent on the picture.

'Who the devil are ye, sir?' cries the doctor; 'are ye
a printer's man or are ye not?' he pronounced it like *naught*.

'Your reverence needn't raise the devil to ask who I am,'
says Colonel Esmond. 'Did you ever hear of Dr. Faustus,
little Tommy? or Friar Bacon, who invented gunpowder,
and set the Thames on fire?'

Mr. Swift turned quite red, almost purple. 'I did not
intend any offence, sir,' says he.

'I daresay, sir, you offended without meaning,' says the
other drily.

'Who are ye, sir? Do you know who I am, sir? You
are one of the pack of Grub-Street scribblers that my friend
Mr. Secretary hath laid by the heels. How dare ye, sir,
speak to me in this tone?' cries the doctor, in a great fume.

'I beg your honour's humble pardon if I have offended
your honour,' says Esmond, in a tone of great humility.

' Rather than be sent to the Compter,* or be put in the
pillory, there's nothing I wouldn't do. But Mrs. Leach,
the printer's lady, told me to mind Tommy whilst she went
for her husband to the tavern, and I daren't leave the child
lest he should fall into the fire ; but if your reverence will
hold him——— '

' I take the little beast ! ' says the doctor, starting back.
' I am engaged to your betters, fellow. Tell Mr. Leach that
when he makes an appointment with Dr. Swift he had
best keep it, do ye hear ? And keep a respectful tongue
in your head, sir, when you address a person like me.'

' I'm but a poor broken-down soldier,' says the colonel,
' and I've seen better days, though I am forced now to turn
my hand to writing. We can't help our fate, sir.'

' You're the person that Mr. Leach hath spoken to me of,
I presume. Have the goodness to speak civilly when you
are spoken to—and tell Leach to call at my lodgings in
Bury Street, and bring the papers with him to-night at ten
o'clock. And the next time you see me, you'll know me,
and be civil, Mr. Kemp.'*

Poor Kemp, who had been a lieutenant at the beginning
of the war, and fallen into misfortune, was the writer of
the *Post-Boy*, and now took honest Mr. Leach's pay in
place of her Majesty's. Esmond had seen this gentleman,
and a very ingenious, hard-working honest fellow he was,
toiling to give bread to a great family, and watching up
many a long winter night to keep the wolf from his door.
And Mr. St. John, who had liberty always on his tongue,
had just sent a dozen of the Opposition writers into prison,
and one actually into the pillory, for what he called libels,
but libels not half so violent as those writ on our side.
With regard to this very piece of tyranny, Esmond had
remonstrated strongly with the secretary, who laughed and
said, the rascals were served quite right ; and told Esmond
a joke of Swift's regarding the matter. Nay, more, this
Irishman, when St. John was about to pardon a poor
wretch condemned to death for rape, absolutely prevented
the secretary from exercising this act of good nature, and
boasted that he had had the man hanged ;* and great as
the doctor's genius might be, and splendid his ability,
Esmond for one would affect no love for him, and never
desired to make his acquaintance. The doctor was at
Court every Sunday assiduously enough, a place the colonel

frequented but rarely, though he had a great inducement to go there in the person of a fair maid of honour of her Majesty's; and the airs and patronage Mr. Swift gave himself, forgetting gentlemen of his country whom he knew perfectly, his loud talk at once insolent and servile, nay, perhaps his very intimacy with lord treasurer and the secretary, who indulged all his freaks and called him Jonathan, you may be sure, were remarked by many a person of whom the proud priest himself took no note, during that time of his vanity and triumph.

'Twas but three days after, the 15th of November, 1712 (Esmond minds him well of the date), that he went by invitation to dine with his general, the foot of whose table he used to take on these festive occasions, as he had done at many a board, hard and plentiful, during the campaign. This was a great feast, and of the latter sort; the honest old gentleman loved to treat his friends splendidly: his grace of Ormonde, before he joined his army as general-issimo, my Lord Viscount Bolingbroke, one of her Majesty's secretaries of state, my Lord Orkney, that had served with us abroad, being of the party. His grace of Hamilton, master of the ordnance, and in whose honour the feast had been given, upon his approaching departure as ambassador to Paris, had sent an excuse to General Webb at two o'clock, but an hour before the dinner: nothing but the most immediate business, his grace said, should have prevented him having the pleasure of drinking a parting glass to the health of General Webb. His absence disappointed Esmond's old chief, who suffered much from his wounds besides; and though the company was grand, it was rather gloomy. St. John came last, and brought a friend with him:—'I'm sure,' says my general, bowing very politely, 'my table hath always a place for Dr. Swift.'

Mr. Esmond went up to the doctor with a bow and a smile:—'I gave Dr. Swift's message,' says he, 'to the printer: I hope he brought your pamphlet to your lodgings in time.' Indeed poor Leach had come to his house very soon after the doctor left it, being brought away rather tipsy from the tavern by his thrifty wife; and he talked of cousin Swift in a maudlin way, though of course Mr. Esmond did not allude to this relationship. The doctor scowled, blushed, and was much confused, and said scarce a word during the whole of dinner. A very little stone will sometimes knock down these Goliaths of wit ; and this one was often discomfited when met by a man of any spirit ; he took his place sulkily, put water in his wine that the others drank plentifully, and scarce said a word.

The talk was about the affairs of the day, or rather about persons than affairs : my Lady Marlborough's fury, her daughters in old clothes and mob-caps looking out from their windows and seeing the company pass to the Drawing-room ; the gentleman-usher's horror when the Prince of Savoy was introduced to her Majesty in a tie-wig, no man out of a full-bottomed periwig ever having kissed the royal hand before ; about the Mohawks and the damage they were doing, rushing through the town, killing and murdering. Some one said the ill-omened face of Mohun had been seen at the theatre the night before, and Macartney and Meredith with him. Meant to be a feast, the meeting, in spite of drink, and talk, was as dismal as a funeral. Every topic started subsided into gloom. His grace of Ormonde went away because the conversation got upon Denain, where we had been defeated in the last campaign. Esmond's general was affected at the allusion to this action too, for his comrade of Wynendael, the Count of Nassau-Woudenberg, had been slain there. Mr. Swift, when Esmond pledged him, said he drank no wine, and took his hat from the peg and went away, beckoning my Lord Bolingbroke to follow him ; but the other bade him take his chariot and save his coach-hire, he had to speak with Colonel Esmond ; and when the rest of the company withdrew to cards, these two remained behind in the dark.

Bolingbroke always spoke freely when he had drunk freely. His enemies could get any secret out of him in that condition ; women were even employed to ply him, and take his words down. I have heard that my Lord Stair,* three years after, when the secretary fled to France and became the pretender's minister, got all the information he wanted by putting female spies over St. John in his cups. He spoke freely now :—' Jonathan knows nothing of this for certain, though he suspects it, and by George, Webb will take an archbishopric, and Jonathan a—no, damme— Jonathan will take an archbishopric from James, I warrant me, gladly enough. Your duke hath the string of the whole matter in his hand,' the secretary went on. ' We have that which will force Marlborough to keep his distance, and he goes out of London in a fortnight. Prior hath his business ; he left me this morning, and mark me, Harry, should fate carry off our august, our beloved, our most gouty and plethoric queen, and defender of the faith, *la bonne cause triomphera.* *A la santé de la bonne cause !* Everything good comes from France. Wine comes from France ; give us another bumper to the *bonne cause.*' We drank it together.

'Will the *bonne cause* turn Protestant ?' asked Mr. Esmond.

'No, hang it,' says the other, ' he'll defend our faith as in duty bound, but he'll stick by his own. The Hind and the Panther*shall run in the same car, by Jove. Righteousness and peace shall kiss each other ; and we'll have Father Massillon to walk down the aisle of St. Paul's, cheek by jowl, with Dr. Sacheverel. Give us more wine ; here's a health to the *bonne cause*, kneeling—damme, let's drink it kneeling.' He was quite flushed and wild with wine as he was talking.

'And suppose,' says Esmond, who always had this gloomy apprehension, ' the *bonne cause* should give us up to the French, as his father and uncle did before him ?'

'Give us up to the French !' starts up Bolingbroke ; ' is there any English gentleman that fears that ? You who have seen Blenheim and Ramillies, afraid of the French ! Your ancestors and mine, and brave old Webb's yonder, have met them in a hundred fields, and our children will be ready to do the like. Who's he that wishes for more men from England ? My cousin Westmoreland ?* Give us up to the French, pshaw !'

'His uncle did,' says Mr. Esmond.

'And what happened to his grandfather ?' broke out St. John, filling out another bumper. 'Here's to the greatest monarch England ever saw ; here's to the Englishman that made a kingdom of her. Our great king came from Huntingdon, not Hanover ; our fathers didn't look for a Dutchman to rule us. Let him come and we'll keep him, and we'll show him Whitehall. If he's a traitor let us have him here to deal with him ; and then there are spirits here as great as any that have gone before. There are men here that can look at danger in the face and not be frightened at it. Traitor, treason ! what names are these to scare you and me ? Are all Oliver's men dead, or his glorious name forgotten in fifty years ? Are there

no men equal to him, think you, as good—aye, as good ?
God save the king ! and, if the monarchy fails us, God
save the British republic ! '

He filled another great bumper, and tossed it up and
drained it wildly, just as the noise of rapid carriage-wheels
approaching was stopped at our door, and after a hurried
knock and a moment's interval, Mr. Swift came into the
hall, ran upstairs to the room we were dining in, and entered
it with a perturbed face.   St. John, excited with drink,
was making some wild quotation out of *Macbeth*, but Swift
stopped him.

'Drink no more, my lord, for God's sake,' says he,
' I come with the most dreadful news.'

' Is the queen dead ? ' cries out Bolingbroke, seizing on
a water-glass.

' No, Duke Hamilton is dead, he was murdered an hour
ago by Mohun and Macartney ; they had a quarrel this
morning ; they gave him not so much time as to write
a letter.   He went for a couple of his friends, and he is
dead, and Mohun, too, the bloody villain, who was set on
him.   They fought in Hyde Park just before sunset ; the
duke killed Mohun, and Macartney came up and stabbed
him, and the dog is fled.   I have your chariot below ; send
to every part of the country and apprehend that villain ;
come to the duke's house and see if any life be left in him.'

' O Beatrix, Beatrix,' thought Esmond, ' and here ends
my poor girl's ambition ! '

CHAPTER VI

POOR BEATRIX

THERE had been no need to urge upon Esmond the necessity
of a separation between him and Beatrix : Fate had done
that completely ; and I think from the very moment poor
Beatrix had accepted the duke's offer, she began to assume
the majestic air of a duchess, nay, queen elect, and to
carry herself as one sacred and removed from us common
people.   Her mother and kinsman both fell into her ways,
the latter scornfully perhaps, and uttering his usual gibes
at her vanity and his own.   There was a certain charm

about this girl of which neither Colonel Esmond nor his fond mistress could forgo the fascination ; in spite of her faults and her pride and wilfulness, they were forced to love her ; and, indeed, might be set down as the two chief flatterers of the brilliant creature's court.

Who, in the course of his life, hath not been so bewitched, and worshipped some idol or another ? Years after this passion hath been dead and buried, along with a thousand other worldly cares and ambitions, he who felt it can recall it out of its grave, and admire, almost as fondly as he did in his youth, that lovely queenly creature. I invoke that beautiful spirit from the shades and love her still ; or rather I should say such a past is always present to a man; such a passion once felt forms a part of his whole being, and cannot be separated from it ; it becomes a portion of the man of to-day, just as any great faith or conviction, the discovery of poetry, the awakening of religion, ever afterward influence him ; just as the wound I had at Blenheim, and of which I wear the scar, hath become part of my frame and influenced my whole body, nay spirit, subsequently, though 'twas got and healed forty years ago. Parting and forgetting ! What faithful heart can do these ? Our great thoughts, our great affections, the Truths of our life, never leave us. Surely, they cannot separate from our consciousness ; shall follow it whithersoever that shall go ; and are of their nature divine and immortal.

With the horrible news of this catastrophe, which was confirmed by the weeping domestics at the duke's own door, Esmond rode homewards as quick as his lazy coach would carry him, devising all the time how he should break the intelligence to the person most concerned in it ; and if a satire upon human vanity could be needed, that poor soul afforded it in the altered company and occupations in which Esmond found her. For days before, her chariot had been rolling the street from mercer to toyshop—from goldsmith to laceman : her taste was perfect, or at least the fond bridegroom had thought so, and had given entire authority over all tradesmen, and for all the plate, furniture, and equipages, with which his grace the ambassador wished to adorn his splendid mission. She must have her picture by Kneller, a duchess not being complete without a portrait, and a noble one he made, and actually sketched in, on a cushion, a coronet which she was about to wear. She

vowed she would wear it at King James the Third's coronation, and never a princess in the land would have become
ermine better. Esmond found the antechamber crowded
with milliners and toyshop women, obsequious goldsmiths
with jewels, salvers, and tankards ; and mercer's men with
hangings, and velvets, and brocades. My lady duchess
elect was giving audience to one famous silversmith from
Exeter'Change, who brought with him a great chased salver,
of which he was pointing out the beauties as Colonel Esmond
entered. ' Come,' says she, ' cousin, and admire the taste
of this pretty thing.' I think Mars and Venus were lying
in the golden bower, that one gilt Cupid carried off the war-
god's casque—another his sword—another his great buckler,
upon which my Lord Duke Hamilton's arms with ours
were to be engraved—and a fourth was kneeling down to
the reclining goddess with the ducal coronet in his hands,
God help us ! The next time Mr. Esmond saw that piece
of plate, the arms were changed, the ducal coronet had been
replaced by a viscount's ; it formed part of the fortune of
the thrifty goldsmith's own daughter, when she married
my Lord Viscount Squanderfield two years after.

' Isn't this a beautiful piece ? ' says Beatrix, examining
it, and she pointed out the arch graces of the Cupids, and
the fine carving of the languid prostrate Mars. Esmond
sickened as he thought of the warrior dead in his chamber,
his servants and children weeping around him ; and of this
smiling creature attiring herself, as it were, for that nuptial
death-bed. ' 'Tis a pretty piece of vanity,' says he, looking
gloomily at the beautiful creature : there were flambeaux
in the room lighting up the brilliant mistress of it. She
lifted up the great gold salver with her fair arms.

' Vanity ! ' says she haughtily. ' What is vanity in you,
sir, is propriety in me. You ask a Jewish price for it, Mr.
Graves ; but have it I will, if only to spite Mr. Esmond.'

' O Beatrix, lay it down ! ' says Mr. Esmond. ' Herodias !
you know not what you carry in the charger.'

She dropped it with a clang ; the eager goldsmith running
to seize his fallen ware. The lady's face caught the fright
from Esmond's pale countenance, and her eyes shone out
like beacons of alarm :—' What is it, Henry ? ' says she,
running to him, and seizing both his hands. ' What do
you mean by your pale face and gloomy tones ? '

' Come away, come away ! ' says Esmond, leading her :

she clung frightened to him, and he supported her upon his heart, bidding the scared goldsmith leave them. The man went into the next apartment, staring with surprise, and hugging his precious charger.

'O my Beatrix, my sister!' says Esmond, still holding in his arms the pallid and affrighted creature, 'you have the greatest courage of any woman in the world; prepare to show it now, for you have a dreadful trial to bear.'

She sprang away from the friend who would have protected her :—'Hath he left me?' says she. 'We had words this morning: he was very gloomy, and I angered him: but he dared not, he dared not!' As she spoke a burning blush flushed over her whole face and bosom. Esmond saw it reflected in the glass by which she stood, with clenched hands, pressing her swelling heart.

'He has left you,' says Esmond, wondering that rage rather than sorrow was in her looks.

'And he is alive,' cries Beatrix, 'and you bring me this commission! He has left me, and you haven't dared to avenge me! You, that pretend to be the champion of our house, have let me suffer this insult! Where is Castlewood? I will go to my brother.'

'The duke is not alive, Beatrix,' said Esmond.

She looked at her cousin wildly, and fell back to the wall as though shot in the breast :—'And you come here, and—and—you killed him?'

'No; thank Heaven,' her kinsman said, 'the blood of that noble heart doth not stain my sword! In its last hour it was faithful to thee, Beatrix Esmond. Vain and cruel woman! kneel and thank the awful Heaven which awards life and death, and chastises pride, that the noble Hamilton died true to you; at least that 'twas not your quarrel, or your pride, or your wicked vanity, that drove him to his fate. He died by the bloody sword which already had drank your own father's blood. O woman, O sister! to that sad field where two corpses are lying—for the murderer died too by the hand of the man he slew—can you bring no mourners but your revenge and your vanity? God help and pardon thee, Beatrix, as He brings this awful punishment to your hard and rebellious heart.'

Esmond had scarce done speaking, when his mistress came in. The colloquy between him and Beatrix had lasted but a few minutes, during which time Esmond's servant

had carried the disastrous news through the household.
The army of Vanity Fair, waiting without, gathered up
all their fripperies and fled aghast. Tender Lady Castlewood
had been in talk above with Dean Atterbury, the pious
creature's almoner and director ; and the dean had entered
with her as a physician whose place was at a sick-bed.
Beatrix's mother looked at Esmond and ran towards her
daughter, with a pale face and open heart and hands, all
kindness and pity. But Beatrix passed her by, nor would
she have any of the medicaments of the spiritual physician.
' I am best in my own room and by myself,' she said. Her
eyes were quite dry ; nor did Esmond ever see them otherwise, save once, in respect to that grief. She gave him
a cold hand as she went out : ' Thank you, brother,' she
said, in a low voice, and with a simplicity more touching
than tears ; ' all you have said is true and kind, and I will
go away and ask pardon.' The three others remained
behind, and talked over the dreadful story. It affected
Dr. Atterbury more even than us, as it seemed. The death
of Mohun, her husband's murderer, was more awful to my
mistress than even the duke's unhappy end. Esmond gave
at length what particulars he knew*of their quarrel, and the
cause of it. The two noblemen had long been at war with
respect to the Lord Gerard's property, whose two daughters
my lord duke and Mohun had married. They had met
by appointment that day at the lawyer's in Lincoln's Inn
Fields ; had words which, though they appeared very
trifling to those who heard them, were not so to men
exasperated by long and previous enmity. Mohun asked
my lord duke where he could see his grace's friends, and
within an hour had sent two of his own to arrange this
deadly duel. It was pursued with such fierceness, and
sprung from so trifling a cause, that all men agreed at the
time that there was a party, of which these three notorious
brawlers were but agents, who desired to take Duke Hamilton's life away. They fought three on a side, as in that
tragic meeting twelve years back, which hath been recounted
already, and in which Mohun performed his second murder.
They rushed in, and closed upon each other at once without
any feints or crossing of swords even, and stabbed one at
the other desperately, each receiving many wounds ; and
Mohun having his death-wound, and my lord duke lying
by him, Macartney came up and stabbed his grace as he

lay on the ground, and gave him the blow of which he died. Colonel Macartney denied this, of which the horror and indignation of the whole kingdom would nevertheless have him guilty, and fled the country, whither he never returned.

What was the real cause of the Duke Hamilton's death— a paltry quarrel that might easily have been made up, and with a ruffian so low, base, profligate, and degraded with former crimes and repeated murders, that a man of such a renown and princely rank as my lord duke might have disdained to sully his sword with the blood of such a villain. But his spirit was so high that those who wished his death knew that his courage was like his charity, and never turned any man away ; and he died by the hands of Mohun, and the other two cut-throats that were set on him. The queen's ambassador to Paris died, the loyal and devoted servant of the House of Stuart, and a royal prince of Scotland himself, and carrying the confidence, the repentance of Queen Anne along with his own open devotion, and the goodwill of millions in the country more, to the queen's exiled brother and sovereign.

That party to which Lord Mohun belonged had the benefit of his service, and now were well rid of such a ruffian. He, and Meredith, and Macartney, were the Duke of Marlborough's men ; and the two colonels had been broke but the year before for drinking perdition to the Tories. His grace was a Whig now and a Hanoverian, and as eager for war as Prince Eugene himself. I say not that he was privy to Duke Hamilton's death, I say that his party profited by it ; and that three desperate and bloody instruments were found to effect that murder.

As Esmond and the dean walked away from Kensington discoursing of this tragedy, and how fatal it was to the cause which they both had at heart ; the street-criers were already out with their broadsides, shouting through the town the full, true, and horrible account of the death of Lord Mohun and Duke Hamilton in a duel. A fellow had got to Kensington, and was crying it in the square there at very early morning, when Mr. Esmond happened to pass by. He drove the man from under Beatrix's very window, whereof the casement had been set open. The sun was shining though 'twas November : he had seen the market-carts rolling into London, the guard relieved at the Palace, the labourers trudging to their work in the gardens between

Kensington and the City—the wandering merchants and hawkers filling the air with their cries. The world was going to its business again, although dukes lay dead and ladies mourned for them ; and kings, very likely, lost their chances. So night and day pass away, and to-morrow comes, and our place knows us not. Esmond thought of the courier, now galloping on the north road to inform him, who was Earl of Arran yesterday, that he was Duke of Hamilton to-day, and of a thousand great schemes, hopes, ambitions, that were alive in the gallant heart, beating a few hours since, and now in a little dust quiescent.

CHAPTER VII

I VISIT CASTLEWOOD ONCE MORE

THUS, for a third time, Beatrix's ambitious hopes were circumvented, and she might well believe that a special malignant fate watched and pursued her, tearing her prize out of her hand just as she seemed to grasp it, and leaving her with only rage and grief for her portion. Whatever her feelings might have been of anger or of sorrow (and I fear me that the former emotion was that which most tore her heart), she would take no confidant, as people of softer natures would have done under such a calamity ; her mother and her kinsman knew that she would disdain their pity, and that to offer it would be but to infuriate the cruel wound which fortune had inflicted. We knew that her pride was awfully humbled and punished by this sudden and terrible blow ; she wanted no teaching of ours to point out the sad moral of her story. Her fond mother could give but her prayers, and her kinsman his faithful friendship and patience to the unhappy stricken creature ; and it was only by hints, and a word or two uttered months afterwards, that Beatrix showed she understood their silent commiseration, and on her part was secretly thankful for their forbearance. The people about the Court said there was that in her manner which frightened away scoffing and condolence : she was above their triumph and their pity, and acted her part in that dreadful tragedy greatly and courageously ; so that those who liked her least were yet forced to admire her. We, who watched her after her disaster, could not but respect the indomitable courage and majestic calm with which she bore it. ' I would rather see her tears than her pride,' her mother said, who was accustomed to bear her sorrows in a very different way, and to receive them as the stroke of God, with an awful submission and meekness. But Beatrix's nature was different to that tender parent's ; she seemed to accept her grief, and to defy it ; nor would she allow it (I believe not even in private, and in her own chamber) to extort from her the confession of even a tear of humiliation or a cry of pain. Friends and children of our race, who come after me, in which way will you bear your trials ? I know one that prays God will give you love rather than pride, and that the Eye all-seeing shall find you in the humble place. Not that we should judge proud spirits otherwise than charitably. 'Tis nature hath fashioned some for ambition and dominion, as it hath formed others for obedience and gentle submission. The leopard follows his nature as the lamb does, and acts after leopard law ; she can neither help her beauty, nor her courage, nor her cruelty ; nor a single spot on her shining coat ; nor the conquering spirit which impels her ; nor the shot which brings her down.

During that well-founded panic the Whigs had, lest the queen should forsake their Hanoverian prince, bound by oaths and treaties as she was to him, and recall her brother, who was allied to her by yet stronger ties of nature and duty ; the Prince of Savoy, and the boldest of that party of the Whigs, were for bringing the young Duke of Cambridge* over, in spite of the queen and the outcry of her Tory servants, arguing that the electoral prince, a peer and prince of the blood-royal of this realm too, and in the line of succession to the crown, had a right to sit in the Parliament whereof he was a member, and to dwell in the country which he one day was to govern. Nothing but the strongest ill will expressed by the queen, and the people about her, and menaces of the royal resentment, should this scheme be persisted in, prevented it from being carried into effect.

The boldest on our side were, in like manner, for having our prince into the country. The undoubted inheritor of

the right divine ; the feelings of more than half the nation,
of almost all the clergy, of the gentry of England and
Scotland with him ; entirely innocent of the crime for
which his father suffered—brave, young, handsome, unfortunate—who in England would dare to molest the prince
should he come among us, and fling himself upon British
generosity, hospitality, and honour ? An invader with an
army of Frenchmen behind him, Englishmen of spirit would
resist to the death, and drive back to the shores whence
he came ; but a prince, alone, armed with his right only,
and relying on the loyalty of his people, was sure, many
of his friends argued, of welcome, at least of safety, among
us. The hand of his sister the queen, of the people his
subjects, never could be raised to do him a wrong. But
the queen was timid by nature, and the successive ministers
she had, had private causes for their irresolution. The
bolder and honester men, who had at heart the illustrious
young exile's cause, had no scheme of interest of their own
to prevent them from seeing the right done, and, provided
only he came as an Englishman, were ready to venture
their all to welcome and defend him.

St. John and Harley both had kind words in plenty for
the prince's adherents, and gave him endless promises of
future support : but hints and promises were all they
could be got to give ; and some of his friends were for
measures much bolder, more efficacious, and more open.
With a party of these, some of whom are yet alive, and some
whose names Mr. Esmond has no right to mention, he found
himself engaged the year after that miserable death of
Duke Hamilton, which deprived the prince of his most
courageous ally in this country. Dean Atterbury was one
of the friends whom Esmond may mention, as the brave
bishop is now beyond exile and persecution, and to him,
and one or two more, the colonel opened himself of a
scheme of his own, that, backed by a little resolution on
the prince's part, could not fail of bringing about the
accomplishment of their dearest wishes.

My young Lord Viscount Castlewood had not come to
England to keep his majority, and had now been absent
from the country for several years. The year when his sister
was to be married and Duke Hamilton died, my lord was
kept at Bruxelles by his wife's lying-in. The gentle
Clotilda could not bear her husband out of her sight ;

perhaps she mistrusted the young scapegrace should he ever get loose from her leading-strings ; and she kept him by her side to nurse the baby and administer posset to the gossips. Many a laugh poor Beatrix had had about Frank's uxoriousness : his mother would have gone to Clotilda when her time was coming, but that the mother-in-law was already in possession, and the negotiations for poor Beatrix's marriage were begun. A few months after the horrid catastrophe in Hyde Park, my mistress and her daughter retired to Castlewood, where my lord, it was expected, would soon join them. But, to say truth, their quiet household was little to his taste ; he could be got to come to Walcote but once after his first campaign ; and then the young rogue spent more than half his time in London, not appearing at Court, or in public under his own name and title, but frequenting plays, bagnios, and the very worst company, under the name of Captain Esmond (whereby his innocent kinsman got more than once into trouble) ; and so under various pretexts, and in pursuit of all sorts of pleasures, until he plunged into the lawful one of marriage, Frank Castlewood had remained away from this country, and was unknown, save amongst the gentlemen of the army, with whom he had served abroad. The fond heart of his mother was pained by this long absence. 'Twas all that Henry Esmond could do to soothe her natural mortification, and find excuses for his kinsman's levity.

In the autumn of the year 1713, Lord Castlewood thought of returning home. His first child had been a daughter ; Clotilda was in the way of gratifying his lordship with a second, and the pious youth thought that, by bringing his wife to his ancestral home, by prayers to St. Philip of Castlewood, and what not, Heaven might be induced to bless him with a son this time, for whose coming the expectant mamma was very anxious.

The long-debated peace had been proclaimed this year at the end of March ; and France was open to us. Just as Frank's poor mother had made all things ready for Lord Castlewood's reception, and was eagerly expecting her son, it was by Colonel Esmond's means that the kind lady was disappointed of her longing, and obliged to defer once more the darling hope of her heart.

Esmond took horses to Castlewood. He had not seen its ancient grey towers and well-remembered woods for

nearly fourteen years, and since he rode thence with my
lord, to whom his mistress with her young children by her
side waved an adieu, what ages seem to have passed since
then, what years of action and passion, of care, love, hope,
disaster ! The children were grown up now, and had stories
of their own. As for Esmond, he felt to be a hundred
years old ; his dear mistress only seemed unchanged ; she
looked and welcomed him quite as of old. There was the
fountain in the court babbling its familiar music, the old
hall and its furniture, the carved chair my late lord used,
the very flagon he drank from. Esmond's mistress knew
he would like to sleep in the little room he used to occupy ;
'twas made ready for him, and wall-flowers and sweet herbs
set in the adjoining chamber, the chaplain's room.

In tears of not unmanly emotion, with prayers of submission to the awful Dispenser of death and life, of good
and evil fortune, Mr. Esmond passed a part of that first
night at Castlewood, lying awake for many hours as the
clock kept tolling (in tones so well remembered), looking
back, as all men will, that revisit their home of childhood,
over the great gulf of time, and surveying himself on the
distant bank yonder, a sad little melancholy boy, with his
lord still alive—his dear mistress, a girl yet, her children
sporting around her. Years ago, a boy on that very bed,
when she had blessed him and called him her knight, he
had made a vow to be faithful and never desert her dear
service. Had he kept that fond boyish promise ? Yes,
before Heaven ; yes, praise be to God ! His life had been
hers ; his blood, his fortune, his name, his whole heart
ever since had been hers and her children's. All night long
he was dreaming his boyhood over again, and waking
fitfully ; he half fancied he heard Father Holt calling to
him from the next chamber, and that he was coming in
and out from the mysterious window.

Esmond rose up before the dawn, passed into the next
room, where the air was heavy with the odour of the wall-
flowers ; looked into the brasier where the papers had been
burnt, into the old presses where Holt's books and papers
had been kept, and tried the spring, and whether the
window worked still. The spring had not been touched
for years, but yielded at length, and the whole fabric of
the window sank down. He lifted it and it relapsed into
its frame ; no one had ever passed thence since Holt used
it sixteen years ago.

Esmond remembered his poor lord saying, on the last day of his life, that Holt used to come in and out of the house like a ghost, and knew that the father liked these mysteries, and practised such secret disguises, entrances, and exits; this was the way the ghost came and went, his pupil had always conjectured. Esmond closed the casement up again as the dawn was rising over Castlewood village; he could hear the clinking at the blacksmith's forge yonder among the trees, across the green, and past the river, on which a mist still lay sleeping.

Next Esmond opened that long cupboard over the woodwork of the mantelpiece, big enough to hold a man, and in which Mr. Holt used to keep sundry secret properties of his. The two swords he remembered so well as a boy, lay actually there still, and Esmond took them out and wiped them, with a strange curiosity of emotion. There were a bundle of papers here, too, which no doubt had been left at Holt's last visit to the place, in my lord viscount's life, that very day when the priest had been arrested and taken to Hexham Castle. Esmond made free with these papers, and found treasonable matter of King William's reign, the names of Charnock and Perkins, Sir John Fenwick and Sir John Friend, Rookwood and Lodwick, Lords Montgomery and Ailesbury, Clarendon and Yarmouth, that had all been engaged in plots against the usurper; a letter from the Duke of Berwick too, and one from the king at St. Germains, offering to confer upon his trusty and well-beloved Francis Viscount Castlewood the titles of Earl and Marquis of Esmond, bestowed by patent royal, and in the fourth year of his reign, upon Thomas Viscount Castlewood and the heirs male of his body, in default of which issue the ranks and dignities were to pass to Francis aforesaid.

This was the paper, whereof my lord had spoken, which Holt showed him the very day he was arrested, and for an answer to which he would come back in a week's time. I put these papers hastily into the crypt whence I had taken them, being interrupted by a tapping of a light finger at the ring of the chamber-door: 'twas my kind mistress, with her face full of love and welcome. She, too, had passed the night wakefully, no doubt; but neither asked the other how the hours had been spent. There are things we divine without speaking, and know though they happen out of our sight. This fond lady hath told me that she knew both days when I was wounded abroad. Who shall say how far sympathy reaches, and how truly love can prophesy ? ' I looked into your room,' was all she said ; ' the bed was vacant, the little old bed ! I knew I should find you here.' And tender and blushing faintly with a benediction in her eyes, the gentle creature kissed him.

They walked out, hand-in-hand, through the old court, and to the terrace-walk, where the grass was glistening with dew, and the birds in the green woods above were singing their delicious choruses under the blushing morning sky. How well all things were remembered ! The ancient towers and gables of the hall darkling against the east, the purple shadows on the green slopes, the quaint devices and carvings of the dial, the forest-crowned heights, the fair yellow plain cheerful with crops and corn, the shining river rolling through it towards the pearly hills beyond ; all these were before us, along with a thousand beautiful memories of our youth, beautiful and sad, but as real and vivid in our minds as that fair and always-remembered scene our eyes beheld once more. We forget nothing. The memory sleeps, but awakens again ; I often think how it shall be when, after the last sleep of death, the réveillé shall arouse us for ever, and the past in one flash of self-consciousness rush back, like the soul, revivified.

The house would not be up for some hours yet (it was July, and the dawn was only just awake), and here Esmond opened himself to his mistress, of the business he had in hand, and what part Frank was to play in it. He knew he could confide anything to her, and that the fond soul would die rather than reveal it ; and bidding her keep the secret from all, he laid it entirely before his mistress (always as stanch a little loyalist as any in the kingdom), and indeed was quite sure that any plan of his was secure of her applause and sympathy. Never was such a glorious scheme to her partial mind, never such a devoted knight to execute it. An hour or two may have passed whilst they were having their colloquy. Beatrix came out to them just as their talk was over ; her tall beautiful form robed in sable (which she wore without ostentation ever since last year's catastrophe), sweeping over the green terrace, and casting its shadows before her across the grass.

She made us one of her grand curtsies smiling, and called

us 'the young people'. She was older, paler, and more majestic than in the year before ; her mother seemed the youngest of the two. She never once spoke of her grief, Lady Castlewood told Esmond, or alluded, save by a quiet word or two, to the death of her hopes.

When Beatrix came back to Castlewood she took to visiting all the cottages and all the sick. She set up a school of children, and taught singing to some of them. We had a pair of beautiful old organs in Castlewood Church, on which she played admirably, so that the music there became to be known in the country for many miles round, and no doubt people came to see the fair organist as well as to hear her. Parson Tusher and his wife were established at the vicarage, but his wife had brought him no children wherewith Tom might meet his enemies at the gate.* Honest Tom took care not to have many such, his great shovel-hat was in his hand for everybody. He was profuse of bows and compliments. He behaved to Esmond as if the colonel had been a commander-in-chief ; he dined at the hall that day, being Sunday, and would not partake of pudding except under extreme pressure. He deplored my lord's perversion, but drank his lordship's health very devoutly ; and an hour before at church sent the colonel to sleep, with a long, learned, and refreshing sermon.

Esmond's visit home was but for two days ; the business he had in hand calling him away and out of the country. Ere he went, he saw Beatrix but once alone, and then she summoned him out of the long tapestry room, where he and his mistress were sitting, quite as in old times, into the adjoining chamber, that had been Viscountess Isabel's sleeping-apartment, and where Esmond perfectly well remembered seeing the old lady sitting up in the bed, in her night-rail, that morning when the troop of guard came to fetch her. The most beautiful woman in England lay in that bed now, whereof the great damask hangings were scarce faded since Esmond saw them last.

Here stood Beatrix in her black robes, holding a box in her hand ; 'twas that which Esmond had given her before her marriage, stamped with a coronet which the disappointed girl was never to wear ; and containing his aunt's legacy of diamonds.

'You had best take these with you, Harry,' says she ; 'I have no need of diamonds any more.' There was not the least token of emotion in her quiet low voice. She held out the black shagreen-case with her fair arm, that did not shake in the least. Esmond saw she wore a black velvet bracelet on it, with my lord duke's picture in enamel; he had given it her but three days before he fell.

Esmond said the stones were his no longer, and strove to turn off that proffered restoration with a laugh: 'Of what good,' says he, 'are they to me? The diamond loop to his hat did not set off Prince Eugene, and will not make my yellow face look any handsomer.'

'You will give them to your wife, cousin,' says she. 'My cousin, your wife has a lovely complexion and shape.'

'Beatrix,' Esmond burst out, the old fire flaming out as it would at times, 'will you wear those trinkets at your marriage? You whispered once you did not know me: you know me better now: how I sought, what I have sighed for, for ten years, what forgone!'

'A price for your constancy, my lord!' says she; 'such a *preux chevalier* wants to be paid. Oh fie, cousin!'

'Again,' Esmond spoke out, 'if I do something you have at heart; something worthy of me and you; something that shall make me a name with which to endow you; will you take it? There was a chance for me once, you said; is it impossible to recall it? Never shake your head, but hear me: say you will hear me a year hence. If I come back to you and bring you fame, will that please you? If I do what you desire most—what he who is dead desired most—will that soften you?'

'What is it, Henry?' says she, her face lighting up; 'what mean you?'

'Ask no questions,' he said, 'wait, and give me but time; if I bring back that you long for, that I have a thousand times heard you pray for, will you have no reward for him who has done you that service? Put away those trinkets, keep them: it shall not be at my marriage, it shall not be at yours, but if man can do it, I swear a day shall come when there shall be a feast in your house, and you shall be proud to wear them. I say no more now; put aside these words, and lock away yonder box until the day when I shall remind you of both. All I pray of you now is, to wait and to remember.'

'You are going out of the country?' says Beatrix, in some agitation.

' Yes, to-morrow,' says Esmond.

' To Lorraine, cousin ? ' says Beatrix, laying her hand on his arm ; 'twas the hand on which she wore the duke's bracelet. ' Stay, Harry ! ' continued she, with a tone that had more despondency in it than she was accustomed to show. ' Hear a last word. I do love you. I do admire you —who would not, that has known such love as yours has been for us all ? But I think I have no heart ; at least, I have never seen the man that could touch it ; and, had I found him, I would have followed him in rags had he been a private soldier, or to sea, like one of those buccaneers you used to read to us about when we were children. I would do anything for such a man, bear anything for him : but I never found one. You were ever too much of a slave to win my heart ; even my lord duke could not command it. I had not been happy had I married him. I knew that three months after our engagement—and was too vain to break it. O Harry ! I cried once or twice, not for him, but with tears of rage because I could not be sorry for him. I was frightened to find I was glad of his death ; and were I joined to you, I should have the same sense of servitude, the same longing to escape. We should both be unhappy, and you the most, who are as jealous as the duke was himself. I tried to love him ; I tried, indeed I did : affected gladness when he came : submitted to hear when he was by me, and tried the wife's part I thought I was to play for the rest of my days. But half an hour of that complaisance wearied me, and what would a lifetime be ? My thoughts were away when he was speaking ; and I was thinking, Oh that this man would drop my hand, and rise up from before my feet ! I knew his great and noble qualities, greater and nobler than mine a thousand times, as yours are, cousin, I tell you, a million and a million times better. But 'twas not for these I took him. I took him to have a great place in the world, and I lost it. I lost it, and do not deplore him—and I often thought, as I listened to his fond vows and ardent words, Oh, if I yield to this man, and meet *the other*, I shall hate him and leave him ! I am not good, Harry : my mother is gentle and good like an angel. I wonder how she should have had such a child. She is weak, but she would die rather than do a wrong ; I am stronger than she, but I would do it out of defiance. I do not care for what the parsons tell me with their droning sermons :

I used to see them at Court as mean and as worthless as the
meanest woman there. Oh, I am sick and weary of the
world ! I wait but for one thing, and when 'tis done, I will
take Frank's religion and your poor mother's, and go into
a nunnery, and end like her. Shall I wear the diamonds
then ?—they say the nuns wear their best trinkets the day
they take the veil. I will put them away as you bid me ;
farewell, cousin, mamma is pacing the next room, racking
her little head to know what we have been saying. She is
jealous, all women are. I sometimes think that is the only
womanly quality I have.'

' Farewell. Farewell, brother ! ' She gave him her cheek
as a brotherly privilege. The cheek was as cold as marble.

Esmond's mistress showed no signs of jealousy when he
returned to the room where she was. She had schooled
herself so as to look quite inscrutably, when she had a mind.
Amongst her other feminine qualities she had that of being
a perfect dissembler.

He rid away from Castlewood to attempt the task he was
bound on, and stand or fall by it ; in truth his state of mind
was such, that he was eager for some outward excitement
to counteract that gnawing malady which he was inwardly
enduring.

CHAPTER VIII

I TRAVEL TO FRANCE AND BRING HOME A PORTRAIT OF RIGAUD

MR. ESMOND did not think fit to take leave at Court, or to
inform all the world of Pall Mall and the coffee-houses, that
he was about to quit England ; and chose to depart in the
most private manner possible. He procured a pass as for
a Frenchman, through Dr. Atterbury, who did that business
for him, getting the signature even from Lord Bolingbroke's
office, without any personal application to the secretary.
Lockwood, his faithful servant, he took with him to Castlewood, and left behind there : giving out ere he left London
that he himself was sick, and gone to Hampshire for
country air, and so departed as silently as might be upon
his business.

As Frank Castlewood's aid was indispensable for Mr.
Esmond's scheme, his first visit was to Bruxelles (passing

by way of Antwerp, where the Duke of Marlborough was in
exile), and in the first-named place Harry found his dear
young Benedict, the married man,* who appeared to be
rather out of humour with his matrimonial chain, and
clogged with the obstinate embraces which Clotilda kept
round his neck. Colonel Esmond was not presented to her ;
but Monsieur Simon was, a gentleman of the Royal Cravat
(Esmond bethought him of the regiment of his honest Irishman, whom he had seen that day after Malplaquet, when
he first set eyes on the young king) ; and Monsieur Simon
was introduced to the Viscountess Castlewood, *née* Comp-
tesse Wertheim ; to the numerous counts, the Lady Clotilda's tall brothers ; to her father the chamberlain ; and
to the lady his wife, Frank's mother-in-law, a tall and
majestic person of large proportions, such as became the
mother of such a company of grenadiers as her warlike sons
formed. The whole race were at free quarters in the
little castle nigh to Bruxelles which Frank had taken ; rode
his horses ; drank his wine ; and lived easily at the poor
lad's charges. Mr. Esmond had always maintained a perfect
fluency in the French, which was his mother tongue ; and
if this family (that spoke French with the twang which the
Flemings use) discovered any inaccuracy in Mr. Simon's
pronunciation, 'twas to be attributed to the latter's long
residence in England, where he had married and remained
ever since he was taken prisoner at Blenheim. His story
was perfectly pat ; there were none there to doubt it save
honest Frank, and he was charmed with his kinsman's
scheme, when he became acquainted with it ; and, in truth,
always admired Colonel Esmond with an affectionate
fidelity, and thought his cousin the wisest and best of all
cousins and men. Frank entered heart and soul into the
plan, and liked it the better as it was to take him to Paris,
out of reach of his brothers, his father, and his mother-in-
law, whose attentions rather fatigued him.

Castlewood, I have said, was born in the same year as
the Prince of Wales ; had not a little of the prince's air,
height, and figure ; and, especially since he had seen the
Chevalier de St. George on the occasion before named,
took no small pride in his resemblance to a person so
illustrious ; which likeness he increased by all the means in
his power, wearing fair brown periwigs, such as the prince
wore, and ribbons, and so forth, of the chevalier's colour.

This resemblance was, in truth, the circumstance on which Mr. Esmond's scheme was founded ; and, having secured Frank's secrecy and enthusiasm, he left him to continue his journey, and see the other personages on whom its success depended. The place whither Mr. Simon next travelled was Bar, in Lorraine, where that merchant arrived with a consignment of broadcloths, valuable laces from Malines, and letters for his correspondent there.

Would you know how a prince, heroic from misfortunes, and descended from a line of kings, whose race seemed to be doomed like the Atridae* of old—would you know how he was employed, when the envoy who came to him through danger and difficulty beheld him for the first time ? The young king, in a flannel jacket, was at tennis with the gentlemen of his suite, crying out after the balls, and swearing like the meanest of his subjects. The next time Mr. Esmond saw him, 'twas when Monsieur Simon took a packet of laces to Miss Oglethorpe ;* the prince's antechamber in those days, at which ignoble door men were forced to knock for admission to his Majesty. The admission was given, the envoy found the king and the mistress together ; the pair were at cards, and his Majesty was in liquor. He cared more for three honours than three kingdoms ; and a half-dozen glasses of ratafia made him forget all his woes and his losses, his father's crown, and his grandfather's head.

Mr. Esmond did not open himself to the prince then. His Majesty was scarce in a condition to hear him ; and he doubted whether a king who drank so much could keep a secret in his fuddled head ; or whether a hand that shook so, was strong enough to grasp at a crown. However at last, and after taking counsel with the prince's advisers, amongst whom were many gentlemen, honest and faithful, Esmond's plan was laid before the king, and her actual Majesty Queen Oglethorpe, in council. The prince liked the scheme well enough ; 'twas easy and daring, and suited to his reckless gaiety and lively youthful spirit. In the morning after he had slept his wine off, he was very gay, lively, and agreeable. His manner had an extreme charm of archness, and a kind simplicity ; and, to do her justice, her Oglethorpean Majesty was kind, acute, resolute, and of good counsel ; she gave the prince much good advice that he was too weak to follow, and loved him with a fidelity which he returned with an ingratitude quite royal.

Having his own forebodings regarding his scheme should it ever be fulfilled, and his usual sceptic doubts as to the benefit which might accrue to the country by bringing a tipsy young monarch back to it, Colonel Esmond had his audience of leave and quiet. Monsieur Simon took his departure. At any rate the youth at Bar was as good as the older Pretender at Hanover ; if the worst came to the worst, the Englishman could be dealt with as easy as the German. Monsieur Simon trotted on that long journey from Nancy to Paris, and saw that famous town, stealthily and like a spy, as in truth he was ; and where, sure, more magnifi cence and more misery is heaped together, more rags and lace, more filth and gilding, than in any city in this world. Here he was put in communication with the king's best friend, his half-brother, the famous Duke of Berwick ; Esmond recognized him as the stranger who had visited Castlewood now near twenty years ago. His grace opened to him when he found that Mr. Esmond was one of Webb's brave regiment, that had once been his grace's own. He was the sword and buckler indeed of the Stuart cause : there was no stain on his shield except the bar across it, which Marlborough's sister left him. Had Berwick been his father's heir, James the Third had assuredly sat on the English throne. He could dare, endure, strike, speak, be silent. The fire and genius, perhaps, he had not (that were given to baser men), but except these he had some of the best qualities of a leader. His grace knew Esmond's father and history ; and hinted at the latter in such a way as made the colonel to think he was aware of the particulars of that story. But Esmond did not choose to enter on it, nor did the duke press him. Mr. Esmond said, ' No doubt he should come by his name if ever greater people came by theirs.'

What confirmed Esmond in his notion that the Duke of Berwick knew of his case was, that when the colonel went to pay his duty at St. Germains, her Majesty once addressed him by the title of Marquis. He took the queen the dutiful remembrances of her goddaughter, and the lady whom, in the days of her prosperity, her Majesty had befriended. The queen remembered Rachel Esmond perfectly well, had heard of my Lord Castlewood's conversion, and was much edified by that act of Heaven in his favour. She knew that others of that family had been of the only true Church too :

' Your father and your mother, *monsieur le marquis*,' her Majesty said (that was the only time she used the phrase). Monsieur Simon bowed very low, and said he had found other parents than his own who had taught him differently ; but these had only one king : on which her Majesty was pleased to give him a medal blessed by the Pope, which had been found very efficacious in cases similar to his own, and to promise she would offer up prayers for his conversion and that of the family : which no doubt this pious lady did, though up to the present moment, and after twenty-seven years, Colonel Esmond is bound to say that neither the medal nor the prayers have had the slightest known effect upon his religious convictions.

As for the splendour of Versailles, Monsieur Simon, the merchant, only beheld them as a humble and distant spectator, seeing the old king but once, when he went to feed his carps ; and asking for no presentation at his Majesty's Court.

By this time my Lord Viscount Castlewood was got to Paris, where, as the London prints presently announced, her ladyship was brought to bed of a son and heir. For a long while afterwards she was in a delicate state of health, and ordered by the physicians not to travel ; otherwise 'twas well known that the Viscount Castlewood proposed returning to England, and taking up his residence at his own seat.

Whilst he remained at Paris, my Lord Castlewood had his picture done by the famous French painter Monsieur Rigaud, a present for his mother in London ; and this piece Monsieur Simon took back with him when he returned to that city, which he reached about May, in the year 1714, very soon after which time my Lady Castlewood and her daughter, and their kinsman, Colonel Esmond, who had been at Castlewood all this time, likewise returned to London ; her ladyship occupying her house at Kensington, Mr. Esmond returning to his lodgings at Knightsbridge, nearer the town, and once more making his appearance at all public places, his health greatly improved by his long stay in the country.

The portrait of my lord, in a handsome gilt frame, was hung up in the place of honour in her ladyship's drawing-room. His lordship was represented in his scarlet uniform of Captain of the Guard, with a light-brown periwig, a cuirass under his coat, a blue ribbon, and a fall of Bruxelles lace. Many of her ladyship's friends admired the piece beyond measure, and flocked to see it ; Bishop Atterbury, Mr. Lesly,* good old Mr. Collier, and others amongst the clergy, were delighted with the performance, and many among the first quality examined and praised it ; only I must own that Dr. Tusher happening to come up to London, and seeing the picture (it was ordinarily covered by a curtain, but on this day Miss Beatrix happened to be looking at it when the doctor arrived), the Vicar of Castlewood vowed he could not see any resemblance in the piece to his old pupil, except perhaps, a little about the chin and the periwig ; but we all of us convinced him, that he had not seen Frank for five years or more ; that he knew no more about the fine arts than a ploughboy, and that he must be mistaken ; and we sent him home assured that the piece was an excellent like-ness. As for my Lord Bolingbroke, who honoured her ladyship with a visit occasionally, when Colonel Esmond showed him the picture he burst out laughing, and asked what devilry he was engaged on ? Esmond owned simply that the portrait was not that of Viscount Castlewood, besought the secretary on his honour to keep the secret, said that the ladies of the house were enthusiastic Jacobites, as was well known ; and confessed that the picture was that of the Chevalier St. George.

The truth is, that Mr. Simon, waiting upon Lord Castle-wood one day at Monsieur Rigaud's, whilst his lordship was sitting for his picture, affected to be much struck with a piece representing the chevalier, whereof the head only was finished, and purchased it of the painter for a hundred crowns. It had been intended, the artist said, for Miss Oglethorpe, the prince's mistress, but that young lady quitting Paris, had left the work on the artist's hands ; and taking this piece home, when my lord's portrait arrived, Colonel Esmond, alias Monsieur Simon, had copied the uniform and other accessories from my lord's picture to fill up Rigaud's incomplete canvas : the colonel all his life having been a practitioner of painting, and especially followed it during his long residence in the cities of Flanders, among the masterpieces of Vandyck and Rubens. My grandson hath the piece, such as it is, in Virginia now.

At the commencement of the month of June, Miss Beatrix Esmond, and my lady viscountess, her mother, arrived from Castlewood; the former to resume her service at Court, which had been interrupted by the fatal catastrophe of Duke Hamilton's death. She once more took her place, then, in her Majesty's suite and at the maids' table, being always a favourite with Mrs. Masham, the queen's chief woman, partly perhaps on account of her bitterness against the Duchess of Marlborough, whom Miss Beatrix loved no better than her rival did. The gentlemen about the Court, my Lord Bolingbroke amongst others, owned that the young lady had come back handsomer than ever, and that the serious and tragic air, which her face now involuntarily wore, became her better than her former smiles and archness.

All the old domestics at the little house of Kensington Square were changed; the old steward that had served the family any time these five-and-twenty years, since the birth of the children of the house, was dispatched into the kingdom of Ireland to see my lord's estate there: the housekeeper, who had been my lady's woman time out of mind, and the attendant of the young children, was sent away grumbling to Walcote, to see to the new painting and preparing of that house, which my lady dowager intended to occupy for the future, giving up Castlewood to her daughter-in-law, that might be expected daily from France. Another servant the viscountess had was dismissed too—with a gratuity—on the pretext that her ladyship's train of domestics must be diminished; so, finally, there was not left in the household a single person who had belonged to it during the time my young Lord Castlewood was yet at home.

For the plan which Colonel Esmond had in view, and the stroke he intended, 'twas necessary that the very smallest number of persons should be put in possession of his secret. It scarce was known, except to three or four out of his family, and it was kept to a wonder.

On the 10th of June, 1714, there came by Mr. Prior's messenger from Paris, a letter from my Lord Viscount Castlewood to his mother, saying that he had been foolish in regard of money matters, that he was ashamed to own he had lost at play, and by other extravagances; and that instead of having great entertainments as he had hoped at Castlewood this year, he must live as quiet as he could, and make every effort to be saving. So far every word of poor Frank's letter was true, nor was there a doubt that he and his tall brothers-in-law had spent a great deal more than they ought, and engaged the revenues of the Castle-wood property, which the fond mother had husbanded and improved so carefully during the time of her guardianship.

His ' Clotilda ', Castlewood went on to say, ' was still delicate, and the physicians thought her lying-in had best take place at Paris. He should come without her ladyship, and be at his mother's house about the 17th or 18th day of June, proposing to take horse from Paris immediately, and bringing but a single servant with him ; and he requested that the lawyers of Gray's Inn might be invited to meet him with their account, and the land-steward come from Castlewood with his, so that he might settle with them speedily, raise a sum of money whereof he stood in need, and be back to his viscountess by the time of her lying-in.' Then his lordship gave some of the news of the town, sent his remembrance to kinsfolk, and so the letter ended. 'Twas put in the common post, and no doubt the French police and the English there had a copy of it, to which they were exceeding welcome.

Two days after another letter was dispatched by the public post of France, in the same open way, and this, after giving news of the fashion at Court there, ended by the following sentences, in which, but for those that had the key, 'twould be difficult for any man to find any secret lurked at all :—

(The king will take) medicine on Thursday. His Majesty is better than he hath been of late, though incommoded by indigestion from his too great appetite. Madame Maintenon continues well. They have performed a play of Mons. Racine at St. Cyr. The Duke of Shrewsbury and Mr. Prior, our envoy, and all the English nobility here were present at it. (The Viscount Castlewood's pass-ports) were refused to him, 'twas said ; his lordship being sued by a goldsmith for *Vaisselle plate,* and a pearl necklace supplied to Mademoiselle Meruel of the French Comedy. 'Tis a pity such news should get abroad (and travel to England) about our young nobility here. Mademoiselle Meruel has been sent to the Fort l'Evesque ; they say she has ordered not only plate, but furniture, and a chariot and horses (under that lord's name), of which extrava-gance his unfortunate viscountess knows nothing.

(His majesty will be) eighty-two years of age on his next birth-day. The Court prepares to celebrate it with a great feast. Mr. Prior is in a sad way about their refusing at home to send him his plate. All here admired my lord viscount's portrait, and said it was a masterpiece of Rigaud. Have you seen it ? It is (at the Lady

Castlewood's house in Kensington Square).   I think no English painter could produce such a piece.

Our poor friend the abbé hath been at the Bastille, but is now transported to the Conciergerie (where his friends may visit him. They are to ask for) a remission of his sentence soon.   Let us hope the poor rogue will have repented in prison.

(The Lord Castlewood) has had the affair of the plate made up, and departs for England.

Is not this a dull letter ? I have a cursed headache with drinking with Mat and some more overnight, and tipsy or sober am

Thine ever ——.

All this letter, save some dozen of words which I have put above between brackets, was mere idle talk, though the substance of the letter was as important as any letter well could be.   It told those that had the key, that *the king will take the Viscount Castlewood's passports and travel to England under that lord's name.   His Majesty will be at the Lady Castlewood's house in Kensington Square, where his friends may visit him ; they are to ask for the Lord Castlewood*.   This note may have passed under Mr. Prior's eyes, and those of our new allies the French, and taught them nothing ; though it explains sufficiently to persons in London what the event was which was about to happen, as 'twill show those who read my memoirs a hundred years hence, what was that errand on which Colonel Esmond of late had been busy.   Silently and swiftly to do that about which others were conspiring, and thousands of Jacobites all over the country, clumsily caballing ; alone to effect that which the leaders here were only talking about ; to bring the Prince of Wales into the country openly in the face of all, under Bolingbroke's very eyes, the walls placarded with the proclamation signed with the secretary's name, and offering five hundred pounds reward for his apprehension : this was a stroke, the playing and winning of which might well give any adventurous spirit pleasure : the loss of the stake might involve a heavy penalty, but all our family were eager to risk that for the glorious chance of winning the game.

Nor should it be called a game, save perhaps with the chief player, who was not more or less sceptical than most public men with whom he had acquaintance in that age. (Is there ever a public man in England that altogether believes in his party ? Is there one, however doubtful, that will not fight for it ?) Young Frank was ready to

fight without much thinking, he was a Jacobite as his
father before him was ; all the Esmonds were Royalists.
Give him but the word, he would cry, ' God save King
James ! ' before the palace guard, or at the Maypole in
the Strand ; and with respect to the women, as is usual
with them, 'twas not a question of party but of faith ;
their belief was a passion ; either Esmond's mistress or
her daughter would have died for it cheerfully. I have
laughed often, talking of King William's reign, and said
I thought Lady Castlewood was disappointed the king
did not persecute the family more ; and those who know
the nature of women may fancy for themselves, what
needs not here be written down, the rapture with which
these neophytes received the mystery when made known
to them ; the eagerness with which they looked forward to
its completion ; the reverence which they paid the minister
who initiated them into that secret Truth, now known
only to a few, but presently to reign over the world. Sure
there is no bound to the trustingness of women. Look at
Arria worshipping the drunken clodpate of a husband who
beats her ; look at Cornelia treasuring as a jewel in her
maternal heart the oaf her son ;* I have known a woman
preach Jesuit's bark, and afterwards Dr. Berkeley's tar-
water,* as though to swallow them were a divine decree,
and to refuse them no better than blasphemy.

On his return from France Colonel Esmond put himself
at the head of this little knot of fond conspirators. No
death or torture he knew would frighten them out of their
constancy. When he detailed his plan for bringing the
king back, his elder mistress thought that that restoration
was to be attributed under Heaven to the Castlewood
family and to its chief, and she worshipped and loved
Esmond, if that could be, more than ever she had done.
She doubted not for one moment of the success of his
scheme, to mistrust which would have seemed impious in
her eyes. And as for Beatrix, when she became acquainted
with the plan, and joined it, as she did with all her heart,
she gave Esmond one of her searching bright looks : ' Ah,
Harry,' says she, ' why were you not the head of our house ?
You are the only one fit to raise it ; why do you give
that silly boy the name and the honour ? But 'tis so in
the world ; those get the prize that don't deserve or care
for it. I wish I could give you *your* silly prize, cousin,

but I can't ; I have tried and I can't.'   And she went away, shaking her head mournfully, but always, it seemed to Esmond, that her liking and respect for him was greatly increased, since she knew what capability he had both to act and bear ; to do and to forgo.

CHAPTER ·IX

THE ORIGINAL OF THE PORTRAIT COMES TO ENGLAND*

'TWAS announced in the family that my Lord Castlewood would arrive, having a confidential French gentleman in his suite, who acted as secretary to his lordship, and who being a Papist, and a foreigner of a good family, though now in rather a menial place, would have his meals served in his chamber, and not with the domestics of the house. The viscountess gave up her bedchamber contiguous to her daughter's, and having a large convenient closet attached to it, in which a bed was put up, ostensibly for Monsieur Baptiste, the Frenchman ; though, 'tis needless to say, when the doors of the apartments were locked, and the two guests retired within it, the young viscount became the servant of the illustrious prince whom he entertained, and gave up gladly the more convenient and airy chamber and bed to his master.   Madam Beatrix also retired to the upper region, her chamber being converted into a sitting-room for my lord.   The better to carry the deceit, Beatrix affected to grumble before the servants, and to be jealous that she was turned out of her chamber to make way for my lord.

No small preparations were made, you may be sure, and no slight tremor of expectation caused the hearts of the gentle ladies of Castlewood to flutter, before the arrival of the personages who were about to honour their house. The chamber was ornamented with flowers ;   the bed covered with the very finest of linen ; the two ladies insisting on making it themselves, and kneeling down at the bedside and kissing the sheets out of respect for the web that was to hold the sacred person of a king.   The toilet was of silver and crystal ;   there was a copy of *Eikon Basilike** laid on the writing-table ;   a portrait of the martyred king hung always over the mantel, having a sword of my poor Lord Castlewood underneath it, and a little picture or emblem which the widow loved always to have before her eyes on waking, and in which the hair of her lord and her two children was worked together. Her books of private devotions, as they were all of the English Church, she carried away with her to the upper apartment which she destined for herself. The ladies showed Mr. Esmond, when they were completed, the fond preparations they had made. 'Twas then Beatrix knelt down and kissed the linen sheets. As for her mother, Lady Castlewood made a curtsy at the door, as she would have done to the altar on entering a church, and owned that she considered the chamber in a manner sacred.

The company in the servants' hall never for a moment supposed that these preparations were made for any other person than the young viscount, the lord of the house, whom his fond mother had been for so many years without seeing. Both ladies were perfect housewives, having the greatest skill in the making of confections, scented waters, &c., and keeping a notable superintendence over the kitchen. Calves enough were killed to feed an army of prodigal sons, Esmond thought, and laughed when he came to wait on the ladies, on the day when the guests were to arrive, to find two pairs of the finest and roundest arms to be seen in England (my Lady Castlewood was remarkable for this beauty of her person), covered with flour up above the elbows, and preparing paste, and turning rolling-pins in the housekeeper's closet. The guest would not arrive till supper-time, and my lord would prefer having that meal in his own chamber. You may be sure the brightest plate of the house was laid out there, and can understand why it was that the ladies insisted that they alone would wait upon the young chief of the family.

Taking horse, Colonel Esmond rode rapidly to Rochester, and there awaited the king in that very town where his father had last set his foot on the English shore. A room had been provided at an inn there for my Lord Castlewood and his servant; and Colonel Esmond timed his ride so well that he had scarce been half an hour in the place, and was looking over the balcony into the yard of the inn, when two travellers rode in at the inn-gate, and the colonel running down, the next moment embraced his dear young lord.

My lord's companion, acting the part of a domestic, dismounted, and was for holding the viscount's stirrup ; but Colonel Esmond, calling to his own man, who was in the court, bade him take the horses and settle with the lad who had ridden the post along with the two travellers, crying out in a cavalier tone in the French language to my lord's companion, and affecting to grumble that my lord's fellow was a Frenchman, and did not know the money or habits of the country :—' My man will see to the horses, Baptiste,' says Colonel Esmond : ' do you understand English ? ' ' Very leetle.' ' So, follow my lord and wait upon him at dinner in his own room.' The landlord and his people came up presently bearing the dishes ; 'twas well they made a noise and stir in the gallery, or they might have found Colonel Esmond on his knee before Lord Castlewood's servant, welcoming his Majesty to his kingdom, and kissing the hand of the king. We told the landlord that the Frenchman would wait on his master ; and Esmond's man was ordered to keep sentry in the gallery without the door. The prince dined with a good appetite, laughing and talking very gaily, and condescendingly bidding his two companions to sit with him at table. He was in better spirits than poor Frank Castlewood, who Esmond thought might be wobegone on account of parting with his divine Clotilda ; but the prince wishing to take a short siesta after dinner, and retiring to an inner chamber where there was a bed, the cause of poor Frank's discomfiture came out ; and bursting into tears, with many expressions of fondness, friendship, and humiliation, the faithful lad gave his kinsman to understand that he now knew all the truth, and the sacrifices which Colonel Esmond had made for him.

Seeing no good in acquainting poor Frank with that secret, Mr. Esmond had entreated his mistress also not to reveal it to her son. The prince had told the poor lad all as they were riding from Dover : ' I had as lief he had shot me, cousin,' Frank said : ' I knew you were the best and the bravest, and the kindest of all men ' (so the enthusiastic young fellow went on) ; ' but I never thought I owed you what I do, and can scarce bear the weight of the obligation.'

' I stand in the place of your father,' says Mr. Esmond kindly, ' and sure a father may dispossess himself in favour of his son. I abdicate the twopenny crown, and invest you with the kingdom of Brentford ;* don't be a fool and cry ; you make a much taller and handsomer viscount than ever I could.' But the fond boy with oaths and protestations, laughter and incoherent outbreaks of passionate emotion, could not be got, for some little time, to put up with Esmond's raillery ; wanted to kneel down to him, and kissed his hand ; asked him and implored him to order something, to bid Castlewood give his own life up or take somebody else's ; anything, so that he might show his gratitude for the generosity Esmond showed him.

'The k——, *he* laughed,' Frank said, pointing to the door where the sleeper was, and speaking in a low tone, 'I don't think he should have laughed as he told me the story. As we rode along from Dover, talking in French, he spoke about you, and your coming to him at Bar ; he called you "*le grand sérieux*", Don Bellianis of Greece,* and I don't know what names ; mimicking your manner' (here Castlewood laughed himself)—'and he did it very well. He seems to sneer at everything. He is not like a king : somehow, Harry, I fancy you are like a king. He does not seem to think what a stake we are all playing. He would have stopped at Canterbury to run after a barmaid there, had I not implored him to come on. He hath a house at Chaillot where he used to go and bury himself for weeks away from the queen, and with all sorts of bad company,' says Frank, with a demure look ; 'you may smile, but I am not the wild fellow I was ; no, no, I have been taught better,' says Castlewood devoutly, making a sign on his breast.

'Thou art my dear brave boy,' says Colonel Esmond, touched at the young fellow's simplicity, 'and there will be a noble gentleman at Castlewood so long as my Frank is there.'

The impetuous young lad was for going down on his knees again, with another explosion of gratitude, but that we heard the voice from the next chamber of the august sleeper, just waking, calling out :—' Eh, *La-Fleur, un verre d'eau* ' ; his Majesty came out yawning :—' A pest,' says he, ' upon your English ale ; 'tis so strong that, *ma foi*, it hath turned my head.'

The effect of the ale was like a spur upon our horses, and we rode very quickly to London, reaching Kensington at nightfall. Mr. Esmond's servant was left behind at

Rochester, to take care of the tired horses, whilst we had fresh beasts provided along the road. And galloping by the prince's side the colonel explained to the Prince of Wales what his movements had been ; who the friends were that knew of the expedition ; whom, as Esmond conceived, the prince should trust ; entreating him, above all, to maintain the very closest secrecy until the time should come when his royal highness should appear. The town swarmed with friends of the prince's cause ; there were scores of correspondents with St. Germains ; Jacobites known and secret ; great in station and humble ; about the Court and the queen ; in the Parliament, Church, and among the merchants in the City. The prince had friends numberless in the army, in the Privy Council, and the officers of state. The great object, as it seemed, to the small band of persons who had concerted that bold stroke, who had brought the queen's brother into his native country, was, that his visit should remain unknown till the proper time came, when his presence should surprise friends and enemies alike ; and the latter should be found so unprepared and disunited, that they should not find time to attack him. We feared more from his friends than from his enemies. The lies, and tittle-tattle sent over to St. Germains by the Jacobite agents about London, had done an incalculable mischief to his cause, and wofully misguided him, and it was from these especially, that the persons engaged in the present venture were anxious to defend the chief actor in it.[1]

The party reached London by nightfall, leaving their horses at the Posting-House over against Westminster, and being ferried over the water where Lady Esmond's coach was already in waiting. In another hour we were all landed at Kensington, and the mistress of the house had that satisfaction which her heart had yearned after for many years, once more to embrace her son, who on his side, with all his waywardness, ever retained a most tender affection for his parent.

[1] The managers were the bishop, who cannot be hurt by having his name mentioned, a very active and loyal Nonconformist divine, a lady in the highest favour at Court, with whom Beatrix Esmond had communication, and two noblemen of the greatest rank, and a Member of the House of Commons, who was implicated in more transactions than one in behalf of the Stuart family. ·

She did not refrain from this expression of her feeling, though the domestics were by, and my Lord Castlewood's attendant stood in the hall. Esmond had to whisper to him in French to take his hat off. Monsieur Baptiste was constantly neglecting his part with an inconceivable levity : more than once on the ride to London, little observations of the stranger, light remarks, and words betokening the greatest ignorance of the country the prince came to govern, had hurt the susceptibility of the two gentlemen forming his escort ; nor could either help owning in his secret mind that they would have had his behaviour otherwise, and that the laughter and the lightness, not to say licence, which characterized his talk, scarce befitted such a great prince, and such a solemn occasion. Not but that he could act at proper times with spirit and dignity. He had behaved, as we all knew, in a very courageous manner on the field. Esmond had seen a copy of the letter the prince writ with his own hand when urged by his friends in England to abjure his religion, and admired that manly and magnanimous reply by which he refused to yield to the temptation. Monsieur Baptiste took off his hat, blushing at the hint Colonel Esmond ventured to give him, and said :—' *Tenez, elle est jolie, la petite mère ; Foi-de-Chevalier ! elle est charmante ; mais l'autre, qui est cette nymphe, cet astre qui brille, cette Diane qui descend sur nous ?* ' And he started back, and pushed forward, as Beatrix was descending the stair. She was in colours for the first time at her own house ; she wore the diamonds Esmond gave her ; it had been agreed between them, that she should wear these brilliants on the day when the king should enter the house, and a queen she looked, radiant in charms, and magnificent and imperial in beauty.

Castlewood himself was startled by that beauty and splendour ; he stepped back and gazed at his sister as though he had not been aware before (nor was he, very likely) how perfectly lovely she was, and I thought blushed as he embraced her. The prince could not keep his eyes off her ; he quite forgot his menial part, though he had been schooled to it, and a little light portmanteau prepared expressly that he should carry it. He pressed forward before my lord viscount. 'Twas lucky the servants' eyes were busy in other directions, or they must have seen that this was no servant, or at least a very insolent and rude one.

Again Colonel Esmond was obliged to cry out, 'Baptiste', in a loud imperious voice, 'have a care to the valise'; at which hint the wilful young man ground his teeth together with something very like a curse between them, and then gave a brief look of anything but pleasure to his Mentor. Being reminded, however, he shouldered the little portmanteau, and carried it up the stair, Esmond preceding him, and a servant with lighted tapers. He flung down his burden sulkily in the bedchamber :—'A prince that will wear a crown must wear a mask,' says Mr. Esmond, in French.

'*Ah, peste !* I see how it is,' says Monsieur Baptiste, continuing the talk in French. 'The Great Serious is seriously '—' alarmed for Monsieur Baptiste,' broke in the colonel. Esmond neither liked the tone with which the prince spoke of the ladies, nor the eyes with which he regarded them.

The bedchamber and the two rooms adjoining it, the closet and the apartment which was to be called my lord's parlour, were already lighted and awaiting their occupier ; and the collation laid for my lord's supper. Lord Castlewood and his mother and sister came up the stair a minute afterwards, and, so soon as the domestics had quitted the apartment, Castlewood and Esmond uncovered, and the two ladies went down on their knees before the prince, who graciously gave a hand to each. He looked his part of prince much more naturally than that of servant, which he had just been trying, and raised them both with a great deal of nobility, as well as kindness in his air. 'Madam,' says he, 'my mother will thank your ladyship for your hospitality to her son ; for you, madam,' turning to Beatrix, 'I cannot bear to see so much beauty in such a posture. You will betray Monsieur Baptiste if you kneel to him ; sure 'tis his place rather to kneel to you.'

A light shone out of her eyes ; a gleam bright enough to kindle passion in any breast. There were times when this creature was so handsome, that she seemed, as it were, like Venus revealing herself a goddess in a flash of brightness. She appeared so now ; radiant, and with eyes bright with a wonderful lustre. A pang, as of rage and jealousy, shot through Esmond's heart, as he caught the look she gave the prince ; and he clenched his hand involuntarily and looked across to Castlewood, whose eyes answered his

alarm-signal, and were also on the alert. The prince gave
his subjects an audience of a few minutes, and then the two
ladies and Colonel Esmond quitted the chamber. Lady
Castlewood pressed his hand as they descended the stair,
and the three went down to the lower rooms, where they
waited awhile till the travellers above should be refreshed
and ready for their meal.

Esmond looked at Beatrix, blazing with her jewels on
her beautiful neck. ' I have kept my word,' says he :
' And I mine,' says Beatrix, looking down on the diamonds.

' Were I the Mogul emperor,' says the colonel, ' you
should have all that were dug out of Golconda.'

' These are a great deal too good for me,' says Beatrix,
dropping her head on her beautiful breast,—' so are you
all, all : ' and when she looked up again, as she did in a
moment, and after a sigh, her eyes, as they gazed at her
cousin, wore that melancholy and inscrutable look which
'twas always impossible to sound.

When the time came for the supper, of which we were
advertised by a knocking overhead, Colonel Esmond and
the two ladies went to the upper apartment, where the prince
already was, and by his side the young viscount, of exactly
the same age, shape, and with features not dissimilar,
though Frank's were the handsomer of the two. The
prince sat down, and bade the ladies sit. The gentlemen
remained standing ; there was, indeed, but one more cover
laid at the table :—' Which of you will take it ? ' says he.

' The head of our house,' says Lady Castlewood, taking
her son's hand, and looking towards Colonel Esmond with
a bow and a great tremor of the voice ; ' the Marquis of
Esmond will have the honour of serving the king.'

' I shall have the honour of waiting on his royal highness,'
says Colonel Esmond, filling a cup of wine, and, as the fashion
of that day was, he presented it to the king on his knee.

' I drink to my hostess and her family,' says the prince,
with no very well-pleased air ; but the cloud passed immediately off his face, and he talked to the ladies in a lively,
rattling strain, quite undisturbed by poor Mr. Esmond's
yellow countenance, that I dare say looked very glum.

When the time came to take leave, Esmond marched
homewards to his lodgings, and met Mr. Addison on the
road that night, walking to a cottage he had at Fulham,
the moon shining on his handsome serene face :—' What

cheer, brother?' says Addison, laughing; I thought it
was a footpad advancing in the dark, and behold 'tis an
old friend. We may shake hands, colonel, in the dark,
'tis better than fighting by daylight. Why should we
quarrel, because I am a Whig and thou art a Tory? Turn
thy steps and walk with me to Fulham, where there is
a nightingale still singing in the garden, and a cool bottle
in a cave I know of; you shall drink to the Pretender if
you like, and I will drink my liquor my own way: I have
had enough of good liquor?—no, never! There is no such
word as enough as a stopper for good wine. Thou wilt
not come? Come any day, come soon. You know I remember *Simois* and the *Sigeia tellus*, and the *praelia mixta mero,
mixta mero*,'* he repeated, with ever so slight a touch of
merum in his voice, and walked back a little way on the
road with Esmond, bidding the other remember he was
always his friend, and indebted to him for his aid in the
Campaign poem. And very likely Mr. Under Secretary
would have stepped in and taken t'other bottle at the
colonel's lodgings, had the latter invited him, but Esmond's
mood was none of the gayest, and he bade his friend an
inhospitable good-night at the door.

'I have done the deed,' thought he, sleepless, and looking
out into the night; 'he is here, and I have brought him;
he and Beatrix are sleeping under the same roof now.
Whom did I mean to serve in bringing him? Was it the
prince, was it Henry Esmond? Had I not best have
joined the manly creed of Addison yonder, that scouts the
old doctrine of right divine, that boldly declares that
Parliament and people consecrate the sovereign, not bishops,
nor genealogies, nor oils, nor coronations.' The eager gaze
of the young prince, watching every movement of Beatrix,
haunted Esmond and pursued him. The prince's figure
appeared before him in his feverish dreams many times
that night. He wished the deed undone, for which he had
laboured so. He was not the first that has regretted his
own act, or brought about his own undoing. Undoing?
Should he write that word in his late years? No, on his
knees before Heaven, rather be thankful for what then he
deemed his misfortune, and which hath caused the whole
subsequent happiness of his life.

Esmond's man, honest John Lockwood, had served his
master and the family all his life, and the colonel knew that

he could answer for John's fidelity as for his own. John returned with the horses from Rochester betimes the next morning, and the colonel gave him to understand that on going to Kensington, where he was free of the servants' hall, and indeed courting Mrs. Beatrix's maid, he was to ask no questions, and betray no surprise, but to vouch stoutly that the young gentleman he should see in a red coat there was my Lord Viscount Castlewood, and that his attendant in grey was Monsieur Baptiste the Frenchman. He was to tell his friends in the kitchen such stories as he remembered of my lord viscount's youth at Castlewood ; what a wild boy he was ; how he used to drill Jack and cane him, before ever he was a soldier; everything, in fine, he knew respecting my lord viscount's early days. Jack's ideas of painting had not been much cultivated during his residence in Flanders with his master ; and, before my young lord's return, he had been easily got to believe that the picture brought over from Paris, and now hanging in Lady Castlewood's drawing-room, was a perfect likeness of her son, the young lord. And the domestics having all seen the picture many times, and catching but a momentary imperfect glimpse of the two strangers on the night of their arrival, never had a reason to doubt the fidelity of the portrait ; and next day, when they saw the original of the piece habited exactly as he was represented in the painting, with the same periwig, ribbon, and uniform of the Guard, quite naturally addressed the gentleman as my Lord Castlewood, my lady viscountess's son.

The secretary of the night previous was now the viscount ; the viscount wore the secretary's grey frock ; and John Lockwood was instructed to hint to the world below stairs that my lord being a Papist, and very devout in that religion, his attendant might be no other than his chaplain from Bruxelles ; hence, if he took his meals in my lord's company there was little reason for surprise. Frank was further cautioned to speak English with a foreign accent, which task he performed indifferently well, and this caution was the more necessary because the prince himself scarce spoke our language like a native of the island ; and John Lockwood laughed with the folks below stairs at the manner in which my lord, after five years abroad, sometimes forgot his own tongue and spoke it like a Frenchman. ' I warrant,' says he, ' that with the English beef and beer, his lordship will

soon get back the proper use of his mouth ; ' and, to do his
new lordship justice, he took to beer and beef very kindly.

The prince drank so much, and was so loud and imprudent
in his talk after his drink, that Esmond often trembled for
him. His meals were served as much as possible in his own
chamber, though frequently he made his appearance in
Lady Castlewood's parlour and drawing-room, calling
Beatrix ' sister ', and her ladyship ' mother ', or 'madam ',
before the servants. And, choosing to act entirely up to
the part of brother and son, the prince sometimes saluted
Mrs. Beatrix and Lady Castlewood with a freedom which
his secretary did not like, and which, for his part, set
Colonel Esmond tearing with rage.

The guests had not been three days in the house when
poor Jack Lockwood came with a rueful countenance to
his master, and said : ' My lord, that is—the gentleman,
has been tampering with Mrs. Lucy' (Jack's sweetheart),
' and given her guineas and a kiss.' I fear that Colonel
Esmond's mind was rather relieved than otherwise, when
he found that the ancillary beauty was the one whom the
prince had selected. His royal tastes were known to lie
that way, and continued so in after-life. The heir of one
of the greatest names, of the greatest kingdoms, and of
the greatest misfortunes in Europe, was often content to
lay the dignity of his birth and grief at the wooden shoes
of a French chambermaid, and to repent afterwards (for
he was very devout) in ashes taken from the dustpan. 'Tis
for mortals such as these that nations suffer, that parties
struggle, that warriors fight and bleed. A year afterwards
gallant heads were falling, and Nithsdale in escape, and
Derwentwater on the scaffold ;* whilst the heedless ingrate,
for whom they risked and lost all, was tippling with his
seraglio of mistresses in his *petite maison* of Chaillot.

Blushing to be forced to bear such an errand, Esmond
had to go to the prince and warn him that the girl whom
his highness was bribing, was John Lockwood's sweetheart,
an honest resolute man, who had served in six campaigns,
and feared nothing, and who knew that the person, calling
himself Lord Castlewood, was not his young master : and
the colonel besought the prince to consider what the effect
of a single man's jealousy might be, and to think of other
designs he had in hand, more important than the seduction
of a waiting-maid, and the humiliation of a brave man.

Ten times, perhaps, in the course of as many days, Mr. Esmond had to warn the royal young adventurer of some imprudence or some freedom. He received these remonstrances very testily, save perhaps in this affair of poor Lockwood's, when he deigned to burst out a-laughing, and said, ' What ! the *soubrette* has peached to the *amoureux*, and Crispin* is angry, and Crispin has served, and Crispin has been a corporal, has he ? Tell him we will reward his valour with a pair of colours, and recompense his fidelity.'

Colonel Esmond ventured to utter some other words of entreaty, but the prince, stamping imperiously, cried out, ' *Assez, milord : je m'ennuye à la prêche ;* I am not come to London to go to the sermon.' And he complained afterwards to Castlewood, that ' *le petit jaune, le noir colonel, le Marquis Misanthrope* ' (by which facetious names his royal highness was pleased to designate Colonel Esmond), ' fatigued him with his grand airs and virtuous homilies.'

The Bishop of Rochester, and other gentlemen engaged in the transaction which had brought the prince over, waited upon his royal highness, constantly asking for my Lord Castlewood on their arrival at Kensington, and being openly conducted to his royal highness in that character, who received them either in my lady's drawing-room below, or above in his own apartment ; and all implored him to quit the house as little as possible, and to wait there till the signal should be given for him to appear. The ladies entertained him at cards, over which amusement he spent many hours in each day and night. He passed many hours more in drinking, during which time he would rattle and talk very agreeably, and especially if the colonel was absent, whose presence always seemed to frighten him ; and the poor ' *Colonel Noir* ' took that hint as a command accordingly, and seldom intruded his black face upon the convivial hours of this august young prisoner. Except for those few persons of whom the porter had the list, Lord Castlewood was denied to all friends of the house who waited on his lordship. The wound he had received had broke out again from his journey on horseback, so the world and the domestics were informed. And Doctor A——,[1] his physician (I shall not mention his name, but he was physician to the Queen of the Scots nation, and a man remarkable

[1] There can be very little doubt that the doctor, mentioned by my dear father, was the famous Dr. Arbuthnot.—R. E. W.

for his benevolence as well as his wit), gave orders that he should be kept perfectly quiet until the wound should heal. With this gentleman, who was one of the most active and influential of our party, and the others before spoken of, the whole secret lay ; and it was kept with so much faithfulness, and the story we told so simple and natural, that there was no likelihood of a discovery except from the imprudence of the prince himself, and an adventurous levity that we had the greatest difficulty to control.   As for Lady Castlewood, although she scarce spoke a word, 'twas easy to gather from her demeanour, and one or two hints she dropped, how deep her mortification was at finding the hero whom she had chosen to worship all her life (and whose restoration had formed almost the most sacred part of her prayers), no more than a man, and not a good one.   She thought misfortune might have chastened him ; but that instructress had rather rendered him callous than humble. His devotion, which was quite real, kept him from no sin he had a mind to.   His talk showed good-humour, gaiety, even wit enough ; but there was a levity in his acts and words that he had brought from among those libertine devotees with whom he had been bred, and that shocked the simplicity and purity of the English lady, whose guest he was.   Esmond spoke his mind to Beatrix pretty freely about the prince, getting her brother to put in a word of warning. Beatrix was entirely of their opinion ; she thought he was very light, very light and reckless ; she could not even see the good looks Colonel Esmond had spoken of. The prince had bad teeth, and a decided squint. How could we say he did not squint ? His eyes were fine, but there was certainly a cast in them. She rallied him at table with wonderful wit ; she spoke of him invariably as of a mere boy ; she was more fond of Esmond than ever, praised him to her brother, praised him to the prince, when his royal highness was pleased to sneer at the colonel, and warmly espoused his cause : ' And if your Majesty does not give him the Garter his father had, when the Marquis of Esmond comes to your Majesty's Court, I will hang myself in my own garters, or will cry my eyes out.' ' Rather than lose those,' says the prince, ' he shall be made archbishop and colonel of the Guard ' (it was Frank Castlewood who told me of this conversation over their supper).

' Yes,' cries she, with one of her laughs,—(I fancy I hear

it now; thirty years afterwards I hear that delightful music)—'yes, he shall be Archbishop of Esmond and Marquis of Canterbury.'

'And what will your ladyship be ?' says the prince; 'you have but to choose your place.'

'I,' says Beatrix, ' will be mother of the maids to the queen of his Majesty King James the Third—*Vive le Roy !* ' and she made him a great curtsy, and drank a part of a glass of wine in his honour.

'The prince seized hold of the glass and drank the last drop of it,' Castlewood said, ' and my mother, looking very anxious, rose up and asked leave to retire. But that 'Trix is my mother's daughter, Harry,' Frank continued, 'I don't know what a horrid fear I should have of her. I wish— I wish this business were over. You are older than I am, and wiser, and better, and I owe you everything, and would die for you—before George I would ; but I wish the end of this were come.'

Neither of us very likely passed a tranquil night ; horrible doubts and torments racked Esmond's soul ; 'twas a scheme of personal ambition, a daring stroke for a selfish end—he knew it. What cared he, in his heart, who was king ? Were not his very sympathies and secret convictions on the other side—on the side of People, Parliament, Freedom ? And here was he, engaged for a prince, that had scarce heard the word 'liberty'; that priests and women, tyrants by nature both, made a tool of. The misanthrope was in no better humour after hearing that story, and his grim face more black and yellow than ever.

CHAPTER X

WE ENTERTAIN A VERY DISTINGUISHED GUEST AT KENSINGTON

SHOULD any clue be found to the dark intrigues at the latter end of Queen Anne's time, or any historian be inclined to follow it, 'twill be discovered, I have little doubt, that not one of the great personages about the queen had a defined scheme of policy, independent of that private and selfish interest which each was bent on pursuing ; St. John was for St. John, and Harley for Oxford, and Marlborough for John Churchill, always ; and according

as they could get help from St. Germains or Hanover, they
sent over proffers of allegiance to the princes there, or
betrayed one to the other : one cause, or one sovereign,
was as good as another to them, so that they could hold
the best place under him ; and like Lockit and Peachem,
the Newgate chiefs in the *Rogues' Opera** Mr. Gay wrote
afterwards, had each in his hand documents and proofs
of treason which would hang the other, only he did not
dare to use the weapon, for fear of that one which his
neighbour also carried in his pocket. Think of the great
Marlborough, the greatest subject in all the world, a conqueror of princes, that had marched victorious over Germany,
Flanders, and France, that had given the law to sovereigns
abroad, and been worshipped as a divinity at home, forced
to sneak out of England—his credit, honours, places, all
taken from him ; his friends in the army broke and ruined ;
and flying before Harley, as abject and powerless as a poor
debtor before a bailiff with a writ. A paper, of which
Harley got possession, and showing beyond doubt that the
duke was engaged with the Stuart family, was the weapon
with which the treasurer drove Marlborough out of the
kingdom. He fled to Antwerp, and began intriguing instantly on the other side, and came back to England, as
all know, a Whig and a Hanoverian.

Though the treasurer turned out of the army and office
every man, military or civil, known to be the duke's friend,
and gave the vacant posts among the Tory party ; he,
too, was playing the double game between Hanover and
St. Germains, awaiting the expected catastrophe of the
queen's death to be master of the state, and offer it to either
family that should bribe him best, or that the nation should
declare for. Whichever the king was, Harley's object was
to reign over him ; and to this end he supplanted the former
famous favourite, decried the actions of the war which had
made Marlborough's name illustrious, and disdained no
more than the great fallen competitor of his, the meanest
arts, flatteries, intimidations, that would secure his power.
If the greatest satirist the world ever hath seen had writ
against Harley, and not for him, what a history had he
left behind of the last years of Queen Anne's reign ! But
Swift, that scorned all mankind, and himself not the least
of all, had this merit of a faithful partisan, that he loved
those chiefs who treated him well, and stuck by Harley

bravely in his fall, as he gallantly had supported him in his better fortune.

Incomparably more brilliant, more splendid, eloquent, accomplished, than his rival, the great St. John could be as selfish as Oxford was, and could act the double part as skilfully as ambidextrous Churchill. He whose talk was always of liberty, no more shrunk from using persecution and the pillory against his opponents, than if he had been at Lisbon and Grand Inquisitor. This lofty patriot was on his knees at Hanover and St. Germains too; notoriously of no religion, he toasted Church and queen as boldly as the stupid Sacheverel, whom he used and laughed at; and to serve his turn, and to overthrow his enemy, he could intrigue, coax, bully, wheedle, fawn on the Court favourite, and creep up the back-stair as silently as Oxford who supplanted Marlborough, and whom he himself supplanted. The crash of my Lord Oxford happened at this very time whereat my history is now arrived. He was come to the very last days of his power, and the agent whom he employed to overthrow the conqueror of Blenheim, was now engaged to upset the conqueror's conqueror, and hand over the staff of government to Bolingbroke, who had been panting to hold it.

In expectation of the stroke that was now preparing, the Irish regiments in the French service were all brought round about Boulogne in Picardy, to pass over if need were with the Duke of Berwick; the soldiers of France no longer, but subjects of James the Third of England and Ireland King. The fidelity of the great mass of the Scots (though a most active, resolute, and gallant Whig party, admirably and energetically ordered and disciplined, was known to be in Scotland too) was notoriously unshaken in their king. A very great body of Tory clergy, nobility, and gentry, were public partisans of the exiled prince; and the indifferents might be counted on to cry King George or King James, according as either should prevail. The queen, especially in her latter days, inclined towards her own family. The prince was lying actually in London, within a stone's-cast of his sister's palace; the first minister toppling to his fall, and so tottering that the weakest push of a woman's finger would send him down; and as for Bolingbroke, his successor, we knew on whose side his power and his splendid eloquence would be on the day when the queen should appear openly before her council and say :—' This, my lords, is my brother ; here is my father's heir, and mine after me.'

During the whole of the previous year the queen had had many and repeated fits of sickness, fever, and lethargy, and her death had been constantly looked for by all her attendants. The Elector of Hanover had wished to send his son, the Duke of Cambridge—to pay his court to his cousin the queen, the Elector said ;—in truth, to be on the spot when death should close her career. Frightened perhaps to have such a *memento mori* under her royal eyes, her Majesty had angrily forbidden the young prince's coming into England. Either she desired to keep the chances for her brother open yet ; or the people about her did not wish to close with the Whig candidate till they could make terms with him. The quarrels of her ministers before her face at the Council board, the pricks of conscience very likely, the importunities of her ministers, and constant turmoil and agitation round about her, had weakened and irritated the princess extremely ; her strength was giving way under these continual trials of her temper, and from day to day it was expected she must come to a speedy end of them. Just before Viscount Castlewood and his companion came from France, her Majesty was taken ill. The St. Anthony's fire* broke out on the royal legs ; there was no hurry for the presentation of the young lord at Court, or that person who should appear under his name ; and my lord viscount's wound breaking out opportunely, he was kept conveniently in his chamber until such time as his physician should allow him to bend his knee before the queen. At the commencement of July, that influential lady, with whom it has been mentioned that our party had relations, came frequently to visit her young friend, the maid of honour, at Kensington, and my lord viscount (the real or supposititious), who was an invalid at Lady Castlewood's house.

On the 27th day of July, the lady in question, who held the most intimate post about the queen, came in her chair from the palace hard by, bringing to the little party in Kensington Square, intelligence of the very highest importance. The final blow had been struck, and my Lord of Oxford and Mortimer was no longer treasurer. The staff was as yet given to no successor, though my Lord Boling-

broke would undoubtedly be the man.   And now the time
was come, the queen's Abigail said : and now my Lord
Castlewood ought to be presented to the sovereign.

After that scene which Lord Castlewood witnessed and
described to his cousin, who passed such a miserable night
of mortification and jealousy as he thought over the transaction ; no doubt the three persons who were set by
nature as protectors over Beatrix came to the same conclusion, that she must be removed from the presence of
a man whose desires towards her were expressed only too
clearly ; and who was no more scrupulous in seeking to
gratify them than his father had been before him.   I suppose Esmond's mistress, her son, and the colonel himself,
had been all secretly debating this matter in their minds, for
when Frank broke out, in his blunt way, with :—' I think
Beatrix had best be anywhere but here,'—Lady Castlewood
said :—' I thank you, Frank, I have thought so too ' ; and
Mr. Esmond, though he only remarked that it was not for
him to speak, showed plainly, by the delight on his countenance, how very agreeable that proposal was to him.

' One sees that you think with us, Henry,' says the
viscountess, with ever so little of sarcasm in her tone :
' Beatrix is best out of this house whilst we have our guest
in it, and as soon as this morning's business is done, she
ought to quit London.'

' What morning's business ? ' asked Colonel Esmond, not
knowing what had been arranged, though in fact the stroke
next in importance to that of bringing the prince, and of
having him acknowledged by the queen, was now being
performed at the very moment we three were conversing
together.

The Court-lady with whom our plan was concerted, and
who was a chief agent in it, the Court-physician, and the
Bishop of Rochester, who were the other two most active
participators in our plan, had held many councils in our
house at Kensington and elsewhere, as to the means best
to be adopted for presenting our young adventurer to his
sister the queen.   The simple and easy plan proposed by
Colonel Esmond had been agreed to by all parties, which
was that on some rather private day, when there were not
many persons about the Court, the prince should appear
there as my Lord Castlewood, should be greeted by his
sister-in-waiting, and led by that other lady into the closet

of the queen.   And according to her Majesty's health or humour, and the circumstances that might arise during the interview ; it was to be left to the discretion of those present at it, and to the prince himself, whether he should declare that it was the queen's own brother, or the brother of Beatrix Esmond, who kissed her royal hand.   And this plan being determined on, we were all waiting in very much anxiety for the day and signal of execution.

Two mornings after that supper, it being the 27th day of July, the Bishop of Rochester breakfasting with Lady Castlewood and her family, and the meal scarce over, Dr. A——'s coach drove up to our house at Kensington, and the doctor appeared amongst the party there, enlivening a rather gloomy company ; for the mother and daughter had had words in the morning in respect to the transactions of that supper, and other adventures perhaps, and on the day succeeding.   Beatrix's haughty spirit brooked remonstrances from no superior, much less from her mother, the gentlest of creatures, whom the girl commanded rather than obeyed.   And feeling she was wrong, and that by a thousand coquetries (which she could no more help exercising on every man that came near her, than the sun can help shining on great and small) she had provoked the prince's dangerous admiration, and allured him to the expression of it, she was only the more wilful and imperious the more she felt her error.

To this party, the prince being served with chocolate in his bedchamber, where he lay late sleeping away the fumes of his wine, the doctor came, and by the urgent and startling nature of his news, dissipated instantly that private and minor unpleasantry under which the family of Castlewood was labouring.

He asked for the guest ;   the guest was above in his own apartment :   he bade *Monsieur Baptiste* go up to his master instantly, and requested that *my Lord Viscount Castlewood* would straightway put his uniform on, and come away in the doctor's coach now at the door.

He then informed Madam Beatrix what her part of the comedy was to be :—' In half an hour,' says he, ' her Majesty and her favourite lady will take the air in the cedar-walk behind the new banqueting-house.   Her Majesty will be drawn in a garden-chair, Madam Beatrix Esmond and *her brother*, *my Lord Viscount Castlewood*, will be walking in the private garden (here is Lady Masham's key), and will come unawares upon the royal party. The man that draws the chair will retire, and leave the queen, the favourite, and the maid of honour and her brother together ; Mrs. Beatrix will present her brother, and then ! —and then, my lord bishop will pray for the result of the interview, and his Scots clerk will say Amen ! Quick, put on your hood, Madam Beatrix ; why doth not his Majesty come down ? Such another chance may not present itself for months again.'

The prince was late and lazy, and indeed had all but lost that chance through his indolence. The queen was actually about to leave the garden just when the party reached it ; the doctor, the bishop, the maid of honour and her brother went off together in the physician's coach, and had been gone half an hour when Colonel Esmond came to Kensington Square.

The news of this errand, on which Beatrix was gone, of course for a moment put all thoughts of private jealousy out of Colonel Esmond's head. In half an hour more the coach returned ; the bishop descended from it first, and gave his arm to Beatrix, who now came out. His lordship went back into the carriage again, and the maid of honour entered the house alone. We were all gazing at her from the upper window, trying to read from her countenance the result of the interview from which she had just come.

She came into the drawing-room in a great tremor and very pale ; she asked for a glass of water as her mother went to meet her, and after drinking that and putting off her hood, she began to speak :—' We may all hope for the best,' says she ; ' it has cost the queen a fit. Her Majesty was in her chair in the cedar-walk accompanied only by Lady ——, when we entered by the private wicket from the west side of the garden, and turned towards her, the doctor following us. They waited in a side-walk hidden by the shrubs, as we advanced towards the chair. My heart throbbed so I scarce could speak ; but my prince whispered, " Courage, Beatrix ", and marched on with a steady step. His face was a little flushed, but he was not afraid of the danger. He who fought so bravely at Malplaquet fears nothing.' Esmond and Castlewood looked at each other at this compliment, neither liking the sound of it.

'The prince uncovered,' Beatrix continued, 'and I saw the queen turning round to Lady Masham, as if asking who these two were. Her Majesty looked very pale and ill, and then flushed up; the favourite made us a signal to advance, and I went up, leading my prince by the hand, quite close to the chair: "Your Majesty will give my lord viscount your hand to kiss," says her lady, and the queen put out her hand, which the prince kissed, kneeling on his knee, he who should kneel to no mortal man or woman.

'"You have been long from England, my lord," says the queen: "why were you not here to give a home to your mother and sister?"

'"I am come, madam, to stay now, if the queen desires me," says the prince, with another low bow.

'"You have taken a foreign wife, my lord, and a foreign religion; was not that of England good enough for you?"

'"In returning to my father's Church," says the prince, "I do not love my mother the less, nor am I the less faithful servant of your Majesty."

'Here,' says Beatrix, 'the favourite gave me a little signal with her hand to fall back, which I did, though I died to hear what should pass; and whispered something to the queen, which made her Majesty start and utter one or two words in a hurried manner, looking towards the prince, and catching hold with her hand of the arm of her chair. He advanced still nearer towards it; he began to speak very rapidly; I caught the words, "Father, blessing, forgiveness,"—and then presently the prince fell on his knees; took from his breast a paper he had there, handed it to the queen, who, as soon as she saw it, flung up both her arms with a scream, and took away that hand nearest the prince, and which he endeavoured to kiss. He went on speaking with great animation of gesture, now clasping his hands together on his heart, now opening them as though to say: "I am here, your brother, in your power." Lady Masham ran round on the other side of the chair, kneeling too, and speaking with great energy. She clasped the queen's hand on her side, and picked up the paper her Majesty had let fall. The prince rose and made a further speech as though he would go; the favourite on the other hand urging her mistress, and then, running back to the prince, brought him back once more close to

the chair. Again he knelt down and took the queen's
hand, which she did not withdraw, kissing it a hundred
times ; my lady all the time, with sobs and supplications,
speaking over the chair. This while the queen sat with
a stupefied look, crumpling the paper with one hand, as
my prince embraced the other ; then of a sudden she
uttered several piercing shrieks, and burst into a great fit
of hysteric tears and laughter. " Enough, enough, sir, for
this time," I heard Lady Masham say ; and the chairman,
who had withdrawn round the banqueting-room, came back,
alarmed by the cries : " Quick," says Lady Masham, " get
some help," and I ran towards the doctor, who, with the
Bishop of Rochester, came up instantly. Lady Masham
whispered the prince he might hope for the very best ;
and to be ready to-morrow ; and he hath gone away to
the Bishop of Rochester's house, to meet several of his
friends there. And so the great stroke is struck,' says
Beatrix, going down on her knees, and clasping her hands,
' God save the King : God save the King ! '

Beatrix's tale told, and the young lady herself calmed
somewhat of her agitation, we asked with regard to the
prince, who was absent with Bishop Atterbury, and were
informed that 'twas likely he might remain abroad the
whole day. Beatrix's three kinsfolk looked at one another
at this intelligence ; 'twas clear the same thought was
passing through the minds of all.

But who should begin to break the news ? Monsieur
Baptiste, that is Frank Castlewood, turned very red, and
looked towards Esmond ; the colonel bit his lips, and fairly
beat a retreat into the window : it was Lady Castlewood
that opened upon Beatrix with the news which we knew
would do anything but please her.

' We are glad,' says she, taking her daughter's hand,
and speaking in a gentle voice, ' that the guest is away.'

Beatrix drew back in an instant, looking round her at
us three, and as if divining a danger. ' Why glad ? ' says
she, her breast beginning to heave ; ' are you so soon tired
of him ? '

' We think one of us is devilishly too fond of him,' cries
out Frank Castlewood.

' And which is it—you, my lord, or is it mamma, who
is jealous because he drinks my health ? or is it the head
of the family ' (here she turned with an imperious look

towards Colonel Esmond), ' who has taken of late to preach
the king sermons ? '

' We do not say you are too free with his Majesty.'

' I thank you, madam,' says Beatrix, with a toss of the
head and a curtsy.

But her mother continued, with very great calmness and
dignity—' At least we have not said so, though we might,
were it possible for a mother to say such words to her own
daughter, your father's daughter.'

' Eh ! mon père,' breaks out Beatrix, ' was no better
than other persons' fathers ; ' and again she looked towards
the colonel.

We all felt a shock as she uttered those two or three
French words ; her manner was exactly imitated from that
of our foreign guest.

' You had not learned to speak French a month ago,
Beatrix,' says her mother, sadly, ' nor to speak ill of your
father.'

Beatrix, no doubt, saw that slip she had made in her
flurry, for she blushed crimson : ' I have learnt to honour
the king,' says she, drawing up, ' and 'twere as well that
others suspected neither his Majesty nor me.'

' If you respected your mother a little more,' Frank said,
' 'Trix, you would do yourself no hurt.'

' I am no child,' says she, turning round on him ; ' we
have lived very well these five years without the benefit of
your advice or example, and I intend to take neither now.
Why does not the head of the house speak ? ' she went on ;
' he rules everything here. When his chaplain has done
singing the psalms, will his lordship deliver the sermon ?
I am tired of the psalms.' The prince had used almost the
very same words, in regard to Colonel Esmond, that the
imprudent girl repeated in her wrath.

' You show yourself a very apt scholar, madam,' says the
colonel ; and, turning to his mistress, ' Did your guest use
these words in your ladyship's hearing, or was it to Beatrix
in private that he was pleased to impart his opinion regarding my tiresome sermon ? '

' Have you seen him alone ? ' cries my lord, starting up
with an oath : ' by God, have you seen him alone ? '

' Were he here, you wouldn't dare so to insult me ; no,
you would not dare ! ' cries Frank's sister. ' Keep your
oaths, my lord, for your wife ; we are not used here to such

language. 'Till you came, there used to be kindness between
me and mamma, and I cared for her when you never did,
when you were away for years with your horses, and your
mistress, and your Popish wife.'

' By ——,' says my lord, rapping out another oath,
' Clotilda is an angel; how dare you say a word against
Clotilda ? '

Colonel Esmond could not refrain from a smile, to see how
easy Frank's attack was drawn off by that feint :—' I fancy
Clotilda is not the subject in hand,' says Mr. Esmond,
rather scornfully ; ' her ladyship is at Paris, a hundred
leagues off, preparing baby-linen. It is about my Lord
Castlewood's sister, and not his wife, the question is.'

' He is not my Lord Castlewood,' says Beatrix, ' and he
knows he is not ; he is Colonel Francis Esmond's son, and
no more, and he wears a false title ; and he lives on another
man's land, and he knows it.' Here was another desperate
sally of the poor beleaguered garrison, and an *alerte* in
another quarter. ' Again, I beg your pardon,' says Esmond.
' If there are no proofs of my claim, I have no claim. If
my father acknowledged no heir, yours was his lawful
successor, and my Lord Castlewood hath as good a right
to his rank and small estate as any man in England. But
that again is not the question, as you know very well :
let us bring our talk back to it, as you will have me meddle
in it.   And I will give you frankly my opinion, that a house
where a prince lies all day, who respects no woman, is no
house for a young unmarried lady ; that you were better
in the country than here ; that he is here on a great end,
from which no folly should divert him ; and that having
nobly done your part of this morning, Beatrix, you should
retire off the scene awhile, and leave it to the other actors
of the play.'

As the colonel spoke with a perfect calmness and politeness, such as 'tis to be hoped he hath always shown to
women,[1] his mistress stood by him on one side of the table,

---

[1] My dear father saith quite truly, that his manner towards our
sex was uniformly courteous. From my infancy upwards, he
treated me with an extreme gentleness, as though I was a little lady.
I can scarce remember (though I tried him often) ever hearing a rough
word from him, nor was he less grave and kind in his manner to the
humblest negresses on his estate. He was familiar with no one
except my mother, and it was delightful to witness up to the very

and Frank Castlewood on the other, hemming in poor Beatrix, that was behind it, and, as it were, surrounding her with our approaches.

Having twice sallied out and been beaten back, she now, as I expected, tried the *ultima ratio* of women, and had recourse to tears. Her beautiful eyes filled with them; I never could bear in her, nor in any woman, that expression of pain :—' I am alone,' sobbed she ; ' you are three against me—my brother, my mother, and you. What have I done, that you should speak and look so unkindly at me ? Is it my fault that the prince should, as you say, admire me ? Did I bring him here ? Did I do aught but what you bade me, in making him welcome ? Did you not tell me that our duty was to die for him ? Did you not teach me, mother, night and morning, to pray for the king, before even ourselves ? What would you have of me, cousin, for you are the chief of the conspiracy against me ; I know you are, sir, and that my mother and brother are acting but as you bid them; whither would you have me go?'

' I would but remove from the prince,' says Esmond gravely, ' a dangerous temptation ; Heaven forbid I should say you would yield : I would only have him free of it. Your honour needs no guardian, please God, but his imprudence doth. He is so far removed from all women by his rank, that his pursuit of them cannot but be unlawful. We would remove the dearest and fairest of our family from the chance of that insult, and that is why we would have you go, dear Beatrix.'

' Harry speaks like a book,' says Frank, with one of his oaths, ' and, by ——, every word he saith is true. You can't help being handsome, 'Trix ; no more can the prince help following you. My council is that you go out of harm's way ; for, by the Lord, were the prince to play any tricks with you, king as he is, or is to be, Harry Esmond and I would have justice of him.'

last days the confidence between them. He was obeyed eagerly by all under him ; and my mother and all her household lived in a constant emulation to please him, and quite a terror lest in any way they should offend him. He was the humblest man, with all this ; the least exacting, the most easily contented ; and Mr. Benson, our minister at Castlewood, who attended him at the last, ever said— ' I know not what Colonel Esmond's doctrine was, but his life and death were those of a devout Christian.'—R. E. W.

'Are not two such champions enough to guard me ?' says Beatrix, something sorrowfully ; 'sure, with you two watching, no evil could happen to me.'

'In faith, I think not, Beatrix,' says Colonel Esmond ; 'nor if the prince knew us would he try.'

'But does he know you ?' interposed Lady Esmond, very quiet : 'he comes of a country where the pursuit of kings is thought no dishonour to a woman. Let us go, dearest Beatrix. Shall we go to Walcote or to Castlewood? We are best away from the city ; and when the prince is acknowledged, and our champions have restored him, and he hath his own house at St. James's or Windsor, we can come back to ours here. Do you not think so, Harry and Frank ?'

Frank and Harry thought with her, you may be sure.

'We will go, then,' says Beatrix, turning a little pale ; 'Lady Masham is to give me warning to-night how her Majesty is, and to-morrow——'

'I think we had best go to-day, my dear,' says my Lady Castlewood ; 'we might have the coach and sleep at Hounslow, and reach home to-morrow. 'Tis twelve o'clock ; bid the coach, cousin, be ready at one.'

'For shame !' burst out Beatrix, in a passion of tears and mortification. 'You disgrace me by your cruel precautions ; my own mother is the first to suspect me, and would take me away as my gaoler. I will not go with you, mother ; I will go as no one's prisoner. If I wanted to deceive, do you think I could find no means of evading you ? My family suspects me. As those mistrust me that ought to love me most, let me leave them ; I will go, but I will go alone : to Castlewood, be it. I have been unhappy there and lonely enough ; let me go back, but spare me at least the humiliation of setting a watch over my misery, which is a trial I can't bear. Let me go when you will, but alone, or not at all. You three can stay and triumph over my unhappiness, and I will bear it as I have borne it before. Let my gaoler-in-chief go order the coach that is to take me away. I thank you, Henry Esmond, for your share in the conspiracy. All my life long I'll thank you, and remember you ; and you, brother, and you, mother, how shall I show my gratitude to you for your careful defence of my honour ?'

She swept out of the room with the air of an empress,

flinging glances of defiance at us all, and leaving us conquerors of the field, but scared, and almost ashamed of
our victory. It did indeed seem hard and cruel that we
three should have conspired the banishment and humiliation
of that fair creature. We looked at each other in silence ;
'twas not the first stroke by many of our actions in that
unlucky time, which, being done, we wished undone. We
agreed it was best she should go alone, speaking stealthily
to one another, and under our breaths, like persons engaged
in an act they felt ashamed in doing.

In a half-hour, it might be, after our talk she came back,
her countenance wearing the same defiant air which it had
borne when she left us. She held a shagreen-case in her
hand ; Esmond knew it as containing his diamonds which
he had given to her for her marriage with Duke Hamilton,
and which she had worn so splendidly on the inauspicious
night of the prince's arrival. ' I have brought back,' says
she, ' to the Marquis of Esmond the present he deigned to
make me in days when he trusted me better than now.
I will never accept a benefit or a kindness from Henry
Esmond more, and I give back these family diamonds,
which belonged to one king's mistress, to the gentleman
that suspected I would be another. Have you been upon
your message of coach-caller, my lord marquis ; will you
send your valet to see that I do not run away ? ' We were
right, yet, by her manner, she had put us all in the wrong ;
we were conquerors, yet the honours of the day seemed
to be with the poor oppressed girl.

That luckless box containing the stones had first been
ornamented with a baron's coronet, when Beatrix was
engaged to the young gentleman from whom she parted,
and afterwards the gilt crown of a duchess figured on the
cover, which also poor Beatrix was destined never to wear.
Lady Castlewood opened the case mechanically and scarce
thinking what she did ; and behold, besides the diamonds,
Esmond's present, there lay in the box the enamelled
miniature of the late duke, which Beatrix had laid aside
with her mourning when the king came into the house ;
and which the poor heedless thing very likely had forgotten.

' Do you leave this, too, Beatrix ? ' says her mother,
taking the miniature out and with a cruelty she did not
very often show ; but there are some moments when the

tenderest women are cruel, and some triumphs which angels can't forgo.[1]

Having delivered this stab, Lady Esmond was frightened at the effect of her blow. It went to poor Beatrix's heart; she flushed up and passed a handkerchief across her eyes, and kissed the miniature, and put it into her bosom :— ' I had forgot it,' says she; ' my injury made me forget my grief, my mother has recalled both to me. Farewell, mother, I think I never can forgive you; something hath broke between us that no tears nor years can repair. I always said I was alone; you never loved me, never— and were jealous of me from the time I sat on my father's knee. Let me go away, the sooner the better; I can bear to be with you no more.'

' Go, child,' says her mother, still very stern; ' go and bend your proud knees and ask forgiveness; go, pray in solitude for humility and repentance. 'Tis not your reproaches that make me unhappy, 'tis your hard heart, my poor Beatrix; may God soften it, and teach you one day to feel for your mother ! '

If my mistress was cruel, at least she never could be got to own as much. Her haughtiness quite overtopped Beatrix's; and, if the girl had a proud spirit, I very much fear it came to her by inheritance.

CHAPTER XI

OUR GUEST QUITS US AS NOT BEING HOSPITABLE ENOUGH

Beatrix's departure took place within an hour, her maid going with her in the post-chaise, and a man armed on the coach-box to prevent any danger of the road. Esmond and Frank thought of escorting the carriage, but she indignantly refused their company, and another man was sent to follow the coach, and not to leave it till it had passed over Hounslow Heath on the next day. And these two forming the whole of Lady Castlewood's male domestics,

[1] This remark shows how unjustly and contemptuously even the best of men will sometimes judge of our sex. Lady Esmond had no intention of triumphing over her daughter; but from a sense of duty alone pointed out her deplorable wrong.—R. E.

Mr. Esmond's faithful John Lockwood came to wait on his mistress during their absence, though he would have preferred to escort Mrs. Lucy, his sweetheart, on her journey into the country.

We had a gloomy and silent meal; it seemed as if a darkness was over the house, since the bright face of Beatrix had been withdrawn from it. In the afternoon came a message from the favourite to relieve us somewhat from this despondency. 'The queen hath been much shaken,' the note said; 'she is better now, and all things will go well. Let *my Lord Castlewood* be ready against we send for him.'

At night there came a second billet: 'There hath been a great battle in Council; lord treasurer hath broke his staff, and hath fallen never to rise again; no successor is appointed. Lord B—— receives a great Whig company to-night at Golden Square. If he is trimming, others are true; the queen hath no more fits, but is abed now, and more quiet. Be ready against morning, when I still hope all will be well.'

The prince came home shortly after the messenger who bore this billet had left the house. His royal highness was so much the better for the bishop's liquor, that to talk affairs to him now was of little service. He was helped to the royal bed; he called Castlewood familiarly by his own name; he quite forgot the part upon the acting of which his crown, his safety, depended. 'Twas lucky that my Lady Castlewood's servants were out of the way, and only those heard him who would not betray him. He inquired after the adorable Beatrix, with a royal hiccup in his voice; he was easily got to bed, and in a minute or two plunged in that deep slumber and forgetfulness with which Bacchus rewards the votaries of that god. We wished Beatrix had been there to see him in his cups. We regretted, perhaps, that she was gone.

One of the party at Kensington Square was fool enough to ride to Hounslow that night, *coram latronibus,*[*] and to the inn which the family used ordinarily in their journeys out of London. Esmond desired my landlord not to acquaint Madam Beatrix with his coming, and had the grim satisfaction of passing by the door of the chamber where she lay with her maid, and of watching her chariot set forth in the early morning. He saw her smile and slip money into the man's hand who was ordered to ride behind the coach as far as Bagshot. The road being open, and the other servant armed, it appeared she dispensed with the escort of a second domestic ; and this fellow, bidding his young mistress adieu with many bows, went and took a pot of ale in the kitchen, and returned in company with his brother servant, John Coachman, and his horses, back to London.

They were not a mile out of Hounslow when the two worthies stopped for more drink, and here they were scared by seeing Colonel Esmond gallop by them. The man said in reply to Colonel Esmond's stern question, that his young mistress had sent her duty ; only that, no other message : she had had a very good night, and would reach Castlewood by nightfall. The colonel had no time for further colloquy, and galloped on swiftly to London, having business of great importance there, as my reader very well knoweth. The thought of Beatrix riding away from the danger soothed his mind not a little. His horse was at Kensington Square (honest Dapple knew the way thither well enough) before the tipsy guest of last night was awake and sober.

The account of the previous evening was known all over the town early next day. A violent altercation had taken place before the queen in the Council-chamber ; and all the coffee-houses had their version of the quarrel. The news brought my lord bishop early to Kensington Square, where he awaited the waking of his royal master above stairs, and spoke confidently of having him proclaimed as Prince of Wales and heir to the throne before that day was over. The bishop had entertained on the previous afternoon certain of the most influential gentlemen of the true British party. His royal highness had charmed all, both Scots and English, Papists and Churchmen : ' Even Quakers,' says he, ' were at our meeting ; and, if the stranger took a little too much British punch and ale, he will soon grow more accustomed to those liquors ; and my Lord Castlewood,' says the bishop, with a laugh, ' must bear the cruel charge of having been for once in his life a little tipsy. He toasted your lovely sister a dozen times, at which we all laughed,' says the bishop, ' admiring so much fraternal affection.—Where is that charming nymph, and why doth she not adorn your ladyship's tea-table with her bright eyes? '

Her ladyship said, drily, that Beatrix was not at home that morning; my lord bishop was too busy with great affairs to trouble himself much about the presence or absence of any lady, however beautiful.

We were yet at table when Dr. A—— came from the Palace with a look of great alarm; the shocks the queen had had the day before had acted on her severely; he had been sent for, and had ordered her to be blooded. The surgeon of Long Acre had come to cup the queen, and her Majesty was now more easy and breathed more freely. What made us start at the name of Mr. Aymé ?* '*Il faut être aimable pour être aimé*,' says the merry doctor; Esmond pulled his sleeve, and bade him hush. It was to Aymé's house, after his fatal duel, that my dear Lord Castlewood, Frank's father, had been carried to die.

No second visit could be paid to the queen on that day at any rate; and when our guest above gave his signal that he was awake, the doctor, the bishop, and Colonel Esmond waited upon the prince's levee, and brought him their news, cheerful or dubious. The doctor had to go away presently, but promised to keep the prince constantly acquainted with what was taking place at the palace hard by. His counsel was, and the bishop's, that as soon as ever the queen's malady took a favourable turn, the prince should be introduced to her bedside; the Council summoned; the guard at Kensington and St. James's, of which two regiments were to be entirely relied on, and one known not to be hostile, would declare for the prince, as the queen would before the lords of her Council, designating him as the heir to her throne.

With locked doors, and Colonel Esmond acting as secretary, the prince and his lordship of Rochester passed many hours of this day composing Proclamations and Addresses to the Country, to the Scots, to the Clergy, to the People of London and England; announcing the arrival of the exile descendant of three sovereigns, and his acknowledgement by his sister as heir to the throne. Every safeguard for their liberties the Church and People could ask was promised to them. The bishop could answer for the adhesion of very many prelates, who besought of their flocks and brother ecclesiastics to recognize the sacred right of the future sovereign, and to purge the country of the sin of rebellion.

During the composition of these papers, more messengers than one came from the Palace regarding the state of the august patient there lying. At midday she was somewhat better; at evening the torpor again seized her, and she wandered in her mind. At night Dr. A—— was with us again, with a report rather more favourable: no instant danger at any rate was apprehended. In the course of the last two years her Majesty had had many attacks similar, but more severe.

By this time we had finished a half-dozen of Proclamations (the wording of them so as to offend no parties, and not to give umbrage to Whigs or Dissenters, required very great caution), and the young prince, who had indeed shown, during a long day's labour, both alacrity at seizing the information given him, and ingenuity and skill in turning the phrases which were to go out signed by his name, here exhibited a good humour and thoughtfulness that ought to be set down to his credit.

'Were these papers to be mislaid,' says he, 'or our scheme to come to mishap, my Lord Esmond's writing would bring him to a place where I heartily hope never to see him; and so, by your leave, I will copy the papers myself, though I am not very strong in spelling; and if they are found they will implicate none but the person they most concern;' and so, having carefully copied the Proclamations out, the prince burned those in Colonel Esmond's handwriting: 'And now, and now, gentlemen,' says he, 'let us go to supper, and drink a glass with the ladies. My Lord Esmond, you will sup with us to-night; you have given us of late too little of your company.'

The prince's meals were commonly served in the chamber which had been Beatrix's bedroom, adjoining that in which he slept. And the dutiful practice of his entertainers was to wait until their royal guest bade them take their places at table before they sat down to partake of the meal. On this night, as you may suppose, only Frank Castlewood and his mother were in waiting when the supper was announced to receive the prince; who had passed the whole of the day in his own apartment, with the bishop as his minister of state, and Colonel Esmond officiating as secretary of his Council.

The prince's countenance wore an expression by no means pleasant; when looking towards the little company assembled, and waiting for him, he did not see Beatrix's bright face there as usual to greet him. He asked Lady Esmond for his fair introducer of yesterday : her ladyship only cast her eyes down, and said quietly, Beatrix could not be of the supper that night ; nor did she show the least sign of confusion, whereas Castlewood turned red, and Esmond was no less embarrassed. I think women have an instinct of dissimulation ; they know by nature how to disguise their emotions far better than the most consummate male courtiers can do. Is not the better part of the life of many of them spent in hiding their feelings, in cajoling their tyrants, in masking over with fond smiles and artful gaiety their doubt, or their grief, or their terror ?

Our guest swallowed his supper very sulky ; it was not till the second bottle his highness began to rally. When Lady Castlewood asked leave to depart, he sent a message to Beatrix, hoping she would be present at the next day's dinner, and applied himself to drink, and to talk afterwards, for which there was subject in plenty.

The next day, we heard from our informer at Kensington that the queen was somewhat better, and had been up for an hour, though she was not well enough yet to receive any visitor.

At dinner a single cover was laid for his royal highness ; and the two gentlemen alone waited on him. We had had a consultation in the morning with Lady Castlewood, in which it had been determined that, should his highness ask further questions about Beatrix, he should be answered by the gentlemen of the house.

He was evidently disturbed and uneasy, looking towards the door constantly, as if expecting some one. There came, however, nobody, except honest John Lockwood, when he knocked with a dish, which those within took from him ; so the meals were always arranged, and I believe the council in the kitchen were of opinion that my young lord had brought over a priest, who had converted us all into Papists, and that Papists were like Jews, eating together, and not choosing to take their meals in the sight of Christians.

The prince tried to cover his displeasure ; he was but a clumsy dissembler at that time, and when out of humour could with difficulty keep a serene countenance ; and having made some foolish attempts at trivial talk, he came to his point presently, and in as easy a manner as he could, saying

to Lord Castlewood, he hoped, he requested, his lordship's
mother and sister would be of the supper that night. As
the time hung heavy on him, and he must not go abroad,
would not Miss Beatrix hold him company at a game of
cards ?

At this, looking up at Esmond, and taking the signal
from him, Lord Castlewood informed his royal highness [1]
that his sister Beatrix was not at Kensington ; and that
her family had thought it best she should quit the town.

' Not at Kensington ! ' says he ; ' is she ill ? she was
well yesterday ; wherefore should she quit the town ?
Is it at your orders, my lord, or Colonel Esmond's, who
seems the master of this house ? '

' Not of this, sir,' says Frank very nobly, ' only of our house
in the country, which he hath given to us. This is my
mother's house, and Walcote is my father's, and the Marquis
of Esmond knows he hath but to give his word, and I return
his to him.'

' The Marquis of Esmond !—the Marquis of Esmond,'
says the prince, tossing off a glass, ' meddles too much with
my affairs, and presumes on the service he hath done me.
If you want to carry your suit with Beatrix, my lord, by
blocking her up in gaol, let me tell you that is not the way
to win a woman.'

' I was not aware, sir, that I had spoken of my suit to
Madam Beatrix to your royal highness.'

' Bah, bah, monsieur ! we need not be a conjurer to see
that. It makes itself seen at all moments. You are
jealous, my lord, and the maid of honour cannot look at
another face without yours beginning to scowl. That
which you do is unworthy, monsieur ; is inhospitable—is,
is *lâche*, yes *lâche :* ' (he spoke rapidly in French, his rage
carrying him away with each phrase :) ' I come to your
house ; I risk my life ; I pass it in ennui ; I repose myself
on your fidelity ; I have no company but your lordship's
sermons or the conversations of that adorable young lady,
and you take her from me ; and you, you rest ! *Merci,
monsieur !* I shall thank you when I have the means ;
I shall know to recompense a devotion a little importunate,
my lord—a little importunate. For a month past your
airs of protector have annoyed me beyond measure. You

[1] In London we addressed the prince as royal highness invariably;
though the women persisted in giving him the title of king.

deign to offer me the crown, and bid me take it on my knees like King John—eh! I know my history, monsieur, and mock myself of frowning barons. I admire your mistress, and you send her to a Bastile of the Province; I enter your house, and you mistrust me. I will leave it, monsieur; from to-night I will leave it. I have other friends whose loyalty will not be so ready to question mine. If I have Garters to give away, 'tis to noblemen who are not so ready to think evil. Bring me a coach and let me quit this place, or let the fair Beatrix return to it. I will not have your hospitality at the expense of the freedom of that fair creature.'

This harangue was uttered with rapid gesticulations such as the French use, and in the language of that nation. The prince striding up and down the room; his face flushed, and his hands trembling with anger. He was very thin and frail from repeated illness and a life of pleasure. Either Castlewood or Esmond could have broke him across their knee, and in half a minute's struggle put an end to him; and here he was insulting us both, and scarce deigning to hide from the two, whose honour it most concerned, the passion he felt for the young lady of our family. My Lord Castlewood replied to the prince's tirade very nobly and simply.

'Sir,' says he, 'your royal highness is pleased to forget that others risk their lives, and for your cause. Very few Englishmen, please God, would dare to lay hands on your sacred person, though none would ever think of respecting ours. Our family's lives are at your service, and everything we have except our honour.'

'Honour! bah, sir, who ever thought of hurting your honour?' says the prince, with a peevish air.

'We implore your royal highness never to think of hurting it,' says Lord Castlewood, with a low bow. The night being warm, the windows were open both towards the gardens and the square. Colonel Esmond heard through the closed door the voice of the watchman calling the hour, in the square on the other side. He opened the door communicating with the prince's room; Martin, the servant that had rode with Beatrix to Hounslow, was just going out of the chamber as Esmond entered it, and when the fellow was gone, and the watchman again sang his cry of 'Past ten o'clock, and a starlight night,' Esmond spoke to the prince in a low voice, and said—' Your royal highness hears that man ? '

' *Après, monsieur ?* ' says the prince.

' I have but to beckon him from the window, and send him fifty yards, and he returns with a guard of men, and I deliver up to him the body of the person calling himself James the Third, for whose capture Parliament hath offered a reward of 5,000*l.*, as your royal highness saw on our ride from Rochester. I have but to say the word, and, by the Heaven that made me, I would say it if I thought the prince, for his honour's sake, would not desist from insulting ours. But the first gentleman of England knows his duty too well to forget himself with the humblest, or peril his crown for a deed that were shameful if it were done.'

' Has your lordship anything to say,' says the prince, turning to Frank Castlewood, and quite pale with anger ; ' any threat or any insult, with which you would like to end this agreeable night's entertainment ? '

' I follow the head of our house,' says Castlewood, bowing gravely. ' At what time shall it please the prince that we should wait upon him in the morning ? '

' You will wait on the Bishop of Rochester early, you will bid him bring his coach hither ; and prepare an apartment for me in his own house, or in a place of safety. The king will reward you handsomely, never fear, for all you have done in his behalf. I wish you a good night, and shall go to bed, unless it pleases the Marquis of Esmond to call his colleague, the watchman, and that I should pass the night with the Kensington guard. Fare you well, be sure I will remember you. My Lord Castlewood, I can go to bed to-night without need of a chamberlain.' And the prince dismissed us with a grim bow, locking one door as he spoke, that into the supping-room, and the other through which we passed, after us. It led into the small chamber which Frank Castlewood or *Monsieur Baptiste* occupied, and by which Martin entered when Colonel Esmond but now saw him in the chamber.

At an early hour next morning the bishop arrived, and was closeted for some time with his master in his own apartment, where the prince laid open to his counsellor the wrongs which, according to his version, he had received from the gentlemen of the Esmond family. The worthy prelate came out from the conference with an air of great satisfaction ; he was a man full of resources, and of a most assured fidelity, and possessed of genius, and a hundred good qualities ; but captious and of a most jealous temper, that could not help exulting at the downfall of any favourite; and he was pleased in spite of himself to hear that the Esmond ministry was at an end.

' I have soothed your guest,' says he, coming out to the two gentlemen and the widow, who had been made acquainted with somewhat of the dispute of the night before. (By the version we gave her, the prince was only made to exhibit anger because we doubted of his intentions in respect to Beatrix ; and to leave us, because we questioned his honour.) ' But I think, all things considered, 'tis as well he should leave this house ; and then, my Lady Castlewood,' says the bishop, ' my pretty Beatrix may come back to it.'

' She is quite as well at home at Castlewood,' Esmond's mistress said, ' till everything is over.'

' You shall have your title, Esmond, that I promise you,' says the good bishop, assuming the airs of a prime minister. ' The prince hath expressed himself most nobly in regard of the little difference of last night, and I promise you he hath listened to my sermon, as well as to that of other folks,' says the doctor archly ; ' he hath every great and generous quality, with perhaps a weakness for the sex which belongs to his family, and hath been known in scores of popular sovereigns from King David downwards.'

' My lord, my lord,' breaks out Lady Esmond, ' the levity with which you speak of such conduct towards our sex shocks me, and what you call weakness I call deplorable sin.'

' Sin it is, my dear creature,' says the bishop, with a shrug, taking snuff ; ' but consider what a sinner King Solomon was, and in spite of a thousand of wives too.'

' Enough of this, my lord,' says Lady Castlewood, with a fine blush, and walked out of the room very stately.

The prince entered it presently with a smile on his face, and if he felt any offence against us on the previous night, at present exhibited none. He offered a hand to each gentleman with great courtesy. ' If all your bishops preach so well as Dr. Atterbury,' says he, ' I don't know, gentlemen, what may happen to me. I spoke very hastily, my lords, last night, and ask pardon of both of you. But I must not stay any longer,' says he, ' giving umbrage to good friends, or keeping pretty girls away from their homes. My lord bishop hath found a safe place for me, hard by at a curate's house, whom the bishop can trust, and whose wife is so ugly as to be beyond all danger ; we will decamp into those new quarters, and I leave you, thanking you for a hundred kindnesses here. Where is my hostess, that I may bid her farewell ? to welcome her in a house of my own, soon I trust, where my friends shall have no cause to quarrel with me.'

Lady Castlewood arrived presently, blushing with great grace, and tears filling her eyes as the prince graciously saluted her. She looked so charming and young, that the doctor, in his bantering way, could not help speaking of her beauty to the prince ; whose compliment made her blush, and look more charming still.

CHAPTER XII

A GREAT SCHEME, AND WHO BALKED IT

As characters written with a secret ink come out with the application of fire, and disappear again and leave the paper white, so soon as it is cool ; a hundred names of men, high in repute and favouring the prince's cause, that were writ in our private lists, would have been visible enough on the great roll of the conspiracy, had it ever been laid open under the sun. What crowds would have pressed forward, and subscribed their names and protested their loyalty, when the danger was over ! What a number of Whigs, now high in place and creatures of the all-powerful minister, scorned Mr. Walpole then ! If ever a match was gained by the manliness and decision of a few at a moment of danger ; if ever one was lost by the treachery and imbecility of those that had the cards in their hands, and might have played them, it was in that momentous game which was enacted in the next three days, and of which the noblest crown in the world was the stake.

From the conduct of my Lord Bolingbroke, those who were interested in the scheme we had in hand, saw pretty well that he was not to be trusted. Should the prince prevail, it was his lordship's gracious intention to declare for him : should the Hanoverian party bring in their sovereign, who more ready to go on his knee, and cry ' God save King George ' ? And he betrayed the one prince and the other ; but exactly at the wrong time. When he should have struck for King James, he faltered and coquetted with the Whigs ; and having committed himself by the most monstrous professions of devotion, which the Elector rightly scorned, he proved the justness of their contempt for him by flying and taking renegado service with St. Germains, just when he should have kept aloof : and that Court despised him, as the manly and resolute men who established the Elector in England had before done. He signed his own name to every accusation of insincerity his enemies made against him ; and the king and the pretender alike could show proofs of St. John's treachery under his own hand and seal.

Our friends kept a pretty close watch upon his motions, as on those of the brave and hearty Whig party, that made little concealment of theirs. They would have in the Elector, and used every means in their power to effect their end. My Lord Marlborough was now with them. His expulsion from power by the Tories had thrown that great captain at once on the Whig side. We heard he was coming from Antwerp ; and in fact, on the day of the queen's death, he once more landed on English shore. A great part of the army was always with their illustrious leader ; even the Tories in it were indignant at the injustice of the persecution which the Whig officers were made to undergo. The chiefs of these were in London, and at the head of them one of the most intrepid men in the world, the Scots Duke of Argyle, whose conduct, on the second day after that to which I have now brought down my history, ended, as such honesty and bravery deserved to end, by establishing the present royal race on the English throne.

Meanwhile there was no slight difference of opinion amongst the councillors surrounding the prince, as to the plan his highness should pursue. His female minister at Court, fancying she saw some amelioration in the queen, was for waiting a few days, or hours it might be, until he could be brought to her bedside, and acknowledged as her heir. Mr. Esmond was for having him march thither, escorted by a couple of troops of Horse Guards, and openly presenting himself to the Council. During the whole of the night of the 29th–30th July, the colonel was engaged with gentlemen of the military profession, whom 'tis needless here to name ; suffice it to say that several of them had exceeding high rank in the army, and one of them in especial was a general, who, when he heard the Duke of Marlborough was coming on the other side, waved his crutch over his head with a huzzah, at the idea that he should march out and engage him. Of the three secretaries of state, we knew that one was devoted to us. The Governor of the Tower was ours : the two companies on duty at Kensington barrack were safe ; and we had intelligence, very speedy and accurate, of all that took place at the Palace within.

At noon, on the 30th of July, a message came to the prince's friends that the Committee of Council was sitting at Kensington Palace, their graces of Ormonde and Shrewsbury, the Archbishop of Canterbury and the three Secretaries of State, being there assembled. In an hour afterwards, hurried news was brought that the two great Whig dukes, Argyle and Somerset, had broke into the Council-chamber without a summons, and taken their seat at table. After holding a debate there, the whole party proceeded to the chamber of the queen, who was lying in great weakness, but still sensible, and the lords recommended his grace of Shrewsbury as the fittest person to take the vacant place of lord treasurer ; her Majesty gave him the staff, as all know. ' And now,' writ my messenger from Court, ' *now or never is the time.*'

Now or never was the time indeed. In spite of the Whig dukes, our side had still the majority in the Council, and Esmond, to whom the message had been brought (the personage at Court not being aware that the prince had quitted his lodging in Kensington Square), and Esmond's gallant young aide de camp, Frank Castlewood, putting on sword and uniform, took a brief leave of their dear lady, who embraced and blessed them both ; and went to her chamber to pray for the issue of the great event which was then pending.

Castlewood sped to the barrack to give warning to the captain of the guard there ; and then went to the ' King's Arms ' tavern at Kensington, where our friends were assembled, having come by parties of twos and threes, riding or in coaches, and were got together in the upper chamber,

fifty-three of them; their servants, who had been instructed
to bring arms likewise, being below in the garden of the
tavern, where they were served with drink. Out of this
garden is a little door that leads into the road of the Palace,
and through this it was arranged that masters and servants
were to march; when that signal was given, and that
Personage appeared, for whom all were waiting. There was
in our company the famous officer next in command to the
Captain-General of the Forces, his grace the Duke of
Ormonde, who was within at the Council. There were with
him two more lieutenant-generals, nine major-generals and
brigadiers, seven colonels, eleven peers of Parliament, and
twenty-one members of the House of Commons. The guard
was with us within and without the Palace: the queen was
with us; the Council (save the two Whig dukes, that must
have succumbed); the day was our own, and with a beating
heart Esmond walked rapidly to the Mall of Kensington,
where he had parted with the prince on the night before.
For three nights the colonel had not been to bed: the last
had been passed summoning the prince's friends together,
of whom the great majority had no sort of inkling of the
transaction pending until they were told that he was actually
on the spot, and were summoned to strike the blow. The
night before and after the altercation with the prince, my
gentleman, having suspicions of his royal highness, and
fearing lest he should be minded to give us the slip, and fly
off after his fugitive beauty, had spent, if the truth must
be told, at the 'Greyhound' tavern, over against my Lady
Esmond's house in Kensington Square, with an eye on the
door, lest the prince should escape from it. The night before
that he had passed in his boots at the 'Crown' at Hounslow,
where he must watch forsooth all night, in order to get one
moment's glimpse of Beatrix in the morning. And fate had
decreed that he was to have a fourth night's ride and wake-
fulness before his business was ended.

He ran to the curate's house in Kensington Mall, and
asked for Mr. Bates, the name the prince went by. The
curate's wife said Mr. Bates had gone abroad very early in
the morning in his boots, saying he was going to the Bishop
of Rochester's house at Chelsea. But the bishop had been
at Kensington himself two hours ago to seek for Mr. Bates,
and had returned in his coach to his own house, when he
heard that the gentleman was gone thither to seek him.

This absence was most unpropitious, for an hour's delay might cost a kingdom ; Esmond had nothing for it but to hasten to the 'King's Arms', and tell the gentlemen there assembled that Mr. George (as we called the prince there) was not at home, but that Esmond would go fetch him ; and taking a general's coach that happened to be there, Esmond drove across the country to Chelsea, to the bishop's house there.

The porter said two gentlemen were with his lordship, and Esmond ran past this sentry up to the locked door of the bishop's study, at which he rattled, and was admitted presently. Of the bishop's guests one was a brother prelate, and the other the Abbé G——.

'Where is Mr. George ?' says Mr. Esmond ; 'now is the time.' The bishop looked scared ; 'I went to his lodging,' he said, 'and they told me he was come hither. I returned as quick as coach would carry me ; and he hath not been here.'

The colonel burst out with an oath ; that was all he could say to their reverences ; ran down the stairs again, and bidding the coachman, an old friend and fellow-campaigner, drive as if he was charging the French with his master at Wynendael—they were back at Kensington in half an hour.

Again Esmond went to the curate's house. Mr. George had not returned. The colonel had to go with this blank errand to the gentlemen at the 'King's Arms', that were grown very impatient by this time.

Out of the window of the tavern, and looking over the garden-wall, you can see the green before Kensington Palace, the Palace gate (round which the ministers' coaches were standing), and the barrack building. As we were looking out from this window in gloomy discourse, we heard presently trumpets blowing, and some of us ran to the window of the front room, looking into the High Street of Kensington, and saw a regiment of horse coming.

'It's Ormonde's Guards,' says one.

'No, by God, it's Argyle's old regiment !' says my general, clapping down his crutch.

It was, indeed, Argyle's regiment that was brought from Westminster, and that took the place of the regiment at Kensington on which we could rely.

'Oh, Harry !' says one of the generals there present, 'you were born under an unlucky star ; I begin to think that there's no Mr. George, nor Mr. Dragon either. 'Tis not the peerage I care for, for our name is so ancient and famous, that merely to be called Lord Lydiard would do me no good; but 'tis the chance you promised me of fighting Marlborough.'

As we were talking, Castlewood entered the room with a disturbed air.

'What news, Frank?' says the colonel, 'is Mr. George coming at last?'

'Damn him, look here!' says Castlewood, holding out a paper. 'I found it in the book—the what you call it, *Eikum Basilikum*,—that villain Martin put it there—he said his young mistress bade him. It was directed to me, but it was meant for him I know, and I broke the seal and read it.'

The whole assembly of officers seemed to swim away before Esmond's eyes as he read the paper; all that was written on it was:—'Beatrix Esmond is sent away to prison, to Castlewood, where she will pray for happier days.'

'Can you guess where he is?' says Castlewood.

'Yes,' says Colonel Esmond. He knew full well, Frank knew full well: our instinct told whither that traitor had fled.

He had courage to turn to the company and say, 'Gentlemen, I fear very much that Mr. George will not be here to-day; something hath happened—and—and—I very much fear some accident may befall him, which must keep him out of the way. Having had your noon's draught, you had best pay the reckoning and go home; there can be no game where there is no one to play it.'

Some of the gentlemen went away without a word, others called to pay their duty to her Majesty and ask for her health. The little army disappeared into the darkness out of which it had been called; there had been no writings, no paper to implicate any man. Some few officers and members of Parliament had been invited overnight to breakfast at the 'King's Arms', at Kensington; and they had called for their bill and gone home.

CHAPTER XIII

AUGUST 1ST, 1714

' Does my mistress know of this ? ' Esmond asked of Frank, as they walked along.

' My mother found the letter in the book, on the toilet-table. She had writ it ere she had left home,' Frank said. ' Mother met her on the stairs, with her hand upon the door, trying to enter, and never left her after that till she went away. He did not think of looking at it there, nor had Martin the chance of telling him. I believe the poor devil meant no harm, though I half killed him ; he thought 'twas to Beatrix's brother he was bringing the letter.'

Frank never said a word of reproach to me, for having brought the villain amongst us. As we knocked at the door I said ; ' When will the horses be ready ? ' Frank pointed with his cane, they were turning the street that moment.

We went up and bade adieu to our mistress ; she was in a dreadful state of agitation by this time, and that bishop was with her whose company she was so fond of.

' Did you tell him, my lord,' says Esmond, ' that Beatrix was at Castlewood ? ' The bishop blushed and stammered : ' Well,' says he, ' I—— '

' You served the villain right,' broke out Mr. Esmond, ' and he has lost a crown by what you told him.'

My mistress turned quite white. ' Henry, Henry,' says she, ' do not kill him.'

' It may not be too late,' says Esmond ; ' he may not have gone to Castlewood ; pray God, it is not too late.' The bishop was breaking out with some *banales* phrases about loyalty and the sacredness of the sovereign's person : but Esmond sternly bade him hold his tongue, burn all papers, and take care of Lady Castlewood ; and in five minutes he and Frank were in the saddle, John Lockwood behind them, riding towards Castlewood at a rapid pace.

We were just got to Alton, when who should meet us but old Lockwood, the porter from Castlewood, John's father, walking by the side of the Hexham flying-coach, who slept the night at Alton. Lockwood said his young mistress had arrived at home on Wednesday night, and this morning, Friday, had dispatched him with a packet for my lady at Kensington, saying the letter was of great importance.

We took the freedom to break it, while Lockwood stared with wonder, and cried out his ' Lord bless me's ', and ' Who'd a thought it's ', at the sight of his young lord, whom he had not seen these seven years.

The packet from Beatrix contained no news of importance at all. It was written in a jocular strain, affecting to make light of her captivity. She asked whether she might have leave to visit Mrs. Tusher, or to walk beyond the court and the garden-wall. She gave news of the peacocks, and a fawn she had there. She bade her mother send her certain gowns and smocks by old Lockwood ; she sent her duty to a certain person, if certain other persons permitted her to take such a freedom ; how that, as she was not able to play cards with him, she hoped he would read good books, such as Dr. Atterbury's sermons and *Eikon Basilike :* she was going to read good books : she thought her pretty mamma would like to know she was not crying her eyes out.

' Who is in the house besides you, Lockwood ? ' says the colonel.

' There be the laundry-maid, and the kitchen-maid, Madam Beatrix's maid, the man from London, and that be all ; and he sleepeth in my lodge away from the maids,' says old Lockwood.

Esmond scribbled a line with a pencil on the note, giving it to the old man, and bidding him go on to his lady. We knew why Beatrix had been so dutiful on a sudden, and why she spoke of *Eikon Basilike.* She writ this letter to put the prince on the scent, and the porter out of the way.

' We have a fine moonlight night for riding on,' says Esmond ; ' Frank, we may reach Castlewood in time yet.' All the way along they made inquiries at the post-houses, when a tall young gentleman in a grey suit, with a light-brown periwig, just the colour of my lord's, had been seen to pass. He had set off at six that morning, and we at three in the afternoon. He rode almost as quickly as we had done ; he was seven hours ahead of us still when we reached the last stage.

We rode over Castlewood Downs before the breaking of dawn. We passed the very spot where the car was upset fourteen years since ; and Mohun lay. The village was not up yet, nor the forge lighted, as we rode through it, passing by the elms, where the rooks were still roosting, and by the church, and over the bridge. We got off our horses at the bridge and walked up to the gate.

' If she is safe,' says Frank, trembling, and his honest eyes filling with tears, ' a silver statue to Our Lady ! ' He was going to rattle at the great iron knocker on the oak gate ; but Esmond stopped his kinsman's hand. He had his own fears, his own hopes, his own despairs and griefs, too : but he spoke not a word of these to his companion, or showed any signs of emotion.

He went and tapped at the little window at the porter's lodge, gently, but repeatedly, until the man came to the bars.

' Who's there ? ' says he, looking out ; it was the servant from Kensington.

' My Lord Castlewood and Colonel Esmond,' we said, from below. ' Open the gate and let us in without any noise.'

' My Lord Castlewood ? ' says the other ; ' my lord's here, and in bed.'

' Open, d—n you,' says Castlewood, with a curse.

' I shall open to no one,' says the man, shutting the glass window as Frank drew a pistol. He would have fired at the porter, but Esmond again held his hand.

' There are more ways than one,' says he, ' of entering such a great house as this.' Frank grumbled that the west gate was half a mile round. ' But I know of a way that's not a hundred yards off,' says Mr. Esmond ; and leading his kinsman close along the wall, and by the shrubs, which had now grown thick on what had been an old moat about the house, they came to the buttress, at the side of which the little window was, which was Father Holt's private door. Esmond climbed up to this easily, broke a pane that had been mended, and touched the spring inside, and the two gentlemen passed in that way, treading as lightly as they could ; and so going through the passage into the court, over which the dawn was now reddening, and where the fountain plashed in the silence.

They sped instantly to the porter's lodge, where the fellow had not fastened his door that led into the court ;

and pistol in hand came upon the terrified wretch, and
bade him be silent. Then they asked him (Esmond's head
reeled, and he almost fell as he spoke) when Lord Castlewood had arrived ? He said on the previous evening,
about eight of the clock.—' And what then ? '—His lordship supped with his sister.—' Did the man wait ? ' Yes,
he and my lady's maid both waited : the other servants
made the supper ; and there was no wine, and they could
give his lordship but milk, at which he grumbled ; and—
and Madam Beatrix kept Miss Lucy always in the room
with her. And there being a bed across the court in the
chaplain's room, she had arranged my lord was to sleep
there. Madam Beatrix had come downstairs laughing with
the maids, and had locked herself in, and my lord had
stood for a while talking to her through the door, and
she laughing at him. And then he paced the court awhile,
and she came again to the upper window ; and my lord
implored her to come down and walk in the room ; but
she would not, and laughed at him again, and shut the
window ; and so my lord uttering what seemed curses, but
in a foreign language, went to the chaplain's room to bed.

' Was this all ? '—' All,' the man swore upon his honour ;
' all as he hoped to be saved.—Stop, there was one thing
more. My lord, on arriving, and once or twice during
supper, did kiss his sister as was natural, and she kissed
him.' At this Esmond ground his teeth with rage, and
wellnigh throttled the amazed miscreant who was speaking,
whereas Castlewood, seizing hold of his cousin's hand, burst
into a great fit of laughter.

' If it amuses thee,' says Esmond in French, ' that your
sister should be exchanging of kisses with a stranger, I fear
poor Beatrix will give thee plenty of sport.'—Esmond
darkly thought, how Hamilton, Ashburnham, had before
been masters of those roses that the young prince's lips
were now feeding on. He sickened at that notion. Her
cheek was desecrated, her beauty tarnished ; shame and
honour stood between it and him. The love was dead
within him ; had she a crown to bring him with her love,
he felt that both would degrade him.

But this wrath against Beatrix did not lessen the angry
feelings of the colonel against the man who had been the
occasion if not the cause of the evil. Frank sat down on
a stone bench in the courtyard, and fairly fell asleep, while

Esmond paced up and down the court, debating what should ensue. What mattered how much or how little had passed between the prince and the poor faithless girl ? They were arrived in time perhaps to rescue her person, but not her mind ; had she not instigated the young prince to come to her ; suborned servants, dismissed others, so that she might communicate with him ? The treacherous heart within her had surrendered, though the place was safe ; and it was to win this that he had given a life's struggle and devotion ; this, that she was ready to give away for the bribe of a coronet or a wink of the prince's eye.

When he had thought his thoughts out he shook up poor Frank from his sleep, who rose yawning, and said he had been dreaming of Clotilda. ' You must back me,' says Esmond, ' in what I am going to do. I have been thinking that yonder scoundrel may have been instructed to tell that story, and that the whole of it may be a lie ; if it be, we shall find it out from the gentleman who is asleep yonder. See if the door leading to my lady's rooms ' (so we called the rooms at the north-west angle of the house), ' see if the door is barred as he saith.' We tried ; it was indeed as the lackey had said, closed within.

' It may have been open and shut afterwards,' says poor Esmond ; ' the foundress of our family let our ancestor in in that way.'

' What will you do, Harry, if—if what that fellow saith should turn out untrue ? ' The young man looked scared and frightened into his kinsman's face ; I dare say it wore no very pleasant expression.

' Let us first go see whether the two stories agree,' says Esmond ; and went in at the passage and opened the door into what had been his own chamber now for wellnigh five-and-twenty years. A candle was still burning, and the prince asleep dressed on the bed—Esmond did not care for making a noise. The prince started up in his bed, seeing two men in his chamber : ' Qui est là ? ' says he, and took a pistol from under his pillow.

' It is the Marquis of Esmond,' says the colonel, ' come to welcome his Majesty to his house of Castlewood, and to report of what hath happened in London. Pursuant to the king's orders, I passed the night before last, after leaving his Majesty, in waiting upon the friends of the king. It is a pity that his Majesty's desire to see the country and to visit our poor house should have caused the king to quit London without notice yesterday, when the opportunity happened which in all human probability may not occur again; and had the king not chosen to ride to Castlewood, the Prince of Wales might have slept at St. James's.'

' 'Sdeath! gentlemen,' says the prince, starting off his bed, whereon he was lying in his clothes, ' the doctor was with me yesterday morning, and after watching by my sister all night, told me I might not hope to see the queen.'

'It would have been otherwise,' says Esmond, with another bow; ' as, by this time, the queen may be dead in spite of the doctor. The Council was met, a new treasurer was appointed, the troops were devoted to the king's cause; and fifty loyal gentlemen of the greatest names of this kingdom were assembled to accompany the Prince of Wales, who might have been the acknowledged heir of the throne, or the possessor of it by this time, had your Majesty not chosen to take the air. We were ready; there was only one person that failed us, your Majesty's gracious—— '

' *Morbleu! monsieur*, you give me too much Majesty,' said the prince; who had now risen up and seemed to be looking to one of us to help him to his coat. But neither stirred.

' We shall take care,' says Esmond, ' not much oftener to offend in that particular.'

' What mean you, my lord?' says the prince, and muttered something about a *guet-à-pens*, which Esmond caught up.

' The snare, sir,' said he, ' was not of our laying; it is not we that invited you. We came to avenge, and not to compass, the dishonour of our family.'

' Dishonour! *Morbleu!* there has been no dishonour,' says the prince, turning scarlet, ' only a little harmless playing.'

' That was meant to end seriously.'

' I swear,' the prince broke out impetuously, ' upon the honour of a gentleman, my lords—— '

' That we arrived in time. No wrong hath been done, Frank,' says Colonel Esmond, turning round to young Castlewood, who stood at the door as the talk was going

on. ' See ! here is a paper whereon his Majesty hath
deigned to commence some verses in honour, or dishonour,
of Beatrix. Here is *madame* and *flamme, cruelle* and
rebelle, and *amour* and *jour,* in the royal writing and
spelling. Had the gracious lover been happy, he had not
passed his time in sighing.' In fact, and actually as he
was speaking, Esmond cast his eyes down towards the
table, and saw a paper on which my young prince had
been scrawling a madrigal, that was to finish his charmer
on the morrow.

' Sir,' says the prince, burning with rage (he had assumed
his royal coat unassisted by this time), ' did I come here
to receive insults ? '

' To confer them, may it please your Majesty,' says the
colonel, with a very low bow, ' and the gentlemen of our
family are come to thank you.'

' *Malédiction !* ' says the young man, tears starting into
his eyes with helpless rage and mortification. ' What will
you with me, gentlemen ? '

' If your Majesty will please to enter the next apartment,'
says Esmond, preserving his grave tone, ' I have some
papers there which I would gladly submit to you, and by
your permission I will lead the way ; ' and, taking the
taper up, and backing before the prince with very great
ceremony, Mr. Esmond passed into the little chaplain's
room, through which we had just entered into the house :—
' Please to set a chair for his Majesty, Frank,' says the
colonel to his companion, who wondered almost as much
at this scene, and was as much puzzled by it, as the other
actor in it. Then going to the crypt over the mantelpiece,
the colonel opened it, and drew thence the papers which so
long had lain there.

' Here, may it please your Majesty,' says he, ' is the
patent of Marquis sent over by your royal father at St.
Germains to Viscount Castlewood, my father : here is the
witnessed certificate of my father's marriage to my mother,
and of my birth and christening ; I was christened of that
religion of which your sainted sire gave all through life so
shining example. These are my titles, dear Frank, and this
what I do with them : here go baptism and marriage,
and here the marquisate and the august sign-manual, with
which your predecessor was pleased to honour our race.'
And as Esmond spoke he set the papers burning in the

brasier. ' You will please, sir, to remember,' he continued,
' that our family hath ruined itself by fidelity to yours :
that my grandfather spent his estate, and gave his blood
and his son to die for your service ; that my dear lord's
grandfather (for lord you are now, Frank, by right and
title too) died for the same cause ; that my poor kinswoman,
my father's second wife, after giving away her honour to
your wicked perjured race, sent all her wealth to the king ;
and got in return that precious title that lies in ashes, and
this inestimable yard of blue ribbon. I lay this at your
feet and stamp upon it : I draw this sword, and break it
and deny you ; and, had you completed the wrong you
designed us, by Heaven I would have driven it through
your heart, and no more pardoned you than your father
pardoned Monmouth. Frank will do the same, won't you,
cousin ? '

Frank, who had been looking on with a stupid air at the
papers as they flamed in the old brasier, took out his sword
and broke it, holding his head down :—' I go with my
cousin,' says he, giving Esmond a grasp of the hand.
' Marquis or not, by ——, I stand by him any day. I beg
your Majesty's pardon for swearing ; that is—that is—I'm
for the Elector of Hanover. . It's all your Majesty's own
fault. The queen's dead most likely by this time. And
you might have been king if you hadn't come dangling
after 'Trix '.

' Thus to lose a crown,' says the young prince, starting
up, and speaking French in his eager way ; ' to lose the
loveliest woman in the world ; to lose the loyalty of such
hearts as yours, is not this, my lords, enough of humiliation ?—Marquis, if I go on my knees will you pardon me ?—
No, I can't do that, but I can offer you reparation, that
of honour, that of gentlemen. Favour me by crossing the
sword with mine : yours is broke—see, yonder in the
armoire are two ; ' and the prince took them out as eager
as a boy, and held them towards Esmond :—' Ah ! you will ?
Merci, monsieur, merci ! '

Extremely touched by this immense mark of condescen-
sion and repentance for wrong done, Colonel Esmond bowed
down so low as almost to kiss the gracious young hand
that conferred on him such an honour, and took his guard
in silence. The swords were no sooner met, than Castlewood knocked up Esmond's with the blade of his own,

which he had broke off short at the shell ; and the colonel
falling back a step dropped his point with another very
low bow, and declared himself perfectly satisfied.

' *Eh bien, vicomte,*' says the young prince, who was
a boy, and a French boy, ' *il ne nous reste qu'une chose
à faire :* ' he placed his sword upon the table, and the fingers
of his two hands upon his breast :—' We have one more
thing to do,' says he ; ' you do not divine it ? ' He stretched
out his arms :—' *Embrassons nous !* '

The talk was scarce over when Beatrix entered the
room :—What came she to seek there ? She started and
turned pale at the sight of her brother and kinsman, drawn
swords, broken sword-blades, and papers yet smouldering
in the brasier.

' Charming Beatrix,' says the prince, with a blush which
became him very well, ' these lords have come a-horseback
from London, where my sister lies in a despaired state, and
where her successor makes himself desired. Pardon me
for my escapade of last evening. I had been so long a
prisoner, that I seized the occasion of a promenade on
horseback, and my horse naturally bore me towards you.
I found you a queen in your little court, where you deigned
to entertain me. Present my homages to your maids of
honour. I sighed as you slept, under the window of your
chamber, and then retired to seek rest in my own. It was
there that these gentlemen agreeably roused me. Yes,
milords, for that is a happy day that makes a prince
acquainted, at whatever cost to his vanity, with such a noble
heart as that of the Marquis of Esmond. Mademoiselle,
may we take your coach to town ? I saw it in the hangar,
and this poor marquis must be dropping with sleep.'

' Will it please the king to breakfast before he goes ? '
was all Beatrix could say. The roses had shuddered out
of her cheeks ; her eyes were glaring ; she looked quite old.
She came up to Esmond and hissed out a word or two :—
' If I did not love you before, cousin,' says she, ' think how
I love you now.' If words could stab, no doubt she would
have killed Esmond ; she looked at him as if she could.

But her keen words gave no wound to Mr. Esmond ; his
heart was too hard. As he looked at her, he wondered
that he could ever have loved her. His love of ten years
was over ; it fell down dead on the spot, at the Kensington
tavern, where Frank brought him the note out of *Eikon*

Basilike. The prince blushed and bowed low, as she gazed at him, and quitted the chamber. I have never seen her from that day.

Horses were fetched and put to the chariot presently. My lord rode outside, and as for Esmond he was so tired that he was no sooner in the carriage than he fell asleep, and never woke till night, as the coach came into Alton.

As we drove to the ' Bell Inn ' comes a mitred coach with our old friend Lockwood beside the coachman. My Lady Castlewood and the bishop were inside ; she gave a little scream when she saw us. The two coaches entered the inn almost together ; the landlord and people coming out with lights to welcome the visitors.

We in our coach sprang out of it, as soon as ever we saw the dear lady, and above all, the doctor in his cassock. What was the news ? Was there yet time ? Was the queen alive ? These questions were put hurriedly, as Boniface stood waiting before his noble guests to bow them up the stair.

' Is she safe ? ' was what Lady Castlewood whispered in a flutter to Esmond.

' All's well, thank God,' says he, as the fond lady took his hand and kissed it, and called him her preserver and her dear. *She* wasn't thinking of queens and crowns.

The bishop's news was reassuring : at least all was not lost ; the queen yet breathed or was alive when they left London, six hours since. (' It was Lady Castlewood who insisted on coming,' the doctor said ;) Argyle had marched up regiments from Portsmouth, and sent abroad for more ; the Whigs were on the alert, a pest on them (I am not sure but the bishop swore as he spoke), and so too were our people. And all might be saved, if only the prince could be at London in time. We called for horses, instantly to return to London. We never went up poor crestfallen Boniface's stairs, but into our coaches again. The prince and his prime minister in one, Esmond in the other, with only his dear mistress as a companion.

Castlewood galloped forwards on horseback to gather the prince's friends, and warn them of his coming. We travelled through the night. Esmond discoursing to his mistress of the events of the last twenty-four hours ; of Castlewood's ride and his ; of the prince's generous behaviour and their reconciliation. The night seemed short enough ; and the starlit hours passed away serenely in that fond company.

So we came along the road ; the bishop's coach heading ours ; and, with some delays in procuring horses, we got to Hammersmith about four o'clock on Sunday morning, the first of August, and half an hour after, it being then bright day, we rode by my Lady Warwick's house, and so down the street of Kensington.

Early as the hour was, there was a bustle in the street, and many people moving to and fro. Round the gate leading to the palace, where the guard is, there was especially a great crowd. And the coach ahead of us stopped, and the bishop's man got down to know what the concourse meant ?

There presently came from out of the gate : Horse Guards with their trumpets, and a company of heralds with their tabards. The trumpets blew, and the herald-at-arms came forward and proclaimed GEORGE, by the grace of God, of Great Britain, France, and Ireland,. King, Defender of the Faith. And the people shouted, ' God save the King ! '

Among the crowd shouting and waving their hats, I caught sight of one sad face, which I had known all my life, and seen under many disguises. It was no other than poor Mr. Holt's, who had slipped over to England to witness the triumph of the good cause ; and now beheld its enemies victorious, amidst the acclamations of the English people. The poor fellow had forgot to huzzah or to take his hat off, until his neighbours in the crowd remarked his want of loyalty, and cursed him for a Jesuit in disguise, when he ruefully uncovered and began to cheer. Sure he was the most unlucky of men : he never played a game but he lost it ; or engaged in a conspiracy but 'twas certain to end in defeat. I saw him in Flanders after this, whence he went to Rome to the head quarters of his Order ; and actually reappeared among us in America, very old, and busy, and hopeful. I am not sure that he did not assume the hatchet and moccasins there ; and, attired in a blanket and war-paint, skulk about a missionary amongst the Indians. He lies buried in our neighbouring province of Maryland now, with a cross over him, and a mound of earth above him ; under which that unquiet spirit is for ever at peace.

With the sound of King George's trumpets, all the vain hopes of the weak and foolish young pretender were blown away ; and with that music, too, I may say, the drama of my own life was ended. That happiness, which hath subsequently crowned it, cannot be written in words ; 'tis of its nature sacred and secret, and not to be spoken of, though the heart be ever so full of thankfulness, save to Heaven and the One Ear alone—to one fond being, the truest and tenderest and purest wife ever man was blessed with. As I think of the immense happiness which was in store for me, and of the depth and intensity of that love which, for so many years, hath blessed me, I own to a transport of wonder and gratitude for such a boon—nay, am thankful to have been endowed with a heart capable of feeling and knowing the immense beauty and value of the gift which God hath bestowed upon me. Sure, love *vincit omnia ;* is immeasurably above all ambition, more precious than wealth, more noble than name. He knows not life who knows not that : he hath not felt the highest faculty of the soul who hath not enjoyed it. In the name of my wife I write the completion of hope, and the summit of happiness. To have such a love is the one blessing, in comparison of which all earthly joy is of no value ; and to think of her, is to praise God.

It was at Bruxelles, whither we retreated after the failure of our plot—our Whig friends advising us to keep out of the way—that the great joy of my life was bestowed upon me, and that my dear mistress became my wife. We had been so accustomed to an extreme intimacy and confidence, and had lived so long and tenderly together, that we might have gone on to the end without thinking of a closer tie ; but circumstances brought about that event which so prodigiously multiplied my happiness and hers (for which I humbly thank Heaven), although a calamity befell us, which, I blush to think, hath occurred more than once in our house. I know not what infatuation of ambition urged the beautiful and wayward woman, whose name hath occupied so many of these pages, and who was served by me with ten years of such a constant fidelity and passion ; but ever after that day at Castlewood, when we rescued her, she persisted in holding all her family as her enemies, and left us, and escaped to France, to what a fate I disdain to tell. Nor was her son's house a home for my dear mistress ; my poor Frank was weak, as perhaps all our race hath been, and led by women. Those around him were imperious, and in a terror of his mother's influence over him, lest he should recant, and deny the creed which he had adopted by their persuasion. The difference of their religion separated the son and the mother : my dearest mistress felt that she was severed from her children and alone in the world— alone but for one constant servant on whose fidelity, praised be Heaven, she could count. 'Twas after a scene of ignoble quarrel on the part of Frank's wife and mother (for the poor lad had been made to marry the whole of that German family with whom he had connected himself), that I found my mistress one day in tears, and then besought her to confide herself to the care and devotion of one who, by God's help, would never forsake her. And then the tender matron, as beautiful in her autumn, and as pure as virgins in their spring, with blushes of love and ' eyes of meek surrender ',* yielded to my respectful importunity, and consented to share my home. Let the last words I write thank her, and bless her who hath blessed it.

By the kindness of Mr. Addison, all danger of prosecution, and every obstacle against our return to England, was removed ; and my son Frank's gallantry in Scotland made his peace with the king's Government. But we two cared no longer to live in England ; and Frank formally and joyfully yielded over to us the possession of that estate which we now occupy, far away from Europe and its troubles, on the beautiful banks of the Potomac, where we have built a new Castlewood, and think with grateful hearts of our old home. In our Transatlantic country we have a season, the calmest and most delightful of the year, which we call the Indian summer : I often say the autumn of our life resembles that happy and serene weather, and am thankful for its rest and its sweet sunshine. Heaven hath blessed us with a child, which each parent loves for her resemblance to the other. Our diamonds are turned into ploughs and axes for our plantations ; and into negroes, the happiest and merriest, I think, in all this country : and the only jewel by which my wife sets any store, and from which she hath never parted, is that gold button she took from my arm on the day when she visited me in prison, and which she wore ever after, as she told me, on the tenderest heart in the world.

APPENDIX

Book I, chap. viii, p. 80, line 9 : ' mist ' was wrongly altered in revised edition to ' midst '.

Book I, chap. xii, p. 130, line 2 from foot : ' through ' was wrongly altered in revised edition to ' to '.

Book II, chap. ii, p. 179, line 7 from foot : ' guests,' though never altered, should clearly be ' hosts '.

Book II, chap. xv, p. 307, line 8 : the following passage was omitted in the edition of 1858 :—

> ' I always thought that paper was Mr. Congreve's,' cries Mr. St. John, showing that he knew more about the subject than he pretended to Mr. Steele, and who was the original Mr. Bickerstaffe drew.
>
> ' Tom Boxer said so in his *Observator*. But Tom's oracle is often making blunders,' cries Steele.
>
> ' Mr. Boxer and my husband were friends once, and when the captain was ill with the fever, no man could be kinder than Mr. Boxer, who used to come to his bedside every day, and actually brought Dr. Arbuthnot who cured him,' whispered Mrs. Steele.
>
> ' Indeed, madam ! How very interesting,' says Mr. St. John.
>
> ' But when the captain's last comedy came out, Mr. Boxer took no notice of it—you know he is Mr. Congreve's man, and won't ever give a word to the other house—and this made my husband angry.'
>
> ' Oh ! Mr. Boxer is Mr. Congreve's man ! ' says Mr. St. John.
>
> ' Mr. Congreve has wit enough of his own,' cries out Mr. Steele. ' No one ever heard me grudge him or any other man his share.'

Book III, chap. i, p. 326, line 19 : for ' Frank ', Thackeray by an interesting reminiscence of *Pendennis* wrote ' Arthur '.

GENEALOGY OF THE ESMOND FAMILY

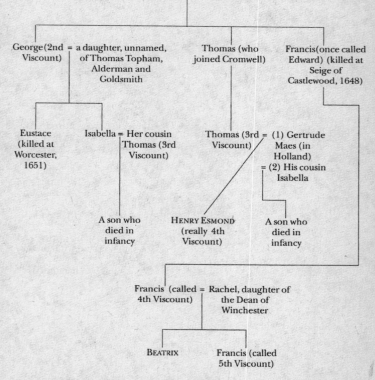

Edward, Earl and Marquis of Esmond, and Lord of Castlewood

Dorothea = Henry Poyns, gent. (1581)

Francis (took his mother's name, and made Knight and Baronet by James I. Fought for the Elector Palatine, and made Warden of the Butteries and Groom of the King's Posset. Created Viscount Castlewood by Charles I in 1643)

George (2nd = a daughter, unnamed,   Thomas (who   Francis (once called
Viscount)   of Thomas Topham,   joined Cromwell)   Edward) (killed at
               Alderman and   Seige of
               Goldsmith   Castlewood, 1648)

Eustace   Isabella = Her cousin   Thomas (3rd = (1) Gertrude
(killed   Thomas (3rd   Viscount)   Maes (in
at Worcester,   Viscount)   Holland)
1651)   = (2) His cousin
                                             Isabella

               A son who   HENRY ESMOND   A son who
               died in   (really 4th   died in
               infancy   Viscount)   infancy

Francis (called = Rachel, daughter of
4th Viscount)   the Dean of
                   Winchester

BEATRIX   Francis (called
               5th Viscount)

Reproduced from *The History of Henry Esmond*, ed. T. C. and William Snow (Oxford, 2nd edition, 1915).

EXPLANATORY NOTES

IN my notes I owe much, including many of the translations from Latin, to *Henry Esmond* edited by T. C. and William Snow (Oxford: Clarendon Press, 1909; revised edition, 1915). That edition contains comprehensive annotation, chronological tables, biographies of the principal historical figures, and an index. I also acknowledge the assistance I have had from Gordon N. Ray's edition of Thackeray's *Letters and Private Papers* and from Mr T. E. Kinsey (for the note on Euripides on p. 97). In my explanations, I have used modern conventional spellings of proper names.

1   *et sibi constet*: 'See it be wrought on one consistent plan, | And end the same creation it began' (Horace, *Art of Poetry*, 126–7, trans. John Conington). Horace's reference to the creation of a character may also be intended by Thackeray as a reference to the construction of *Henry Esmond* as a whole. See Andrew Sanders, *The Victorian Historical Novel 1840–1880* (Basingstoke and London, 1978), p. 109.

5   *Lord Ashburton*: the 2nd Baron (1799–1864), whose first wife, Harriet (1805–57), the friend of Carlyle and Thackeray, tried to effect a reconciliation between Thackeray and the Brookfields after the breach between them.

8   *Rochambeau*: the comte de Rochambeau (1725–1807) commanded a force of 6,000 men in support of Washington.

10   *Dawley*: Bolingbroke's estate in Buckinghamshire (near Uxbridge) where he temporarily settled in 1725. Henry St John, 1st Viscount Bolingbroke (1678–1751), entered the House of Commons in 1701 and had a turbulent political career. As Secretary of State, he was the most prominent statesman towards the end of Queen Anne's reign. (See Historical Background.) After a period in the service of the exiled Prince James Edward, he returned to England, writing many attacks on Walpole and the Whigs. He retired again to France in 1735 and wrote *The Patriot King* in 1738.

After 1739, his political effectiveness came to an end. In 1743 he finally returned to England.

Sachem: the supreme head or chief of some American Indian tribes (*OED*).

Pocahontas: an American Indian princess (*c.*1595–1617), who reputedly saved Captain John Smith's life in Virginia, married John Rolfe in 1614, and died at Gravesend. See *The Virginians*, ch. 80.

Lord Stair: Sir John Dalrymple, 1st Earl of Stair (1648–1707), general and diplomat.

13   *Mr. Dryden's words*: perhaps reminiscences of Shakespeare's phrase in *Twelfth Night*, I. i. 4, Dryden's 'The soft complaining flute | In dying notes discovers | The woes of hopeless lovers' (*A Song for St. Cecilia's Day, 1687*, 33–5) and Pope's 'The strains decay, | And melt away | In a dying, dying fall' (*Ode for Music, on St. Cecilia's Day*, 19–21).

15   *Cato*: Addison's blank-verse tragedy (1713), which Thackeray described as a 'prodigious poem' in *The English Humourists*.

Ostade or Mieris: Adriaen Van Ostade (1610–84) and presumably Frans Van Mieris (1635–81), Dutch painters of low-life 'genre' subjects.

Your Knellers and Le Bruns: Sir Godfrey Kneller (1649?–1723) and Charles Lebrun (1619–90), painters at the English and French courts respectively. Thackeray called the former painter 'the wonderful Kneller' in *The English Humourists*.

16   *his last journey to Tyburn*: Thackeray is recalling the 11th and 12th engravings in Hogarth's series, *Industry and Idleness* (1747): 'The Idle 'Prentice Executed at Tyburn' and 'The Industrious 'Prentice Lord-Mayor of London'.

Castlewood Hall: the titles of this chapter and Chapter II should be transposed.

Mr. Dobson: Van Dyck (1599–1641) and William Dobson (1610–46) were both court painters in the service of Charles I.

17　*Dea certè*: 'a goddess manifest' (Virgil, *Aeneid*, i. 328).

20　*when the sweetmeats were brought*: '[The chaplain] might fill himself with the corned beef and the carrots: but, as soon as the tarts and the cheesecakes made their appearance, he quitted his seat, and stood aloof till he was summoned to return thanks for the repast, from a great part of which he had been excluded' (Macaulay, *History of England*, ch. 3).

23·　*Jack Churchill*: John Churchill, 1st Duke of Marlborough (1650–1722), was educated at St Paul's School. He married Sarah Jennings in 1678; their only son died in 1703 (p. 232). He served James II and William and Mary as a military commander, and was raised to the peerage in 1682. Sarah Churchill became Queen Anne's influential favourite, and her husband was created Duke of Marlborough in 1702. His great triumphs in the campaigns against the French raised him to the height of fame, but he was eventually dismissed from his command. (See Historical Background.) Although he returned to England under the reign of George I, he never regained his former powerful position, and ended his days suffering from the effects of a stroke and senile decay.

　　your sister: Arabella Churchill (1648–1730), the mistress of the Duke of York (later, James II), by whom she had two daughters and two sons, including the Duke of Berwick (1670–1734).

24　*Alsatia and the Friars*: the disreputable area in Whitefriars, London, where thieves, debtors, and other criminals could find sanctuary.

　　toy-shops: shops 'for the sale of trinkets, knick-knacks, or small ornamental articles' (*OED*).

　　Mr. Killigrew: Thomas Killigrew (1612–83), playwright, theatre manager, and wit.

25　*Mr. Wycherley*: William Wycherley (1640?–1716), the Restoration playwright.

26　*Lady Dorchester*: Catherine, Countess of Dorchester (1657–1717), a mistress of the Duke of York's, was, in fact, the daughter of Sir Charles Sedley, the poet, playwright, and wit.

our elderly Vashti: King Ahasuerus chose Esther, a humble maiden, as his queen in place of his beautiful, disobedient wife, Vashti (Esther, 2: 17).

27 *No-Popery Cry*: this had also become a popular cry just before the publication of *Henry Esmond* because of the fear of 'papal aggression' associated with the restoration of the Catholic hierarchy in Britain in 1850. Thackeray would have known his friend John Leech's famous *Punch* cartoon of Lord John Russell, with its caption, 'This is the boy who chalked up "No Popery!"—and then ran away!!!' (22 March 1851).

30 *noverca*: stepmother (Latin).

31 *lions and bears in the moats*: a menagerie of wild animals was kept at the Tower of London from the reign of Henry III to 1834.

36 *the land of his youth*: when Aeneas landed in Italy, after the fall of Troy, he found that Helenus, who had preceded him there, had given places Trojan names (Virgil, *Aeneid*, iii. 349–57).

41 *his valet de chambre*: 'Il n'y a point de héros pour son valet de chambre', attributed to Mme Bigot de Cornuel (1605–94), among others.

42 *News Letter or the Grand Cyrus*: the *News Letter* was a periodical that ran from 7 January to 3 March 1716; it is in the Burney collection of periodicals in the British Library, almost certainly used by Thackeray in his reading for *Henry Esmond*. *Artamène, ou le Grand Cyrus* (1649–53), a vast 'heroic romance' by Mlle de Scudéry, is included in the lady's library described by Addison (*The Spectator*, No. 37, 12 April 1711).

Mr. Shadwell's: Thomas Shadwell (1642?–92), author of seventeen plays, including the lively comedies, *The Sullen Lovers* and *The Squire of Alsatia*.

50 *quinquina*: 'Peruvian or Jesuits' bark; the bark of several species of cinchona, yielding quinine and other febrifugal

alkaloids' (*OED*), first brought to Europe *c.*1650 by the Jesuits.

53 *of Queen's Crawley*: Lord Sark and Sir Wilmot Crawley are both fictional names. The latter is intended as the ancestor of the Crawleys in *Vanity Fair*.

Ginckel: Godert de Ginkel (1630–1703), the 1st Earl of Athlone, was a Dutch general in the service of William III.

60 *Sir John Fenwick and Mr. Coplestone*: Fenwick (1645?–97) was beheaded for conspiring against William III. Coplestone is unidentifiable. Further references to the conspiracy are on pp. 120, 121, and 393, below.

62 *Dick the Scholar*: Richard Steele (1672–1729) did not join the army until 1694. But though Thackeray's portrait of Steele is inaccurate in detail, 'it is very vivid, very human, and in most essentials could scarcely be disproved' (Austin Dobson, *Richard Steele*, 1888, p. 217). Steele became a gentleman waiter to Prince George of Denmark, Queen Anne's husband, in 1706. His notable literary works include the *Christian Hero* (p. 157). Most famous of all are his essays for *The Tatler* (1709–11), by the supposed Isaac Bickerstaff, and for *The Spectator* (1711–12); he was closely associated with Addison on these periodicals. Steele also engaged in political pamphleteering on behalf of the Whigs and was an MP for a short period (1713–14) before his expulsion from the House of Commons. He wrote a number of sentimental comedies, including *The Conscious Lovers* (1722). Thackeray's colourful depiction of his second wife, Mary Scurlock (pp. 304–8), has some basis in fact, since she was 'imperious and exacting' (Austin Dobson in the *DNB*). He was notoriously improvident.

63 *a sermon of Mr. Cudworth's*: the Revd. James Brogden had called Thackeray's attention to Ralph Cudworth's 'noble sermon', preached in English before the House of Commons on 31 March 1647. Shortly after the publication of *Henry Esmond*, Brogden dedicated an edition of the sermon to Thackeray (Cambridge, 1852).

65 *as upon certain Paradise*: in *The Present State of the Ottoman Empire* (1668), Sir Paul Rycaut wrote of 'that persuasion and principle . . . that the souls of those who die in the wars against the Christians . . . are immediately transported to Paradise' (Book II, ch. 3).

66 *Joe Addison*: Joseph Addison (1672–1719), the poet and essayist, was educated at Charterhouse (where Steele and Thackeray also went) and at The Queen's College and Magdalen College, Oxford. His composition of his poem, *The Campaign*, is described in Book II, Ch. XI. A Whig, Addison held a number of political appointments and became an MP in 1708. He was associated with Richard Steele in writing essays for *The Tatler* (1709–11) and *The Spectator* (1711–12; 1714); in the latter periodical, he created his famous character, Sir Roger de Coverley. His tragedy, *Cato* (1713), also brought him great fame (pp. 15, 343). He married the Countess of Warwick in 1716.

    deteriora sequi: 'Video meliora proboque; | deteriora sequor': 'I see the better course, and approve it; I follow the worse' (Ovid, *Metamorphoses*, vii. 20–1).

69 *unicum filium suum dilectissimum*: his only and beloved son.

70 *I ever knew*: most of this reminiscence is reproduced virtually verbatim from *The Tatler*, No. 181, 6 June 1710.

71 *maxima debetur pueris reverentia*: correctly, 'maxima debetur puero reverentia': 'the greatest reverence is due to a child' (Juvenal, *Satires*, xiv. 47).

75 *vacuae sedes et inania arcana*: correctly, 'vacuam sedem et inania arcana': 'the shrine tenantless and the secret chamber empty' (Tacitus, *History of Rome*, v. 9).

76 *aught in malice*: '. . . nothing extenuate, | Nor set down aught in malice' (*Othello*, v. ii. 345–6).

79 *inoculation from Turkey*: Lady Mary Wortley Montagu (1689–1762), letter-writer and traveller, introduced inoculation for smallpox soon after her return to England in 1718 from Constantinople, where her husband had been ambassador.

80 *Waller*: Edmund Waller (1606–87), poet, MP, and a favourite at the courts of Charles II and James II.

88 *can upset an empire*: William III died a few days after he was thrown from his horse, Sorrell, which stumbled on a molehill in Hampton Court Park.

90 *Mr. Prior's pretty poem*: 'I saw and kissed her in her shroud' (Matthew Prior, 'The Garland,' 36). Thackeray quotes four stanzas from this poem in his lecture on 'Prior, Gay, and Pope' in *The English Humourists*.

93 *Mr. Thomas Parr*: 'Old Parr', of Alderbury, near Shrewsbury, was reputed to have lived from *c.*1483 to 1635.

94 *Ovid's epistles*: these epistles, in elegiac verse, include letters from Oenone to Paris (No. 5) and from Medea to Jason (No. 12).

95 *indocilis pauperiem pati*: 'not schooled to suffer poverty' (Horace, *Odes*, i. 1. 18).

96 *Corderius and Lily*: the former is the Latinized surname of Mathurin Cordier (*c.*1480–1564), whose *Colloquia* was used as a Latin textbook in schools for 300 years. William Lily's Latin Grammar, compiled in the 1520s, also became a standard textbook, which was the basis of the Eton Latin Grammar.

pudet haec opprobria dicere nobis: 'it is a shame to tell us of such scandals' (adapted from Ovid, *Metamorphoses*, i. 758).

97 *the lady of Mr. Addison's opera*: Rosamond, Henry II's mistress, was the heroine of Addison's opera of that name, with music by Thomas Clayton, first performed on 2 April 1706. Queen Eleanor approaches Rosamond 'with a bowl in one hand, and a dagger in the other', offering her a choice of deaths (Act II, scene 6).

certain lines out of Euripides: presumably from *Medea*. An appropriate extract would be Medea's plea to Creon not to banish her from Corinth. Jason has deserted her and is about to marry Creon's daughter.

100 *our great English schoolmen*: the divines cited here, not always

appropriately, are William Wake (1657–1737), Archbishop of Canterbury; William Sherlock (1641–1709), Dean of St Paul's; Edward Stillingfleet (1635–99), Bishop of Worcester; Simon Patrick (1626–1727), Bishop of Ely; Jeremy Taylor (1613–67), the author of *Holy Living* (1650) and *Holy Dying* (1651); Richard Baxter (1615–91), presbyterian divine; and William Law (1686–1761), the author of the *Serious Call* (1728).

106   *Alnaschar*: Antoine Galland's French translation of the *Arabian Nights* was published in 1704–17. In the 'Barber's Fifth Brother', Alnaschar inadvertently smashes the glassware in his basket, while dreaming that he is already rich. 'In the years after he lost his fortune the story of Alnaschar and his tray of glass . . . became for Thackeray a symbol of his own history' (Ray, *Letters* i. 297 n.).

107   *Sir Peter Lely*: Lely (1618–80) was Principal Painter to Charles II.

108   *than my lord himself had ever done*: a pensioner was a Cambridge undergraduate who paid his own expenses. A junior soph was an undergraduate in his second year. John Montague was Master of Trinity College, Cambridge, 1683–99. Sir Isaac Newton attended Trinity College, as did Thackeray (as a pensioner).

110   *Don Dismallo*: the name applied by Tory writers to the 2nd Earl of Nottingham (1647–1730), as in Steele's reference to a 'Don Diego Dismallo' in *The Tatler*, No. 21, 28 May 1709.

     to procure it: this story, which appears in Spence's *Anecdotes*, is repeated in Macaulay's *History of England*, ch. 4.

111   *Calliope*: in Greek mythology, the muse of epic poetry and eloquence.

     Hobbs and Bayle: the famous work of William Chillingworth (1602–44), the religious controversialist, is *The Religion of Protestants a Safe Way to Salvation* (1637). Esmond also probably read *Leviathan* (1651) by Thomas Hobbes (1588–1679). But the *Dictionnaire historique et critique* (1697) by Pierre Bayle (1647–1706) appeared after Esmond had left Cambridge.

113   *he had borne a part*: various wars waged by France in the seventeenth century, with Turenne (1611–75) and Condé (1621–81) as the outstanding commanders.

escrime: fencing, which Thackeray himself practised for a while at Cambridge.

114   *Lord Mohun*: the first reference to the nobleman who plays such a prominent part in the novel. Charles, 4th Baron Mohun (1675?–1712), was 'a young nobleman whose life was one long revel and brawl' (Macaulay, *History of England*, ch. 19). At the age of 17, he was involved in the murder of William Mountfort, stabbed by Captain Richard Hill; he was tried by his peers but acquitted. After at least three further duels and brawls and a period of distinguished military service in Flanders (1694–6), Mohun, with the Earl of Warwick and others, was involved in an affray in November 1698 in Leicester Field, London, which resulted in the death of Captain Coote. Again, he was tried and acquitted. Thackeray, who describes this incident in his lecture on Steele in *The English Humourists*, used it as the basis for the episode in Book I, Ch. XIV. Mohun attended the Earl of Macclesfield on his embassy to Sophia, the Electress-Dowager (p. 192). A complex lawsuit with the crown and the Duke of Hamilton resulted in the fatal duel between him and Hamilton on 15 November 1712. Thackeray departs in several instances from the facts of Mohun's life for his fictional purposes. His renaming him 'Harry' is especially noteworthy (see p. 147). See Robert Stanley Forsythe, *A Noble Rake: the Life of Charles, Fourth Lord Mohun* (Cambridge, Mass., 1928), which is 'a study in the historical background of Thackeray's *Henry Esmond*'.

116   *abi in pace*: go in peace (Latin).

Baucis and Philemon: an old woman and her husband who despite their poverty were hospitable to Zeus and Hermes. After their deaths, they were transformed into trees with intertwining boughs (Ovid, *Metamorphoses*, viii).

118   *in corpore vili*: literally, 'on a worthless body', though Thackeray intends the plural.

119 *the Malabar wives*: the practice of suttee, as in Malabar, a district on the west coast of India.

121 *at the gallows' foot*: Jeremy Collier (1650–1726), the nonjuring clergyman and author of the *Short View of the Immorality and Profaneness of the English Stage* (1689), performed this function at the execution on 3 April 1696 of Sir John Friend and Sir William Parkyns for their part in the conspiracy.

130 *the 'Rose'*: a tavern in Russell Street, Covent Garden.

132 *Spring Garden*: a pleasure garden of some ill-repute at Vauxhall. Sir Roger de Coverley 'told the mistress of the house, who sat at the bar, that he should be a better customer to her garden, if there were more nightingales, and fewer strumpets' (Addison, *The Spectator*, No. 383, 20 May 1712).

perhaps overthrows us: the image is Pascal's in *Pensées*, 176, referring to Cromwell: 'Cromwell allait ravager toute la chrétienté; la famille royale était perdue, et la sienne à jamais puissante, sans un petit grain de sable qui se mit dans son urètre' ('Cromwell was about to ravage all Christendom; the royal family was undone, and his own for ever established, save for a little grain of sand which formed in his ureter', trans. W. F. Trotter, Everyman's Library edition).

133 *'bright particular star'*: *All's Well That Ends Well*, I. i. 80.

134 *has written so nobly*: The Latin phrase describes Fortune as loving her 'cruel game' (Horace, *Odes*, iii. 29. 49). Dryden, the 'great poet', uses the phrase 'malicious joy' in his version of the poem. For further references to this Ode, see pp. 172 and 258, below.

137 *Amurath*: a version of Murad, the name of five Sultans of Turkey.

139 *Beati pacifici*: blessed are the peacemakers.

140 *Mohocks*: 'aristocratic ruffians who infested the streets of London at night in the early years of the 18th century' (*OED*), described by Steele in *The Spectator*, No. 324, 12 March 1712.

141 *your favourite Bishop Taylor*: John Tillotson (1630–94), Arch-bishop of Canterbury, whose sermons were widely published. For Taylor, see note to p. 100, above.

143 *medicine it away*: 'Not poppy, nor mandragora, | Nor all the drowsy syrups of the world, | Shall ever medicine thee to that sweet sleep | Which thou owed'st yesterday' (*Othello*, III, iii. 334–7).

145 *botte de Jésuite*: a thrust or lunge in fencing, as taught to Henry Esmond by the supposed 'Jesuit in disguise', pp. 112–13, above.

151 *Doctor Cheyne*: George Cheyne (1671–1743), MD, a popular and influential physician, whose numerous publications included an *Essay on Health and Long Life* (1724).

152 *Mr. Betterton*: Thomas Betterton (1635?–1710), the leading actor of his time, was a member of the Duke's Company, which Thackeray has confused with Duke Street.

as the play says: '. . . and then to breakfast with | What appetite you have' (*King Henry VIII*, III. ii. 202–3).

156 *Mrs. Bracegirdle*: Anne Bracegirdle (1663?–1748), the most famous actress of the period, is here performing the part of Fidelia in Wycherley's *The Plain Dealer*, not *Love in a Wood*.

bad news from Bullock Fair: perhaps a reference to Shallow's question in *King Henry IV, Part II*, III. ii. 37–8: 'How a good yoke of bullocks at Stamford fair?'

Captain Macartney: George MacCartney (1660?–1730), later a general. See pp. 380, 382, and 387, below.

157 *a mischievous fatal look*: it was said that Captain Hill had killed Mountfort as a rival for Mrs Bracegirdle's affections.

Christian Hero: Steele's treatise on morals was published in 1701.

159 *Mons and Namur*: Mons was besieged and taken by the French in 1691. Namur was besieged and taken by William in 1695.

160 *who kept a bath*: Henry Ayme kept 'The Queen's Bagnio', where it was 'convenient for both sexes to sweat and bathe . . .

and to be cupped' (advertisement in *The Tatler*, No. 95, 17 November 1709).

161   *Mr. Atterbury*: Francis Atterbury (1662–1732), who became Bishop of Rochester and Dean of Westminster in 1713, was a friend of contemporary men of letters, including Swift and Pope. He had strongly Jacobite sympathies.

163   *Benedicti benedicentes*: blessed are they who bless.

171   *Dr. Ken*: George Herbert (1593–1633), poet and Rector of Bemerton, Wiltshire; Thomas Ken (1637–1711), one of the Seven Bishops, who refused to read James II's Declaration of Indulgence (1688).

172   *virtute sua*: an allusion to Horace, *Odes*, iii. 29. 53–5, where the 'goddess' is Fortune: 'Si celeres quatit | pennas, resigno, quae dedit, et mea | virtute me involvo': 'But let her shake | Those wings, her presents I resign, | Cloak me in native worth' (trans. Conington). 'Virtute sua', adapted from the above lines, is 'his native worth'.

173   *Reficimus rates quassas*: correctly, 'reficit rates | quassas': 'he refits his battered craft' (Horace, *Odes*, i. 1. 17–18, trans. Conington).

174   *of the English army*: Lieutenant-General Lord Cutts (1661–1707), who had a distinguished military career, including heroic conduct at the Siege of Namur (1695).

176   *a weeping Belvidera*: after the killing of her children, Niobe was metamorphosed by Zeus into a perpetually weeping stone. Sigismunda and Belvidera are the tragic heroines of one of Boccaccio's stories in the *Decameron* (IV. i.) and Thomas Otway's *Venice Preserv'd*, respectively.

matre pulcra filia pulcrior: 'O lovelier than the lovely dame | That bore you' (Horace, *Odes*, i. 16. 1, trans. Conington).

177   *imo pectore*: from the bottom of his heart (Latin).

182   *Her Grace of Portsmouth*: Louise Renée de Keroualle (1649–1734), Duchess of Portsmouth and Aubigny, was one of Charles II's mistresses.

Isabelle Vicomptesse d'Esmond: to those who know French, the misspellings explain themselves, with perhaps the following exceptions: ayscrimme = escrime; vouseluy = vous et lui; ansamb = ensemble; veux = veut; milfoy = mille fois; trotar = trop tard; sentéraysent = s'intéressent; fi = fils. *Costé* and *estes* are not misspellings, but the normal spelling of the time, which is also true of the *c* in *sceu, scay, scavay*, except that in the two latter words it should be *ç*. (Note from the Snows' edition.) 'M. le Compte de Varique' is the Earl of Warwick and 'M. de Moon' is Lord Mohun. 'la Reine Anne' should be 'la Princesse Anne'; presumably this was a slip on Thackeray's part.

184   *'dropping odours'*: a phrase from Milton's *Comus*, 106.

    the towers of Cybele: Cybele, the goddess and the wife of Saturn, is conventionally depicted with turrets or a tower covering her head.

189   *had swallow for them all*: Thackeray's list of 'marvellous tales' comes from 'An Extract of several miraculous cures performed by the intercession of the late James the Second, King of Great Britain', in James Macpherson's *Original Papers* (1775), i. 598–9.

190   *Mr. Fox*: George Fox (1624–91), the founder of the Quakers.

    εχουσιν: 'Lo you now, how vainly do mortal men blame the gods, for of us they say comes evil, whereas they, even of themselves, through the blindness of their own hearts, have sorrows beyond that which is ordained' (Homer, *Odyssey*, i. 32–4, trans. Butcher and Lang).

192   *from the queen*: just before his death, the 2nd Earl of Macclesfield (1659?–1701) went to Hanover to present the Electress-Dowager Sophia with a copy of the Act of Succession.

193   *weak courts*: see *Gulliver's Travels*, Part 1, chs. 6 and 7. Jonathan Swift (1667–1745), the prose writer, poet, and clergyman, first achieved literary fame with his prose satires, *A Tale of a Tub* (1696) and the *Battle of the Books* (1697). He later wrote much in support of the Tory cause. His *Journal to*

Stella (1710–13) is an invaluable, gossipy record of the political and social life of the time. He was appointed Dean of St Patrick's, Dublin in 1713. His masterpiece, *Gulliver's Travels*, was published in 1726.

198   *and Smell Powder*: a combined fleet of English and Dutch ships, with Sir George Rooke as Commander-in-Chief and Sir Thomas Hopsonn as second-in-command, overwhelmed the French and Spanish in Vigo Bay on 12 October 1702, following the inglorious events Thackeray describes.

Captain Avory or Captain Kid: John (?) Avory was a pirate notorious for levying tolls on vessels entering and leaving the Red Sea in 1695. William Kidd (d. 1701) was also active as a pirate in the 1690s; his doings are colourfully described by Macaulay in his *History of England*, ch. 25.

201   *'Mori pro patria'*: '[dulce et decorum est] mori pro patria': 'it is sweet and fitting to die for one's country' (Horace, *Odes*, iii. 2. 13).

202   *General Lumley*: Henry Lumley (1660–1722) continued his military career until 1717, when he resigned the command of his regiment. See p. 232, below, where Thackeray seems to have forgotten this first reference to Esmond and the General.

204   *secretly pleasant to us*: 'Dans l'adversité de nos meilleurs amis, nous trouvons toujours quelque chose qui ne nous deplaît pas': 'In the misfortunes of our best friends, we find something not unpleasing.'

a great reconciler: 'Sweet are the uses of adversity; | Which, like the toad, ugly and venomous, | Wears yet a precious jewel in his head' (*As You Like It*, ii. i. 12–14).

208   *and Hamilton*: Sir George Etherege (1635–91), Restoration dramatist; Sir Charles Sedley (1639?–1701), poet and dramatist; John Wilmot, 2nd Earl of Rochester (1647–80), poet; Henry Jermyn, the Earl of St Albans (d. 1684), courtier; Anthony Hamilton (1636?–1720), author, soldier, and Jacobite. Thackeray has grouped them together as typically 'rakish' authors and courtiers.

our Lady of Chaillot: the shrine of the Virgin Mary at the Convent of the Visitation at Chaillot, near Paris, where the heart of James II was buried.

209 *Monsieur Rigaud's portrait*: Hyacinth Rigaud y Ros (1649–1743), court painter to Louis XIV and Louis XV.

211 *Reddas incolumem precor*: 'Give him back safe, I pray' (Horace, *Odes*, i. 3. 7).

Septimi, Gades aditure mecum: 'Septimius, who with me would brave far Gades [i.e. Cadiz]' (Horace, *Odes*, ii. 6. 1, trans. Conington).

213 *bringing his sheaves with him*: a not completely accurate quotation from Psalm 126: 1, 6–7 (*Book of Common Prayer*), sung at Evening Prayer on the 27th day of the month. Psalms 142 and 143 should be sung on 29 December, but Thackeray has chosen appropriately for his purposes.

214 *Non omnis moriar*: 'Not all of me will die' (Horace, *Odes*, iii. 30. 6).

the holy Advent season: it is, of course, the Christmas season. Advent had ended on 24 December.

217 *Milton*: for example, '. . . he in delight | Both of her beauty and submissive charms | Smiled with superior love' (*Paradise Lost*, iv. 497–9).

220 *Lindamiras and Ardelias*: Steele refers to Lindamira, a 'masterpiece of Nature' (*The Spectator*, No. 41, 17 April 1711), and Swift wrote a poem, 'Apollo Outwitted, to the Honourable Mrs Finch, under her Name of Ardelia' (1709).

223 *Grammont*: Philibert, comte de Grammont (1621–1707), courtier at both the French and English courts, whose *Memoirs*, written by Anthony Hamilton and published in 1713, remain a fascinating source of gossip and information.

Dr. Hare: Francis Hare (1671–1740), DD, tutor at Cambridge to Robert Walpole and Marlborough's son, the Marquis of Blandford.

232 *the Campaign of 1704*: the central event of this chapter is the Battle of Blenheim, which took place on 13 August 1704.

Brigadier Webb's regiment of Fusiliers: John Richmond Webb (1667?–1724), who plays a heroic and leading role in this part of the novel. Thackeray explained in a letter to S. N. Rowland on 2 May 1855 the reason for the prominence he gives to Webb: 'When I wrote "Esmond" I thought (for so the tradition was in our family) that I was a lineal descendant of the General . . . but I am sorry to say the General is not in *my* direct line. We branch from a common ancestor in Charles II's time, two generations off' (Ray, *Letters*, iii. 446).

233 *our seamen went down*: in the great storm of November 1703, which caused terrible destruction and numerous deaths. For Addison's poem, *The Campaign*, from which the quotation comes, see pp. 250–60, below.

General Churchill: Charles Churchill (1656–1714), a younger brother of the Duke of Marlborough.

234 *the famous Prince of Savoy*: Prince Eugene (1663–1736), who was Marlborough's allied commander in the campaigns against the French.

235 *the drama of war*: parts of Thackeray's description were possibly suggested by Robert Southey's poem, 'The Battle of Blenheim' (1798).

who live at home at ease: 'You gentlemen of England | Who live at home at ease, | How little do you think | On the dangers of the seas' (Martin Parker, d. 1656, 'The Valiant Sailors').

236 *when she cuts it*: of the Three Fates, Clotho held the spindle carrying the thread of life, Lachesis drew out the thread, and Atropos cut it off.

240 *vana somnia*: empty dreams (Latin).

deserved a Gloriana: Amadis of Gaul, the hero of a 15th-century Spanish romance, married Oriana, whom Thackeray has confused with the Gloriana of Spenser's *Faerie Queene*.

241 *desipere in loco*: '[dulce est] desipere in loco': ' 'tis sweet the fool to play' (Horace, *Odes*, iv. 12. 28, trans. Conington).

242 *like Hector brave*: slightly misquoted, with one couplet

omitted, from the *Battel of Audenard*, published anonymously (London, 1708).

Maison-du-Roy: the household troops, of high rank, in the French army.

Vendosme and Villeroy: Louis-Joseph, Duc de Vendôme (1654–1712) and Francois, Duc de Villeroi (1644–1730), military commanders.

245 *Dr. Bentley*: Richard Bentley (1662–1742), the classical scholar and controversialist, became Master of Trinity College, Cambridge, on 1 February 1700.

246 *Bathyllus*: a beautiful youth of Samos, beloved by Anacreon, the Greek lyric poet.

247 *Nicolini*: Nicolo Grimaldi (1673–1731), known as Nicolini, the celebrated alto castrato: 'the greatest performer in dramatic music that is now living, or that perhaps ever appeared upon a stage' (Addison, *The Spectator*, No. 405, 14 June 1712).

248 *remedium amoris*: a remedy for love (adapted from the title of a poem by Ovid, 'Remedia Amoris').

249 *Observator*: a Whig periodical founded by John Tutchin and issued from 1702 to 1712.

Mr. Prior: Matthew Prior (1664–1721), the poet, diplomat, and MP, who played a leading part in negotiating the Treaty of Utrecht (1713). See p. 90, above, and pp. 373, 381, below.

250 *The Famous Mr. Joseph Addison*: when Godolphin, the Lord Treasurer, wanted a poet to celebrate the victory at Blenheim, Lord Halifax recommended Addison. Henry Boyle, the Chancellor of the Exchequer, negotiated with him. The result was *The Campaign* (1704) and the appointment of Addison to a Commissionership of Appeal in the Excise. Macaulay gives a characteristically graphic account of the episode in his essay on Addison (1843), which Thackeray may be recalling in this chapter.

252 *admired them*: Esmond has quoted the opening of Addison's Latin poem, 'Ad D. D. Hannes, Isignissimum Medicum et

Poetam' ('O thou who drawest thy tuneful strain more sweetly than the singer Orpheus').

254   *the lines*: lines 227–38 of *The Campaign*. Thackeray or the printer has reversed the order of the 3rd and 4th lines and has changed Addison's singular verbs, 'turns' and 'burns', into the plural.

256   *Si parva licet*: 'si parva licet componere magnis': 'if it is permitted to compare the small with the great' (Virgil, *Georgics*, iv. 176).

      plebeia favori: 'Bringer of peace to the Rhine and Danube . . . In his single person the strife of differing ranks has ceased; in him the knight is glad, the senator makes his boast, and the plebeian's prayer rivals the patrician's devotion' (Claudian, *De Laudibus Stilichonis*, iii. 13. 48–50). This amalgamation of lines is the epigraph to *The Campaign*.

257   *in the poem of the Campaign*: lines 279–92, which praise Marlborough's serenity amidst the storm of battle.

      hic est Sigeia tellus: 'here the Simois flowed . . . here is the land of Sigeium' (slightly misquoted from Ovid, *Heroides*, i. 33).

      aliquo praelia mixta mero: 'battles mixed with wine' (possibly an imperfect reminiscence of Ovid, *Heroides*, i. 36).

258   *where to rage*: The Campaign, 285–6.

      'I puff the prostitute away': from Dryden's version of Horace, *Odes*, iii. 29.

260   *the 'Toy'*: a popular inn at Hampton Court.

261   *Mrs. Mountford*: the widow of William Mountfort. See note to p. 114, above.

      the famous 23rd of May, 1706: according to Keith Feiling, in his *History of England* (1950), this was Marlborough's 'happiest day, for never were seen better the simplicity of his design, his brilliance of decision, or the fighting power of British, Danes, and Dutch' (p. 608).

263   *afflavit Deus, et dissipati sunt*: 'God blew, and they were

scattered' (the legend on medals celebrating the defeat of the Spanish Armada in 1588).

the Grand Signor's Janizaries: the Sultan of Turkey's guards.

264 *'Over the hills and far away'*: the songs are 'Our 'prentice Tom may now refuse' (Farquhar, *The Recruiting Officer*, ii. 3) and 'Were I laid on Greenland's coast' (Gay, *The Beggar's Opera*, i. 13). But the latter 'comedy' did not appear until 1728.

265 *meminisse juvat*: 'Forsan et haec olim meminisse iuvabit': 'Perhaps one day it will be sweet to recall even this' (Virgil, *Aeneid*, i. 203).

267 *Pandour*: a Serbo-Croatian or Hungarian guard or armed retainer.

269 *who knows where*: '[the Jesuits] were to be found in the garb of Mandarins superintending the observatory at Pekin. They were to be found, spade in hand, teaching the rudiments of agriculture to the savages of Paraguay' (Macaulay, *History of England*, ch. 6).

whom her parents should find for her: this story was told of George I's sister, not his daughter. It appears in Thackeray's lecture, 'George the First', in *The Four Georges*.

270 *Oudenarde*: the Battle of Oudenarde, 11 July 1708.

271 *Villar's own guinguette*: François, duc de Rohan-Rohan, known as the Prince of Soubise (1669–1749), courtier and soldier; Claude Louis Hector, duc de Villars (1653–1749), the great French general.

279 *Mrs. Masham*: Abigail Masham (d. 1734), who supplanted her cousin Sarah, Duchess of Marlborough, as Queen Anne's favourite. Robert Harley, 1st Earl of Oxford (1661–1724), entered the House of Commons in 1689 and soon established himself as a powerful Tory politician. He secretly worked to undermine the influence of the Marlboroughs at the royal court, with the help of Mrs. Masham, who was related to him. Queen Anne dismissed him from office just before her death. (See Historical Background.) In the reign of George I, he was impeached on charges including that of secretly favouring the Old Pretender, but he was acquitted.

when so convinced: 'He that complies against his will, | Is of his own opinion still' (Butler, *Hudibras*, III. iii. 547–8).

Galway: Henri de Marsue de Ruvigny, 1st Earl of Galway (1648–1720), defeated at Almanza.

280 *Cadogan's share*: William, 1st Earl Cadogan (1675–1720), general.

284 *Abbé of Savoy*: Louis XIV had refused to grant a commission to Prince Eugene, who was known as the 'abbé' at the French court because he had been destined for the Church. This refusal caused Eugene to have a lifelong resentment against the King.

286 *Wynendael*: the battle took place on 28 September 1708. Thackeray thought that it 'was one of the most brilliant and timely actions ever fought by British men' (Ray, *Letters*, iii. 446).

289 *Cardonnel*: Adam Cardonnel (d. 1719), secretary to the Duke of Marlborough.

290 *Order of Generosity*: founded in 1665 by Friedrich Wilhelm of Brandenburg, the Great Elector.

298 *Mr. Jervas*: Charles Jervas (1675–1739), a portrait painter of high reputation at the time.

299 *Mrs. Tofts*: Catherine Tofts (1685?–1756), soprano, described in Grove's *Dictionary* as 'the first English prima donna'.

302 *the Prince of Savoy's mother*: Olympe Mancini, one of Mazarin's nieces, married the comte de Soissons.

306 *the Scots Duke of Hamilton*: James Douglas, 4th Duke of Hamilton (1658–1712), served Charles II and James II in various capacities; on the accession of William and Mary, he was briefly imprisoned in the Tower. He went on, however, to play an active part in politics and was awarded the Order of the Garter in 1712. Before the conclusion of the Treaty of Utrecht, Hamilton was appointed ambassador extraordinary to France. But he was killed on 15 November 1712 in the duel with Mohun after a prolonged legal dispute over property. He was married first to Lady Anne Spencer and

secondly to Elizabeth, the daughter and heiress of Digby, Lord Gerard (who long outlived him). As with Mohun, Thackeray has virtually created a fictional character in his portrayal of Hamilton.

Lord Ashburnham: the 3rd baron (1687–1737), later created an earl.

a liberal education: Steele's description of Aspasia (Lady Elizabeth Hastings, a daughter of the Earl of Huntingdon) appeared in *The Tatler*, No. 49, 2 August 1709.

309   *Tom Boxer*: see p. 464 for the omitted passage from the first edition, which refers to Tom Boxer. The passage was a coded attack on John Forster, who had adversely reviewed Thackeray's lectures on the English Humourists and who had mistakenly attributed Steele's 'To love her is a liberal education' to Congreve. Steele and Boxer represent Thackeray and Forster; *The Observator* is *The Examiner*, which Forster edited; Congreve and Arbuthnot are Dickens and Dr John Elliotson (Ray, *Letters*, ii. 779–80).

315   *Monsieur Gauthier by name*: François Gautier (d. 1720), chaplain to the French embassy in London, and a go-between for Bolingbroke and de Torcy (see p. 323, below).

316   *Sir Josiah Child*: Thackeray has confused Sir Josiah Child (1630–99), a writer on trade and chairman of the East India Company, with Sir Francis Child (1684?–1740), a banker and Lord Mayor of London.

317   *aweary of the sun*: *Macbeth*, v. iv. 49.

318   *Malplaquet*: fought on 11 September 1709.

320   *General Uriah*: David ordered Joab to ensure the death of Uriah, the husband of Bathsheba, by setting him 'in the forefront of the hottest battle' (2 Samuel II: 15).

322   *Dr. Sacheverel*: Henry Sacheverell (1674?–1724), the Tory and High Church preacher, whose violently expressed, uncompromising opinions led to his impeachment in 1710.

323   *Monsieur de Torcy*: Jean-Baptiste Colbert, marquis de Torcy

(1665–1746), French diplomat and the minister for foreign affairs.

Mr. Tunstal: an agent of Prince James Edward's. Thackeray would have read a letter from him to the Earl of Middleton and the latter's reply in Macpherson's *Original Papers*, ii. 228–33.

325   *11th of September last year*: i.e. the date of the Battle of Malplaquet.

Mr. Sterne: Roger Sterne, the father of Laurence Sterne. In his Memoirs, Laurence Sterne writes that his father was a lieutenant in Handyside's regiment and that he was 'a little smart man . . . somewhat rapid and hasty, but of a kindly sweet disposition'.

334   *Post-Boy*: the leading Tory newspaper of the period.

336   *Guiscard, that stabbed Mr. Harvy*: Guiscard was a French refugee, formerly the abbé de Bourlie and subsequently known as the marquis de Guiscard, who stabbed Harley with a penknife on 8 March 1711. 'Harvy' is a misprint for 'Harley'.

339   *Lais*: the name of two Greek courtesans, of the 5th and 4th centuries BC.

October Club: a 'set of above a hundred [Tory] parliament-men of the country' (Swift, *Journal to Stella*, 18 February 1711). They met at the Bell Tavern, King Street, Westminster.

342   *Lord Peterborow*: Charles Mordaunt, 3rd Earl of Peterborough (1658–1735), whose 'life was a wild romance made up of mysterious intrigues, both political and amorous' (Macaulay, *History of England*, ch. 7).

343   *Mr. Dennis, the great critic*: John Dennis (1657–1734), the prolific and combative critic, chiefly remembered today for his attacks on Addison and Pope.

Mr. Wilks: Robert Wilks (1665?–1732), a versatile actor who created many roles, mostly at Drury Lane. He was celebrated by Steele in *The Spectator*, No. 369, 3 May 1712. Cibber's *Apology* (1740) contains much detail about him.

344 *Spectator*: the actual paper 341 was by Eustace Budgell. Thackeray has chosen the date for obvious reasons. Austin Dobson pointed out that 'Mr. Esmond, to his very apposite Latin epigraph, unluckily appended an English translation,— a concession to the country gentlemen from which both Addison and Steele deliberately abstained, holding that their distinctive mottoes were (in Addison's own phrase) "words to the wise," of no concern to unlearned persons' (*De Libris*, 1908, pp. 184–5).

346 *angel that visited the pool*: 'For an angel went down at a certain season into the pool [of Bethesda] and troubled the water' (John 5: 4). The words occur in the Second Lesson for Morning Prayer on 16 May.

  Dr. Swift's pun: 'I tell you a good pun; a fellow hard by pretends to cure Agues, and has set out a sign, and spells it Egoes; a gentleman and I observing it, he said, How does that fellow pretend to cure Agues? I said, I did not know, but I was sure it was not by a Spell' (*Journal to Stella*, 25 December 1710).

356 *upon his shoulders*: as Aeneas carried his father out of burning Troy (Virgil, *Aeneid*, ii).

364 *'Gawrie'*: an anachronistic reference to Robert Paltock's fantasy, *Peter Wilkins* (1751), in which the hero finds himself among a people who can fly. 'Gawry' was their word for 'woman'.

366 *in all England*: 'On her white breast a sparkling cross she wore' (Pope, *Rape of the Lock*, ii. 7).

370 *Sword of Honour*: Queen Anne presented the diamond-covered sword to Prince Eugene in London on her birthday, 6 February 1712. Sir Roger de Coverley came to London 'and made me promise to get him a stand in some convenient place where he might have a full sight of that extraordinary man, whose presence does so much honour to the British nation' (Addison, *The Spectator*, No. 269, 8 January 1712).

our defeat at Denain: on 24 July 1712 Villars decisively defeated Prince Eugene's army at Denain.

373   *the Doctors Garth and Arbuthnot*: Samuel Garth (1661–1719), physician and poet, who wrote *The Dispensary* (1699), a burlesque poem; John Arbuthnot (1667–1735), physician, writer, and friend of Swift, Pope, and Gay.

Button's: the coffee-house in Russell Street, Covent Garden, frequented by Addison, Steele, Congreve, and many other writers and wits.

nunc prescribere longum est: 'It is too long to give the list' (from the *Eton Grammar*). The correct verb is *perscribere*.

374   *'vidi tantum'*: 'I only just saw him' (Ovid, *Tristia*, iv. 10. 51).

of Handyside's: i.e. Roger Sterne. See p. 325, above.

375   *Omphale and Delilah*: Hercules was desperately in love with Omphale, Queen of Lydia, who made him wear a woman's dress and spin flax. Samson's infatuation with Delilah brought about his servitude among the Philistines (Judges 16).

376   *Wills's*: the coffee-house at No. 1 Bow Street, Covent Garden.

Bouchain: Marlborough's final victory was his capture of Bouchain on 14 September 1711.

377   *at which he looks very fierce*: the ensuing scene can be compared with some of Thackeray's comments in his lecture on Swift in *The English Humourists*: 'If you had been his inferior in parts . . . his equal in mere social station, he would have bullied, scorned, and insulted you; if, undeterred by his great reputation, you had met him like a man, he would have quailed before you, and not had the pluck to reply, and gone home, and years after written a foul epigram about you . . .'

Mr. Leach: Dryden Leach, printer, and a distant relation of Swift and Dryden.

378   *Compter*: the name given to various London prisons (that were originally debtors' prisons).

Kemp: probably an invented name.

he had had the man hanged: '. . . besides, he was a fiddler, and consequently a rogue, and deserved hanging for something else' (*Journal to Stella*, 25 July 1711). Quoted in one of the footnotes to Thackeray's lecture on Swift in *The English Humourists*.

380   *Lord Stair*: the 2nd Earl of Stair (1673–1747), son of the Lord Stair mentioned on p. 10, above. He became the English ambassador to France.

381   *The Hind and the Panther*: the Catholic Church and the Church of England respectively, as depicted in Dryden's poem of that name (1687).

My cousin Westmoreland: see *King Henry V*, IV, iii. 16–20.

386   *what particulars he knew*: Thackeray's account agrees with the contemporary narratives, where they agree, except in two points. (1) They did not fight 'three on a side', but two, the Duke and his cousin, Captain Hamilton, against Mohun and Macartney (p. 387). (2) The Duchess was a cousin, not a sister of Lady Mohun. (Note in the Snows' edition.)

389   *the young Duke of Cambridge*: the Electoral Prince of Hanover, later George II.

395   *his enemies at the gate*: 'thy seed shall possess the gate of his enemies' (Genesis 22: 17).

399   *Benedict, the married man*: a phrase used twice in *Much Ado About Nothing* (V. i. and V. ii).

400   *Atridae*: Agamemnon and Menelaus, whose 'doomed race' was portrayed by Aeschylus in his tragedies.

Miss Oglethorpe: Anne Oglethorpe, the beautiful daughter of Sir Theophilus Oglethorpe, the general and Jacobite, said to be a mistress of the Old Pretender.

403   *Mr. Lesly*: the Revd. Charles Leslie (1650–1722), a nonjuror and religious pamphleteer.

407   *the oaf her son*: when Arria's husband hesitated to commit suicide, she stabbed herself as an example to him, and then handed him the dagger (AD 42). Cornelia, the widowed

mother of the Gracchi, proudly called them her 'jewels' (2nd century BC).

Dr. Berkeley's tar-water: for 'Jesuit's bark', see note to p. 50, above. The enthusiasm of Bishop Berkeley, the philosopher, for tar-water was expressed in his *Siris* (1744). This is therefore an anachronistic reference.

408   *The Original of the Portrait Comes to England*: 'Of course the latter part of the book about the Pretender's coming to England is fabulous, but there was a meeting at Kensington, and there was a famous General to be set up in opposition to Marlborough, and this one, I think, was most likely John Richmond Webb' (Thackeray, letter to S. N. Rowland, 2 May 1855; Ray, *Letters*, iii. 447).

Eikon Basilike: the title of a book (literally, 'Royal Image'), published at the time of Charles I's execution in 1649 and supposedly containing the King's meditations.

411   *the kingdom of Brentford*: the two Kings of Brentford enter, hand in hand, in the Duke of Buckingham's burlesque, *The Rehearsal* (1672). Among Thackeray's poems are 'The King of Brentford's Testament' and two versions of 'The King of Brentford'.

Don Bellianis of Greece: a Spanish romance (1547), with additional parts written later by Gerónimo Fernández, popular in various translations and versions in seventeenth- and eighteenth-century England.

416   *mixta mero*: see above, p. 257.

418   *Derwentwater on the scaffold*: the 5th Earl of Nithsdale (1676–1744) and the 3rd Earl of Derwentwater (1689–1716) both took part in the 1715 rebellion. Nithsdale escaped from the Tower of London but Derwentwater was beheaded.

419   *Crispin*: an impudent valet in French comedy, as in Le Sage's *Crispin rival de son maître* (1707).

422   *Rogues' Opera*: i.e. *The Beggar's Opera*.

424   *St. Anthony's fire*: erysipelas.

436   *coram latronibus*: in sight of the robbers. Adapted from Juvenal, *Satires*, x. 22.

438   *Aymé*: see note to p. 160, above.

463   '*eyes of meek surrender*': *Paradise Lost*, iv. 494.

THE WORLD'S CLASSICS

A Select List

JANE AUSTEN: Emma
Edited by James Kinsley and David Lodge

WILLIAM BECKFORD: Vathek
Edited by Roger Lonsdale

JOHN BUNYAN: The Pilgrim's Progress
Edited by N. H. Keeble

THOMAS CARLYLE: The French Revolution
Edited by K. J. Fielding and David Sorensen

GEOFFREY CHAUCER: The Canterbury Tales
Translated by David Wright

CHARLES DICKENS: Christmas Books
Edited by Ruth Glancy

BENJAMIN DISRAELI: Coningsby
Edited by Sheila M. Smith

MARIA EDGEWORTH: Castle Rackrent
Edited by George Watson

SUSAN FERRIER: Marriage
Edited by Herbert Foltinek

ELIZABETH GASKELL: Cousin Phillis and Other Tales
Edited by Angus Easson

THOMAS HARDY: A Pair of Blue Eyes
Edited by Alan Manford

HOMER: The Iliad
Translated by Robert Fitzgerald
Introduction by G. S. Kirk

HENRIK IBSEN: An Enemy of the People, The Wild Duck,
Rosmersholm
Edited and Translated by James McFarlane

HENRY JAMES: The Ambassadors
Edited by Christopher Butler

A complete list of Oxford Paperbacks, including The World's Classics, OPUS, Past Masters, Oxford Authors, Oxford Shakespeare, and Oxford Paperback Reference, is available in the UK from the Arts and Reference Publicity Department (RS), Oxford University Press, Walton Street, Oxford OX2 6DP.

In the USA, complete lists are available from the Paperbacks Marketing Manager, Oxford University Press, 200 Madison Avenue, New York, NY 10016.

Oxford Paperbacks are available from all good bookshops. In case of difficulty, customers in the UK can order direct from Oxford University Press Bookshop, Freepost, 116 High Street, Oxford, OX1 4BR, enclosing full payment. Please add 10 per cent of published price for postage and packing.